CW00493442

ROME

ÉMILE ZOLA

ROME

TRANSLATED BY ERNEST ALFRED VIZETELLY

ALAN SUTTON

First published in 1896

First published in this edition in the United Kingdom in 1993
Alan Sutton Publishing Ltd
Phoenix Mill · Far Thrupp · Stroud · Gloucestershire

First published in this edition in the United States of America in 1993
Alan Sutton Publishing Inc · 83 Washington Street · Dover · NH 03820

Copyright © in this edition
Alan Sutton Publishing Ltd, 1993

All rights reserved. No part of this publication may be reproduced, stored in a retrieval system, or transmitted, in any form or by any means, electronic, mechanical, photocopying, recording or otherwise, without the prior permission of the publisher and copyright holder.

British Library Cataloguing in Publication Data
A catalogue record for this book is available from the British Library

ISBN 0-7509-0451-8

Library of Congress Cataloging in Publication Data applied for

Cover picture: The Castell St Angelo, Rome *by Andreas Achenbach (Courtesy Mensing Gallery, Hamm-Rhynem, Germany; Photograph: Fine Art Photographic Library Ltd)*

Typeset in 9/10 Bembo.
Typesetting and origination by
Alan Sutton Publishing Limited.
Printed in Great Britain by
The Guernsey Press Company Limited,
Guernsey, Channel Islands.

CONTENTS

INTRODUCTION

In 1893, after twenty-five years' involvement, Zola brought his cycle of *Rougon-Macquart* novels to a triumphant and no doubt relieved conclusion. The task of remaining referentially accurate and avoiding anachronisms in his depiction of the historical period of the Second Empire (1852–70) had become increasingly difficult under the pressure of contemporary events, with novels such as *Au Bonheur des Dames, Germinal* and *L'Argent* showing signs of the need felt by the author to synthesize more recent stages of development in mass merchandising, revolutionary syndicalism and financial market manipulation. A dozen years earlier, Zola had predicted to his friend Paul Alexis that after the *Rougon-Macquart* he might occupy himself with a history of French literature, write children's stories, or even do nothing at all. But the undermining of previously held convictions, such as his belief in social Darwinism, led him to think again, and to address social problems of immediate relevance to the final decade of the century.

That a substantial body of readers should be eager to see the new direction his thoughts were taking in *Lourdes*, the novel on the documentary research for which he was known to be proceeding in his usual assiduous fashion, was greatly to the credit of a man whose failure to obtain the enabling *baccalauréat* meant that he lacked credible academic qualifications. Émile Zola was born near the Paris Bourse in 1840, to a Venetian engineer father and a French mother from the grain-growing plain of the Beauce, to the south-west of the city. The family moved in 1843 to Aix-en-Provence, where Francesco was involved in a bold project to ensure the town's water supply via an aqueduct, but died in 1847, leaving them in a state of

poverty relieved only by the gentle climate. They returned to
Paris in 1858, thereby disrupting Émile's secondary school
studies at a critical time; after failing his exams, he was obliged
to find low-grade clerical employment and, abandoning this, led
an impecunious bohemian existence in a succession of dismal
apartments. Here he read omnivorously, penned epic poetry
and contemplated other literary projects.

At length he was found a post in the publicity department of
the progressive publishing house of Hachette. His job
description in 1862 included menial tasks such as the packing
and despatch of books, but his natural talent for writing blurbs
and synopses soon flourished, and he made personal contact
with distinguished authors and standard-bearers of scientific
positivism such as Michelet, Taine and Sainte-Beuve. He began
to write reviews and art criticism for newspapers, championing
the objectivity and modernity of painters like Manet and
novelists like the Goncourts, and to find publishers willing to
print his fiction, beginning with a volume of short stories,
Contes à Ninon. The sexual frankness of his novels, particularly
Thérèse Raquin (1867), led to brushes with imperial censorship,
and his political outspokenness would have landed him in court
for incitement to military disobedience if the Franco-Prussian
War of 1870 had not intervened.

The *débâcle* of Sedan and Emperor Napoléon III's flight from
France provided Zola with the 'terrible but necessary ending'
he had openly wished for the cycle of novels that he had offered
two years earlier to the publisher Lacroix. This was to become
Les Rougon-Macquart, a natural and social history of a family
during the Second Empire, in which the two major scientific
determinants of heredity and environment were to be seen in
their effect on the legitimate issue of Adélaïde Fouque's
marriage to Rougon, a solid citizen, and the illegitimate
progeny of her liaison with a criminal degenerate, Macquart.
The original plan provided for the opening *La Fortune des
Rougon* and another nine novels, but soon it was expanded to a
list of seventeen, and the ultimate total of twenty could have
been higher but for a somewhat uneasy conflation of subject-
matter in *La Bête Humaine*. The novels enjoyed unremarkable

sales until 1877, when the seventh in the series, *L'Assommoir*, his first total immersion in a study of working-class life, gave Zola both commercial and critical success. Fame and fortune then allowed him to buy his house at Médan, today a Zola museum, where he entertained the young writers, including Huysmans and Maupassant, who were to immortalize the setting in the anthology of antimilitaristic short stories, *Les Soirées de Médan* (1880).

This collection owed much of its acclaim to a by now well-oiled publicity machine that had given maximum exposure to Zola's theories on literary and dramatic naturalism, most trenchantly and truculently formulated in the collection of essays, *Le Roman Expérimental*, which appeared in the same year. His sustained polemical comparison between the novelist's craft and the experimental scientist's pursuit of working hypotheses provoked lively controversy on the intellectual scene in France. Bold paradoxes such as 'the Republic will be naturalist, or will not exist' commended his ideas to the attention of arch-opponents such as Brunetière, and Balzac, Stendhal and Flaubert were lauded in essays reprinted under the title of *Les Romanciers Naturalistes* that established them as forebears of Zola's movement, though the honour more properly belonged to the Goncourt brothers, whose *Soeur Philomène* (1861) and *Germinie Lacerteux* (1864) had been a major influence on the uncompromisingly deterministic *Thérèse Raquin*.

The year 1880 was also marked by a series of bereavements: the writer Duranty was followed by Flaubert, and finally Zola's mother. Depression, insomnia and psychosomatic disorders overcame the author, and Lazare of *La Joie de Vivre* (1883) seems an uncomfortably close fictional incarnation. But such Schopenhauerian pessimism was more constant in Maupassant than in Zola: his robust secular faith in human qualities that triumph over biological determinism suffuses the endings of *Germinal* (1885), *La Terre* (1887), *L'Argent* (1890), *La Débâcle* (1892) and *Le Docteur Pascal* (1893). It is a faith that, respectfully rather than arrogantly asserted, continues to be manifest in the *Three Cities* (1894–8), but one that was to be put to the severest of tests by the Dreyfus Affair. Zola's brave crusade was a result of the unjust conviction and deportation of a French officer accused of spying, mainly on the grounds that he was Jewish whereas the more circumstantially guilty Esterhazy was not. In *J'Accuse* (*L'Aurore*, 13 January 1898), an open letter condemning the anti-Semitic prejudice of those who had engineered this travesty of justice, the accusation of libel was deliberately provoked in the hope that aspects of the case would be reopened during the consequent criminal proceedings. After a second trial Zola was convicted and, while the appeal was pending, forced to flee to England, where he stayed for nearly a year until moves to obtain a pardon for Dreyfus had gained momentum. It was in exile that he began to write the *Four Gospels*, which are notable because, in spite of all that could have caused him personally to despair, such matters are regarded as but a minor setback in the victorious forward march of mankind, described with visionary enthusiasm in scenarios anticipating the ultimate defeat of retrograde obscurantism in all its forms. Only the first three of these – *Fécondité, Travail,* and *Vérité* – had been completed before his untimely death by carbon monoxide poisoning in 1902. A few preparatory notes exist for the last, and its title – *Justice* – denotes Zola's greatest desire, and one shared by the central protagonist of the *Three Cities*.

F.W.J. Hemmings notes that up to *Nana*, the ninth of the *Rougon-Macquart* cycle, Zola's novels are gratuitous, almost decorative, with the twin goals of environmental reconstruction and precise historical depiction predominating. After this, though, they become functional, beginning to address themselves to more specific and timeless dilemmas and problems without descending to the special pleading or the artificial, allegorical construction of the *roman à thèse*, and hence displaying both social consciousness and creative vitality in a delicate balancing act. But strain was already apparent in *Le Docteur Pascal*, that bends beneath the burden of recapitulation, and the *Three Cities* and the *Four Gospels* will subsequently prove to be fairly mechanically assembled, with plot subservient to ideas. Characters now tend to be stereotypes or mouthpieces, and to recur not in the Balzacian sense – from novel to novel –

but at regular and predictable intervals within each.

The boundless confidence in science of the mid-1860s had given way, by the 1890s, to a 'moral and intellectual uneasiness amidst which the end of the century is struggling' (*Rome*, I, 1). A revival of religious faith was being experienced by a younger generation of intellectuals, stimulated by Pope Leo XIII, whose encyclicals, such as *Rerum Novarum* (1891), sought to reconquer the moral high ground. Brunetière, an adversary who had sought no quarrel with Zola's agnosticism but rather with the unimaginative crudity of his naturalist aesthetics, was ostentatiously converted to Catholicism; in the *Revue des Deux Mondes* of 1 January 1895, he claimed to have done so because of the 'bankruptcy of science'. More pertinently to Zola, perhaps, the greater depth of the Russian novel, with its spiritually tormented protagonists such as Dostoevsky's Alyosha (*The Brothers Karamazov*), had been proclaimed in influential critical essays by Count Eugène-Melchior de Vogüé. Religious preoccupations had not been absent from the *Rougon-Macquart* novels (*La Conquête de Plassans, La Faute de l'Abbé Mouret, La Joie de Vivre, Le Rêve*), but it could be argued that the triumph of scientific rationalism over narrow dogmatism had been hitherto unproblematical. The one-off novel about Lourdes developed into a cities trilogy, in which Zola endeavoured to sustain his appeal to the following generation by asserting his naturalist principles in a more tender and humanitarian way.

Rome (1896) narrates the second leg of l'Abbé Pierre Froment's urban sociological investigation. Whereas Zola could expect no better than to find his fiction, even the new-style *Lourdes*, placed (within a month of publication) on the Vatican Index of prohibited works, such a condemnation is offensive to Pierre, whose *New Rome*, written after his visit to Lourdes, was intended to be a serious discussion of the future of papal authority. He envisages the head of a *risorgimento* of Christian socialism as being of such potential moral prestige that the squabbles with the Italian monarchy over temporal power, pitting 'black' faction against 'white', will be seen to be futile and unnecessary. He therefore resolves to seek an audience with

the Pope in order to have the decision reversed, little realizing
that his enlightened interpretation of *Rerum Novarum* in fact
runs counter to the Vatican's most deep-seated territorial
imperatives. Months of Kafkaesque delaying tactics will be
employed to bring him voluntarily to condemn and disavow his
book; he will not do so, however, in a state of grateful
submission to Leo XIII's wisdom, but in the conviction that
Catholicism is doomed if it has to rely on such arcane political
manoeuvring.

The stalemates encountered by Pierre as he is shuffled from
one influential ecclesiastical dignitary to another, by
subordinates full of unction or bristling with paranoia regarding
an international Jesuit conspiracy, give him leisure to reflect on
the Italian national character and, from Sistine Chapel to
neglected Tiber and Trastevere slums, to visit Rome
extensively. The vast, panoramic cityscapes that are described,
somewhat in the manner of the vistas of Paris from Passy in *Une
Page d'Amour*, result from Zola's six-week visit of 1894. He was
armed with the indispensable Baedeker, and as was his wont
spent much time interviewing cultural attachés (such as Narcisse
Habert) and newspaper correspondents, but this was not
sufficient to gain him the superior comprehension of a Stendhal
(*Promenades dans Rome*), born of much longer acquaintance. His
predecessor's *Chroniques Italiennes* may also be mentioned, for
Zola invents a similarly melodramatic Renaissance poisoning
plot designed to eliminate Pierre's host, Cardinal Boccanera,
from succession to the papacy. This fails to strike its intended
victim, and leads instead to a baroque *Liebestod* in which the
Boccanera cousins, a dying Dario and a Benedetta determined
to belong only to him, undergo a symbolic enactment of sex,
whereupon she too expires, perhaps of pulmonary failure. This
idea of 'Italian' female fidelity unto death (for the males enjoy
the privilege of the double standard) is no doubt poetic, and a
fantasy satisfaction for the author reminiscent of the carnal act
that takes place between the entombed Étienne and Catherine
in *Germinal*, but is bizarre in context here. The degree of
recycling of materials that has been referred to in this paragraph
bears witness to the fact that Zola is beginning to reach a

creative impasse; the problem is admittedly less serious when, in the concluding *Three Cities* novel, he returns to the familiar ground of Paris, but will return with a vengeance in the dull and formulaically repetitive *Four Gospels*, in accordance with the truism that good literature is rarely born of worthy sentiments.

The translator, Ernest Alfred Vizetelly, may have had rather more knowledge of the Italian national character than, in spite of his descent, did Zola. Brother Edward had been a war correspondent and knew Garibaldi, who appears in the fervently nationalistic reminiscences of Pierre Froment's truest friend in Rome, Orlando Prada. An uncle, Frank Vizetelly, 'whose bones lie bleaching somewhere in the Soudan', was war artist for the *Illustrated London News* and constant companion of the Italian general during his campaigns.

GEOFF WOOLLEN

ROME

I

THE train had been greatly delayed during the night between Pisa and Civita Vecchia, and it was close upon nine o'clock in the morning when, after a fatiguing journey of twenty-five hours' duration, Abbé Pierre Froment at last reached Rome. He had brought only a valise with him, and, springing hastily out of the railway carriage amidst the scramble of the arrival, he brushed the eager porters aside, intent on carrying his trifling luggage himself, so anxious was he to reach his destination, to be alone, and look around him. And almost immediately, on the Piazza dei Cinquecento, in front of the railway station, he climbed into one of the small open cabs ranged alongside the footwalk, and placed the valise near him after giving the driver this address :

'Via Giulia, Palazzo Boccanera.'[1]

It was a Monday, the 3rd of September,- a beautifully bright and mild morning, with a clear sky overhead. The cabby, a plump little man with sparkling eyes and white teeth, smiled on realising by Pierre's accent that he had to deal with a French priest. Then he whipped up his lean horse, and the vehicle started off at the rapid pace customary to the clean and cheerful cabs of Rome. However, on reaching the Piazza delle Terme, after skirting the greenery of a little public garden, the man turned round, still smiling, and, pointing to some ruins with his whip,

'The baths of Diocletian,' said he in broken French, like an obliging driver who is anxious to court favour with foreigners in order to secure their custom.

[1] Boccanera mansion, Julia Street.

Then, at a fast trot, the vehicle descended the rapid slope of the Via Nazionale, which dips down from the summit of the Viminalis,[1] where the railway station is situated. And from that moment the driver scarcely ceased turning round and pointing at the monuments with his whip. In this broad new thoroughfare there were only buildings of recent erection. Still, the wave of the cabman's whip became more pronounced and his voice rose to a higher key, with a somewhat ironical inflection, when he gave the name of a huge and still chalky pile on his left, a gigantic erection of stone, overladen with sculptured work—pediments and statues.

'The National Bank!' he said.

Pierre, however, during the week which had followed his resolve to make the journey, had spent wellnigh every day in studying Roman topography in maps and books. Thus he could have directed his steps to any given spot without inquiring his way, and he anticipated most of the driver's explanations. At the same time he was disconcerted by the sudden slopes, the perpetually recurring hills, on which certain districts rose, house above house, in terrace fashion. On his right-hand clumps of greenery were now climbing a height, and above them stretched a long bare yellow building of barrack or convent-like aspect.

'The Quirinal, the King's palace,' said the driver.

Lower down, as the cab turned across a triangular square, Pierre, on raising his eyes, was delighted to perceive a sort of aërial garden high above him—a garden which was upheld by a lofty smooth wall, and whence the elegant and vigorous silhouette of a parasol pine, many centuries old, rose aloft into the limpid heavens. At this sight he realised all the pride and grace of Rome.

'The Villa Aldobrandini,' the cabman called.

Then, yet lower down, there came a fleeting vision which decisively impassioned Pierre. The street again made a sudden bend, and in one corner, beyond a short dim alley, there was a blazing gap of light. On a lower level appeared a white square, a well of sunshine, filled with a blinding golden dust; and amidst all that morning glory there arose a gigantic marble column, gilt from base to summit on the side which the sun in rising had laved with its beams for wellnigh eighteen

[1] One of the seven hills on which Rome is built. The other six are the Capitoline, Aventine, Quirinal, Esquiline, Cœlian, and Palatine. These names will perforce frequently occur in the present narrative.

hundred years. And Pierre was surprised when the cabman
told him the name of the column, for in his mind he had
never pictured it soaring aloft in such a dazzling cavity with
shadows all around. It was the column of Trajan.

The Via Nazionale turned for the last time at the foot of
the slope. And then other names fell hastily from the driver's
lips as his horse went on at a fast trot. There was the Palazzo
Colonna, with its garden edged by meagre cypresses; the
Palazzo Torlonia almost ripped open by recent 'improvements'; the Palazzo di Venezia, bare and fearsome, with its
crenelated walls, its stern and tragic appearance, that of some
fortress of the middle ages, forgotten there amidst the commonplace life of nowadays. Pierre's surprise increased at the
unexpected aspect which certain buildings and streets presented; and the keenest blow of all was dealt him when the
cabman with his whip triumphantly called his attention to
the Corso, a long narrow thoroughfare, about as broad as Fleet
Street,[1] white with sunshine on the left, and black with shadows on the right, whilst at the far end the Piazza del Popolo
(the Square of the People) showed like a bright star. Was
this, then, the heart of the city, the vaunted promenade, the
street brimful of life, whither flowed all the blood of Rome?

However, the cab was already entering the Corso Vittorio
Emanuele, which follows the Via Nazionale, these being the
two piercings effected right across the olden city from the
railway station to the bridge of St'. Angelo. On the left-hand
the rounded apsis of the Gesù church looked quite golden in
the morning brightness. Then, between the church and the
heavy Altieri palace which the 'improvers' had not dared to
demolish, the street became narrower, and one entered into
cold, damp shade. But a moment afterwards, before the façade
of the Gesù, when the square was reached, the sun again appeared, dazzling, throwing golden sheets of light around;
whilst afar off at the end of the Via di Ara Cœli, steeped
in shadow, a glimpse could be caught of some sunlit palm-
trees.

'That's the Capitol yonder,' said the cabman.

The priest hastily leant to the left, but only espied the
patch of greenery at the end of the dim corridor-like street.
The sudden alternations of warm light and cold shade made

[1] M. Zola likens the Corso to the Rue St. Honoré in Paris, but I have
thought that an English comparison would be preferable in the present
version.—*Trans.*

him shiver. In front of the Palazzo di Venezia, and in front
of the Gesù, it had seemed to him as if all the night of
ancient times were falling icily upon his shoulders; but at
each fresh square, each broadening of the new thoroughfares,
there came a return to light, to the pleasant warmth and
gaiety of life. The yellow sunflashes, in falling from the
house fronts, sharply outlined the violescent shadows. Strips
of sky, very blue and very benign, could be perceived between
the roofs. And it seemed to Pierre that the air he breathed
had a particular savour, which he could not yet quite define,
but it was like that of fruit, and increased the feverishness
which had possessed him ever since his arrival.

The Corso Vittorio Emanuele is, in spite of its irregu-
larity, a very fine modern thoroughfare; and for a time Pierre
might have fancied himself in any great city full of huge
houses let out in flats. But when he passed before the
Cancelleria,[1] Bramante's masterpiece, the typical monument
of the Roman Renascence, his astonishment came back to
him and his mind returned to the mansions which he had
previously espied, those bare, huge, heavy edifices, those vast
cubes of stonework resembling hospitals or prisons. Never
would he have imagined that the famous Roman 'palaces'
were like that, destitute of all grace and fancy and external
magnificence. However, they were considered very fine and
must be so; he would doubtless end by understanding things,
but for that he would require reflection.[2]

All at once the cab turned out of the populous Corso
Vittorio Emanuele into a succession of winding alleys,
through which it had difficulty in making its way. Quietude
and solitude now came back again; the olden city, cold and
somniferous, followed the new city with its bright sunshine
and its crowds. Pierre remembered the maps which he had
consulted, and realised that he was drawing near to the Via
Giulia, and thereupon his curiosity, which had been steadily
increasing, augmented to such a point that he suffered from
it, full of despair at not seeing more and learning more at
once. In the feverish state in which he had found himself
ever since leaving the station, his astonishment at not finding
things such as he had expected, the many shocks that his
imagination had received, aggravated his passion beyond

[1] Formerly the residence of the Papal Vice-Chancellors.
[2] It is as well to point out at once that a palazzo is not a palace
as we understand the term, but rather a mansion.—*Trans.*

endurance, and brought him an acute desire to satisfy himself immediately. Nine o'clock had struck but a few minutes previously, he had the whole morning before him to repair to the Boccanera palace, so why should he not at once drive to the classic spot, the summit whence one perceives the whole of Rome spread out upon her seven hills? And when once this thought had entered into his mind it tortured him until he was at last compelled to yield to it.

The driver no longer turned his head, so that Pierre rose up to give him this new address: 'To San Pietro in Montorio!'

On hearing him the man at first looked astonished, unable to understand. He indicated with his whip that San Pietro was yonder, far away. However, as the priest insisted, he again smiled complacently, with a friendly nod of his head. All right! For his own part he was quite willing.

The horse then went on at a more rapid pace through the maze of narrow streets. One of these was pent between high walls, and the daylight descended into it as into a deep trench. But at the end came a sudden return to light, and the Tiber was crossed by the antique bridge of Sextus IV, right and left of which stretched the new quays, amidst the ravages and fresh plaster work of recent erections. On the other side of the river the Trastevere district also was ripped open, and the vehicle ascended the slope of the Janiculum by a broad thoroughfare where large slabs bore the name of Garibaldi. For the last time the driver made a gesture of good-natured pride as he named this triumphal route.

'Via Garibaldi!'

The horse had been obliged to slacken its pace, and Pierre, mastered by childish impatience, turned round to look at the city as by degrees it spread out and revealed itself behind him. The ascent was a long one; fresh districts were ever rising up, even to the most distant hills. Then, in the increasing emotion which made his heart beat, the young priest felt that he was spoiling the contentment of his desire by thus gradually satisfying it, slowly and but partially effecting his conquest of the horizon. He wished to receive the shock full in the face, to behold all Rome at one glance, to gather the holy city together, and embrace the whole of it at one grasp. And thereupon he mustered sufficient strength of mind to refrain from turning round any more, in spite of the impulses of his whole being.

There is a spacious terrace on the summit of the incline. The church of San Pietro in Montorio stands there, on the spot where, as some say, St. Peter was crucified. The square is bare and brown, baked by the hot summer suns; but a little further away in the rear, the clear and noisy waters of the Acqua Paola fall bubbling from the three basins of a monumental fountain amidst sempiternal freshness. And alongside the terrace parapet, on the very crown of the Trastevere, there are always rows of tourists, slim Englishmen and square-built Germans, agape with traditional admiration, or consulting their guide-books in order to identify the monuments.

Pierre sprang lightly from the cab, leaving his valise on the seat, and making a sign to the driver, who went to join the row of waiting cabs, and remained philosophically seated on his box in the full sunlight, his head drooping like that of his horse, both resigning themselves to the customary long stoppage.

Meantime Pierre, erect against the parapet in his tight black cassock, and with his bare feverish hands nervously clenched, was gazing before him with all his eyes, with all his soul. Rome! Rome! the city of the Cæsars, the city of the Popes, the Eternal City which has twice conquered the world, the predestined city of the glowing dream in which he had indulged for months! At last it was before him, at last his eyes beheld it! During the previous days some rain-storms had abated the intense August heat, and on that lovely September morning the air had freshened under the pale blue of the spotless far-spreading heavens. And the Rome that Pierre beheld was a Rome steeped in mildness, a visionary Rome which seemed to evaporate in the clear sun-shine. A fine bluey haze, scarcely perceptible, as delicate as gauze, hovered over the roofs of the low-lying districts; whilst the vast Campagna, the distant hills, died away in a pale pink flush. At first Pierre distinguished nothing, sought no particular edifice or spot, but gave sight and soul alike to the whole of Rome, to the living colossus spread out below him, on a soil compounded of the dust of generations. Each century had renewed the city's glory as with the sap of immortal youth. And that which struck Pierre, that which made his heart leap within him, was that he found Rome such as he had desired to find her, fresh and youthful, with a volatile, almost incorporeal, gaiety of aspect, smiling as at the hope of a new life in the pure dawn of a lovely day.

And standing motionless before the sublime vista, with his hands still clenched and burning, Pierre in a few minutes again lived the last three years of his life. Ah! what a terrible year had the first been, spent in his little house at Neuilly, with doors and windows ever closed, burrowing there like some wounded animal suffering unto death. He had come back from Lourdes with his soul desolate, his heart bleeding, with nought but ashes within him. Silence and darkness fell upon the ruins of his love and his faith. Days and days went by, without a pulsation of his veins, without the faintest gleam arising to brighten the gloom of his abandonment. His life was a mechanical one; he awaited the necessary courage to resume the tenor of existence in the name of sovereign reason, which had imposed upon him the sacrifice of everything. Why was he not stronger, more resistant, why did he not quietly adapt his life to his new opinions? As he was unwilling to cast off his cassock, through fidelity to the love of one and disgust of backsliding, why did he not seek occupation in some science suited to a priest, such as astronomy or archæology? The truth was that something, doubtless his mother's spirit, wept within him, an infinite, distracted love which nothing had yet satisfied and which ever despaired of attaining contentment. Therein lay the perpetual suffering of his solitude: beneath the lofty dignity of reason regained, the wound still lingered, raw and bleeding.

One autumn evening, however, under a dismal rainy sky, chance brought him into relations with an old priest, Abbé Rose, who was curate at the church of Ste. Marguerite, in the Faubourg St. Antoine. He went to see Abbé Rose in the Rue de Charonne, where in the depths of a damp ground floor he had transformed three rooms into an asylum for abandoned children, whom he picked up in the neighbouring streets. And from that moment Pierre's life changed, a fresh and all-powerful source of interest had entered into it, and by degrees he became the old priest's passionate helper. It was a long way from Neuilly to the Rue de Charonne, and at first he only made the journey twice a week. But afterwards he bestirred himself every day, leaving home in the morning and not returning until night. As the three rooms no longer sufficed for the asylum, he rented the first floor of the house, reserving for himself a chamber in which ultimately he often slept. And all his modest income was expended there, in the prompt succouring of poor children; and the old priest, delighted,

touched to tears by the young devoted help which had come
to him from heaven, would often embrace Pierre, weeping,
and call him a child of God.

It was then that Pierre knew want and wretchedness—
wicked, abominable wretchedness ; then that he lived amidst
it for two long years. The acquaintance began with the poor
little beings whom he picked up on the pavements, or whom
kind-hearted neighbours brought to him now that the asylum
was known in the district—little boys, little girls, tiny mites
stranded on the streets whilst their fathers and mothers were
toiling, drinking, or dying. The father had often disappeared,
the mother had gone wrong, drunkenness and debauchery had
followed slack times into the home ; and then the brood was
swept into the gutter, and the younger ones half perished of
cold and hunger on the footways whilst their elders betook
themselves to courses of vice and crime. One evening Pierre
rescued from the wheels of a stone-dray two little nippers,
brothers, who could not even give him an address, tell him
whence they had come. On another evening he returned to
the asylum with a little girl in his arms, a fair-haired little
angel, barely three years old, whom he had found on a bench,
and who sobbed, saying that her mother had left her there.
And by a logical chain of circumstances, after dealing with
the fleshless, pitiful fledgelings ousted from their nests, he came
to deal with the parents, to enter their hovels, penetrating
each day further and further into a hellish sphere, and ultimately acquiring knowledge of all its frightful horror, his
heart meantime bleeding, rent by terrified anguish and impotent charity.

Oh ! the grievous City of Misery, the bottomless abyss of
human suffering and degradation—how frightful were his
journeys through it during those two years which distracted
his whole being ! In that Ste. Marguerite district of Paris, in
the very heart of that Faubourg St. Antoine, so active and so
brave for work, however hard, he discovered no end of sordid
dwellings, whole lanes and alleys of hovels without light or air,
cellar-like in their dampness, and where a multitude of
wretches wallowed and suffered as from poison. All the way
up the shaky staircases one's feet slipped upon filth. On
every story there was the same destitution, dirt, and promiscuity. Many windows were paneless, and in swept the wind
howling, and the rain pouring torrentially. Many of the inmates slept on the bare tiled floors, never unclothing them-

selves. There was neither furniture nor linen, the life led
there was essentially an animal life, a commingling of either
sex and of every age—humanity lapsing into animality through
lack of even indispensable things, through indigence of so
complete a character that men, women, and children fought
even with tooth and nail for the very crumbs swept from the
tables of the rich. And the worst of it all was the degradation of the human being; this was no case of the free naked
savage, hunting and devouring his prey in the primeval forests;
here civilised man was found, sunk into brutishness, with all
the stigmas of his fall, debased, disfigured, and enfeebled,
amidst the luxury and refinement of that city of Paris which
is one of the queens of the world.

In every household Pierre heard the same story. There
had been youth and gaiety at the outset, brave acceptance of
the law that one must work. Then weariness had come; what
was the use of always toiling if one were never to get rich?
And so, by way of snatching a share of happiness, the husband
turned to drink; the wife neglected her home, also drinking
at times, and letting the children grow up as they might.
Sordid surroundings, ignorance, and overcrowding did the rest.
In the great majority of cases, prolonged lack of work was
mostly to blame; for this not only empties the drawers of the
savings hidden away in them, but exhausts human courage,
and tends to confirmed habits of idleness. During long weeks
the workshops empty, and the arms of the toilers lose strength.
In all Paris, so feverishly inclined to action, it is impossible to
find the slightest thing to do. And then the husband comes
home in the evening with tearful eyes, having vainly offered
his arms everywhere, having failed even to get a job at street-
sweeping, for that employment is much sought after, and to
secure it one needs influence and protectors. Is it not monstrous to see a man seeking work that he may eat, and finding
no work and therefore no food in this great city resplendent
and resonant with wealth? The wife does not eat, the children do not eat. And then comes black famine, brutishness,
and finally revolt and the snapping of all social ties under the
frightful injustice meted out to poor beings who by their weakness are condemned to death. And the old workman, he whose
limbs have been worn out by half a century of hard toil, without possibility of saving a copper, on what pallet of agony, in
what dark hole must he not sink to die? Should he then be
finished off with a mallet, like a crippled beast of burden, on

the day when ceasing to work he also ceases to eat ? Almost
all pass away in the hospitals, others disappear, unknown,
swept off by the muddy flow of the streets. One morning, on
some rotten straw in a loathsome hovel, Pierre found a poor
devil who had died of hunger and had been forgotten there for
a week. The rats had devoured his face.

But it was particularly on an evening of the last winter
that Pierre's heart had overflowed with pity. Awful in winter
time are the sufferings of the poor in their fireless hovels,
where the snow penetrates by every chink. The Seine rolls
blocks of ice, the soil is frost-bound, in all sorts of callings
there is an enforced cessation of work. Bands of urchins,
barefooted, scarcely clad, hungry and racked by coughing,
wander about the ragpickers' 'rents' and are carried off by sudden hurricanes of consumption. Pierre found families, women
with five and six children, who had not eaten for three days,
and who huddled together in heaps to try to keep themselves
warm. And on that terrible evening, before anybody else, he
went down a dark passage and entered a room of terror, where
he found that a mother had just committed suicide with her
five little ones—driven to it by despair and hunger—a tragedy
of misery which for a few hours would make all Paris shudder !
There was not an article of furniture or linen left in the place ;
it had been necessary to sell everything bit by bit to a neighbouring dealer. There was nothing but the stove where the
charcoal was still smoking and a half-emptied palliasse on
which the mother had fallen, suckling her last-born, a babe
but three months old. And a drop of blood had trickled from
the nipple of her breast, towards which the dead infant still
protruded its eager lips. Two little girls, three and five years
old, two pretty little blondes, were also lying there, sleeping
the eternal sleep side by side ; whilst of the two boys, who
were older, one had succumbed crouching against the wall with
his head between his hands, and the other had passed through
the last throes on the floor, struggling as though he had sought
to crawl on his knees to the window in order to open it. Some
neighbours, hurrying in, told Pierre the fearful, commonplace
story : slow ruin, the father unable to find work, perchance
taking to drink, the landlord weary of waiting, threatening the
family with expulsion, and the mother losing her head, thirsting for death and prevailing on her little ones to die with her,
while her husband, who had been out since the morning, was
vainly scouring the streets. Just as the Commissary of Police

arrived to verify what had happened, the poor devil returned, and when he had seen and understood things, he fell to the ground like a stunned ox, and raised a prolonged, plaintive howl, such a poignant cry of death that the whole terrified street wept at it.

Both in his ears and in his heart Pierre carried away with him that horrible cry, the plaint of a condemned race expiring amidst abandonment and hunger; and that night he could neither eat nor sleep. Was it possible that such abomination, such absolute destitution, such black misery leading straight to death should exist in the heart of that great city of Paris, brimful of wealth, intoxicated with enjoyment, flinging millions out of the windows for mere pleasure? What! there should on one side be such colossal fortunes, so many foolish fancies gratified, with lives endowed with every happiness, whilst on the other was found inveterate poverty, lack even of bread, absence of every hope, and mothers killing themselves with their babes, to whom they had nought to offer but the blood of their milkless breasts! And a feeling of revolt stirred Pierre; he was for a moment conscious of the derisive futility of charity. What indeed was the use of doing that which he did—picking up the little ones, succouring the parents, prolonging the sufferings of the aged? The very foundations of the social edifice were rotten; all would soon collapse amid mire and blood. A great act of justice alone could sweep the old world away in order that the new world might be built. And at that moment he realised so keenly how irreparable was the breach, how irremediable the evil, how deathly the cancer of misery, that he understood the actions of the violent, and was himself ready to accept the devastating and purifying whirlwind, the regeneration of the world by flame and steel, even as when in the dim ages Jehovah in His wrath sent fire from heaven to cleanse the accursed cities of the plains.

However, on hearing him sob that evening, Abbé Rose came up to remonstrate in fatherly fashion. The old priest was a saint, endowed with infinite gentleness and infinite hope. Why despair indeed when one had the Gospel? Did not the divine commandment, ' Love one another,' suffice for the salvation of the world? He, Abbé Rose, held violence in horror and was wont to say that, however great the evil, it would soon be overcome if humanity would but turn backward to the age of humility, simplicity, and purity, when Christians lived together in innocent brotherhood. What a delightful picture

he drew of evangelical society, of whose second coming he spoke
with quiet gaiety as though it were to take place on the very
morrow! And Pierre, anxious to escape from his frightful
recollections, ended by smiling, by taking pleasure in Abbé
Rose's bright consoling tale. They chatted until a late hour,
and on the following days reverted to the same subject of conversation, one which the old priest was very fond of, ever
supplying new particulars, and speaking of the approaching
reign of love and justice with the touching confidence of a good
if simple man, who is convinced that he will not die till he
shall have seen the Deity descend upon earth.

And now a fresh evolution took place in Pierre's mind.
The practice of benevolence in that poor district had developed
infinite compassion in his breast, his heart failed him, distracted,
rent by contemplation of the misery which he despaired of
healing. And in this awakening of his feelings he often thought
that his reason was giving way, he seemed to be retracing his
steps towards childhood, to that need of universal love which
his mother had implanted in him, and dreamt of chimerical
solutions, awaiting help from the unknown powers. Then his
fears, his hatred of the brutality of facts at last brought him
an increasing desire to work salvation by love. No time should
be lost in seeking to avert the frightful catastrophe which
seemed inevitable, the fratricidal war of classes which would
sweep the old world away beneath the accumulation of its
crimes. Convinced that injustice had attained its apogee, that
but little time remained before the vengeful hour when the
poor would compel the rich to part with their possessions, he
took pleasure in dreaming of a peaceful solution, a kiss of peace
exchanged by all men, a return to the pure morals of the Gospel
as it had been preached by Jesus.

Doubts tortured him at the outset. Could olden Catholicism
be rejuvenated, brought back to the youth and candour of
primitive Christianity? He set himself to study things, reading
and questioning, and taking a more and more passionate interest
in that great problem of Catholic socialism which had made
no little noise for some years past. And quivering with pity
for the wretched, ready as he was for the miracle of fraternisa-
tion, he gradually lost such scruples as intelligence might have
prompted, and persuaded himself that once again Christ would
work the redemption of suffering humanity. At last a precise
idea took possession of him, a conviction that Catholicism
purified, brought back to its original state, would prove the one

pact, the supreme law that might save society by averting the sanguinary crisis which threatened it.

When he had quitted Lourdes two years previously, revolted by all its gross idolatry, his faith for ever dead, but his mind worried by the everlasting need of the divine which tortures human creatures, a cry had arisen within him from the deepest recesses of his being: ' A new religion! a new religion! ' And it was this new religion, or rather this revived religion which he now fancied he had discovered in his desire to work social salvation—ensuring human happiness by means of the only moral authority that was erect, the distant outcome of the most admirable implement ever devised for the government of nations.

During the period of slow development through which Pierre passed, two men, apart from Abbé Rose, exercised great influence on him. A benevolent action brought him into intercourse with Monseigneur Bergerot, a bishop whom the Pope had recently created a cardinal, in reward for a whole life of charity, and this in spite of the covert opposition of the papal *curia* which suspected the French prelate to be a man of open mind, governing his diocese in paternal fashion. Pierre became more impassioned by his intercourse with this apostle, this shepherd of souls, in whom he detected one of the good simple leaders that he desired for the future community. However, his apostolate was influenced even more decisively by meeting Viscount Philibert de la Choue at the gatherings of certain working-men's Catholic associations. A handsome man, with military manners, and a long noble-looking face, spoilt by a small and broken nose which seemed to presage the ultimate defeat of a badly balanced mind, the Viscount was one of the most active agitators of Catholic socialism in France. He was the possessor of vast estates, a vast fortune, though it was said that some unsuccessful agricultural enterprises had already reduced his wealth by nearly one half. In the department where his property was situated he had been at great pains to establish model farms, at which he had put his ideas on Christian socialism into practice, but success did not seem to follow him. However, it had all helped to secure his election as a deputy, and he spoke in the Chamber, unfolding the programme of his party in long and stirring speeches.

Unwearying in his ardour, he also led pilgrimages to Rome, presided over meetings, and delivered lectures, devoting himself particularly to the people, the conquest of whom, so he privately

remarked, could alone ensure the triumph of the Church. And
thus he exercised considerable influence over Pierre, who in him
admired qualities which himself did not possess—an organising
spirit and a militant if somewhat blundering will, entirely applied to the revival of Christian society in France. However,
though the young priest learnt a good deal by associating with
him, he nevertheless remained a sentimental dreamer, whose
imagination, disdainful of political requirements, straightway
winged its flight to the future abode of universal happiness ;
whereas the Viscount aspired to complete the downfall of the
liberal ideas of 1789 by utilising the disillusion and anger of
the democracy to work a return towards the past.

Pierre spent some delightful months. Never before had
neophyte lived so entirely for the happiness of others. He
was all love, consumed by the passion of his apostolate. The
sight of the poor wretches whom he visited, the men without
work, the women, the children without bread, filled him with
a keener and keener conviction that a new religion must arise
to put an end to all the injustice which otherwise would bring
the rebellious world to a violent death. And he was resolved
to employ all his strength in effecting and hastening the
intervention of the Divine, the resuscitation of primitive
Christianity. His Catholic faith remained dead ; he still had
no belief in dogmas, mysteries, and miracles ; but a hope
sufficed him, the hope that the Church might yet work good,
by connecting itself with the irresistible modern democratic
movement, so as to save the nations from the social catastrophe which impended. His soul had grown calm since he
had taken on himself the mission of replanting the Gospel in
the hearts of the hungry and growling people of the Faubourgs. He was now leading an active life, and suffered less
from the frightful void which he had brought back from
Lourdes ; and as he no longer questioned himself, the anguish
of uncertainty no longer tortured him. It was with the
serenity which attends the simple accomplishment of duty
that he continued to say his mass. He even finished by
thinking that the mystery which he thus celebrated—indeed,
that all the mysteries and all the dogmas were but symbols—
rites requisite for humanity in its childhood, which would be
got rid of later on, when enlarged, purified, and instructed
humanity should be able to support the brightness of naked
truth.

And in his zealous desire to be useful, his passion to pro-

claim his belief aloud, Pierre one morning found himself at
his table writing a book. This had come about quite naturally; the book proceeded from him like a heart-cry, without
any literary idea having crossed his mind. One night, whilst
he lay awake, its title suddenly flashed before his eyes in the
darkness: 'NEW ROME.' That expressed everything, for
must not the new redemption of the nations originate in
eternal and holy Rome? The only existing authority was
found there; rejuvenescence could only spring from the
sacred soil where the old Catholic oak had grown. He wrote
his book in a couple of months, having unconsciously prepared
himself for the work by his studies in contemporary socialism
during a year past. There was a bubbling flow in his brain
as in a poet's; it seemed to him sometimes as if he dreamt
those pages, as if an internal distant voice dictated them to
him.

When he read passages written on the previous day to
Viscount Philibert de la Choue, the latter often expressed
keen approval of them from a practical point of view, saying
that one must touch the people in order to lead them, and
that it would also be a good plan to compose pious and yet
amusing songs for singing in the workshops. As for Monseigneur Bergerot, without examining the book from the
dogmatic standpoint, he was deeply touched by the glowing
breath of charity which every page exhaled, and was even
guilty of the imprudence of writing an approving letter to the
author, which letter he authorised him to insert in his work
by way of preface. And yet now the Congregation of the
Index Expurgatorius was about to place this book, issued in
the previous June, under interdict; and it was to defend it
that the young priest had hastened to Rome, inflamed by
the desire to make his ideas prevail, and resolved to plead his
cause in person before the Holy Father, having, he was convinced of it, simply given expression to the pontiff's views.

Pierre had not stirred whilst thus living his three last
years afresh; he still stood erect before the parapet, before
Rome, which he had so often dreamt of and had so keenly
desired to see. There was a constant succession of arriving
and departing vehicles behind him; the slim Englishmen and
the heavy Germans passed away after bestowing on the classic
view the five minutes prescribed by their guide-books; whilst
the driver and the horse of Pierre's cab remained waiting complacently, each with his head drooping under the bright sun,

which was heating the valise on the seat of the vehicle. And
Pierre, in his black cassock, seemed to have grown slimmer
and elongated, very slight of build as he stood there motionless, absorbed in the sublime spectacle. He had lost flesh
after his journey to Lourdes, his features too had become less
pronounced. Since his mother's part in his nature had
regained ascendency, the broad, straight forehead, the intellectual air which he owed to his father seemed to have grown
less conspicuous, while his kind and somewhat large mouth,
and his delicate chin, bespeaking infinite affection, dominated,
revealing his soul, which also glowed in the kindly sparkle of
his eyes.

Ah ! how tender and glowing were the eyes with which he
gazed upon the Rome of his book, the new Rome that he had
dreamt of ! If, first of all, the *ensemble* had claimed his
attention in the soft and somewhat veiled light of that lovely
morning, at present he could distinguish details, and let his
glance rest upon particular edifices. And it was with childish
delight that he identified them, having long studied them in
maps and collections of photographs. Beneath his feet, at
the bottom of the Janiculum, stretched the Trastevere district
with its chaos of old ruddy houses, whose sunburnt tiles hid
the course of the Tiber. He was somewhat surprised by the
flattish aspect of everything as seen from the terraced summit.
It was as though this bird's-eye view levelled the city, the
famous hills merely showing like bosses, swellings scarcely
perceptible amidst the spreading sea of house fronts. Yonder,
on the right, distinct against the distant blue of the Alban
mountains, was certainly the Aventine with its three churches
half-hidden by foliage; there, too, was the discrowned Palatine, edged as with black fringe by a line of cypresses. In the
rear, the Cœlian hill faded away, showing only the trees of
the Villa Mattei paling in the golden sunshine. The slender
spire and two little domes of Sta. Maria Maggiore alone indicated the summit of the Esquiline, right in front and far
away at the other end of the city; whilst on the heights of
the neighbouring Viminal Pierre only perceived a confused
mass of whitish blocks, steeped in light and streaked with fine
brown lines—recent erections, no doubt, which at that distance
suggested an abandoned stone quarry. He long sought the
Capitol without being able to discover it ; he had to take his
bearings, and ended by convincing himself that the square
tower, modestly lost among surrounding house-roofs, which

he saw in front of Sta. Maria Maggiore was its campanile. Next, on the left, came the Quirinal, recognisable by the long façade of the royal palace, a barrack or hospital-like façade, flat, crudely yellow in hue, and pierced by an infinite number of regularly disposed windows. However, as Pierre was completing the circuit, a sudden vision made him stop short. Without the city, above the trees of the Botanical Garden, the dome of St. Peter's appeared to him. It seemed to be poised upon the greenery, and rose up into the pure blue sky, sky-blue itself and so ethereal that it mingled with the azure of the infinite. The stone lantern which surmounts it, white and dazzling, looked as though it were suspended on high.

Pierre did not weary, and his glances incessantly travelled from one end of the horizon to the other. They lingered on the noble outlines, the proud gracefulness of the town-sprinkled Sabine and Alban mountains, whose girdle limited the expanse. The Roman Campagna spread out in far stretches, bare and majestic, like a desert of death, with the glaucous green of a stagnant sea ; and he ended by distinguishing ' the stern round tower ' of the tomb of Cæcilia Metella, behind which a thin pale line indicated the ancient Appian Way. Remnants of aqueducts strewed the short herbage amidst the dust of the fallen worlds. And, bringing his glance nearer in, the city again appeared with its jumble of edifices, on which his eyes lighted at random. Close at hand, by its loggia turned towards the river, he recognised the huge tawny cube of the Palazzo Farnese. The low cupola, farther away and scarcely visible, was probably that of the Pantheon. Then by sudden leaps came the freshly whitened walls of San Paolo-fuori-le-Mura,[1] similar to those of some huge barn, and the statues crowning San Giovanni in Laterano, delicate, scarcely as big as insects. Next the swarming of domes, that of the Gesù, that of San Carlo, that of St'. Andrea della Valle, that of San Giovanni dei Fiorentini ; then a number of other sites and edifices, all quivering with memories, the castle of St'. Angelo with its glittering statue of the Destroying Angel, the Villa Medici dominating the entire city, the terrace of the Pincio with its marbles showing whitely among its scanty verdure ; and the thick foliaged trees of the Villa Borghese, whose green crests bounded the horizon. Vainly, however, did Pierre seek the Colosseum.

The north wind, which was blowing very mildly, had now

[1] St. Paul-beyond-the-walls.

begun to dissipate the morning haze. Whole districts
vigorously disentangled themselves, and showed against the
vaporous distance like promontories in a sunlit sea. Here
and there, in the indistinct swarming of houses, a strip of
white wall glittered, a row of window panes flared, or a garden
supplied a black splotch, of wondrous intensity of hue. And
all the rest, the medley of streets and squares, the endless
blocks of buildings, scattered about on either hand, mingled
and grew indistinct in the living glory of the sun, whilst long
coils of white smoke, which had ascended from the roofs,
slowly traversed the pure sky.

Guided by a secret influence, however, Pierre soon ceased
to take interest in all but three points of the mighty panorama. That line of slender cypresses which set a black
fringe on the height of the Palatine yonder filled him with
emotion: beyond it he only saw a void: the palaces of the
Cæsars had disappeared, had fallen, had been razed by time ;
and he evoked their memory, he fancied he could see them
rise like vague, trembling phantoms of gold amidst the purple
of that splendid morning. Then his glances reverted to St.
Peter's, and there the dome yet soared aloft, screening the
Vatican which he knew was beside the colossus, clinging to
its flanks. And that dome, of the same colour as the heavens,
appeared so triumphant, so full of strength, so vast, that it
seemed to him like a giant king, dominating the whole city
and seen from every spot throughout eternity. Then he fixed
his eyes on the height in front of him, on the Quirinal, and
there the King's palace no longer appeared aught but a flat
low barracks bedaubed with yellow paint.

And for him all the secular history of Rome, with its constant convulsions and successive resurrections, found embodi-
ment in that symbolical triangle, in those three summits
gazing at one another across the Tiber. Ancient Rome
blossoming forth in a piling up of palaces and temples, the
monstrous florescence of imperial power and splendour ; Papal
Rome, victorious in the middle ages, mistress of the world,
bringing that colossal church, symbolical of beauty regained,
to weigh upon all Christendom ; and the Rome of to-day,
which he knew nothing of, which he had neglected, and
whose royal palace, so bare and so cold, brought him disparaging
ideas—the idea of some out-of-place, bureaucratic effort, some
sacrilegious attempt at modernity in an exceptional city
which should have been left entirely to the dreams of the

future. However, he shook off the almost painful feelings
which the importunate present brought to him, and would not
let his eyes rest on a pale new district, quite a little town, in
course of erection, no doubt, which he could distinctly see near
St. Peter's on the margin of the river. He had dreamt of his
own new Rome, and still dreamt of it, even in front of the
Palatine whose edifices had crumbled in the dust of centuries,
of the dome of St. Peter's whose huge shadow lulled the
Vatican to sleep, of the Palace of the Quirinal repaired and
repainted, reigning in homely fashion over the new districts
which swarmed on every side, while with its ruddy roofs the
olden city, ripped up by improvements, coruscated beneath the
bright morning sun.

Again did the title of his book, 'NEW ROME,' flare before
Pierre's eyes, and another reverie carried him off; he lived his
book afresh even as he had just lived his life. He had
written it amid a flow of enthusiasm, utilising the *data* which
he had accumulated at random; and its division into three
parts, past, present, and future, had at once forced itself upon
him.

The PAST was the extraordinary story of primitive
Christianity, of the slow evolution which had turned this
Christianity into present-day Catholicism. He showed that
an economical question is invariably hidden beneath each
religious evolution, and that, upon the whole, the everlasting evil, the everlasting struggle, has never been aught
but one between the rich and the poor. Among the Jews,
when their nomadic life was over, and they had conquered
the land of Canaan, and ownership and property came into
being, a class warfare at once broke out. There were rich
and there were poor; thence arose the social question. The
transition had been sudden, and the new state of things so
rapidly went from bad to worse that the poor suffered keenly,
and protested with the greater violence as they still remembered the golden age of the nomadic life. Until the time of
Jesus the prophets are but rebels who surge from out the
misery of the people, proclaim its sufferings, and vent their
wrath upon the rich, to whom they prophesy every evil in
punishment for their injustice and their harshness. Jesus
Himself appears as the claimant of the rights of the poor.
The prophets, whether socialists or anarchists, had preached
social equality, and called for the destruction of the world if it
were unjust. Jesus likewise brings to the wretched hatred of

the rich. All His teaching threatens wealth and property ;
and if by the Kingdom of Heaven which He promised one
were to understand peace and fraternity upon this earth, there
would only be a question of returning to a life of pastoral
simplicity, to the dream of the Christian community, such as
after Him it would seem to have been realised by His disciples.
During the first three centuries each Church was an experiment in communism, a real association whose members
possessed all in common—wives excepted. This is shown to
us by the apologists and early fathers of the Church.
Christianity was then but the religion of the humble and the
poor, a form of democracy, of socialism struggling against
Roman society. And when the latter toppled over, rotted by
money, it succumbed far more beneath the results of frantic
speculation, swindling banks, and financial disasters, than
beneath the onslaught of barbarian hordes and the stealthy,
termite-like working of the Christians.

The money question will always be found at the bottom of
everything. And a new proof of this was supplied when
Christianity, at last triumphing by virtue of historical, social,
and human causes, was proclaimed a State religion. To
ensure itself complete victory it was forced to range itself on
the side of the rich and the powerful ; and one should see by
means of what artfulness and sophistry the fathers of the
Church succeeded in discovering a defence of property and
wealth in the Gospel of Jesus. All this, however, was a vital
political necessity for Christianity ; it was only at this price
that it became Catholicism, the universal religion. From that
time forth the powerful machine, the weapon of conquest and
rule, was reared aloft : up above were the powerful and the
wealthy, those whose duty it was to share with the poor, but
who did not do so ; while down below were the poor, the
toilers, who were taught resignation and obedience, and
promised the kingdom of futurity, the divine and eternal
reward—an admirable monument which has lasted for ages,
and which is entirely based on the promise of life beyond life,
on the inextinguishable thirst for immortality and justice that
consumes mankind.

Pierre had completed this first part of his book, this history
of the past, by a broad sketch of Catholicism until the present
time. First appeared St. Peter, ignorant and anxious, coming
to Rome by an inspiration of genius, there to fulfil the ancient
oracles which had predicted the eternity of the Capitol. Then

came the first popes, mere heads of burial associations, the slow rise of the all-powerful papacy ever struggling to conquer the world, unremittingly seeking to realise its dream of universal domination. At the time of the great popes of the middle ages it thought for a moment that it had attained its goal, that it was the sovereign master of the nations. Would not absolute truth and right consist in the pope being both pontiff and ruler of the world, reigning over both the souls and the bodies of all men, even like the Deity whose vicar he is? This, the highest and mightiest of all ambitions, one, too, that is perfectly logical, was attained by Augustus, emperor and pontiff, master of all the known world; and it is the glorious figure of Augustus, ever rising anew from among the ruins of ancient Rome, which has always haunted the popes; it is his blood which has pulsated in their veins.

But power had become divided into two parts amidst the crumbling of the Roman empire; it was necessary to content oneself with a share, and leave temporal government to the emperor, retaining over him, however, the right of coronation by divine grant. The people belonged to God, and in God's name the pope gave the people to the emperor, and could take it from him; an unlimited power whose most terrible weapon was excommunication, a superior sovereignty, which carried the papacy towards real and final possession of the empire. Looking at things broadly, the everlasting quarrel between the pope and the emperor was a quarrel for the people, the inert mass of humble and suffering ones, the great silent multitude whose irremediable wretchedness was only revealed by occasional covert growls. It was disposed of, for its good, as one might dispose of a child. Yet the Church really contributed to civilisation, rendered constant services to humanity, diffused abundant alms. In the convents, at any rate, the old dream of the Christian community was ever coming back: one-third of the wealth accumulated for the purposes of worship, the adornment and glorification of the shrine, one-third for the priests, and one-third for the poor. Was not this a simplification of life, a means of rendering existence possible to the faithful who had no earthly desires, pending the marvellous contentment of heavenly life? Give us, then, the whole earth, and we will divide terrestrial wealth into three such parts, and you shall see what a golden age will reign amidst the resignation and the obedience of all!

However, Pierre went on to show how the papacy was

assailed by the greatest dangers on emerging from its all-powerfulness of the middle ages. It was almost swept away amidst the luxury and excesses of the Renascence, the bubbling of living sap which then gushed from eternal nature, downtrodden and regarded as dead for ages past. More threatening still were the stealthy awakenings of the people, of the great silent multitude whose tongue seemed to be loosening. The Reformation burst forth like the protest of reason and justice, like a recall to the disregarded truths of the Gospel ; and to escape total annihilation Rome needed the stern defence of the Inquisition, the slow stubborn labour of the Council of Trent, which strengthened the dogmas and ensured the temporal power. And then the papacy entered into two centuries of peace and effacement, for the strong absolute monarchies which had divided Europe among themselves could do without it, and had ceased to tremble at the harmless thunderbolts of excommunication or to look on the pope as aught but a master of ceremonies, controlling certain rites. The possession of the people was no longer subject to the same rules. Allowing that the kings still held the people from God, it was the pope's duty to register the donation once for all, without ever intervening, whatever the circumstances, in the government of states. Never was Rome farther away from the realisation of its ancient dream of universal dominion. And when the French Revolution burst forth, it may well have been imagined that the proclamation of the rights of man would kill that papacy to which the exercise of divine right over the nations had been committed. And so how great at first was the anxiety, the anger, the desperate resistance with which the Vatican opposed the idea of freedom, the new *credo* of liberated reason, of humanity regaining self-possession and control. It was the apparent *dénouement* of the long struggle between the pope and the emperor for possession of the people : the emperor vanished, and the people, henceforward free to dispose of itself, claimed to escape from the pope—an unforeseen solution, in which it seemed as though all the ancient scaffolding of the Catholic world must fall to the very ground.

At this point Pierre concluded the first part of his book by contrasting primitive Christianity with present-day Catholicism, which is the triumph of the rich and the powerful. That Roman society which Jesus had come to destroy in the name of the poor and the humble, had not Catholic Rome steadily continued rebuilding it through all the centuries, by its policy of cupidity and pride? And what bitter irony it was to find, after eighteen hundred years of the Gospel, that the world was again collapsing through frantic speculation, rotten banks, financial disasters, and the frightful injustice of a few men gorged with wealth whilst thousands of their brothers were dying of hunger! The whole redemption of the wretched had to be worked afresh. However, Pierre gave expression to all these terrible things in words so softened by charity, so steeped in hope, that they lost their revolutionary danger. Moreover, he nowhere attacked the dogmas. His book, in its sentimental, somewhat poetic form, was but the cry of an apostle glowing with love for his fellow-men.

Then came the second part of the work, the PRESENT, a study of Catholic society as it now exists. Here Pierre had painted a frightful picture of the misery of the poor, the misery of a great city, which he knew so well and bled for, through having laid his hands upon its poisonous wounds. The present-day injustice could no longer be tolerated, charity was becoming powerless, and so frightful was the suffering that all hope was dying away from the hearts of the people. And was it not the monstrous spectacle presented by Christendom, whose abominations corrupted the people, and maddened it with hatred and vengeance, that had largely destroyed its faith? However, after this picture of rotting and crumbling society, Pierre returned to history, to the period of the French Revolution, to the mighty hope with which the idea of freedom had filled the world. The middle classes, the great Liberal party, on attaining power had undertaken to bring happiness to one and all. But after a century's experience it really seemed that liberty had failed to bring any happiness whatever to the outcasts. In the political sphere illusions were departing. At all events, if the reigning third estate declares itself satisfied, the fourth estate, that of the toilers,[1] still suffers and continues to demand its share of fortune. The working classes have been proclaimed free; political equality has been granted them, but the gift has been valueless, for economically they are still bound to servitude, and only enjoy, as they did formerly, the liberty of dying of hunger. All the socialist revendications have come from that; between

---

[1] In England we call the press the fourth estate, but in France and elsewhere the term is applied to the working classes, and in that sense must be taken here.—*Trans.*

labour and capital rests the terrifying problem, the solution of which threatens to sweep away society. When slavery disappeared from the olden world to be succeeded by salaried employment the revolution was immense, and certainly the Christian principle was one of the great factors in the destruction of slavery. Nowadays, therefore, when the question is to replace salaried employment by something else, possibly by the participation of the workman in the profits of his work, why should not Christianity again seek a new principle of action? The fatal and proximate accession of the democracy means the beginning of another phase in human history, the creation of the society of to-morrow. And Rome cannot keep away from the arena; the papacy must take part in the quarrel if it does not desire to disappear from the world like a piece of mechanism that has become altogether useless.

Hence it followed that Catholic socialism was legitimate. On every side the socialist sects were battling with their various solutions for the privilege of ensuring the happiness of the people, and the Church also must offer her solution of the problem. Here it was that New Rome appeared, that the evolution spread into a renewal of boundless hope. Most certainly there was nothing contrary to democracy in the principles of the Roman Catholic Church. Indeed she had only to return to the evangelical traditions, to become once more the Church of the humble and the poor, to re-establish the universal Christian community. She is undoubtedly of democratic essence, and if she sided with the rich and the powerful when Christianity became Catholicism, she only did so perforce, that she might live by sacrificing some portion of her original purity; so that if to-day she should abandon the condemned governing classes in order to make common cause with the multitude of the wretched, she would simply be drawing nearer to Christ, thereby securing a new lease of youth and purifying herself of all the political compromises which she formerly was compelled to accept. Without renouncing aught of her absolutism the Church has at all times known how to bow to circumstances; but she reserves her perfect sovereignty, simply tolerating that which she cannot prevent, and patiently waiting, even through long centuries, for the time when she shall again become the mistress of the world.

Might not that time come in the crisis which was now at hand? Once more, all the powers are battling for possession of the people. Since the people, thanks to liberty and education, has become strong, since it has developed consciousness and will, and claimed its share of fortune, all rulers have been seeking to attach it to themselves, to reign by it, and even with it, should that be necessary. Socialism, therein lies the future, the new instrument of government; and the kings tottering on their thrones, the middle-class presidents of anxious republics, the ambitious plotters who dream of power, all dabble in socialism! They all agree that the capitalist organisation of the State is a return to pagan times, to the olden slave-market; and they all talk of breaking for ever the iron law by which the labour of human beings has become so much merchandise, subject to supply and demand, with wages calculated on an estimate of what is strictly necessary to keep a workman from dying of hunger. And, down in the sphere below, the evil increases, the workmen agonise with hunger and exasperation, while above them discussion still goes on, systems are bandied about, and well-meaning persons exhaust themselves in attempting to apply ridiculously inadequate remedies. There is much stir without any progress, all the wild bewilderment which precedes great catastrophes. And among the many, Catholic socialism, quite as ardent as Revolutionary socialism, enters the lists and strives to conquer.

After these explanations Pierre gave an account of the long efforts made by Catholic socialism throughout the Christian world. That which particularly struck one in this connection was that the warfare became keener and more victorious whenever it was waged in some land of propaganda, as yet not completely conquered by Roman Catholicism. For instance, in the countries where Protestantism confronted the latter, the priests fought with wondrous passion, as for dear life itself, contending with the schismatical clergy for possession of the people by dint of daring, by unfolding the most audacious democratic theories. In Germany, the classic land of socialism, Mgr. Ketteler was one of the first to speak of adequately taxing the rich; and later he fomented a widespread agitation which the clergy now directs by means of numerous associations and newspapers. In Switzerland Mgr. Mermillod pleaded the cause of the poor so loudly that the bishops there now almost make common cause with the democratic socialists, whom they doubtless hope to convert when the day for sharing arrives. In England, where socialism penetrates so very slowly, Cardinal Manning achieved considerable success, stood by the working classes on the occasion of a famous strike, and helped on a popular movement, which was signalised by numerous conversions. But it was particularly in the United States of America that Catholic socialism proved triumphant, in a sphere of democracy where the bishops, like Mgr. Ireland, were forced to set themselves at the head of the working-class agitation. And there across the Atlantic a new Church seems to be germinating, still in confusion but overflowing with sap, and upheld by intense hope, as at the aurora of the rejuvenated Christianity of to-morrow.

Passing thence to Austria and Belgium, both Catholic countries, one found Catholic socialism mingling in the first instance with anti-semitism, while in the second it had no precise sense. And all movement ceased and disappeared when one came to Spain and Italy, those old lands of faith. The former with its intractable bishops who contented themselves with hurling excommunication at unbelievers as in the days of the Inquisition, seemed to be abandoned to the violent theories of revolutionaries, whilst Italy, immobilised in the traditional courses, remained without possibility of initiative, reduced to silence and respect by the presence of the Holy See. In France, however, the struggle remained keen, but it was more particularly a struggle of ideas. On the whole, the war was there being waged against the revolution, and to some it seemed as though it would suffice to re-establish the old organisation of monarchical times in order to revert to the golden age. It was thus that the question of working-class corporations had become the one problem, the panacea for all the ills of the toilers. But people were far from agreeing; some, those Catholics who rejected State interference and favoured purely moral action, desired that the corporations should be free; whilst others, the young and impatient ones, bent on action, demanded that they should be obligatory, each with capital of its own, and recognised and protected by the State.

Viscount Philibert de la Choue had by pen and speech carried on a vigorous campaign in favour of the obligatory corporations; and his great grief was that he had so far failed to prevail on the Pope to say whether in his opinion these corporations should be closed or open. According to the Viscount, herein lay the fate of society, a peaceful solution of the social question or the frightful catastrophe which must sweep everything away. In reality, though he refused to own it, the Viscount had ended by adopting State socialism. And, despite the lack of agreement, the agitation remained very great; attempts, scarcely happy in their results, were made; co-operative associations, companies for erecting workmen's dwellings, popular savings' banks were started; many more or less disguised efforts to revert to the old Christian community organisation were tried; while day by day, amidst the prevailing confusion, in the mental perturbation and political difficulties through which the country passed, the militant Catholic party felt its hopes increasing, even to the blind conviction of soon resuming sway over the whole world.

The second part of Pierre's book concluded by a picture of the moral and intellectual uneasiness amidst which the end of the century is struggling. While the toiling multitude suffers from its hard lot and demands that in any fresh division of wealth it shall be ensured at least its daily bread, the *élite* is no better satisfied, but complains of the void induced by the freeing of its reason and the enlargement of its intelligence. It is the famous bankruptcy of rationalism, of positivism, of science itself which is in question. Minds consumed by need of the absolute grow weary of groping, weary of the delays of science which recognises only proven truths; doubt tortures them, they need a complete and immediate synthesis in order to sleep in peace; and they fall on their knees, overcome by the roadside, distracted by the thought that science will never tell them all, and preferring the Deity, the mystery revealed and affirmed by faith. Even to-day, it must be admitted, science calms neither our thirst for justice, our desire for safety, nor our everlasting idea of happiness after life in an eternity of enjoyment. To one and all it only brings the austere duty to live, to be a mere contributor in the universal toil; and how well one can understand that hearts should revolt and sigh for the Christian heaven, peopled with lovely angels, full of light and music and perfumes! Ah! to embrace one's dead, to tell oneself that one will meet them again, that one will live with them once more in glorious immortality! And to possess the certainty of sovereign equity to enable one to support the abominations of terrestrial life! And in this wise to trample on the frightful thought of annihilation, to escape the horror of the disappearance of the *ego*, and to tranquillise oneself with that unshakable faith which postpones until the portal

of death be crossed the solution of all the problems of destiny !
This dream will be dreamt by the nations for ages yet. And
this it is which explains why, in these last days of the
century, excessive mental labour and the deep unrest of
humanity, pregnant with a new world, have awakened
religious feeling, anxious, tormented by thoughts of the ideal
and the infinite, demanding a moral law and an assurance of
superior justice. Religions may disappear, but religious
feelings will always create new ones, even with the help of
science. A new religion! a new religion! Was it not the
ancient Catholicism, which in the soil of the present day,
where all seemed conducive to a miracle, was about to spring
up afresh, throw out green branches and blossom in a young
yet mighty florescence ?

At last, in the third part of his book and in the glowing
language of an apostle, Pierre depicted the Future : Catholicism rejuvenated, and bringing health and peace, the
forgotten golden age of primitive Christianity, back to expiring society. He began with an emotional and sparkling
portrait of Leo XIII, the ideal Pope, the Man of Destiny
entrusted with the salvation of the nations. He had
conjured up a presentment of him and beheld him thus in
his feverish longing for the advent of a pastor who should
put an end to human misery. It was perhaps not a close
likeness, but it was a portrait of the needed saviour, with
open heart and mind, and inexhaustible benevolence, such as
he had dreamed. At the same time he had certainly
searched documents, studied encyclical letters, based his
sketch upon facts : first Leo's religious education at Rome,
then his brief nunciature at Brussels, and afterwards his long
episcopate at Perugia. And as soon as Leo became pope in
the difficult situation bequeathed by Pius IX, the duality of
his nature appeared : on one hand was the firm guardian of
dogmas, on the other the supple politician resolved to carry
conciliation to its utmost limits. We see him flatly severing
all connection with modern philosophy, stepping backward
beyond the Renascence to the middle ages and reviving
Christian philosophy, as expounded by 'the angelic doctor,'
St. Thomas Aquinas, in Catholic schools. Then the dogmas
being in this wise sheltered, he adroitly maintains himself in
equilibrium by giving securities to every power, striving to
utilise every opportunity. He displays extraordinary activity,
reconciles the Holy See with Germany, draws nearer to

Russia, contents Switzerland, seeks the friendship of Great Britain, and writes to the Emperor of China begging him to protect the missionaries and Christians in his dominions. Later on, too, he intervenes in France and acknowledges the legitimacy of the Republic.

From the very outset an idea becomes apparent in all his actions, an idea which will place him among the great papal politicians. It is moreover the ancient idea of the papacy— the conquest of every soul, Rome capital and mistress of the world. Thus Leo XIII has but one desire, one object, that of unifying the Church, of drawing all the dissident communities to it in order that it may be invincible in the coming social struggle. He seeks to obtain recognition of the moral authority of the Vatican in Russia; he dreams of disarming the Anglican Church and of drawing it into a sort of fraternal truce; and he particularly seeks to come to an understanding with the Schismatical Churches of the East, which he regards as sisters, simply living apart, whose return his paternal heart entreats. Would not Rome indeed dispose of victorious strength if she exercised uncontested sway over all the Christians of the earth?

And here the social ideas of Leo XIII come in. Whilst yet Bishop of Perugia he wrote a pastoral letter in which a vague humanitarian socialism appeared. As soon, however, as he had assumed the triple crown his opinions changed, and he anathematised the revolutionaries whose audacity was terrifying Italy. But almost at once he corrected himself, warned by events and realising the great danger of leaving socialism in the hands of the enemies of the Church. Then he listened to the bishops of the lands of propaganda, ceased to intervene in the Irish quarrel, withdrew the excommunications which he had launched against the American ' knights of labour,' and would not allow the bold works of Catholic socialist writers to be placed in the Index. This evolution towards democracy may be traced through his most famous encyclical letters : *Immortale Dei*, on the constitution of States; *Libertas*, on human liberty ; *Sapientiæ*, on the duties of Christian citizens ; *Rerum novarum*, on the condition of the working classes ; and it is particularly this last which would seem to have rejuvenated the Church. The Pope herein chronicles the undeserved misery of the toilers, the undue length of the hours of labour, the insufficiency of salaries. All men have the right to live, and all contracts extorted by threat of starvation are unjust.

Elsewhere he declares that the workman must not be left
defenceless in presence of a system which converts the misery
of the majority into the wealth of a few. Compelled to deal
vaguely with questions of organisation, he contents himself
with encouraging the corporative movement, placing it under
State patronage; and after thus contributing to restore the secular power, he reinstates the Deity on the throne of sovereignty,
and discerns the path to salvation more particularly in moral
measures, in the ancient respect due to family ties and ownership. Nevertheless, was not the helpful hand which the august
Vicar of Christ thus publicly tendered to the poor and the
humble, the certain token of a new alliance, the announcement
of a new reign of Jesus upon earth? Thenceforward the people
knew that it was not abandoned. And from that moment too
how glorious became Leo XIII, whose sacerdotal jubilee and
episcopal jubilee were celebrated by all Christendom amidst
the coming of a vast multitude, of endless offerings, and of
flattering letters from every sovereign!

Pierre next dealt with the question of the temporal power,
and this he thought he might treat freely. Naturally, he was
not ignorant of the fact that the Pope in his quarrel with
Italy upheld the rights of the Church over Rome as stubbornly
as his predecessor; but he imagined that this was merely a
necessary conventional attitude, imposed by political considerations, and destined to be abandoned when the times were
ripe. For his own part he was convinced that if the Pope
had never appeared greater than he did now, it was to the loss
of the temporal power that he owed it: for thence had come
the great increase of his authority, the pure splendour of moral
omnipotence which he diffused.

What a long history of blunders and conflicts had been
that of the possession of the little kingdom of Rome during
fifteen centuries! Constantine quits Rome in the fourth
century, only a few forgotten functionaries remaining on the
deserted Palatine, and the Pope naturally rises to power, and
the life of the city passes to the Lateran. However, it is only
four centuries later that Charlemagne recognises accomplished
facts and formally bestows the States of the Church upon the
papacy. From that time warfare between the spiritual power
and the temporal powers has never ceased; though often latent
it has at times become acute, breaking forth with blood and
fire. And to-day, in the midst of Europe in arms, is it not
unreasonable to dream of the papacy ruling a strip of terri-

tory where it would be exposed to every vexation, and where it could only maintain itself by the help of a foreign army? What would become of it in the general massacre which is apprehended? Is it not far more sheltered, far more dignified, far more lofty when disentangled from all terrestrial cares, reigning over the world of souls?

In the early times of the Church the papacy from being merely local, merely Roman, gradually became catholicised, universalised, slowly acquiring dominion over all Christendom. In the same way the Sacred College, at first a continuation of the Roman Senate, acquired an international character, and in our time has ended by becoming the most cosmopolitan of assemblies, in which representatives of all the nations have seats. And is it not evident that the Pope, thus leaning on the cardinals, has become the one great international power which exercises the greater authority since it is free from all monarchical interests, and can speak not merely in the name of country but in that of humanity itself? The solution so often sought amidst such long wars surely lies in this: Either give the Pope the temporal sovereignty of the world, or leave him only the spiritual sovereignty. Vicar of the Deity, absolute and infallible sovereign by divine delegation, he can but remain in the sanctuary if, ruler already of the human soul, he is not recognised by every nation as the one master of the body also—the king of kings.

But what a strange affair was this new incursion of the papacy into the field sown by the French Revolution, an incursion conducting it perhaps towards the domination, which it has striven for with a will that has upheld it for centuries! For now it stands alone before the people. The kings are down. And as the people is henceforth free to give itself to whomsoever it pleases, why should it not give itself to the Church? The depreciation which the idea of liberty has certainly undergone renders every hope permissible. The liberal party appears to be vanquished in the sphere of economics. The toilers, dissatisfied with 1789, complain of the aggravation of their misery, bestir themselves, seek happiness despairingly. On the other hand the new *régimes* have increased the international power of the Church; Catholic members are numerous in the parliaments of the republics and the constitutional monarchies. All circumstances seem therefore to favour this extraordinary return of fortune, Catholicism reverting to the vigour of youth in its old age. Even

science, remember, is accused of bankruptcy, a charge which
saves the *Syllabus* from ridicule, troubles the minds of men,
and throws the limitless sphere of mystery and impossibility
open once more. And then a prophecy is recalled, a prediction that the papacy shall be mistress of the world on the day
when she marches at the head of the democracy after reuniting
the Schismatical Churches of the East to the Catholic, Apostolic, and Roman Church. And, in Pierre's opinion, assuredly
the times had come since Pope Leo XIII, dismissing the great
and the wealthy of the world, left the kings driven from their
thrones in exile to place himself like Jesus on the side of the food-
less toilers and the beggars of the high roads. Yet a few more
years, perhaps, of frightful misery, alarming confusion, fearful
social danger, and the people, the great silent multitude which
others have so far disposed of, will return to the cradle, to the
unified Church of Rome, in order to escape the destruction
which threatens human society.

Pierre concluded his book with a passionate evocation of
New Rome, the spiritual Rome which would soon reign over
the nations, reconciled and fraternising as in another golden
age. Herein he even saw the end of superstitions. Without
making a direct attack on dogma, he allowed himself to dream
of an enlargement of religious feeling, freed from rites, and
absorbed in the one satisfaction of human charity. And still
smarting from his journey to Lourdes, he felt the need of
contenting his heart. Was not that gross superstition of
Lourdes the hateful symptom of the excessive suffering of the
times? On the day when the Gospel should be universally
diffused and practised, suffering ones would cease seeking an
illusory relief so far away, assured as they would be of finding
assistance, consolation, and cure in their homes amidst their
brothers. At Lourdes there was an iniquitous displacement
of wealth, a spectacle so frightful as to make one doubt of
God, a perpetual conflict which would disappear in the truly
Christian society of to-morrow. Ah ! that society, that Christian community, all Pierre's work ended in an ardent longing
for its speedy advent : Christianity becoming once more the
religion of truth and justice which it had been before it allowed itself to be conquered by the rich and the powerful !
The little ones and the poor ones reigning, sharing the wealth
of earth, and owing obedience to nought but the levelling law
of work ! The Pope alone erect at the head of the federation
of nations, prince of peace, with the simple mission of sup-

plying the moral rule, the link of charity and love which was
to unite all men ! And would not this be the speedy realisation of the promises of Christ ? The times were near accomplishment, secular and religious society would mingle so closely
that they would form but one ; and it would be the age of
triumph and happiness predicted by all the prophets, no more
struggles possible, no more antagonism between the mind and
the body, but a marvellous equilibrium which would kill evil
and set the kingdom of heaven upon earth. New Rome, the
centre of the world, bestowing on the world the new religion !

Pierre felt that tears were coming to his eyes, and with an
unconscious movement, never noticing how much he astonished
the slim Englishmen and thick-set Germans passing along
the terrace, he opened his arms and extended them towards
the *real* Rome, steeped in such lovely sunshine and stretched
out at his feet. Would she prove responsive to his dream ?
Would he, as he had written, find within her the remedy for
our impatience and our alarms ? Could Catholicism be renewed, could it return to the spirit of primitive Christianity,
become the religion of the democracy, the faith which the
modern world, overturned and in danger of perishing, awaits
in order to be pacified and to live ?

Pierre was full of generous passion, full of faith. He again
beheld good Abbé Rose weeping with emotion as he read his
book. He heard Viscount Philibert de la Choue telling him
that such a book was worth an army. And he particularly
felt strong in the approval of Cardinal Bergerot, that apostle
of inexhaustible charity. Why should the Congregation of
the Index threaten his work with interdiction ? Since he had
been officiously advised to go to Rome if he desired to defend
himself, he had been turning this question over in his mind
without being able to discover which of his pages were
attacked. To him indeed they all seemed to glow with the
purest Christianity. However, he had arrived quivering with
enthusiasm and courage : he was all eagerness to kneel before
the Pope, and place himself under his august protection,
assuring him that he had not written a line without taking
inspiration from his ideas, without desiring the triumph of
his policy. Was it possible that condemnation should be
passed on a book in which he imagined in all sincerity that
he had exalted Leo XIII by striving to help him in his work
of Christian reunion and universal peace ?

For a moment longer Pierre remained standing before the

parapet. He had been there for nearly an hour, unable to
drink in enough of the grandeur of Rome, which, given all
the unknown things she hid from him, he would have liked
to possess at once. Oh! to seize hold of her, know her,
ascertain at once the true word which he had come to seek
from her! This again, like Lourdes, was an experiment, but
a graver one, a decisive one, whence he would emerge either
strengthened or overcome for evermore. He no longer sought
the simple, perfect faith of the little child, but the superior
faith of the intellectual man, raising himself above rites and
symbols, working for the greatest happiness of humanity as
based on its need of certainty. His temples throbbed responsive to his heart. What would be the answer of Rome?

The sunlight had increased and the higher districts now
stood out more vigorously against the fiery background.
Far away the hills became gilded and empurpled, whilst the
nearer house-fronts grew very distinct and bright with their
thousands of windows sharply outlined. However, some
morning haze still hovered around; light veils seemed to rise
from the lower streets, blurring the summits for a moment,
and then evaporating in the ardent heavens where all was
blue. For a moment Pierre fancied that the Palatine had
vanished, for he could scarcely see the dark fringe of cypresses;
it was as though the dust of its ruins concealed the hill. But
the Quirinal was even more obscured; the royal palace
seemed to have faded away in a fog, so paltry did it look
with its low flat front, so vague in the distance that he no
longer distinguished it; whereas above the trees on his left
the dome of St. Peter's had grown yet larger in the limpid
gold of the sunshine, and appeared to occupy the whole sky
and dominate the whole city!

Ah! the Rome of that first meeting, the Rome of early
morning, whose new districts he had not even noticed in the
burning fever of his arrival—with what boundless hopes did
she not inspirit him, this Rome which he believed he should
find alive, such indeed as he had dreamed! And whilst he
stood there in his thin black cassock, thus gazing on her that
lovely day, what a shout of coming redemption seemed to
arise from her house-roofs, what a promise of universal peace
seemed to issue from that sacred soil, twice already Queen of
the world! It was the third Rome, it was New Rome whose
maternal love was travelling across the frontiers to all the
nations to console them and reunite them in a common

embrace. In the passionate candour of his dream he beheld her, he heard her, rejuvenated, full of the gentleness of child-hood, soaring, as it were, amidst the morning freshness into the vast pure heavens.

But at last Pierre tore himself away from the sublime spectacle. The driver and the horse, their heads drooping under the broad sunlight, had not stirred. On the seat the valise was almost burning, hot with the rays of the sun which was already heavy. And once more Pierre got into the vehicle and gave this address:

' Via Giulia, Palazzo Boccanera.'

II

THE Via Giulia, which runs in a straight line over a distance of five hundred yards from the Farnese palace to the church of St. John of the Florentines, was at that hour steeped in bright sunlight, the glow streaming from end to end and whitening the small square paving stones. The street had no footways, and the cab rolled along it almost to the farther extremity, passing the old grey sleepy and deserted residences whose large windows were barred with iron, while their deep porches revealed sombre courts resembling wells. Laid out by Pope Julius II, who had dreamt of lining it with magnifi-cent palaces, the street, then the most regular and handsome in Rome, had served as Corso [1] in the sixteenth century. One could tell that one was in a former luxurious district, which had lapsed into silence, solitude, and abandonment, instinct with a kind of religious gentleness and discretion. The old house-fronts followed one after another, their shutters closed and their gratings occasionally decked with climbing plants. At some doors cats were seated, and dim shops, appropriated to humble trades, were installed in certain dependencies. But little traffic was apparent. Pierre only noticed some bareheaded women dragging children behind them, a hay cart drawn by a mule, a superb monk draped in drugget, and a bicyclist speeding along noiselessly, his machine sparkling in the sun.

At last the driver turned and pointed to a large square building at the corner of a lane running towards the Tiber.

[1] The Corso was so called on account of the horse-races held in it at carnival time.—*Trans.*

'Palazzo Boccanera.'

Pierre raised his head and was pained by the severe aspect of the structure, so bare and massive and blackened by age. Like its neighbours the Farnese and the Sacchetti palaces, it had been built by Antonio da Sangallo in the early part of the sixteenth century, and, as with the former of those residences, the tradition ran that in raising the pile the architect had made use of stones pilfered from the Colosseum and the Theatre of Marcellus. The vast, square-looking façade had three upper stories, each with seven windows, and the first one very lofty and noble. Down below, the only sign of decoration was that the high ground-floor windows, barred with huge projecting gratings as though from fear of siege, rested upon large consoles, and were crowned by attics which smaller consoles supported. Above the monumental entrance, with folding doors of bronze, there was a balcony in front of the central first-floor window. And at the summit of the façade against the sky appeared a sumptuous entablature, whose frieze displayed admirable grace and purity of ornamentation. This frieze, the consoles, the attics, and the door-case were of white marble, but marble whose surface had so crumbled and so darkened that it now had the rough yellowish grain of stone. Right and left of the entrance were two antique seats upheld by griffons also of marble; and incrusted in the wall at one corner, a lovely Renascence fountain, its source dried up, still lingered; and on it a cupid riding a dolphin could with difficulty be distinguished, to such a degree had the wear and tear of time eaten into the sculpture.

Pierre's eyes, however, had been more particularly attracted by an escutcheon carved above one of the ground-floor windows, the escutcheon of the Boccaneras, a winged dragon venting flames, and underneath it he could plainly read the motto which had remained intact: '*Bocca nera, Alma rossa*' ('Black mouth, Red Soul'). Above another window, as a pendant to the escutcheon, there was one of those little shrines which are still common in Rome, a satin robed statuette of the Blessed Virgin, before which a lantern burnt in the full daylight.

The cabman was about to drive through the dim and gaping porch, according to custom, when the young priest, overcome by timidity, stopped him. 'No, no,' he said; 'don't go in, it's useless.'

Then he alighted from the vehicle, paid the man, and, valise in hand, found himself first under the vaulted roof, and then in the central court, without having met a living soul.

It was a square and fairly spacious court, surrounded by a porticus like a cloister. Some remnants of statuary, marbles discovered in excavating, an armless Apollo, and the trunk of a Venus, were ranged against the walls under the dismal arcades; and some fine grass had sprouted between the pebbles which paved the soil as with a black and white mosaic. It seemed as if the sunrays could never reach that paving, mouldy with damp. A dimness and a silence instinct with departed grandeur and infinite mournfulness reigned there.

Surprised by the emptiness of this silent mansion, Pierre continued seeking somebody, a porter, a servant; and, fancying that he saw a shadow flit by, he decided to pass through another arch which led to a little garden fringing the Tiber. On this side the façade of the building was quite plain, displaying nothing beyond its three rows of symmetrically disposed windows. However, the abandonment reigning in the garden brought Pierre yet a keener pang. In the centre some large box-plants were growing in the basin of a fountain which had been filled up; while among the mass of weeds, some orange trees with golden, ripening fruit alone indicated the tracery of the paths which they had once bordered. Between two huge laurel bushes, against the right-hand wall, there was a sarcophagus of the second century—with fauns offering violence to nymphs, one of those wild *baccanali*, those scenes of eager passion which Rome in its decline was wont to depict on the tombs of its dead; and this marble sarcophagus, crumbling with age and green with moisture, served as a tank into which a streamlet of water fell from a large tragic mask incrusted in the wall. Facing the Tiber there had formerly been a sort of colonnaded loggia, a terrace whence a double flight of steps descended to the river. For the construction of the new quays, however, the river bank was being raised, and the terrace was already lower than the new ground level, and stood there crumbling and useless amidst piles of rubbish and blocks of stone, all the wretched chalky confusion of the improvements which were ripping up and overturning the district.

Pierre, however, was suddenly convinced that he could see somebody crossing the court. So he returned thither and found a woman somewhat short of stature, who must have been nearly fifty, though as yet she had not a white hair, but

looked very bright and active. At sight of the priest, however, an expression of distrust passed over her round face and
clear eyes.

Employing the few words of broken Italian which he knew,
Pierre at once sought to explain matters : ' I am Abbé Pierre
Froment, madam——' he began.

However, she did not let him continue, but exclaimed in
fluent French, with the somewhat thick and lingering accent
of the province of the Ile-de-France : ' Ah ! yes, Monsieur
l'Abbé, I know, I know—I was expecting you, I received orders
about you.' And then, as he gazed at her in amazement, she
added : ' Oh ! I'm a Frenchwoman ! I've been here for five
and twenty years, but I haven't yet been able to get used to
their horrible lingo ! '

Pierre thereupon remembered that Viscount Philibert de
la Choue had spoken to him of this servant, one Victorine
Bosquet, a native of Auneau in La Beauce, who, when two and
twenty, had gone to Rome with a consumptive mistress. The
latter's sudden death had left her in as much terror and
bewilderment as if she had been alone in some land of savages ;
and so she had gratefully devoted herself to the Countess
Ernesta Brandini, a Boccanera by birth, who had, so to say,
picked her up in the streets. The Countess had at first employed her as nurse to her daughter Benedetta, hoping in this
way to teach the child some French ; and Victorine—remaining
for five and twenty years with the same family—had by
degrees raised herself to the position of housekeeper, whilst
still remaining virtually illiterate, so destitute indeed of any
linguistic gift that she could only jabber a little broken Italian,
just sufficient for her needs in her intercourse with the other
servants.

' And is Monsieur le Vicomte quite well ? ' she resumed
with frank familiarity. ' He is so very pleasant, and we are
always so pleased to see him. He stays here, you know, each
time he comes to Rome. I know that the Princess and the
Contessina received a letter from him yesterday announcing
you.'

It was indeed Viscount Philibert de la Choue who had
made all the arrangements for Pierre's sojourn in Rome. Of
the ancient and once vigorous race of the Boccaneras, there
now only remained Cardinal Pio Boccanera, the Princess his
sister, an old maid who from respect was called ' Donna '
Serafina, their niece Benedetta—whose mother Ernesta had

followed her husband, Count Brandini, to the tomb—and finally
their nephew, Prince Dario Boccanera, whose father, Prince
Onofrio, was likewise dead, and whose mother, a Montefiori,
had married again. It so chanced that the Viscount de la
Choue was connected with the family, his younger brother
having married a Brandini, sister to Benedetta's father; and
thus, with the courtesy rank of uncle, he had, in Count
Brandini's time, frequently sojourned at the mansion in the
Via Giulia. He had also become attached to Benedetta,
especially since the advent of a private family drama, consequent upon an unhappy marriage which the young woman
had contracted, and which she had petitioned the Holy Father
to annul. Since Benedetta had left her husband to live with
her aunt Serafina and her uncle the Cardinal, M. de la Choue
had often written to her and sent her parcels of French books.
Among others he had forwarded her a copy of Pierre's book,
and the whole affair had originated in that wise. Several
letters on the subject had been exchanged when at last
Benedetta sent word that the work had been denounced to
the Congregation of the Index, and that it was advisable the
author should at once repair to Rome, where she graciously
offered him the hospitality of the Boccanera mansion.

The Viscount was quite as much astonished as the young
priest at these tidings, and failed to understand why the book
should be threatened at all; however, he prevailed on Pierre
to make the journey as a matter of good policy, becoming
himself impassioned for the achievement of a victory which he
counted in anticipation as his own. And so it was easy to
understand the bewildered condition of Pierre, on tumbling
into this unknown mansion, launched into an heroic adventure, the reasons and circumstances of which were beyond
him.

Victorine, however, suddenly resumed: 'But I am leaving
you here, Monsieur l'Abbé. Let me conduct you to your
rooms. Where is your luggage?'

Then, when he had shown her his valise which he had
placed on the ground beside him, and explained that having
no more than a fortnight's stay in view he had contented
himself with bringing a second cassock and some linen, she
seemed very much surprised.

'A fortnight! You only expect to remain here a fortnight?
Well, well, you'll see.'

And then summoning a big devil of a lackey who had

ended by making his appearance, she said: 'Take that up into the red room, Giacomo. Will you kindly follow me, Monsieur l'Abbé?'

Pierre felt quite comforted and inspirited by thus unexpectedly meeting such a lively, good-natured compatriot in this gloomy Roman 'palace.' Whilst crossing the court he listened to her as she related that the Princess had gone out, and that the Contessina—as Benedetta from motives of affection was still called in the house, despite her marriage—had not yet shown herself that morning, being rather poorly. However, added Victorine, she had her orders.

The staircase was in one corner of the court, under the porticus. It was a monumental staircase with broad, low steps, the incline being so gentle that a horse might easily have climbed it. The stone walls, however, were quite bare, the landings empty and solemn, and a deathlike mournfulness fell from the lofty vault above.

As they reached the first floor, noticing Pierre's emotion, Victorine smiled. The mansion seemed to be uninhabited; not a sound came from its closed chambers. Simply pointing to a large oaken door on the right hand, the housekeeper remarked: 'The wing overlooking the court and the river is occupied by his Eminence. But he doesn't use a quarter of the rooms. All the reception rooms on the side of the street have been shut. How could one keep up such a big place, and what, too, would be the use of it? We should need somebody to lodge.'

With her lithe step she continued ascending the stairs. She had remained essentially a foreigner, a Frenchwoman, too different from those among whom she lived to be influenced by her environment. On reaching the second floor she resumed: 'There, on the left, are Donna Serafina's rooms, those of the Contessina are on the right. This is the only part of the house where there's a little warmth and life. Besides, it's Monday to-day, the Princess will be receiving visitors this evening. You'll see.'

Then, opening a door, beyond which was a second and very narrow staircase, she went on: 'We others have our rooms on the third floor. I must ask Monsieur l'Abbé to let me go up before him.'

The grand staircase ceased at the second floor, and Victorine explained that the third story was reached exclusively by this servants' staircase, which led from the lane running down

to the Tiber on one side of the mansion. There was a small
private entrance in this lane, which was very convenient.

At last, reaching the third story, she hurried along a passage, again calling Pierre's attention to various doors. 'These
are the apartments of Don Vigilio, his Eminence's secretary.
These are mine. And these will be yours. Monsieur le Vicomte will never have any other rooms when he comes to spend
a few days in Rome. He says that he enjoys more liberty up
here, as he can come in and go out as he pleases. I gave
him a key to the door in the lane, and I'll give you one too.
And, besides, you'll see what a nice view there is from here!'

Whilst speaking she had gone in. The apartments comprised two rooms: a somewhat spacious *salon*, with wall-paper
of a large scroll pattern on a red ground, and a bed chamber,
where the paper was of a flax grey, studded with faded blue
flowers. The sitting-room was in one corner of the mansion
overlooking the lane and the Tiber, and Victorine at once went
to the windows, one of which afforded a view over the distant
lower part of the river, while the other faced the Trastevere
and the Janiculum across the water.

'Ah! yes, it's very pleasant!' said Pierre, who had followed
and stood beside her.

Giacomo, who did not hurry, came in behind them with
the valise. It was now past eleven o'clock; and seeing that
the young priest looked tired, and realising that he must be
hungry after such a journey, Victorine offered to have some
breakfast served at once in the sitting-room. He would then
have the afternoon to rest or go out, and would only meet the
ladies in the evening at dinner. At the mere suggestion of
resting, however, Pierre began to protest, declaring that he
should certainly go out, not wishing to lose an entire afternoon. The breakfast he readily accepted, for he was indeed
dying of hunger.

However, he had to wait another full half-hour. Giacomo,
who served him under Victorine's orders, did everything in a
most leisurely way. And Victorine, lacking confidence in the
man, remained with the young priest to make sure that everything he might require was provided.

'Ah! Monsieur l'Abbé,' said she, 'what people! What a
country! You can't have an idea of it. I should never get
accustomed to it even if I were to live here for a hundred
years. Ah! if it were not for the Contessina, but she's so
good and beautiful.'

Then, whilst placing a dish of figs on the table, she astonished Pierre by adding that a city where nearly everybody was
a priest could not possibly be a good city. Thereupon the
presence of this gay, active, unbelieving servant in the queer
old palace again scared him.

'What! you are not religious?' he exclaimed.

'No, no, Monsieur l'Abbé, the priests don't suit me,' said
Victorine; 'I knew one in France when I was very little, and
since I've been here I've seen too many of them. It's all
over. Oh! I don't say that on account of his Eminence,
who is a holy man worthy of all possible respect. And besides,
everybody in the house knows that I've nothing to reproach
myself with. So why not leave me alone, since I'm fond of
my employers and attend properly to my duties?'

She burst into a frank laugh. 'Ah!' she resumed, 'when
I was told that another priest was coming, just as if we hadn't
enough already, I couldn't help growling to myself. But you
look like a good young man, Monsieur l'Abbé, and I feel sure
we shall get on well together. . . . I really don't know why
I'm telling you all this—probably it's because you've come
from yonder, and because the Contessina takes an interest in
you. At all events, you'll excuse me, won't you, Monsieur
l'Abbé? And take my advice, stay here and rest to-day; don't
be so foolish as to go running about their tiring city. There's
nothing very amusing to be seen in it, whatever they may say
to the contrary.'

When Pierre found himself alone, he suddenly felt overwhelmed by all the fatigue of his journey coupled with the
fever of enthusiasm that had consumed him during the morning. And as though dazed, intoxicated by the hasty meal
which he had just made—a couple of eggs and a cutlet—he
flung himself upon the bed with the idea of taking half an hour's
rest. He did not fall asleep immediately, but for a time
thought of those Boccaneras, with whose history he was
partly acquainted, and of whose life in that deserted and silent
palace, instinct with such dilapidated and melancholy grandeur,
he began to dream. But at last his ideas grew confused,
and by degrees he sank into sleep amidst a crowd of shadowy
forms, some tragic and some sweet, with vague faces which
gazed at him with enigmatical eyes as they whirled before him
in the depths of dreamland.

The Boccaneras had supplied two popes to Rome, one in
the thirteenth, the other in the fifteenth century, and from

those two favoured ones, those all-powerful masters, the family
had formerly derived its vast fortune—large estates in the
vicinity of Viterbo, several palaces in Rome, enough works of
art to fill numerous spacious galleries, and a pile of gold
sufficient to cram a cellar. The family passed as being the
most pious of the Roman *patriziato*, a family of burning faith
whose sword had always been at the service of the Church;
but if it were the most believing family it was also the most
violent, the most disputatious, constantly at war, and so
fiercely savage that the anger of the Boccaneras had become
proverbial. And thence came their arms, the winged dragon
spitting flames, and the fierce, glowing motto, with its play on
the name '*Bocca nera, Alma rossa*' (black mouth, red soul),
the mouth darkened by a roar, the soul flaming like a brazier
of faith and love.

Legends of endless passion, of terrible deeds of justice and
vengeance still circulated. There was the duel fought by
Onfredo, the Boccanera by whom the present palazzo had
been built in the sixteenth century on the site of the demolished antique residence of the family. Onfredo, learning that
his wife had allowed herself to be kissed on the lips by young
Count Costamagna, had caused the Count to be kidnapped one
evening and brought to the palazzo bound with cords. And
there in one of the large halls, before freeing him, he compelled him to confess himself to a monk. Then he severed
the cords with a stiletto, threw the lamps over and extinguished them, calling to the Count to keep the stiletto and
defend himself. During more than an hour in complete
obscurity, in this hall full of furniture, the two men sought
one another, fled from one another, seized hold of one another,
and pierced one another with their blades. And when the
doors were broken down and the servants rushed in they found
among the pools of blood, among the overturned tables and
broken seats, Costamagna with his nose sliced off and his hips
pierced with two and thirty wounds, whilst Onfredo had lost
two fingers of his right hand, and had both shoulders riddled
with holes! The wonder was that neither died of the encounter.

A century later, on that same bank of the Tiber, a daughter
of the Boccaneras, a girl barely sixteen years of age, the lovely
and passionate Cassia, filled all Rome with terror and admiration. She loved Flavio Corradini, the scion of a rival and
hated house, whose alliance her father, Prince Boccanera,

roughly rejected, and whom her elder brother, Ercole, swore to slay should he ever surprise him with her. Nevertheless the young man came to visit her in a boat, and she joined him by the little staircase descending to the river. But one evening Ercole, who was on the watch, sprang into the boat and planted his dagger full in Flavio's heart. Later on the subsequent incidents were unravelled ; it was understood that Cassia, wrathful and frantic with despair, unwilling to survive her love and bent on wreaking justice, had thrown herself upon her brother, had seized both murderer and victim with the same grasp whilst overturning the boat; for when the three bodies were recovered Cassia still retained her hold upon the two men, pressing their faces one against the other with her bare arms, which had remained as white as snow.

But those were vanished times. Nowadays, if faith remained, blood violence seemed to be departing from the Boccaneras. Their huge fortune also had been lost in the slow decline which for a century past has been ruining the Roman *patriziato*. It had been necessary to sell the estates; the palace had emptied, gradually sinking to the mediocrity and bourgeois life of the new times. For their part the Boccaneras obstinately declined to contract any alien alliances, proud as they were of the purity of their Roman blood. And poverty was as nothing to them ; they found contentment in their immense pride, and without a plaint sequestered themselves amidst the silence and gloom in which their race was dwindling away.

Prince Ascanio, dead since 1848, had left four children by his wife, a Corvisieri ; first Pio, the Cardinal ; then Serafina, who, in order to remain with her brother, had not married ; and finally Ernesta and Onofrio, both of whom were deceased. As Ernesta had merely left a daughter, Benedetta, behind her, it followed that the only male heir, the only possible continuator of the family name was Onofrio's son, young Prince Dario, now some thirty years of age. Should he die without posterity, the Boccaneras, once so full of life and whose deeds had filled Roman history in papal times, must fatally disappear.

Dario and his cousin Benedetta had been drawn together by a deep, smiling, natural passion ever since childhood. They seemed born one for the other ; they could not imagine that they had been brought into the world for any other purpose than that of becoming husband and wife as soon as they should be old enough to marry. When Prince Onofrio—an amiable man of forty, very popular in Rome, where he spent his modest fortune as his heart listed—espoused La Montefiori's daughter, the little Marchesa Flavia, whose superb beauty, suggestive of a youthful Juno, had maddened him, he went to reside at the Villa Montefiori, the only property, indeed the only belonging, that remained to the two ladies. It was in the direction of St'. Agnese-fuori-le-Mura,[1] and there were vast grounds, a perfect park in fact, planted with centenarian trees, among which the villa, a somewhat sorry building of the seventeenth century, was falling into ruins.

Unfavourable reports were circulated about the ladies, the mother having almost lost caste since she had become a widow, and the girl having too bold a beauty, too conquering an air. Thus the marriage had not met with the approval of Serafina, who was very rigid, or of Onofrio's elder brother Pio, at that time merely a *Cameriere segreto* of the Holy Father and a Canon of the Vatican basilica. Only Ernesta kept up a regular intercourse with Onofrio, fond of him as she was by reason of his gaiety of disposition; and thus, later on, her favourite diversion was to go each week to the Villa Montefiori with her daughter Benedetta, there to spend the day. And what a delightful day it always proved to Benedetta and Dario, she ten years old and he fifteen, what a fraternal loving day in that vast and almost abandoned garden with its parasol pines, its giant box plants, and its clumps of evergreen oaks, amidst which one lost oneself as in a virgin forest.

The poor stifled soul of Ernesta was a soul of pain and passion. Born with a mighty longing for life, she thirsted for the sun—for a free, happy, active existence in the full daylight. She was noted for her large limpid eyes and the charming oval of her gentle face. Extremely ignorant, like all the daughters of the Roman nobility, having learnt the little she knew in a convent of French nuns, she had grown up cloistered in the black Boccanera palace, having no knowledge of the world than by those daily drives to the Corso and the Pincio on which she accompanied her mother. Eventually, when she was five and twenty, and was already weary and desolate, she contracted the customary marriage of her caste, espousing Count Brandini, the last-born of a very noble, very numerous and poor family, who had to come and live in the Via Giulia mansion, where an entire wing of the second floor was

[1] St. Agnes without the Walls, N.E. of Rome.

got ready for the young couple. And nothing changed, Ernesta
continued to live in the same cold gloom, in the midst of the
same dead past, the weight of which, like that of a tombstone,
she felt pressing more and more heavily upon her.

The marriage was, on either side, a very honourable one.
Count Brandini soon passed as being the most foolish and
haughty man in Rome. A strict, intolerant formalist in
religious matters, he became quite triumphant when, after
innumerable intrigues, secret plottings which lasted ten long
years, he at last secured the appointment of grand equerry to
the Holy Father. With this appointment it seemed as if all
the dismal majesty of the Vatican entered his household.
However, Ernesta found life still bearable in the time of
Pius IX—that is until the latter part of 1870—for she might
still venture to open the windows overlooking the street,
receive a few lady friends otherwise than in secrecy, and
accept invitations to festivities. But when the Italians had
conquered Rome and the Pope declared himself a prisoner, the
mansion in the Via Giulia became a sepulchre. The great
doors were closed and bolted, even nailed together in token of
mourning; and during ten years the inmates only went out
and came in by the little staircase communicating with the
lane. It was also forbidden to open the window shutters of
the façade. This was the sulking, the protest of the black
world, the mansion sinking into deathlike immobility, complete seclusion; no more receptions, barely a few shadows,
the intimates of Donna Serafina who on Monday evenings
slipped in by the little door in the lane which was scarcely
set ajar. And during those ten lugubrious years, overcome
by secret despair, the young woman wept every night, suffered
untold agony at thus being buried alive.

Ernesta had given birth to her daughter Benedetta rather
late in life, when three and thirty years of age. At first the
little one helped to divert her mind. But afterwards her
wonted existence, like a grinding mill-stone, again seized hold
of her, and she had to place the child in the charge of the
French nuns, by whom she herself had been educated, at the
convent of the Sacred Heart of La Trinità de' Monti. When
Benedetta left the convent, grown up, nineteen years of age,
she was able to speak and write French, knew a little arith-
metic and her catechism, and possessed a few hazy notions of
history. Then the life of the two women was resumed, the
life of a *gynæceum*, suggestive of the Orient; never an excur-

sion with husband or father, but day after day spent in closed,
secluded rooms, with nought to cheer one but the sole, everlasting, obligatory promenade, the daily drive to the Corso and
the Pincio.

At home, absolute obedience was the rule; the tie of
relationship possessed an authority, a strength, which made
both women bow to the will of the Count, without possible
thought of rebellion ; and to the Count's will was added that
of Donna Serafina and that of Cardinal Pio, both of whom
were stern defenders of the old-time customs. Since the
Pope had ceased to show himself in Rome, the post of grand
equerry had left the Count considerable leisure, for the number
of equipages in the pontifical stables had been very largely
reduced ; nevertheless, he was constant in his attendance at
the Vatican, where his duties were now a mere matter of
parade, and ever increased his devout zeal as a mark of protest
against the usurping monarchy installed at the Quirinal.
However, Benedetta had just attained her twentieth year,
when one evening her father returned coughing and shivering
from some ceremony at St. Peter's. A week later he died,
carried off by inflammation of the lungs. And despite their
mourning, the loss was secretly considered a deliverance by
both women, who now felt that they were free.

Thenceforward Ernesta had but one thought, that of
saving her daughter from that awful life of immurement and
entombment. She herself had sorrowed too deeply : it was no
longer possible for her to remount the current of existence;
but she was unwilling that Benedetta should in her turn lead a
life contrary to nature, in a voluntary grave. Moreover,
similar lassitude and rebellion were showing themselves
among other patrician families, which, after the sulking of the
first years, were beginning to draw nearer to the Quirinal.
Why indeed should the children, eager for action, liberty, and
sunlight, perpetually keep up the quarrel of the fathers ? And
so, though no reconciliation could take place between the
black world and the white world,[1] intermediate tints were
already appearing, and some unexpected matrimonial alliances
were contracted.

Ernesta for her part was indifferent to the political question ; she knew next to nothing about it ; but that which she
passionately desired was that her race might at last emerge

---

[1] The 'blacks' are the supporters of the Papacy, the 'whites' those
of the King of Italy.—*Trans.*

from that hateful sepulchre, that black, silent Boccanera
mansion, where her woman's joys had been frozen by so long
a death. She had suffered very grievously in her heart, as
girl, as lover, and as wife, and yielded to anger at the thought
that her life should have been so spoiled, so lost through idiotic
resignation. Then, too, her mind was greatly influenced by the
choice of a new confessor at this period; for she had remained
very religious, practising all the rites of the Church, and ever
docile to the advice of her spiritual director. To free herself
the more, however, she now quitted the Jesuit Father whom
her husband had chosen for her, and in his stead took Abbé
Pisoni, the rector of the little church of Sta. Brigida, on the
Piazza Farnese, close by. He was a man of fifty, very gentle,
and very good-hearted, of a benevolence seldom found in the
Roman world; and archæology, a passion for the old stones of
the past, had made him an ardent patriot. Humble though
his position was, folks whispered that he had on several occasions served as an intermediary in delicate matters between
the Vatican and the Quirinal. And, becoming confessor not
only of Ernesta but of Benedetta also, he was fond of discoursing to them about the grandeur of Italian unity, the
triumphant sway that Italy would exercise when the Pope and
the King should agree together.

Meantime Benedetta and Dario loved as on the first day,
patiently, with the strong, tranquil love of those who know that
they belong to one another. But it happened that Ernesta
threw herself between them and stubbornly opposed their
marriage. No, no! her daughter must not espouse that
Dario, that cousin, the last of the name, who in his turn
would immure his wife in the black sepulchre of the
Boccanera palace! Their union would be a prolongation of
entombment, an aggravation of ruin, a repetition of the
haughty wretchedness of the past, of the everlasting peevish
sulking which depressed and benumbed one! She was well
acquainted with the young man's character; she knew that
he was egotistical and weak, incapable of thinking and acting,
predestined to bury his race with a smile on his lips, to let
the last remnant of the house crumble about his head without
attempting the slightest effort to found a new family. And
that which she desired was fortune in another guise, a new
birth for her daughter with wealth and the florescence of life
amid the victors and powerful ones of to-morrow.

From that moment the mother did not cease her stubborn

efforts to ensure her daughter's happiness despite herself.
She told her of her tears, entreated her not to renew her own
deplorable career. Yet she would have failed, such was the
calm determination of the girl who had for ever given her
heart, if certain circumstances had not brought her into connection with such a son-in-law as she dreamt of. At that
very Villa Montefiori where Benedetta and Dario had plighted
their troth, she met Count Prada, son of Orlando, one of the
heroes of the reunion of Italy. Arriving in Rome from Milan,
with his father, when eighteen years of age, at the time of the
occupation of the city by the Italian Government, Prada had
first entered the Ministry of Finances as a mere clerk, whilst
the old warrior, his sire, created a senator, lived scantily on a
petty income, the last remnant of a fortune spent in his
country's service. The fine, warlike madness of the former
comrade of Garibaldi had, however, in the son turned into a
fierce appetite for booty, so that the young man became one
of the real conquerors of Rome, one of those birds of prey
that dismembered and devoured the city. Engaged in vast
speculations on land, already wealthy according to popular
report, he had—at the time of meeting Ernesta—just become
intimate with Prince Onofrio, whose head he had turned by suggesting to him the idea of selling the far-spreading grounds of
the Villa Montefiori for the erection of a new suburban district
on the site. Others averred that he was the lover of the
princess, the beautiful Flavia, who, although nine years his
senior, was still superb. And, truth to tell, he was certainly
a man of violent desires, with an eagerness to rush on the
spoils of conquest which rendered him utterly unscrupulous
with regard either to the wealth or to the wives of others.

From the first day that he beheld Benedetta he desired her.
But she, at any rate, could only become his by marriage.
And he did not for a moment hesitate, but broke off all connection with Flavia, eager as he was for the pure virgin beauty,
the patrician youth of the other. When he realised that
Ernesta, the mother, favoured him, he asked her daughter's
hand, feeling certain of success. And the surprise was great,
for he was some fifteen years older than the girl. However,
he was a count, he bore a name which was already historical,
he was piling up millions, he was regarded with favour at the
Quirinal, and none could tell to what heights he might not
attain. All Rome became impassioned.

Never afterwards was Benedetta able to explain to herself

how it happened that she had eventually consented. Six
months sooner, six months later, such a marriage would certainly have been impossible, given the fearful scandal which
it raised in the black world. A Boccanera, the last maiden of
that antique papal race, given to a Prada, to one of the despoilers of the Church! Was it credible? In order that the
wild project might prove successful it had been necessary that
it should be formed at a particular brief moment—a moment
when a supreme effort was being made to conciliate the Vatican
and the Quirinal. A report circulated that an agreement was
on the point of being arrived at, that the King consented to
recognise the Pope's absolute sovereignty over the Leonine
City,[1] and a narrow band of territory extending to the sea.
And if such were the case would not the marriage of Benedetta
and Prada become, so to say, a symbol of union, of national
reconciliation? That lovely girl, the pure lily of the black
world, was she not the acquiescent sacrifice, the pledge granted
to the whites?

For a fortnight nothing else was talked of; people discussed the question, allowed their emotion rein, indulged in
all sorts of hopes. The girl, for her part, did not enter into
the political reasons, but simply listened to her heart, which she
could not bestow since it was hers no more. From morn till
night, however, she had to encounter her mother's prayers
entreating her not to refuse the fortune, the life which offered.
And she was particularly exercised by the counsels of her confessor, good Abbé Pisoni, whose patriotic zeal now burst forth.
He weighed upon her with all his faith in the Christian destinies of Italy, and returned heartfelt thanks to Providence for
having chosen one of his penitents as the instrument for
hastening the reconciliation which would work God's triumph
throughout the world. And her confessor's influence was
certainly one of the decisive factors in shaping Benedetta's
decision, for she was very pious, very devout, especially with
regard to a certain Madonna whose image she went to adore
every Sunday at the little church on the Piazza Farnese.
One circumstance in particular struck her: Abbé Pisoni
related that the flame of the lamp before the image in question
whitened each time that he himself knelt there to beg the

---

[1] The Vatican suburb of Rome, called the *Civitas Leonina*, because
Leo IV, to protect it from the Saracens and Arabs, enclosed it with walls
in the 9th century.—*Trans.*

Virgin to incline his penitent to the all-redeeming marriage. And thus superior forces intervened; and she yielded in obedience to her mother, whom the Cardinal and Donna Serafina had at first opposed, but whom they left free to act when the religious question arose.

Benedetta had grown up in such absolute purity and ignorance, knowing nothing of herself, so shut off from existence, that marriage with another than Dario was to her simply the rupture of a long-kept promise of life in common. It was not the violent wrenching of heart and flesh that it would have been in the case of a woman who knew the facts of life. She wept a good deal, and then in a day of self-surrender she married Prada, lacking the strength to continue resisting everybody, and yielding to a union which all Rome had conspired to bring about.

But the clap of thunder came on the very night of the nuptials. Was it that Prada, the Piedmontese, the Italian of the North, the man of conquest, displayed towards his bride the same brutality that he had shown towards the city he had sacked? Or was it that the revelation of married life filled Benedetta with repulsion since nothing in her own heart responded to the passion of this man? On that point she never clearly explained herself; but with violence she shut the door of her room, locked it and bolted it, and refused to admit her husband. For a month Prada was maddened by her scorn. He felt outraged; both his pride and his passion bled; and he swore to master her, even as one masters a colt, with the whip. But all his virile fury was impotent against the indomitable determination which had sprung up one evening behind Benedetta's small and lovely brow. The spirit of the Boccaneras had awoke within her; nothing in the world, not even the fear of death, would have induced her to become her husband's wife.[1] And then, love being at last revealed to her, there came a return of her heart to Dario, a conviction that she must reserve herself for him alone, since it was to him that she had promised herself.

Ever since that marriage, which he had borne like a bereavement, the young man had been travelling in France.

---

[1] Many readers will doubtless remember that the situation as here described is somewhat akin to that of the earlier part of M. George Ohnet's *Ironmaster*, which, in its form as a novel, I translated into English many years ago. However, all resemblance between *Rome* and the *Ironmaster* is confined to this one point.—*Trans.*

She did not hide the truth from him, but wrote to him, again vowing that she would never be another's. And meantime her piety increased, her resolve to reserve herself for the lover she had chosen mingled in her mind with constancy of religious faith. The ardent heart of a great *amorosa* had ignited within her, she was ready for martyrdom for faith's sake. And when her despairing mother with clasped hands entreated her to resign herself to her conjugal duties, she replied that she owed no duties, since she had known nothing when she married. Moreover, the times were changing; the attempts to reconcile the Quirinal and the Vatican had failed, so completely, indeed, that the newspapers of the rival parties had, with renewed violence, resumed their campaign of mutual insult and outrage; and thus that triumphal marriage, to which everyone had contributed as to a pledge of peace, crumbled amid the general smash-up, became but a ruin the more added to so many others.

Ernesta died of it. She had made a mistake. Her spoilt life—the life of a joyless wife—had culminated in this supreme maternal error. And the worst was that she alone had to bear all the responsibility of the disaster, for both her brother, the Cardinal, and her sister, Donna Serafina, overwhelmed her with reproaches. For consolation she had but the despair of Abbé Pisoni, whose patriotic hopes had been destroyed, and who was consumed with grief at having contributed to such a catastrophe. And one morning Ernesta was found, icy white and cold, in her bed. Folks talked of the rupture of a blood-vessel, but grief had been sufficient, for she had suffered frightfully, secretly, without a plaint, as indeed she had suffered all her life long.

At this time Benedetta had been married about a twelve-month: still strong in her resistance to her husband, but remaining under the conjugal roof in order to spare her mother the terrible blow of a public scandal. However, her aunt Serafina had brought influence to bear on her, by opening to her the hope of a possible nullification of her marriage, should she throw herself at the feet of the Holy Father and entreat his intervention. And Serafina ended by persuading her of this, when, deferring to certain advice, she removed her from the spiritual control of Abbé Pisoni, and gave her the same confessor as herself. This was a Jesuit father named Lorenza, a man scarce five and thirty, with bright eyes, grave and amiable manners, and great persuasive powers.

However, it was only on the morrow of her mother's death that Benedetta made up her mind, and returned to the Palazzo Boccanera, to occupy the apartments where she had been born, and where her mother had just passed away.

Immediately afterwards proceedings for annulling the marriage were instituted, in the first instance, for inquiry, before the Cardinal Vicar charged with the diocese of Rome. It was related that the Contessina had only taken this step after a secret audience with his Holiness, who had shown her the most encouraging sympathy. Count Prada at first spoke of applying to the law courts to compel his wife to return to the conjugal domicile ; but, yielding to the entreaties of his old father Orlando, whom the affair greatly grieved, he eventually consented to accept the ecclesiastical jurisdiction. He was infuriated, however, to find that the nullification of the marriage was solicited on the ground of its non-consummation through *impotentia mariti* ; this being one of the most valid and decisive pleas on which the Church of Rome consents to part those whom she has joined. And far more unhappy marriages than might be imagined are severed on these grounds, though the world only gives attention to those cases in which people of title or renown are concerned, as it did, for instance, with the famous Martinez Campos suit.

In Benedetta's case, her counsel, Consistorial-Advocate Morano, one of the leading authorities of the Roman bar, simply neglected to mention, in his memoir, that if she was still merely a wife in name, this was entirely due to herself. In addition to the evidence of friends and servants, showing on what terms the husband and wife had lived since their marriage, the advocate produced a certificate of a medical character, showing that the non-consummation of the union was certain. And the Cardinal Vicar, acting as Bishop of Rome, had thereupon remitted the case to the Congregation of the Council. This was a first success for Benedetta, and matters remained in this position. She was waiting for the Congregation to deliver its final pronouncement, hoping that the ecclesiastical dissolution of the marriage would prove an irresistible argument in favour of the divorce which she meant to solicit of the civil courts. And meantime, in the icy rooms where her mother Ernesta, submissive and desolate, had lately died, the Contessina resumed her girlish life, showing herself calm, yet very firm in her passion, having vowed that she would belong to none but Dario, and that she would not belong to

him until the day when a priest should have joined them
together in God's holy name.

As it happened, some six months previously, Dario also
had taken up his abode at the Boccanera palace in consequence of the death of his father and the catastrophe which
had ruined him. Prince Onofrio, after adopting Prada's
advice and selling the Villa Montefiori to a financial company
for ten million *lire*,[1] had, instead of prudently keeping his
money in his pockets, succumbed to the fever of speculation
which was consuming Rome. He began to gamble, buying
back his own land, and ending by losing everything in the
formidable *Krach* which was swallowing up the wealth of the
entire city. Totally ruined, somewhat deeply in debt even,
the Prince nevertheless continued to promenade the Corso,
like the handsome, smiling, popular man he was, when he
accidentally met his death through falling from his horse ; and
four months later his widow, the ever-beautiful Flavia—who
had managed to save a modern villa and a personal income of
forty thousand *lire* [2] from the disaster—was re-married to a man
of magnificent presence, her junior by some ten years. This
was a Swiss named Jules Laporte, originally a sergeant in the
Papal Swiss Guard, then a traveller for a shady business in
' relics,' and finally Marchese Montefiore, having secured that
title in securing his wife, thanks to a special brief of the Holy
Father. Thus the Princess Boccanera had again become the
Marchioness Montefiori.

It was then that Cardinal Boccanera, feeling greatly hurt,
insisted on his nephew Dario coming to live with him, in a
small apartment on the first floor of the *palazzo*. In the
heart of that holy man, who seemed dead to the world, there
still lingered pride of name and lineage, with a feeling of
affection for his young slightly-built nephew, the last of the
race, the only one by whom the old stock might blossom
anew. Moreover, he was not opposed to Dario's marriage with
Benedetta, whom he also loved with a paternal affection ; and
so proud was he of the family honour, and so convinced of the
young people's pious rectitude, that, in taking them to live with
him, he absolutely scorned the abominable rumours which
Count Prada's friends in the white world had begun to
circulate ever since the two cousins had resided under the
same roof. Donna Serafina guarded Benedetta, like he, the
Cardinal, guarded Dario, and in the silence and the gloom of

the vast deserted mansion, ensanguined of olden time by so many tragic deeds of violence, there now only remained these four with their restrained, stilled passions, last survivors of a crumbling world upon the threshold of a new one.

When Abbé Pierre Froment all at once awoke from sleep, his head heavy with painful dreams, he was worried to find that the daylight was already waning. His watch, which he hastened to consult, pointed to six o'clock. Intending to rest for an hour at the utmost, he had slept on for nearly seven hours, overcome beyond power of resistance. And even on awaking he remained on the bed, helpless, as though he were conquered before he had fought. Why, he wondered, did he experience this prostration, this unreasonable discouragement, this quiver of doubt which had come he knew not whence during his sleep, and which was annihilating his youthful enthusiasm of the morning? Had the Boccaneras any connection with this sudden weakening of his powers? He had espied dim disquieting figures in the black night of his dreams; and the anguish which they had brought him continued, and he again evoked them, scared as he was at thus awaking in a strange room, full of uneasiness in presence of the unknown. Things no longer seemed natural to him. He could not understand why Benedetta should have written to Viscount Philibert de la Choue to tell him that his, Pierre's, book had been denounced to the Congregation of the Index. What interest too could she have had in his coming to Rome to defend himself; and with what object had she carried her amiability so far as to desire that he should take up his quarters in the mansion? Pierre's stupefaction indeed arose from his being there, on that bed in that strange room, in that palace whose deep, death-like silence encompassed him. As he lay there, his limbs still overpowered and his brain seemingly empty, a flash of light suddenly came to him, and he realised that there must be certain circumstances that he knew nothing of—that, simple though things appeared, they must really hide some complicated intrigue. However, it was only a fugitive gleam of enlightenment; his suspicions faded; and he rose up shaking himself and accusing the gloomy twilight of being the sole cause of the shivering and the despondency of which he felt ashamed.

In order to bestir himself, Pierre began to examine the two rooms. They were furnished simply, almost meagrely, in mahogany, there being scarcely any two articles alike, though all dated from the beginning of the century. Neither the bed nor the windows nor the doors had any hangings. On the floor of bare tiles, coloured red and polished, there were merely some little foot-mats in front of the various seats. And at sight of this middle-class bareness and coldness Pierre ended by remembering a room where he had slept in childhood—a room at Versailles, at the abode of his grandmother, who had kept a little grocer's shop there in the days of Louis Philippe. However, he became interested in an old painting which hung in the bedroom, on the wall facing the bed, amidst some childish and valueless engravings. But partially discernible in the waning light, this painting represented a woman seated on some projecting stone work, on the threshold of a great stern building, whence she seemed to have been driven forth. The folding doors of bronze had for ever closed behind her, yet she remained there in a mere drapery of white linen; whilst scattered articles of clothing, thrown forth chancewise with a violent hand, lay upon the massive granite steps. Her feet were bare, her arms were bare, and her hands, distorted by bitter agony, were pressed to her face—a face which one saw not, veiled as it was by the tawny gold of her rippling, streaming hair. What nameless grief, what fearful shame, what hateful abandonment was thus being hidden by that rejected one, that lingering victim of love, of whose unknown story one might for ever dream with tortured heart? It could be divined that she was adorably young and beautiful in her wretchedness, in the shred of linen draped about her shoulders; but mystery enveloped everything else—her passion, possibly her misfortune, perhaps even her transgression—unless, indeed, she were there merely as a symbol of all that shivers and that weeps visageless before the ever-closed portal of the unknown. For a long time Pierre looked at her, and so intently that he at last imagined he could distinguish her profile, divine in its purity and expression of suffering. But this was only an illusion; the painting had greatly suffered, blackened by time and neglect; and he asked himself whose work it might be that it should move him so intensely. On the adjoining wall a picture of a Madonna, a bad copy of an eighteenth-century painting, irritated him by the banality of its smile.

Night was falling faster and faster, and, opening the sitting-room window, Pierre leant out. On the other bank of the Tiber facing him arose the Janiculum, the height whence

he had gazed upon Rome that morning. But at this dim
hour Rome was no longer the city of youth and dreamland soaring into the early sunshine. The night was raining
down, grey and ashen; the horizon was becoming blurred,
vague, and mournful. Yonder, to the left, beyond the sea of
roofs, Pierre could still divine the presence of the Palatine;
and yonder, to the right, there still arose the Dome of St.
Peter's, now grey like slate against the leaden sky; whilst
behind him the Quirinal, which he could not see, must also
be fading away into the misty night. A few minutes went by,
and everything became yet more blurred; he realised that
Rome was fading, departing in its immensity of which he
knew nothing. Then his causeless doubt and disquietude
again came on him so painfully that he could no longer remain
at the window. He closed it and sat down, letting the darkness submerge him with its flood of infinite sadness. And
his despairing reverie only ceased when the door gently
opened and the glow of a lamp enlivened the room.

It was Victorine who came in quietly, bringing the light.
'Ah! so you are up, Monsieur l'Abbé,' said she; 'I came in
at about four o'clock but I let you sleep on. You have done
quite right to take all the rest you required.'

Then, as he complained of pains and shivering, she became
anxious. 'Don't go catching their nasty fevers,' she said.
'It isn't at all healthy near their river, you know. Don
Vigilio, his Eminence's secretary, is always having the fever,
and I assure you that it isn't pleasant.'

She accordingly advised him to remain upstairs and
lie down again. She would excuse his absence to the Princess
and the Contessina. And he ended by letting her do as she
desired, for he was in no state to have any will of his own.
By her advice he dined, partaking of some soup, a wing of
a chicken, and some preserves, which Giacomo, the big
lackey, brought up to him. And the food did him a great
deal of good; he felt so restored that he refused to go to bed,
desiring, said he, to thank the ladies that very evening for
their kindly hospitality. As Donna Serafina received on
Mondays he would present himself before her.

'Very good,' said Victorine approvingly. 'As you are all
right again it can do you no harm, it will even enliven you.
The best thing will be for Don Vigilio to come for you at
nine o'clock and accompany you. Wait for him here.'

Pierre had just washed and put on the new cassock he had

brought with him, when, at nine o'clock precisely, he heard
a discreet knock at his door. A little priest came in, a man
scarcely thirty years of age, but thin and debile of build, with
a long, seared, saffron-coloured face. For two years past
attacks of fever, coming on every day at the same hour, had
been consuming him. Nevertheless, whenever he forgot to
control the black eyes which lighted his yellow face, they
shone out ardently with the glow of his fiery soul. He bowed,
and then in fluent French introduced himself in this simple
fashion : ' Don Vigilio, Monsieur l'Abbé, who is entirely at
your service. If you are willing, we will go down.'

Pierre immediately followed him, expressing his thanks,
and Don Vigilio, relapsing into silence, answered his remarks
with a smile. Having descended the small staircase, they
found themselves on the second floor, on the spacious landing
of the grand staircase. And Pierre was surprised and saddened by the scanty illumination, which, as in some dingy
lodging-house, was limited to a few gas-jets, placed far apart,
their yellow splotches but faintly relieving the deep gloom of
the lofty, endless corridors. All was gigantic and funereal.
Even on the landing, where was the entrance to Donna
Serafina's apartments, facing those occupied by her niece,
nothing indicated that a reception was being held that
evening. The door remained closed, not a sound came from
the rooms, a death-like silence arose from the whole palace.
And Don Vigilio did not even ring, but, after a fresh bow,
discreetly turned the door-handle.

A single petroleum lamp, placed on a table, lighted the
anteroom, a large apartment with bare fresco-painted walls,
simulating hangings of red and gold, draped regularly all
around in the antique fashion. A few men's overcoats and
two ladies' mantles lay on the chairs, whilst a pier table was
littered with hats, and a servant sat there dozing, with his
back to the wall.

However, as Don Vigilio stepped aside to allow Pierre to
enter a first reception room, hung with red *brocatelle*, a room
but dimly lighted and which he imagined to be empty, the
young priest found himself face to face with an apparition in
black, a woman whose features he could not at first distinguish.
Fortunately he heard his companion say, with a low bow,
' Contessina, I have the honour to present to you Monsieur
l'Abbé Pierre Froment, who arrived from France this morning.'

Then, for a moment, Pierre remained alone with Benedetta

in that deserted *salone*, in the sleepy glimmer of two lace-veiled lamps. At present, however, a sound of voices came from a room beyond, a larger apartment whose doorway, with folding doors thrown wide open, described a parallelogram of brighter light.

The young woman at once showed herself very affable, with perfect simplicity of manner: 'Ah! I am happy to see you, Monsieur l'Abbé. I was afraid that your indisposition might be serious. You are quite recovered now, are you not?'

Pierre listened to her, fascinated by her slow and rather thick voice, in which restrained passion seemed to mingle with much prudent good sense. And at last he saw her, with her hair so heavy and so dark, her skin so white, the whiteness of ivory. She had a round face, with somewhat full lips, a small refined nose, features as delicate as a child's. But it was especially her eyes that lived, immense eyes, whose infinite depths none could fathom. Was she slumbering? Was she dreaming? Did her motionless face conceal the ardent tension of a great saint and a great *amorosa*? So white, so young, and so calm, her every movement was harmonious, her appearance at once very staid, very noble, and very rhythmical. In her ears she wore two large pearls of matchless purity, pearls which had come from a famous necklace of her mother's, known thoughout Rome.

Pierre apologised and thanked her. 'You see me in confusion, madame,' said he; 'I should have liked to express to you this morning my gratitude for your great kindness.'

He had hesitated to call her madame, remembering the plea brought forward in the suit for the dissolution of her marriage. But plainly enough everybody must call her madame. Moreover, her face had retained its calm and kindly expression.

'Consider yourself at home here, Monsieur l'Abbé,' she responded, wishing to put him at his ease. 'It is sufficient that our relative, Monsieur de la Choue, should be fond of you, and take interest in your work. I have, you know, much affection for him.' Then her voice faltered slightly, for she realised that she ought to speak of the book, the one reason of Pierre's journey and her proffered hospitality. 'Yes,' she added, ' the Viscount sent me your book. I read it and found it very beautiful. It disturbed me. But I am only an ignoramus, and certainly failed to understand everything in it.

We must talk it over together; you will explain your ideas to me, won't you, Monsieur l'Abbé?'

In her large clear eyes, which did not know how to lie, Pierre then read the surprise and emotion of a child's soul when confronted by disquieting and undreamt-of problems. So it was not she who had become impassioned and had desired to have him near her that she might sustain him and assist his victory. Once again, and this time very keenly, he suspected a secret influence, a hidden hand which was directing everything towards some unknown goal. However, he was charmed by so much simplicity and frankness in so beautiful, young, and noble a creature; and he gave himself to her after the exchange of those few words, and was about to tell her that she might absolutely dispose of him, when he was interrupted by the advent of another woman, whose tall, slight figure, also clad in black, stood out strongly against the luminous background of the further reception room as seen through the open doorway.

'Well, Benedetta, have you sent Giacomo up to see?' asked the newcomer. 'Don Vigilio has just come down and he is quite alone. It is improper.'

'No, no, aunt. Monsieur l'Abbé is here,' was the reply of Benedetta, hastening to introduce the young priest. 'Monsieur l'Abbé Pierre Froment—The Princess Boccanera.'

Ceremonious salutations were exchanged. The Princess must have been nearly sixty, but she laced herself so tightly that from behind one might have taken her for a young woman. This tight lacing, however, was her last coquetry. Her hair, though still plentiful, was quite white, her eyebrows alone remaining black in her long, wrinkled face, from which projected the large obstinate nose of the family. She had never been beautiful, and had remained a spinster, wounded to the heart by the selection of Count Brandini, who had preferred her younger sister, Ernesta. From that moment she had resolved to seek consolation and satisfaction in family pride alone, the hereditary pride of the great name which she bore. The Boccaneras had already supplied two Popes to the Church, and she hoped that before she died her brother would become the third. She had transformed herself into his housekeeper, as it were, remaining with him, watching over him, and advising him, managing all the household affairs herself, and accomplishing miracles in order to conceal the slow ruin which was bringing the ceilings about their heads. If every Monday for thirty years past she had continued receiving a few intimates, all of them folks of the Vatican, it was from high political considerations, so that her drawing-room might remain a meeting place of the black world, a power and a threat.

And Pierre divined by her greeting that she deemed him of little account, petty foreign priest that he was, not even a prelate. This too again surprised him, again brought the puzzling question to the fore : Why had he been invited, what was expected of him in this society from which the humble were usually excluded ? Knowing the Princess to be austerely devout, he at last fancied that she received him solely out of regard for her kinsman, the Viscount, for in her turn she only found these words of welcome : 'We are so pleased to receive good news of Monsieur de la Choue ! He brought us such a beautiful pilgrimage two years ago.'

Passing the first through the doorway, she at last ushered the young priest into the adjoining reception room. It was a spacious square apartment, hung with old yellow *brocatelle* of a flowery Louis XIV pattern. The lofty ceiling was adorned with a very fine panelling, carved and coloured, with gilded roses in each compartment. The furniture, however, was of all sorts. There were some high mirrors, a couple of superb gilded pier-tables, and a few handsome seventeenth-century armchairs ; but all the rest was wretched. A heavy round table of first-empire style, which had come nobody knew whence, caught the eye, with a medley of anomalous articles picked up at some bazaar, and a quantity of cheap photographs littered the costly marble tops of the pier-tables. No interesting article of *virtù* was to be seen. The old paintings on the walls were with two exceptions feebly executed. There was a delightful example of an unknown primitive master, a fourteenth-century Visitation, in which the Virgin had the stature and pure delicacy of a child of ten, whilst the Archangel, huge and superb, inundated her with a stream of dazzling, superhuman love ; and in front of this hung an antique family portrait, depicting a very beautiful young girl in a turban, who was thought to be Cassia Boccanera, the *amorosa* and avengeress who had flung herself into the Tiber with her brother Ercole and the corpse of her lover, Flavio Corradini. Four lamps threw a broad, peaceful glow over the faded room, and, like a melancholy sunset, tinged it with yellow. It looked grave and bare, with not even a flower in a vase to brighten it.

In a few words Donna Serafina at once introduced Pierre to
the company ; and in the silence, the pause which ensued in
the conversation, he felt that every eye was fixed upon him
as upon a promised and expected curiosity.   There were
altogether some ten persons present, among them being
Dario, who stood talking with little Princess Celia Buongiovanni, whilst the elderly relative who had brought the latter
sat whispering to a prelate, Monsignor Nani, in a dim corner.
Pierre, however, had been particularly struck by the name of
Consistorial-Advocate Morano, of whose position in the house
Viscount de la Choue had thought proper to inform him in
order to avert any unpleasant blunder.   For thirty years past
Morano had been Donna Serafina's *amico*.   Their connection,
formerly a guilty one, for the advocate had wife and children
of his own, had in course of time, since he had been left a
widower, become one of those *liaisons* which tolerant people
excuse and except.   Both parties were extremely devout and
had certainly assured themselves of all needful 'indulgences.'
And thus Morano was there in the seat which he had always
taken for a quarter of a century past, a seat beside the chimney-
piece, though as yet the winter fire had not been lighted, and
when Donna Serafina had discharged her duties as mistress
of the house, she returned to her own place in front of him,
on the other side of the chimney.

When Pierre in his turn had seated himself near Don
Vigilio, who, silent and discreet, had already taken a chair,
Dario resumed in a louder voice the story which he had been
relating to Celia.   Dario was a handsome man, of average
height, slim and elegant.   He wore a full beard, dark and
carefully tended, and had the long face and pronounced nose
of the Boccaneras, but the impoverishment of the family
blood over a course of centuries had attenuated, softened as it
were, any sharpness or undue prominence of feature.

'Oh ! a beauty, an astounding beauty !' he repeated
emphatically.

'Whose beauty ?' asked Benedetta, approaching him.

Celia, who resembled the little Virgin of the primitive
master hanging above her head, began to laugh.   'Oh !
Dario's speaking of a poor girl, a work girl whom he met to-
day,' she explained.

Thereupon Dario had to begin his narrative again.   It
appeared that while passing along a narrow street near the
Piazza Navona, he had perceived a tall, shapely girl of

twenty, who was weeping and sobbing violently, prone
upon a flight of steps. Touched particularly by her beauty,
he had approached her and learnt that she had been working
in the house outside which she was, a manufactory of wax
beads, but that, slack times having come, the workshops had
closed and she did not dare to return home, so fearful was
the misery there. Amidst the downpour of her tears she
raised such beautiful eyes to his that he ended by drawing
some money from his pocket. But at this, crimson with
confusion, she sprang to her feet, hiding her hands in the
folds of her skirt, and refusing to take anything. She added,
however, that he might follow her if it so pleased him, and
give the money to her mother. And then she hurried off
towards the Ponte St'. Angelo.[1]

'Yes, she was a beauty, a perfect beauty,' repeated Dario
with an air of ecstasy. 'Taller than I, and slim though sturdy,
with the bosom of a goddess. In fact, a real antique, a Venus
of twenty, her chin rather bold, her mouth and nose of perfect
form, and her eyes wonderfully pure and large! And she was
bare-headed too, with nothing but a crown of heavy black hair,
and a dazzling face, gilded, so to say, by the sun.'

They had all begun to listen to him, enraptured, full of
that passionate admiration for beauty which, in spite of every
change, Rome still retains in her heart.

'Those beautiful girls of the people are becoming very
rare,' remarked Morano. 'You might scour the Trastevere
without finding any. However, this proves that there is at
least one of them left.'

'And what was your goddess's name?' asked Benedetta,
smiling, amused and enraptured like the others.

'Pierina,' replied Dario, also with a laugh.

'And what did you do with her?'

At this question the young man's excited face assumed an
expression of discomfort and fear, like the face of a child on
suddenly encountering some ugly creature amidst its play.

'Oh! don't talk of it,' said he. 'I felt very sorry afterwards. I saw such misery—enough to make one ill.'

Yielding to his curiosity, it seemed, he had followed the
girl across the Ponte St'. Angelo into the new district which
was being built over the former castle meadows;[2] and there,

---

[1] Bridge of St. Angelo.
[2] The meadows around the Castle of St. Angelo. The district, now
covered with buildings, is quite flat, and was formerly greatly subject to
floods. It is known as the Quartiere dei Prati.—*Trans.*

on the first floor of an abandoned house which was already
falling into ruins, though the plaster was scarcely dry, he had
come upon a frightful spectacle which still stirred his heart:
a whole family, father and mother, children, and an infirm old
uncle, dying of hunger and rotting in filth! He selected the
most dignified words he could think of to describe the scene,
waving his hand the while with a gesture of fright, as if to
ward off some horrible vision.

'At last,' he concluded, 'I ran away, and you may be sure
that I shan't go back again.'

A general wagging of heads ensued in the cold, irksome
silence which fell upon the room. Then Morano summed up
the matter in a few bitter words, in which he accused the
despoilers, the men of the Quirinal, of being the sole cause
of all the frightful misery of Rome. Were not people even
talking of the approaching nomination of Deputy Sacco as
Minister of Finances—Sacco, that intriguer who had engaged
in all sorts of underhand practices? His appointment would
be the climax of impudence; bankruptcy would speedily and
infallibly ensue.

Méantime Benedetta, who had fixed her eyes on Pierre,
with his book in her mind, alone murmured: 'Poor people,
how very sad! But why not go back to see them?'

Pierre, out of his element and absent-minded during the
earlier moments, had been deeply stirred by the latter part of
Dario's narrative. His thoughts reverted to his apostolate
amidst the misery of Paris, and his heart was touched with
compassion at being confronted by the story of such fearful
sufferings on the very day of his arrival in Rome. Unwittingly, impulsively, he raised his voice, and said aloud: 'Oh!
we will go to see them together, madame; you will take me.
These questions impassion me so much.'

The attention of everybody was then again turned upon the
young priest. The others questioned him, and he realised that
they were all anxious about his first impressions, his opinion
of their city and of themselves. He must not judge Rome by
mere outward appearances, they said. What effect had the
city produced on him? How had he found it, and what did
he think of it? Thereupon he politely apologised for his
inability to answer them. He had not yet gone out, said he,
and had seen nothing. But this answer was of no avail; they
pressed him all the more keenly, and he fully understood that
their object was to gain him over to admiration and love.

They advised him, adjured him not to yield to any fatal disillusion, but to persist and wait until Rome should have revealed to him her soul.

'How long do you expect to remain among us, Monsieur l'Abbé?' suddenly inquired a courteous voice with a clear but gentle ring.

It was Monsignor Nani, who, seated in the gloom, thus raised his voice for the first time. On several occasions it had seemed to Pierre that the prelate's keen blue eyes were steadily fixed upon him, though all the while he pretended to be attentively listening to the drawling chatter of Celia's aunt. And before replying Pierre glanced at him. In his crimson-edged cassock, with a violet silk sash drawn tightly around his waist, Nani still looked young, although he was over fifty. His hair had remained *blond*, he had a straight refined nose, a mouth very firm yet very delicate of contour, and beautifully white teeth.

'Why, a fortnight or perhaps three weeks, monsignor,' replied Pierre.

But everybody protested. What, three weeks! It was his pretension to know Rome in three weeks! Why, six weeks, twelve months, ten years were required! The first impression was always a disastrous one, and a long sojourn was needed for a visitor to recover from it.

'Three weeks!' repeated Donna Serafina with her disdainful air. 'Is it possible for people to study one another and get fond of one another in three weeks? Those who come back to us are those who have learned to know us.'

Instead of launching into exclamations like the others, Nani had at first contented himself with smiling, and gently waving his shapely hand, which bespoke his aristocratic origin. Then, as Pierre modestly explained himself, saying that he had come to Rome to attend to certain matters and would leave again as soon as those matters should have been concluded, the prelate, still smiling, summed up the argument with the remark: 'Oh! Monsieur l'Abbé will stay with us for more than three weeks; we shall have the happiness of his presence here for a long time, I hope.'

These words, though spoken with quiet cordiality, strangely disturbed the young priest. What was known, what was meant? He leant towards Don Vigilio, who had remained near him, still and ever silent, and in a whisper inquired: 'Who is Monsignor Nani?'

The secretary, however, did not at once reply. His feverish face became yet more livid. Then his ardent eyes glanced round to make sure that nobody was watching him, and in a breath he responded : 'He is the Assessor of the Holy Office.' [1]

This information sufficed, for Pierre was not ignorant of the fact that the assessor, who was present in silence at the meetings of the Holy Office, waited upon his Holiness every Wednesday evening after the sitting, to render him an account of the matters dealt with in the afternoon. This weekly audience, this hour spent with the Pope in a privacy which allowed of every subject being broached, gave the assessor an exceptional position, one of considerable power. Moreover the office led to the cardinalate ; the only 'rise' that could be given to the assessor was his promotion to the Sacred College.

Monsignor Nani, who seemed so perfectly frank and amiable, continued to look at the young priest with such an encouraging air that the latter felt obliged to go and occupy the seat beside him, which Celia's old aunt at last vacated. After all, was there not an omen of victory in meeting, on the very day of his arrival, a powerful prelate whose influence would perhaps open every door to him ? He therefore felt very touched when Monsignor Nani, immediately after the first words, inquired in a tone of deep interest, 'And so, my dear child, you have published a book ? '

After this, gradually mastered by his enthusiasm and forgetting where he was, Pierre unbosomed himself, and recounted the birth and progress of his burning love amidst the sick and the humble, gave voice to his dream of a return to the olden Christian community, and triumphed with the rejuvenescence of Catholicism, developing into the one religion of the universal democracy. Little by little he again raised his voice, and silence fell around him in the stern, antique reception room, every one lending ear to his words with increasing surprise, with a growing coldness of which he remained unconscious.

At last Nani gently interrupted him, still wearing his perpetual smile, the faint irony of which, however, had departed. 'No doubt, no doubt, my dear child,' he said, 'it is very beautiful, oh ! very beautiful, well worthy of the pure and noble imagination of a Christian. But what do you count on doing now ?

[1] Otherwise the Inquisition.

'I shall go straight to the Holy Father to defend myself,' answered Pierre.

A light, restrained laugh went round, and Donna Serafina expressed the general opinion by exclaiming: 'The Holy Father isn't seen as easily as that.'

Pierre, however, was quite impassioned. 'Well, for my part, he rejoined, 'I hope I shall see him. Have I not expressed his views? Have I not defended his policy? Can he let my book be condemned when I believe that I have taken inspiration from all that is best in him?'

'No doubt, no doubt,' Nani again hastily replied, as if he feared that the others might be too brusque with the young enthusiast. 'The Holy Father has such a lofty mind. And of course it would be necessary to see him. Only, my dear child, you must not excite yourself so much; reflect a little; take your time.' And, turning to Benedetta, he added, 'Of course his Eminence has not seen Abbé Froment yet. It would be well, however, that he should receive him to-morrow morning to guide him with his wise counsel.'

Cardinal Boccanera never attended his sister's Monday-evening receptions. Still, he was always there in the spirit, like some absent sovereign master.

'To tell the truth,' replied the Contessina, hesitating, 'I fear that my uncle does not share Monsieur l'Abbé's views.'

Nani again smiled, 'Exactly; he will tell him things which it is good he should hear.'

Thereupon it was at once settled with Don Vigilio that the latter would put down the young priest's name for an audience on the following morning at ten o'clock.

However, at that moment a cardinal came in, clad in town costume—his sash and his stockings red, but his simar black, with a red edging and red buttons. It was Cardinal Sarno, a very old intimate of the Boccaneras; and whilst he apologised for arriving so late, through press of work, the company became silent and deferentially clustered round him. This was the first cardinal Pierre had seen, and he felt greatly disappointed, for the newcomer had none of the majesty, none of the fine port and presence to which he had looked forward. On the contrary, he was short and somewhat deformed, with the left shoulder higher than the right, and a worn, ashen face with lifeless eyes. To Pierre he looked like some old clerk of seventy, half stupefied by fifty years of office work, dulled and bent by incessantly leaning over his writing-desk

ever since his youth. And indeed that was Sarno's story.
The puny child of a petty middle-class family, he had been
educated at the Seminario Romano. Then later he had for
ten years professed Canon Law at that same seminary, afterwards becoming one of the secretaries of the Congregation for
the Propagation of the Faith. Finally, five-and-twenty years
ago, he had been created a cardinal, and the jubilee of his
cardinalate had recently been celebrated. Born in Rome, he
had always lived there ; he was the perfect type of the prelate
who, through growing up in the shade of the Vatican, has
become one of the masters of the world. Although he had
never occupied any diplomatic post, he had rendered such
important services to the Propaganda, by his methodical habits
of work, that he had become president of one of the two com-
missions which furthered the interests of the Church in those
vast countries of the west which are not yet Catholic. And
thus, in the depths of his dim eyes, behind his low, dull-look-
ing brow, the huge map of Christendom was stored away.

Nani himself had risen, full of covert respect for the unobtrusive but terrible man whose hand was everywhere, even
in the most distant corners of the earth, although he had never
left his office. As Nani knew, despite his apparent nullity,
Sarno, with his slow, methodical, ably organised work of conquest, possessed sufficient power to set empires in confusion.

'Has your Eminence recovered from that cold which distressed us so much ? ' asked Nani.

'No, no, I still cough. There is a most malignant passage
at the offices. I feel as cold as ice as soon as I leave my room.'

From that moment Pierre felt quite little, virtually lost.
He was not even introduced to the Cardinal. And yet he had
to remain in the room for nearly another hour, looking around
and observing. That antiquated world then seemed to him
puerile, as though it had lapsed into a mournful second childhood. Under all the apparent haughtiness and proud reserve
he could divine real timidity, unacknowledged distrust, born
of great ignorance. If the conversation did not become
general, it was because nobody dared to speak out frankly ;
and what he heard in the corners was simply so much childish
chatter, the petty gossip of the week, the trivial echoes of
sacristies and drawing-rooms. People saw but little of one
another, and the slightest incidents assumed huge proportions. At last Pierre ended by feeling as though he were
transported into some *salon* of the time of Charles X, in one of

the episcopal cities of the French provinces. No refreshments were served. Celia's old aunt secured possession of Cardinal Sarno; but, instead of replying to her, he simply wagged his head from time to time. Don Vigilio had not opened his mouth the whole evening. However, a conversation in a very low tone was started by Nani and Morano, to whom Donna Serafina listened, leaning forward and expressing her approval by slowly nodding her head. They were doubtless speaking of the dissolution of Benedetta's marriage, for they glanced at the young woman gravely from time to time. And in the centre of the spacious room, in the sleepy glow of the lamps, there were only the young people, Benedetta, Dario, and Celia, who seemed to be at all alive, chattering in undertones and occasionally repressing a burst of laughter.

All at once Pierre was struck by the great resemblance between Benedetta and the portrait of Cassia hanging on the wall. Each displayed the same delicate youth, the same passionate mouth, the same large, unfathomable eyes, set in the same round, sensible, healthy-looking face. In each there was certainly the same upright soul, the same heart of flame. Then a recollection came to Pierre, that of a painting by Guido Reni, the adorable, candid head of Beatrice Cenci, which, at that moment and to his thinking, the portrait of Cassia closely resembled. This resemblance stirred him and he glanced at Benedetta with anxious sympathy, as if all the fierce fatality of race and country were about to fall on her. But no, it could not be; she looked so calm, so resolute, and so patient! Besides, ever since he had entered that room he had noticed none other than signs of gay fraternal tenderness between her and Dario, especially on her side, for her face ever retained the bright serenity of a love which may be openly confessed. At one moment, it is true, Dario in a joking way had caught hold of her hands and pressed them; but while he began to laugh rather nervously, with a brighter gleam darting from his eyes, she on her side, all composure, slowly freed her hands, as though theirs was but the play of old and affectionate friends. She loved him, though, it was visible, with her whole being and for her whole life.

At last when Dario, after stifling a slight yawn and glancing at his watch, had slipped off to join some friends who were playing cards at a lady's house, Benedetta and Celia sat down together on a sofa near Pierre; and the latter, without wishing to listen, overheard a few words of their confidential

chat. The little Princess was the eldest daughter of Prince
Matteo Buongiovanni, who was already the father of five
children by an English wife, a Mortimer, to whom he was
indebted for a dowry of two hundred thousand pounds. Indeed, the Buongiovannis were known as one of the few
patrician families of Rome that were still rich, still erect
among the ruins of the past, now crumbling on every side.
They also numbered two popes among their forerunners, yet
this had not prevented Prince Matteo from lending support
to the Quirinal without quarrelling with the Vatican. Son of an
American woman, no longer having the pure Roman blood in his
veins, he was a more supple politician than other aristocrats,
and was also, folks said, extremely grasping, struggling to be
one of the last to retain the wealth and power of olden times,
which he realised were condemned to death. Yet it was in his
family, renowned for its superb pride and its continued magnificence, that a love romance had lately taken birth, a romance
which was the subject of endless gossip : Celia had suddenly
fallen in love with a young lieutenant to whom she had never
spoken ; her love was reciprocated, and the passionate attachment of the officer and the girl only found vent in the glances
they exchanged on meeting each day during the usual drive
through the Corso. Nevertheless Celia displayed a tenacious
will, and after declaring to her father that she would never
take any other husband, she was waiting, firm and resolute,
in the certainty that she would ultimately secure the man of
her choice. The worst of the affair was that the lieutenant,
Attilio Sacco, happened to be the son of Deputy Sacco, a
parvenu whom the black world looked down upon, as upon
one sold to the Quirinal and ready to undertake the very
dirtiest jobs.

'It was for me that Morano spoke just now,' Celia murmured in Benedetta's ear. 'Yes, yes, when he spoke so
harshly of Attilio's father and that ministerial appointment
which people are talking about. He wanted to give me a
lesson.'

The two girls had sworn eternal affection in their school-
days, and Benedetta, the elder by five years, showed herself
maternal. 'And so,' she said, 'you've not become a whit
more reasonable. You still think of that young man ?'

'What! are you going to grieve me too, dear ?' replied
Celia. 'I love Attilio and mean to have him. Yes, him and

not another! I want him and I'll have him, because I love
him and he loves me. It's simple enough.'

Pierre glanced at her thunderstruck. With her gentle
virgin face she was like a candid, budding lily. A brow and
a nose of blossom-like purity; a mouth all innocence with its
lips closing over pearly teeth, and eyes like spring water,
clear and fathomless. And not a quiver passed over her
cheeks of satiny freshness, no sign, however faint, of anxiety
or inquisitiveness appeared in her candid glance. Did she
think? Did she know? Who could have answered? She
was virginity personified with all its redoubtable mystery.

'Ah! my dear,' resumed Benedetta, 'don't begin my sad
story over again. One doesn't succeed in marrying the Pope
and the King.'

All tranquillity, Celia responded: 'But you didn't love
Prada, whereas I love Attilio. Life lies in that: one must
love.'

These words, spoken so naturally by that ignorant child,
disturbed Pierre to such a point that he felt tears rising to
his eyes. Love! yes, therein lay the solution of every quarrel,
the alliance between the nations, the reign of peace and joy
throughout the world! However, Donna Serafina had now
risen, shrewdly suspecting the nature of the conversation which
was impassioning the two girls. And she gave Don Vigilio a
glance, which the latter understood, for he came to tell Pierre
in an undertone that it was time to retire. Eleven o'clock was
striking, and Celia went off with her aunt. Advocate Morano,
however, doubtless desired to retain Cardinal Sarno and Nani
for a few moments in order that they might privately discuss
some difficulty which had arisen in the divorce proceedings.
On reaching the outer reception room, Benedetta, after kissing
Celia on both cheeks, took leave of Pierre with much good
grace.

'In answering the Viscount to-morrow morning,' said she,
'I shall tell him how happy we are to have you with us, and
for longer than you think. Don't forget to come down at ten
o'clock to see my uncle, the Cardinal.'

Having climbed to the third floor again, Pierre and Don
Vigilio, each carrying a candlestick which the servant had
handed to them, were about to part for the night, when the
former could not refrain from asking the secretary a question
which had been worrying him for hours: 'Is Monsignor Nani
a very influential personage?'

Don Vigilio again became quite scared, and simply replied by a gesture, opening his arms as if to embrace the world. Then his eyes flashed, and in his turn he seemed to yield to inquisitiveness. 'You already knew him, didn't you?' he inquired.

'I? not at all!'

'Really! Well, he knows you very well. Last Monday I heard him speak of you in such precise terms that he seemed to be acquainted with the slightest particulars of your career and your character.'

'Why, I never even heard his name before.'

'Then he must have procured information.'

Thereupon Don Vigilio bowed and entered his room; whilst Pierre, surprised to find his door open, saw Victorine come out with her calm active air.

'Ah! Monsieur l'Abbé, I wanted to make sure that you had everything you were likely to want. There are candles, water, sugar, and matches. And what do you take in the morning, please? Coffee? No, a cup of milk with a roll. Very good; at eight o'clock, eh? And now rest and sleep well. I was awfully afraid of ghosts during the first nights I spent in this old palace! But I never saw a trace of one. The fact is, when people are dead, they are too well pleased, and don't want to break their rest!'

Then off she went, and Pierre at last found himself alone, glad to be able to shake off the strain imposed on him, to free himself from the discomfort which he had felt in that reception room, among those people who in his mind still mingled and vanished like shadows in the sleepy glow of the lamps. Ghosts, thought he, are the old dead ones of long ago whose distressed spirits return to love and suffer in the breasts of the living of to-day. And, despite his long afternoon rest, he had never felt so weary, so desirous of slumber, confused and foggy as was his mind, full of the fear that he had hitherto not understood things aright. When he began to undress, his astonishment at being in that room returned to him with such intensity that he almost fancied himself another person. What did all those people think of his book? Why had he been brought to this cold dwelling whose hostility he could divine? Was it for the purpose of helping him or conquering him? And again in the yellow glimmer, the dismal sunset of the drawing-room, he perceived Donna Serafina and Advocate Morano on either side of the chimney-piece, whilst behind

the calm yet passionate visage of Benedetta appeared the
smiling face of Monsignor Nani, with cunning eyes and lips
bespeaking indomitable energy.

He went to bed, but soon got up again, stifling, feeling
such a need of fresh, free air that he opened the window wide
in order to lean out. But the night was black as ink, the
darkness had submerged the horizon. A mist must have
hidden the stars in the firmament; the vault above seemed
opaque and heavy like lead; and yonder in front the houses
of the Trastevere had long since been asleep. Not one of all
their windows glittered; there was but a single gas-light
shining, all alone and far away, like a lost spark. In vain did
Pierre seek the Janiculum. In the depths of that ocean of
nihility all sunk and vanished, Rome's four and twenty centuries, the ancient Palatine and the modern Quirinal, even
the giant dome of St. Peter's, blotted out from the sky by the
flood of gloom. And below him he could not see, he could
not even hear the Tiber, the dead river flowing past the dead
city.

III

AT a quarter to ten o'clock on the following morning Pierre
came down to the first floor of the mansion for his audience
with Cardinal Boccanera. He had awoke free of all fatigue
and again full of courage and candid enthusiasm; nothing
remaining of his strange despondency of the previous night,
the doubts and suspicions which had then come over him. The
morning was so fine, the sky so pure and so bright, that his
heart once more palpitated with hope.

On the landing he found the folding doors of the first
anteroom wide open. While closing the gala saloons which
overlooked the street, and which were rotting with old age and
neglect, the Cardinal still used the reception rooms of one of
his grand-uncles, who in the eighteenth century had risen to
the same ecclesiastical dignity as himself. There was a suite
of four immense rooms, each sixteen feet high, with windows
facing the lane which sloped down towards the Tiber; and the
sun never entered them, shut off as it was by the black houses
across the lane. Thus the installation, in point of space, was
in keeping with the display and pomp of the old-time princely
dignitaries of the Church. But no repairs were ever made,
no care was taken of anything, the hangings were frayed and

ragged, and dust preyed on the furniture, amidst an unconcern
which seemed to betoken some proud resolve to stay the course
of time.

Pierre experienced a slight shock as he entered the first
room, the servants' antechamber. Formerly two pontifical
gente d'armi in full uniform had always stood there amidst a
stream of lackeys; and the single servant now on duty seemed
by his phantom-like appearance to increase the melancholiness
of the vast and gloomy hall. One was particularly struck by
an altar facing the windows, an altar with red drapery surmounted by a *baldacchino* with red hangings, on which appeared
the escutcheon of the Boccaneras, the winged dragon spitting
flames with the device, *Bocca nera, Alma rossa.* And the
grand-uncle's red hat, the old huge ceremonial hat, was also
there, with the two cushions of red silk, and the two antique
parasols which were taken in the coach each time his Eminence
went out. And in the deep silence it seemed as if one could
almost hear the faint noise of the termites preying for a
century past upon all this dead splendour, which would have
fallen into dust at the slightest touch of a feather broom.

The second anteroom, that was formerly occupied by the
secretary, was also empty, and it was only in the third one,
the *anticamera nobile*, that Pierre found Don Vigilio. With
his retinue reduced to what was strictly necessary, the Cardinal
had preferred to have his secretary near him—at the door, so to
say, of the old throne-room, where he gave audience. And
Don Vigilio, so thin and yellow, and quivering with fever, sat
there like one lost, at a small, common, black table covered
with papers. Raising his head from among a batch of documents, he recognised Pierre, and in a low voice, a faint
murmur amidst the silence, he said, 'His Eminence is
engaged. Please wait.'

Then he again turned to his reading, doubtless to escape
all attempts at conversation.

Not daring to sit down, Pierre examined the apartment.
It looked perhaps yet more dilapidated than the others, with
its hangings of green damask worn by age and resembling the
faded moss on ancient trees. The ceiling, however, had
remained superb. Within a frieze of gilded and coloured ornaments was a fresco representing the Triumph of Amphitrite,
the work of one of Raffaelle's pupils And, according to antique
usage, it was here that the *berretta*, the red cap, was placed,
on a credence, below a large crucifix of ivory and ebony.

As Pierre grew used to the half-light, however, his attention was more particularly attracted by a recently painted full-length portrait of the Cardinal in ceremonial costume—cassock of red moire, rochet of lace, and *cappa* thrown like a royal mantle over his shoulders. In these vestments of the Church the tall old man of seventy retained the proud bearing of a prince, clean shaven, but still boasting an abundance of white hair which streamed in curls over his shoulders. He had the commanding visage of the Boccaneras, a large nose and a large thin-lipped mouth in a long face intersected by broad lines; and the eyes which lighted his pale countenance were indeed the eyes of his race, very dark, yet sparkling with ardent life under bushy brows which had remained quite black. With laurels about his head he would have resembled a Roman emperor, very handsome and master of the world, as though indeed the blood of Augustus pulsated in his veins.

Pierre knew his story which this portrait recalled. Educated at the College of the Nobles, Pio Boccanera had but once absented himself from Rome, and that when very young, hardly a deacon, but nevertheless appointed ablegate to convey a *berretta* to Paris. On his return his ecclesiastical career had continued in sovereign fashion. Honours had fallen on him naturally, as by right of birth. Ordained by Pius IX himself, afterwards becoming a Canon of the Vatican Basilica, and *Cameriere segreto*, he had risen to the post of Majordomo about the time of the Italian occupation, and in 1874 had been created a Cardinal. For the last four years, moreover, he had been Papal Chamberlain (*Camerlingo*), and folks whispered that Leo XIII had appointed him to that post, even as he himself had been appointed to it by Pius IX, in order to lessen his chance of succeeding to the pontifical throne; for although the conclave in choosing Leo had set aside the old tradition that the Camerlingo was ineligible for the papacy, it was not probable that it would again dare to infringe that rule. Moreover, people asserted that, even as had been the case in the reign of Pius, there was a secret warfare between the Pope and his Camerlingo, the latter remaining on one side, condemning the policy of the Holy See, holding radically different opinions on all things, and silently waiting for the death of Leo, which would place power in his hands with the duty of summoning the conclave, and provisionally watching over the affairs and interests of the Church until a new Pope should be elected. Behind Cardinal Pio's broad, stern brow, however, in the glow of his dark eyes, might there not also be the ambition of actually rising to the papacy, of repeating the career of Gioachino Pecci, Camerlingo and then Pope, all tradition notwithstanding ? With the pride of a Roman prince Pio knew but Rome ; he almost gloried in being totally ignorant of the modern world ; and verily he showed himself very pious, austerely religious, with a full firm faith into which the faintest doubt could never enter.

But a whisper drew Pierre from his reflections. Don Vigilio, in his prudent way, invited him to sit down : 'You may have to wait some time : take a stool.'

Then he began to cover a large sheet of yellowish paper with fine writing, while Pierre seated himself on one of the stools ranged alongside the wall in front of the portrait. And again the young man fell into a reverie, picturing in his mind a renewal of all the princely pomp of the old-time cardinals in that antique room. To begin with, as soon as nominated, a cardinal gave public festivities, which were sometimes very splendid. During three days the reception rooms remained wide open, all could enter, and from room to room ushers repeated the names of those who came—patricians, people of the middle class, poor folks, all Rome indeed, whom the new cardinal received with sovereign kindliness, as a king might receive his subjects. Then there was quite a princely retinue ; some cardinals carried five hundred people about with them, had no fewer than sixteen distinct offices in their households, lived, in fact, amidst a perfect court. Even when life subsequently became simplified, a cardinal, if he were a prince, still had a right to a gala train of four coaches drawn by black horses. Four servants preceded him in liveries, emblazoned with his arms, and carried his hat, cushion, and parasols. He was also attended by a secretary in a mantle of violet silk, a train-bearer in a gown of violet woollen stuff, and a gentleman in waiting, wearing an Elizabethan style of costume, and bearing the *berretta* with gloved hands. Although the household had then become smaller, it still comprised an *auditore* specially charged with the congregational work, a secretary employed exclusively for correspondence, a chief usher who introduced visitors, a gentleman in attendance for the carrying of the *berretta*, a train-bearer, a chaplain, a majordomo and a *valet de chambre*, to say nothing of a flock of underlings, lackeys, cooks, coachmen, grooms, quite a population, which filled the vast mansions with bustle. And with these attendants Pierre mentally sought to fill the three spacious anterooms now so deserted; the stream of lackeys in blue liveries broidered with emblazonry, the world of abbés and prelates in silk mantles appeared before him, again setting magnificent and passionate life under the lofty ceilings, illumining all the semi-gloom with resuscitated splendour.

But nowadays—particularly since the Italian occupation of Rome—nearly all the great fortunes of the Roman princes have been exhausted, and the pomp of the great dignitaries of the Church has disappeared. The ruined patricians have kept aloof from badly remunerated ecclesiastical offices to which little renown attaches, and have left them to the ambition of the petty *bourgeoisie*. Cardinal Boccanera, the last prince of ancient nobility invested with the purple, received scarcely more than 30,000 *lire* [1] a year to enable him to sustain his rank, that is 22,000 *lire*,[2] the salary of his post as Camerlingo, and various small sums derived from other functions. And he would never have made both ends meet had not Donna Serafina helped him with the remnants of the former family fortune which he had long previously surrendered to his sisters and his brother. Donna Serafina and Benedetta lived apart, in their own rooms, having their own table, servants and personal expenses. The Cardinal only had his nephew Dario with him, and he never gave a dinner or held a public reception. His greatest source of expense was his carriage, the heavy pair-horse coach, which ceremonial usage compelled him to retain, for a cardinal cannot go on foot through the streets of Rome. However, his coachman, an old family servant, spared him the necessity of keeping a groom by insisting on taking entire charge of the carriage and the two black horses, which, like himself, had grown old in the service of the Boccaneras. There were two footmen, father and son, the latter born in the house. And the cook's wife assisted in the kitchen. However, yet greater reductions had been made in the anterooms, where the staff, once so brilliant and numerous, was now simply composed of two petty priests, Don Vigilio, who was at once secretary, *auditore*, and majordomo, and Abbé Paparelli, who acted as train-bearer, chaplain, and chief usher. There, where a crowd of salaried people of all ranks had once moved to and fro, filling the vast halls with bustle and colour, one now only beheld two little black cossacks gliding noise-

lessly along, two unobtrusive shadows flitting about amidst
the deep gloom of the lifeless rooms.

And Pierre now fully understood the haughty unconcern of
the Cardinal, who suffered time to complete its work of destruction in that ancestral mansion, to which he was powerless to
restore the glorious life of former times ! Built for that shining
life, for the sovereign display of a sixteenth-century prince,
it was now deserted and empty, crumbling about the head of
its last master, who had no servants left him to fill it, and
would not have known how to pay for the materials which
repairs would have necessitated. And so, since the modern
world was hostile, since religion was no longer sovereign, since
men had changed, and one was drifting into the unknown,
amidst the hatred and indifference of new generations, why
not allow the old world to collapse in the stubborn, motionless
pride born of its ancient glory ? Heroes alone died standing,
without relinquishing aught of their past, preserving the same
faith until their final gasp, beholding, with painfraught bravery
and infinite sadness, the slow last agony of their divinity.
And the Cardinal's tall figure, his pale, proud face, so full of
sovereign despair and courage, expressed that stubborn determination to perish beneath the ruins of the old social edifice
rather than change a single one of its stones.

Pierre was roused by a rustling of furtive steps, a little
mouse-like trot, which made him raise his head. A door in
the wall had just opened, and to his surprise there stood before
him an abbé of some forty years, fat and short, looking like an
old maid in a black skirt, a very old maid in fact, so numerous
were the wrinkles on his flabby face. It was Abbé Paparelli,
the train-bearer and usher, and on seeing Pierre he was about
to question him, when Don Vigilio explained matters.

‘Ah ! very good, very good, Monsieur l'Abbé Froment.
His Eminence will condescend to receive you, but you must
wait, you must wait.’

Then, with his silent rolling walk, he returned to the second
anteroom, where he usually stationed himself.

Pierre did not like his face—the face of an old female
devotee, whitened by celibacy, and ravaged by stern observance
of the rites ; and so, as Don Vigilio—his head weary and his
hands burning with fever—had not resumed his work, the
young man ventured to question him. Oh ! Abbé Paparelli,
he was a man of the liveliest faith, who from simple humility
remained in a modest post in his Eminence's service. On the

other hand, his Eminence was pleased to reward him for his devotion by occasionally condescending to listen to his advice.

As Don Vigilio spoke, a faint gleam of irony, a kind of veiled anger appeared in his ardent eyes. However, he continued to examine Pierre, and gradually seemed reassured, appreciating the evident frankness of this foreigner who could hardly belong to any clique. And so he ended by departing somewhat from his continual sickly distrust, and even engaged in a brief chat.

' Yes, yes,' he said, ' there is a deal of work sometimes, and rather hard work too. His Eminence belongs to several Congregations, the Consistorial, the Holy Office, the Index, the Rites. And all the documents concerning the business which falls to him come into my hands. I have to study each affair, prepare a report on it, clear the way, so to say. Besides which all the correspondence is carried on through me. Fortunately his Eminence is a holy man, and intrigues neither for himself nor for others, and this enables us to taste a little peace.'

Pierre took a keen interest in these particulars of the life led by a prince of the Church. He learnt that the Cardinal rose at six o'clock, summer and winter alike. He said his mass in his chapel, a little room which simply contained an altar of painted wood, and which nobody but himself ever entered. His private apartments were limited to three rooms— a bedroom, dining-room, and study—all very modest and small, contrived indeed by partitioning off portions of one large hall. And he led a very retired life, exempt from all luxury, like one who is frugal and poor. At eight in the morning he drank a cup of cold milk for his breakfast. Then, when there were sittings of the Congregations to which he belonged, he attended them; otherwise he remained at home and gave audience. Dinner was served at one o'clock, and afterwards came the siesta, lasting until five in summer and until four at other seasons—a sacred moment when a servant would not have dared even to knock at the door. On awaking, if it were fine, his Eminence drove out towards the ancient Appian Way, returning at sunset when the *Ave Maria* began to ring. And finally, after again giving audience between seven and nine, he supped and retired into his room, where he worked all alone or went to bed. The cardinals wait upon the Pope on fixed days, two or three times each month, for purposes connected with their functions. For nearly a year, however, the Camerlingo had not been received in private audience by his Holiness, and this was a sign of disgrace, a proof of secret warfare, of which the entire black world spoke in prudent whispers.

'His Eminence is sometimes a little rough,' continued Don Vigilio in a soft voice. 'But you should see him smile when his niece the Contessina, of whom he is very fond, comes down to kiss him. If you have a good reception, you know, you will owe it to the Contessina.'

At this moment the secretary was interrupted. A sound of voices came from the second anteroom, and forthwith he rose to his feet, and bent very low at sight of a stout man in a black cassock, red sash, and black hat, with twisted cord of red and gold, whom Abbé Paparelli was ushering in with a great display of deferential genuflections. Pierre also had risen at a sign from Don Vigilio, who found time to whisper to him, 'Cardinal Sanguinetti, Prefect of the Congregation of the Index.'

Meantime Abbé Paparelli was lavishing attentions on the prelate, repeating with an expression of blissful satisfaction: 'Your most reverend Eminence was expected. I have orders to admit your most reverend Eminence at once. His Eminence the Grand Penitentiary is already here.'

Sanguinetti, loud of voice and sonorous of tread, spoke out with sudden familiarity, 'Yes, yes, I know. A number of importunate people detained me! One can never do as one desires. But I am here at last.'

He was a man of sixty, squat and fat, with a round and highly-coloured face distinguished by a huge nose, thick lips, and bright eyes which were always on the move. But he more particularly struck one by his active, almost turbulent, youthful vivacity, scarcely a white hair as yet showing among his brown and carefully tended locks, which fell in curls about his temples. Born at Viterbo, he had studied at the seminary there before completing his education at the Università Gregoriana in Rome. His ecclesiastical appointments showed how rapidly he had made his way, how supple was his mind: first of all secretary to the nunciature at Lisbon; then created titular Bishop of Thebes, and intrusted with a delicate mission in Brazil; on his return appointed nuncio first at Brussels and next at Vienna; and finally raised to the cardinalate, to say nothing of the fact that he had lately secured the suburban episcopal see of Frascati.[1] Trained to business, having dealt with every nation in Europe, he had nothing

---

[1] Cardinals York and Howard were Bishops of Frascati.—*Trans.*

against him but his ambition, of which he made too open a
display, and his spirit of intrigue, which was ever restless. It
was said that he was now one of the irreconcilables who demanded that Italy should surrender Rome, though formerly
he had made advances to the Quirinal. In his wild passion
to become the next Pope he rushed from one opinion to
the other, giving himself no end of trouble to gain people
from whom he afterwards parted. He had twice already fallen
out with Leo XIII, but had deemed it politic to make his submission. In point of fact, given that he was an almost openly
declared candidate to the papacy, he was wearing himself out
by his perpetual efforts, dabbling in too many things, and
setting too many people agog.

Pierre, however, had only seen in him the Prefect of the
Congregation of the Index ; and the one idea which struck
him was that this man would decide the fate of his book. And
so, when the Cardinal had disappeared and Abbé Paparelli had
returned to the second anteroom, he could not refrain from
asking Don Vigilio, ‘Are their Eminences Cardinal Sanguinetti and Cardinal Boccanera very intimate, then ? ’

An irrepressible smile contracted the secretary’s lips, while
his eyes gleamed with an irony which he could no longer
subdue : ‘ Very intimate—oh ! no, no—they see one another
when they can’t do otherwise.’

Then he explained that considerable deference was shown
to Cardinal Boccanera’s high birth, and that his colleagues
often met at his residence, when, as happened to be the case
that morning, any grave affair presented itself; requiring an
interview apart from the usual official meetings. Cardinal
Sanguinetti, he added, was the son of a petty medical man of
Viterbo. ‘ No, no,’ he concluded, ‘ their Eminences are not
at all intimate. It is difficult for men to agree when they
have neither the same ideas nor the same character, especially
too when they are in each other’s way.’

Don Vigilio spoke these last words in a lower tone, as if
talking to himself and still retaining his sharp smile. But
Pierre scarcely listened, absorbed as he was in his own worries :
‘ Perhaps they have met to discuss some affair connected with
the Index ? ’ said he.

Don Vigilio must have known the object of the meeting.
However, he merely replied that, if the Index had been in
question, the meeting would have taken place at the residence
of the Prefect of that Congregation. Thereupon Pierre, yield-

ing to his impatience, was obliged to put a straight question.
'You know of my affair—the affair of my book,' he said.
'Well, as his Eminence is a member of the Congregation, and
all the documents pass through your hands, you might be able
to give me some useful information. I know nothing as yet
and am so anxious to know!'

At this Don Vigilio relapsed into scared disquietude. He
stammered, saying that he had not seen any documents,
which was true. 'Nothing has yet reached us,' he added; 'I
assure you I know nothing.'

Then, as the other persisted, he signed to him to keep
quiet, and again turned to his writing, glancing furtively
towards the second anteroom as if he believed that Abbé
Paparelli was listening. He had certainly said too much, he
thought, and he made himself very small, crouching over the
table, and melting, fading away in his dim corner.

Pierre again fell into a reverie, a prey to all the mystery
which enveloped him—the sleepy, antique sadness of his surroundings. Long minutes went by; it was nearly eleven when
the sound of a door opening and a buzz of voices roused him.
Then he bowed respectfully to Cardinal Sanguinetti, who went
off accompanied by another cardinal, a very thin and tall
man, with a grey, bony, ascetic face. Neither of them, however, seemed even to see the petty foreign priest who bent
low as they went by. They were chatting aloud in familiar
fashion.

'Yes! the wind is falling; it is warmer than yesterday.'

'We shall certainly have the sirocco to-morrow.'

Then solemn silence again fell on the large, dim room. Don
Vigilio was still writing, but his pen made no noise as it
travelled over the stiff yellow paper. However, the faint
tinkle of a cracked bell was suddenly heard, and Abbé
Paparelli, after hastening into the throne-room for a moment,
returned to summon Pierre, whom he announced in a restrained
voice: 'Monsieur l'Abbé Pierre Froment.'

The spacious throne-room was like the other apartments,
a virtual ruin. Under the fine ceiling of carved and gilded
woodwork, the red wall-hangings of *brocatelle*, with a large
palm pattern, were falling into tatters. A few holes had been
patched, but long wear had streaked the dark purple of the
silk—once of dazzling magnificence—with pale hues. The
curiosity of the room was its old throne, an arm-chair
upholstered in red silk, on which the Holy Father had sat

when visiting Cardinal Pio's grand-uncle. This chair was
surmounted by a canopy, likewise of red silk, under which hung
the portrait of the reigning Pope. And, according to custom,
the chair was turned towards the wall, to show that none
might sit on it. The other furniture of the apartment was
made up of sofas, armchairs, and chairs, with a marvellous
Louis Quatorze table of gilded wood, having a top of mosaic
work representing the rape of Europa.

But at first Pierre only saw Cardinal Boccanera standing
by the table which he used for writing. In his simple black
cassock, with red edging and red buttons, the Cardinal seemed
to him yet taller and prouder than in the portrait which
showed him in ceremonial costume. There was the same
curly white hair, the same long, strongly-marked face, with
large nose and thin lips, and the same ardent eyes, illumining
the pale countenance from under bushy brows which had
remained black. But the portrait did not express the lofty,
tranquil faith which shone in this handsome face, a complete
certainty of what truth was, and an absolute determination to
abide by it for ever.

Boccanera had not stirred, but with black, fixed glance
remained watching his visitor's approach; and the young
priest, acquainted with the usual ceremonial, knelt and kissed
the large ruby which the prelate wore on his hand. However,
the Cardinal immediately raised him.

'You are welcome here, my dear son. My niece spoke to
me about you with so much sympathy that I am happy to
receive you.' With these words Pio seated himself near the
table, as yet not telling Pierre to take a chair, but still examining him whilst speaking slowly and with studied politeness:
'You arrived yesterday morning, did you not, and were very
tired?'

'Your Eminence is too kind—yes, I was worn out, as
much through emotion as fatigue. This journey is one of such
gravity for me.'

The Cardinal seemed indisposed to speak of serious matters
so soon. 'No doubt; it is a long way from Paris to Rome,'
he replied. 'Nowadays the journey may be accomplished with
fair rapidity, but formerly how interminable it was!' Then
speaking yet more slowly: 'I went to Paris once—oh! a long
time ago, nearly fifty years ago—and then for barely a week. A
large and handsome city; yes, yes, a great many people in the
streets, extremely well-bred people, a nation which has accom-

plished great and admirable things. Even in these sad times one cannot forget that France was the eldest daughter of the Church. But since that one journey I have not left Rome——'

Then he made a gesture of quiet disdain, expressive of all he left unsaid. What was the use of journeying to a land of doubt and rebellion? Did not Rome suffice—Rome, which governed the world—the Eternal City which, when the times should be accomplished, would become the capital of the world once more?

Silently glancing at the Cardinal's lofty stature, the stature of one of the violent warlike princes of long ago, now reduced to wearing that simple cassock, Pierre deemed him superb with his proud conviction that Rome sufficed unto herself. But that stubborn resolve to remain in ignorance, that determination to take no account of other nations except-ing to treat them as vassals, disquieted him when he reflected on the motives that had brought him there. And as silence had again fallen he thought it politic to approach the subject he had at heart by words of homage.

'Before taking any other steps,' said he, 'I desired to express my profound respect for your Eminence; for in your Eminence I place my only hope; and I beg your Eminence to be good enough to advise and guide me.'

With a wave of the hand Boccanera thereupon invited Pierre to take a chair in front of him. 'I certainly do not refuse you my counsel, my dear son,' he replied. 'I owe my counsel to every Christian who desires to do well. But it would be wrong for you to rely on my influence. I have none. I live entirely apart from others; I cannot and will not ask for anything. However, this will not prevent us from chat-ting.' Then, approaching the question in all frankness, with-out the slightest artifice, like one of brave and absolute mind who fears no responsibility however great, he continued: 'You have written a book, have you not?—" New Rome," I believe—and you have come to defend this book which has been denounced to the Congregation of the Index. For my own part I have not yet read it. You will understand that I can-not read everything. I only see the works that are sent to me by the Congregation, which I have belonged to since last year; and, besides, I often content myself with the reports which my secretary draws up for me. However, my niece Benedetta has read your book, and has told me that it is not lacking in interest. It first astonished her somewhat, and then greatly moved her. So I promise you that I will go through it and study the incriminated passages with the greatest care.'

Pierre profited by the opportunity to begin pleading his cause. And it occurred to him that it would be best to give his references at once. 'Your Eminence will realise how stupefied I was when I learnt that proceedings were being taken against my book,' he said. 'Monsieur le Vicomte Philibert de la Choue, who is good enough to show me some friendship, does not cease repeating that such a book is worth the best of armies to the Holy See.'

'Oh! De la Choue, De la Choue!' repeated the Cardinal with a pout of good-natured disdain. 'I know that De la Choue considers himself a good Catholic. He is in a slight degree our relative, as you know. And when he comes to Rome and stays here, I willingly see him, on condition, however, that no mention is made of certain subjects on which it would be impossible for us to agree. To tell the truth, the Catholicism preached by De la Choue—worthy, clever man though he is—his Catholicism, I say, with his corporations, his working-class clubs, his cleansed democracy and his vague socialism, is after all merely so much literature!'

This pronouncement struck Pierre, for he realised all the disdainful irony contained in it—an irony which touched himself. And so he hastened to name his other reference, whose authority he imagined to be above discussion: 'His Eminence Cardinal Bergerot has been kind enough to signify his full approval of my book.'

At this Boccanera's face suddenly changed. It no longer wore an expression of derisive blame, tinged with the pity that is prompted by a child's ill-considered action fated to certain failure. A flash of anger now lighted up the Cardinal's dark eyes, and a pugnacious impulse hardened his entire countenance. 'In France,' he slowly resumed, 'Cardinal Bergerot no doubt has a reputation for great piety. We know little of him in Rome. Personally, I have only seen him once, when he came to receive his hat. And I would not therefore allow myself to judge him if his writings and actions had not recently saddened my believing soul. Unhappily, I am not the only one ; you will find nobody here, of the Sacred College, who approves of his doings.' Boccanera paused, then in a firm voice concluded : 'Cardinal Bergerot is a Revolutionary!'

This time Pierre's surprise for a moment forced him to
silence. A Revolutionary—good Heavens ! a Revolutionary—
that gentle pastor of souls, whose charity was inexhaustible,
whose one dream was that Jesus might return to earth to
insure at last the reign of peace and justice ! So words did
not have the same signification in all places ; into what
religion had he now tumbled that the faith of the poor and the
humble should be looked upon as a mere insurrectional, condemnable passion ? As yet unable to understand things aright,
Pierre nevertheless realised that discussion would be both
discourteous and futile, and his only remaining desire was to
give an account of his book, explain and vindicate it. But at
his first words the Cardinal interposed.

'No, no, my dear son. It would take us too long and I
wish to read the passages. Besides, there is an absolute rule.
All books which meddle with the faith are condemnable and
pernicious. Does your book show perfect respect for dogma ? '

'I believe so, and I assure your Eminence that I have had
no intention of writing a work of negation.'

'Good : I may be on your side if that is true. Only, in
the contrary case, I have but one course to advise you, which
is to withdraw your work, condemn it, and destroy it without
waiting until a decision of the Index compels you to do so.
Whosoever has given birth to scandal must stifle it and
expiate it, even if he have to cut into his own flesh. The
only duties of a priest are humility and obedience, the
complete annihilation of self before the sovereign will of the
Church. And, besides, why write at all ? For there is
already rebellion in expressing an opinion of one's own. It
is always the temptation of the devil which puts a pen in an
author's hand. Why, then, incur the risk of being for ever
damned by yielding to the pride of intelligence and domination ? Your book again, my dear son—your book is literature,
literature ! '

This expression again repeated was instinct with so much
contempt that Pierre realised all the wretchedness that
would fall upon the poor pages of his apostolate on meeting
the eyes of this prince who had become a saintly man. With
increasing fear and admiration he listened to him, and beheld
him growing greater and greater.

'Ah ! faith, my dear son, everything is in faith—perfect,
disinterested faith—which believes for the sole happiness of
believing ! How restful it is to bow down before the mysteries

without seeking to penetrate them, full of the tranquil conviction that, in accepting them, one possesses both the
certain and the final! Is not the highest intellectual satisfaction that which is derived from the victory of the divine
over the mind, which it disciplines, and contents so completely
that it knows desire no more? And apart from that perfect
equilibrium, that explanation of the unknown by the divine,
no durable peace is possible for man. If one desires that
truth and justice should reign upon earth, it is in God that
one must place them. He that does not believe is like a
battlefield, the scene of every disaster. Faith alone can
tranquillise and deliver.'

For an instant Pierre remained silent before the great
figure rising up in front of him. At Lourdes he had only
seen suffering humanity rushing thither for health of the
body and consolation of the soul; but here was the intellectual
believer, the mind that needs certainty, finding satisfaction,
tasting the supreme enjoyment of doubting no more. He
had never previously heard such a cry of joy at living in
obedience without anxiety as to the morrow of death. He
knew that Boccanera's youth had been somewhat stormy,
traversed by acute attacks of sensuality, a flaring of the red
blood of his ancestors; and he marvelled at the calm majesty
which faith had at last implanted in this descendant of so
violent a race, who had no passion remaining in him but that
of pride.

'And yet,' Pierre at last ventured to say in a timid, gentle
voice, 'if faith remains essential and immutable, forms
change. From hour to hour evolution goes on in all things—
the world changes.'

'That is not true!' exclaimed the Cardinal, 'the world
does not change. It continually tramps over the same
ground, loses itself, strays into the most abominable courses,
and it continually has to be brought back into the right path.
That is the truth. In order that the promises of Christ may
be fulfilled, is it not necessary that the world should return
to its starting point, its original innocence? Is not the end of
time fixed for the day when men shall be in possession of the
full truth of the Gospel? Yes, truth is in the past, and it is
always to the past that one must cling if one would avoid
the pitfalls which evil imaginations create. All those fine
novelties, those mirages of that famous so-called progress, are
simply traps and snares of the eternal tempter, causes of

perdition and death. Why seek any further, why constantly
incur the risk of error, when for eighteen hundred years the
truth has been known? Truth! why it is in Apostolic
and Roman Catholicism as created by a long succession of
generations! What madness to desire to change it when so
many lofty minds, so many pious souls have made of it the
most admirable of monuments, the one instrument of order in
this world, and of salvation in the next!'

Pierre, whose heart had contracted, refrained from further
protest, for he could no longer doubt that he had before him
an implacable adversary of his most cherished ideas. Chilled
by a covert fear, as though he felt a faint breath, as of a distant wind from a land of ruins, pass over his face, bringing
with it the mortal cold of a sepulchre, he bowed respectfully
whilst the Cardinal, rising to his full height, continued in his
obstinate voice, resonant with proud courage: ' And if Catholicism, as its enemies pretend, be really stricken unto death,
it must die standing and in all its glorious integrality. You
hear me, Monsieur l'Abbé—not one concession, not one surrender, not a single act of cowardice! Catholicism is such as it
is, and cannot be otherwise. No modification of the divine
certainty, the entire truth, is possible. The removal of the
smallest stone from the edifice could only prove a cause of
instability. Is this not evident? You cannot save old houses
by attacking them with the pickaxe under pretence of deco-
rating them. You only enlarge the fissures. Even if it were
true that Rome were on the eve of falling into dust, the only
result of all the repairing and patching would be to hasten
the catastrophe. And instead of a noble death, met unflinch-
ingly, we should then behold the basest of agonies, the death
throes of a coward who struggles and begs for mercy! For
my part I wait. I am convinced that all that people say is
but so much horrible falsehood, that Catholicism has never
been firmer, that it imbibes eternity from the one and only
source of life. But should the heavens indeed fall, on that
day I should be here, amidst these old and crumbling walls,
under these old ceilings whose beams are being devoured by
the worms, and it is here erect, among the ruins, that I
should meet my end, repeating my *credo* for the last time.'

His final words fell more slowly, full of haughty sadness,
whilst with a sweeping gesture he waved his arms towards
the old, silent, deserted palace around him, whence life was
withdrawing day by day. Had an involuntary presentiment

come to him, did the faint cold breath from the ruins also
fan his own cheeks ? All the neglect into which the vast
rooms had fallen was explained by his words; and a superb,
despondent grandeur enveloped this prince and cardinal, this
uncompromising Catholic who, withdrawing into the dim
half-light of the past, braved with a soldier's heart the inevitable downfall of the olden world.

Deeply impressed, Pierre was about to take his leave when,
to his surprise, a little door opened in the hangings. ' What
is it ? Can't I be left in peace for a moment ? ' exclaimed
Boccanera with sudden impatience.

Nevertheless, Abbé Paparelli, fat and sleek, glided into the
room without the faintest sign of emotion. And he whispered
a few words in the ear of the Cardinal, who, on seeing him,
had become calm again. ' What curate ? ' asked Boccanera.
' Oh ! yes, Santobono, the curate of Frascati. I know—tell
him I cannot see him just now.'

Paparelli, however, again began whispering in his soft voice,
though not in so low a key as previously, for some of his words
could be overheard. The affair was urgent, the curate was
compelled to return home, and had only a word or two to say.
And then, without awaiting consent, the train-bearer ushered
in the visitor, a *protégé* of his, whom he had left just outside
the little door. And for his own part he withdrew with the
tranquillity of a retainer who, whatever the modesty of his
office, knows himself to be all powerful.

Pierre, who was momentarily forgotten, looked at the
visitor—a big fellow of a priest, the son of a peasant evidently,
and still near to the soil. He had an ungainly, bony figure,
huge feet and knotted hands, with a seamy tanned face lighted
by extremely keen black eyes. Five and forty and still robust,
his chin and cheeks bristling, and his cassock, overlarge,
hanging loosely about his big projecting bones, he suggested
a bandit in disguise. Still there was nothing base about him ;
the expression of his face was proud. And in one hand he
carried a small wicker basket carefully covered over with fig-
leaves.

Santobono at once bent his knees and kissed the Cardinal's
ring, but with hasty unconcern, as though only some ordinary
piece of civility were in question. Then, with that commingling
of respect and familiarity which the little ones of the world
often evince towards the great, he said, ' I beg your most
reverend Eminence's forgiveness for having insisted. But

there were people waiting, and I should not have been received if my old friend Paparelli had not brought me by way of that door. Oh! I have a very great service to ask of your Eminence, a real service of the heart. But first of all may I be allowed to offer your Eminence a little present?'

The Cardinal listened with a grave expression. He had been well acquainted with Santobono in the years when he had spent the summer at Frascati, at a princely residence which the Boccaneras had possessed there—a villa rebuilt in the seventeenth century, surrounded by a wonderful park, whose famous terrace overlooked the Campagna, stretching far and bare like the sea. This villa, however, had since been sold, and on some vineyards, which had fallen to Benedetta's share, Count Prada, prior to the divorce proceedings, had begun to erect quite a district of little pleasure houses. In former times, when walking out, the Cardinal had condescended to enter and rest in the dwelling of Santobono, who officiated at an antique chapel dedicated to St. Mary of the Fields, without the town. The priest had his home in a half-ruined building adjoining this chapel, and the charm of the place was a walled garden which he cultivated himself with the passion of a true peasant.

'As is my rule every year,' said he, placing his basket on the table, 'I wished that your Eminence might taste my figs. They are the first of the season. I gathered them expressly this morning. You used to be so fond of them, your Eminence, when you condescended to gather them from the tree itself. You were good enough to tell me that there wasn't another tree in the world that produced such fine figs.'

The Cardinal could not help smiling. He was indeed very fond of figs, and Santobono spoke truly, his fig-tree was renowned throughout the district. 'Thank you, my dear Abbé,' said Boccanera, 'you remember my little failings. Well, and what can I do for you?'

Again he became grave, for, in former times, there had been unpleasant discussions between him and the curate, a lack of agreement which had angered him. Born at Nemi, in the core of a fierce district, Santobono belonged to a violent family, and his eldest brother had died of a stab. He himself had always professed ardently patriotic opinions. It was said that he had all but taken up arms for Garibaldi; and, on the day when the Italians had entered Rome, force had been needed to prevent him from raising the flag of Italian unity above his

roof. His passionate dream was to behold Rome mistress
of the world, when the Pope and the King should have embraced and made cause together. Thus the Cardinal looked
on him as a dangerous revolutionary, a renegade who imperilled
Catholicism.

'Oh! what your Eminence can do for me, what your
Eminence can do if only condescending and willing!' repeated
Santobono in an ardent voice, clasping his big knotty hands.
And then, breaking off, he inquired, 'Did not his Eminence
Cardinal Sanguinetti explain my affair to your most reverend
Eminence?'

'No, the Cardinal simply advised me of your visit, saying
that you had something to ask of me.'

Whilst speaking Boccanera's face had clouded over, and it
was with increased sternness of manner that he again waited.
He was aware that the priest had become Sanguinetti's 'client'
since the latter had been in the habit of spending weeks together
at his suburban see of Frascati. Walking in the shadow of
every cardinal who is a candidate to the papacy, there are
familiars of low degree who stake the ambition of their life on
the possibility of that cardinal's election. If he becomes Pope
some day, if they themselves help him to the throne, they enter
the great pontifical family in his train. It was related that
Sanguinetti had once already extricated Santobono from a
nasty difficulty : the priest having one day caught a marauding
urchin in the act of climbing his wall, had beaten the little
fellow with such severity that he had ultimately died of it.
However, to Santobono's credit it must be added that his
fanatical devotion to the Cardinal was largely based upon the
hope that he would prove the Pope whom men awaited,
the Pope who would make Italy the sovereign nation of the
world.

'Well, this is my misfortune,' he said. 'Your Eminence
knows my brother Agostino, who was gardener at the villa for
two years in your Eminence's time. He is certainly a very
pleasant and gentle young fellow, of whom nobody has ever
complained. And so it is hard to understand how such an
accident can have happened to him, but it seems that he has
killed a man with a knife at Genzano, while walking in the
street in the evening. I am dreadfully distressed about it, and
would willingly give two fingers of my right hand to extricate
him from prison. However, it occurred to me that your Eminence would not refuse me a certificate stating that Agostino

was formerly in your Eminence's service, and that your Eminence was always well pleased with his quiet disposition.'

But the Cardinal flatly protested : ' I was not at all pleased with Agostino. He was wildly violent, and I had to dismiss him precisely because he was always quarrelling with the other servants.'

' Oh ! how grieved I am to hear your Eminence say that ! So it is true, then, my poor little Agostino's disposition has really changed ! Still there is always a way out of a difficulty, is there not ? You can still give me a certificate, first arranging the wording of it. A certificate from your Eminence would have such a favourable effect upon the law officers.'

' No doubt,' replied Boccanera ; ' I can understand that, but I will give no certificate.'

' What ! does your most reverend Eminence refuse my prayer ? '

' Absolutely ! I know that you are a priest of perfect morality, that you discharge the duties of your ministry with strict punctuality, and that you would be deserving of high commendation were it not for your political fancies. Only your fraternal affection is now leading you astray. I cannot tell a lie to please you.'

Santobono gazed at him in real stupefaction, unable to understand that a prince, an all-powerful cardinal, should be influenced by such petty scruples, when the entire question was a mere knife thrust, the most commonplace and frequent of incidents in the yet wild land of the old Roman castles.

' A lie ! a lie ! ' he muttered ; ' but surely it isn't lying just to say what is good of a man, leaving out all the rest, especially when a man has good points as Agostino certainly has. In a certificate, too, everything depends on the words one uses.'

He stubbornly clung to that idea ; he could not conceive that a person should refuse to soften the rigour of justice by an ingenious presentation of the facts. However, on acquiring a certainty that he would obtain nothing, he made a gesture of despair, his livid face assuming an expression of violent rancour, whilst his black eyes flamed with restrained passion.

' Well, well ! each looks on truth in his own way,' he said. ' I shall go back to tell his Eminence Cardinal Sanguinetti. And I beg your Eminence not to be displeased with me for having disturbed your Eminence to no purpose. By the way, perhaps the figs are not yet quite ripe ; but I will take the

liberty to bring another basketful towards the end of the
season, when they will be quite nice and sweet. A thousand
thanks and a thousand felicities to your most reverend
Eminence.'

Santobono went off backwards, his big bony figure bend-
ing double with repeated genuflections. Pierre, whom the
scene had greatly interested, in him beheld a specimen of the
petty clergy of Rome and its environs, of whom people had
told him before his departure from Paris. This was not the
scagnozzò, the wretched famished priest whom some nasty
affair brings from the provinces, who seeks his daily bread on
the pavements of Rome; one of the herd of begowned beggars
searching for a livelihood among the crumbs of Church life,
voraciously fighting for chance masses, and mingling with the
lowest orders in taverns of the worst repute. Nor was this
the country priest of distant parts, a man of crass ignorance
and superstition, a peasant among the peasants, treated as an
equal by his pious flock, which is careful not to mistake him
for the Divinity, and which, whilst kneeling in all humility
before the parish saint, does not bend before the man who
from that saint derives his livelihood. At Frascati the officiating minister of a little church may receive a stipend of some
nine hundred *lire* a year,[1] and he has only bread and meat to
buy if his garden yields him wine and fruit and vegetables.
This one, Santobono, was not without education; he knew a
little theology and a little history, especially the history of
the past grandeur of Rome, which had inflamed his patriotic
heart with the mad dream that universal domination would
soon fall to the portion of renascent Rome, the capital of
united Italy. But what an insuperable distance still remained
between this petty Roman clergy, often very worthy and
intelligent, and the high clergy, the high dignitaries of the
Vatican! Nobody that was not at least a prelate seemed to
count.

'A thousand thanks to your most reverend Eminence, and
may success attend all your Eminence's desires.'

With these words Santobono finally disappeared, and the
Cardinal returned to Pierre, who also bowed preparatory to
taking his leave.

'To sum up the matter, Monsieur l'Abbé,' said Boccanera,
'the affair of your book presents certain difficulties. As I have

[1] About 36*l*. One is reminded of Goldsmith's line : 'And passing
rich with forty pounds a year.'—*Trans.*

told you, I have no precise information, I have seen no documents. But knowing that my niece took an interest in you, I said a few words on the subject to Cardinal Sanguinetti, the Prefect of the Index, who was here just now. And he knows little more than I do, for nothing has yet left the secretary's hands. Still he told me that the denunciation emanated from personages of rank and influence, and applied to numerous pages of your work, in which it was said there were passages of the most deplorable character as regards both discipline and dogma.'

Greatly moved by the idea that he had hidden foes, secret adversaries who pursued him in the dark, the young priest responded : ' Oh! denounced, denounced! If your Eminence only knew how that word pains my heart! And denounced, too, for offences which were certainly involuntary, since my one ardent desire was the triumph of the Church! All I can do, then, is to fling myself at the feet of the Holy Father and entreat him to hear my defence.'

Boccanera suddenly became very grave again. A stern look rested on his lofty brow as he drew his haughty figure to its full height. ' His Holiness,' said he, ' can do everything, even receive you, if such be his good pleasure, and absolve you also. But listen to me. I again advise you to withdraw your book yourself, to destroy it, simply and courageously, before embarking in a struggle in which you will reap the shame of being overwhelmed. Reflect on that.'

Pierre, however, had no sooner spoken of the Pope than he had regretted it, for he realised that an appeal to the sovereign authority was calculated to wound the Cardinal's feelings. Moreover, there was no further room for doubt. Boccanera would be against his book, and the utmost that he could hope for was to gain his neutrality by bringing pressure to bear on him through those about him. At the same time he had found the Cardinal very plain spoken, very frank, far removed from all the secret intriguing in which the affair of his book was involved, as he now began to realise ; and so it was with deep respect and genuine admiration for the prelate's strong and lofty character that he took leave of him.

' I am infinitely obliged to your Eminence,' he said, ' and I promise that I will carefully reflect upon all that your Eminence has been kind enough to say to me.'

On returning to the anteroom, Pierre there found five or six persons who had arrived during his audience, and were

now waiting. There was a bishop, a domestic prelate, and
two old ladies, and as he drew near to Don Vigilio before
retiring, he was surprised to find him conversing with a tall,
fair young fellow, a Frenchman, who, also in astonishment, exclaimed, 'What! are you here in Rome, Monsieur
l'Abbé?'

For a moment Pierre had hesitated. 'Ah! I must ask
your pardon, Monsieur Narcisse Habert,' he replied, 'I did not
at first recognise you! It was the less excusable as I knew
that you had been an *attaché* at our embassy here ever since
last year.'

Tall, slim, and elegant of appearance, Narcisse Habert had
a clear complexion, with eyes of a bluish, almost mauvish, hue,
a fair frizzy beard, and long curling fair hair cut short over
the forehead in the Florentine fashion. Of a wealthy family
of militant Catholics, chiefly members of the bar or bench, he
had an uncle in the diplomatic profession, and this had decided
his own career. Moreover, a place at Rome was marked out
for him, for he there had powerful connections. He was a
nephew by marriage of Cardinal Sarno, whose sister had
married another of his uncles, a Paris notary; and he was
also cousin german of Monsignor Gamba del Zoppo, a *cameriere
segreto*, and son of one of his aunts, who had married an
Italian colonel. And in some measure for these reasons he
had been attached to the embassy to the Holy See, his superiors
tolerating his somewhat fantastic ways, his everlasting passion
for art which sent him wandering hither and thither through
Rome. He was moreover very amiable and extremely well-
bred; and it occasionally happened, as was the case that
morning, that with his weary and somewhat mysterious air
he came to speak to one or another of the cardinals on some
real matter of business in the ambassador's name.

So as to converse with Pierre at his ease, he drew him into
the deep embrasure of one of the windows. 'Ah! my dear
Abbé, how pleased I am to see you!' said he. 'You must
remember what pleasant chats we had when we met at Cardinal
Bergerot's! I told you about some paintings which you were
to see for your book, some miniatures of the fourteenth and
fifteenth centuries. And now, you know, I mean to take
possession of you. I'll show you Rome as nobody else
could show it to you. I've seen and explored everything.
Ah! there are treasures, such treasures! But in truth there
is only one supreme work; one always comes back to one's

particular passion. The Botticelli in the Sixtine Chapel—ah, the Botticelli!'

His voice died away, and he made a faint gesture as if overcome by admiration. Then Pierre had to promise that he would place himself in his hands and accompany him to the Sixtine Chapel. 'You know why I am here,' at last said the young priest. 'Proceedings have been taken against my book; it has been denounced to the Congregation of the Index.'

'Your book! is it possible?' exclaimed Narcisse: 'a book like that with pages recalling the delightful St. Francis of Assisi!' And thereupon he obligingly placed himself at Pierre's disposal. 'But our ambassador will be very useful to you,' he said. 'He is the best man in the world, of charming affability, and full of the old French spirit. I will present you to him this afternoon or to-morrow morning at the latest; and since you desire an immediate audience with the Pope, he will endeavour to obtain one for you. His position naturally designates him as your intermediary. Still, I must confess that things are not always easily managed. Although the Holy Father is very fond of him, there are times when his Excellency fails, for the approaches are so extremely intricate.'

Pierre had not thought of employing the ambassador's good offices, for he had naïvely imagined that an accused priest who came to defend himself would find every door open. However, he was delighted with Narcisse's offer, and thanked him as warmly as if the audience were already obtained.

'Besides,' the young man continued, 'if we encounter any difficulties I have relatives at the Vatican, as you know. I don't mean my uncle the Cardinal, who would be of no use to us, for he never stirs out of his office at the Propaganda, and will never apply for anything. But my cousin, Monsignor Gamba del Zoppo, is very obliging, and he lives in intimacy with the Pope, his duties requiring his constant attendance on him. So, if necessary, I will take you to see him, and he will no doubt find a means of procuring you an interview, though his extreme prudence keeps him perpetually afraid of compromising himself. However, it's understood, you may rely on me in every respect.'

'Ah! my dear sir,' exclaimed Pierre, relieved and happy, 'I heartily accept your offer. You don't know what balm your words have brought me; for ever since my arrival everybody has been discouraging me, and you are the first to restore my strength by looking at things in the true French way.'

Then, lowering his voice, he told the *attaché* of his interview with Cardinal Boccanera, of his conviction that the latter would not help him, of the unfavourable information which had been given by Cardinal Sanguinetti, and of the rivalry which he had divined between the two prelates. Narcisse listened, smiling, and in his turn began to gossip confidentially. The rivalry which Pierre had mentioned, the premature contest for the tiara which Sanguinetti and Boccanera were waging, impelled to it by a furious desire to become the next Pope, had for a long time been revolutionising the black world. There was incredible intricacy in the depths of the affair; none could exactly tell who was pulling the strings, conducting the vast intrigue. As regards generalities, it was simply known that Boccanera represented absolutism—the Church freed from all compromises with modern society, and waiting in immobility for the Deity to triumph over Satan, for Rome to be restored to the Holy Father, and for repentant Italy to perform penance for its sacrilege; whereas Sanguinetti, extremely politic and supple, was reported to harbour bold and novel ideas: permission to vote to be granted to all true Catholics,[1] a majority to be gained by this means in the Legislature; then, as a fatal corollary, the downfall of the House of Savoy, and the proclamation of a kind of republican federation of all the former petty States of Italy under the august protectorate of the Pope. On the whole, the struggle was between these two antagonistic elements—the first bent on upholding the Church by a rigorous maintenance of the old traditions, and the other predicting the fall of the Church if it did not follow the bent of the coming century. But all was steeped in so much mystery that people ended by thinking that, if the present Pope should live a few years longer, his successor would certainly be neither Boccanera nor Sanguinetti.

All at once Pierre interrupted Narcisse: 'And Monsignor Nani, do you know him? I spoke with him yesterday evening. And there he is coming in now!'

Nani was indeed just entering the anteroom with his usual

[1] Since the occupation of Rome by the Italian authorities, the supporters of the Church, obedient to the prohibition of the Vatican, have abstained from taking part in the political elections, this being their protest against the new order of things which they do not recognise. Various attempts have been made, however, to induce the Pope to give them permission to vote, many members of the Roman aristocracy considering the present course impolitic and even harmful to the interests of the Church.—*Trans,*

smile on his amiable pink face. His cassock of fine texture,
and his sash of violet silk shone with discreet soft luxury.
And he showed himself very amiable to Abbé Paparelli, who
accompanying him in all humility, begged him to be kind
enough to wait until his Eminence should be able to receive
him.

'Oh! Monsignor Nani,' muttered Narcisse, becoming serious, 'he is a man whom it is advisable to have for a friend.'

Then, knowing Nani's history, he related it in an undertone. Born at Venice, of a noble but ruined family which had
produced heroes, Nani, after first studying under the Jesuits,
had come to Rome to perfect himself in philosophy and theology at the Collegio Romano, which was then also under Jesuit
management. Ordained when three-and-twenty, he had at
once followed a nuncio to Bavaria as private secretary ; and
then had gone as *auditore* to the nunciatures of Brussels and
Paris, in which latter city he had lived for five years. Everything seemed to predestine him to diplomacy, his brilliant
beginnings and his keen and encyclopædical intelligence, but
all at once he had been recalled to Rome, where he was soon
afterwards appointed Assessor to the Holy Office. It was
asserted at the time that this was done by the Pope himself,
who, being well acquainted with Nani, and desirous of having
a person he could depend upon at the Holy Office, had given
instructions for his recall, saying that he could render far
more services at Rome than abroad. Already a domestic prelate, Nani had also lately become a Canon of St. Peter's and
an apostolic prothonotary, with the prospect of obtaining a
cardinal's hat whenever the Pope should find some other
favourite who would please him better as assessor.

'Oh, Monsignor Nani !' continued Narcisse. 'He's a
superior man, thoroughly well acquainted with modern
Europe, and at the same time a very saintly priest, a sincere
believer, absolutely devoted to the Church, with the substantial faith of an intelligent politician—a belief different, it is
true, from the narrow, gloomy theological faith which we know
so well in France. And this is one of the reasons why you will
hardly understand things here at first. The Roman prelates
leave the Deity in the sanctuary and reign in His name,
convinced that Catholicism is the human expression of the
government of God, the only perfect and eternal government,
beyond the pales of which nothing but falsehood and social
danger can be found. While we in our country lag behind,

furiously arguing whether there be a God or not, they do not
admit that God's existence can be doubted, since they themselves are His delegated ministers; and they entirely devote
themselves to playing their parts as ministers whom none
can dispossess, exercising their power for the greatest good of
humanity, and devoting all their intelligence, all their energy
to maintaining themselves as the accepted masters of the
nations. As for Monsignor Nani, after being mixed up in
the politics of the whole world, he has for ten years been
discharging the most delicate functions in Rome, taking part
in the most varied and most important affairs. He sees all
the foreigners who come to Rome, knows everything, has a
hand in everything. Add to this that he is extremely discreet
and amiable, with a modesty which seems perfect, though
none can tell whether, with his light silent footstep, he is not
really marching towards the highest ambition, the purple of
sovereignty.'

'Another candidate for the tiara,' thought Pierre, who had
listened passionately; for this man Nani interested him,
caused him an instinctive disquietude, as though behind his
pink and smiling face he could divine an infinity of obscure
things. At the same time, however, the young priest but ill
understood his friend, for he again felt bewildered by all
this strange Roman world, so different from what he had
expected.

Nani had perceived the two young men, and came towards
them with his hand cordially outstretched : 'Ah! Monsieur
l'Abbé Froment, I am happy to meet you again. I won't ask
you if you have slept well, for people always sleep well at
Rome. Good-day, Monsieur Habert; your health has kept
good, I hope, since I met you in front of Bernini's Santa
Teresa, which you admire so much.[1] I see that you know
one another. That is very nice. I must tell you, Monsieur
l'Abbé, that Monsieur Habert is a passionate lover of our city ;
he will be able to show you all its finest sights.'

Then, in his affectionate way, he at once asked for information respecting Pierre's interview with the Cardinal. He
listened attentively to the young man's narrative, nodding
his head at certain passages, and occasionally restraining his
sharp smile. The Cardinal's severity and Pierre's conviction

---

[1] The allusion is to a statue representing St. Theresa in ecstasy, with
the Angel of Death descending to transfix her with his dart. It stands
in a transept of Sta. Maria della Vittoria.—*Trans.*

that he would accord him no support did not at all astonish
Nani. It seemed as if he had expected that result. However, on hearing that Cardinal Sanguinetti had been there
that morning, and had pronounced the affair of the book to
be very serious, he appeared to lose his self-control for a
moment, for he spoke out with sudden vivacity :

'It can't be helped, my dear child, my intervention came
too late. Directly I heard of the proceedings I went to his
Eminence Cardinal Sanguinetti to tell him that the result
would be an immense advertisement for your book. Was it
sensible ? What was the use of it ? We know that you are
inclined to be carried away by your ideas, that you are an
enthusiast, and are prompt to do battle. So what advantage
should we gain by embarrassing ourselves with the revolt of
a young priest who might wage war against us with a book
of which some thousands of copies have been sold already ?
For my part I desired that nothing should be done. And I
must say that the Cardinal, who is a man of sense, was of the
same mind. He raised his arms to heaven, went into a
passion, and exclaimed that he was never consulted, that the
blunder was already committed beyond recall, and that it was
impossible to prevent process from taking its course since the
matter had already been brought before the Congregation, in
consequence of denunciations from authoritative sources,
based on the gravest motives. Briefly, as he said, the
blunder was committed, and I had to think of something
else.'

All at once Nani paused. He had just noticed that
Pierre's ardent eyes were fixed upon his own, striving to
penetrate his meaning. A faint flush then heightened the
pinkiness of his complexion, whilst in an easy way he
continued, unwilling to reveal how annoyed he was at having
said too much : 'Yes, I thought of helping you with all the
little influence I possess, in order to extricate you from the
worries in which this affair will certainly land you.'

An impulse of revolt was stirring Pierre, who vaguely felt
that he was perhaps being made game of. Why should he not
be free to declare his faith, which was so pure, so free from
personal considerations, so full of glowing Christian charity ?
'Never,' said he, 'will I withdraw ; never will I myself suppress
my book, as I am advised to do. It would be an act of
cowardice and falsehood, for I regret nothing, I disown nothing.
If I believe that my book brings a little truth to light I cannot

destroy it without acting criminally both towards myself and towards others. No, never! You hear me—never!'

Silence fell. But almost immediately he resumed: 'It is at the knees of the Holy Father that I desire to make that declaration. He will understand me, he will approve me.'

Nani no longer smiled; henceforth his face remained as it were closed. He seemed to be studying the sudden violence of the young priest with curiosity; then sought to calm him with his own tranquil kindliness. 'No doubt, no doubt,' said he. 'There is certainly great sweetness in obedience and humility. Still I can understand that, before anything else, you should desire to speak to his Holiness. And afterwards you will see—is that not so?—you will see——'

Then he evinced a lively interest in the suggested application for an audience. He expressed keen regret that Pierre had not forwarded that application from Paris, before even coming to Rome: in that course would have rested the best chance of a favourable reply. Pother of any kind was not liked at the Vatican, and if the news of the young priest's presence in Rome should only spread abroad, and the motives of his journey be discussed, all would be lost. Then, on learning that Narcisse had offered to present Pierre to the French ambassador, Nani seemed full of anxiety, and deprecated any such proceeding: 'No, no! don't do that—it would be most imprudent. In the first place you would run the risk of embarrassing the ambassador, whose position is always delicate in affairs of this kind. And then, too, if he failed—and my fear is that he might fail—yes, if he failed it would be all over; you would no longer have the slightest chance of obtaining an audience by any other means. For the Vatican would not like to hurt the ambassador's feelings by yielding to other influence after resisting his.'

Pierre anxiously glanced at Narcisse, who wagged his head, embarrassed and hesitating. 'The fact is,' the *attaché* at last murmured, 'we lately solicited an audience for a high French personage and it was refused, which was very unpleasant for us. Monsignor is right. We must keep our ambassador in reserve, and only utilise him when we have exhausted all other means.' Then, noticing Pierre's disappointment, he added obligingly: 'Our first visit therefore shall be for my cousin at the Vatican.'

Nani, his attention again roused, looked at the young man

in astonishment. 'At the Vatican? You have a cousin there?'

'Why, yes—Monsignor Gamba del Zoppo.'

'Gamba! Gamba! Yes, yes, excuse me, I remember now. Ah! so you thought of Gamba to bring influence to bear on his Holiness? That's an idea, no doubt; one must see—one must see.'

He repeated these words again and again as if to secure time to see into the matter himself, to weigh the *pros* and *cons* of the suggestion. Monsignor Gamba del Zoppo was a worthy man who played no part at the Papal Court, whose nullity indeed had become a byword at the Vatican. His childish stories, however, amused the Pope, whom he greatly flattered, and who was fond of leaning on his arm while walking in the gardens. It was during these strolls that Gamba easily secured all sorts of little favours. However, he was a remarkable poltroon, and had such an intense fear of losing his influence that he never risked a request without having convinced himself by long meditation that no possible harm could come to him through it.

'Well, do you know, the idea is not a bad one,' Nani at last declared. 'Yes, yes, Gamba can secure the audience for you, if he is willing. I will see him myself and explain the matter.'

At the same time Nani did not cease advising extreme caution. He even ventured to say that it was necessary to be on one's guard with the papal *entourage*, for, alas! it was a fact his Holiness was so good, and had such a blind faith in the goodness of others, that he had not always chosen his familiars with the critical care which he ought to have displayed. Thus one never knew to what sort of man one might be applying, or in what trap one might be setting one's foot. Nani even allowed it to be understood that on no account ought any direct application to be made to his Eminence the Secretary of State, for even his Eminence was not a free agent, but found himself encompassed by intrigues of such intricacy that his best intentions were paralysed. And as Nani went on discoursing in this fashion, in a very gentle, extremely unctuous manner, the Vatican appeared like some enchanted castle, guarded by jealous and treacherous dragons— a castle where one must not take a step, pass through a doorway, risk a limb, without having carefully assured oneself that one would not leave one's whole body there to be devoured.

Pierre continued listening, feeling colder and colder at heart, and again sinking into uncertainty. 'Mon Dieu!' he exclaimed, 'I shall never know how to act. You discourage me, Monsignor.'

At this Nani's cordial smile reappeared. 'I, my dear child? I should be sorry to do so. I only want to repeat to you that you must wait and do nothing. Avoid all feverishness especially. There is no hurry, I assure you, for it was only yesterday that a *consultore* was chosen to report upon your book, so you have a good full month before you. Avoid everybody, live in such a way that people shall be virtually ignorant of your existence, visit Rome in peace and quietness —that is the best course you can adopt to forward your interests.' Then, taking one of the priest's hands between both his own, so aristocratic, soft, and plump, he added: 'You will understand that I have my reasons for speaking to you like this. I should have offered my own services; I should have made it a point of honour to take you straight to his Holiness, had I thought it advisable. But I do not wish to mix myself up in the matter at this stage; I realise only too well that at the present moment we should simply make sad work of it. Later on—you hear me—later on, in the event of nobody else succeeding, I myself will obtain you an audience; I formally promise it. But meanwhile, I entreat you, refrain from using those words "a new religion," which, unfortunately, occur in your book, and which I heard you repeat again only last night. There can be no new religion, my dear child; there is but one eternal religion, which is beyond all surrender and compromise—the Catholic, Apostolic, and Roman religion. And at the same time leave your Paris friends to themselves. Don't rely too much on Cardinal Bergerot, whose lofty piety is not sufficiently appreciated in Rome. I assure you that I am speaking to you as a friend.'

Then, seeing how disabled Pierre appeared to be, half overcome already, no longer knowing in what direction to begin his campaign, he again strove to comfort him: 'Come, come, things will right themselves; everything will end for the best, both for the welfare of the Church and your own. And now you must excuse me, I must leave you; I shall not be able to see his Eminence to-day, for it is impossible for me to wait any longer.'

Abbé Paparelli, whom Pierre had noticed prowling around with his ears cocked, now hastened forward and declared to

Monsignor Nani that there were only two persons to be received
before him. But the prelate very graciously replied that he
would come back again at another time, for the affair which
he wished to lay before his Eminence was in no wise pressing.
Then he withdrew, courteously bowing to everybody.

Narcisse Habert's turn came almost immediately afterwards. However, before entering the throne-room he pressed
Pierre's hand, repeating, ' So it is understood. I will go to
see my cousin at the Vatican to-morrow, and directly I get a
reply I will let you know. We shall meet again soon, I hope.'

It was now past twelve o'clock, and the only remaining
visitor was one of the two old ladies who seemed to have
fallen asleep. At his little secretarial table Don Vigilio still
sat covering huge sheets of yellow paper with fine hand-
writing, from which he only lifted his eyes at intervals to
glance about him distrustfully, and make sure that nothing
threatened him.

In the mournful silence which fell around, Pierre lingered
for yet another moment in the deep embrasure of the window.
Ah! what anxiety consumed his poor tender, enthusiastic
heart! On leaving Paris things had seemed so simple, so
natural to him! He was unjustly accused, and he started off
to defend himself, arrived and flung himself at the feet of the
Holy Father, who listened to him indulgently. Did not the
Pope personify living religion, intelligence to understand,
justice based upon truth? And was he not, before aught else,
the Father, the delegate of Divine forgiveness and mercy,
with arms outstretched towards all the children of the Church,
even the guilty ones? Was it not meet, then, that he should
leave his door wide open so that the humblest of his sons
might freely enter to relate their troubles, confess their transgressions, explain their conduct, imbibe comfort from the
source of eternal lovingkindness? And yet on the very first
day of his, Pierre's, arrival, the doors closed upon him with a
bang; he felt himself sinking into a hostile sphere, full of traps
and pitfalls. One and all cried out to him ' Beware! ' as if he
were incurring the greatest dangers in setting one foot before
the other. His desire to see the Pope became an extraordinary
pretension, so difficult of achievement that it set the interests
and passions and influences of the whole Vatican agog. And
there was endless conflicting advice, long discussed manœu-
vring, all the strategy of generals leading an army to victory,
and fresh complications ever arising in the midst of a dim

stealthy swarming of intrigues. Ah! good Lord! how different all this was from the charitable reception that Pierre had anticipated: the pastor's house standing open beside the high road for the admission of all the sheep of the flock, both those that were docile and those that had gone astray!

That which began to frighten Pierre, however, was the evil, the wickedness, which he could divine vaguely stirring in the gloom: Cardinal Bergerot suspected, dubbed a Revolutionary, deemed so compromising that he, Pierre, was advised not to mention his name again! The young priest once more saw Cardinal Boccanera's pout of disdain while speaking of his colleague. And then Monsignor Nani had warned him not to repeat those words ' a new religion,' as if it were not clear to everybody that they simply signified the return of Catholicism to the primitive purity of Christianity! Was that one of the crimes denounced to the Congregation of the Index? He had begun to suspect who his accusers were, and felt alarmed, for he was now conscious of secret subterranean plotting, a great stealthy effort to strike him down and suppress his work. All that surrounded him became suspicious. If he listened to advice and temporised, it was solely to follow the same politic course as his adversaries, to learn to know them before acting. He would spend a few days in meditation, in surveying and studying that black world of Rome which to him had proved so unexpected. But, at the same time, in the revolt of his apostle-like faith, he swore, even as he had said to Nani, that he would never yield, never change either a page or a line of his book, but maintain it in its integrity in the broad daylight as the unshakable testimony of his belief. Even were the book condemned by the Index, he would not tender submission, withdraw aught of it. And should it become necessary he would quit the Church, he would go even as far as schism, continuing to preach the new religion and writing a new book, 'Real Rome,' such as he now vaguely began to espy.

However, Don Vigilio had ceased writing, and gazed so fixedly at Pierre that the latter at last stepped up to him politely in order to take leave. And then the secretary, yielding, despite his fears, to a desire to confide in him, murmured, 'He came simply on your account, you know; he wanted to ascertain the result of your interview with his Eminence.'

It was not necessary for Don Vigilio to mention Nani by

name; Pierre understood. 'Really, do you think so?' he
asked.

'Oh! there is no doubt of it. And if you take my advice
you will do what he desires with a good grace, for it is absolutely certain that you will do it later on.'

These words brought Pierre's disquietude and exasperation
to a climax. He went off with a gesture of defiance. They
would see if he would ever yield.

The three anterooms which he again crossed appeared to
him blacker, emptier, more lifeless than ever. In the second
one Abbé Paparelli saluted him with a little silent bow; in
the first the sleepy lackey did not even seem to see him. A
spider was weaving its web between the tassels of the great
red hat under the *baldacchino*. Would not the better course
have been to set the pick at work amongst all that rotting
past, now crumbling into dust, so that the sunlight might
stream in freely and restore to the purified soil the fruitfulness
of youth?

IV

ON the afternoon of that same day Pierre, having leisure before
him, at once thought of beginning his peregrinations through
Rome by a visit on which he had set his heart. Almost
immediately after the publication of 'New Rome' he had been
deeply moved and interested by a letter addressed to him from
the Eternal City by old Count Orlando Prada, the hero of
Italian independence and reunion, who, although unacquainted
with him, had written spontaneously after a first hasty perusal
of his book. And the letter had been a flaming protest, a cry
of the patriotic faith still young in the heart of that aged
man, who accused him of having forgotten Italy and claimed
Rome, the new Rome, for the country which was at last free and
united. Correspondence had ensued, and the priest, while
clinging to his dream of Neo-Catholicism saving the world, had
from afar grown attached to the man who wrote to him with
such glowing love of country and freedom. He had eventually
informed him of his journey, and promised to call upon
him. But the hospitality which he had accepted at the
Boccanera mansion now seemed to him somewhat of an
impediment; for after Benedetta's kindly, almost affectionate,
greeting, he felt that he could not, on the very first day and

without warning her, sally forth to visit the father of the man from whom she had fled and from whom she now asked the Church to part her for ever. Moreover, old Orlando was actually living with his son in a little palazzo which the latter had erected at the farther end of the Via Venti Settembre.

Before venturing on any step Pierre resolved to confide in the Contessina herself; and this seemed the easier as Viscount Philibert de la Choue had told him that the young woman still retained a filial feeling, mingled with admiration, for the old hero. And indeed, at the very first words which he uttered after lunch, Benedetta promptly retorted : 'But go, Monsieur l'Abbé, go at once ! Old Orlando, you know, is one of our national glories—you must not be surprised to hear me call him by his Christian name. All Italy does so, from pure affection and gratitude. For my part I grew up among people who hated him, who likened him to Satan. It was only later that I learned to know him, and then I loved him, for he is certainly the most just and gentle man in the world.'

She had begun to smile, but timid tears were moistening her eyes at the recollection, no doubt, of the year of suffering she had spent in her husband's house, where her only peaceful hours had been those passed with the old man. And in a lower and somewhat tremulous voice she added: 'As you are going to see him, tell him from me that I still love him, and, whatever happens, shall never forget his goodness.'

So Pierre set out, and whilst he was driving in a cab towards the Via Venti Settembre, he recalled to mind the heroic story of old Orlando's life which had been told him in Paris. It was like an epic poem, full of faith, bravery, and the disinterestedness of another age.

Born of a noble house of Milan, Count Orlando Prada had learnt to hate the foreigner at such an early age that, when scarcely fifteen, he already formed part of a secret society, one of the ramifications of the antique Carbonarism. This hatred of Austrian domination had been transmitted from father to son through long years, from the olden days of revolt against servitude, when the conspirators met by stealth in abandoned huts, deep in the recesses of the forests ; and it was rendered the keener by the eternal dream of Italy delivered, restored to herself, transformed once more into a great sovereign nation, the worthy daughter of those who had conquered and ruled the world. Ah ! that land of whilom glory, that unhappy, dismembered, parcelled Italy, the prey of a crowd of petty

tyrants, constantly invaded and appropriated by neighbouring
nations—how superb and ardent was that dream to free her
from such long opprobrium ! To defeat the foreigner, drive
out the despots, awaken the people from the base misery of
slavery, to proclaim Italy free and Italy united—such was the
passion which then inflamed the young with inextinguishable
ardour, which made the youthful Orlando's heart leap with
enthusiasm. He spent his early years consumed by holy
indignation, proudly and impatiently longing for an opportunity to give his blood for his country, and to die for her if
he could not deliver her.

Quivering under the yoke, wasting his time in sterile con-
spiracies, he was living in retirement in the old family residence
at Milan, when, shortly after his marriage and his twenty-
fifth birthday, tidings came to him of the flight of Pius IX
and the Revolution of Rome.[1] And at once he quitted everything, wife and hearth, and hastened to Rome as if summoned
thither by the call of destiny. This was the first time
that he set out scouring the roads for the attainment of
independence ; and how frequently, yet again and again, was
he to start upon fresh campaigns, never wearying, never dis-
heartened ! And now it was that he became acquainted with
Mazzini, and for a moment was inflamed with enthusiasm
for that mystical unitarian republican. He himself indulged
in an ardent dream of a Universal Republic, adopted the
Mazzinian device, 'Dio e popolo' (God and the people), and
followed the procession which wended its way with great
pomp through insurrectionary Rome. The time was one of
vast hopes, one when people already felt a need of renovated
religion, and looked to the coming of a humanitarian Christ
who would redeem the world yet once again. But before long
a man, a captain of the ancient days, Giuseppe Garibaldi,
whose epic glory was dawning, made Orlando entirely his own,
transformed him into a soldier whose sole cause was freedom
and union. Orlando loved Garibaldi as though the latter
were a demi-god, fought beside him in defence of Republican
Rome, took part in the victory of Rieti over the Neapolitans,
and followed the stubborn patriot in his retreat when he
sought to succour Venice, compelled as he was to relinquish
the Eternal City to the French army of General Oudinot, who

[1] It was on November 24, 1848, that the Pope fled to Gaeta, consequent
upon the insurrection which had broken out nine days previously.—
Trans.

came thither to reinstate Pius IX. And what an extraordinary and madly heroic adventure was that of Garibaldi and Venice! Venice, which Manin, another great patriot, a martyr, had again transformed into a republican city, and which for long months had been resisting the Austrians! And Garibaldi starts with a handful of men to deliver the city, charters thirteen fishing barks, loses eight in a naval engagement, is compelled to return to the Roman shores, and there in all wretchedness is bereft of his wife, Anita, whose eyes he closes before returning to America, where, once before, he had awaited the hour of insurrection. Ah! that land of Italy, which in those days rumbled from end to end with the internal fire of patriotism, where men of faith and courage arose in every city, where riots and insurrections burst forth on all sides like eruptions—it continued, in spite of every check, its invincible march to freedom!

Orlando returned to his young wife at Milan, and for two years lived there, almost in concealment, devoured by impatience for the glorious morrow which was so long in coming. Amidst his fever a gleam of happiness softened his heart; a son, Luigi, was born to him, but the birth killed the mother, and joy was turned into mourning. Then, unable to remain any longer at Milan, where he was spied upon, tracked by the police, suffering also too grievously from the foreign occupation, Orlando decided to realise the little fortune remaining to him, and to withdraw to Turin, where an aunt of his wife took charge of the child. Count di Cavour, like a great statesman, was then already seeking to bring about independence, preparing Piedmont for the decisive *rôle* which it was destined to play. It was the time when King Victor Emmanuel evinced flattering cordiality towards all the refugees who came to him from every part of Italy, even those whom he knew to be republicans, compromised and flying the consequences of popular insurrection. The rough, shrewd House of Savoy had long been dreaming of bringing about Italian unity to the profit of the Piedmontese monarchy, and Orlando well knew under what master he was taking service; but in him the republican already went behind the patriot, and indeed he had begun to question the possibility of a united republican Italy, placed under the protectorate of a liberal Pope, as Mazzini had at one time dreamed. Was that not indeed a chimera beyond realisation which would devour generation after generation if one obstinately continued to pursue it? For his

part, he did not wish to die without having slept in Rome as
one of the conquerors. Even if liberty was to be lost, he
desired to see his country united and erect, returning once
more to life in the full sunlight. And so it was with feverish
happiness that he enlisted at the outset of the war of 1859 ;
and his heart palpitated with such force as almost to rend his
breast, when, after Magenta, he entered Milan with the French
army—Milan which he had quitted eight years previously, like
an exile, in despair. The treaty of Villafranca which followed
Solferino proved a bitter deception : Venetia was not secured,
Venice remained enthralled. Nevertheless the Milanese was
conquered from the foe, and then Tuscany and the duchies of
Parma and Modena voted for annexation. So, at all events,
the nucleus of the Italian star was formed ; the country had
begun to build itself up afresh around victorious Piedmont.

Then, in the following year, Orlando plunged into epopœia
once more. Garibaldi had returned from his two sojourns in
America, with the halo of a legend round him—paladin-like
feats in the pampas of Uruguay, an extraordinary passage
from Canton to Lima—and he had returned to take part in
the war of 1859, forestalling the French army, overthrowing
an Austrian marshal, and entering Como, Bergamo, and
Brescia. And now, all at once, folks heard that he had
landed at Marsala with only a thousand men—the Thousand
of Marsala, the ever illustrious handful of braves ! Orlando
fought in the first rank, and Palermo after three days' resistance was carried. Becoming the dictator's favourite lieutenant, he helped him to organise a government, then crossed
the straits with him, and was beside him on the triumphal
entry into Naples, whose king had fled. There was mad
audacity and valour at that time, an explosion of the inevitable ;
and all sorts of supernatural stories were current—Garibaldi
invulnerable, protected better by his red shirt than by the
strongest armour, Garibaldi routing opposing armies like an
archangel, by merely brandishing his flaming sword ! The
Piedmontese on their side had defeated General Lamoricière
at Castelfidardo, and were invading the States of the Church.
And Orlando was there when the dictator, abdicating power,
signed the decree which annexed the Two Sicilies to the
Crown of Italy ; even as subsequently he took part in that
forlorn attempt on Rome, when the rageful cry was ' Rome or
Death ! '—an attempt which came to a tragic issue at
Aspromonte, when the little army was dispersed by the Italian

troops, and Garibaldi, wounded, was taken prisoner, and sent back to the solitude of his island of Caprera, where he became but a fisherman and a tiller of the rocky soil.[1]

Six years of waiting again went by, and Orlando still dwelt at Turin, even after Florence has been chosen as the new capital. The Senate had acclaimed Victor Emmanuel, King of Italy; and Italy was indeed almost built, it lacked only Rome and Venice. But the great battles seemed all over, the epic era was closed; Venice was to be won by defeat. Orlando took part in the unlucky battle of Custozza, where he received two wounds, full of furious grief at the thought that Austria should be triumphant. But at that same moment the latter, defeated at Sadowa, relinquished Venetia, and five months later Orlando satisfied his desire to be in Venice participating in the joy of triumph, when Victor Emmanuel made his entry amidst the frantic acclamations of the people. Rome alone remained to be won, and wild impatience urged all Italy towards the city; but friendly France had sworn to maintain the Pope, and this acted as a check. Then, for the third time, Garibaldi dreamt of renewing the feats of the old-world legends, and threw himself upon Rome like a soldier of fortune illumined by patriotism and free from every tie. And for the third time Orlando shared in that fine heroic madness destined to be vanquished at Mentana by the Pontifical Zouaves supported by a small French corps. Again wounded, he came back to Turin in almost a dying condition. But, though his spirit quivered, he had to resign himself; the situation seemed to have no outlet; only an upheaval of the nations could give Rome to Italy.

All at once the thunderclap of Sedan, of the downfall of France, resounded through the world; and then the road to Rome lay open, and Orlando, having returned to service in the regular army, was with the troops who took up position in the Campagna to insure the safety of the Holy See, as was said in the letter which Victor Emmanuel wrote to Pius IX.

---

[1] M. Zola's brief but glowing account of Garibaldi's glorious achievements has stirred many memories in my mind. My uncle, Frank Vizetelly, the war artist of the *Illustrated London News*, whose bones lie bleaching somewhere in the Soudan, was one of Garibaldi's constant companions throughout the memorable campaign of the Two Sicilies, and afterwards he went with him to Caprera. Later, in 1870, my brother, Edward Vizetelly, acted as orderly-officer to the general when he offered the help of his sword to France.—*Trans.*

There was, however, but the shadow of an engagement : General Kanzler's Pontifical Zouaves were compelled to fall back, and Orlando was one of the first to enter the city by the breach of the Porta Pia. Ah ! that twentieth of September— that day when he experienced the greatest happiness of his life—a day of delirium, of complete triumph, which realised the dream of so many years of terrible contest, the dream for which he had sacrificed rest and fortune, and given both body and mind !

Then came more than ten happy years in conquered Rome —in Rome adored, flattered, treated with all tenderness, like a woman in whom one has placed one's entire hope. From her he awaited so much national vigour, such a marvellous resurrection of strength and glory for the endowment of the young nation. Old Republican, old insurrectional soldier that he was, he had been obliged to adhere to the monarchy, and accept a senatorship. But then did not Garibaldi himself— Garibaldi his divinity—likewise call upon the king and sit in parliament ? Mazzini alone, rejecting all compromises, was unwilling to rest content with a united and independent Italy that was not republican. Moreover, another consideration influenced Orlando, the future of his son Luigi, who had attained his eighteenth birthday shortly after the occupation of Rome. Though he, Orlando, could manage with the crumbs which remained of the fortune he had expended in his country's service, he dreamt of a splendid destiny for the child of his heart. Realising that the heroic age was over, he desired to make a great politician of him, a great administrator, a man who should be useful to the mighty nation of the morrow ; and it was on this account that he had not rejected royal favour, the reward of long devotion, desiring, as he did, to be in a position to help, watch, and guide Luigi. Besides, was he himself so old, so used-up, as to be unable to assist in organisation, even as he had assisted in conquest? Struck by his son's quick intelligence in business matters, perhaps also instinctively divining that the battle would now continue on financial and economic grounds, he obtained him employment at the Ministry of Finances. And again he himself lived on dreaming, still enthusiastically believing in a splendid future, overflowing with boundless hope, seeing Rome double her population, grow and spread with a wild vegetation of new districts, and once more, in his loving, enraptured eyes, become the queen of the world.

But all at once came a thunderbolt. One morning, as he was going downstairs, Orlando was stricken with paralysis. Both his legs suddenly became lifeless, as heavy as lead. It was necessary to carry him up again, and never since had he set foot on the street pavement. At that time he had just completed his fifty-sixth year, and for fourteen years since he had remained in his armchair, as motionless as stone, he who had so impetuously trod every battlefield of Italy. It was a pitiful business, the collapse of a hero. And worst of all, from that room where he was for ever imprisoned, the old soldier beheld the slow crumbling of all his hopes, and fell into dismal melancholy, full of unacknowledged fear for the future. Now that the intoxication of action no longer dimmed his eyes, now that he spent his long and empty days in thought, his vision became clear. Italy, which he had desired to see so powerful, so triumphant in her unity, was acting madly, rushing to ruin, possibly to bankruptcy. Rome, which to him had ever been the one necessary capital, the city of unparalleled glory, requisite for the sovereign people of to-morrow, seemed unwilling to take upon herself the part of a great modern metropolis ; heavy as a corpse she weighed with all her centuries on the bosom of the young nation. Moreover, his son Luigi distressed him. Rebellious to all guidance, the young man had become one of the devouring offsprings of conquest, eager to despoil that Italy, that Rome, which his father seemed to have desired solely in order that he might pillage them and batten on them. Orlando had vainly opposed Luigi's departure from the ministry, his participation in the frantic speculations on land and house property to which the mad building of the new districts had given rise. But at the same time he loved his son, and was reduced to silence, especially now when everything had succeeded with Luigi, even his most risky financial ventures, such as the transformation of the Villa Montefiori into a perfect town—a colossal enterprise in which many of great wealth had been ruined, but whence he himself had emerged with millions. And it was in part for this reason that Orlando, sad and silent, had obstinately restricted himself to one small room on the third floor of the little palazzo erected by Luigi in the Via Venti Settembre—a room where he lived cloistered with a single servant, subsisting on his own scanty income, and accepting nothing but that modest hospitality from his son.

As Pierre reached that new Via Venti Settembre [1] which
climbs the side and summit of the Viminal hill, he was struck
by the heavy sumptuousness of the new 'palaces,' which
betokened among the moderns the same taste for the huge
that marked the ancient Romans. In the warm afternoon
glow, blent of purple and old gold, the broad, triumphant
thoroughfare, with its endless rows of white housefronts, bore
witness to new Rome's proud hope of futurity and sovereign
power. And Pierre fairly gasped when he beheld the Palazzo
delle Finanze, or Treasury, a gigantic erection, a cyclopean
cube with a profusion of columns, balconies, pediments, and
sculptured work, to which the building mania had given birth
in a day of immoderate pride. And on the other side of the
street, a little higher up, before reaching the Villa Bonaparte,
stood Count Prada's little palazzo.

After discharging his driver, Pierre for a moment remained
somewhat embarrassed. The door was open, and he entered
the vestibule ; but, as at the mansion in the Via Giulia, no
door porter or servant was to be seen. So he had to make up
his mind to ascend the monumental stairs, which with their
marble balustrades seemed to be copied, on a smaller scale,
from those of the Palazzo Boccanera. And there was much
the same cold bareness, tempered, however, by a carpet and
red door-hangings, which contrasted vividly with the white
stucco of the walls. The reception rooms, sixteen feet high,
were on the first floor, and as a door chanced to be ajar he
caught a glimpse of two salons, one following the other, and
both displaying quite modern richness, with a profusion of
silk and velvet hangings, gilt furniture, and lofty mirrors
reflecting a pompous assemblage of stands and tables. And
still there was nobody, not a soul, in that seemingly forsaken
abode, which exhaled nought of woman's presence. Indeed
Pierre was on the point of going down again to ring, when a
footman at last presented himself.

'Count Prada, if you please.'

The servant silently surveyed the little priest, and seemed
to understand. 'The father or the son ? ' he asked.

'The father, Count Orlando Prada.'

'Oh! that's on the third floor.' And he condescended to
add : 'The little door on the right-hand side of the landing.
Knock loudly if you wish to be admitted.'

[1] The name—Twentieth September Street—was given to the
thoroughfare to commemorate the date of the occupation of Rome by
Victor Emmanuel's army.—*Trans.*

Pierre indeed had to knock twice, and then a little withered old man of military appearance, a former soldier who had remained in the Count's service, opened the door and apologised for the delay by saying that he had been attending to his master's legs. Immediately afterwards he announced the visitor, and the latter, after passing through a dim and narrow anteroom, was lost in amazement on finding himself in a relatively small chamber, extremely bare and bright, with wall-paper of a light hue studded with tiny blue flowers. Behind a screen was an iron bedstead, the soldier's pallet, and there was no other furniture than the armchair in which the cripple spent his days, with a table of black wood placed near him, and covered with books and papers, and two old straw-seated chairs which served for the accommodation of the infrequent visitors. A few planks, fixed to one of the walls, did duty as book-shelves. However, the broad, clear, curtain-less window overlooked the most admirable panorama of Rome that could be desired.

Then the room disappeared from before Pierre's eyes, and with a sudden shock of deep emotion he only beheld old Orlando, the old blanched lion, still superb, broad and tall. A forest of white hair crowned his powerful head, with its thick mouth, fleshy broken nose, and large, sparkling black eyes. A long white beard streamed down with the vigour of youth, curling like that of an ancient god. By that leonine muzzle one divined what great passions had growled within ; but all, carnal and intellectual alike, had erupted in patriotism, in wild bravery, and riotous love of independence. And the old stricken hero, his torso still erect, was fixed there on his straw-seated armchair, with lifeless legs buried beneath a black wrapper. Alone did his arms and hands live, and his face beam with strength and intelligence.

Orlando turned towards his servant, and gently said to him : 'You can go away, Bastista. Come back in a couple of hours.' Then, looking Pierre full in the face, he exclaimed in a voice which was still sonorous despite his seventy years : ' So it's you at last, my dear Monsieur Froment, and we shall be able to chat at our ease. There, take that chair, and sit down in front of me.'

He had noticed the glance of surprise which the young priest had cast upon the bareness of the room, and he gaily added : ' You will excuse me for receiving you in my cell. Yes, I live here like a monk, like an old invalided soldier, henceforth withdrawn from active life. My son long begged me to take one of the fine rooms downstairs. But what would have been the use of it ? I have no needs, and I scarcely care for feather beds, for my old bones are accustomed to the hard ground. And then too I have such a fine view up here, all Rome presenting herself to me, now that I can no longer go to her.'

With a wave of the hand towards the window he sought to hide the embarrassment, the slight flush which came to him each time that he thus excused his son ; unwilling as he was to tell the true reason, the scruple of probity which had made him obstinately cling to his bare pauper's lodging.

'But it is very nice, the view is superb ! ' declared Pierre, in order to please him. 'I am for my own part very glad to see you, very glad to be able to grasp your valiant hands, which accomplished so many great things.'

Orlando made a fresh gesture, as though to sweep the past away. 'Pooh ! pooh ! all that is dead and buried. Let us talk about you, my dear Monsieur Froment, you who are young and represent the present ; and especially about your book, which represents the future ! Ah ! if you only knew how angry your book, your "New Rome," made me first of all !'

He began to laugh, and took the book from off the table near him ; then, tapping on its cover with his big broad hand, he continued : 'No, you cannot imagine with what starts of protest I read your book. The Pope, and again the Pope, and always the Pope ! New Rome to be created by the Pope and for the Pope, to triumph thanks to the Pope, to be given to the Pope, and to fuse its glory in the glory of the Pope ! But what about us ? What about Italy ? What about all the millions which we have spent in order to make Rome a great capital ? Ah ! only a Frenchman, and a Frenchman of Paris, could have written such a book ! But let me tell you, my dear sir, if you are ignorant of it, that Rome has become the capital of the kingdom of Italy, that we here have King Humbert, and the Italian people, a whole nation which must be taken into account, and which means to keep Rome—glorious, resuscitated Rome—for itself ! '

This juvenile ardour made Pierre laugh in turn : ' Yes, yes,' said he, ' you wrote me that. Only what does it matter from my point of view ? Italy is but one nation, a part of humanity, and I desire concord and fraternity among all the

nations, mankind reconciled, believing and happy. Of what
consequence, then, is any particular form of government,
monarchy or republic, of what consequence is any question of
a united and independent country, if all mankind forms but
one free people subsisting on truth and justice ? '

To only one word of this enthusiastic outburst did Orlando
pay attention. In a lower tone, and with a dreamy air, he
resumed : ' Ah ! a republic. In my youth I ardently desired
one. I fought for one ; I conspired with Mazzini, a saintly
man, a believer, who was shattered by collision with the
absolute. And then, too, one had to bow to practical necessities ; the most obstinate ended by submitting. And nowadays would a republic save us ? In any case it would differ
but little from our parliamentary monarchy. Just think
of what goes on in France ! And so why risk a revolution
which would place power in the hands of the extreme revolu-
tionists, the anarchists ? We fear all that, and this explains
our resignation. I know very well that a few think they can
detect salvation in a republican federation, a reconstitution of
all the former little states in so many republics, over which
Rome would preside. The Vatican would gain largely by any
such transformation ; still one cannot say that it endeavours
to bring it about ; it simply regards the eventuality without
disfavour. But it is a dream, a dream ! '

At this Orlando's gaiety came back to him, with even a
little gentle irony : ' You don't know, I suppose, what it was
that took my fancy in your book—for, in spite of all my pro-
tests, I have read it twice. Well, what pleased me was that
Mazzini himself might almost have written it at one time.
Yes ! I found all my youth again in your pages, all the wild
hope of my twenty-fifth year, the new religion of a humanitarian Christ, the pacification of the world effected by the
Gospel ! Are you aware that, long before your time, Mazzini
desired the renovation of Christianity ? He set dogma and
discipline on one side and only retained morals. And it was
new Rome, the Rome of the people, which he would have
given as see to the universal Church, in which all the churches
of the past were to be fused—Rome, the eternal and predestined city, the mother and queen, whose domination was
to arise anew to insure the definitive happiness of mankind !
Is it not curious that all the present-day neo-Catholicism, the
vague spiritualistic awakening, the evolution towards communion and Christian charity, with which some are making so

much stir, should be simply a return of the mystical and humanitarian ideas of 1848? Alas! I saw all that, I believed and burned, and I know in what a fine mess those flights into the azure of mystery landed us! So it cannot be helped, I lack confidence.'

Then, as Pierre on his side was growing impassioned and sought to reply, he stopped him: 'No, let me finish. I only want to convince you how absolutely necessary it was that we should take Rome and make her the capital of Italy. Without Rome new Italy could not have existed; Rome represented the glory of ancient time; in her dust lay the sovereign power which we wished to re-establish; she brought strength, beauty, eternity to those who possessed her. Standing in the middle of our country, she was its heart, and must assuredly become its life as soon as she should be awakened from the long sleep of ruin. Ah! how we desired her, amidst victory and amidst defeat, through years and years of frightful impatience! For my part I loved her, and longed for her, far more than for any woman, with my blood burning, and in despair that I should be growing old. And when we possessed her, our folly was a desire to behold her huge, magnificent, and commanding all at once, the equal of the other great capitals of Europe—Berlin, Paris, and London. Look at her! she is still my only love, my only consolation now that I am virtually dead, with nothing alive in me but my eyes.'

With the same gesture as before, he directed Pierre's attention to the window. Under the glowing sky Rome stretched out in its immensity, empurpled and gilded by the slanting sunrays. Across the horizon, far, far away, the trees of the Janiculum stretched a green girdle, of a limpid emerald hue, whilst the dome of St. Peter's, more to the left, showed palely blue, like a sapphire bedimmed by too bright a light. Then came the low town, the old ruddy city, baked as it were by centuries of burning summers, soft to the eye and beautiful with the deep life of the past, an unbounded chaos of roofs, gables, towers, *campanili*, and cupolas. But, in the foreground under the window, there was the new city—that which had been building for the last five and twenty years— huge blocks of masonry piled up side by side, still white with plaster, neither the sun nor history having as yet robed them in purple. And in particular the roofs of the colossal Palazzo delle Finanze had a disastrous effect, spreading out like far, bare steppes of cruel hideousness. And it was upon the desolation and abomination of all the newly-erected piles that the eyes of the old soldier of conquest at last rested.

Silence ensued. Pierre felt the faint chill of hidden, unacknowledged sadness pass by, and courteously waited.

'I must beg your pardon for having interrupted you just now,' resumed Orlando; 'but it seems to me that we cannot talk about your book to any good purpose until you have seen and studied Rome closely. You only arrived yesterday, did you not? Well, stroll about the city, look at things, question people, and I think that many of your ideas will change. I shall particularly like to know your impression of the Vatican since you have come here solely to see the Pope and defend your book against the Index. Why should we discuss things to-day, if facts themselves are calculated to bring you to other views, far more readily than the finest speeches which I might make? It is understood, you will come to see me again, and we shall then know what we are talking about, and, maybe, agree together.'

'Why certainly, you are too kind,' replied Pierre. 'I only came to-day to express my gratitude to you for having read my book so attentively, and to pay homage to one of the glories of Italy.'

Orlando was not listening, but remained for a moment absorbed in thought, with his eyes still resting upon Rome. And overcome, despite himself, by secret disquietude, he resumed in a low voice as though making an involuntary confession : ' We have gone too fast, no doubt. There were expenses of undeniable utility—the roads, ports, and railways. And it was necessary to arm the country also; I did not at first disapprove of the heavy military burden. But since then how crushing has been the war budget—a war which has never come, and the long wait for which has ruined us. Ah ! I have always been the friend of France. I only reproach her with one thing, that she has failed to understand the position in which we were placed, the vital reasons which compelled us to ally ourselves with Germany. And then there are the thousand millions of *lire*[1] swallowed up in Rome ! That was the real madness ; pride and enthusiasm led us astray. Old and solitary as I've been for many years now, given to deep reflection, I was one of the first to divine the pitfall, the frightful financial crisis, the deficit which would bring about the collapse of the nation. I shouted it from the housetops, to

my son, to all who came near me; but what was the use?
They didn't listen; they were mad, still buying and selling
and building, with no thought but for gambling booms and
bubbles. But you'll see, you'll see. And the worst is that
we are not situated as you are; we haven't a reserve of men
and money in a dense peasant population, whose thrifty
savings are always at hand to fill up the gaps caused by big
catastrophes. There is no social rise among our people as yet;
fresh men don't spring up out of the lower classes to re-invi-
gorate the national blood, as they constantly do in your country.
And, besides, the people are poor; they have no stockings to
empty. The misery is frightful, I must admit it. Those
who have any money prefer to spend it in the towns in a
petty way rather than to risk it in agricultural or manufac-
turing enterprise. Factories are but slowly built, and the land
is almost everywhere tilled in the same primitive manner as
it was two thousand years ago. And then, too, take Rome—
Rome, which didn't make Italy, but which Italy made its
capital to satisfy an ardent, overpowering desire—Rome, which
is still but a splendid bit of scenery, picturing the glory of the
centuries, and which, apart from its historical splendour, has
only given us its degenerate papal population, swollen with
ignorance and pride! Ah! I loved Rome too well, and I
still love it too well to regret being now within its walls. But,
good heavens! what insanity its acquisition brought us,
what piles of money it has cost us, and how heavily and
triumphantly it weighs us down! Look! look!'

He waved his hand as he spoke towards the livid roofs of
the Palazzo delle Finanze, that vast and desolate steppe, as
though he could see the harvest of glory all stripped off and
bankruptcy appear with its fearful, threatening bareness.
Restrained tears were dimming his eyes, and he looked
superbly pitiful with his expression of baffled hope and
grievous disquietude, with his huge white head, the muzzle
of an old blanched lion henceforth powerless and caged in that
bare, bright room, whose poverty-stricken aspect was instinct
with so much pride that it seemed, as it were, a protest
against the monumental splendour of the whole surrounding
district! So those were the purposes to which the conquest
had been put! And to think that he was impotent, henceforth unable to give his blood and his soul as he had done in
the days gone by.

'Yes, yes,' he exclaimed in a final outburst; 'one gave

everything, heart and brain, one's whole life indeed, so long as it was a question of making the country one and independent. But, now that the country is ours, just try to stir up enthusiasm for the reorganisation of its finances! There's no ideality in that! And this explains why, whilst the old ones are dying off, not a new man comes to the front among the young ones——'

All at once he stopped, looking somewhat embarrassed, yet smiling at his feverishness. ' Excuse me,' he said, ' I'm off again, I'm incorrigible. But it's understood, we'll leave that subject alone, and you'll come back here, and we'll chat together when you've seen everything.'

From that moment he showed himself extremely pleasant, and it was apparent to Pierre that he regretted having said so much, by the seductive affability and growing affection which he now displayed. He begged the young priest to prolong his sojourn, to abstain from all hasty judgments on Rome, and to rest convinced that, at bottom, Italy still loved France. And he was also very desirous that France should love Italy, and displayed genuine anxiety at the thought that perhaps she loved her no more. As at the Boccanera mansion, on the previous evening, Pierre realised that an attempt was being made to persuade him to admiration and affection. Like a susceptible woman with secret misgivings respecting the attractive power of her beauty, Italy was all anxiety with regard to the opinion of her visitors, and strove to win and retain their love.

However, Orlando again became impassioned when he learnt that Pierre was staying at the Boccanera mansion, and he made a gesture of extreme annoyance on hearing, at that very moment, a knock at the outer door. ' Come in! ' he called ; but at the same time he detained Pierre, saying, ' No, no, don't go yet ; I wish to know——'

But a lady came in—a woman of over forty, short and extremely plump, and still attractive with her small features and pretty smile swamped in fat. She was a blonde, with green limpid eyes ; and, fairly well dressed in a sober, nicely fitting mignonette gown, she looked at once pleasant, modest, and shrewd.

' Ah! it's you, Stefana,' said the old man, letting her kiss him.

' Yes, uncle, I was passing by and came up to see how you were getting on.'

The visitor was the Signora Sacco, niece of Prada and a Neapolitan by birth, her mother having quitted Milan to marry a certain Pagani, a Neapolitan banker, who had afterwards failed. Subsequent to that disaster Stefana had married Sacco, then merely a petty post-office clerk. He, later on, wishing to revive his father-in-law's business, had launched into all sorts of terrible, complicated, suspicious affairs, which by unforeseen luck had ended in his election as a deputy. Since he had arrived in Rome, to conquer the city in his turn, his wife had been compelled to assist his devouring ambition by dressing well and opening a *salon*; and, although she was still a little awkward, she rendered him many real services, being very economical and prudent, a thorough good housewife, with all the sterling substantial qualities of Northern Italy which she had inherited from her mother, and which showed conspicuously beside the turbulence and carelessness of her husband, in whom flared Southern Italy with its perpetual, rageful appetite.

Despite his contempt for Sacco, old Orlando had retained some affection for his niece, in whose veins flowed blood similar to his own. He thanked her for her kind inquiries, and then at once spoke of an announcement which he had read in the morning papers, for he suspected that the deputy had sent his wife to ascertain his opinion.

' Well, and that ministry ? ' he asked.

The Signora had seated herself and made no haste to reply, but glanced at the newspapers strewn over the table. ' Oh ! nothing is settled yet,' she at last responded ; ' the newspapers spoke out too soon. The Prime Minister sent for Sacco, and they had a talk together. But Sacco hesitates a good deal ; he fears that he has no aptitude for the Department of Agriculture. Ah ! if it were only the Finances——— However, in any case, he would not have come to a decision without consulting you. What do you think of it, uncle ? '

He interrupted her with a violent wave of the hand : ' No, no, I won't mix myself up in such matters ! '

To him the rapid success of that adventurer Sacco, that schemer and gambler who had always fished in troubled waters, was an abomination, the beginning of the end. His son Luigi certainly distressed him ; but it was even worse to think that— whilst Luigi, with his great intelligence and many remaining fine qualities, was nothing at all—Sacco, on the other hand, Sacco, blunderhead and ever-famished battener that he was, had not merely slipped into Parliament, but was now, it seemed, on the point of securing office! A little, swarthy, dry man he was, with big round eyes, projecting cheekbones, and prominent chin. Ever dancing and chattering, he was gifted with a showy eloquence, all the force of which lay in his voice—a voice which at will became admirably powerful or gentle! And withal an insinuating man, profiting by every opportunity, wheedling and commanding by turn.

'You hear, Stefana,' said Orlando; 'tell your husband that the only advice I have to give him is to return to his clerkship at the post-office, where perhaps he may be of use.'

What particularly filled the old soldier with indignation and despair was that such a man, a Sacco, should have fallen like a bandit on Rome—on that Rome whose conquest had cost so many noble efforts. And in his turn Sacco was conquering the city, was carrying it off from those who had won it by such hard toil, and was simply using it to satisfy his wild passion for power and its attendant enjoyments. Beneath his wheedling air there was the determination to devour everything. After the victory, while the spoil lay there, still warm, the wolves had come. It was the North that had made Italy, whereas the South, eager for the quarry, simply rushed upon the country, preyed upon it. And beneath the anger of the old stricken hero of Italian unity there was indeed all the growing antagonism of the North towards the South—the North industrious, economical, shrewd in politics, enlightened, full of all the great modern ideas, and the South ignorant and idle, bent on enjoying life immediately, amidst childish disorder in action, and an empty show of fine sonorous words.

Stefana had begun to smile in a placid way while glancing at Pierre, who had approached the window. 'Oh, you say that, uncle,' she responded; 'but you love us well all the same, and more than once you have given me myself some good advice, for which I'm very thankful to you. For instance, there's that affair of Attilio's——'

She was alluding to her son, the lieutenant, and his love affair with Celia, the little Princess Buongiovanni, of which all the drawing-rooms, white and black alike, were talking.

'Attilio—that's another matter!' exclaimed Orlando. 'He and you are both of the same blood as myself, and it's wonderful how I see myself again in that fine fellow. Yes, he is just the same as I was at his age, good-looking and brave and enthusiastic! I'm paying myself compliments, you see.

But, really now, Attilio warms my heart, for he is the future, and brings me back some hope. Well, and what about his affair?'

'Oh! it gives us a lot of worry, uncle. I spoke to you about it before, but you shrugged your shoulders, saying that in matters of that kind all that the parents had to do was to let the lovers settle their affairs between them. Still, we don't want everybody to repeat that we are urging our son to get the little princess to elope with him, so that he may afterwards marry her money and title.'

At this Orlando indulged in a frank outburst of gaiety: 'That's a fine scruple! Was it your husband who instructed you to tell me of it? I know, however, that he affects some delicacy in this matter. For my own part, I believe myself to be as honest as he is, and I can only repeat that, if I had a son like yours, so straightforward and good, and candidly loving, I should let him marry whomsoever he pleased in his own way. The Buongiovannis—good heavens! the Buongiovannis—why, despite all their rank and lineage and the money they still possess, it will be a great honour for them to have a handsome young man with a noble heart as their son-in-law!'

Again did Stefana assume an expression of placid satisfaction. She had certainly only come there for approval. 'Very well, uncle,' she replied, 'I'll repeat that to my husband, and he will pay great attention to it; for if you are severe towards him he holds you in perfect veneration. And as for that ministry—well, perhaps nothing will be done, Sacco will decide according to circumstances.'

She rose and took her leave, kissing the old soldier very affectionately as on her arrival. And she complimented him on his good looks, declaring that she found him as handsome as ever, and making him smile by speaking of a lady who was still madly in love with him. Then, after acknowledging the young priest's silent salutation by a slight bow, she went off, once more wearing her modest and sensible air.

For a moment Orlando, with his eyes turned towards the door, remained silent, again sad, reflecting no doubt on all the difficult, equivocal present, so different from the glorious past. But all at once he turned to Pierre, who was still waiting. 'And so, my friend,' said he, 'you are staying at the Palazzo Boccanera? Ah! what a grievous misfortune there has been on that side too!'

However, when the priest had told him of his conversation with Benedetta, and of her message that she still loved him and would never forget his goodness to her, no matter whatever happened, he appeared moved and his voice trembled: ' Yes, she has a good heart, she has no spite. But what would you have ? She did not love Luigi, and he was possibly violent. There is no mystery about the matter now, and I can speak to you freely, since to my great grief everybody knows what has happened.'

Then Orlando abandoned himself to his recollections, and related how keen had been his delight on the eve of the marriage at the thought that so lovely a creature would become his daughter, and set some youth and charm around his invalid's armchair. He had always worshipped beauty, and would have had no other love than woman, if his country had not seized upon the best part of him. And Benedetta on her side loved him, revered him, constantly coming up to spend long hours with him, sharing his poor little room, which at those times became resplendent with all the divine grace that she brought with her. With her fresh breath near him, the pure scent she diffused, the caressing womanly tenderness with which she surrounded him, he lived anew. But, immediately afterwards, what a frightful drama and how his heart had bled at his inability to reconcile the husband and the wife ! He could not possibly say that his son was in the wrong in desiring to be the loved and accepted spouse. At first indeed he had hoped to soften Benedetta, and throw her into Luigi's arms. But when she had confessed herself to him in tears, owning her old love for Dario, and her horror of belonging to another, he realised that she would never yield. And a whole year had then gone by ; he had lived for a whole year imprisoned in his armchair, with that poignant drama progressing beneath him in those luxurious rooms whence no sound even reached his ears. How many times had he not listened, striving to hear, fearing atrocious quarrels, in despair at his inability to prove still useful by creating happiness. He knew nothing by his son, who kept his own counsel ; he only learnt a few particulars from Benedetta at intervals when emotion left her defenceless ; and that marriage in which he had for a moment espied the much needed alliance between old and new Rome, that unconsummated marriage filled him with despair, as if it were indeed the defeat of every hope, the final collapse of the dream which had

filled his life. And he himself had ended by desiring the
divorce, so unbearable had become the suffering caused by
such a situation.

'Ah! my friend!' he said to Pierre; 'never before did I so
well understand the fatality of certain antagonism, the
possibility of working one's own misfortune and that of others,
even when one has the most loving heart and upright mind!'

But at that moment the door again opened, and this time,
without knocking, Count Luigi Prada came in. And after
rapidly bowing to the visitor, who had risen, he gently took
hold of his father's hands and felt them, as if fearing that
they might be too warm or too cold.

'I've just arrived from Frascati, where I had to sleep,'
said he; 'for the interruption of all that building gives me
a lot of worry. And I'm told that you spent a bad night!'

'No, I assure you.'

'Oh! I knew you wouldn't own it. But why will you
persist in living up here without any comfort? All this
isn't suited to your age. I should be so pleased if you
would accept a more comfortable room where you might sleep
better.'

'No, no—I know that you love me well, my dear Luigi.
But let me do as my old head tells me. That's the only way
to make me happy.'

Pierre was much struck by the ardent affection which
sparkled in the eyes of the two men as they gazed at one
another, face to face. This seemed to him very touching
and beautiful, knowing as he did how many contrary ideas
and actions, how many moral divergencies separated them.
And he next took an interest in comparing them physically.
Count Luigi Prada, shorter, more thick-set than his father,
had, however, much the same strong energetic head, crowned
with coarse black hair, and the same frank but somewhat
stern eyes set in a face of clear complexion, barred by thick
moustaches. But his mouth differed—a sensual, voracious
mouth it was, with wolfish teeth—a mouth of prey made for
nights of rapine, when the only question is to bite, and tear,
and devour others. And for this reason, when some praised
the frankness of his eyes, another would retort: 'Yes, but I
don't like his mouth.' His feet were large, his hands plump
and overbroad, but admirably cared for.

And Pierre marvelled at finding him such as he had
anticipated. He knew enough of his story to picture in him

a hero's son spoilt by conquest, eagerly devouring the harvest
garnered by his father's glorious sword. And he particularly
studied how the father's virtues had deflected and become
transformed into vices in the son—the most noble qualities
being perverted, heroic and disinterested energy lapsing into a
ferocious appetite for possession, the man of battle leading to
the man of booty, since the great gusts of enthusiasm no
longer swept by, since men no longer fought, since they
remained there resting, pillaging, and devouring amidst the
heaped-up spoils. And the pity of it was that the old hero,
the paralytic, motionless father beheld it all—beheld the degeneration of his son, the speculator and company promoter
gorged with millions !

However, Orlando introduced Pierre. 'This is Monsieur
l'Abbé Pierre Froment, whom I spoke to you about,' he said,
'the author of the book which I gave you to read.'

Luigi Prada showed himself very amiable, at once talking
of Rome with an intelligent passion like one who wished to
make the city a great modern capital. He had seen Paris
transformed by the Second Empire ; he had seen Berlin
enlarged and embellished after the German victories ; and,
according to him, if Rome did not follow the movement, if it
did not become the inhabitable capital of a great people, it
was threatened with prompt death : either a crumbling
museum or a renovated, resuscitated city—those were the
alternatives.[1]

Greatly struck, almost gained over already, Pierre listened
to this clever man, charmed with his firm, clear mind. He
knew how skilfully Prada had manoeuvred in the affair of the
Villa Montefiori, enriching himself when every one else
was ruined, having doubtless foreseen the fatal catastrophe
even while the gambling passion was maddening the entire
nation. However, the young priest could already detect marks
of weariness, precocious wrinkles and a fall of the lips, on that
determined, energetic face, as though its possessor were growing tired of the continual struggle that he had to carry on
amidst surrounding downfalls, the shock of which threatened

---

[1] Personally I should have thought the example of Berlin a great
deterrent. The enlargement and embellishment of the Prussian capital,
after the war of 1870, was attended by far greater roguery and wholesale
swindling than even the previous transformation of Paris. Thousands
of people too were ruined, and instead of an increase of prosperity the
result was the very reverse.—*Trans.*

to bring the most firmly established fortunes to the ground.
It was said that Prada had recently had grave cause for
anxiety; and indeed there was no longer any solidity to be
found; everything might be swept away by the financial crisis
which day by day was becoming more and more serious. In
the case of Luigi, sturdy son though he was of Northern Italy,
a sort of degeneration had set in, a slow rot, caused by the
softening, perversive influence of Rome. He had there
rushed upon the satisfaction of every appetite, and prolonged
enjoyment was exhausting him. This, indeed, was one of
the causes of the deep silent sadness of Orlando, who was
compelled to witness the swift deterioration of his conquering
race, whilst Sacco, the Italian of the South—served as it were
by the climate, accustomed to the voluptuous atmosphere, the
life of those sun-baked cities compounded of the dust of antiquity—bloomed there like the natural vegetation of a soil
saturated with the crimes of history, and gradually grasped
everything, both wealth and power.

As Orlando spoke of Stefana's visit to his son, Sacco's name
was mentioned. Then, without another word, the two men
exchanged a smile. A rumour was current that the Minister
of Agriculture, lately deceased, would perhaps not be replaced
immediately, and that another minister would take charge of
the department pending the next session of the Chamber.

Next the Palazzo Boccanera was mentioned, and Pierre,
his interest awakened, became more attentive. 'Ah!' exclaimed Count Luigi, turning to him, 'so you are staying in
the Via Giulia? All the Rome of olden time sleeps there in
the silence of forgetfulness.'

With perfect ease he went on to speak of the Cardinal and
even of Benedetta—'the Countess,' as he called her. But,
although he was careful to let no sign of anger escape him,
the young priest could divine that he was secretly quivering,
full of suffering and spite. In him the enthusiastic energy of
his father appeared in a baser, degenerate form. Quitting the
yet handsome Princess Flavia in his passion for Benedetta,
her divinely beautiful niece, he had resolved to make the latter
his own at any cost; determined to marry her, to struggle
with her and overcome her, although he knew that she loved
him not, and that he would almost certainly wreck his entire
life. Rather than relinquish her, however, he would have set
Rome on fire. And thus his hopeless suffering was now great
indeed: this woman was but his wife in name, and so torturing

was the thought of her disdain, that at times, however calm his outward demeanour, he was consumed by a jealous, vindictive, sensual madness that did not even recoil from the idea of crime.

'Monsieur l'Abbé is acquainted with the situation,' sadly murmured old Orlando.

His son responded by a wave of the hand, as though to say that everybody was acquainted with it. 'Ah! father,' he added, 'but for you I should never have consented to take part in those proceedings for annulling the marriage! The Countess would have found herself compelled to return here, and would not now-a-days be deriding us with her lover, that cousin of hers, Dario!'

At this Orlando also waved his hand, as if in protest.

'Oh! it's a fact, father,' continued Luigi. 'Why did she flee from here if it wasn't to go and live with her lover? And indeed, in my opinion, it's scandalous that a cardinal's palace should shelter such goings-on!'

This was the report which he spread abroad, the accusation which he everywhere levelled against his wife of publicly carrying on a shameless *liaison*. In reality, however, he did not believe a word of it, being too well acquainted with Benedetta's firm rectitude, and her determination to belong to none but the man she loved, and to him only in marriage. However, in David's eyes such accusations were not only fair play but also very efficacious.

And now, although he turned pale with covert exasperation, and laughed a hard, vindictive, cruel laugh, he went on to speak in a bantering tone of the proceedings for annulling the marriage, and in particular of the plea put forward by Benedetta's advocate Morano. And at last his language became so free that Orlando, with a glance towards the priest, gently interposed: 'Luigi! Luigi!'

'Yes, you are right, father, I'll say no more,' thereupon added the young Count. 'But it's really abominable and ridiculous. Lisbeth, you know, is highly amused at it.'

Orlando again looked displeased, for when visitors were present he did not like his son to refer to the person whom he had just named. Lisbeth Kauffmann, very *blonde* and pink and merry, was barely thirty years of age, and belonged to the Roman foreign colony. For two years past she had been a widow, her husband having died at Rome, whither he had come to nurse a complaint of the lungs. Thenceforward free, and sufficiently well off, she had remained in the city by taste, having a marked predilection for art, and painting a little, herself. In the Via Principe Amadeo, in the new Viminal district, she had purchased a little palazzo, and transformed a large apartment on its second floor into a studio hung with old stuffs, and balmy in every season with the scent of flowers. The place was well known to tolerant and intellectual society. Lisbeth was there found in perpetual jubilation, clad in a long blouse, somewhat of a *gamine* in her ways, trenchant too and often bold of speech, but nevertheless capital company, and as yet compromised with nobody but Prada. Their *liaison* had begun some four months after his wife had left him, and now Lisbeth was near the time of becoming a mother. This she in no wise concealed, but displayed such candid tranquillity and happiness that her numerous acquaintances continued to visit her as if there were nothing in question, so facile and free indeed is the life of the great cosmopolitan continental cities. Under the circumstances which his wife's suit had created, Prada himself was not displeased at the turn which events had taken with regard to Lisbeth, but none the less his incurable wound still bled. There could be no compensation for the bitterness of Benedetta's disdain, it was she for whom his heart burned, and he dreamt of one day wreaking on her a tragic punishment.

Pierre, knowing nothing of Lisbeth, failed to understand the allusions of Orlando and his son. But realising that there was some embarrassment between them, he sought to take countenance by picking from off the littered table a thick book which, to his surprise, he found to be a French educational work, one of those manuals for the *baccalauréat*,[1] containing a digest of the knowledge which the official programmes require. It was but an humble, practical, elementary work, yet it necessarily dealt with all the mathematical, physical, chemical, and natural sciences, thus broadly outlining the intellectual conquests of the century, the present phase of human knowledge.

'Ah!' exclaimed Orlando, well pleased with the diversion, 'you are looking at the book of my old friend Théophile Morin. He was one of the thousand of Marsala, you know,

[1] The examination for the degree of bachelor, which degree is the necessary passport to all the liberal professions in France. M. Zola, by the way, failed to secure it, being ploughed for 'insufficiency in literature'!—*Trans.*

and helped us to conquer Sicily and Naples. A hero! But
for more than thirty years now he has been living in France
again, absorbed in the duties of his petty professorship which
hasn't made him at all rich. And so he lately published that
book, which sells very well in France it seems ; and it occurred
to him that he might increase his modest profits on it by
issuing translations, an Italian one among others. He and I
have remained brothers, and thinking that my influence
would prove decisive, he wishes to utilise it. But he is mistaken ; I fear, alas! that I shall be unable to get anybody to
take up his book.'

At this, Luigi Prada, who had again become very composed
and amiable, shrugged his shoulders slightly, full as he was of
the scepticism of his generation which desired to maintain
things as they were in order to derive the greatest profit
from them. 'What would be the good of it?' he murmured ;
'there are too many books already!'

'No, no!' the old man passionately retorted, 'there can
never be too many books! We still and ever require fresh
ones! It's by literature, not by the sword, that mankind will
overcome falsehood and injustice and attain to the final peace
of fraternity among the nations—Oh! you may smile ; I know
that you call these ideas my fancies of '48, the fancies of a
grey beard, as people say in France. But it is none the less
true that Italy is doomed, if the problem be not attacked from
down below, if the people be not properly fashioned. And
there is only one way to make a nation, to create men, and
that is to educate them, to develop by educational means the
immense lost force which now stagnates in ignorance and
idleness. Yes, yes, Italy is made, but let us make an Italian
nation. And give us more and more books, and let us ever go
more and more forward into science and into light, if we wish
to live and to be healthy, good, and strong!'

With his torso erect, with his powerful leonine muzzle
flaming with the white brightness of his beard and hair, old
Orlando looked superb. And in that simple, candid chamber,
so touching with its intentional poverty, he raised his cry of
hope with such intensity of feverish faith, that before the
young priest's eyes there arose another figure—that of Cardinal
Boccanera, erect and black save for his snow-white hair, and
likewise glowing with heroic beauty in his crumbling palace
whose gilded ceilings threatened to fall about his head! Ah!
the magnificent stubborn men of the past, the believers, the

old men who still show themselves more virile, more ardent
than the young! Those two represented the opposite poles
of belief; they had not an idea, an affection in common, and
in that ancient city of Rome, where all was being blown away
in dust, they alone seemed to protest, indestructible, face to
face like two parted brothers, standing motionless on either
horizon. And to have seen them thus, one after the other, so
great and grand, so lonely, so detached from ordinary life, was
to fill one's day with a dream of eternity.

Luigi, however, had taken hold of the old man's hands to
calm him by an affectionate filial clasp. 'Yes, yes, you are
right, father, always right, and I'm a fool to contradict you.
Now, pray don't move about like that, for you are uncovering
yourself, and your legs will get cold again.'

So saying, he knelt down and very carefully arranged the
wrapper; and then remaining on the floor like a child, albeit
he was two-and-forty, he raised his moist eyes, full of mute,
entreating worship towards the old man who, calmed and
deeply moved, caressed his hair with a trembling touch.

Pierre had been there for nearly two hours, when he at
last took leave, greatly struck and affected by all that he had
seen and heard. And again he had to promise that he would
return and have a long chat with Orlando. Once out of doors
he walked along at random. It was barely four o'clock, and
it was his idea to ramble in this wise, without any predeter-
mined programme, through Rome at that delightful hour when
the sun sinks in the refreshed and far blue atmosphere.
Almost immediately, however, he found himself in the Via
Nazionale, along which he had driven on arriving the previous
day. And he recognised the huge livid Banca d'Italia, the
green gardens climbing to the Quirinal, and the heaven-soar-
ing pines of the Villa Aldobrandini. Then, at the turn of the
street, as he halted in order that he might again contemplate the column of Trajan which now rose up darkly from its
low piazza, already full of twilight, he was surprised to see a
victoria suddenly stop, and a young man courteously beckon
to him.

'Monsieur l'Abbé Froment! Monsieur l'Abbé Froment!'

It was young Prince Dario Boccanera, on the way to his
daily drive along the Corso. He now virtually subsisted on
the liberality of his uncle the Cardinal, and was almost always
short of money. But, like all the Romans, he would, if necessary, have rather lived on bread and water than have for-

gone his carriage, horse, and coachman. An equipage, indeed, is the one indispensable luxury of Rome.

'If you will come with me, Monsieur l'Abbé Froment,' said the young Prince, ' I will show you the most interesting part of our city.'

He doubtless desired to please Benedetta, by behaving amiably towards her protégé. Idle as he was, too, it seemed to him a pleasant occupation to initiate that young priest, who was said to be so intelligent, into what he deemed the inimitable side, the true florescence of Roman life.

Pierre was compelled to accept, although he would have preferred a solitary stroll. Yet he was interested in this young man, the last born of an exhausted race, who, while seemingly incapable of either thought or action, was none the less very seductive with his high-born pride and indolence. Far more a Roman than a patriot, Dario had never had the faintest inclination to rally to the new order of things, being well content to live apart and do nothing; and passionate though he was, he indulged in no follies, being very practical and sensible at heart, as are all his fellow-citizens, despite their apparent impetuosity. As soon as his carriage, after crossing the Piazza di Venezia, entered the Corso, he gave rein to his childish vanity, his desire to shine, his passion for gay, happy life in the open under the lovely sky. All this, indeed, was clearly expressed in the simple gesture which he made whilst exclaiming : ' The Corso ! '

As on the previous day, Pierre was filled with astonishment. The long narrow street again stretched before him as far as the white dazzling Piazza del Popolo, the only difference being that the right-hand houses were now steeped in sunshine, whilst those on the left were black with shadow. What ! was that the Corso then, that semi-obscure trench, close pressed by high and heavy house-fronts, that mean roadway where three vehicles could scarcely pass abreast, and which serried shops lined with gaudy displays ? There was neither space, nor far horizon, nor refreshing greenery such as the fashionable drives of Paris could boast ! Nothing but jostling, crowding, and stifling on the little footways under the narrow strip of sky. And although Dario named the pompous and historical palaces, Bonaparte, Doria, Odescalchi, Sciarra, and Chigi ; although he pointed out the column of Marcus Aurelius on the Piazza Colonna, the most lively square of the whole city with its everlasting throng of lounging, gazing, chattering people ;

although, all the way to the Piazza del Popolo, he never
ceased calling attention to churches, houses, and side-streets,
notably the Via dei Condotti, at the far end of which the
Trinità de' Monti, all golden in the glory of the sinking sun,
appeared above that famous flight of steps, the triumphal Scala
di Spagna—Pierre still and ever retained the impression of
disillusion which the narrow, airless thoroughfare had conveyed to him : the 'palaces' looked to him like mournful
hospitals or barracks, the Piazza Colonna suffered terribly
from a lack of trees, and the Trinità de' Monti alone took his
fancy by its distant radiance of fairyland.

But it was necessary to come back from the Piazza del
Popolo to the Piazza di Venezia, then return to the former
square, and come back yet again, following the entire Corso
three and four times without wearying. The delighted Dario
showed himself and looked about him, exchanging salutations.
On either footway was a compact crowd of promenaders whose
eyes roamed over the equipages and whose hands could have
shaken those of the carriage folks. So great at last became
the number of vehicles that both lines were absolutely unbroken,
crowded to such a point that the coachmen could do no more
than walk their horses. Perpetually going up and coming
down the Corso, people scrutinised and jostled one another.
It was open-air promiscuity, all Rome gathered together in the
smallest possible space, the folks who knew one another and
who met here as in a friendly drawing-room, and the folks belonging to adverse parties who did not speak together but who
elbowed each other, and whose glances penetrated to each
other's soul. Then a revelation came to Pierre, and he suddenly
understood the Corso, the ancient custom, the passion and
glory of the city. Its pleasure lay precisely in the very
narrowness of the street, in that forced elbowing which facilitating not only desired meetings but the satisfaction of curiosity, the display of vanity, and the garnering of endless tittle-
tattle. All Roman society met here each day, displayed itself,
spied on itself, offering itself in spectacle to its own eyes, with
such an indispensable need of thus beholding itself that the
man of birth who missed the Corso was like one out of his
element, destitute of newspapers, living like a savage. And
withal the atmosphere was delightfully balmy, and the narrow
strip of sky between the heavy, rusty mansions displayed an
infinite azure purity.

Dario never ceased smiling, and slightly inclining his head

while he repeated to Pierre the names of princes and princesses, dukes and duchesses—high-sounding names whose flourish had filled history, whose sonorous syllables conjured up the shock of armour on the battle-field and the splendour of papal pomp with robes of purple, tiaras of gold, and sacred vestments sparkling with precious stones. And as Pierre listened and looked he was pained to see merely some corpulent ladies or undersized gentlemen, bloated or shrunken beings, whose ill-looks seemed to be increased by their modern attire. However, a few pretty women went by, particularly some young, silent girls with large, clear eyes. And just as Dario had pointed out the Palazzo Buongiovanni, a huge seventeenth-century façade, with windows encompassed by foliaged ornamentation deplorably heavy in style, he added gaily :

'Ah! look—that's Attilio there on the footway. Young Lieutenant Sacco—you know, don't you?'

Pierre signed that he understood. Standing there in uniform, Attilio, so young, so energetic and brave of appearance, with a frank countenance softly illumined by blue eyes like his mother's, at once pleased the priest. He seemed indeed the very personification of youth and love, with all their enthusiastic, disinterested hope in the future.

'You'll see by and by, when we pass the palace again,' said Dario. 'He'll still be there and I'll show you something.'

Then he began to talk gaily of the girls of Rome, the little princesses, the little duchesses, so discreetly educated at the convent of the Sacred Heart, quitting it for the most part so ignorant and then completing their education beside their mothers, never going out but to accompany the latter on the obligatory drive to the Corso, and living through endless days, cloistered, imprisoned in the depths of sombre mansions. Nevertheless what tempests raged in those mute souls to which none had ever penetrated! what stealthy growth of will suddenly appeared from under passive obedience, apparent unconsciousness of surroundings! How many there were who stubbornly set their minds on carving out their lives for themselves, on choosing the man who might please them, and securing him despite the opposition of the entire world! And the lover was chosen there from among the stream of young men promenading the Corso, the lover hooked with a glance during the daily drive, those candid eyes speaking aloud and sufficing for confession and the gift of all, whilst not a breath was wafted from the lips so chastely closed. And afterwards there came love letters, furtively exchanged in church, and the winning-over of maids to facilitate stolen meetings, at first so innocent. In the end, a marriage often resulted.

Celia, for her part, had determined to win Attilio on the very first day when their eyes had met. And it was from a window of the Palazzo Buongiovanni that she had perceived him one afternoon of mortal weariness. He had just raised his head, and she had taken him for ever and given herself to him with those large, pure eyes of hers as they rested on his own. She was but an *amorosa*—nothing more ; he pleased her ; she had set her heart on him—him and none other. She would have waited twenty years for him, but she relied on winning him at once by quiet stubbornness of will. People declared that the terrible fury of the Prince, her father, had proved impotent against her respectful, obstinate silence. He, man of mixed blood as he was, son of an American woman, and husband of an English woman, laboured but to retain his own name and fortune intact amidst the downfall of others ; and it was rumoured that as the result of a quarrel which he had picked with his wife, whom he accused of not sufficiently watching over their daughter, the Princess had revolted, full not only of the pride of a foreigner who had brought a huge dowry in marriage, but also of such plain, frank egotism that she had declared she no longer found time enough to attend to herself, let alone another. Had she not already done enough in bearing him five children ? She thought so ; and now she spent her time in worshipping herself, letting Celia do as she listed, and taking no further interest in the household through which swept stormy gusts.

However, the carriage was again about to pass the Buongiovanni mansion, and Dario forewarned Pierre. 'You see,' said he, 'Attilio has come back. And now look up at the third window on the first floor.'

It was at once rapid and charming. Pierre saw the curtain slightly drawn aside and Celia's gentle face appear. Closed, candid lily, she did not smile, she did not move. Nothing could be read on those pure lips, or in those clear but fathomless eyes of hers. Yet she was taking Attilio to herself, and giving herself to him without reserve. And soon the curtain fell once more.

'Ah, the little mask !' muttered Dario. 'Can one ever tell what there is behind so much innocence ?'

As Pierre turned round he perceived Attilio, whose head was still raised, and whose face was also motionless and pale, with closed mouth, and widely opened eyes. And the young priest was deeply touched, for this was love, absolute love in its sudden omnipotence, true love, eternal and juvenescent, in which ambition and calculation played no part.

Then Dario ordered the coachman to drive up to the Pincio; for, before or after the Corso, the round of the Pincio is obligatory on fine, clear afternoons. First came the Piazza del Popolo, the most airy and regular square of Rome, with its conjunction of thoroughfares, its churches and fountains, its central obelisk, and its two clumps of trees facing one another at either end of the small white paving-stones, betwixt the severe and sun-gilt buildings. Then, turning to the right, the carriage began to climb the inclined way to the Pincio—a magnificent winding ascent, decorated with bas-reliefs, statues, and fountains—a kind of apotheosis of marble, a commemoration of ancient Rome, rising amidst greenery. Up above, however, Pierre found the garden small, little better than a large square, with just the four necessary roadways to enable the carriages to drive round and round as long as they pleased. An uninterrupted line of busts of the great men of ancient and modern Italy fringed these roadways. But what Pierre most admired was the trees—trees of the most rare and varied kinds, chosen and tended with infinite care, and nearly always evergreens, so that in winter and summer alike the spot was adorned with lovely foliage of every imaginable shade of verdure. And beside these trees, along the fine, breezy roadways, Dario's victoria began to turn, following the continuous, unwearying stream of the other carriages.

Pierre remarked one young woman of modest demeanour and attractive simplicity who sat alone in a dark blue victoria, drawn by a well-groomed, elegantly harnessed horse. She was very pretty, short, with chestnut hair, a creamy complexion, and large gentle eyes. Quietly robed in dead-leaf silk, she wore a large hat, which alone looked somewhat extravagant. And seeing that Dario was staring at her, the priest inquired her name, whereat the young Prince smiled. Oh! she was nobody, La Tonietta was the name that people gave her; she was one of the few *demi-mondaines* that Roman society talked of. Then, with the freeness and frankness which his race displays in such matters, Dario added some particulars. La Tonietta's origin was obscure; some said that she was the

daughter of an innkeeper of Tivoli, and others that of a Neapolitan banker. At all events, she was very intelligent, had
educated herself, and knew thoroughly well how to receive and
entertain people at the little palazzo in the Via dei Mille,
which had been given to her by old Marquis Manfredi now
deceased. She made no scandalous show, had but one protector at a time, and the princesses and duchesses who paid
attention to her at the Corso every afternoon considered her
nice-looking. One peculiarity had made her somewhat notorious. There was some one whom she loved and from whom
she never accepted aught but a bouquet of white roses; and
folks would smile indulgently when at times for weeks together
she was seen driving round the Pincio with those pure, white
bridal flowers on the carriage seat.

Dario, however, suddenly paused in his explanations to
address a ceremonious bow to a lady who, accompanied by a
gentleman, drove by in a large landau. Then he simply said
to the priest : ' My mother.'

Pierre already knew of her. Viscount de la Choue had
told him her story, how, after Prince Onofrio Boccanera's
death, she had married again although she was already fifty ;
how at the Corso, just like some young girl, she had hooked
with her eyes a handsome man to her liking—one, too, who
was fifteen years her junior. And Pierre also knew who that
man was, a certain Jules Laporte, an ex-sergeant of the papal
Swiss Guard, an ex-traveller in relics, compromised in an
extraordinary ' false relic ' fraud ; and he was further aware
that Laporte's wife had made a fine-looking Marquis Montefiori of him, the last of the fortunate adventurers of romance,
triumphing as in the legendary lands where shepherds are
wedded to queens.

At the next turn, as the large landau again went by, Pierre
looked at the couple. The Marchioness was really wonderful,
blooming with all the classical Roman beauty, tall, opulent,
and very dark, with the head of a goddess and regular if somewhat massive features, nothing as yet betraying her age except the down upon her upper lip. And the Marquis, the
Romanised Swiss of Geneva, really had a proud bearing, with
his sturdy soldierly figure and long wavy moustaches. People
said that he was in no wise a fool but, on the contrary, very
gay and very supple, just the man to please women. His wife
so gloried in him that she dragged him about and displayed
him everywhere, having begun life afresh with him as if she

were still but twenty, spending on him the little fortune which she had saved from the Villa Montefiori disaster, and so completely forgetting her son that she only saw the latter now and again at the promenade and acknowledged his bow like that of some chance acquaintance.

'Let us go to see the sun set behind St. Peter's,' all at once said Dario, conscientiously playing his part as a showman of curiosities.

The victoria thereupon returned to the terrace where a military band was now playing with a terrific blare of brass instruments. In order that their occupants might hear the music, a large number of carriages had already drawn up, and a growing crowd of loungers on foot had assembled there. And from that beautiful terrace so broad and lofty one of the most wonderful views of Rome was offered to the gaze. Beyond the Tiber, beyond the pale chaos of the new district of the castle meadows,[1] and between the greenery of Monte Mario and the Janiculum arose St. Peter's. Then on the left came all the olden city, an endless stretch of roofs, a rolling sea of edifices as far as the eye could reach. But one's glances always came back to St. Peter's, towering into the azure with pure and sovereign grandeur. And, seen from the terrace, the slow sunsets in the depths of the vast sky behind the colossus were sublime.

Sometimes there are topplings of sanguineous clouds, battles of giants hurling mountains at one another and succumbing beneath the monstrous ruins of flaming cities. Sometimes only red streaks or fissures appear on the surface of a sombra lake, as if a net of light has been flung to fish the submerged orb from amidst the seaweed. Sometimes, too, there is a rosy mist, a kind of delicate dust which falls, streaked with pearls by a distant shower, whose curtain is drawn across the mystery of the horizon. And sometimes there is a triumph, a cortège of gold and purple chariots of cloud rolling along a highway of fire, galleys floating upon an azure sea, fantastic and extravagant pomps slowly sinking into the less and less fathomable abyss of the twilight.

But that night the sublime spectacle presented itself to Pierre with a calm, blinding, desperate grandeur. At first, just above the dome of St. Peter's, the sun, descending in a spotless, deeply limpid sky, proved yet so resplendent that one's eyes could not face its brightness. And in this resplen-

[1] See *ante*, p. 63, note.

dency the dome seemed to be incandescent, you would have
said a dome of liquid silver; whilst the surrounding districts,
the house-roofs of the Borgo, were as though changed into a
lake of live embers.   Then, as the sun was by degrees inclined,
it lost some of its blaze, and one could look; and soon afterwards sinking with majestic slowness it disappeared behind
the dome, which showed forth darkly blue, while the orb, now
entirely hidden, set an aureola around it, a glory like a crown
of flaming rays.   And then began the dream, the dazzling
symbol, the singular illumination of the row of windows beneath the cupola which were transpierced by the light and
looked like the ruddy mouths of furnaces, in such wise that
one might have imagined the dome to be poised upon a brazier,
isolated, in the air, as though raised and upheld by the
violence of the fire.   It all lasted barely three minutes.
Down below the jumbled roofs of the Borgo became steeped
in violet vapour, sank into increasing gloom, whilst from the
Janiculum to Monte Mario the horizon showed its firm black
line.   And it was the sky then which became all purple and
gold, displaying the infinite placidity of a supernatural radiance
above the earth which faded into nihility.   Finally the last
window reflections were extinguished, the glow of the heavens
departed, and nothing remained but the vague, fading roundness
of the dome of St. Peter's amidst the all-invading night.

And, by some subtle connection of ideas, Pierre at that
moment once again saw rising before him the lofty, sad,
declining figures of Cardinal Boccanera and old Orlando.
On the evening of that day when he had learnt to know them,
one after the other, both so great in the obstinacy of their
hope, they seemed to be there, erect on the horizon above
their annihilated city, on the fringe of the heavens which
death apparently was about to seize.   Was everything then
to crumble with them? was everything to fade away and disappear in the falling night following upon accomplished
Time?

V

ON the following day Narcisse Habert came in great worry to
tell Pierre that Monsignor Gamba del Zoppo complained of
being unwell, and asked for a delay of two or three days before
receiving the young priest and considering the matter of his

audience. Pierre was thus reduced to inaction, for he dared
not make any attempt elsewhere in view of seeing the Pope.
He had been so frightened by Nani and others that he feared
he might jeopardise everything by inconsiderate endeavours.
And so he began to visit Rome in order to occupy his leisure.

His first visit was for the ruins of the Palatine. Going
out alone one clear morning at eight o'clock, he presented
himself at the entrance in the Via San Teodoro, an iron gateway flanked by the lodges of the keepers. One of the latter
at once offered his services, and though Pierre would have
preferred to roam at will, following the bent of his dream, he
somehow did not like to refuse the offer of this man, who
spoke French very distinctly, and smiled in a very good-
natured way. He was a squatly-built little man, a former
soldier, some sixty years of age, and his square-cut, ruddy
face was barred by thick white moustaches.

'Then will you please follow me, Monsieur l'Abbé,' said
he. 'I can see that you are French, Monsieur l'Abbé. I'm a
Piedmontese myself, but I know the French well enough ; I
was with them at Solferino. Yes, yes, whatever people may
say, one can't forget old friendships. Here, this way, please,
to the right.'

Raising his eyes, Pierre had just perceived the line of
cypresses edging the plateau of the Palatine on the side of
the Tiber ; and in the delicate blue atmosphere the intense
greenery of these trees showed like a black fringe. They alone
attracted the eye ; the slope, of a dusty, dirty grey, stretched out
bare and devastated, dotted by a few bushes, among which
peeped fragments of ancient walls. All was instinct with the
ravaged, leprous sadness of a spot handed over to excavation,
and where only men of learning could wax enthusiastic.

'The palaces of Tiberius, Caligula and the Flavians are
up above,' resumed the guide. 'We must keep them for the
end and go round.' Nevertheless he took a few steps to the
left, and pausing before an excavation, a sort of grotto in the
hillside, exclaimed : 'This is the Lupercal den where the
wolf suckled Romulus and Remus. Just here at the entry
used to stand the Ruminal fig-tree which sheltered the twins.'

Pierre could not restrain a smile, so convinced was the
tone in which the old soldier gave these explanations, proud
as he was of all the ancient glory, and wont to regard the
wildest legends as indisputable facts. However, when the
worthy man pointed out some vestiges of Roma Quadrata—

remnants of walls which really seemed to date from the
foundation of the city—Pierre began to feel interested, and a
first touch of emotion made his heart beat. This emotion was
certainly not due to any beauty of scene, for he merely beheld
a few courses of tufa blocks, placed one upon the other and
uncemented. But a past which had been dead for seven and
twenty centuries seemed to rise up before him, and those
crumbling, blackened blocks, the foundation of such a mighty
edifice of power and splendour, acquired extraordinary majesty.

Continuing their inspection, they went on, skirting the
hillside. The outbuildings of the palaces must have descended to this point; fragments of porticoes, fallen beams,
columns and friezes set up afresh, edged the rugged path which
wound through wild weeds, suggesting a neglected cemetery;
and the guide repeated the words which he had used day
by day for ten years past, continuing to enunciate supposi-
tions as facts, and giving a name, a destination, a history, to
every one of the fragments.

'The house of Augustus,' he said at last, pointing towards
some masses of earth and rubbish.

Thereupon Pierre, unable to distinguish anything, ventured
to inquire: 'Where do you mean?'

'Oh!' said the man, 'it seems that the walls were still
to be seen at the end of the last century. But it was
entered from the other side, from the Sacred Way. On this
side there was a huge balcony which overlooked the Circus
Maximus so that one could view the sports. However, as you
can see, the greater part of the palace is still buried under that
big garden up above, the garden of the Villa Mills. When
there's money for fresh excavations it will be found again,
together with the temple of Apollo and the shrine of Vesta
which accompanied it.'

Turning to the left, he next entered the Stadium, the arena
erected for foot-racing, which stretched beside the palace of
Augustus; and the priest's interest was now once more
awakened. It was not that he found himself in presence of
well-preserved and monumental remains, for not a column
had remained erect, and only the right-hand walls were still
standing. But the entire plan of the building had been traced,
with the goals at either end, the porticus round the course, and
the colossal imperial tribune which, after being on the left, annexed to the house of Augustus, had afterwards opened on the
right, fitting into the palace of Septimius Severus. And while

Pierre looked on all the scattered remnants, his guide went on chattering, furnishing the most copious and precise information, and declaring that the gentlemen who directed the excavations had mentally reconstructed the Stadium in each and every particular, and were even preparing a most exact plan of it, showing all the columns in their proper order and the statues in their niches, and actually specifying the divers sorts of marble which had covered the walls.

'Oh! the directors are quite at ease,' the old soldier eventually added with an air of infinite satisfaction. 'There will be nothing for the Germans to pounce on here. They won't be allowed to set things topsy-turvy as they did at the Forum, where everybody's at sea since they came along with their wonderful science!'

Pierre—a Frenchman—smiled, and his interest increased when, by broken steps and wooden bridges thrown over gaps, he followed the guide into the great ruins of the palace of Severus. Rising on the southern point of the Palatine, this palace had overlooked the Appian Way and the Campagna as far as the eye could reach. Nowadays, almost the only remains are the sub-structures, the subterranean halls contrived under the arches of the terraces, by which the plateau of the hill was enlarged; and yet these dismantled sub-structures suffice to give some idea of the triumphant palace which they once upheld, so huge and powerful have they remained in their indestructible massiveness. Near by arose the famous Septizonium, the tower with the seven tiers of arcades, which only finally disappeared in the sixteenth century. One of the palace terraces yet juts out upon cyclopean arches and from it the view is splendid. But all the rest is a commingling of massive yet crumbling walls, gaping depths whose ceilings have fallen, endless corridors and vast halls of doubtful destination. Well cared for by the new administration, swept and cleansed of weeds, the ruins have lost their romantic wildness and assumed an aspect of bare and mournful grandeur. However, flashes of living sunlight often gild the ancient walls, penetrate by their breaches into the black halls, and animate with their dazzlement the mute melancholy of all this dead splendour now exhumed from the earth in which it slumbered for centuries. Over the old ruddy masonry, stripped of its pompous marble covering, is the purple mantle of the sunlight, draping the whole with imperial glory once more.

For more than two hours already Pierre had been walking on, and yet he still had to visit all the earlier palaces on the north and east of the plateau. 'We must go back,' said the guide, 'the gardens of the Villa Mills and the convent of San Bonaventura stop the way. We shall only be able to pass on this side when the excavations have made a clearance. Ah! Monsieur l'Abbé, if you had walked over the Palatine merely some fifty years ago! I've seen some plans of that time. There were only some vineyards and little gardens with hedges then, a real campagna, where not a soul was to be met. And to think that all these palaces were sleeping underneath!'

Pierre followed him, and after again passing the house of Augustus, they ascended the slope and reached the vast Flavian palace,[1] still half buried by the neighbouring villa, and composed of a great number of halls large and small, on the nature of which scholars are still arguing. The aula regia, or throne room, the basilica, or hall of justice, the triclinium or dining-room, and the peristylium seem certainties; but for all the rest, and especially the small chambers of the private part of the structure, only more or less fanciful conjectures can be offered. Moreover, not a wall is entire; merely foundations peep out of the ground, mutilated bases describing the plan of the edifice. The only ruin preserved, as if by miracle, is the house on a lower level which some assert to have been that of Livia,[2] a house which seems very small beside all the huge palaces, and where are three halls comparatively intact, with mural paintings of mythological scenes, flowers and fruits, still wonderfully fresh. As for the palace of Tiberius, not one of its stones can be seen; its remains lie buried beneath a lovely public garden; whilst of the neighbouring palace of Caligula, overhanging the Forum, there are only some huge sub-structures, akin to those of the house of Severus—buttresses, lofty arcades, which upheld the palace, vast basements, so to say, where the prætorians were posted and gorged themselves with continual junketings. And thus this lofty plateau dominating the city merely offered some scarcely recognisable vestiges to the view, stretches of grey bare soil turned up by the pick, and dotted

---

[1] Begun by Vespasian and finished by Domitian.—*Trans.*

[2] Others assert it to have been the house of Germanicus, father of Caligula.—*Trans.*

with fragments of old walls; and it needed a real effort of scholarly imagination to conjure up the ancient imperial splendour which once had triumphed there.

Nevertheless Pierre's guide, with quiet conviction, persisted in his explanations, pointing to empty space as though the edifices still rose before him. 'Here,' said he, 'we are in the Area Palatina. Yonder, you see, is the façade of Domitian's palace, and there you have that of Caligula's palace, while on turning round the temple of Jupiter Stator is in front of you. The Sacred Way came up as far as here, and passed under the Porta Mugonia, one of the three gates of primitive Rome.'

He paused and pointed to the north-west portion of the height. 'You will have noticed,' he resumed, 'that the Cæsars didn't build yonder. And that was evidently because they had to respect some very ancient monuments dating from before the foundation of the city and greatly venerated by the people. There stood the temple of Victory built by Evander and his Arcadians, the Lupercal grotto which I showed you, and the humble hut of Romulus constructed of reeds and clay. Oh! everything has been found again, Monsieur l'Abbé; and, in spite of all that the Germans say, there isn't the slightest doubt of it.'

Then, quite abruptly, like a man suddenly remembering the most interesting thing of all, he exclaimed: 'Ah! to wind up we'll just go to see the subterranean gallery where Caligula was murdered.'

Thereupon they descended into a long crypto-porticus, through the breaches of which the sun now casts bright rays. Some ornaments of stucco and fragments of mosaic-work are yet to be seen. Still the spot remains mournful and desolate, well fitted for tragic horror. The old soldier's voice had become graver as he related how Caligula, on returning from the Palatine games, had been minded to descend all alone into this gallery to witness certain sacred dances which some youths from Asia were practising there. And then it was that the gloom gave Cassius Chæreas, the chief of the conspirators, an opportunity to deal him the first thrust in the abdomen. Howling with pain, the emperor sought to flee; but the assassins, his creatures, his dearest friends, rushed upon him, threw him down, and dealt him blow after blow, whilst he, mad with rage and fright, filled the dim, deaf gallery with the howling of a slaughtered beast. When he had expired, silence fell once more, and the frightened murderers fled.

The classical visit to the Palatine was now over, and when Pierre came up into the light again, he wished to rid himself of his guide and remain alone in the pleasant dreamy garden on the summit of the height. For three hours he had been tramping about with the guide's voice buzzing in his ears. The worthy man was now talking of his friendship for France and relating the battle of Magenta in great detail. He smiled as he took the piece of silver which Pierre offered him, and then started on the battle of Solferino. Indeed, it seemed impossible to stop him, when fortunately a lady came up to ask for some information. And, thereupon, he went off with her. 'Good evening, Monsieur l'Abbé,' he said; 'you can go down by way of Caligula's palace.'

Delightful was Pierre's relief when he was at last able to rest for a moment on one of the marble seats in the garden. There were but few clumps of trees, cypresses, box-trees, palms, and some fine evergreen oaks; but the latter, sheltering the seat, cast a dark shade of exquisite freshness around. The charm of the spot was also largely due to its dreamy solitude, to the low rustle which seemed to come from that ancient soil saturated with resounding history. Here formerly had been the pleasure grounds of the Villa Farnese which still exists though greatly damaged, and the grace of the Renascence seems to linger here, its breath passing caressingly through the shiny foliage of the old evergreen oaks. You are, as it were, enveloped by the soul of the past, an ethereal conglomeration of visions, and overhead is wafted the straying breath of innumerable generations buried beneath the sod.

After a time, however, Pierre could no longer remain seated, so powerful was the attraction of Rome, scattered all around that august summit. So he rose and approached the balustrade of a terrace; and beneath him appeared the Forum, and beyond it the Capitoline hill. To the eye the latter now only presented a commingling of grey buildings, lacking both grandeur and beauty. On the summit one saw the rear of the Palace of the Senator, flat, with little windows, and surmounted by a high square campanile. The large, bare, rusty-looking walls hid the church of Santa Maria in Ara Cœli and the spot where the temple of Capitoline Jove had formerly stood, radiant in all its royalty. On the left, some ugly houses rose terrace-wise upon the slope of Monte Caprino, where goats were pastured in the middle ages; while the few fine trees in the grounds of the Caffarelli Palace, the present German embassy, set some greenery above the ancient Tarpeian rock now scarcely to be found, lost, hidden as it is, by buttress walls. Yet this was the Mount of the Capitol, the most glorious of the seven hills, with its citadel and its temple, the temple to which universal dominion was promised, the St. Peter's of Pagan Rome; this indeed was the hill—steep on the side of the Forum, and a precipice on that of the Campus Martius—where the thunder of Jupiter fell, where in the dimmest of the far-off ages the Asylum of Romulus rose with its sacred oaks, a spot of infinite savage mystery. Here, later, were preserved the public documents of Roman grandeur inscribed on tablets of brass; hither climbed the heroes of the trebly hundred triumphs; and here the emperors became gods, erect in statues of marble. And nowadays the eye inquires wonderingly how so much history and so much glory can have had for their scene so small a space, such a rugged, jumbled pile of paltry buildings, a mole-hill, looking no bigger, no loftier than a hamlet perched between two valleys.

Then another surprise for Pierre was the Forum, starting from the Capitol and stretching out below the Palatine: a narrow square, close pressed by the neighbouring hills, a hollow where Rome in growing had been compelled to rear edifice close to edifice till all stifled for lack of breathing space. It was necessary to dig very deep—some fifty feet—to find the venerable republican soil, and now all you see is a long, clean, livid trench, cleared of ivy and bramble, and where the fragments of paving, the bases of columns, and the piles of foundations appear like bits of bone. Level with the ground the Basilica Julia, entirely mapped out, looks like an architect's ground plan. On that side the arch of Septimius Severus alone rears itself aloft virtually intact, whilst of the temple of Vespasian only a few isolated columns remain still standing, as if by miracle, amidst the general downfall, soaring with a proud elegance, with sovereign audacity of equilibrium, so slender and so gilded, into the blue heavens. The column of Phocas is also erect; and you see some portions of the Rostra fitted together out of fragments discovered near by. But if the eye seeks a sensation of extraordinary vastness, it must travel beyond the three columns of the temple of Castor and Pollux, beyond the vestiges of the house of the Vestals, beyond the temple of Faustina, in which the Christian

Church of San Lorenzo has so composedly installed itself, and
even beyond the round temple of Romulus, to light upon the
Basilica of Constantine with its three colossal, gaping arch-
ways. From the Palatine they look like porches built for a nation
of giants, so massive that a fallen fragment resembles some
huge rock hurled by a whirlwind from a mountain summit.
And there, in that illustrious, narrow, overflowing Forum the
history of the greatest of nations held for centuries, from the
legendary time of the Sabine women, reconciling their relatives
and their ravishers, to that of the proclamation of public liberty,
so slowly wrung from the patricians by the plebeians. Was
not the Forum at once the market, the exchange, the tribunal,
the open-air hall of public meeting? The Gracchi there
defended the cause of the humble; Sylla there set up the
lists of those whom he proscribed; Cicero there spoke, and
there, against the rostra, his bleeding head was hung. Then,
under the emperors, the old renown was dimmed, the centuries
buried the monuments and temples with such piles of dust
that all that the Middle Ages could do was to turn the spot into
a cattle market! Respect has come back once more, a respect
which violates tombs, which is full of feverish curiosity and
science, which is dissatisfied with mere hypotheses, which loses
itself amidst this historical soil where generations rise one
above the other, and hesitates between the fifteen or twenty
restorations of the Forum that have been planned on paper,
each of them as plausible as the other. But to the mere passer-
by, who is not a professional scholar and has not recently
re-perused the history of Rome, the details have no significance.
All he sees on this searched and scoured spot is a city's cemetery where old exhumed stones are whitening, and whence
rises the intense sadness that envelops dead nations. Pierre,
however, noting here and there fragments of the Sacred Way,
now turning, now running down, and now ascending with
their pavement of silex indented by the chariot-wheels, thought
of the triumphs, of the ascent of the triumpher, so sorely
shaken as his chariot jolted over that rough pavement of
glory.

But the horizon expanded towards the south-east, and
beyond the arches of Titus and Constantine he perceived the
Colosseum. Ah! that colossus, only one half or so of which
has been destroyed by time as with the stroke of a mighty
scythe, it rises in its enormity and majesty like a stone
lace-work, with hundreds of empty bays agape against the blue

of heaven! There is a world of halls, stairs, landings, and
passages, a world where one loses oneself amidst deathlike
silence and solitude. The furrowed tiers of seats, eaten into
by the atmosphere, are like shapeless steps leading down into
some old extinct crater, some natural circus excavated by the
force of the elements in indestructible rock. The hot suns of
eighteen hundred years have baked and scorched this ruin,
which has reverted to a state of nature, bare and golden-brown
like a mountain-side, since it has been stripped of its vegetation, the flora which once made it like a virgin forest. And
what an evocation when the mind sets flesh and blood and life
again on all that dead osseous framework, fills the circus with
the 90,000 spectators which it could hold, marshals the games
and the combats of the arena, gathers a whole civilisation
together, from the emperor and the dignitaries to the surging
plebeian sea, all aglow with the agitation and brilliancy of an
impassioned people, assembled under the ruddy reflection of
the giant purple *velum*. And then, yet further, on the horizon,
were other cyclopean ruins, the baths of Caracalla, standing
there like relics of a race of giants long since vanished from
the world: halls extravagantly and inexplicably spacious and
lofty; vestibules large enough for an entire population; a
frigidarium, where five hundred people could swim together; a
tepidarium and a *calidarium* [1] on the same proportions, born of
a wild craving for the huge; and then the terrific massiveness
of the structures, the thickness of the piles of brickwork, such
as no feudal castle ever knew; and, in addition the general
immensity which makes passing visitors look like lost ants;
such an extraordinary riot of the great and the mighty that
one wonders for what men, for what multitudes, this monstrous edifice was reared. To-day, you would say a mass of
rocks in the rough, thrown from some height for building
the abode of Titans.

And as Pierre gazed, he became more and more immersed
in the limitless past which encompassed him. On all sides
history rose up like a surging sea. Those bluey plains on the
north and west were ancient Etruria; those jagged crests on
the east were the Sabine Mountains; while southward, the
Alban Mountains and Latium spread out in the streaming
gold of the sunshine. Alba Longa was there, and so was
Monte Cavo, with its crown of old trees, and the convent
which has taken the place of the ancient temple of Jupiter.

[1] *Tepidarium*, warm bath; *calidarium*, vapour bath.—*Trans.*

Then beyond the Forum, beyond the Capitol, the greater part
of Rome stretched out, whilst behind Pierre, on the margin of
the Tiber, was the Janiculum. And a voice seemed to come
from the whole city, a voice which told him of Rome's eternal
life, resplendent with past greatness. He remembered just
enough of what he had been taught at school to realise
where he was; he knew just what everyone knows of Rome
with no pretension to scholarship, and it was more particularly his artistic temperament which awoke within him and
gathered warmth from the flame of memory. The present
had disappeared, and the ocean of the past was still rising,
buoying him up, carrying him away.

And then his mind involuntarily pictured a resurrection
instinct with life. The grey, dismal Palatine, razed like some
accursed city, suddenly became animated, peopled, crowned
with palaces and temples. There had been the cradle of the
eternal city, founded by Romulus on that summit overlooking
the Tiber. There assuredly the seven kings of its two and a
half centuries of monarchical rule had dwelt, enclosed within
high, strong walls, which had but three gateways. Then the
five centuries of republican sway spread out, the greatest, the
most glorious of all the centuries, those which brought the
Italic peninsula and finally the known world under Roman
dominion. During those victorious years of social and warlike
struggle, Rome grew and peopled the seven hills, and the
Palatine became but a venerable cradle with legendary temples,
and was even gradually invaded by private residences. But
at last Cæsar, the incarnation of the power of his race, after
Gaul and after Pharsalia triumphed in the name of the whole
Roman people, having completed the colossal task by which
the five following centuries of imperialism were to profit, with
a pompous splendour and a rush of every appetite. And then
Augustus could ascend to power; glory had reached its climax;
millions of gold were waiting to be filched from the depths of
the provinces; and the imperial gala was to begin in the
world's capital, before the eyes of the dazzled and subjected
nations. Augustus had been born on the Palatine, and after
Actium had given him the empire, he set his pride in reigning
from the summit of that sacred mount, venerated by the
people. He bought up private houses and there built his
palace with luxurious splendour: an atrium upheld by four
pilasters and eight columns; a peristylium encompassed by
fifty-six Ionic columns; private apartments all around, and all

in marble; a profusion of marble, brought at great cost from
foreign lands, and of the brightest hues, resplendent like gems.
And he lodged himself with the gods, building near his own
abode a large temple of Apollo and a shrine of Vesta in order
to ensure himself divine and eternal sovereignty. And then
the seed of the imperial palaces was sown; they were to spring
up, grow and swarm, and cover the entire mount.

Ah! the all-powerfulness of Augustus, his four and forty
years of total, absolute, superhuman power, such as no despot
has known even in his dreams! He had taken to himself
every title, united every magistracy in his person. Imperator
and consul, he commanded the armies and exercised executive
power; pro-consul, he was supreme in the provinces; perpetual censor and princeps, he reigned over the senate; tribune, he was the master of the people. And, formerly called
Octavius, he had caused himself to be declared Augustus,
sacred, god among men, having his temples and his priests,
worshipped in his lifetime like a divinity deigning to visit the
earth. And finally he had resolved to be supreme pontiff,
annexing religious to civil power, and thus by a stroke of
genius attaining to the most complete dominion to which
man can climb. As the supreme pontiff could not reside in a
private house, he declared his abode to be State property. As
the supreme pontiff could not leave the vicinity of the temple
of Vesta, he built a temple to that goddess near his own dwelling, leaving the guardianship of the ancient altar below the
Palatine to the Vestal virgins. He spared no effort, for he
well realised that human omnipotence, the mastery of mankind
and the world, lay in that reunion of sovereignty, in being
both king and priest, emperor and pope. All the sap of a
mighty race, all the victories achieved, and all the favours of
fortune yet to be garnered, blossomed forth in Augustus, in a
unique splendour which was never again to shed such brilliant
radiance. He was really the master of the world, amidst the
conquered and pacified nations, encompassed by immortal glory
in literature and in art. In him would seem to have been
satisfied the old intense ambition of his people, the ambition
which it had pursued through centuries of patient conquest, to
become the people-king. The blood of Rome, the blood of
Augustus, at last coruscated in the sunlight, in the purple of
empire. And the blood of Augustus, of the divine, triumphant, absolute sovereign of bodies and souls, of the man in
whom seven centuries of national pride had culminated, was

to descend through the ages, through an innumerable posterity with a heritage of boundless pride and ambition. For it was fatal: the blood of Augustus was bound to spring into life once more and pulsate in the veins of all the successive masters of Rome, ever haunting them with the dream of ruling the whole world. And later on, after the decline and fall, when power had once more become divided between the king and the priest, the popes—their hearts burning with the red, devouring blood of their great forerunner—had no other passion, no other policy, through the centuries, than that of attaining to civil dominion, to the totality of human power.

But Augustus being dead, his palace having been closed and consecrated, Pierre saw that of Tiberius spring up from the soil. It had stood where his feet now rested, where the beautiful evergreen oaks sheltered him. He pictured it with courts, porticoes, and halls both substantial and grand, despite the gloomy bent of the emperor who betook himself far from Rome to live amongst informers and debauchees, with his heart and brain poisoned by power to the point of crime and most extraordinary insanity. Then the palace of Caligula followed, an enlargement of that of Tiberius, with arcades set up to increase its extent, and a bridge thrown over the Forum to the Capitol, in order that the prince might go thither at his ease to converse with Jove, whose son he claimed to be. And sovereignty also rendered this one ferocious—a madman with omnipotence to do as he listed! Then, after Claudius, Nero, not finding the Palatine large enough, seized upon the delightful gardens climbing the Esquiline in order to set up his Golden House, a dream of sumptuous immensity which he could not complete and the ruins of which disappeared in the troubles following the death of this monster whom pride demented. Next, in eighteen months, Galba, Otho, and Vitellius fell one upon the other, in mire and in blood, the purple converting them also into imbeciles and monsters, gorged like unclean beasts at the trough of imperial enjoyment. And afterwards came the Flavians, at first a respite, with common-sense and human kindness: Vespasian; next Titus, who built but little on the Palatine; but then Domitian, in whom the sombre madness of omnipotence burst forth anew amidst a *régime* of fear and spying, idiotic atrocities and crimes, debauchery contrary to nature, and building enterprises born of insane vanity instinct with a desire to outvie the temples of the gods. The palace

of Domitian, parted by a lane from that of Tiberius, arose
colossal-like—a palace of fairyland. There was the hall of
audience, with its throne of gold, its sixteen columns of
Phrygian and Numidian marble, and its eight niches containing
colossal statues; there were the hall of justice, the vast
dining-room, the peristylium, the sleeping apartments, where
granite, porphyry, and alabaster overflowed, carved and decorated by the most famous artists, and lavished on all sides
in order to dazzle the world. And finally, many years later,
a last palace was added to all the others—that of Septimius
Severus: again a building of pride, with arches supporting
lofty halls, terraced storeys, towers o'ertopping the roofs, a
perfect Babylonian pile, rising up at the extreme point of the
mount in view of the Appian Way, so that the emperor's
compatriots—those from the province of Africa, where he was
born—might, on reaching the horizon, marvel at his fortune
and worship him in his glory.

And now Pierre beheld all those palaces which he had
conjured up around him, resuscitated, resplendent in the full
sunlight. They were as if linked together, parted merely by
the narrowest of passages. In order that not an inch of that
precious summit might be lost they had sprouted thickly like
the monstrous florescence of strength, power, and unbridled
pride which satisfied itself at the cost of millions, bleeding
the whole world for the enjoyment of one man. And in
truth there was but one palace altogether, a palace enlarged
as soon as one emperor died and was placed among the deities,
and another, shunning the consecrated pile where possibly
the shadow of death frightened him, experienced an imperious
need to build a house of his own and perpetuate in everlasting stone the memory of his reign. All the emperors were
seized with this building craze; it was like a disease which
the very throne seemed to carry from one occupant to another
with growing intensity, a consuming desire to excel all prede-
cessors by thicker and higher walls, by a more and more wonderful profusion of marbles, columns and statues. And among
all these princes there was the idea of a glorious survival, of
leaving a testimony of their greatness to dazzled and stupefied
generations, of perpetuating themselves by marvels which
would not perish but for ever weigh heavily upon the earth,
when their own light ashes should long since have been
swept away by the winds. And thus the Palatine became
but the venerable base of a monstrous edifice, a thick vegeta-

tion of adjoining buildings, each new pile being like a fresh eruption of feverish pride ; while the whole, now showing the snowy brightness of white marble and now the glowing hues of coloured marble, ended by crowning Rome and the world with the most extraordinary and most insolent abode of sovereignty—whether palace, temple, basilica, or cathedral— that omnipotence and dominion have ever reared under the heavens.

But death lurked beneath this excess of strength and glory. Seven hundred and thirty years of monarchy and republic had sufficed to make Rome great ; and in five centuries of imperial sway the people-king was to be devoured down to its last muscles. There was the immensity of the territory, the more distant provinces gradually pillaged and exhausted ; there was the fisc consuming everything, digging the pit of fatal bankruptcy ; and there was the degeneration of the people, poisoned by the scenes of the circus and the arena, fallen to the sloth and debauchery of their masters, the Cæsars, while mercenaries fought the foe and tilled the soil. Already at the time of Constantine, Rome had a rival, Byzantium ; disruption followed with Honorius ; and then some ten emperors sufficed for decomposition to be complete, for the bones of the dying prey to be picked clean, the end coming with Romulus Augustulus, the sorry creature whose name is, so to say, a mockery of the whole glorious history, a buffet for both the founder of Rome and the founder of the empire.

The palaces, the colossal assemblage of walls, storeys, terraces, and gaping roofs, still remained on the deserted Palatine; many ornaments and statues, however, had already been removed to Byzantium. And the empire, having become Christian, had afterwards closed the temples and extinguished the fire of Vesta, whilst yet respecting the ancient Palladium. But in the fifth century the Barbarians rush upon Rome, sack and burn it, and carry the spoils spared by the flames away in their chariots. As long as the city was dependent on Byzantium a custodian of the imperial palaces remained there watching over the Palatine. Then all fades and crumbles in the night of the middle ages. It would really seem that the popes then slowly took the place of the Cæsars, succeeding them both in their abandoned marble halls and their ever-subsisting passion for domination. Some of them assuredly dwelt in the palace of Septimius Severus ; a council of the Church was held in the Septizonium ; and, later on, Gelasius II was elected in a neighbouring monastery on the sacred mount. It was as if Augustus were again rising from the tomb, once more master of the world, with a Sacred College of Cardinals resuscitating the Roman Senate. In the twelfth century the Septizonium belonged to some Benedictine monks, and was sold by them to the powerful Frangipani family, who fortified it as they had already fortified the Colosseum and the arches of Constantine and Titus, thus forming a vast fortress round about the venerable cradle of the city. And the violent deeds of civil war and the ravages of invasion swept by like whirl-winds, throwing down the walls, razing the palaces and towers. And afterwards successive generations invaded the ruins, in-stalled themselves in them by right of trover and conquest, turned them into cellars, store places for forage, and stables for mules. Kitchen gardens were formed, vines were planted on the spots where fallen soil had covered the mosaics of the imperial halls. All around nettles and brambles grew up, and ivy preyed on the overturned porticoes, till there came a day when the colossal assemblage of palaces and temples, which marble was to have rendered eternal, seemed to dive beneath the dust, to disappear under the surging soil and vegetation which impassive Nature threw over it. And then, in the hot sunlight, among the wild flowerets, only big buzzing flies remained, whilst herds of goats strayed in freedom through the throne room of Domitian and the fallen sanctuary of Apollo.

A great shudder passed through Pierre. To think of so much strength, pride, and grandeur, and such rapid ruin—a world for ever swept away ! He wondered how entire palaces, yet peopled by admirable statuary, could thus have been gradually buried without anyone thinking of protecting them. It was no sudden catastrophe which had swallowed up those masterpieces, subsequently to be disinterred with exclamations of admiring wonder ; they had been drowned, as it were—caught progressively by the legs, the waist, and the neck, till at last the head had sunk beneath the rising tide. And how could one explain that generations had heedlessly witnessed such things without thought of putting forth a helping hand ? It would seem as if, at a given moment, a black curtain were suddenly drawn across the world, as if mankind began afresh, with a new and empty brain which needed moulding and furnishing. Rome had become depopulated ; men ceased to repair the ruins left by fire and sword ; the edifices which by their very immensity had become useless were utterly neglected,

allowed to crumble and fall. And then, too, the new religion
everywhere hunted down the old one, stole its temples, overturned its gods. Earthy deposits probably completed the
disaster—there were, it is said, both earthquakes and inunda-
tions—and the soil was ever rising, the alluvia of the young
Christian world buried the ancient pagan society. And after
the pillaging of the temples, the theft of the bronze roofs and
marble columns, the climax came with the filching of the
stones torn from the Colosseum and the Theatre of Marcellus,
with the pounding of the statuary and sculpture work, thrown
into kilns to procure the lime needed for the new monuments
of Catholic Rome.

It was nearly one o'clock, and Pierre awoke as from a
dream. The sun-rays were streaming in a golden rain between
the shiny leaves of the ever-green oaks above him, and down
below Rome lay dozing, overcome by the great heat. Then
he made up his mind to leave the garden, and went stumbling
over the rough pavement of the Clivus Victoriæ, his mind
still haunted by blinding visions. To complete his day, he
had resolved to visit the old Appian Way during the afternoon,
and, unwilling to return to the Via Giulia, he lunched at a
suburban tavern, in a large, dim room, where, alone with the
buzzing flies, he lingered for more than two hours, awaiting
the sinking of the sun.

Ah! that Appian Way, that ancient queen of the highroads, crossing the Campagna in a long straight line with
rows of proud tombs on either hand—to Pierre it seemed like
a triumphant prolongation of the Palatine. He there found
the same passion for splendour and domination, the same
craving to eternise the memory of Roman greatness in marble
and daylight. Oblivion was vanquished; the dead refused to
rest, and remained for ever erect among the living, on either
side of that road which was traversed by multitudes from the
entire world. The deified images of those who were now but
dust still gazed on the passers-by with empty eyes; the
inscriptions still spoke, proclaiming names and titles. In
former times the rows of sepulchres must have extended without interruption along all the straight, level miles between the
tomb of Cæcilia Metella and that of Casale Rotondo, forming
an elongated cemetery where the powerful and wealthy com-
peted as to who should leave the most colossal and lavishly
decorated mausoleum : such, indeed, was the craving for survival, the passion for pompous immortality, the desire to deify

death by lodging it in temples; whereof the present day
monumental splendour of the Genoese Campo Santo and the
Roman Campo Verano is, so to say, a remote inheritance.
And what a vision it was to picture all the tremendous tombs
on the right and left of the glorious pavement which the
legions trod on their return from the conquest of the world!
That tomb of Cæcilia Metella, with its bond-stones so huge,
its walls so thick that the middle ages transformed it into the
battlemented keep of a fortress! And then all the tombs
which follow, the modern structures erected in order that the
marble fragments discovered might be set in place, the old
blocks of brick and concrete, despoiled of their sculptured work
and rising up like seared rocks, yet still suggesting their
original shapes as shrines, *cippi*, and *sarcophagi*. There is a
wondrous succession of high reliefs figuring the dead in groups
of three and five; statues in which the dead live deified, erect;
seats contrived in niches in order that wayfarers may rest and
bless the hospitality of the dead; laudatory epitaphs celebrating the dead, both the known and the unknown, the children
of Sextus Pompeius Justus, the departed Marcus Servilius
Quartus, Hilarius Fuscus, Rabirius Hermodorus; without
counting the sepulchres venturously ascribed to Seneca and
the Horatii and Curiatii. And finally there is the most
extraordinary and gigantic of all the tombs, that known as
Casale Rotondo, which is so large that it has been possible to
establish a farmhouse and an olive garden on its substructures,
which formerly upheld a double rotunda, adorned with
Corinthian pilasters, large candelabra, and scenic masks.[1]

Pierre, having driven in a cab as far as the tomb of Cæcilia
Metella, continued his excursion on foot, going slowly towards
Casale Rotondo. In many places the old pavement appears—
large blocks of basaltic lava, worn into deep ruts that jolt the
best-hung vehicles. Among the ruined tombs on either hand
run bands of grass, the neglected grass of cemeteries, scorched
by the summer suns and sprinkled with big violet thistles and
tall sulphur-wort. Parapets of dry stones, breast high, enclose
the russet roadsides, which resound with the crepitation of
grasshoppers; and, beyond, the Campagna stretches, vast and
bare, as far as the eye can see. A parasol pine, a eucalyptus,

---

[1] Some believe this tomb to have been that of Messalla Corvinus, the
historian and poet, a friend of Augustus and Horace; others ascribe it
to his son, Aurelius Messallinus Cotta.—*Trans.*

some olive or fig trees, white with dust, alone rise up near the
road at infrequent intervals.   On the left the ruddy arches of
the Acqua Claudia show vigorously in the meadows, and
stretches of poorly cultivated land, vineyards and little farms,
extend to the blue and lilac Sabine and Alban hills, where
Frascati, Rocca di Papa, and Albano set bright spots, which
grow and whiten as one gets nearer to them.   Then, on the
right, towards the sea, the houseless, treeless plain grows and
spreads with vast, broad ripples, extraordinary ocean-like
simplicity and grandeur, a long, straight line alone parting it
from the sky.   At the height of summer all burns and flares
on this limitless prairie, then of a ruddy gold; but in
September a green tinge begins to suffuse the ocean of
herbage, which dies away in the pink and mauve and vivid
blue of the fine sunsets.

As Pierre, quite alone and in a dreary mood, slowly paced
the endless, flat highway, that resurrection of the past which
he had beheld on the Palatine again confronted his mind's eye.
On either hand the tombs once more rose up intact, with
marble of dazzling whiteness.   Had not the head of a colossal
statue been found, mingled with fragments of huge sphinxes,
at the foot of yonder vase-shaped mass of bricks?   He seemed
to see the entire colossal statue standing again between the
huge, crouching beasts.   Farther on a beautiful headless
statue of a woman had been discovered in the cella of a
sepulchre, and he beheld it, again whole, with features
expressive of grace and strength smiling upon life.   The
inscriptions also became perfect; he could read and understand them at a glance, as if living among those dead ones of
two thousand years ago.   And the road, too, became peopled:
the chariots thundered, the armies tramped along, the people
of Rome jostled him with the feverish agitation of great
communities.   It was a return of the times of the Flavians or
the Antonines, the palmy years of the Empire, when the pomp
of the Appian Way, with its grand sepulchres, carved and
adorned like temples, attained its apogee.   What a monumental Street of Death, what an approach to Rome, that
highway, straight as an arrow, where, with the extraordinary
pomp of their pride, which had survived their dust, the great
dead greeted the traveller, ushered him into the presence
of the living!   He may well have wondered among what
sovereign people, what masters of the world, he was about
to find himself—a nation which had committed to its dead

the duty of telling strangers that it allowed nothing whatever to perish—that its dead, like its city, remained eternal
and glorious in monuments of extraordinary vastness! To
think of it—the foundations of a fortress, and a tower sixty
feet in diameter, that one woman might be laid to rest! And
then, far away, at the end of the superb, dazzling highway, bordered with the marble of its funereal palaces, Pierre,
turning round, distinctly beheld the Palatine, with the marble
of its imperial palaces—the huge assemblage of palaces whose
omnipotence had dominated the world!

But suddenly he started : two carabiniers had just appeared
among the ruins. The spot was not safe ; the authorities
watched over tourists even in broad daylight. And later on
came another meeting which caused him some emotion. He
perceived an ecclesiastic, a tall old man, in a black cassock,
edged and girt with red ; and was surprised to recognise
Cardinal Boccanera, who had quitted the roadway, and was
slowly strolling along the band of grass, among the tall
thistles and sulphur-wort. With his head lowered and his
feet brushing against the fragments of the tombs, the Cardinal
did not even see Pierre. The young priest courteously turned
aside, surprised to find him so far from home and alone.
Then, on perceiving a heavy coach, drawn by two black
horses, behind a building, he understood matters. A footman
in black livery was waiting motionless beside the carriage, and
the coachman had not quitted his box. And Pierre remembered that the Cardinals were not expected to walk in Rome,
so that they were compelled to drive into the country when
they desired to take exercise. But what haughty sadness,
what solitary and so-to-say ostracised grandeur there was
about that tall, thoughtful old man, thus forced to seek the
desert, and wander among the tombs, in order to breathe a
little of the evening air!

Pierre had lingered there for long hours ; the twilight was
coming on, and once again he witnessed a lovely sunset. On
his left the Campagna became blurred, and assumed a slaty
hue, against which the yellowish arcades of the aqueduct
showed very plainly, while the Alban hills, far away, faded
into pink. Then, on the right, towards the sea, the planet
sank among a number of cloudlets, figuring an archipelago of
gold in an ocean of dying embers. And excepting the sapphire
sky, studded with rubies, above the endless line of the Campagna, which was likewise changed into a sparkling lake, the

dull green of the herbage turning to a liquid emerald tint,
there was nothing to be seen, neither a hillock nor a flock—
nothing, indeed, but Cardinal Boccanera's black figure, erect
among the tombs, and looking, as it were, enlarged as it stood
out against the last purple flush of the sunset.

Early on the following morning Pierre, eager to see everything, returned to the Appian Way in order to visit the cata-
comb of St. Calixtus, the most extensive and remarkable of
the old Christian cemeteries, and one, too, where several of
the early popes were buried. You ascend through a scorched
garden, past olives and cypresses, reach a shanty of boards
and plaster in which a little trade in 'articles of piety' is
carried on, and there a modern and fairly easy flight of steps
enables you to descend. Pierre fortunately found there some
French Trappists, who guard these catacombs and show them
to strangers. One brother was on the point of going down
with two French ladies, the mother and daughter, the former
still comely and the other radiant with youth. They stood
there smiling, though already slightly frightened, while the
monk lighted some long, slim candles. He was a man with a
bossy brow, the large, massive jaw of an obstinate believer and
pale eyes bespeaking an ingenuous soul.

'Ah! Monsieur l'Abbé,' he said to Pierre, 'you've come
just in time. If the ladies are willing, you had better come
with us; for three brothers are already below with people,
and you would have a long time to wait. This is the great
season for visitors.'

The ladies politely nodded, and the Trappist handed a
candle to the priest. In all probability neither mother nor
daughter was devout, for both glanced askance at their new
companion's cassock, and suddenly became serious. Then
they all went down and found themselves in a narrow subterranean corridor. 'Take care, mesdames,' repeated the Trappist, lighting the ground with his candle. 'Walk slowly, for
there are projections and slopes.'

Then, in a shrill voice full of extraordinary conviction, he
began his explanations. Pierre had descended in silence, his
heart beating with emotion. Ah! how many times, indeed,
in his innocent seminary days, had he not dreamt of those
catacombs of the early Christians, those asylums of the primitive faith! Even recently, while writing his book, he had often
thought of them as of the most ancient and venerable remains
of that community of the lowly and simple, for the return of

which he called. But his brain was full of pages written by poets and great prose writers. He had beheld the catacombs through the magnifying glass of those imaginative authors, and had believed them to be vast, similar to subterranean cities, with broad highways and spacious halls, fit for the accommodation of vast crowds. And now how poor and humble the reality!

'Well, yes,' said the Trappist in reply to the ladies' questions, 'the corridor is scarcely more than a yard in width; two persons could not pass along side by side. How they dug it? Oh! it was simple enough. A family or a burial association needed a place of sepulchre. Well, a first gallery was excavated with pickaxes in soil of this description—granular tufa, as it is called—a reddish substance, as you can see, both soft and yet resistant, easy to work and at the same time waterproof. In a word, just the substance that was needed, and one, too, that has preserved the remains of the buried in a wonderful way.' He paused and brought the flamelet of his candle near to the compartments excavated on either hand of the passage. 'Look,' he continued, 'these are the *loculi*. Well, a subterranean gallery was dug, and on both sides these compartments were hollowed out, one above the other. The bodies of the dead were laid in them, for the most part simply wrapped in shrouds. Then the aperture was closed with tiles or marble slabs, carefully cemented. So, as you can see, everything explains itself. If other families joined the first one, or the burial association became more numerous, fresh galleries were added to those already filled. Passages were excavated on either hand, in every sense; and, indeed, a second and lower storey, at times even a third, was dug out. And here, you see, we are in a gallery which is certainly thirteen feet high. Now, you may wonder how they raised the bodies to place them in the compartments of the top tier. Well, they did not raise them to any such height; in all their work they kept on going lower and lower, removing more and more of the soil as the compartments became filled. And in this wise, in these catacombs of St. Calixtus, in less than four centuries, the Christians excavated more than ten miles of galleries, in which more than a million of their dead must have been laid to rest. Now, there are dozens of catacombs; the environs of Rome are honeycombed with them. Think of that, and perhaps you will be able to form some idea of the vast number of people who were buried in this manner.'

Pierre listened, feeling greatly impressed. He had once visited a coal pit in Belgium, and he here found the same narrow passages, the same heavy, stifling atmosphere, the same nihility of darkness and silence. The flamelets of the candles showed merely like stars in the deep gloom ; they shed no radiance around. And he at last understood the character of this funereal, termite-like labour—these chance burrowings, continued according to requirements, without art, method, or symmetry. The rugged soil was ever ascending and descending, the sides of the gallery snaked : neither plumb-line nor square had been used. All this, indeed, had simply been a work of charity and necessity, wrought by simple, willing grave-diggers, illiterate craftsmen, with the clumsy handiwork of the decline and fall. Proof thereof was furnished by the inscriptions and emblems on the marble slabs. They reminded one of the childish drawings which street urchins scrawl upon blank walls.

'You see,' the Trappist continued, 'most frequently there is merely a name ; and sometimes there is no name, but simply the words *In Pace*. At other times there is an emblem, the dove of purity, the palm of martyrdom, or else the fish whose name in Greek is composed of five letters which, as initials, signify : "Jesus Christ, Son of God, Saviour."'

He again brought his candle near to the marble slabs, and the palm could be distinguished : a central stroke, whence started a few oblique lines ; and then came the dove or the fish, roughly outlined, a zigzag indicating a tail, two bars representing the bird's feet, while a round point simulated an eye. And the letters of the short inscriptions were all askew, of various sizes, often quite misshapen, as in the coarse hand-writing of the ignorant and simple.

However, they reached a crypt, a sort of little hall, where the graves of several popes had been found ; among others that of Sixtus II, a holy martyr, in whose honour there was a superbly engraved metrical inscription set up by Pope Damasus. Then, in another hall, a family vault of much the same size, decorated, at a later stage, with naïve mural paintings, the spot where St. Cecilia's body had been discovered was shown. And the explanations continued. The Trappist dilated on the paintings, drawing from them a confirmation of every dogma and belief, baptism, the Eucharist, the resurrection, Lazarus arising from the tomb, Jonas cast up by the whale, Daniel in the lions' den, Moses drawing water from the rock, and Christ

—shown beardless, as was the practice in the early ages—
accomplishing His various miracles.

'You see,' repeated the Trappist, 'all those things are
shown there ; and remember that none of the paintings was
specially prepared : they are absolutely authentic.'

At a question from Pierre, whose astonishment was increasing, he admitted that the catacombs had been mere
cemeteries at the outset, when no religious ceremonies had been
celebrated in them. It was only later, in the fourth century,
when the martyrs were honoured, that the crypts were utilised
for worship. And in the same way they only became places
of refuge during the persecutions, when the Christians had to
conceal the entrances to them. Previously they had remained
freely and legally open. This was indeed their true history :
cemeteries four centuries old becoming places of asylum, ravaged
at times during the persecutions ; afterwards held in veneration till the eighth century ; then despoiled of their holy relics,
and subsequently blocked up and forgotten, so that they remained buried during more than seven hundred years, people
thinking of them so little that at the time of the first
searches in the fifteenth century they were considered an
extraordinary discovery—an intricate historical problem—one,
moreover, which only our own age has solved.

'Please, stoop, mesdames,' resumed the Trappist. 'In
this compartment here is a skeleton which has not been
touched. It has been lying here for sixteen or seventeen
hundred years, and will show you how the bodies were laid
out. Savants say that it is the skeleton of a female, probably a young girl. It was still quite perfect last spring ;
but the skull, as you can see, is now split open. An American
broke it with his walking stick to make sure that it was
genuine.'

The ladies leaned forward, and the flickering light
illumined their pale faces, expressive of mingled fright and
compassion. Especially noticeable was the pitiful, pain-fraught
look which appeared on the countenance of the daughter, so
full of life with her red lips and large black eyes. Then all
relapsed into gloom, and the little candles were borne aloft
and went their way through the heavy darkness of the galleries.
The visit lasted another hour, for the Trappist did not spare
a detail, fond as he was of certain nooks and corners, and as
zealous as if he desired to work the redemption of his visitors.

While Pierre followed the others a complete evolution

took place within him. As he looked about him, and formed
a more and more complete idea of his surroundings, his first
stupefaction at finding the reality so different from the
embellished accounts of story-tellers and poets, his disillusion
at being plunged into such rudely excavated mole-burrows,
gave way to fraternal emotion. It was not that he thought
of the fifteen hundred martyrs whose sacred bones had rested
there. But how humble, resigned, yet full of hope had been
those who had chosen such a place of sepulchre! Those low,
darksome galleries were but temporary sleeping places for the
Christians. If they did not burn the bodies of their dead, as
the Pagans did, it was because, like the Jews, they believed
in the resurrection of the body; and it was that lovely idea
of sleep, of tranquil rest after a just life, whilst awaiting the
celestial reward, which imparted such intense peacefulness,
such infinite charm, to the black, subterranean city. Everything there spoke of calm and silent night; everything there
slumbered in rapturous quiescence, patient until the far-off
awakening. What could be more touching than those terra-
cotta tiles, those marble slabs, which bore not even a name—
nothing but the words *In Pace*—at peace. Ah! to be at
peace—life's work at last accomplished; to sleep in peace, to
hope in peace for the advent of heaven! And the peacefulness
seemed the more delightful as it was enjoyed in such deep
humility. Doubtless the diggers worked chancewise and
clumsily; the craftsmen no longer knew how to engrave a
name or carve a palm or a dove. Art had vanished; but all
the feebleness and ignorance were instinct with the youth of
a new humanity. Poor and lowly and meek ones swarmed
there, reposing beneath the soil, whilst up above the sun continued its everlasting task. You found there charity and
fraternity in death; husband and wife often lying together
with their offspring at their feet; the great mass of the unknown submerging the personage, the bishop, or the martyr;
the most touching equality—that springing from modesty—
prevailing amidst all that dust, with compartments ever
similar and slabs destitute of ornament, so that rows and
rows of the sleepers mingled without distinctive sign. The
inscriptions seldom ventured on a word of praise, and then
how prudent, how delicate it was: the men were very worthy,
very pious: the women very gentle, very beautiful, very
chaste. A perfume of infancy arose, unlimited human affection spread: this was death as understood by the primitive

Christians—death which hid itself to await the resurrection, and dreamt no more of the empire of the world !

And all at once before Pierre's eyes arose a vision of the sumptuous tombs of the Appian Way, displaying the domineering pride of a whole civilisation in the sunlight—tombs of vast dimensions, with a profusion of marbles, grandiloquent inscriptions, and masterpieces of sculptured work. Ah ! what an extraordinary contrast between that pompous avenue of death, conducting, like a highway of triumph, to the regal, eternal city, when compared with the subterranean necropolis of the Christians, that city of hidden death, so gentle, so beautiful, and so chaste ! Here only quiet slumber, desired and accepted night, resignation and patience were to be found. Millions of human beings had here laid themselves to rest in all humility, had slept for centuries, and would still be sleeping here, lulled by the silence and the gloom, if the living had not intruded on their desire to remain in oblivion so long as the trumpets of the Judgment Day did not awaken them. Death had then spoken of Life : nowhere had there been more intimate and touching life than in these buried cities of the unknown, lowly dead. And a mighty breath had formerly come from them—the breath of a new humanity destined to renew the world. With the advent of meekness, contempt for the flesh, terror and hatred of nature, relinquishment of terrestrial joys, and a passion for death, which delivers and opens the portals of Paradise, another world had begun. And the blood of Augustus, so proud of purpling in the sunlight, so fired by the passion for sovereign dominion, seemed for a moment to disappear, as if, indeed, the new world had sucked it up in the depths of its gloomy sepulchres.

However, the Trappist insisted on showing the ladies the steps of Diocletian, and began to tell them the legend. ' Yes,' said he, ' it was a miracle. One day, under that emperor, some soldiers were pursuing several Christians, who took refuge in these catacombs ; and when the soldiers followed them inside the steps suddenly gave way, and all the persecutors were hurled to the bottom. The steps remain broken to this day. Come and see them ; they are close by.'

But the ladies were quite overcome, so affected by their prolonged sojourn in the gloom and by the tales of death which the Trappist had poured into their ears that they insisted on going up again. Moreover, the candles were coming to an end. They were all dazzled when they found

themselves once more in the sunlight, outside the little hut
where articles of piety and souvenirs were sold. The girl
bought a paper weight, a piece of marble on which was
engraved the fish symbolical of 'Jesus Christ, Son of God,
Saviour of Mankind.'

On the afternoon of that same day Pierre decided to visit
St. Peter's. He had as yet only driven across the superb
piazza with its obelisk and twin fountains, encircled by
Bernini's colonnades, those four rows of columns and
pilasters which form a girdle of monumental majesty. At the
far end rises the basilica, its façade making it look smaller
and heavier than it really is, but its sovereign dome nevertheless filling the heavens.

Pebbled, deserted inclines stretched out, and steps followed
steps, worn and white, under the burning sun; but at last
Pierre reached the door and went in. It was three o'clock.
Broad sheets of light streamed in through the high square
windows, and some ceremony—the vesper service, no doubt—
was beginning in the Cappella Clementina on the left. Pierre,
however, heard nothing; he was simply struck by the immensity of the edifice, as with raised eyes he slowly walked along.
At the entrance came the giant basins for holy water with
their boy-angels as chubby as Cupids; then the nave, vaulted
and decorated with sunken coffers; then the four cyclopean
buttress-piers upholding the dome, and then again the transepts and apsis, each as large as one of our churches. And the
proud pomp, the dazzling, crushing splendour of everything,
also astonished him: he marvelled at the cupola, looking like
a planet, resplendent with the gold and bright colours of its
mosaic work, at the sumptuous *baldacchino* of bronze, crowning the high altar raised above the very tomb of St. Peter, and
whence descend the double steps of the Confession, illumined
by seven and eighty lamps, which are always kept burning.
And finally he was lost in astonishment at the extraordinary
profusion of marble, both white and coloured. Oh! those
polychromatic marbles, Bernini's luxurious passion! The
splendid pavement reflecting the entire edifice, the facings of
the pilasters with their medallions of popes, the tiara and the
keys borne aloft by chubby angels, the walls covered with
emblems, particularly the dove of Innocent X, the niches with
their colossal statues uncouth in taste, the *loggie* and their
balconies, the balustrade and double steps of the Confession, the
rich altars and yet richer tombs—all, nave, aisles, transepts,

and apsis, were in marble, resplendent with the wealth of marble ; not a nook small as the palm of one's hand appearing but it showed the insolent opulence of marble. And the basilica triumphed, beyond discussion, recognised and admired by every one as the largest and most splendid church in the whole world—the personification of hugeness and magnificence combined.

Pierre still wandered on, gazing, overcome, as yet not distinguishing details. He paused for a moment before the bronze statue of St. Peter, seated in a stiff, sacerdotalal attitude on a marble pedestal. A few of the faithful were there kissing the large toe of the Saint's right foot. Some of them carefully wiped it before applying their lips ; others, with no thought of cleanliness, kissed it, pressed their foreheads to it, and then kissed it again. Next, Pierre turned into the transept on the left, where stand the confessionals. Priests are ever stationed there, ready to confess penitents in every language. Others wait, holding long staves, with which they lightly tap the heads of kneeling sinners, who thereby obtain thirty days' indulgence. However, there were few people present, and inside the small wooden boxes the priests occupied their leisure time in reading and writing, as if they were at home. Then Pierre again found himself before the Confession, and gazed with interest at the eighty lamps, scintillating like stars. The high altar, at which the Pope alone can officiate, seemed wrapped in the haughty melancholy of solitude under its gigantic, flowery *baldacchino*, the casting and gilding of which cost two and twenty thousand pounds. But suddenly Pierre remembered the ceremony in the Cappella Clementina, and felt astonished, for he could hear nothing of it. As he drew near a faint breath, like the far-away piping of a flute, was wafted to him. Then the volume of sound slowly increased, but it was only on reaching the chapel that he recognised an organ peal. The sunlight here filtered through red curtains drawn before the windows, and thus the chapel glowed like a furnace whilst resounding with the grave music. But in that huge pile all became so slight, so weak, that at sixty paces neither voice nor organ could be distinguished.

On entering the basilica Pierre had fancied that it was quite empty and lifeless. There were, however, some people there, but so few and far between that their presence was not noticed. A few tourists wandered about wearily, guide-book

in hand. In the grand nave a painter with his easel was
taking a view, as in a public gallery. Then a French seminary
went by, conducted by a prelate who named and explained the
tombs. But in all that space these fifty or a hundred people
looked merely like a few black ants who had lost themselves
and were vainly seeking their way. And Pierre pictured himself in some gigantic gala hall or tremendous vestibule in an
immeasurable palace of reception. The broad sheets of sunlight streaming through the lofty square windows of plain
white glass illumined the church with blending radiance.
There was not a single stool or chair : nothing but the superb,
bare pavement, such as you might find in a museum, shining
mirror-like under the dancing shower of sun-rays. Nor was
there a single corner for solitary reflection, a nook of gloom
and mystery, where one might kneel and pray. In lieu thereof
the sumptuous, sovereign dazzlement of broad daylight prevailed upon every side. And, on thus suddenly finding himself in this deserted opera-house, all aglow with flaring gold
and purple, Pierre could but remember the quivering gloom of
the Gothic cathedrals of France, where dim crowds sob and
supplicate amidst a forest of pillars. In presence of all this
ceremonial majesty—this huge, empty pomp, which was all
Body—he recalled with a pang the emaciate architecture and
statuary of the middle ages, which were all Soul. He vainly
sought for some poor, kneeling woman, some creature swayed
by faith or suffering, yielding in a modest half-light to thoughts
of the unknown, and with closed lips holding communion with
the invisible. These he found not : there was but the weary
wandering of the tourists, and the bustle of the prelates conducting the young priests to the obligatory stations ; while
the vesper service continued in the left-hand chapel, nought
of it reaching the ears of the visitors save, perhaps, a confused
vibration, as of the peal of a bell penetrating from outside
through the vaults above.

And Pierre then understood that this was the splendid
skeleton of a colossus whence life was departing. To fill it,
to animate it with a soul, all the gorgeous display of great
religious ceremonies was needed ; the eighty thousand worshippers which it could hold, the great pontifical pomps, the
festivals of Christmas and Easter, the processions and *cortèges*
displaying all the luxury of the Church amidst operatic scenery
and appointments. And he tried to conjure up a picture of
the past magnificence—the basilica overflowing with an idola-

trous multitude, and the superhuman *cortège* passing along
whilst every head was lowered ; the cross and the sword opening the march, the cardinals going two by two, like twin
divinities, in their rochets of lace and their mantles and robes
of red moire, which train-bearers held up behind them ; and
at last, with Jove-like pomp, the Pope, carried on a stage
draped with red velvet, seated in an arm-chair of red velvet
and gold, and dressed in white velvet, with cope of gold, stole
of gold, and tiara of gold. The bearers of the ' *Sedia gestatoria* '[1] shone bravely in red tunics broidered with gold. Above
the one and only Sovereign Pontiff of the world the *flabelli*
waved those huge fans of feathers which formerly were waved
before the idols of pagan Rome. And around the seat of
triumph what a dazzling, glorious court there was ! The
whole pontifical family, the stream of assistant prelates, the
patriarchs, the archbishops, and the bishops, with vestments
and mitres of gold, the *camerieri segreti partecipanti* in violet
silk, the *camerieri partecipanti* of the cape and the sword in
black velvet Renascence costumes, with ruffs and golden
chains, the whole innumerable ecclesiastical and laical suite,
which not even a hundred pages of the ' Gerarchia ' can completely enumerate, the prothonotaries, the chaplains, the prelates of every class and degree, without mentioning the military household, the gendarmes with their busbies, the Palatine
Guards in blue trousers and black tunics, the Swiss Guards
costumed in red, yellow, and black, with breastplates of silver,
suggesting the men at arms of some drama of the Romantic
school, and the Noble Guards, superb in their high boots,
white pigskins, red tunics, gold lace, epaulets and helmets !
However, since Rome had become the capital of Italy the
doors were no longer thrown wide open ; on the rare occasions
when the Pope yet came down to officiate, to show himself as
the supreme representative of the Divinity on earth, the
basilica was filled with chosen ones. To enter it you needed
a card of invitation. You no longer saw the people—a throng
of fifty, even eighty, thousand Christians—flocking to the
church and swarming within it promiscuously ; there was but
a select gathering, a congregation of friends convened as for a
private function. Even when, by dint of effort, thousands were
collected together there, they formed but a picked audience
invited to the performance of a monster concert.

---

[1] The chair and stage are known by that name.—*Trans.*

And as Pierre strolled among the bright, crude marbles in
that cold if gorgeous museum, the feeling grew upon him that
he was in some pagan temple raised to the deity of Light and
Pomp. The larger temples of ancient Rome were certainly
similar piles, upheld by the same precious columns, with walls
covered with the same polychromatic marbles and vaulted
ceilings having the same gilded panels. And his feeling was
destined to become yet more acute after his visits to the other
basilicas, which could but reveal the truth to him. First one
found the Christian church quietly, audaciously quartering
itself in a pagan church, as, for instance, San Lorenzo in
Miranda installed in the temple of Antoninus and Faustina,
and retaining the latter's rare porticus in *cipollino* marble
and its handsome white marble entablature. Then there was
the Christian church springing from the ruins of the destroyed
pagan edifice, as, for example, San Clemente, beneath which
centuries of contrary beliefs are stratified : a very ancient
edifice of the time of the kings or the republic, then another
of the days of the empire identified as a temple of Mithras,
and next a basilica of the primitive faith. Then, too, there was
the Christian church typified by that of Saint Agnes beyond
the walls which had been built on exactly the same pattern as
the Roman secular basilica—that Tribunal and Exchange
which accompanied every Forum. And, in particular, there
was the Christian church erected with materials stolen from
the demolished pagan temples. To this testified the sixteen
superb columns of that same Saint Agnes, columns of various
marbles filched from various gods ; the one and twenty columns
of Santa Maria in Trastevere, columns of all sorts of orders
torn from a temple of Isis and Serapis, who even now are
represented on their capitals ; also the six and thirty white
marble ionic columns of Santa Maria Maggiore derived from
the temple of Juno Lucina ; and the two and twenty columns
of Santa Maria in Ara Cœli, these varying in substance, size,
and workmanship, and certain of them said to have been stolen
from Jove himself, from the famous temple of Jupiter
Capitolinus which rose upon the sacred summit. In addition,
the temples of the opulent Imperial period seemed to resuscitate
in our times at San Giovanni in Laterano and San Paolo
fuori le mura. Was not that Basilica of San Giovanni—'the
Mother and Head of all the churches of the city and the earth'
—like the abode of honour of some pagan divinity whose
splendid kingdom was of this world ? It boasted five naves,

parted by four rows of columns; it was a profusion of bas-reliefs, friezes, and entablatures, and its twelve colossal statues of the Apostles looked like subordinate deities lining the approach to the master of the gods! And did not San Paolo, lately completed, its new marbles shimmering like mirrors, recall the abode of the Olympian immortals, typical temple as it was with its majestic colonnade, its flat, gilt-panelled ceiling, its marble pavement incomparably beautiful both in substance and workmanship, its violet columns with white bases and capitals, and its white entablature with violet frieze: everywhere, indeed, you found the mingling of those two colours so divinely carnal in their harmony. And there, as at St. Peter's, not one patch of gloom, not one nook of mystery where one might peer into the invisible, could be found! And, withal, St. Peter's remained the monster, the colossus, larger than the largest of all others, an extravagant testimony of what the mad passion for the huge can achieve when human pride, by dint of spending millions, dreams of lodging the divinity in an over-vast, over-opulent palace of stone, where in truth that pride itself, and not the divinity, triumphs!

And to think that after long centuries that gala colossus had been the outcome of the fervour of primitive faith! You found there a blossoming of that ancient sap, peculiar to the soil of Rome, which in all ages has thrown up preposterous edifices, of exaggerated hugeness and dazzling and ruinous luxury. It would seem as if the absolute masters successively ruling the city brought that passion for cyclopean building with them, derived it from the soil in which they grew, for they transmitted it one to the other, without a pause, from civilization to civilization, however diverse and contrary their minds. It has all been, so to say, a continuous blossoming of human vanity, a passionate desire to set one's name on an imperishable wall, and, after being master of the world, to leave behind one an indestructible trace, a tangible proof of one's passing glory, an eternal edifice of bronze and marble fit to attest that glory until the end of time. At the bottom the spirit of conquest, the proud ambition to dominate the world, subsists; and when all has crumbled, and a new society has sprung up from the ruins of its predecessor, men have erred in imagining it to be cured of the sin of pride, steeped in humility once more, for it has had the old blood in its veins, and has yielded to the same insolent madness as its ancestors, a prey to all the violence of its heredity directly it has become great

and strong. Among the illustrious popes there has not been
one that did not seek to build, did not revert to the traditions of
the Cæsars, eternising their reigns in stone and raising temples
for resting-places, so as to rank among the gods. Ever the
same passion for terrestrial immortality has burst forth : it
has been a battle as to who should leave the highest, most
substantial, most gorgeous monument ; and so acute has been
the disease that those who, for lack of means and opportunity,
have been unable to build, and have been forced to content
themselves with repairing, have, nevertheless, desired to bequeath the memory of their modest achievements to subsequent
generations by commemorative marble slabs engraved with
pompous inscriptions ! These slabs are to be seen on every
side : not a wall has ever been strengthened but some pope
has stamped it with his arms, not a ruin has been restored,
not a palace repaired, not a fountain cleaned, but the reigning
pope has signed the work with his Roman and pagan title of
' Pontifex Maximus.' It is a haunting passion, a form of involuntary debauchery, the fated florescence of that compost of
ruins, that dust of edifices whence new edifices are ever arising.
And given the perversion with which the old Roman soil almost
immediately tarnished the doctrines of Jesus, that resolute passion for domination and that desire for terrestrial glory which
wrought the triumph of Catholicism in scorn of the humble
and pure, the fraternal and simple ones of the primitive
Church, one may well ask whether Rome has ever been
Christian at all !

And whilst Pierre was for the second time walking round
the huge basilica, admiring the tombs of the popes, truth, like
a sudden illumination, burst upon him and filled him with its
glow. Ah ! those tombs ! Yonder in the full sunlight, in the
rosy Campagna, on either side of the Appian Way—that
triumphal approach to Rome, conducting the stranger to the
august Palatine with its crown of circling palaces—there arose
the gigantic tombs of the powerful and wealthy, tombs of unparalleled artistic splendour, perpetuating in marble the pride
and pomp of a strong race that had mastered the world. Then,
near at hand, beneath the sod, in the shrouding night of
wretched mole holes, other tombs were hidden—the tombs of
the lowly, the poor, and the suffering—tombs destitute of art or
display, but whose very humility proclaimed that a breath of
affection and resignation had passed by, that One had come
preaching love and fraternity, the relinquishment of the wealth

of the earth for the everlasting joys of a future life, and committing to the soil the good seed of His Gospel, sowing the
new humanity which was to transform the olden world. And,
behold, from that seed, buried in the soil for centuries, behold,
from those humble, unobtrusive tombs, where martyrs slept
their last and gentle sleep whilst waiting for the glorious call,
yet other tombs had sprung, tombs as gigantic and as pompous
as the ancient, destroyed sepulchres of the idolaters, tombs
uprearing their marbles among a pagan-temple-like splendour,
proclaiming the same superhuman pride, the same mad passion for universal sovereignty. At the time of the Renascence
Rome became pagan once more ; the old imperial blood frothed
up and swept Christianity away with the greatest onslaught
ever directed against it. Ah ! those tombs of the popes at St.
Peter's, with their impudent, insolent glorification of the
departed, their sumptuous, carnal hugeness, defying death and
setting immortality upon this earth. There are giant popes
of bronze, allegorical figures and angels of equivocal character
wearing the beauty of lovely girls, of passion-compelling women
with the thighs and the breasts of pagan goddesses !
Paul III is seated on a high pedestal, Justice and Prudence
are almost prostrate at his feet. Urban VIII is between
Prudence and Religion, Innocent XI between Religion and
Justice, Innocent XII between Justice and Charity, Gregory
XIII between Religion and Strength. Attended by Prudence
and Justice, Alexander VII appears kneeling, with Charity
and Truth before him, and a skeleton rises up displaying an
empty hour-glass. Clement XIII, also on his knees, triumphs
above a monumental sarcophagus, against which leans Religion
bearing the Cross ; while the Genius of Death, his elbow resting on the right-hand corner, has two huge, superb lions,
emblems of omnipotence, beneath him. Bronze bespeaks the
eternity of the figures, white marble describes opulent flesh,
and coloured marble winds around in rich draperies, deifying
the monuments under the bright golden glow of nave and
aisles.

And Pierre passed from one tomb to the other on his way
through the magnificent, deserted, sunlit basilica. Yes,
these tombs, so imperial in their ostentation, were meet companions for those of the Appian Way. Assuredly it was
Rome, the soil of Rome, that soil where pride and domination
sprouted like the herbage of the fields that had transformed
the humble Christianity of primitive times, the religion of

faternity, justice, and hope into what it now was: victorious Catholicism, allied to the rich and powerful, a huge implement of government, prepared for the conquest of every nation. The popes had awoke as Cæsars. Remote heredity had acted, the blood of Augustus had bubbled forth afresh, flowing through their veins and firing their minds with immeasurable ambition. As yet none but Augustus had held the empire of the world, had been both emperor and pontiff, master of the body and the soul. And thence had come the eternal dream of the popes in despair at only holding the spiritual power, and obstinately refusing to yield in temporal matters, clinging for ever to the ancient hope that their dream might at last be realised, and the Vatican become another Palatine, whence they might reign with absolute despotism over all the conquered nations.

VI

PIERRE had been in Rome for a fortnight, and yet the affair of his book was no nearer solution. He was still possessed by an ardent desire to see the Pope, but could in no wise tell how to satisfy it, so frequent were the delays and so greatly had he been frightened by Monsignor Nani's predictions of the dire consequences which might attend any imprudent action. And so, foreseeing a prolonged sojourn, he at last betook himself to the Vicariate in order that his 'celebret' might be stamped, and afterwards said his mass each morning at the church of Santa Brigida, where he received a kindly greeting from Abbé Pisoni, Benedetta's former confessor.

One Monday evening he resolved to repair early to Donna Serafina's customary reception in the hope of learning some news and expediting his affairs. Perhaps Monsignor Nani would look in; perhaps he might be lucky enough to come across some cardinal or domestic prelate willing to help him. It was in vain that he had tried to extract any positive information from Don Vigilio, for, after a short spell of affability and willingness, Cardinal Pio's secretary had relapsed into distrust and fear, and avoided Pierre as if he were resolved not to meddle in a business which, all considered, was decidedly suspicious and dangerous. Moreover, for a couple of days past a violent attack of fever had compelled him to keep his room.

Thus the only person to whom Pierre could turn for com-

fort was Victorine Bosquet, the old Beauceronne servant who
had been promoted to the rank of housekeeper, and who still
retained a French heart after thirty years' residence in Rome.
She often spoke to the young priest of Auneau, her native
place, as if she had left it only the previous day; but on that
particular Monday even she had lost her wonted gay vivacity,
and when she heard that he meant to go down in the evening
to see the ladies she wagged her head significantly. 'Ah!
you won't find them very cheerful,' said she. 'My poor
Benedetta is greatly worried. Her divorce suit is not progressing at all well.'

All Rome, indeed, was again talking of this affair. An
extraordinary revival of tittle-tattle had set both white and
black worlds agog. And so there was no need for reticence
on Victorine's part, especially in conversing with a compatriot.
It appeared, then, that, in reply to Advocate Morano's
memoir setting forth that the marriage had not been consummated, there had come another memoir, a terrible one,
emanating from Monsignor Palma, a doctor in theology,
whom the Congregation of the Council had selected to defend
the marriage. As a first point, Monsignor Palma flatly disputed the alleged non-consummation, questioned the certificate
put forward on Benedetta's behalf, and quoted instances
recorded in scientific text-books which showed how deceptive
appearances often were. He strongly insisted, moreover, on
the narrative which Count Prada supplied in another memoir,
a narrative well calculated to inspire doubt; and, further, he
so turned and twisted the evidence of Benedetta's own maid
as to make that evidence also serve against her. Finally
he argued in a decisive way that, even supposing the marriage
had not been consummated, this could only be ascribed to
the resistance of the Countess, who had thus set at defiance
one of the elementary laws of married life, which was that a
wife owed obedience to her husband.

Next had come a fourth memoir, drawn up by the reporter
of the Congregation, who analysed and discussed the three
others, and subsequently the Congregation itself had dealt
with the matter, opining in favour of the dissolution of the
marriage by a majority of one vote—such a bare majority,
indeed, that Monsignor Palma, exercising his rights, had
hastened to demand further inquiry, a course which brought
the whole *procédure* again into question, and rendered a fresh
vote necessary.

'Ah! the poor Contessina!' exclaimed Victorine, 'she'll surely die of grief, for, calm as she may seem, there's an inward fire consuming her. It seems that Monsignor Palma is the master of the situation, and can make the affair drag on as long as he likes. And then a deal of money has already been spent, and one will have to spend a lot more. Abbé Pisoni, whom you know, was very badly inspired when he helped on that marriage; and though I certainly don't want to soil the memory of my good mistress, Countess Ernesta, who was a real saint, it's none the less true that she wrecked her daughter's life when she gave her to Count Prada.'

The housekeeper paused. Then, impelled by an instinctive sense of justice, she resumed: 'It's only natural that Count Prada should be annoyed, for he's really being made a fool of. And, for my part, as there is no end to all the fuss, and this divorce is so hard to obtain, I really don't see why the Contessina shouldn't live with her Dario without troubling any further. Haven't they loved one another ever since they were children? Aren't they both young and handsome, and wouldn't they be happy together, whatever the world might say? Happiness, *mon Dieu!* one finds it so seldom that one can't afford to let it pass.'

Then, seeing how greatly surprised Pierre was at hearing such language, she began to laugh with the quiet composure of one belonging to the humble classes of France, whose only desire is a quiet and happy life, irrespective of matrimonial ties. Next, in more discreet language, she proceeded to lament another worry which had fallen on the household, another result of the divorce affair. A rupture had come about between Donna Serafina and Advocate Morano, who was very displeased with the ill success of his memoir to the congregation, and accused Father Lorenza—the confessor of the Boccanera ladies—of having urged them into a deplorable lawsuit, whose only fruit could be a wretched scandal affecting everybody. And so great had been Morano's annoyance that he had not returned to the Boccanera mansion, but had severed a connection of thirty years' standing, to the stupefaction of all the Roman drawing-rooms, which altogether disapproved of his conduct. Donna Serafina was, for her part, the more grieved as she suspected the advocate of having purposely picked the quarrel in order to secure an excuse for leaving her; his real motive, in her estimation, being a sudden, disgraceful passion for a young and intriguing woman of the middle classes.

That Monday evening, when Pierre entered the drawing-room, hung with yellow brocatelle of a flowery Louis XIV pattern, he at once realised that melancholy reigned in the dim light radiating from the lace-veiled lamps. Benedetta and Celia, seated on a sofa, were chatting with Dario, whilst Cardinal Sarno, ensconced in an arm-chair, listened to the ceaseless chatter of the old relative who conducted the little princess to each Monday gathering. And the only other person present was Donna Serafina, seated all alone in her wonted place on the right-hand side of the chimney-piece, and consumed with secret rage at seeing the chair on the left-hand side unoccupied—that chair which Morano had always taken during the thirty years that he had been faithful to her. Pierre noticed with what anxious and then despairing eyes she observed his entrance, her glance ever straying towards the door, as though she even yet hoped for the fickle one's return. Withal her bearing was erect and proud; she seemed to be more tightly laced than ever; and there was all the wonted haughtiness on her hard-featured face, with its jet black eye-brows and snowy hair.

Pierre had no sooner paid his respects to her than he allowed his own worry to appear by inquiring whether they would not have the pleasure of seeing Monsignor Nani that evening. And thereupon Donna Serafina could not refrain from answering: 'Oh! Monsignor Nani is forsaking us like the others. People always take themselves off when they can be of service.'

She harboured a spite against the prelate for having done so little to further the divorce in spite of his many promises. Beneath his outward show of extreme willingness and caressing affability he doubtless concealed some scheme of his own which he was tenaciously pursuing. However, Donna Serafina promptly regretted the confession which anger had wrung from her, and resumed: 'After all, he will perhaps come. He is so good-natured, and so fond of us.'

In spite of the vivacity of her temperament she really wished to act diplomatically, so as to overcome the bad luck which had recently set in. Her brother the Cardinal had told her how irritated he was by the attitude of the Congregation of the Council; he had little doubt that the frigid reception accorded to his niece's suit had been due in part to

the desire of some of his brother cardinals to be disagreeable
to him. Personally, he desired the divorce, as it seemed to
him the only means of ensuring the perpetuation of the
family; for Dario obstinately refused to marry any other
woman than his cousin. And thus there was an accumulation
of disasters; the Cardinal was wounded in his pride, his
sister shared his sufferings and on her own side was stricken
in the heart, whilst both lovers were plunged in despair at
finding their hopes yet again deferred.

As Pierre approached the sofa where the young folks
were chatting he found that they were speaking of the catastrophe. 'Why should you be so despondent?' asked Celia
in an undertone. 'After all, there was a majority of a vote
in favour of annulling the marriage. Your suit hasn't been
rejected; there is only a delay.'

But Benedetta shook her head. 'No, no! If Monsignor
Palma proves obstinate His Holiness will never consent.
It's all over.'

'Ah! if one were only rich, very rich!' murmured Dario
with such an air of conviction that no one smiled. And,
turning to his cousin, he added in a whisper: 'I must really
have a talk with you. We cannot go on living like this.'

In a breath she responded: 'Yes, you are right. Come
down to-morrow evening at five. I will be here alone.'

Then dreariness set in; the evening seemed to have no
end. Pierre was greatly touched by the evident despair of
Benedetta, who as a rule was so calm and sensible. The deep
eyes which illumined her pure, delicate, infantile face were
now blurred as by restrained tears. He had already formed a
sincere affection for her, pleased as he was with her equable
if somewhat indolent disposition, the semblance of discreet
good sense with which she veiled her soul of fire. That
Monday even she certainly tried to smile while listening to
the pretty secrets confided to her by Celia, whose love affairs
were prospering far more than her own. There was only one
brief interval of general conversation, and that was brought
about by the little princess's aunt, who, suddenly raising her
voice, began to speak of the infamous manner in which the
Italian newspapers referred to the Holy Father. Never, indeed,
had there been so much bad feeling between the Vatican and
the Quirinal. Cardinal Sarno felt so strongly on the subject
that he departed from his wonted silence to announce that on
the occasion of the sacrilegious festivities of the Twentieth of

September, celebrating the capture of Rome, the Pope intended
to cast a fresh letter of protest in the face of all the Christian
powers, whose indifference proved their complicity in the
odious spoliation of the Church.

'Yes, indeed! what folly to try and marry the pope and
the king,' bitterly exclaimed Donna Serafina, alluding to her
niece's deplorable marriage.

The old maid now seemed quite beside herself; it was
already so late that neither Monsignor Nani nor anybody else
was expected. However, at the unhoped-for sound of footsteps her eyes again brightened and turned feverishly towards
the door. But it was only to encounter a final disappointment. The visitor proved to be Narcisse Habert, who
stepped up to her, apologising for making so late a call. It
was Cardinal Sarno, his uncle by marriage, who had introduced him into this exclusive *salon*, where he had received a
cordial reception on account of his religious views, which were
said to be most uncompromising. If, however, despite the
lateness of the hour, he had ventured to call there that evening,
it was solely on account of Pierre, whom he at once drew on
one side.

'I felt sure I should find you here,' he said. 'Just now I
managed to see my cousin, Monsignor Gamba del Zoppo, and
I have some good news for you. He will see us to-morrow
at about eleven in his rooms at the Vatican.' Then, lowering
his voice: 'I think he will endeavour to conduct you to the
Holy Father. Briefly, the audience seems to me assured.'

Pierre was greatly delighted by this promised certainty,
which came to him so suddenly in that dreary drawing-room,
where for a couple of hours he had been gradually sinking into
despair! So at last a solution was at hand!

Meantime Narcisse, after shaking hands with Dario and
bowing to Benedetta and Celia, approached his uncle the
Cardinal, who, having rid himself of the old relation, made up
his mind to talk. But his conversation was confined to the
state of his health, and the weather, and sundry insignificant
anecdotes which he had lately heard. Not a word escaped
him respecting the thousand complicated matters with which
he dealt at the Propaganda. It was as though, once outside
his office, he plunged into the commonplace and the unim-
portant by way of resting from the anxious task of governing
the world. And after he had spoken for a time every one got
up, and the visitors took leave.

'Don't forget,' Narcisse repeated to Pierre, 'you will find me at the Sixtine Chapel to-morrow at ten. And I will show you the Botticellis before we go to our appointment.'

At half-past nine on the following morning Pierre, who had come on foot, was already on the spacious Piazza of St. Peter's; and before turning to the right, towards the bronze gate near one corner of Bernini's colonnade, he raised his eyes and lingered gazing at the Vatican. Nothing to his mind could be less monumental than the jumble of buildings which, without semblance of architectural order or regularity of any kind, had grown up in the shadow cast by the dome of the basilica. Roofs rose one above the other and broad, flat walls stretched out chance-wise, just as wings and storeys had been added. The only symmetry observable above the colonnade was that of the three sides of the court of San Damaso, where the lofty glasswork which now encloses the old *loggie* sparkled in the sun between the ruddy columns and pilasters, suggesting, as it were, three huge conservatories.

And this was the most beautiful palace in the world, the largest of all palaces, comprising no fewer than eleven thousand apartments and containing the most admirable masterpieces of human genius! But Pierre, disillusioned as he was, had eyes only for the lofty façade on the right, over-looking the piazza, for he knew that the second floor windows there were those of the Pope's private apartments. And he contemplated those windows for a long time, and remembered having been told that the fifth one on the right was that of the Pope's bedroom, and that a lamp could always be seen burning there far into the night.

What was there, too, behind that gate of bronze which he saw before him—that sacred portal by which all the kingdoms of the world communicated with the kingdom of heaven, whose august vicar had secluded himself behind those lofty, silent walls? From where he stood Pierre gazed on that gate with its metal panels studded with large square-headed nails, and wondered what it defended, what it con-cealed, what it shut off from the view, with its stern, for-bidding air, recalling that of the gate of some ancient fortress. What kind of world would he find behind it, what treasures of human charity jealously preserved in yonder gloom, what revivifying hope for the new nations hungering for fraternity and justice? He took pleasure in fancying, in picturing the one holy pastor of humanity, ever watching in the depths of that closed palace, and, while the nations strayed into hatred, preparing all for the final reign of Jesus, and at last proclaiming the advent of that reign by transforming our democracies into the one great Christian community promised by the Saviour. Assuredly the world's future was being prepared behind that bronze portal; assuredly it was that future which would issue forth.

But all at once Pierre was amazed to find himself face to face with Monsignor Nani, who had just left the Vatican on his way to the neighbouring Palace of the Inquisition, where, as Assessor, he had his residence.

'Ah! Monseigneur,' said Pierre, 'I am very pleased. My friend Monsieur Habert is going to present me to his cousin, Monsignor Gamba del Zoppo, and I think I shall obtain the audience I so greatly desire.'

Monsignor Nani smiled with his usual amiable yet keen expression. 'Yes, yes, I know.' But, correcting himself as it were, he added: 'I share your satisfaction, my dear son. Only, you must be prudent.' And then, as if fearing that the young priest might have understood by his first words that he had just seen Monsignor Gamba, the most easily terrified prelate of the whole prudent pontifical family, he related that he had been running about since an early hour on behalf of two French ladies, who likewise were dying of a desire to see the Pope. However, he greatly feared that the help he was giving them would not prove successful.

'I will confess to you, Monseigneur,' replied Pierre, 'that I myself was getting very discouraged. Yes, it is high time I should find a little comfort, for my sojourn here is hardly calculated to brace my soul.'

He went on in this strain, allowing it to be seen that the sights of Rome were finally destroying his faith. Such days as those which he had spent on the Palatine and along the Appian Way, in the Catacombs and at St. Peter's, grievously disturbed him, spoilt his dream of Christianity rejuvenated and triumphant. He emerged from them full of doubt and growing lassitude, having already lost much of his usually rebellious enthusiasm.

Still smiling, Monsignor Nani listened and nodded approvingly. Yes, no doubt that was the fatal result. He seemed to have foreseen it, and to be well satisfied thereat. 'At all events, my dear son,' said he, 'everything is going on well, since you are now certain that you will see his Holiness.'

'That is true, Monseigneur; I have placed my only hope
in the very just and perspicacious Leo XIII. He alone can
judge me, since he alone can recognise in my book his own
ideas, which I think I have very faithfully set forth. Ah!
if he be willing he will, in Jesus' name and by democracy and
science, save this old world of ours!'

Pierre's enthusiasm was returning again, and Nani, smiling
more and more affably with his piercing eyes and thin lips,
again expressed approval : 'Certainly; quite so, my dear son.
You will speak to him, you will see.'

Then, as they both raised their heads and looked towards
the Vatican, Nani carried his amiability so far as to undeceive
Pierre with respect to the Pope's bedroom. No, the window
where a light was seen every evening was simply that of a
landing where the gas was kept burning almost all night.
The window of his Holiness's bed-chamber was the second
one farther on. Then both relapsed into silence, equally
grave as they continued to gaze at the façade.

'Well, till we meet again, my dear son,' said Nani at last.
'You will tell me of your interview, I hope.'

As soon as Pierre was alone he went in by the bronze
portal, his heart beating violently, as if he were entering some
redoubtable sanctuary where the future happiness of mankind
was elaborated. A sentry was on duty there, a Swiss guard,
who walked slowly up and down in a grey-blue cloak, below
which one only caught a glimpse of his baggy, red, black
and yellow breeches; and it seemed as if that cloak of sober
hue were purposely cast over a disguise in order to conceal
its strangeness, which had become irksome. Then, on the
right hand, came the covered stairway conducting to the
Court of San Damaso; but to reach the Sixtine Chapel it
was necessary to follow a long gallery, with columns on either
hand, and ascend the royal staircase, the Scala Regia. And
in this realm of the gigantic, where every dimension is exaggerated and replete with overpowering majesty, Pierre's
breath came short as he ascended the broad steps.

He was much surprised on entering the Sixtine Chapel,
for it at first seemed to him small, a sort of rectangular and
lofty hall, with a delicate screen of white marble separating
the part where guests congregate on the occasion of great
ceremonies from the choir where the cardinals sit on simple
oaken benches, while the inferior prelates remain standing
behind them. On a low platform to the right of the soberly

adorned altar is the pontifical throne; while in the wall on the left opens the narrow singing gallery with its balcony of marble. And for everything suddenly to spread out and soar into the infinite one must raise one's head, allow one's eyes to ascend from the huge fresco of the Last Judgment, occupying the whole of the end wall, to the paintings which cover the vaulted ceiling down to the cornice extending between the twelve windows of white glass, six on either hand.

Fortunately there were only three or four quiet tourists there; and Pierre at once perceived Narcisse Habert occupying one of the cardinals' seats above the steps where the train-bearers crouch. Motionless, and with his head somewhat thrown back, the young man seemed to be in ecstasy. But it was not the work of Michael Angelo that he thus contemplated. His eyes never strayed from one of the earlier frescoes below the cornice; and on recognising the priest he contented himself with murmuring: 'Ah! my friend, just look at the Botticelli.' Then, with dreamy eyes, he relapsed into a state of rapture.

Pierre, for his part, had received a great shock both in heart and in mind, overpowered as he was by the superhuman genius of Michael Angelo. The rest vanished; there only remained, up yonder, as in a limitless heaven, the extraordinary creations of the master's art. That which at first surprised one was that the painter should have been the sole artisan of the mighty work. No marble cutters, no bronze workers, no gilders, no one of another calling had intervened. The painter with his brush had sufficed for all—for the pilasters, columns, and cornices of marble, for the statues and the ornaments of bronze, for the *fleurons* and roses of gold, for the whole of the wondrously rich decorative work which surrounded the frescoes. And Pierre imagined Michael Angelo on the day when the bare vault was handed over to him, covered with plaster, offering only a flat white surface, hundreds of square yards to be adorned. And he pictured him face to face with that huge white page, refusing all help, driving all inquisitive folks away, jealously, violently shutting himself up alone with his gigantic task, spending four and a half years in fierce solitude, and day by day adding to his colossal work of creation. Ah! that mighty work, a task to fill a whole lifetime, a task which he must have begun with quiet confidence in his own will and power, drawing, as it were, an entire world from his brain and flinging it there with the ceaseless flow of creative virility in the full heyday of its omnipotence.

And Pierre was yet more overcome when he began to examine these presentments of humanity, magnified as by the eyes of a visionary, overflowing in mighty sympathetic pages of cyclopean symbolisation. Royal grace and nobility, sovereign peacefulness and power—every beauty shone out like natural florescence. And there was perfect science, the most audacious foreshortening risked with the certainty of success—an everlasting triumph of technique over the difficulty which an arched surface presented. And, in particular, there was wonderful simplicity of medium ; matter was reduced almost to nothingness ; a few colours were used broadly without any studied search for effect or brilliancy. Yet that sufficed, the blood seethed freely, the muscles projected, the figures became animated and stood out of their frames with such energy and dash that it seemed as if a flame were flashing by aloft, endowing all those beings with superhuman and immortal life. Life, aye, it was life, which burst forth and triumphed— mighty, swarming life, miraculous life, the creation of one sole hand possessed of the supreme gift—simplicity blended with power.

That a philosophical system, a record of the whole of human destiny, should have been found therein, with the creation of the world, of man, and of woman, the fall, the chastisement, then the redemption, and finally God's judgment on the last day—this was a matter on which Pierre was unable to dwell at this first visit in the wondering stupor into which the paintings threw him. But he could not help noticing how the human body, its beauty, its power, and its grace were exalted ! Ah ! that regal Jehovah, at once terrible and paternal, carried off amid the whirlwind of his creation, his arms outstretched and giving birth to worlds ! And that superb and nobly outlined Adam with extended hand, whom Jehovah, though he touch him not, animates with his finger—a wondrous and admirable gesture, leaving a sacred space between the finger of the Creator and that of the created—a tiny space, in which, nevertheless, abides all the infinite of the invisible and the mysterious. And then that powerful yet adorable Eve, that Eve with the sturdy flanks fit for the bearing of humanity, that Eve with the proud, tender grace of a woman bent on being loved even to perdition, that Eve embodying the whole of woman with her fecundity, her seductiveness, her empire! Moreover, even the decorative figures of the pilasters at the corners of the frescoes celebrate the triumph of the flesh: there are the twenty young men radiant in their nakedness, with incomparable splendour of torso and of limb, and such intensity of life that a craze for motion seems to carry them off, bend them, throw them over in superb attitudes. And between the windows are the giants, the prophets and the sibyls—man and woman deified, with inordinate wealth of muscle and grandeur of intellectual expression. There is Jeremiah with his elbow resting on his knee and his chin on his hand, plunged as he is in reflection—in the very depths of his visions and his dreams; there is the Sibylla Erythræa, so pure of profile, so young despite the opulence of her form, and with one finger resting on the open book of destiny; there is Isaiah with the thick lips of truth, virile and haughty, his head half turned and his hand raised with a gesture of command; there is the Sibylla Cumæa, terrifying with her science and her old age, her wrinkled countenance, her vulture's nose, her square protruding chin; there is Jonah cast forth by the whale, and wondrously foreshortened, his torso twisted, his arms bent, his head thrown back, and his mouth agape and shouting: and there are the others, all of the same full-blown, majestic family, reigning with the sovereignty of eternal health and intelligence, and typifying the dream of a broader, loftier, and indestructible humanity. Moreover, in the lunettes and the arches over the windows other figures of grace, power, and beauty appear and throng, the ancestors of the Christ, thoughtful mothers with lovely nude infants, men with wondering eyes peering into the future, representatives of the punished weary race longing for the promised Redeemer; while in the pendentives of the four corners various biblical episodes, the victories of Israel over the Spirit of Evil, spring into life. And finally there is the gigantic fresco at the far end, the Last Judgment with its swarming multitude, so numerous that days and days are needed to see each figure aright, a distracted crowd, full of the hot breath of life, from the dead rising in response to the furious trumpeting of the angels, from the fearsome groups of the damned whom the demons fling into hell, even to Jesus the justiciar, surrounded by the saints and apostles, and to the radiant concourse of the blessed who ascend upheld by angels, whilst higher and still higher other angels, bearing the instruments of the Passion, triumph as in full glory. And yet, above this gigantic composition, painted thirty years subsequently, in the full ripeness of age, the ceiling retains its ethereality, its unquestionable superiority, for on it the artist bestowed all his virgin power, his whole youth, the first great flare of his genius.

And Pierre found but one word to express his feelings: Michael Angelo was the monster dominating and crushing all others. Beneath his immense achievement you had only to glance at the works of Perugino, Pinturicchio, Roselli, Signorelli and Botticelli, those earlier frescoes, admirable in their way, which below the cornice spread out around the chapel.

Narcisse for his part had not raised his eyes to the overpowering splendour of the ceiling. Wrapt in ecstasy, he did not allow his gaze to stray from one of the three frescoes of Botticelli. 'Ah! Botticelli,' he at last murmured; 'in him you have the elegance and the grace of the mysterious; a profound feeling of sadness even in the midst of voluptuousness, a divination of the whole modern soul, with the most troublous charm that ever attended artist's work.'

Pierre glanced at him in amazement, and then ventured to inquire: 'You come here to see the Botticellis?'

'Yes, certainly,' the young man quietly replied; 'I only come here for him, and five hours every week I only look at his work. There, just study that fresco, Moses and the daughters of Jethro. Isn't it the most penetrating work that human tenderness and melancholy have produced?'

Then, with a faint, devout quiver in his voice and the air of a priest initiating another into the delightful but perturbing atmosphere of a sanctuary, he went on repeating the praises of Botticelli's art; his women with long, sensual, yet candid faces, supple bearing, and rounded forms showing from under light drapery; his young men, his angels of doubtful sex, blending stateliness of muscle with infinite delicacy of outline; next the mouths he painted, fleshy, fruit-like mouths, at times suggesting irony, at others pain, and often so enigmatical with their sinuous curves that one knew not whether the words they left unuttered were words of purity or filth; then, too, the eyes which he bestowed on his figures, eyes of languor and passion, of carnal or mystical rapture, their joy at times so instinct with grief as they peer into the nihility of human things that no eyes in the world could be more impenetrable. And finally there were Botticelli's hands, so carefully and delicately painted, so full of life, wantoning so to say in a free atmosphere, now joining, caressing, and even, as it were, speaking, the whole evincing such intense solicitude for gracefulness that at times there seems to be undue mannerism, though every hand has its particular expression, each varying expression of the enjoyment or pain which the sense of touch can bring. And yet there was nothing effeminate or false about the painter's work: on all sides a sort of virile pride was apparent, an atmosphere of superb passionate motion, absolute concern for truth, direct study from life, conscientiousness, veritable realism, corrected and elevated by a genial strangeness of feeling and character that imparted a never-to-be-forgotten charm even to ugliness itself.

Pierre's stupefaction, however, increased as he listened to Narcisse, whose somewhat studied elegance, whose curly hair cut in the Florentine fashion, and whose blue, mauvish eyes paling with enthusiasm he now for the first time remarked. 'Botticelli,' he at last said, 'was no doubt a marvellous artist, only it seems to me that here, at any rate, Michael Angelo——'

But Narcisse interrupted him almost with violence. 'No! no! Don't talk of him! He spoilt everything, ruined everything! A man who harnessed himself to his work like an ox, who laboured at his task like a navvy, at the rate of so many square yards a day! And a man, too, with no sense of the mysterious and the unknown, who saw everything so huge as to disgust one with beauty, painting girls like the trunks of oak-trees, women like giant butchers, with heaps and heaps of stupid flesh, and never a gleam of a divine or infernal soul! He was a mason—a colossal mason, if you like—but he was nothing more.'

Weary 'modern' that Narcisse was, spoilt by the pursuit of the original and the rare, he thus unconsciously gave rein to his fated hate of health and power. That Michael Angelo who brought forth without an effort, who had left behind him the most prodigious of all artistic creations, was the enemy. And his crime precisely was that he had created life, produced life in such excess that all the petty creations of others, even the most delightful among them, vanished in presence of the overflowing torrent of human beings flung there all alive in the sunlight.

'Well, for my part,' Pierre courageously declared, 'I'm not of your opinion. I now realise that life is everything in art; that real immortality belongs only to those who create. The case of Michael Angelo seems to me decisive, for he is the superhuman master, the monster who overwhelms all others, precisely because he brought forth that magnificent living flesh which offends your sense of delicacy. Those who are inclined to the curious, those who have minds of a pretty turn, whose intellects are ever seeking to penetrate things, may try to improve on the equivocal and invisible, and set all the charm of art in some elaborate stroke or symbolisation; but, none the less, Michael Angelo remains the all-powerful, the maker of men, the master of clearness, simplicity, and health.'

At this Narcisse smiled with indulgent and courteous disdain. And he anticipated further argument by remarking: 'It's already eleven. My cousin was to have sent a servant here as soon as he could receive us. I am surprised to have seen nobody as yet. Shall we go up to see the *Stanze* of Raffaelle while we wait?'

Once in the rooms above, he showed himself perfect, both lucid in his remarks and just in his appreciations, having recovered all his easy intelligence as soon as he was no longer upset by his hatred of colossal labour and cheerful decoration.

It was unfortunate that Pierre should have first visited the Sixtine Chapel; for it was necessary he should forget what he had just seen and accustom himself to what he now beheld in order to enjoy its pure beauty. It was as if some potent wine had confused him, and prevented any immediate relish of a lighter vintage of delicate fragrance. Admiration did not here fall upon one with lightning speed; it was slowly, irresistibly that one grew charmed. And the contrast was like that of Racine beside Corneille, Lamartine beside Hugo, the eternal pair, the masculine and feminine genius coupled through centuries of glory. With Raffaelle it is nobility, grace, exquisiteness and correctness of line, and divineness of harmony that triumph. You do not find in him merely the materialist symbolism so superbly thrown off by Michael Angelo; he introduces psychological analysis of deep penetration into the painter's art. Man is shown more purified, idealised; one sees more of that which is within him. And though one may be in presence of an artist of sentimental bent, a feminine genius whose quiver of tenderness one can feel, it is also certain that admirable firmness of workmanship confronts one, that the whole is very strong and very great. Pierre gradually yielded to such sovereign masterliness, such virile elegance, such a vision of supreme beauty set in supreme perfection. But if the 'Dispute on the Sacrament' and the so-called 'School of Athens,' both prior to the paintings of the Sixtine Chapel, seemed to him to be Raffaelle's masterpieces, he felt that in the 'Burning of the Borgo,' and particularly in the 'Expulsion of Heliodorus from the Temple,' and 'Pope St. Leo staying Attila at the gates of Rome,' the artist had lost the flower of his divine grace, through the deep impression which the overwhelming grandeur of Michael Angelo had wrought upon him. How crushing indeed had been the blow when the Sixtine Chapel was thrown open and the rivals entered! The creations of the monster then appeared, and the greatest of the humanisers lost some of his soul at sight of them, thenceforward unable to rid himself of their influence.

From the *stanze* Narcisse took Pierre to the *loggie*, those glazed galleries which are so high and so delicately decorated. But here you only find work which pupils executed after designs left by Raffaelle at his death. The fall was sudden and complete, and never had Pierre better understood that genius is everything—that when it disappears the school collapses. The man of genius sums up his period; at a given hour he throws forth all the sap of the social soil, which afterwards remains exhausted often for centuries. So Pierre became more particularly interested in the fine view that the *loggie* afford, and all at once he noticed that the papal apartments were in front of him, just across the Court of San Damaso. This court, with its porticus, fountain, and white pavement, had an aspect of empty, airy, sunlit solemnity which surprised him. There was none of the gloom or pent-up religious mystery that he had dreamt of with his mind full of the surroundings of the old northern cathedrals. Right and left of the steps conducting to the rooms of the Pope and the Cardinal Secretary of State four or five carriages were ranged, the coachmen stiffly erect and the horses motionless in the brilliant light; and nothing else peopled that vast square desert of a court which, with its bareness gilded by the coruscations of its glasswork and the ruddiness of its stones, suggested a pagan temple dedicated to the sun. But what more particularly struck Pierre was the splendid panorama of Rome, for he had not hitherto imagined that the

Pope from his windows could thus behold the entire city
spread out before him as if he merely had to stretch forth his
hand to make it his own once more.

While Pierre contemplated the scene a sound of voices
caused him to turn ; and he perceived a servant in black livery
who, after repeating a message to Narcisse, was retiring with
a deep bow. Looking much annoyed, the *attaché* approached
the young priest. 'Monsignor Gamba del Zoppo,' said he,
'has sent word that he can't see us this morning. Some unexpected duties require his presence.' However, Narcisse's
embarrassment showed that he did not believe in the excuse,
but rather suspected some one of having so terrified his cousin
that the latter was afraid of compromising himself. Obliging
and courageous as Habert himself was, this made him indignant. Still he smiled and resumed : 'Listen, perhaps there's
a means of forcing an entry. If your time is your own we can
lunch together and then return to visit the Museum of Antiquities. I shall certainly end by coming across my cousin,
and we may, perhaps, be lucky enough to meet the Pope should
he go down to the gardens.'

At the news that his audience was yet again postponed
Pierre had felt keenly disappointed. However, as the whole
day was at his disposal, he willingly accepted the *attaché's*
offer. They lunched in front of St. Peter's, in a little restaurant of the Borgo, most of whose customers were pilgrims, and
the fare, as it happened, was far from good. Then, at about
two o'clock, they set off for the museum, skirting the basilica
by way of the Piazza della Sagrestia. It was a bright, deserted,
burning district ; and again, but in a far greater degree, did
the young priest experience that sensation of bare, tawny, sun-
baked majesty which had come upon him while gazing into
the Court of San Damaso. Then, as he passed the apse of St.
Peter's, the enormity of the colossus was brought home to
him more strongly than ever : it rose like a giant bouquet of
architecture edged by empty expanses of pavement sprinkled
with fine weeds. And in all the silent immensity there were
only two children playing in the shadow of a wall. The old
papal mint, the Zecca, now an Italian possession, and guarded
by soldiers of the royal army, is on the left of the passage
leading to the museums, while on the right, just in front, is
one of the entrances of honour to the Vatican where the papal
Swiss Guard keeps watch and ward ; and this is the entrance

by which, according to etiquette, the pair-horse carriages convey the Pope's visitors into the Court of San Damaso.

Following the long lane which ascends between a wing of the palace and its garden wall, Narcisse and Pierre at last reached the Museum of Antiquities. Ah! what a museum it is, with galleries innumerable, a museum compounded of three museums, the Pio-Clementino, the Chiaramonti, and the Braccio-Nuovo, and containing a whole world found beneath the soil, then exhumed, and now glorified in full sunlight. For more than two hours Pierre went from one hall to another, dazzled by the masterpieces, bewildered by the accumulation of genius and beauty. It was not only the celebrated examples of statuary—the Laocoon and the Apollo of the cabinets of the Belvedere, the Meleager, or even the torso of Hercules—that astonished him. He was yet more impressed by the *ensemble*, by the innumerable quantities of Venuses, Bacchuses, and deified emperors and empresses, by the whole superb growth of beautiful or august flesh celebrating the immortality of life. Three days previously he had visited the Museum of the Capitol, where he had admired the Venus, the dying Gaul,[1] the marvellous Centaurs of black marble, and the extraordinary collection of busts, but here his admiration became intensified into stupor by the inexhaustible wealth of the galleries. And, with more curiosity for life than for art, perhaps, he again lingered before the busts which so powerfully resuscitate the Rome of history—the Rome which, whilst incapable of realising the ideal beauty of Greece, was certainly well able to create life. The emperors, the philosophers, the learned men, the poets are all there, and live such as they really were, studied and portrayed in all scrupulousness with their deformities, their blemishes, the slightest peculiarities of their features. And from this extreme solicitude for truth springs a wonderful wealth of character and an incomparable vision of the past. Nothing, indeed, could be loftier: the very men live once more, and retrace the history of their city, that history which has been so falsified that the teaching of it has caused generations of schoolboys to hold antiquity in horror. But on seeing the men, how well one understands, how fully one can sympathise! And indeed the smallest bits of marble, the maimed statues, the bas-reliefs in fragments, even the isolated

---

[1] Best known in England, through Byron's lines, as the dying Gladiator, though that appellation is certainly erroneous.—*Trans.*

limbs—whether the divine arm of a nymph or the sinewy, shaggy thigh of a satyr—evoke the splendour of a civilisation full of light, grandeur, and strength.

At last Narcisse brought Pierre back into the Gallery of the Candelabra, three hundred feet in length and full of fine examples of sculpture. 'Listen, my dear Abbé,' said he. 'It is scarcely more than four o'clock, and we will sit down here for a while, as I am told that the Holy Father sometimes passes this way to go down to the gardens. It would be really lucky if you could see him, perhaps even speak to him—who can tell? At all events, it will rest you, for you must be tired out.'

Narcisse was known to all the attendants, and his relationship to Monsignor Gamba gave him the run of almost the entire Vatican, where he was fond of spending his leisure time. Finding two chairs, they sat down, and the *attaché* again began to talk of art.

How astonishing had been the destiny of Rome, what a singular, borrowed royalty had been hers! She seemed like a centre whither the whole world converged, but where nothing grew from the soil itself, which from the outset appeared to be stricken with sterility. The arts required to be acclimatised there ; it was necessary to transplant the genius of neighbouring nations, which, once there, however, flourished magnificently. Under the emperors, when Rome was the queen of the earth, the beauty of her monuments and sculpture came to her from Greece. Later, when Christianity arose in Rome, it there remained impregnated with paganism ; it was on another soil that it produced Gothic art, the Christian art *par excellence*. Later still, at the Renascence, it was certainly at Rome that the age of Julius II and Leo X shone forth ; but the artists of Tuscany and Umbria prepared the evolution, brought it to Rome that it might thence expand and soar. For the second time, indeed, art came to Rome from without, and gave her the royalty of the world by blossoming so triumphantly within her walls. Then occurred the extraordinary awakening of antiquity, Apollo and Venus resuscitated, worshipped by the popes themselves, who from the time of Nicholas V dreamt of making papal Rome the equal of the imperial city. After the precursors, so sincere, tender, and strong in their art—Fra Angelico, Perugino, Botticelli, and so many others—came the two sovereigns, Michael Angelo and Raffaelle, the superhuman and the divine. Then the fall was

sudden, years elapsed before the advent of Caravaggio with
power of colour and modelling, all that the science of painting
could achieve when bereft of genius. And afterwards the
decline continued until Bernini was reached—Bernini the real
creator of the Rome of the present popes, the prodigal child who
at twenty could already show a galaxy of colossal marble
wenches, the universal architect who with fearful activity finished
the façade, built the colonnade, decorated the interior of St.
Peter's, and raised fountains, churches, and palaces innumerable. And that was the end of all, for since then Rome
has little by little withdrawn from life, from the modern world,
as though she, who always lived on what she derived from
others, were dying of her inability to take anything more from
them in order to convert it to her own glory.

'Ah! Bernini, that delightful Bernini!' continued Narcisse
with his rapturous air. 'He is both powerful and exquisite,
his *verve* always ready, his ingenuity invariably awake, his
fecundity full of grace and magnificence. As for their
Bramante with his masterpiece, that cold, correct Cancelleria,
we'll dub him the Michael Angelo and Raffaelle of architecture and say no more about it. But Bernini, that exquisite
Bernini, why, there is more delicacy and refinement in his
pretended bad taste than in all the hugeness and perfection of
the others! Our own age ought to recognise itself in his
art, at once so varied and so deep, so triumphant in its
mannerisms, so full of a perturbing solicitude for the artificial
and so free from the baseness of reality. Just go to the Villa
Borghese to see the group of Apollo and Daphne which
Bernini executed when he was eighteen,[1] and in particular see
his statue of Santa Teresa in ecstasy at Santa Maria della
Vittoria! Ah! that Santa Teresa! It is like heaven opening, with the quiver that only a purely divine enjoyment can
set in woman's flesh, the rapture of faith carried to the point
of spasm, the creature losing breath and dying of pleasure in
the arms of the Divinity! I have spent hours and hours before
that work without exhausting the infinite scope of its precious,
burning symbolisation.'

Narcisse's voice died away, and Pierre, no longer astonished

---

[1] There is also at the Villa Borghese Bernini's *Anchises carried by
Æneas*, which he sculptured when only *sixteen*. No doubt his faults
were many; but it was his misfortune to belong to a decadent period.—
Trans.

at his covert, unconscious hatred of health, simplicity, and strength, scarcely listened to him. The young priest himself was again becoming absorbed in the idea he had formed of pagan Rome resuscitating in Christian Rome and turning it into Catholic Rome, the new political, sacerdotal, domineering centre of earthly government. Apart from the primitive age of the catacombs, had Rome ever been Christian? The thoughts that had come to him on the Palatine, in the Appian Way, and in St. Peter's were gathering confirmation. Genius that morning had brought him fresh proof. No doubt the paganism which reappeared in the art of Michael Angelo and Raffaelle was tempered, transformed by the Christian spirit. But did it not still remain the basis? Had not the former master peered across Olympus when snatching his great nudities from the terrible heavens of Jehovah? Did not the ideal figures of Raffaelle reveal the superb, fascinating flesh of Venus beneath the chaste veil of the Virgin? It seemed so to Pierre, and some embarrassment mingled with his despondency, for all those beautiful forms glorifying the ardent passions of life, were in opposition to his dream of rejuvenated Christianity giving peace to the world and reviving the simplicity and purity of the early ages.

All at once he was surprised to hear Narcisse, by what transition he could not tell, speaking to him of the daily life of Leo XIII. 'Yes, my dear Abbé, at eighty-four [1] the Holy Father shows the activity of a young man and leads a life of determination and hard work such as neither you nor I would care for! At six o'clock he is already up, says his mass in his private chapel, and drinks a little milk for breakfast. Then, from eight o'clock till noon, there is a ceaseless procession of cardinals and prelates, all the affairs of the congregations passing under his eyes, and none could be more numerous or intricate. At noon the public and collective audiences usually begin. At two he dines. Then comes the siesta which he has well earned, or else a promenade in the gardens until six o'clock. The private audiences then sometimes keep him for an hour or two. He sups at nine and scarcely eats, lives on nothing, in fact, and is always alone at his little table. What do you think, eh, of the etiquette which compels him to such loneliness? There you have a man who for eighteen years has

[1] The reader should remember that the period selected for this narrative is the year 1894. Leo XIII was born in 1810.—*Trans.*

never had a guest at his table, who day by day sits all alone
in his grandeur! And as soon as ten o'clock strikes, after
saying the Rosary with his familiars, he shuts himself up in
his room. But, although he may go to bed, he sleeps very
little; he is frequently troubled by insomnia, and gets up and
sends for a secretary to dictate memoranda or letters to him.
When any interesting matter requires his attention he gives
himself up to it heart and soul, never letting it escape his
thoughts. And his life, his health, lies in all this. His mind
is always busy; his will and strength must always be exerting
themselves. You may know that he long cultivated Latin
verse with affection; and I believe that in his days of struggle
he had a passion for journalism, inspired the articles of the
newspapers he subsidised, and even dictated some of them
when his most cherished ideas were in question.'

Silence fell. At every moment Narcisse craned his neck
to see if the little papal *cortège* were not emerging from the
Gallery of the Tapestries to pass them on its way to the gardens.
'You are perhaps aware,' he resumed, 'that his Holiness is
brought down on a low chair which is small enough to pass
through every doorway. It's quite a journey, more than a
mile, through the Loggie, the Stanze of Raffaelle, the painting and sculpture galleries, not to mention the numerous staircases, before he reaches the gardens, where a pair-horse carriage
awaits him. It's quite fine this evening, so he will surely
come. We must have a little patience.'

Whilst Narcisse was giving these particulars Pierre again
sank into a reverie and saw the whole extraordinary history
pass before him. First came the worldly, ostentatious popes
of the Renascence, those who resuscitated antiquity with so
much passion and dreamt of draping the Holy See with the
purple of Empire once more. There was Paul II, the magnificent Venetian who built the Palazzo di Venezia; Sixtus IV,
to whom one owes the Sixtine Chapel; and Julius II and Leo
X, who made Rome a city of theatrical pomp, prodigious festivities, tournaments, ballets, hunts, masquerades and banquets. At
that time the papacy had just rediscovered Olympus amidst
the dust of buried ruins, and as though intoxicated by the
torrent of life which arose from the ancient soil, it founded
the museums, thus reviving the superb temples of the pagan
age, and restoring them to the cult of universal admiration.
Never had the Church been in such peril of death, for if
the Christ was still honoured at St. Peter's, Jupiter and

all the other gods and goddesses, with their beauteous, triumphant flesh, were enthroned in the halls of the Vatican. Then, however, another vision passed before Pierre, one of the modern popes prior to the Italian occupation—notably Pius IX, who, whilst yet free, often went into his good city of Rome. His huge red and gold coach was drawn by six horses, surrounded by Swiss Guards and followed by Noble Guards; but now and again he would alight in the Corso, and continue his promenade on foot, and then the mounted men of the escort galloped forward to give warning and stop the traffic. The carriages drew up, the gentlemen had to alight and kneel on the pavement, whilst the ladies simply rose and devoutly inclined their heads, as the Holy Father, attended by his Court, slowly wended his way to the Piazza del Popolo, smiling and blessing at every step. And now had come Leo XIII, the voluntary prisoner, shut up in the Vatican for eighteen years, and he, behind the high, silent walls, in the unknown sphere where each of his days flowed by so quietly, had acquired a more exalted majesty, instinct with sacred and redoubtable mysteriousness.

Ah! that Pope whom you no longer meet or see, that Pope hidden from the common of mankind like some terrible divinity whom the priests alone dare to approach! It is in that sumptuous Vatican which his forerunners of the Renascence built and adorned for giant festivities that he has secluded himself; it is there he lives, far from the crowd, in prison with the handsome men and the lovely women of Michael Angelo and Raffaelle, with the gods and goddesses of marble, with the whole of resplendent Olympus celebrating around him the religion of life and light. With him the entire Papacy is there steeped in paganism. What a spectacle when the slender, weak old man, all soul, so purely white, passes along the galleries of the Museum of Antiquities on his way to the gardens. Right and left the statues behold him pass with all their bare flesh. There is Jupiter, there is Apollo, there is Venus the *dominatrix*, there is Pan the universal god in whose laugh the joys of earth ring out. Nereids bathe in transparent water. Bacchantes roll, unveiled, in the warm grass. Centaurs gallop by carrying lovely girls, faint with rapture, on their steaming haunches. Ariadne is surprised by Bacchus, Ganymede fondles the eagle, Adonis fires youth and maiden with his flame. And on and on passes the weak, white old man, swaying on his low chair, amidst that splendid triumph, that display and glorification of the flesh, which shouts aloud the omnipotence of Nature, of everlasting matter! Since they have found it again, exhumed it and honoured it, that it is which once more reigns there imperishable; and in vain have they set vine leaves on the statues, even as they have swathed the huge figures of Michael Angelo; sex still flares on all sides, life overflows, its germs course in torrents through the veins of the world. Near by, in that Vatican library of incomparable wealth, where all human science lies slumbering, there lurks a yet more terrible danger—the danger of an explosion which would sweep away everything, Vatican and St. Peter's also, if one day the books in their turn were to awake and speak aloud as speak the beauty of Venus and the manliness of Apollo. But the white, diaphanous old man seems neither to see nor to hear, and the huge heads of Jupiter, the trunks of Hercules, the equivocal statues of Antinous continue to watch him as he passes on!

However, Narcisse had become impatient, and, going in search of an attendant, he learnt from him that his Holiness had already gone down. To shorten the distance, indeed, the *cortège* often passes along a kind of open gallery leading towards the Mint. 'Well, let us go down as well,' said Narcisse to Pierre; 'I will try to show you the gardens.'

Down below, in the vestibule, a door of which opened on to a broad path, he spoke to another attendant, a former pontifical soldier whom he personally knew. The man at once let him pass with Pierre, but was unable to tell him whether Monsignor Gamba del Zoppo had accompanied his Holiness that day.

'No matter,' resumed Narcisse when he and his companion were alone in the path; 'I don't despair of meeting him—and these, you see, are the famous gardens of the Vatican.'

They are very extensive grounds, and the Pope can go quite two and a half miles by passing along the paths of the wood, the vineyard, and the kitchen garden. Occupying the plateau of the Vatican hill, which the mediæval wall of Leo IV still girdles, the gardens are separated from the neighbouring valleys as by a fortified rampart. The wall formerly stretched to the castle of Sant' Angelo, thereby forming what was known as the Leonine City. No inquisitive eyes can peer into the grounds excepting from the dome of St. Peter's, which casts its huge shadow over them during the hot summer weather. They are, too, quite a little world, which each pope has taken pleasure in embellishing. There is a large parterre with lawns of geometrical patterns, planted with handsome palms and adorned with lemon and orange trees in pots; there is a less formal, a shadier garden, where, amidst deep plantations of yoke-elms, you find Giovanni Vesanzio's fountain, the Aquilone, and Pius IV's old Casino; then, too, there are the woods with their superb evergreen oaks, their thickets of plane trees, acacias, and pines, intersected by broad avenues, which are delightfully pleasant for leisurely strolls; and finally, on turning to the left, beyond other clumps of trees, come the kitchen garden and the vineyard, the last well tended.

Whilst walking through the wood Narcisse told Pierre of the life led by the Holy Father in these gardens. He strolls in them every second day when the weather allows. Formerly the popes left the Vatican for the Quirinal, which is cooler and healthier, as soon as May arrived; and spent the dog days at Castle Gandolfo on the margins of the Lake of Albano. But nowadays the only summer residence possessed by his Holiness is a virtually intact tower of the old rampart of Leo IV. He here spends the hottest days, and has even erected a sort of pavilion beside it for the accommodation of his suite. Narcisse, like one at home, went in and secured permission for Pierre to glance at the one room occupied by the Pope, a spacious round chamber with semispherical ceiling, on which are painted the heavens with symbolical figures of the constellations; one of the latter, the lion, having two stars for eyes— stars which a system of lighting causes to sparkle during the night. The walls of the tower are so thick that after blocking up a window, a kind of room, for the accommodation of a couch, has been contrived in the embrasure. Besides this couch the only furniture is a large work-table, a dining-table with flaps, and a large regal arm-chair, a mass of gilding, one of the gifts of the Pope's episcopal jubilee. And you dream of the days of solitude and perfect silence, spent in that low donjon hall, where the coolness of a tomb prevails whilst the heavy suns of August are scorching overpowered Rome.

An astronomical observatory has been installed in another tower, surmounted by a little white cupola, which you espy amidst the greenery; and under the trees there is also a Swiss chalet, where Leo XIII is fond of resting. He sometimes goes on foot to the kitchen garden, and takes much interest in the vineyard, visiting it to see if the grapes are ripening and if

the vintage will be a good one. What most astonished
Pierre, however, was to learn that the Holy Father had been
very fond of ' sport ' before age had weakened him. He was
indeed passionately addicted to bird snaring. Broad-meshed
nets were hung on either side of a path on the fringe of a
plantation, and in the middle of the path were placed cages
containing the decoys, whose songs soon attracted all the birds
of the neighbourhood—red-breasts, white-throats, black-caps,
nightingales, fig-peckers of all sorts. And when a numerous
company of them was gathered together Leo XIII, seated out
of sight and watching, would suddenly clap his hands and
startle the birds, which flew up and were caught by the wings
in the meshes of the nets. All that then remained to be done
was to take them out of the nets and stifle them by a touch of
the thumb. Roast fig-peckers are delicious.[1]

As Pierre came back through the wood he had another
surprise. He suddenly lighted on a ' Grotto of Lourdes,' a
miniature imitation of the original, built of rocks and blocks
of cement. And such was his emotion at the sight that he
could not conceal it. ' It's true, then ! ' said he. ' I was told
of it, but I thought that the Holy Father was of loftier mind
—free from all such base superstitions ! '

' Oh ! ' replied Narcisse, ' I fancy that the grotto dates
from Pius IX, who evinced especial gratitude to our Lady of
Lourdes. At all events, it must be a gift, and Leo XIII
simply keeps it in repair.'

For a few moments Pierre remained motionless and silent
before that imitative grotto, that childish plaything. Some
zealously devout visitors had left their visiting cards in the
cracks of the cement work ! For his part, he felt very sad, and
followed his companion with bowed head, lamenting the
wretched idiocy of the world. Then, on emerging from the
wood, on again reaching the parterre, he raised his eyes.

Ah ! how exquisite in spite of everything was that decline
of a lovely day, and what a victorious charm ascended from
the soil in that part of the gardens. There, in front of that
bare, noble, burning parterre, far more than under the
languishing foliage of the wood or among the fruitful vines,
Pierre realised the strength of Nature. Above the grass
growing meagrely over the compartments of geometrical

[1] Perhaps so ; but what a delightful pastime for the Vicar of the
Divinity !—*Trans.*

pattern which the pathways traced there were barely a few
low shrubs, dwarf roses, aloes, rare tufts of withering flowers.
Some green bushes still described the escutcheon of Pius IX
in accordance with the strange taste of former times. And
amidst the warm silence one only heard the faint crystalline
murmur of the water trickling from the basin of the central
fountain. But all Rome, its ardent heavens, sovereign grace,
and conquering voluptuousness, seemed with their own soul to
animate this vast rectangular patch of decorative gardening,
this mosaic of verdure, which in its semi-abandonment and
scorched decay assumed an aspect of melancholy pride,
instinct with the ever returning quiver of a passion of fire
that could not die. Some antique vases and statues, whitely
nude under the setting sun, skirted the parterres. And
above the aroma of eucalyptus and of pine, stronger even
than that of the ripening oranges, there rose the odour of the
large, bitter box-shrubs, so laden with pungent life that it
disturbed one as one passed as if indeed it were the very scent
of the fecundity of that ancient soil saturated with the dust of
generations.

'It's very strange that we have not met his Holiness,'
exclaimed Narcisse. 'Perhaps his carriage took the other
path through the wood while we were in the tower.'

Then, reverting to Monsignor Gamba del Zoppo, the
attaché explained that the functions of *Coppiere*, or papal
cupbearer, which his cousin should have discharged as one of
the four *camerieri segreti partecipanti*, had become purely
honorary since the dinners offered to diplomatists or in honour
of newly consecrated bishops had been given by the Cardinal
Secretary of State. Monsignor Gamba, whose cowardice and
nullity were legendary, seemed therefore to have no other
rôle than that of enlivening Leo XIII, whose favour he had
won by his incessant flattery and the anecdotes which he was
ever relating about both the black and the white worlds. Indeed
this fat, amiable man, who could even be obliging when his
interests were not in question, was a perfect newspaper, brimful of tittle-tattle, disdaining no item of gossip whatever,
even if it came from the kitchens. And thus he was quietly
marching towards the cardinalate, certain of obtaining the
hat without other exertion than that of bringing a budget of
gossip to beguile the pleasant hours of the promenade. And
Heaven knew that he was always able to garner an abundant
harvest of news in that closed Vatican swarming with prelates

of every kind, in that womanless pontifical family of old begowned bachelors, all secretly exercised by vast ambitions, covert and revolting rivalries, and ferocious hatreds, which, it is said, are still sometimes carried as far as the good old poison of ancient days.

All at once Narcisse stopped. 'Ah!' he exclaimed, 'I was certain of it. There's the Holy Father! But we are not in luck. He won't even see us; he is about to get into his carriage again.'

As he spoke a carriage drew up at the verge of the wood, and a little *cortège*, emerging from a narrow path, went towards it.

Pierre felt as if he had received a great blow in the heart. Motionless beside his companion, and half-hidden by a lofty vase containing a lemon tree, it was only from a distance that he was able to see the white old man, looking so frail and slender in the wavy folds of his white cassock, and walking so very slowly with short, gliding steps. The young priest could scarcely distinguish the emaciated face of old diaphanous ivory, emphasized by a large nose which jutted out above thin lips. However, the pontiff's black eyes were glittering with an inquisitive smile, while his right ear was inclined towards Monsignor Gamba del Zoppo, who was doubtless finishing some story at once rich and short, flowery and dignified. And on the left walked a Noble Guard; and two other prelates followed.

It was but a familiar apparition; Leo XIII was already climbing into the closed carriage. And Pierre, in the midst of that large, odiferous, burning garden, again experienced the singular emotion which had come upon him in the Gallery of the Candelabra while he was picturing the Pope on his way between the Apollos and Venuses radiant in their triumphant nudity. There, however, it was only pagan art which had celebrated the eternity of life, the superb, almighty powers of Nature. But here he had beheld the pontiff steeped in nature itself, in nature clad in the most lovely, most voluptuous, most passionate guise. Ah! that Pope, that old man strolling with his Divinity of grief, humility and renunciation along the paths of those gardens of love, in the languid evenings of the hot summer days, beneath the caressing scents of pine and eucalyptus, ripe oranges, and tall, acrid box-shrubs! Pan, the great god Pan, enveloped him with the sovereign effluvia of his powers. How pleasant was the

thought of living there, amidst that magnificence of heaven
and of earth, of loving the beauty of woman and of rejoicing
in the fruitfulness of all! And suddenly the decisive truth
burst forth that from a land of such joy and light it was only
possible for a temporal religion of conquest and political
domination to rise; not the mystical, pain-fraught religion of
the north—the religion of the soul!

However, Narcisse led the young priest away, telling him
other anecdotes as they went—anecdotes of the occasional
bonhomie of Leo XIII., who would stop to chat with the
gardeners, and question them about the health of the trees
and the sale of the oranges. And he also mentioned the
Pope's former passion for a pair of gazelles, sent him from
Africa, two graceful creatures which he had been fond of
caressing, and at whose death he had shed tears. But Pierre
no longer listened. When they found themselves on the
Piazza of St. Peter's he turned round and gazed at the
Vatican once more.

His eyes had fallen on the gate of bronze, and he remembered having wondered that morning what there might be
behind these metal panels ornamented with big nails. And
he did not yet dare to answer the question, and decide if the
new nations thirsting for fraternity and justice would really
find there the religion necessary for the democracies of to-
morrow; for he had not been able to probe things, and only
carried a first impression away with him. But how keen it
was, and how ill it boded for his dream! A gate of bronze!
Yes, a hard, impregnable gate, so completely shutting the
Vatican off from the rest of the world that nothing new had
entered the palace for three hundred years. Behind that
portal the old centuries, as far as the sixteenth, remained
immutable. Time seemed to have stayed its course there for
ever; nothing more stirred; the very costumes of the Swiss
Guards, the Noble Guards, and the prelates themselves were
unchanged; and you found yourself in the world of three
hundred years ago, with its etiquette, its costumes, and its
ideas. That the popes in a spirit of haughty protest should
for five and twenty years have voluntarily shut themselves up
in their palace was already regrettable; but this imprisonment
of centuries within the past, within the grooves of tradition,
was far more serious and dangerous. It was all Catholicism
which was thus imprisoned, whose dogmas and sacerdotal
organisation were obstinately immobilised. Perhaps, in spite

of its apparent flexibility, Catholicism was really unable to yield in anything, under peril of being swept away, and therein lay both its weakness and its strength. And then what a terrible world was there, how great the pride and ambition, how numerous the hatreds and rivalries! And how strange the prison, how singular the company assembled behind the bars—the Crucified by the side of Jupiter Capitolinus, all pagan antiquity fraternising with the Apostles, all the splendours of the Renascence surrounding the pastor of the Gospel who reigns in the name of the humble and the poor!

The sun was sinking, the gentle, luscious sweetness of the Roman evenings was falling from the limpid heavens, and after that splendid day spent with Michael Angelo, Raffaelle, the ancients, and the Pope, in the finest palace of the world, the young priest lingered, distracted, on the Piazza of St. Peter's.

'Well, you must excuse me, my dear Abbé,' concluded Narcisse. 'But I will now confess to you that I suspect my worthy cousin of a fear that he might compromise himself by meddling in your affair. I shall certainly see him again, but you will do well not to put too much reliance on him.'

It was nearly six o'clock when Pierre got back to the Boccanera mansion. As a rule, he passed in all modesty down the lane, and entered by the little side door, a key of which had been given him. But he had that morning received a letter from M. de la Choue, and desired to communicate it to Benedetta. So he ascended the grand staircase, and on reaching the ante-room was surprised to find nobody there. As a rule, whenever the man-servant went out Victorine installed herself in his place and busied herself with some needlework. Her chair was there, and Pierre even noticed some linen which she had left on a little table when probably summoned elsewhere. Then, as the door of the first reception room was ajar, he at last ventured in. It was almost night there already, the twilight was softly dying away, and all at once the young priest stopped short, fearing to take another step, for, from the room beyond, the large yellow *salon*, there came a murmur of feverish, distracted words, ardent entreaties, fierce panting, a rustling and a shuffling of footsteps. And suddenly Pierre no longer hesitated, urged on despite himself by the conviction that the sounds he heard were those of a struggle, and that some one was hard pressed.

And when he darted into the further room he was stupefied,

for Dario was there, no longer showing the degenerate elegance of the last scion of an exhausted race, but maddened by the hot, frantic blood of the Boccaneras which had bubbled up within him. He had clasped Benedetta by the shoulders in a frenzy of passion and was scorching her face with his hot, entreating words : 'But since you say, my darling, that it is all over, that your marriage will never be dissolved—oh ! why should we be wretched for ever ! Love me as you do love me, and let me love you—let me love you ! '

But the Contessina, with an indescribable expression of tenderness and suffering on her tearful face, repulsed him with her outstretched arms, she likewise evincing a fierce energy as she repeated : 'No, no ; I love you, but it must not, it must not be.'

At that moment, amidst the roar of his despair, Dario became conscious that some one was entering the room. He turned and gazed at Pierre with an expression of stupefied insanity, scarce able even to recognise him. Then he carried his two hands to his face, to his bloodshot eyes and his cheeks wet with scalding tears, and fled, heaving a terrible, pain-fraught sigh in which baffled passion mingled with grief and repentance.

Benedetta seated herself, breathing hard, her strength and courage well nigh exhausted. But as Pierre, too much embarrassed to speak, turned towards the door, she addressed him in a calmer voice : 'No, no, Monsieur l'Abbé, do not go away—sit down, I pray you ; I should like to speak to you for a moment.'

He thereupon thought it his duty to account for his sudden entrance, and explained that he had found the door of the first *salon* ajar, and that Victorine was not in the ante-room, though he had seen her work lying on the table there.

'Yes,' exclaimed the Contessina, 'Victorine ought to have been there ; I saw her there but a short time ago. And when my poor Dario lost his head I called her. Why did she not come ? ' Then, with sudden expansion, leaning towards Pierre, she continued : 'Listen, Monsieur l'Abbé, I will tell you what happened, for I don't want you to form too bad an opinion of my poor Dario. It was all in some measure my fault. Last night he asked me for an appointment here in order that we might have a quiet chat, and as I knew that my aunt would be absent at this time to-day I told him to come. It was only natural—wasn't it ?—that we should want to see one another and come to an agreement after the grievous news that my marriage will probably never be annulled. We suffer too much, and must form a decision. And so when he came in this evening we began to weep and embrace, mingling our tears together. I kissed him again and again, telling him how I adored him, how bitterly grieved I was at being the cause of his sufferings, and how surely I should die of grief at seeing him so unhappy. Ah! no doubt I did wrong; I ought not to have caught him to my heart and embraced him as I did, for it maddened him, Monsieur l'Abbé; he lost his head, and would have made me break my vow to the Blessed Virgin.'

She spoke these words in all tranquillity and simplicity, without sign of embarrassment, like a young and beautiful woman who is at once sensible and practical. Then she resumed: 'Oh! I know my poor Dario well, but it does not prevent me from loving him; perhaps, indeed, it only makes me love him the more. He looks delicate, perhaps rather sickly, but in truth he is a man of passion. Yes, the old blood of my people bubbles up in him. I know something of it myself, for when I was a child I sometimes had fits of angry passion which left me exhausted on the floor, and even now, when the gusts arise within me, I have to fight against myself and torture myself in order that I may not act madly. But my poor Dario does not know how to suffer. He is like a child whose fancies must be gratified. And yet at bottom he has a good deal of common sense; he waits for me because he knows that the only real happiness lies with the woman who adores him.'

As Pierre listened he was able to form a more precise idea of the young prince, of whose character he had hitherto had but a vague perception. Whilst dying of love for his cousin, Dario had ever been a man of pleasure. Though he was no doubt very amiable, the basis of his temperament was none the less egotism. And, in particular, he was unable to endure suffering; he loathed suffering, ugliness, and poverty, whether they affected himself or others. Both his flesh and his soul required gaiety, brilliancy, show, life in the full sunlight. And withal he was exhausted, with no strength left him but for the idle life he led, so incapable of thought and will that the idea of joining the new *régime* had not even occurred to him. Yet he had all the unbounded pride of a Roman; sagacity—a keen, practical perception of the real—was mingled with his indolence; while his inveterate love of woman, more frequently displayed in charm of manner, burst forth at times in attacks of frantic sensuality.

'After all he is a man,' concluded Benedetta in a low voice, 'and I must not ask impossibilities of him.' Then, as Pierre gazed at her, his notions of Italian jealousy quite upset, she exclaimed, aglow with passionate adoration: 'No, no. Situated as we are, I am not jealous. I know very well that he will always return to me, and that he will be mine alone whenever I please, whenever it may be possible.'

Silence followed; shadows were filling the room, the gilding of the large pier tables faded away, and infinite melancholy fell from the lofty, dim ceiling and the old hangings, yellow like autumn leaves. But soon, by some chance play of the waning light, a painting stood out above the sofa on which the Contessina was seated. It was the portrait of the beautiful young girl with the turban—Cassia Boccanera the forerunner, the *amorosa* and avengeress. Again was Pierre struck by the portrait's resemblance to Benedetta, and, thinking aloud, he resumed: 'Passion always proves the stronger; there invariably comes a moment when one succumbs——'

But Benedetta violently interrupted him: 'I! I! Ah! you do not know me; I would rather die!' And with extraordinary exaltation, all aglow with love, as if her superstitious faith had fired her passion to ecstasy, she continued: 'I have vowed to the Madonna that I will belong to none but the man I love, and to him only when he is my husband. And hitherto I have kept that vow, at the cost of my happiness, and I will keep it still, even if it cost me my life! Yes, we will die, my poor Dario and I, if it be necessary; but the holy Virgin has my vow, and the angels shall not weep in heaven!'

She was all in those words, her nature all simplicity, intricate, inexplicable though it might seem. She was doubtless swayed by that idea of human nobility which Christianity has set in renunciation and purity; a protest, as it were, against eternal matter, against the forces of nature, the everlasting fruitfulness of life. But there was more than this; she reserved herself, like a divine and priceless gift, to be bestowed on the one being whom her heart had chosen, he who would be her lord and master when God should have united them in marriage. For her everything lay in the blessing of the priest, in the religious solemnisation of matrimony. And thus one understood her long resistance to Prada, whom she did not love, and her despairing, grievous resistance to Dario, whom she did love, but who was not her husband. And how torturing it was for that soul of fire to have to resist her love ; how continual was the combat waged by duty in the Virgin's name against the wild, passionate blood of her race ! Ignorant, indolent though she might be, she was capable of great fidelity of heart, and, moreover, she was not given to dreaming : love might have its immaterial charms, but she desired it complete.

As Pierre looked at her in the dying twilight he seemed to see and understand her for the first time. The duality of her nature appeared in her somewhat full, fleshy lips, in her big black eyes, which suggested a dark, tempestuous night illumined by flashes of lightning, and in the calm, sensible expression of the rest of her gentle, infantile face. And, withal, behind those eyes of flame, beneath that pure, candid skin, one divined the internal tension of a superstitious, proud, and self-willed woman, who was obstinately intent on reserving herself for her one love. And Pierre could well understand that she should be adored, that she should fill the life of the man she chose with passion, and that to his own eyes she should appear like the younger sister of that lovely, tragic Cassia who, unwilling to survive the blow that had rendered self-bestowal impossible, had flung herself into the Tiber, dragging her brother Ercole and the corpse of her lover Flavio with her.

However, with a gesture of kindly affection Benedetta caught hold of Pierre's hands. 'You have been here a fortnight, Monsieur l'Abbé,' said she, 'and I have come to like you very much, for I feel you to be a friend. If at first you do not understand us, at least pray do not judge us too severely. Ignorant as I may be, I always strive to act for the best, I assure you.'

Pierre was greatly touched by her affectionate graciousness, and thanked her whilst for a moment retaining her beautiful hands in his own, for he also was becoming much attached to her. A fresh dream was carrying him off, that of educating her, should he have the time, or, at all events, of not returning home before winning her soul over to his own ideas of future charity and fraternity. Did not that adorable, unoccupied, indolent, ignorant creature, who only knew how to defend her love, personify the Italy of yesterday ? The Italy of yesterday, so lovely and so sleepy, instinct with a dying grace, charming one even in her drowsiness, and retaining so much mystery in the fathomless depths of her black, pas-

sionate eyes! And what a *rôle* would be that of awakening
her, instructing her, winning her over to truth, making her
the rejuvenated Italy of to-morrow such as he had dreamt of!
Even in that disastrous marriage with Count Prada he tried
to see merely a first attempt at revival which had failed, the
modern Italy of the North being over hasty, too brutal in its
eagerness to love and transform that gentle, belated Rome
which was yet so superb and indolent. But might he not
take up the task? Had he not noticed that his book, after the
astonishment of the first perusal, had remained a source of
interest and reflection with Benedetta amidst the emptiness of
her days given over to grief? What! was it really possible
that she might find some appeasement for her own wretchedness by interesting herself in the humble, in the happiness of
the poor? Emotion already thrilled her at the idea, and he,
quivering at the thought of all the boundless love that was
within her and that she might bestow, vowed to himself that
he would draw tears of pity from her eyes.

But the night had now almost completely fallen, and
Benedetta rose to ask for a lamp. Then, as Pierre was about
to take leave, she detained him for another moment in the
gloom. He could no longer see her; he only heard her grave
voice: 'You will not go away with too bad an opinion of us,
will you, Monsieur l'Abbé? We love one another, Dario and
I, and that is no sin when one behaves as one ought. Ah!
yes, I love him, and have loved him for years. I was barely
thirteen, he was eighteen, and we already loved one another
wildly in those big gardens of the Villa Montefiori which are
now all broken up. Ah! what days we spent there, whole
afternoons among the trees, hours in secret hiding-places,
where we kissed like little angels. When the oranges ripened
their perfume intoxicated us. And the large box-plants, ah,
Dio! how they enveloped us, how their strong, acrid scent
made our hearts beat! I can never smell them nowadays
without feeling faint!'

A man-servant brought in the lamp, and Pierre ascended
to his room. But when half-way up the little staircase he
perceived Victorine, who started slightly, as if she had posted
herself there to watch his departure from the *salon*. And
now, as she followed him up, talking and seeking for information, he suddenly realised what had happened. 'Why did you
not go to your mistress instead of running off,' he asked,

'when she called you, while you were sewing in the ante-
room?'

At first she tried to feign astonishment and reply that she
had heard nothing. But her good-natured, frank face did not
know how to lie, and she ended by confessing, with a gay,
courageous air. 'Well,' she said, 'it surely wasn't for me to
interfere between lovers! Besides, my poor little Benedetta
is simply torturing herself to death with those ideas of hers.
Why shouldn't they be happy, since they love one another?
Life isn't so amusing as some may think. And how bitterly
one regrets not having seized hold of happiness when the time
for it has gone!'

Once alone in his room, Pierre suddenly staggered, quite
overcome. The great box-plants, the great box-plants with
their acrid, perturbing perfume! She, Benedetta, like himself, had quivered as she smelt them; and he saw them once
more in a vision of the pontifical gardens, the voluptuous
gardens of Rome, deserted, glowing under the August sun.
And now his whole day, crystallised, assumed clear and full
significance. It spoke to him of the fruitful awakening, of
the eternal protest of nature and life, of Venus and Hercules,
whom one may bury for centuries beneath the soil, but who
nevertheless one day arise from it, and though one may seek
to wall them up within the domineering, stubborn, immutable
Vatican, reign yet even there, and rule the whole wide world
with sovereign power!

VII

On the following day as Pierre, after a long ramble, once
more found himself in front of the Vatican, whither a
harassing attraction ever led him, he again encountered
Monsignor Nani. It was a Wednesday evening, and the
Assessor of the Holy Office had just come from his weekly
audience with the Pope, whom he had acquainted with the
proceedings of the Congregation at its meeting that morning.
'What a fortunate chance, my dear sir,' said he; 'I was thinking of you. Would you like to see his Holiness in public
while you are waiting for a private audience?'

Nani had put on his pleasant expression of smiling civility,
beneath which one would barely detect the faint irony of a

superior man who knew everything, prepared everything, and
could do everything.

'Why, yes, Monseigneur,' Pierre replied, somewhat
astonished by the abruptness of the offer. 'Anything of a
nature to divert one's mind is welcome when one loses one's
time in waiting.'

'No, no, you are not losing your time,' replied the prelate.
'You are looking round you, reflecting, and enlightening
yourself. Well, this is the point. You are doubtless aware
that the great international pilgrimage of the Peter's Pence
Fund will arrive in Rome on Friday, and be received on
Saturday by his Holiness. On Sunday, moreover, the Holy
Father will celebrate mass at the basilica. Well, I have a
few cards left, and here are some very good places for both
ceremonies.' So saying he produced an elegant little pocket-
book bearing a gilt monogram and handed Pierre two cards,
one green and the other pink. 'If you only knew how people
fight for them,' he resumed. 'You remember that I told you
of two French ladies who are consumed by a desire to see his
Holiness. Well, I did not like to support their request for an
audience in too pressing a way, and they have had to content
themselves with cards like these. The fact is, the Holy
Father is somewhat fatigued at the present time. I found
him looking yellow and feverish just now. But he has so
much courage; he nowadays only lives by force of soul.'
Then Nani's smile came back with its almost imperceptible
touch of derision as he resumed: 'Impatient ones ought to
find a great example in him, my dear son. I heard that
Monsignor Gamba del Zoppo had been unable to help you.
But you must not be too much distressed on that account.
This long delay is assuredly a grace of Providence in order
that you may instruct yourself and come to understand certain
things which you French priests do not, unfortunately, realise
when you arrive in Rome. And perhaps it will prevent you
from making certain mistakes. Come, calm yourself, and
remember that the course of events is in the hands of God,
who, in His sovereign wisdom, fixes the hour for all things.'

Thereupon Nani offered Pierre his plump, supple, shapely
hand, a hand soft like a woman's but with the grasp of a vice.
And afterwards he climbed into his carriage, which was waiting for him.

It so happened that the letter which Pierre had received
from Viscount Philibert de la Choue was a long cry of spite

and despair in connection with the great international pilgrimage of the Peter's Pence Fund. The Viscount wrote from his bed, to which he was confined by a very severe attack of gout, and his grief at being unable to come to Rome was the greater as the President of the Committee, who would naturally present the pilgrims to the Pope, happened to be Baron de Fouras, one of his most bitter adversaries of the old conservative Catholic party. M. de la Choue felt certain that the Baron would profit by his opportunity to win the Pope over to the theory of free corporations; whereas he, the Viscount, believed that the salvation of Catholicism and the world could only be worked by a system in which the corporations should be closed and obligatory. And so he urged Pierre to exert himself with such cardinals as were favourable, to secure an audience with the Holy Father whatever the obstacles, and to remain in Rome until he should have secured the pontiff's approbation, which alone could decide the victory. The letter further mentioned that the pilgrimage would be made up of a number of groups headed by bishops and other ecclesiastical dignitaries, and would comprise three thousand people from France, Belgium, Spain, Austria, and even Germany. Two thousand of these would come from France alone. An international committee had assembled in Paris to organise everything and select the pilgrims, which last had proved a delicate task, as a representative gathering had been desired, a commingling of members of the aristocracy, sisterhoods of middle-class ladies, and associations of the working classes, among whom all social differences would be forgotten in the union of a common faith. And the Viscount added that the pilgrimage would bring the Pope a large sum of money, and had settled the date of its arrival in the Eternal City in such wise that it would figure as a solemn protest of the Catholic world against the festivities of September 20, by which the Quirinal had just celebrated the anniversary of the occupation of Rome.

The reception of the pilgrimage being fixed for noon, Pierre in all simplicity thought that he would be sufficiently early if he reached St. Peter's at eleven. The function was to take place in the Hall of Beatifications, which is a large and handsome apartment over the portico, and has been arranged as a chapel since 1890. One of its windows opens on to the central balcony, whence the Popes formerly blessed the people, the city, and the world. To reach the apartment you pass

through two other halls of audience, the Sala Regia and Sala
Ducale, and when Pierre wished to gain the place to which
his green card entitled him he found both those rooms so
extremely crowded that he could only elbow his way forward
with the greatest difficulty. For an hour already the three
or four thousand people assembled there had been stifling, full
of growing emotion and feverishness. At last the young
priest managed to reach the threshold of the third hall, but
was so discouraged at sight of the extraordinary multitude of
heads before him that he did not attempt to go any further.

The apartment, which he could survey at a glance by
rising on tip-toe, appeared to him to be very rich of aspect,
with walls gilded and painted under a severe and lofty ceiling.
On a low platform, where the altar usually stood, facing the
entry, the pontifical throne had now been set: a large arm-
chair upholstered in red velvet with glittering golden back
and arms; whilst the hangings of the *baldacchino*, also of
red velvet, fell behind and spread out on either side like a
pair of huge purple wings. However, what more particularly interested Pierre was the wildly passionate concourse of
people whose hearts he could almost hear beating and whose
eyes sought to beguile their feverish impatience by contemplating and adoring the empty throne. As if it had been some
golden monstrance which the Divinity in person would soon
deign to occupy, that throne dazzled them, disturbed them,
filled them all with devout rapture. Among the throng were
workmen rigged out in their Sunday best, with clear childish
eyes and rough ecstatic faces; ladies of the upper classes
wearing black, as the regulations required, and looking
intensely pale from the sacred awe which mingled with their
excessive desire; and gentlemen in evening dress, who appeared
quite glorious, inflated with the conviction that they were
saving both the Church and the nations. One cluster of dress-
coats, assembled near the throne, was particularly noticeable;
it comprised the members of the International Committee,
headed by Baron de Fouras, a very tall, stout, fair man of
fifty, who bestirred and exerted himself and issued orders like
some commander on the morning of a decisive victory. Then,
amidst the general mass of grey, neutral hue, there gleamed
the violet silk of some bishop's cassock, for each pastor had
desired to remain with his flock; whilst members of various
religious orders, superiors in brown, black, and white habits,
rose up above all others with lofty bearded or shaven heads.

Right and left drooped banners which associations and congregations had brought to present to the Pope. And the sea of pilgrims ever waved and surged with a growing clamour : so much impatient love being exhaled by those perspiring faces, burning eyes, and hungry mouths that the atmosphere, reeking with the odour of the throng, seemed thickened and darkened.

All at once, however, Pierre perceived Monsignor Nani standing near the throne and beckoning him to approach ; and although the young priest replied by a modest gesture, implying that he preferred to remain where he was, the prelate insisted, and even sent an usher to make way for him. Directly the usher had led him forward, Nani inquired : ' Why did you not come to take your place ? Your card entitled you to be here, on the left of the throne.'

' The truth is,' answered the priest, ' I did not like to disturb so many people. Besides, this is an undue honour for me.'

' No, no ; I gave you that place in order that you should occupy it. I want you to be in the first rank, so that you may see everything of the ceremony.'

Pierre could not do otherwise than thank him. Then, on looking round, he saw that several cardinals and many other prelates were likewise waiting on either side of the throne. But it was in vain that he sought Cardinal Boccanera, who only came to St. Peter's and the Vatican on the days when his functions required his presence there. However, he recognised Cardinal Sanguinetti, who, broad and sturdy and red of face, was talking in a loud voice to Baron de Fouras. And Nani, with his obliging air, stepped up again to point out two other Eminences who were high and mighty personages—the Cardinal Vicar, a short, fat man, with a feverish countenance scorched by ambition, and the Cardinal Secretary, who was robust and bony, fashioned as with a hatchet, suggesting a romantic type of Sicilian bandit, who, to other courses, had preferred the discreet, smiling diplomacy of the Church. A few steps further on, and quite alone, the Grand Penitentiary, silent and seemingly suffering, showed his grey, lean, ascetic profile.

Noon had struck. There was a false alarm, a burst of emotion, which swept in like a wave from the other halls. But it was merely the ushers opening a passage for the *cortège*. Then, all at once, acclamations arose in the first hall, gathered

volume, and drew nearer. This time it was the *cortège* itself.
First came a detachment of the Swiss Guard in undress,
headed by a sergeant ; then a party of chair-bearers in red ;
and next the domestic prelates, including the four *camerieri
segreti partecipanti.* And finally, between two rows of Noble
Guards, in semi-gala uniforms, walked the Holy Father, alone,
smiling a pale smile, and slowly blessing the pilgrims on either
hand. In his wake the clamour which had risen in the other
apartments swept into the Hall of Beatifications with the violence of delirious love ; and, under his slender, white, benedic·
tive hand, all those distracted creatures fell upon both knees,
nought remaining but the prostration of a devout multitude,
overwhelmed, as it were, by the apparition of its god.

Quivering, carried away, Pierre had knelt like the others.
Ah ! that omnipotence, that irresistible contagion of faith, of
the redoubtable current from the spheres beyond, increased
tenfold by a *scenario* and a pomp of sovereign grandeur ! Profound silence fell when Leo XIII was seated on the throne
surrounded by the cardinals and his court ; and then the
ceremony proceeded according to rite and usage. First a
bishop spoke, kneeling and laying the homage of the faithful
of all Christendom at his Holiness's feet. The President of
the Committee, Baron de Fouras, followed, remaining erect
whilst he read a long address in which he introduced the pilgrimage and explained its motive, investing it with all the
gravity of a political and religious protest. This stout man
had a shrill and piercing voice, and his words jarred like the
grating of a gimlet as he proclaimed the grief of the Catholic
world at the spoliation which the Holy See had endured for a
quarter of a century, and the desire of all the nations there
represented by the pilgrims to console the supreme and venerated Head of the Church by bringing him the offerings of
rich and poor, even to the mites of the humblest, in order that
the Papacy might retain the pride of independence and be
able to treat its enemies with contempt. And he also spoke of
France, deplored her errors, predicted her return to healthy
traditions, and gave it to be understood that she remained in
spite of everything the most opulent and generous of the Christian nations, the donor whose gold and presents flowed into
Rome in a never-ending stream. At last Leo XIII arose to
reply to the bishop and the baron. His voice was full, with a
strong nasal twang, and surprised one coming from a man
so slight of build. In a few sentences he expressed his grati-

tude, saying how touched he was by the devotion of the nations
to the Holy See. Although the times might be bad, the final
triumph could not be delayed much longer. There were evident signs that mankind was returning to faith, and that
iniquity would soon cease under the universal dominion of the
Christ. As for France, was she not the eldest daughter of the
Church, and had she not given too many proofs of her affection for the Holy See for the latter ever to cease loving her?
Then, raising his arm, he bestowed on all the pilgrims present,
on the societies and enterprises they represented, on their
families and friends, on France, on all the nations of the
Catholic world, his apostolic benediction, in gratitude for the
precious help which they sent him. And whilst he was again
seating himself applause burst forth, frantic salvoes of applause
lasting for ten minutes and mingling with vivats and inarticu-
late cries—a passionate, tempestuous outburst, which made
the very building shake.

Amidst this blast of frantic adoration Pierre gazed at
Leo XIII, now again motionless on his throne. With the
papal cap on his head and the red cape edged with ermine
about his shoulders, he retained in his long white cassock the
rigid, sacerdotal attitude of an idol venerated by two hundred
and fifty millions of Christians. Against the purple background of the hangings of the *baldacchino*, between the wing-
like drapery on either side, enclosing, as it were, a brasier of
glory, he assumed real majesty of aspect. He was no longer
the feeble old man with the slow, jerky walk and the slender,
scraggy neck of a poor ailing bird. The simious ugliness of
his face, the largeness of his nose, the long slit of his mouth,
the hugeness of his ears, the conflicting jumble of his withered
features disappeared. In that waxen countenance you only
distinguished the admirable, dark, deep éyes, beaming with
eternal youth, with extraordinary intelligence and penetration.
And then there was a resolute bracing of his entire person, a
consciousness of the eternity which he represented, a regal
nobility, born of the very circumstance that he was now but a
mere breath, a soul set in so pellucid a body of ivory that it
became visible as though it were already freed from the bonds
of earth. And Pierre realised what such a man—the Sovereign Pontiff, the King obeyed by two hundred and fifty millions of subjects—must be for the devout and dolent creatures
who came to adore him from so far, and who fell at his feet
awestruck by the splendour of the powers incarnate in him.

Behind him, amidst the purple of the hangings, what a gleam
was suddenly afforded of the spheres beyond, what an Infinite
of ideality and blinding glory ! So many centuries of history
from the Apostle Peter downward, so much strength and genius,
so many struggles and triumphs to be summed up in one being,
the Elect, the Unique, the Superhuman ! And what a miracle,
incessantly renewed, was that of Heaven deigning to descend
into human flesh, of the Deity fixing His abode in His chosen
servant, whom He consecrated above and beyond all others,
endowing him with all power and all science ! What sacred
perturbation, what emotion fraught with distracted love might
one not feel at the thought of the Deity being ever there in
the depths of that man's eyes, speaking with his voice and
emanating from his hand each time that he raised it to bless !
Could one imagine the exorbitant absoluteness of that sovereign who was infallible, who disposed of the totality of authority in this world and of salvation in the next ! At all events,
how well one understood that souls consumed by a craving for
faith should fly towards him, that those who at last found the
certainty they had so ardently sought should seek annihilation
in him, the consolation of self-bestowal and disappearance
within the Deity Himself.

Meantime, the ceremony was drawing to an end ; Baron
de Fouras was now presenting the members of the committee
and a few other persons of importance. There was a slow
procession with trembling genuflexions and much greedy
kissing of the papal ring and slipper. Then the banners
were offered, and Pierre felt a pang on seeing that the finest
and richest of them was one of Lourdes, an offering no doubt
from the Fathers of the Immaculate Conception. On one
side of the white gold-broidered silk Our Lady of Lourdes was
painted, while on the other appeared a portrait of Leo XIII.
Pierre saw the Pope smile at the presentment of himself, and
was greatly grieved thereat, as though, indeed, his whole
dream of an intellectual, evangelical Pope, disentangled from
all low superstition, were crumbling away. And just then his
eyes met those of Nani, who from the outset had been watching
him with the inquisitive air of a man who is making an experiment.

' That banner is superb, isn't it ? ' said Nani, drawing near.
' How it must please his Holiness to be so nicely painted in
company with so pretty a Virgin ! ' And as the young priest,
turning pale, did not reply, the prelate added, with an air of

devout enjoyment : ' We are very fond of Lourdes in Rome ; that story of Bernadette is so delightful.'

However, the scene which followed was so extraordinary that for a long time Pierre remained overcome by it. He had beheld never-to-be-forgotten idolatry at Lourdes, incidents of naïve faith and frantic religious passion which yet made him quiver with alarm and grief. But the crowds rushing on the grotto, the sick dying of divine love before the Virgin's statue, the multitudes delirious with the contagion of the miraculous— nothing of all that gave an idea of the blast of madness which suddenly inflamed the pilgrims at the feet of the Pope. Some bishops, superiors of religious orders, and other delegates of various kinds had stepped forward to deposit near the throne the offerings which they brought from the whole Catholic world, the universal 'collection' of St. Peter's Pence. It was the voluntary tribute of the nations to their sovereign : silver, gold, and bank notes in purses, bags, and cases. Ladies came and fell on their knees to offer silk and velvet almsbags which they themselves had embroidered. Others had caused the note cases which they tendered to be adorned with the monogram of Leo XIII in diamonds. And at one moment the enthusiasm became so intense that several women stripped themselves of their adornments, flung their own purses on to the platform, and emptied their pockets even to the very coppers they had about them. One lady, tall and slender, very beautiful and very dark, wrenched her watch from about her neck, pulled off her rings, and threw everything upon the carpet. Had it been possible, they would have torn away their flesh to pluck out their love-burnt hearts and fling them likewise to the demi-god. They would even have flung themselves, have given themselves without reserve. It was a rain of presents, an explosion of the passion which impels one to strip oneself for the object of one's cult, happy at having nothing of one's own that shall not belong to him. And meantime the clamour grew, vivats and shrill cries of adoration arose amidst pushing and jostling of increased violence, one and all yielding to the irresistible desire to kiss the idol !

But a signal was given, and Leo XIII made haste to quit the throne and take his place in the *cortège* in order to return to his apartments. The Swiss Guards energetically thrust back the throng, seeking to open a way through the three halls. But at sight of his Holiness's departure a lamentation arose and spread, as if Heaven's gates had suddenly closed

again and shut out those who had not yet been able to
approach.   What a frightful disappointment—to have beheld
the living manifestation of the Deity and to see it disappear
before gaining salvation by just touching it! So terrible
became the scramble, so extraordinary the confusion, that the
Swiss Guards were swept away.   And ladies were seen to dart
after the Pope, to drag themselves on all fours over the
marble slabs and kiss his footprints and lap up the dust of his
steps! The tall dark lady suddenly fell at the edge of the
platform, raised a loud shriek, and fainted; and two gentlemen
of the committee had to hold her so that she might not do
herself an injury in the convulsions of the hysterical fit which
had come upon her.   Another, a plump *blonde*, was wildly,
desperately kissing one of the golden arms of the throne-
chair, on which the old man's poor bony elbow had just
rested.   And others, on seeing her, came to dispute possession,
seized both arms, gilding and velvet, and pressed their mouths
to woodwork or upholstery, their bodies meanwhile shaking
with their sobs.   Force had to be employed in order to drag
them away.

When it was all over Pierre went off, emerging as it were
from a painful dream, sick at heart, and with his mind revolting.   And again he encountered Nani's glance, which never
left him. 'It was a superb ceremony, was it not?' said the
prelate.   'It consoles one for many iniquities.'

'Yes, no doubt; but what idolatry!' the young priest
murmured despite himself.

Nani, however, merely smiled, as if he had not heard the
last word.   At that same moment the two French ladies
whom he had provided with tickets came up to thank him,
and Pierre was surprised to recognise the mother and daughter
whom he had met at the Catacombs.   Charming, bright, and
healthy as they were, their enthusiasm was only for the
spectacle: they declared that they were well pleased at having
seen it—that it was really astonishing, unique.

As the crowd slowly withdrew Pierre all at once felt a
tap on his shoulder, and, on turning his head, perceived
Narcisse Habert, who also was very enthusiastic. 'I made
signs to you, my dear Abbé,' said he,' but you didn't see me.
Ah! how superb was the expression of that dark woman who
fell rigid beside the platform with her arms outstretched.
She reminded me of a masterpiece of one of the primitives,
Cimabue, Giotto, or Fra Angelico.   And the others, those who

devoured the chair arms with their kisses, what suavity, beauty, and love ! I never miss these ceremonies : there are always some fine scenes, perfect pictures, in which souls reveal themselves.'

The long stream of pilgrims slowly descended the stairs, and Pierre, followed by Nani and Narcisse, who had begun to chat, tried to bring the ideas which were tumultuously throbbing in his brain into something like order. There was certainly grandeur and beauty in that Pope who had shut himself up in his Vatican, and who, the more he became a purely moral, spiritual authority, freed from all terrestrial cares, had grown in the adoration and awe of mankind. Such a flight into the ideal deeply stirred Pierre, whose dream of rejuvenated Christianity rested on the idea of the supreme Head of the Church exercising only a purified, spiritual authority. He had just seen what an increase of majesty and power was in that way gained by the Supreme Pontiff of the spheres beyond, at whose feet the women fainted, and behind whom they beheld a vision of the Deity. But at the same moment the pecuniary side of the question had risen before him and spoilt his joy. If the enforced relinquishment of the temporal power had exalted the Pope by freeing him from the worries of a petty sovereignty which was ever threatened, the need of money still remained like a chain about his feet tying him to earth. As he could not accept the proffered subvention of the Italian government,[1] there was certainly in the Peter's Pence a means of placing the Holy See above all material cares, provided, however, that this Peter's Pence were really the Catholic *sou*, the mite of each believer, levied on his daily income and sent direct to Rome. Such a voluntary tribute paid by the flock to its pastor would, moreover, suffice for the wants of the Church if each of the 250,000,000 of Catholics gave his or her *sou* every week. In this wise the Pope, indebted to each and all of his children, would be indebted to none in particular. A *sou* was so little and so easy to give, and there was also something so touching about the idea. But, unhappily, things were not worked in that way ; the great majority of Catholics gave nothing whatever, while the rich ones sent large sums from motives of political passion ; and a particular objection was

[1] 110,000*l.* per annum. It has never been accepted, and the accumulations lapse to the government every five years, and cannot afterwards be recovered.—*Trans.*

that the gifts were centralised in the hands of certain bishops and religious orders, so that these became ostensibly the benefactors of the papacy, the indispensable cashiers from whom it drew the sinews of life. The lowly and humble whose mites filled the collection boxes were, so to say, suppressed, and the Pope became dependent on the intermediaries, and was compelled to act cautiously with them, listen to their remonstrances, and even at times obey their passions, lest the stream of gifts should suddenly dry up. And so, although he was disburdened of the dead weight of the temporal power, he was not free; but remained the tributary of his clergy, with interests and appetites around him which he must needs satisfy. And Pierre remembered the 'Grotto of Lourdes' in the Vatican gardens, and the banner which he had just seen, and he knew that the Lourdes Fathers levied two hundred thousand francs a year on their receipts to send them as a present to the Holy Father. Was not that the chief reason of their great power? He quivered, and suddenly became conscious that, do what he might, he would be defeated, and his book would be condemned.

At last, as he was coming out on to the Piazza of St. Peter's, he heard Narcisse asking Monsignor Nani: 'Indeed! Do you really think that to-day's gifts exceeded that figure?'

'Yes, more than three millions,[1] I'm convinced of it,' the prelate replied.

For a moment the three men halted under the right-hand colonnade and gazed at the vast sunlit piazza where the pilgrims were spreading out like little black specks hurrying hither and thither—an anthill, as it were, in revolution.

Three millions! The words had rung in Pierre's ears. And, raising his head, he gazed at the Vatican, all golden in the sunlight against the expanse of blue sky, as if he wished to penetrate its walls and follow the steps of Leo XIII returning to his apartments. He pictured him laden with those millions, with his weak, slender arms pressed to his breast, carrying the silver, the gold, the banknotes, and even the jewels which the women had flung him. And almost unconsciously the young priest spoke aloud: 'What will he do with those millions? Where is he taking them?'

Narcisse and even Nani could not help being amused by

[1] All the amounts given on this and the following pages are calculated in francs. The reader will bear in mind that a million francs is equivalent to 40,000*l.*—*Trans.*

this strangely expressed curiosity. It was the young *attaché*
who replied. ' Why, his Holiness is taking them to his room ;
or, at least, is having them carried there before him. Didn't
you see two persons of his suite picking up everything and
filling their pockets ? And now his Holiness has shut himself up quite alone ; and if you could see him you would find
him counting and recounting his treasure with cheerful care,
ranging the rolls of gold in good order, slipping the bank
notes into envelopes in equal quantities, and then putting
everything away in hiding-places which are only known to
himself.'

While his companion was speaking Pierre again raised
his eyes to the windows of the Pope's apartments as if to
follow the scene. Moreover, Narcisse gave further explanations, asserting that the money was put away in a certain
article of furniture, standing against the right-hand wall in
the Holy Father's bedroom. Some people, he added, also
spoke of a writing-table or secrétaire with deep drawers ; and
others declared that the money slumbered in some big padlocked trunks stored away in the depths of the alcove, which
was very roomy. Of course, on the left side of the passage
leading to the Archives there was a large room occupied
by a general cashier and a monumental safe ; but the
funds kept there were simply those of the Patrimony of
St. Peter, the administrative receipts of Rome ; whereas the
Peter's Pence money, the voluntary donations of Christendom,
remained in the hands of Leo XIII : he alone knew the exact
amount of that fund, and lived alone with its millions, which
he disposed of like an absolute master, rendering account to
none. And such was his prudence that he never left his
room when the servants cleaned and set it in order. At
the utmost he would consent to remain on the threshold of
the adjoining apartment in order to escape the dust. And
whenever he meant to absent himself for a few hours, to go
down into the gardens, for instance, he double-locked the
doors and carried the keys away with him, never confiding
them to another.

At this point Narcisse paused and, turning to Nani,
inquired : ' Is not that so, Monseigneur ? These are things
known to all Rome.'

The prelate, ever smiling and wagging his head without
expressing either approval or disapproval, had begun to study
on Pierre's face the effect of these curious stories. ' No doubt,

'no doubt,' he responded; ' so many things are said! I know nothing myself, but you seem to be certain of it all, Monsieur Habert.'

'Oh!' resumed the other, 'I don't accuse his Holiness of sordid avarice, such as is rumoured. Some fabulous stories are current, stories of coffers full of gold in which the Holy Father is said to plunge his hands for hours at a time; treasures which he has heaped up in corners for the sole pleasure of counting them over and over again. Nevertheless, one may well admit that his Holiness is somewhat fond of money for its own sake, for the pleasure of handling it and setting it in order when he happens to be alone—and after all that is a very excusable mania in an old man who has no other pastime. But I must add that he is yet fonder of money for the social power which it brings, the decisive help which it will give to the Holy See in the future, if the latter desires to triumph.'

These words evoked the lofty figure of a wise and prudent Pope, conscious of modern requirements, inclined to utilise the powers of the century in order to conquer it, and for this reason venturing on business and speculation. As it happened, the treasure bequeathed by Pius IX had nearly been lost in a financial disaster, but ever since that time Leo XIII had sought to repair the breach and make the treasure whole again, in order that he might leave it to his successor intact and even enlarged. Economical he certainly was, but he saved for the needs of the Church, which, as he knew, increased day by day; and money was absolutely necessary if Atheism was to be met and fought in the sphere of the schools, institutions, and associations of all sorts. Without money, indeed, the Church would become a vassal at the mercy of the civil powers, the Kingdom of Italy and other Catholic States; and so, although he liberally helped every enterprise which might contribute to the triumph of the Faith, Leo XIII had a contempt for all expenditure without an object, and treated himself and others with stern closeness. Personally, he had no needs. At the outset of his pontificate he had set his small private patrimony apart from the rich patrimony of St. Peter, refusing to take aught from the latter for the purpose of assisting his relatives. Never had pontiff displayed less nepotism : his three nephews and his two nieces had remained poor —in fact, in great pecuniary embarrassment. Still he listened neither to complaints nor accusations, but remained inflexible,

proudly resolved to bequeath the sinews of life, the invincible
weapon money, to the Popes of future times, and therefore
vigorously defending the millions of the Holy See against the
desperate covetousness of one and all.

'But what are the receipts and expenses of the Holy
See ?' inquired Pierre.

In all haste Nani again made his amiable evasive gesture.
'Oh ! I am altogether ignorant in such matters,' he replied.
'Ask Monsieur Habert, who is so well informed.'

'For my part,' responded the *attaché*,' I simply know what
is known to all the embassies here, the matters which are the
subject of common report.   With respect to the receipts there
is, first of all, the treasure left by Pius IX, some twenty millions, invested in various ways and formerly yielding about a
million a year in interest.   But, as I said before, a disaster
happened, and there must then have been a falling off in the
income.   Still, nowadays it is reported that nearly all deficiencies have been made good.   Well, besides the regular
income from the invested money, a few hundred thousand
francs are derived every year from chancellery dues, patents of
nobility, and all sorts of little fees paid to the Congregations.
However, as the annual expenses exceed seven millions, it has
been necessary to find quite six millions every year ; and certainly it is the Peter's Pence Fund that has supplied, not the
six millions, perhaps, but three or four of them, and with these
the Holy See has speculated in the hope of doubling them and
making both ends meet.   It would take me too long just now
to relate the whole story of these speculations, the first huge
gains, then the catastrophe which almost swept everything
away, and finally the stubborn perseverance which is gradually
supplying all deficiencies.   However, if you are anxious on the
subject, I will one day tell you all about it.'

Pierre had listened with deep interest.   'Six millions—
even four ! ' he exclaimed, ' what does the Peter's Pence Fund
bring in, then ? '

'Oh ! I can only repeat that nobody has ever known the
exact figures.   In former times the Catholic Press published
lists giving the amounts of different offerings, and in this way
one could frame an approximate estimate.   But the practice
must have been considered unadvisable, for no documents
nowadays appear, and it is absolutely impossible for people to
form any real idea of what the Pope receives.   He alone
knows the correct amount, keeps the money, and disposes of

it with absolute authority. Still, I believe that in good years the offerings have amounted to between four and five millions. Originally France contributed one half of the sum; but nowadays it certainly gives much less. Then come Belgium and Austria, England and Germany. As for Spain and Italy —oh! Italy——'

Narcisse paused and smiled at Monsignor Nani, who was wagging his head with the air of a man delighted at learning some extremely curious things of which he had previously had no idea.

'Oh, you may proceed, you may proceed, my dear son,' said he.

'Well, then, Italy scarcely distinguishes itself. If the Pope had to provide for his living out of the gifts of the Italian Catholics there would soon be a famine at the Vatican. Far from helping him, indeed, the Roman nobility has cost him dear; for one of the chief causes of his pecuniary losses was his folly in lending money to the princes who speculated. It is really only from France and England that rich people, noblemen and so forth, have sent royal gifts to the imprisoned and martyred pontiff. Among others there was an English nobleman who came to Rome every year with a large offering, the outcome of a vow which he had made in the hope that Heaven would cure his unhappy idiot son. And, of course, I don't refer to the extraordinary harvest garnered during the sacerdotal and the episcopal jubilees—the forty millions which then fell at his Holiness's feet.'

'And the expenses?' asked Pierre.

'Well, as I told you, they amount to about seven millions. We may reckon two of them for the pensions paid to former officials of the pontifical government who were unwilling to take service under Italy; but I must add that this source of expense is diminishing every year as people die off and their pensions become extinguished. Then, broadly speaking, we may put down one million for the Italian sees, another for the Secretariate and the Nunciatures, and another for the Vatican. In this last sum I include the expenses of the pontifical Court, the military establishment, the museums, and the repair of the palace and the basilica. Well, we have reached five millions, and the two others may be set down for the various subsidised enterprises, the Propaganda, and particularly the schools, which Leo XIII, with great practical good sense, subsidises very handsomely, for he is well aware

that the battle and the triumph lie in that direction—among
the children who will be men to-morrow, and who will then
defend their mother the Church, provided that they have been
inspired with horror for the abominable doctrines of the age.'

A spell of silence ensued, and the three men slowly paced
the majestic colonnade. The swarming crowd had gradually
disappeared, leaving the piazza empty, so that only the obelisk
and the twin fountains now arose from the burning desert of
symmetrical paving ; whilst on the entablature of the porticus
across the square a noble line of motionless statues stood out
in the bright sunlight. And Pierre, with his eyes still raised to
the Pope's windows, again fancied that he could see Leo XIII
amidst all the streaming gold that had been spoken of, his
whole, white, pure figure, his poor, waxen, transparent form
steeped amidst those millions which he hid and counted and
expended for the glory of God alone. 'And so,' murmured
the young priest, ' he has no anxiety, he is not in any pecuniary embarrassment.'

' Pecuniary embarrassment ! ' exclaimed Monsignor Nani,
his patience so sorely tried by the remark that he could no
longer retain his diplomatic reserve. ' Oh ! my dear son !
Why, when Cardinal Mocenni, the treasurer, goes to his
Holiness every month, his Holiness always gives him the
sum he asks for ; he would give it, and be able to give it,
however large it might be ! His Holiness has certainly had
the wisdom to effect great economies ; the Treasure of St.
Peter is larger than ever. Pecuniary embarrassment, indeed !
Why, if a misfortune should occur, and the Sovereign Pontiff
were to make a direct appeal to all his children, the
Catholics of the entire world, do you know that in that case
a thousand millions would fall at his feet just like the gold
and the jewels which you saw raining on the steps of his
throne just now ? ' Then suddenly calming himself and recovering his pleasant smile, Nani added : ' At least, that is
what I sometimes hear said ; for, personally, I know nothing,
absolutely nothing ; and it is fortunate that Monsieur Habert
should have been here to give you information. Ah ! Monsieur
Habert, Monsieur Habert ! Why, I fancied that you were
always in the skies absorbed in your passion for art, and far
removed from all base mundane interests ! But you really
understand these things like a banker or a notary. Nothing
escapes you, nothing. It is wonderful.'

Narcisse must have felt the sting of the prelate's delicate

sarcasm. At bottom, beneath this make-believe Florentine all angelicalness, with long curly hair and mauve eyes which grew dim with rapture at sight of a Botticelli, there was a thoroughly practical, business-like young man, who took admirable care of his fortune and was even somewhat miserly. However, he contented himself with lowering his eyelids and assuming a languorous air. 'Oh !' said he, 'I'm all reverie ; my soul is elsewhere.'

'At all events,' resumed Nani, turning towards Pierre, 'I am very glad that you were able to see such a beautiful spectacle. A few more such opportunities and you will understand things far better than you would from all the explanations in the world. Don't miss the grand ceremony at St. Peter's to-morrow. It will be magnificent, and will give you food for useful reflection ; I'm sure of it. And now allow me to leave you, delighted at seeing you in such a fit frame of mind.'

Darting a last glance at Pierre, Nani seemed to have observed with pleasure the weariness and uncertainty which were paling his face. And when the prelate had gone off, and Narcisse also had taken leave with a gentle hand-shake, the young priest felt the ire of protest rising within him. What fit frame of mind did Nani mean ? Did that man hope to weary him and drive him to despair by throwing him into collision with obstacles, so that he might afterwards overcome him with perfect ease ? For the second time Pierre became suddenly and briefly conscious of the stealthy efforts which were being made to invest and crush him. But, believing as he did in his own strength of resistance, pride filled him with disdain. Again he swore that he would never yield, never withdraw his book, no matter what might happen. And then, before crossing the piazza, he once more raised his eyes to the windows of the Vatican, all his impressions crystallising in the thought of that much-needed money which like a last bond still attached the Pope to earth. Its chief evil doubtless lay in the manner in which it was provided ; and if indeed the only question were to devise an improved method of collection, his dream of a pope who should be all soul, the bond of love, the spiritual leader of the world, would not be seriously affected. At this thought, Pierre felt comforted and was unwilling to look on things otherwise than hopefully, moved as he was by the extraordinary scene which he had just beheld, that feeble old man shining forth like the

symbol of human deliverance, obeyed and venerated by the
multitudes, and alone among all men endowed with the moral
omnipotence that might at last set the reign of charity and
peace on earth.

For the ceremony on the following day, it was fortunate
that Pierre held a private ticket which admitted him to a reserved gallery, for the scramble at the entrances to the basilica
proved terrible. The mass, which the Pope was to celebrate
in person, was fixed for ten o'clock, but people began to pour
into St. Peter's four hours earlier, as soon, indeed, as the
gates had been thrown open. The three thousand members
of the International Pilgrimage were increased tenfold by the
arrival of all the tourists in Italy, who had hastened to Rome
eager to witness one of those great pontifical functions which
nowadays are so rare. Moreover, the devotees and partisans
whom the Holy See numbered in Rome itself and in other
great cities of the kingdom, helped to swell the throng, all
alacrity at the prospect of a demonstration. Judging by the
tickets distributed, there would be a concourse of 40,000 people.
And, indeed, at nine o'clock, when Pierre crossed the piazza
on his way to the Canons' Entrance in the Via Santa Marta,
where the holders of pink tickets were admitted, he saw the
portico of the façade still thronged with people who were but
slowly gaining admittance, while several gentlemen in evening
dress, members of some Catholic association, bestirred themselves to maintain order with the help of a detachment of
Pontifical Guards. Nevertheless, violent quarrels broke out
in the crowd, and blows were exchanged amidst the involuntary scramble. Some people were almost stifled, and two
women were carried off half crushed to death.

A disagreeable surprise met Pierre on his entry into the
basilica. The huge edifice was draped ; coverings of old red
damask with bands of gold swathed the columns and pilasters,
seventy-five feet high ; even the aisles were hung with the
same old and faded silk ; and the shrouding of those pompous
marbles, of all the superb dazzling ornamentation of the church,
bespoke a very singular taste, a tawdry affectation of pom-
posity, extremely wretched in its effect. However, he was yet
more amazed on seeing that even the statue of St. Peter was
clad, costumed like a living pope in sumptuous pontifical vestments, with a tiara on its metal head. He had never imagined
that people could garment statues either for their glory or for

the pleasure of the eyes, and the result seemed to him
disastrous.

The Pope was to say mass at the papal altar of the Confession, the high altar which stands under the dome. On a
platform at the entrance of the left hand transept was the
throne on which he would afterwards take his place. Then,
on either side of the nave, tribunes had been erected for the
choristers of the Sixtine Chapel, the Corps Diplomatique, the
Knights of Malta, the Roman nobility, and other guests of
various kinds. And, finally, in the centre before the altar,
there were three rows of benches covered with red rugs, the
first for the cardinals and the other two for the bishops and
the prelates of the pontifical Court. All the rest of the congregation was to remain standing.

Ah! that huge concert-audience, those thirty, forty thousand believers from here, there, and everywhere, inflamed with
curiosity, passion, or faith, bestirring themselves, jostling one
another, rising on tip-toe to see the better! The clamour of
a human sea arose, the crowd was as gay and familiar as if it
had found itself in some heavenly theatre where it was allowable for one to chat aloud and recreate oneself with the spectacle of religious pomp! At first Pierre was thunderstruck,
he who only knew of nervous, silent kneeling in the depths of
dim cathedrals, who was not accustomed to that religion of
light, whose brilliancy transformed a religious celebration into
a morning festivity. Around him, in the same tribune as
himself, were gentlemen in dress-coats and ladies gowned in
black, carrying glasses as in an opera-house. There were
German and English women, and numerous Americans, all
more or less charming, displaying the grace of thoughtless,
chirruping birds. In the tribune of the Roman nobility on
the left he recognised Benedetta and Donna Serafina, and
there the simplicity of the regulation attire for ladies was relieved by large lace veils rivalling one another in richness and
elegance. Then on the right was the tribune of the Knights
of Malta, where the Grand Master stood amidst a group of
commanders: while across the nave rose the diplomatic tribune where Pierre perceived the ambassadors of all the
Catholic nations, resplendent in gala uniforms covered with
gold lace. However, the young priest's eyes were ever returning to the crowd, the great surging throng in which the three
thousand pilgrims were lost amidst the multitude of other
spectators. And yet, as the basilica was so vast that it could

easily contain eighty thousand people, it did not seem to be
more than half full. People came and went along the aisles
and took up favourable positions without impediment. Some
could be seen gesticulating, and calls rang out above the
ceaseless rumble of voices. From the lofty windows of plain
white glass fell broad sheets of sunlight, which set a gory glow
upon the faded damask hangings, and these cast a reflection
as of fire upon all the tumultuous, feverish, impatient faces.
The multitude of candles, and the seven-and-eighty lamps
of the Confession paled to such a degree that they seemed
but glimmering night-lights in the blinding radiance ; and
everything proclaimed the worldly gala of the imperial Deity
of Roman pomp.

All at once there came a premature shock of delight, a
false alarm. Cries burst forth and circulated through the
crowd : '*Eccolo ! eccolo !* Here he comes !' And then
there was pushing and jostling, eddying which made the
human sea whirl and surge, all craning their necks, raising
themselves to their full height, darting forward in a frenzied
desire to see the Holy Father and the *cortège*. But only a
detachment of Noble Guards marched by and took up position
right and left of the altar. A flattering murmur accompanied
them, their fine impassive bearing, with its exaggerated military stiffness, provoking the admiration of the throng. An
American woman declared that they were superb-looking
fellows ; and a Roman lady gave an English friend some
particulars about the select corps to which they belonged.
Formerly, said she, young men of the aristocracy had greatly
sought the honour of forming part of it, for the sake of wearing its rich uniform and caracoling in front of the ladies. But
recruiting was now such a difficult matter that one had to
content oneself with good-looking young men of doubtful or
ruined nobility, whose only care was for the meagre 'pay'
which just enabled them to live.

When another quarter of an hour of chatting and scrutinising had elapsed, the papal *cortège* at last made its appearance, and no sooner was it seen than applause burst forth as
in a theatre—furious applause it was which rose and rolled
along under the vaulted ceilings, suggesting the acclamations
which ring out when some popular, idolised actor makes his
entry on the stage. As in a theatre, too, everything had been
very skilfully contrived so as to produce all possible effect
amidst the magnificent scenery of the basilica. The *cortège*

was formed in the wings, that is in the Cappella della Pietà, the first chapel of the right aisle, and, in order to reach it, the Holy Father, coming from his apartments by the way of the Chapel of the Blessed Sacrament, had been stealthily carried behind the hangings of the aisle which served the purpose of a drop-scene. Awaiting him in all readiness in the Cappella della Pietà were the cardinals, archbishops, and bishops, the whole pontifical prelacy, hierarchically classified and grouped. And then, as at a signal from a ballet master, the *cortège* made its entry, reaching the nave and ascending it in triumph from the closed Porta Santa to the altar of the Confession. On either hand were the rows of spectators whose applause at the sight of so much magnificence grew louder and louder as their delirious enthusiasm increased.

It was the *cortège* of the olden solemnities, the cross and sword, the Swiss Guard in full uniform, the valets in scarlet simars, the Knights of the Cape and the Sword in Renascence costumes, the canons in rochets of lace, the superiors of the religious communities, the apostolic prothonotaries, the archbishops and bishops, all the pontifical prelates in violet silk, the cardinals, each wearing the *cappa magna* and draped in purple, walking solemnly two by two with long intervals between each pair. Finally, around his Holiness were grouped the officers of the military household, the chamber prelates, Monsignor the Majordomo, Monsignor the Grand Chamberlain, and all the other high dignitaries of the Vatican, with the Roman Prince assistant of the throne, the traditional, symbolical defender of the Church. And on the *Sedia gestatoria*, screened by the *flabelli* with their lofty triumphal fans of feathers and carried on high by the bearers in red tunics broidered with silk, sat the Pope, clad in the sacred vestments which he had assumed in the Chapel of the Blessed Sacrament, the amict, the alb, the stole, and the white chasuble and white mitre enriched with gold, two gifts of extraordinary sumptuousness that had come from France. And, as his Holiness drew near, all hands were raised and clapped yet more loudly amidst the waves of living sunlight which streamed from the lofty windows.

Then a new and different impression of Leo XIII came to Pierre. The Pope, as he now beheld him, was no longer the familiar, tired, inquisitive old man, leaning on the arm of a talkative prelate as he strolled through the loveliest gardens in the world. He no longer recalled the Holy Father, in red

cape and papal cap, giving a paternal welcome to a pilgrimage
which brought him a fortune. He was here the Sovereign
Pontiff, the all-powerful Master whom Christendom adored.
His slim waxen form seemed to have stiffened within his white
vestments, heavy with golden broidery, as in a reliquary of
precious metal; and he retained a rigid, haughty, hieratic
attitude, like that of some idol, gilded, withered for centuries
past by the smoke of sacrifices. Amidst the mournful stiffness
of his face only his eyes lived—eyes like black sparkling diamonds gazing afar, beyond earth, into the infinite. He gave
not a glance to the crowd, he lowered his eyes neither to
right nor to left, but remained soaring in the heavens, ignoring
all that took place at his feet.

And as that seemingly embalmed idol, deaf and blind, in
spite of the brilliancy of its eyes, was carried through the
frantic multitude which it appeared neither to hear nor to
see, it assumed fearsome majesty, disquieting grandeur, all the
rigidity of dogma, all the immobility of tradition exhumed
with its *fasciæ* which alone kept it erect. Still Pierre fancied
he could detect that the Pope was ill and weary, suffering from
the attack of fever which Nani had spoken of when glorifying
the courage of that old man of eighty-four, whom strength
of soul alone now kept alive.

The service began. Alighting from the *Sedia gestatoria*
before the altar of the Confession, his Holiness slowly celebrated a low mass, assisted by four prelates and the pro-prefect
of the ceremonies. When the time came for washing his
fingers, Monsignor the Majordomo and Monsignor the Grand
Chamberlain, accompanied by two cardinals, poured the
water on his august hands; and shortly before the elevation
of the host all the prelates of the pontifical court, each holding a lighted taper, came and knelt around the altar. There
was a solemn moment, the forty thousand believers there assembled shuddered as if they could feel the terrible yet delicious blast of the invisible sweeping over them when during
the elevation the silver clarions sounded the famous chorus of
angels which invariably makes some women swoon. Almost
immediately an aerial chant descended from the cupola, from
a lofty gallery where one hundred and twenty choristers were
concealed, and the enraptured multitude marvelled as though
the angels had indeed responded to the clarion call. The
voices descended, taking their flight under the vaulted ceilings
with the airy sweetness of celestial harps; then in suave har-

mony they died away, reascended to the heavens as with a
faint flapping of wings. And, after the mass, his Holiness,
still standing at the altar, in person started the *Te Deum*,
which the singers of the Sixtine Chapel and the other choristers took up, each party chanting a verse alternately. But
soon the whole congregation joined them, forty thousand
voices were raised, and the hymn of joy and glory spread
through the vast nave with incomparable splendour of effect.
And then the scene became one of extraordinary magnificence :
there was Bernini's triumphal, flowery, gilded *baldacchino*,
surrounded by the whole pontifical court with the lighted
tapers showing like starry constellations, there was the Sovereign Pontiff in the centre, radiant like a planet in his gold-
broidered chasuble, there were the benches crowded with
cardinals in purple and archbishops and bishops in violet silk,
there were the tribunes glittering with official finery, the gold
lace of the diplomatists, the variegated uniforms of foreign
officers, and then there was the throng flowing and eddying
on all sides, rolling billows after billows of heads from the
most distant depths of the basilica. And the hugeness of the
temple increased one's amazement ; and even the glorious
hymn which the multitude repeated became colossal, ascended
like a tempest blast amidst the great marble tombs, the superhuman statues and gigantic pillars, till it reached the vast
vaulted heavens of stone, and penetrated into the firmament
of the cupola where the Infinite seemed to open resplendent
with the gold work of the mosaics.

A long murmur of voices followed the *Te Deum*, whilst
Leo XIII, after donning the tiara in lieu of the mitre, and
exchanging the chasuble for the pontifical cope, went to occupy
his throne on the platform at the entry of the left transept.
He thence dominated the whole assembly through which a
quiver sped when after the prayers of the ritual, he once more
rose erect. Beneath the symbolic, triple crown, in the golden
sheathing of his cope, he seemed to have grown taller.
Amidst sudden and profound silence, which only feverish
heart-beats interrupted, he raised his arm with a very noble
gesture and pronounced the papal benediction in a slow, loud,
full voice, which seemed, as it were, the very voice of the
Deity, so greatly did its power astonish one, coming from
such waxen lips, from such a bloodless, lifeless frame. And
the effect was prodigious : as soon as the *cortège* re-formed to
return whence it had come, applause again burst forth, a

frenzy of enthusiasm which the clapping of hands could no longer content. Acclamations resounded and gradually gained upon the whole multitude. They began among a group of ardent partisans stationed near the statue of St. Peter: *Evviva il Papa-Rè ! evviva il Papa-Rè !* Long live the Pope-King !' As the *cortège* went by the shout rushed along like leaping fire, inflaming heart after heart, and at last springing from every mouth in a thunderous protest against the theft of the States of the Church. All the faith, all the love of those believers, over-excited by the regal spectacle they had just beheld, returned once more to the dream, to the rageful desire that the Pope should be both King and Pontiff, master of men's bodies as he was of their souls—in one word, the absolute sovereign of the earth. Therein lay the only truth, the only happiness, the only salvation ! Let all be given to him, both mankind and the world ! '*Evviva il Papa-Rè ! evviva il Papa-Rè !* Long live the Pope-King !'

Ah ! that cry, that cry of war which had caused so many errors and so much bloodshed, that cry of self-abandonment and blindness which, realised, would have brought back the old ages of suffering, it shocked Pierre, and impelled him in all haste to quit the tribune where he was in order that he might escape the contagion of idolatry. And while the *cortège* still went its way and the deafening clamour of the crowd continued, he for a moment followed the left aisle amidst the general scramble. This, however, made him despair of reaching the street, and, anxious to escape the crush of the general departure, it occurred to him to profit by a door which he saw open and which led him into a vestibule, whence ascended the steps conducting to the dome. A sacristan standing in the doorway, both bewildered and delighted at the demonstration, looked at him for a moment, hesitating whether he should stop him or not. However, the sight of the young priest's cassock combined with his own emotion rendered the man tolerant. Pierre was allowed to pass, and at once began to climb the staircase as rapidly as he could, in order that he might flee farther and farther away, ascend higher and yet higher into peace and silence.

And the silence suddenly became profound, the walls stifled the cry of the multitude. The staircase was easy and light, with broad paved steps turning within a sort of tower. When Pierre came out upon the roofs of nave and aisles, he was delighted to find himself in the bright sunlight and the pure

keen air which blew there as in the open country. And it
was with astonishment that he gazed upon the huge expanse
of lead, zinc, and stonework, a perfect aerial city living a life
of its own under the blue sky. He saw cupolas, spires,
terraces, even houses and gardens, houses bright with flowers,
the residences of the workmen who live atop of the basilica,
which is ever and ever requiring repair. A little population
here bestirs itself, labours, loves, eats and sleeps. However,
Pierre desired to approach the balustrade so as to get a near
view of the colossal statues of the Saviour and the Apostles
which surmount the façade on the side of the piazza. These
giants, some nineteen feet in height, are constantly being
mended; their arms, legs, and heads, into which the atmosphere is ever eating, nowadays only hold together by the help
of cement, bars, and hooks. And having examined them,
Pierre was leaning forward to glance at the Vatican's
jumble of ruddy roofs, when it seemed to him that the shout
from which he had fled was rising from the piazza, and
thereupon, in all haste, he resumed his ascent within the
pillar conducting to the dome. There was first a staircase,
and then came some narrow, oblique passages, inclines intersected by a few steps, between the inner and outer walls of
the cupola. Yielding to curiosity, Pierre pushed a door open,
and suddenly found himself inside the basilica again, at
nearly 200 feet from the ground. A narrow gallery there
ran round the dome just above the frieze, on which, in
letters five feet high, appeared the famous inscription: *Tu es
Petrus et super hanc petram ædificabo ecclesiam meam et tibi
dabo claves regni cœlorum.*[1] And then, as Pierre leant over to
gaze into the fearful cavity beneath him and the wide open-
ings of nave and aisles and transepts, the cry, the delirious
cry of the multitude, yet clamorously swarming below, struck
him full in the face. He fled once more; but, higher up, yet
a second time he pushed another door open and found another
gallery, one perched above the windows, just where the
splendid mosaics begin, and whence the crowd seemed to him
lost in the depths of a dizzy abyss, altar and *baldacchino*
alike looking no larger than toys. And yet the cry of idolatry
and warfare arose again, and smote him like the buffet of
a tempest which gathers increase of strength the farther it

---

[1] Thou art Peter (*Petrus*) and on that rock (*petram*) will I build my
Church, and to thee will I give the keys of the Kingdom of Heaven.

rushes. So to escape it he had to climb higher still, even to the outer gallery which encircles the lantern, hovering in the very heavens.

How delightful was the relief which that bath of air and sunlight at first brought him! Above him now there only remained the ball of gilt copper into which emperors and queens have ascended, as is testified by the pompous inscriptions in the passages; a hollow ball it is, where the voice crashes like thunder, where all the sounds of space reverberate. As he had emerged on the side of the apse, his eyes at first plunged into the papal gardens, whose clumps of trees seemed mere bushes almost level with the soil; and he could retrace his recent stroll among them, the broad *parterre* looking like a faded Smyrna rug, the large wood showing the deep glaucous greenery of a stagnant pool. Then there were the kitchen garden and the vineyard easily identified and tended with care. The fountains, the observatory, the casino, where the Pope spent the hot days of summer, showed merely like little white spots in those undulating grounds, walled in like any other estate, but with the fearsome rampart of the fourth Leo, which yet retained its fortress-like aspect. However, Pierre took his way round the narrow gallery and abruptly found himself in front of Rome, a sudden and immense expanse, with the distant sea on the west, the uninterrupted mountain chains on the east and the south, the Roman Campagna stretching to the horizon like a bare and greenish desert, while the city, the Eternal City, was spread out at his feet. Never before had space impressed him so majestically. Rome was there, as a bird might see it, within the glance, as distinct as some geographical plan executed in relief. To think of it, such a past, such a history, so much grandeur, and Rome so dwarfed and contracted by distance! Houses as lilliputian and as pretty as toys; and the whole a mere mouldy speck upon the earth's wide face! What impassioned Pierre was that he could at a glance understand the divisions of Rome: the antique city yonder with the Capitol, the Forum, and the Palatine; the papal city in that Borgo which he overlooked, with St. Peter's and the Vatican gazing across the city of the middle ages—which was huddled together in the right angle described by the yellow Tiber—towards the modern city, the Quirinal of the Italian monarchy. And particularly did he remark the chalky girdle with which the new districts encompassed the ancient, central, sun-tanned quarters, thus

symbolising an effort at rejuvenescence, the old heart but
slowly mended, whereas the outlying limbs were renewed as
if by miracle.

In that ardent noontide glow, however, Pierre no longer
beheld the pure ethereal Rome which had met his eyes on the
morning of his arrival in the delightfully soft radiance of the
rising sun. That smiling, unobtrusive city, half veiled by
golden mist, immersed as it were in some dream of childhood,
now appeared to him flooded with a crude light, motionless,
hard of outline and silent like death. The distance was as if
devoured by too keen a flame, steeped in a luminous dust in
which it crumbled. And against that blurred background the
whole city showed with violent distinctness in great patches
of light and shade, their tracery harshly conspicuous. One
might have fancied oneself above some very ancient, abandoned
stone quarry, which a few clumps of trees spotted with dark
green. Of the ancient city one could see the sunburnt tower
of the Capitol, the black cypresses of the Palatine, and the
ruins of the palace of Septimius Severus, suggesting the
white osseous carcase of some fossil monster, left there by a
flood. In front, was enthroned the modern city with the long,
renovated buildings of the Quirinal whose yellow walls stood
forth with wondrous crudity amidst the vigorous crests of
the garden trees. And to right and left on the Viminal,
beyond the palace, the new districts appeared like a city of
chalk and plaster mottled by innumerable windows as with a
thousand touches of black ink. Then here and there were the
Pincio showing like a stagnant mere, the Villa Medici uprearing
its campanili, the castle of Sant' Angelo brown like rust, the
spire of Santa Maria Maggiore aglow like a burning taper, the
three churches of the Aventine drowsy amidst verdure, the
Palazzo Farnese with its summer-baked tiles showing like old
gold, the domes of the Gesù, of Sant' Andrea della Valle, of
San Giovanni dei Fiorentini, and yet other domes and other
domes, all in fusion, incandescent in the brazier of the heavens.
And Pierre again felt a heart-pang in presence of that harsh,
stern Rome, so different from the Rome of his dream, the
Rome of rejuvenescence and hope, which he had fancied he
had found on his first morning, but which had now faded away
to give place to the immutable city of pride and domination, stubborn under the sun even unto death.

And there on high, all alone with his thoughts, Pierre
suddenly understood. It was as if a dart of flaming light fell

on him in that free, unbounded expanse where he hovered.
Had it come from the ceremony which he had just beheld,
from the frantic cry of servitude still ringing in his ears?
Had it come from the spectacle of that city beneath him, that
city which suggested an embalmed Queen still reigning amidst
the dust of her tomb? He knew not; but doubtless both had
acted as factors, and at all events the light which fell upon
his mind was complete: he felt that Catholicism could not
exist without the temporal power, that it must fatally disappear whenever it should no longer be king over this earth.
A first reason of this lay in heredity, in the forces of history,
the long line of the heirs of the Cæsars, the Popes, the great
pontiffs, in whose veins the blood of Augustus, demanding
the empire of the world, had never ceased to flow. Though
they might reside in the Vatican they had come from the
imperial abodes on the Palatine, from the palace of Septimius
Severus, and throughout the centuries their policy had ever
pursued the dream of Roman mastery, of all the nations
vanquished, submissive, and obedient to Rome. If its
sovereignty were not universal, extending alike over bodies
and over souls, Catholicism would lose its *raison d'être;* for
the Church cannot recognise any empire or kingdom otherwise than politically—the emperors and the kings being
purely and simply so many temporary delegates placed in
charge of the nations pending the time when they shall be
called upon to relinquish their trust. All the nations, all
humanity and the whole world belong to the Church to whom
they have been given by God. And if real and effective
possession be not hers to-day, this is only because she yields
to force, compelled to face accomplished facts, but with the
formal reserve that she is in presence of guilty usurpation,
that her possessions are unjustly withheld from her, and that
she awaits the realisation of the promises of the Christ, who,
when the times shall be accomplished, will for ever restore to
her both the earth and mankind. Such is the real future
city which time is to bring: Catholic Rome, sovereign of the
world once more. And Rome the city forms a substantial
part of the dream, Rome whose eternity has been predicted,
Rome whose soil has imparted to Catholicism the inextinguishable thirst of absolute power. And thus the destiny of
the Papacy is linked to that of Rome, to such a point indeed
that a pope elsewhere than at Rome would no longer be a
Catholic pope. The thought of all this frightened Pierre; a

great shudder passed through him, as he leant on the light iron balustrade, gazing down into the abyss where the stern mournful city was even now crumbling away under the fierce sun.

There was, however, evidence of the facts which had dawned on him. If Pius IX and Leo XIII had resolved to imprison themselves in the Vatican it was because necessity bound them to Rome. A pope is not free to leave the city, to be the head of the Church elsewhere; and in the same way a pope, however well he may understand the modern world, has not the right to relinquish the temporal power. This is an inalienable inheritance which he must defend, and it is moreover, a question of life, peremptory, above discussion. And thus Leo XIII has retained the title of Master of the temporal dominions of the Church, and this he has done the more readily since as a cardinal—like all the members of the Sacred College when elected—he swore that he would maintain those dominions intact. Italy may hold Rome as her capital for another century or more, but the coming popes will never cease to protest and claim their kingdom. If ever an understanding should be arrived at, it must be based on the gift of a strip of territory. Formerly, when rumours of reconciliation were current, was it not said that the papacy exacted, as a formal condition, the possession of at least the Leonine city with the neutralisation of a road leading to the sea? Nothing is not enough, one cannot start from nothing to attain to everything, whereas that Civitas Leonina, that bit of a city, would already be a little royal ground, and it would then only be necessary to conquer the rest, first Rome, next Italy, then the neighbouring states, and at last the whole world. Never has the Church despaired, even when, beaten and despoiled, she seemed to be at the last gasp. Never will she abdicate, never will she renounce the promises of the Christ, for she believes in a boundless future and declares herself to be both indestructible and eternal. Grant her but a pebble on which to rest her head, and she will hope to possess, first the field in which that pebble lies, and then the empire in which the field is situated. If one pope cannot achieve the recovery of the inheritance, another pope, ten, twenty other popes will continue the work. The centuries do not count. And this explains why an old man of eighty-four has undertaken colossal enterprises whose achievement requires several lives, certain as he is that his successors will take his place, and that the work will ever and ever be carried forward and completed.

As these thoughts coursed through his mind, Pierre, overlooking that ancient city of glory and domination, so stubbornly clinging to its purple, realised that he was an imbecile with his dream of a purely spiritual pope. The notion seemed to him so different from the reality, so out of place, that he experienced a sort of shame-fraught despair. The new pope, consonant to the teachings of the Gospel, such as a purely spiritual pope reigning over souls alone would be, was virtually beyond the ken of a Roman prelate. At thought of that papal Court congealed in ritual, pride, and authority, Pierre suddenly understood what horror and repugnance such a pastor would inspire. How great must be the astonishment and contempt of the papal prelates for that singular notion of the northern mind, a pope without dominions or subjects, military household or royal honours, a pope who would be, as it were, a spirit, exercising purely moral authority, dwelling in the depths of God's temple, and governing the world solely with gestures of benediction and deeds of kindliness and love! All that was but a misty Gothic invention for this Latin clergy, these priests of light and magnificence, who were certainly pious and even superstitious, but who left the Deity well sheltered within the tabernacle in order to govern in His name, according to what they considered the interests of Heaven. Thence it arose that they employed craft and artifice like mere politicians, and lived by dint of expedients amidst the great battle of human appetites, marching with the prudent, stealthy steps of diplomatists towards the final terrestrial victory of the Christ, who, in the person of the Pope, was one day to reign over all the nations. And how stupéfied must a French prelate have been—a prelate like Monseigneur Bergerot, that apostle of renunciation and charity—when he lighted amidst that world of the Vatican! How difficult must it have been for him to understand and focus things, and afterwards how great his grief at finding himself unable to come to any agreement with those men without country, without fatherland, those 'internationals,' who were ever poring over the maps of both hemispheres, ever absorbed in schemes which were to bring them empire. Days and days were necessary, one needed to live in Rome, and he, Pierre himself, had only seen things clearly after a month's sojourn, whilst labouring under the violent shock of

the royal pomp of St. Peter's, and standing face to face with
the ancient city as it slumbered heavily in the sunlight and
dreamt its dream of eternity.

But on lowering his eyes to the piazza in front of the
basilica he perceived the multitude, the 40,000 believers
streaming over the pavement like insects. And then he
thought that he could hear the cry again rising : ' *Evviva il
Papa-Rè* ! *evviva il Papa-Rè* ! Long live the Pope-King !'
Whilst ascending those endless staircases a moment previously
it had seemed to him as if the colossus of stone were quivering with the frantic shout raised beneath its ceilings. And
now that he had climbed even into cloudland that shout
apparently was traversing space. If the colossal pile beneath
him still vibrated with it, was it not as with a last rise of sap
within its ancient walls, a reinvigoration of that Catholic
blood which formerly had demanded that the pile should be
a stupendous one, the veritable king of temples, and which
now was striving to reanimate it with the powerful breath of
life, and this at the very hour when death was beginning to
fall upon its over-vast, deserted nave and aisles ? The
crowd was still streaming forth, filling the piazza, and Pierre's
heart was wrung by frightful anguish, for that throng with
its shout had just swept his last hope away. On the previous
afternoon, after the reception of the pilgrimage, he had yet
been able to deceive himself by overlooking the necessity for
money which bound the Pope to earth in order that he might
see nought but the feeble old man, all spirituality, resplendent
like the symbol of moral authority. But his faith in such a
pastor of the Gospel, free from all considerations of earthly
wealth, and king of none other than a heavenly kingdom, had
fled. Not only did the Peter's Pence impose hard servitude
upon Leo XIII but he was also the prisoner of papal tradition
—the eternal king of Rome, riveted to the soil of Rome,
unable either to quit the city or to renounce the temporal
power. The fatal end would be collapse on the spot, the dome
of St. Peter's falling even as the temple of Olympian Jupiter
had fallen, Catholicism strewing the grass with its ruins
whilst elsewhere schism burst forth : a new faith for the new
nations. Of this Pierre had a grandiose and tragical vision :
he beheld his dream destroyed, his book swept away amidst
that cry which spread around him as if flying to the four
corners of the Catholic world : ' *Evviva il Papa-Rè* ! *evviva il
Papa-Rè* ! Long live the Pope-King !' But even in that

hour of the Papacy's passing triumph he already felt that the giant of gold and marble on which he stood was oscillating, even as totter all old and rotten societies.

At last he took his way down again, and a fresh shock of emotion came to him as he reached the roofs, that sunlit expanse of lead and zinc, large enough for the site of a town. Monsignor Nani was there, in company with the two French ladies, the mother and the daughter, both looking very happy and highly amused. No doubt the prelate had good-naturedly offered to conduct them to the dome. However, as soon as he recognised the young priest he went towards him : ' Well, my dear son,' he inquired, ' are you pleased ? Have you been impressed, edified ? ' As he spoke, his searching eyes dived into Pierre's soul, as if to ascertain the present result of his experiments. Then, satisfied with what he detected, he began to laugh softly : ' Yes, yes, I see—Come, you are a sensible fellow after all. I begin to think that the unfortunate affair which brought you here will have a happy ending.'

VIII

WHEN Pierre remained in the morning at the Boccanera mansion he often spent some hours in the little neglected garden which had formerly ended with a sort of colonnaded *loggia*, whence two flights of steps descended to the Tiber. This garden was a delightful, solitary nook, perfumed by the ripe fruit of the centenarian orange trees, whose symmetrical lines were the only indication of the former pathways, now hidden beneath rank weeds. And Pierre also found there the acrid scent of the large box-shrubs growing in the old central fountain basin, which had been filled up with loose earth and rubbish.

On those luminous October mornings, full of such tender and penetrating charm, the spot was one where all the joy of living might well be savoured, but Pierre brought thither his northern dreaminess, his concern for suffering, his steadfast feeling of compassion, which rendered yet sweeter the caress of the sunlight pervading that atmosphere of love. He seated himself against the right-hand wall on a fragment of a fallen column over which a huge laurel cast a deep black shadow, fresh and aromatic. In the antique greenish sarcophagus beside him, on which fauns offered violence to nymphs, the streamlet

of water trickling from the mask incrusted in the wall set the
unchanging music of its crystal note, whilst he read the
newspapers and the letters which he received, all the com-
munications of good Abbé Rose, who kept him informed of
his mission among the wretched ones of gloomy Paris, now
already steeped in fog and mud.

One morning, however, Pierre unexpectedly found Benedetta
seated on the fallen column which he usually made his chair.
She raised a light cry of surprise on seeing him, and for a
moment remained embarrassed, for she had with her his
book 'New Rome,' which she had read once already, but had
then imperfectly understood. And overcoming her embarrassment she now hastened to detain him, making him sit
down beside her, and frankly owning that she had come to
the garden in order to be alone and apply herself to an
attentive study of the book, in the same way as some ignorant
schoolgirl. Then they began to chat like a pair of friends,
and the young priest spent a delightful hour. Although
Benedetta did not speak of herself, he realised that it was
her grief alone which brought her nearer to him, as if indeed
her own sufferings enlarged her heart and made her think of
all who suffered in the world. Patrician as she was, regarding
social hierarchy as a divine law, she had never previously
thought of such things, and some pages of Pierre's book
greatly astonished her. What! one ought to take interest in
the lowly, realise that they had the same souls and the same
griefs as oneself, and seek in brotherly or sisterly fashion to
make them happy? She certainly sought to acquire such
an interest, but with no great success, for she secretly
feared that it might lead her into sin, as it could not be right
to alter aught of the social system which had been established
by God and consecrated by the Church. Charitable she undoubtedly was, wont to bestow small sums in alms, but she did
not give her heart, she felt no true sympathy for the humble,
belonging as she did to such a different race, which looked to
a throne in heaven high above the seats of the plebeian elect.

She and Pierre, however, found themselves on other mornings side by side in the shade of the laurels near the trickling,
singing water; and he, lacking occupation, weary of waiting
for a solution which seemed to recede day by day, fervently
strove to animate this young and beautiful woman with some
of his own fraternal feelings. He was impassioned by the
idea that he was catechising Italy herself, the queen of beauty,

who was still slumbering in ignorance, but who would recover all her past glory if she were to awake to the new times with soul enlarged, swelling with pity for men and things. Reading good Abbé Rose's letters to Benedetta, he made her shudder at the frightful wail of wretchedness which ascends from all great cities. With such deep tenderness in her eyes, with the happiness of love reciprocated emanating from her whole being, why should she not recognise, even as he did, that the law of love was the sole means of saving suffering humanity, which, through hatred, incurred the danger of death? And to please him she did try to believe in democracy, in the fraternal remodelling of society, but among other nations only —not at Rome, for an involuntary, gentle laugh came to her lips whenever his words evoked the idea of the poor still remaining in the Trastevere district fraternising with those who yet dwelt in the old princely palaces. No, no, things had been as they were so long; they could not, must not, be altered! And so, after all, Pierre's pupil made little progress: she was, in reality, simply touched by the wealth of ardent love which the young priest had chastely transferred from one alone to the whole of human kind. And between him and her, as those sunlit October mornings went by, a tie of exquisite sweetness was formed; they came to love one another with deep, pure, fraternal affection, amidst the great glowing passion which consumed them both.

Then, one day, Benedetta, her elbow resting on the sarcophagus, spoke of Dario, whose name she had hitherto refrained from mentioning. Ah! poor *amico*, how circumspect and repentant he had shown himself since that fit of brutal insanity! At first, to conceal his embarrassment, he had gone to spend three days at Naples, and it was said that La Tonietta, the sentimental *demi-mondaine*, had hastened to join him there, wildly in love with him. Since his return to the mansion he had avoided all private meetings with his cousin, and scarcely saw her except at the Monday receptions, when he wore a submissive air, and with his eyes silently entreated forgiveness.

'Yesterday, however,' continued Benedetta, 'I met him on the staircase and gave him my hand. He understood that I was no longer angry with him and was very happy. What else could I have done? One must not be severe for ever. Besides, I do not want things to go too far between him and that woman. I want him to remember that I still love him, and am still waiting for him. Oh! he is mine, mine alone. But alas! I cannot say the word: our affairs are in such sorry plight.'

She paused, and two big tears welled into her eyes. The divorce proceedings to which she alluded had now come to a standstill, fresh obstacles ever arising to stay their course.

Pierre was much moved by her tears, for she seldom wept. She herself sometimes confessed, with her calm smile, that she did not know how to weep. But now her heart was melting, and for a moment she remained overcome, leaning on the mossy, crumbling sarcophagus, whilst the clear water falling from the gaping mouth of the tragic mask still sounded its flute-like note. And a sudden thought of death came to the priest as he saw her, so young and so radiant with beauty, half fainting beside that marble resting-place where fauns were rushing upon nymphs in a frantic bacchanal which proclaimed the omnipotence of love—that omnipotence which the ancients were fond of symbolising on their tombs as a token of life's eternity. And meantime a faint, warm breeze passed through the sunlit, silent garden, wafting hither and thither the penetrating scent of box and orange.

'One has so much strength when one loves,' Pierre at last murmured.

'Yes, yes, you are right,' she replied, already smiling again. 'I am childish. But it is the fault of your book. It is only when I suffer that I properly understand it. But all the same I am making progress, am I not? Since you desire it, let all the poor, all those who suffer, as I do, be my brothers and sisters.'

Then for a while they resumed their chat.

On these occasions Benedetta was usually the first to return to the house, and Pierre would linger alone under the laurels, vaguely dreaming of sweet, sad things. Often did he think how hard life proved for poor creatures whose only thirst was for happiness!

One Monday evening, at a quarter-past ten, only the young folks remained in Donna Serafina's reception room. Monsignor Nani had merely put in an appearance that night, and Cardinal Sarno had just gone off. Even Donna Serafina, in her usual seat by the fireplace, seemed to have withdrawn from the others, absorbed as she was in contemplation of the chair which the absent Morano still stubbornly left unoccupied. Chatting and laughing in front of the sofa on which sat

Benedetta and Celia were Dario, Pierre, and Narcisse Habert,
the last of whom had begun to twit the young Prince, having
met him, so he asserted, a few days previously, in the company
of a very pretty girl.

'Oh! don't deny it, my dear fellow,' continued Narcisse,
'for she was really superb. She was walking beside you,
and you turned into a lane together—the Borgo Angelico, I
think.'

Dario listened smiling, quite at his ease and incapable of
denying his passionate predilection for beauty. 'No doubt,
no doubt; it was I, I don't deny it,' he responded. 'Only the
inferences you draw are not correct.' And turning towards
Benedetta, who, without a thought of jealous anxiety, wore as
gay a look as himself, as though delighted that he should
have enjoyed that passing pleasure of the eyes, he went on : 'It
was the girl, you know, whom I found in tears six weeks ago.
Yes, that bead-worker who was sobbing because the workshop
was shut up, and who rushed along, all blushing, to conduct
me to her parents when I offered her a bit of silver. Pierina
her name is, as you, perhaps, remember.'

'Oh! yes, Pierina.'

'Well, since then I've met her in the street on four or five
occasions. And, to tell the truth, she is so very beautiful that
I've stopped and spoken to her. The other day, for instance,
I walked with her as far as a manufacturer's. But she hasn't
yet found any work, and she began to cry, and so, to console
her a little, I kissed her. She was quite taken aback at it, but
she seemed very well pleased.'

At this all the others began to laugh. But suddenly Celia
desisted and said very gravely, 'You know, Dario, she loves
you ; you must not be hard on her.'

Dario, no doubt, was of Celia's opinion, for he again looked
at Benedetta, but with a gay toss of the head, as if to say that,
although the girl might love him, he did not love her. A
bead-worker indeed, a girl of the lowest classes, pooh ! She
might be a Venus, but she could be nothing to him. And he
himself made merry over his romantic adventure, which
Narcisse sought to arrange in a kind of antique sonnet: A
beautiful bead-worker falling madly in love with a young
prince, as fair as sunlight, who, touched by her misfortune,
hands her a silver crown ; then the beautiful bead-worker,
quite overcome at finding him as charitable as handsome,
dreaming of him incessantly, and following him everywhere,

chained to his steps by a link of flame ; and finally the beautiful bead-worker, who has refused the silver crown, so entreating the handsome prince with her soft, submissive eyes, that
he at last deigns to grant her the alms of his heart. This
pastime greatly amused Benedetta ; but Celia, with her angelic
face and the air of a little girl who ought to have been ignorant of everything, remained very grave and repeated sadly,
' Dario, Dario, she loves you ; you must not make her suffer.'

Then the Contessina, in her turn, was moved to pity. 'And
those poor folks are not happy ! ' said she.

' Oh ! ' exclaimed the Prince, ' it's misery beyond belief.
On the day she took me to the Quartiere dei Prati [1] I was quite
overcome ; it was awful, astonishingly awful ! '

' But I remember that we promised to go to see the poor
people,' resumed Benedetta, ' and we have done wrong in
delaying our visit so long. For your studies, Monsieur l'Abbé
Froment, you greatly desired to accompany us and see the
poor of Rome—was that not so ? '

As she spoke she raised her eyes to Pierre, who for a
moment had been silent. He was much moved by her charitable thought, for he realised, by the faint quiver of her voice,
that she desired to appear a docile pupil, progressing in affection for the lowly and the wretched. Moreover, his passion
for his apostolate had at once returned to him. ' Oh ! ' said
he, ' I shall not quit Rome without having seen those who
suffer, those who lack work and bread. Therein lies the
malady which affects every nation ; salvation can only be
attained by the healing of misery. When the roots of the
tree cannot find sustenance the tree dies.'

' Well,' resumed the Contessina, ' we will fix an appointment at once ; you shall come with us to the Quartiere dei Prati
—Dario will take us there.'

At this the Prince, who had listened to the priest with an
air of stupefaction, unable to understand the simile of the tree
and its roots, began to protest distressfully, ' No, no, cousin,
take Monsieur l'Abbé for a stroll there if it amuses you. But
I've been, and don't want to go back. Why, when I got
home the last time I was so upset that I almost took to
my bed. No, no ; such abominations are too awful—it isn't
possible.'

At this moment a voice, bitter with displeasure, arose
from the chimney corner. Donna Serafina was emerging

[1] The district of the castle meadows—see *ante* p. 63 (note).—*Trans.*

from her long silence. 'Dario is quite right! Send your
alms, my dear, and I will gladly add mine. There are other
places where you might take Monsieur l'Abbé, and which it
would be far more useful for him to see. With that idea of
yours you would send him away with a nice recollection of
our city.'

Roman pride rang out amidst the old lady's bad temper.
Why, indeed, show one's sores to foreigners, whose visit is
possibly prompted by hostile curiosity? One always ought
to look beautiful; Rome should not be shown otherwise than
in the garb of glory.

Narcisse, however, had taken possession of Pierre. 'It's
true, my dear Abbé,' said he; 'I forgot to recommend that
stroll to you. You really must visit the new district built
over the castle meadows. It's typical, and sums up all the
others. And you won't lose your time there, I'll warrant you,
for nowhere can you learn more about the Rome of the present
day. It's extraordinary, extraordinary!' Then, addressing
Benedetta, he added, 'Is it decided? Shall we say to-morrow
morning? You'll find the Abbé and me over there, for I
want to explain matters to him beforehand, in order that he
may understand them. What do you say to ten o'clock?'

Before answering him the Contessina turned towards her
aunt and respectfully opposed her views. 'But Monsieur
l'Abbé, aunt, has met enough beggars in our streets already,
so he may well see everything. Besides, judging by his book,
he won't see worse things than he has seen in Paris. As he
says in one passage, hunger is the same all the world over.'
Then, with her sensible air, she gently laid siege to Dario.
'You know, Dario,' said she, 'you would please me very much
by taking me there. We can go in the carriage and join these
gentlemen. It will be a very pleasant outing for us. It is such
a long time since we went out together.'

It was certainly that idea of going out with Dario, of
having a pretext for a complete reconciliation with him, that
enchanted her; he himself realised it, and, unable to escape, he
tried to treat the matter as a joke. 'Ah! cousin,' he said,
'it will be your fault; I shall have the nightmare for a week.
An excursion like that spoils all the enjoyment of life for days
and days.'

The mere thought made him quiver with revolt. However,
laughter again rang out around him, and, in spite of Donna
Serafina's mute disapproval, the appointment was finally fixed

for the following morning at ten o'clock. Celia as she went
off expressed deep regret that she could not form one of the
party; but, with the closed candour of a budding lily, she really
took interest in Pierina alone. As she reached the ante-room
she whispered in her friend's ear: 'Take a good look at that
beauty, my dear, so as to tell me whether she is so very
beautiful—beautiful beyond compare.'

When Pierre met Narcisse near the castle of Sant' Angelo
on the morrow, at nine o'clock, he was surprised to find him
again languid and enraptured, plunged anew in artistic
enthusiasm. At first not a word was said of the excursion.
Narcisse related that he had risen at sunrise in order that he
might spend an hour before Bernini's Santa Teresa. It
seemed that when he did not see that statue for a week he
suffered as acutely as if he were parted from some cherished
mistress. And his adoration varied with the time of day,
according to the light in which he beheld the figure: in the
morning, when the pale glow of dawn steeped it in whiteness,
he worshipped it with quite a mystical transport of the soul,
whilst in the afternoon, when the glow of the declining sun's
oblique rays seemed to permeate the marble, his passion
became as fiery red as the blood of martyrs. 'Ah! my
friend,' said he with a weary air whilst his dreamy eyes faded
to mauve, 'you have no idea how delightful and perturbing her
awakening was this morning—how languorously she opened
her eyes, like a pure, candid virgin, emerging from the embrace
of the Divinity. One could die of rapture at the sight!'

Then, growing calm again when he had taken a few steps,
he resumed in the voice of a practical man who does not lose
his balance in the affairs of life: 'We'll walk slowly towards
the castle fields district—the buildings yonder; and on our
way I'll tell you what I know of the things we shall see there.
It was the maddest affair imaginable, one of those delirious
frenzies of speculation which have a splendour of their own,
just like the superb, monstrous masterpiece of a man of
genius whose mind is unhinged. I was told of it all by some
relatives of mine, who took part in the gambling, and, in point
of fact, made a good deal of money by it.'

Thereupon, with the clearness and precision of a financier,
employing technical terms with perfect ease, he recounted the
extraordinary adventure. That all Italy, on the morrow of
the occupation of Rome, should have been delirious with
enthusiasm at the thought of at last possessing the ancient

and glorious city, the eternal capital to which the empire of the world had been promised, was but natural. It was, so to say, a legitimate explosion of the delight and the hopes of a young nation anxious to show its power. The question was to make Rome a modern capital worthy of a great kingdom, and before aught else there were sanitary requirements to be dealt with : the city needed to be cleansed of all the filth which disgraced it. One cannot nowadays imagine in what abominable putrescence the City of the Popes, the *Roma sporca* which artists regret, was then steeped : the vast majority of the houses lacked even the most primitive arrangements, the public thoroughfares were used for all purposes, noble ruins served as storeplaces for sewage, the princely palaces were surrounded by filth, and the streets were perfect manure beds which fostered frequent epidemics. Thus vast municipal works were absolutely necessary, the question was one of health and life itself. And in much the same way it was only right to think of building houses for the new-comers, who would assuredly flock into the city. There had been a precedent at Berlin, whose population, after the establishment of the German empire, had suddenly increased by some hundreds of thousands. In the same way the population of Rome would certainly be doubled, tripled, quadrupled, for as the new centre of national life the city could necessarily attract all the *vis viva* of the provinces. And at this thought pride stepped in : the fallen government of the Vatican must be shown what Italy was capable of achieving, what splendour she would bestow on the new and third Rome, which, by the magnificence of its thoroughfares and the multitude of its people, would far excel either the imperial or the papal city.

True, during the early years some prudence was observed; wisely enough, houses were only built in proportion as they were required. The population had doubled at one bound, rising from two to four hundred thousand souls, thanks to the arrival of the little world of employees and officials of the public services—all those who live on the State or hope to live on it, without mentioning the idlers and enjoyers of life whom a Court always carries in its train. However, this influx of new-comers was a first cause of intoxication, for everyone imagined that the increase would continue, and, in fact, become more and more rapid. And so the city of the day before no longer seemed large enough ; it was necessary to make immediate preparations for the morrow's need by enlarging Rome on all sides. Folks talked, too, of the Paris of the Second Empire, which had been so extended and transformed into a city of light and health. But unfortunately on the banks of the Tiber there was neither any preconcerted general plan nor any clear-seeing man, master of the situation, supported by powerful financial organisations. And the work, begun by pride, prompted by the ambition of surpassing the Rome of the Cæsars and the Popes, the determination to make the eternal, predestined city the queen and centre of the world once more, was completed by speculation, one of those extra-ordinary gambling frenzies, those tempests which arise, rage, destroy, and carry everything away without premonitory warning or possibility of arresting their course. All at once it was rumoured that land bought at five francs the mètre had been sold again for a hundred francs the mètre; and thereupon the fever arose—the fever of a nation which is passionately fond of gambling. A flight of speculators descending from north Italy swooped down upon Rome, the noblest and easiest of preys. Those needy, famished mountaineers found spoils for every appetite in that voluptuous south where life is so benign, and the very delights of the climate helped to corrupt and hasten moral gangrene. At first, too, it was merely necessary to stoop; money was to be found by the shovelful among the rubbish of the first districts which were opened up. People who were clever enough to scent the course which the new thoroughfares would take and purchase buildings threatened with demolition increased their capital tenfold in a couple of years. And after that the contagion spread, infecting all classes—the princes, burgesses, petty proprietors, even the shop-keepers, bakers, grocers, and boot-makers; the delirium rising to such a pitch that a mere baker subsequently failed for forty-five millions.[1] Nothing, indeed, was left but rageful gambling, in which the stakes were millions, whilst the lands and the houses became mere fictions, mere pretexts for stock-exchange operations. And thus the old hereditary pride, which had dreamt of transforming Rome into the capital of the world, was heated to madness by the high fever of speculation—folks buying, and building, and selling without limit, without a pause, even as one might throw shares upon the market as fast and as long as presses can be found to print them.

No other city in course of evolution has ever furnished such a spectacle. Nowadays, when one strives to penetrate

[1] 1,800,000*l*. See *ante* p. 220 (note).—*Trans.*

things one is confounded. The population had increased to
five hundred thousand, and then seemingly remained stationary; nevertheless, new districts continued to sprout up more
thickly than ever. Yet what folly it was not to wait for a
further influx of inhabitants! Why continue piling up
accommodation for thousands of families whose advent was
uncertain? The only excuse lay in having beforehand pro-
pounded the proposition that the third Rome, the triumphant
capital of Italy, could not count less than a million souls, and
in regarding that proposition as indisputable fact. The people
had not come, but they surely would come: no patriot could
doubt it without being guilty of treason. And so houses were
built and built without a pause, for the half-million citizens
who were coming. There was no anxiety as to the date of
their arrival; it was sufficient that they should be expected.
Inside Rome the companies which had been formed in connection with the new thoroughfares passing through the old,
demolished, pestiferous districts, certainly sold or let their
house property, and thereby realised large profits. But, as the
craze increased, other companies were established for the
purpose of erecting yet more and more districts outside Rome
—veritable little towns, of which there was no need whatever.
Beyond the Porta San Giovanni and the Porta San Lorenzo
suburbs sprang up as by miracle. A town was sketched out
over the vast estate of the Villa Ludovisi, from the Porta Pia
to the Porta Salaria and even as far as Sant' Agnese. And
then came an attempt to make quite a little city, with church,
school, and market, arise all at once on the fields of the
castle of Sant' Angelo. And it was no question of small
dwellings for labourers, modest flats for employees, and others
of limited means; no, it was a question of colossal mansions
three and four storeys high, displaying uniform and endless façades which made these new excentral quarters quite
Babylonian, such districts, indeed, as only capitals endowed
with intense life, like Paris and London, could contrive to
populate. However, such were the monstrous products of
pride and gambling; and what a page of history, what a bitter
lesson now that Rome, financially ruined, is further disgraced
by that hideous girdle of empty, and, for the most part, uncom-
pleted carcases, whose ruins already strew the grassy streets!

The fatal collapse, the disaster proved a frightful one.
Narcisse explained its causes and recounted its phases so
clearly that Pierre fully understood. Naturally enough, nume-

rous financial companies had sprouted up: the Immobiliere, the Società d' Edilizia e Construzione, the Fondaria, the Tiberiana, and the Esquilino. Nearly all of them built, erected huge houses, entire streets of them, for purposes of sale ; but they also gambled in land, selling plots at large profit to petty speculators, who also dreamt of making large profits amidst the continuous, fictitious rise brought about by the growing fever of agiotage. And the worst was that the petty speculators, the middle-class people, the inexperienced shop-keepers without capital, were crazy enough to build in their turn by borrowing of the banks or applying to the companies which had sold them the land for sufficient cash to enable them to complete their structures. As a general rule, to avoid the loss of everything, the companies were one day compelled to take back both land and buildings, incomplete though the latter might be, and from the congestion which resulted they were bound to perish. If the expected million of people had arrived to occupy the dwellings prepared for them the gains would have been fabulous, and in ten years Rome might have become one of the most flourishing capitals of the world. But the people did not come, and the dwellings remained empty. Moreover, the buildings erected by the companies were too large and costly for the average investor inclined to put his money into house property. Heredity had acted, the builders had planned things on too huge a scale, raising a series of magnificent piles whose purpose was to dwarf those of all other ages ; but, as it happened, they were fated to remain lifeless and deserted, testifying with wondrous eloquence to the impotence of pride.

So there was no private capital that dared or could take the place of that of the companies. Elsewhere, in Paris for instance, new districts have been erected and embellishments have been carried out with the capital of the country—the money saved by dint of thrift. But in Rome all was built on the credit system, either by means of bills of exchange at ninety days, or—and this was chiefly the case—by borrowing money abroad. The huge sum sunk in these enterprises is estimated at a milliard, four-fifths of which was French money. The bankers did everything; the French ones lent to the Italian bankers at $3\frac{1}{2}$ or 4 per cent.; and the Italian bankers accommodated the speculators, the Roman builders, at 6, 7, and even 8 per cent. And thus the disaster was great indeed when France, learning of Italy's alliance with Ger-

many, withdrew her 800,000,000 francs in less than two
years. The Italian banks were drained of their specie, and
the land and building companies, being likewise compelled to
reimburse their loans, were compelled to apply to the banks
of issue, those privileged to issue notes. At the same time
they intimidated the government, threatening to stop all
work and throw 40,000 artisans and labourers starving on
the pavement of Rome if it did not compel the banks of
issue to lend them the five or six millions of paper which
they needed. And this the government at last did, appalled
by the possibility of universal bankruptcy. Naturally, however, the five or six millions could not be paid back at
maturity, as the newly-built houses found neither purchasers
nor tenants; and so the great fall began, and continued with
a rush, heaping ruin upon ruin. The petty speculators fell
on the builders, the builders on the land companies, the land
companies on the banks of issue, and the latter on the public
credit, ruining the nation. And that was how a mere
municipal crisis became a frightful disaster: a whole milliard
sunk to no purpose, Rome disfigured, littered with the ruins
of the gaping and empty dwellings which had been prepared
for the five or six hundred thousand inhabitants for whom the
city yet waits in vain!

Moreover, in the breeze of glory which swept by, the
State itself took a colossal view of things. It was a question of at once making Italy triumphant and perfect, of
accomplishing in five and twenty years what other nations
have required centuries to effect. So there was feverish
activity and a prodigious outlay on canals, ports, roads, railway lines, and improvements in all the great cities. Directly
after the alliance with Germany, moreover, the military and
naval estimates began to devour millions to no purpose. And
the ever-growing financial requirements were simply met by
the issue of paper, by a fresh loan each succeeding year. In
Rome alone, too, the building of the Ministry of War cost
ten millions, that of the Ministry of Finances fifteen, whilst
a hundred was spent on the yet unfinished quays, and two
hundred and fifty were sunk on works of defence around the
city. And all this was a flare of the old hereditary pride,
springing from that soil whose sap can only blossom in
extravagant projects; the determination to dazzle and conquer
the world which comes as soon as one has climbed to the
Capitol, even though one's feet rest amidst the accumulated

dust of all the forms of human power which have there
crumbled one above the other.

'And, my dear friend,' continued Narcisse, 'if I could go
into all the stories that are current, that are whispered here
and there, you would be stupefied at the insanity which overcame the whole city amidst the terrible fever to which the
gambling passion gave rise. Folks of small account, and
fools and ignorant people were not the only ones to be ruined ;
nearly all the Roman nobles lost their ancient fortunes, their
gold and their palaces and their galleries of masterpieces,
which they owed to the munificence of the popes. The
colossal wealth which it had taken centuries of nepotism to
pile up in the hands of a few melted away like wax, in less
than ten years, in the levelling fire of modern speculation.'
Then, forgetting that he was speaking to a priest, he went on
to relate one of the whispered stories to which he had alluded :
'There's our good friend Dario, Prince Boccanera, the last of
the name, reduced to live on the crumbs which fall to him
from his uncle the Cardinal, who has little beyond his stipend
left him. Well, Dario would be a rich man had it not been
for that extraordinary affair of the Villa Montefiori. You
have heard of it, no doubt; how Prince Onofrio, Dario's
father, speculated, sold the villa grounds for ten millions,
then bought them back and built on them, and how, at last,
not only the ten millions were lost, but also all that remained
of the once colossal fortune of the Boccaneras. What you
haven't been told, however, is the secret part which Count
Prada—our Contessina's husband—played in the affair. He
was the lover of Princess Boccanera, the beautiful Flavia
Montefiori, who had brought the villa as dowry to the old
Prince. She was a very fine woman, much younger than her
husband, and it is positively said that it was through her that
Prada mastered the Prince—for she held her old doting
husband at arm's length whenever he hesitated to give a
signature or go farther into the affair of which he scented the
danger. And in all this Prada gained the millions which he
now spends, while as for the beautiful Flavia, you are aware,
no doubt, that she saved a little fortune from the wreck and
bought herself a second and much younger husband, whom
she turned into a Marquis Montefiori. In the whole affair
the only victim is our good friend Dario, who is absolutely
ruined, and wishes to marry his cousin, who is as poor as
himself. It's true that she's determined to have him, and

that it's impossible for him not to reciprocate her love. But for that he would have already married some American girl with a dowry of millions, like so many of the ruined princes, on the verge of starvation, have done; that is, unless the Cardinal and Donna Serafina had opposed such a match, which would not have been surprising, proud and stubborn as they are, anxious to preserve the purity of their old Roman blood. However, let us hope that Dario and the exquisite Benedetta will some day be happy together.'

Narcisse paused; but, after taking a few steps in silence, he added in a lower tone: 'I've a relative who picked up nearly three millions in that Villa Montefiori affair. Ah! I regret that I wasn't here in those heroic days of speculation. It must have been very amusing; and what strokes there were for a man of self-possession to make !'

However, all at once, as he raised his head, he saw before him the Quartiere dei Prati—the new district of the castle fields; and his face thereupon changed: he again became an artist, indignant with the modern abominations with which old Rome had been disfigured. His eyes paled, and a curl of his lips expressed the bitter disdain of a dreamer whose passion for the vanished centuries was sorely hurt: 'Look, look at it all !' he exclaimed. 'To think of it, in the city of Augustus, the city of Leo X, the city of eternal power and eternal beauty !'

Pierre himself was thunderstruck. The meadows of the castle of Sant' Angelo, dotted with a few poplar trees, had here formerly stretched alongside the Tiber as far as the first slopes of Monte Mario, thus supplying, to the satisfaction of artists, a foreground of greenery to the Borgo and the dome of St. Peter's. But now, amidst the white, leprous, overturned plain, there stood a town of huge, massive houses, cubes of stone-work, invariably the same, with broad streets intersecting one another at right angles. From end to end similar façades appeared, suggesting series of convents, barracks, or hospitals. Extraordinary and painful was the impression produced by this town so suddenly immobilised whilst in course of erection. It was as if on some accursed morning a wicked magician had with one touch of his wand stopped the works and emptied the noisy stone-yards, leaving the buildings in mournful abandonment. Here on one side the soil had been banked up; there deep pits dug for foundations had remained gaping, overrun with weeds.

There were houses whose walls scarcely rose above the level
of the soil; others which had been raised to a second or third
floor; others, again, which had been carried as high as was
intended, and even roofed in, suggesting skeletons or empty
cages. Then there were houses finished excepting that their
walls had not been plastered, others which had been left
without window frames, shutters, or doors; others, again,
which had their doors and shutters, but were nailed up like
coffins with not a soul inside them; and yet others which were
partly, and in a few cases fully, inhabited—animated by the
most unexpected of populations. And no words could describe
the fearful mournfulness of that City of the Sleeping Beauty,
hushed into mortal slumber before it had even lived, lying
annihilated beneath the heavy sun pending an awakening
which, likely enough, would never come.

Following his companion, Pierre walked along the broad,
deserted streets, where all was still as in a cemetery. Not a
vehicle nor a pedestrian passed by. Some streets had no
footways; weeds were covering the unpaved roads, turning
them once more into fields; and yet there were temporary
gas lamps, mere leaden pipes bound to poles, which had
been there for years. To avoid payment of the door and
window tax, the house owners had generally closed all
apertures with planks: while some houses, of which little
had been built, were surrounded by high palings for fear lest
their cellars should become the dens of all the bandits of the
district. But the most painful sight of all was that of the
young ruins, the proud, lofty structures, which, although
unfinished, were already cracking on all sides, and required
the support of an intricate arrangement of timbers to prevent
them from falling in dust upon the ground. A pang came to
one's heart as though one were in a city which some scourge
had depopulated—pestilence, war, or bombardment, of which
these gaping carcases seem to retain the mark. Then at
the thought that this was abortion, not death—that destruction would complete its work before the dreamt-of, vainly
awaited denizens would bring life to the stillborn houses,
one's melancholy deepened to hopeless discouragement. And
at each corner, moreover, there was the frightful irony of the
magnificent marble slabs which bore the names of the streets,
illustrious historical names, Gracchus, Scipio, Pliny, Pompey,
Julius Cæsar, blazing forth on those unfinished, crumbling
walls like a buffet dealt by the Past to modern incompetency.

Then Pierre was once more struck by this truth—that whosoever possesses Rome is consumed by the building frenzy, the passion for marble, the boastful desire to build and leave his monument of glory to future generations. After the Cæsars and the Popes had come the Italian Government, which was no sooner master of the city than it wished to reconstruct it, make it more splendid, more huge than it had ever been before. It was the fatal suggestion of the soil itself—the blood of Augustus rushing to the brain of these last-comers and urging them to a mad desire to make the third Rome the queen of the earth. Thence had come all the vast schemes such as the cyclopean quays and the mere ministries struggling to outvie the Colosseum; and thence had come all the new districts of gigantic houses which had sprouted like towns around the ancient city. It was not only on the castle fields, but at the Porta San Giovanni, the Porta San Lorenzo, the Villa Ludovisi, and on the heights of the Viminal and the Esquiline that unfinished, empty districts were already crumbling amidst the weeds of their deserted streets. After two thousand years of prodigious fertility the soil really seemed to be exhausted. Even as in very old fruit gardens newly planted plum and cherry trees wither and die, so the new walls, no doubt, found no life in that old dust of Rome, impoverished by the immemorial growth of so many temples, circuses, arches, basilicas, and churches. And thus the modern houses which men had sought to render fruitful, the useless, overhuge houses, swollen with hereditary ambition, had been unable to attain maturity, and remained there sterile like dry bushes on a plot of land exhausted by over-cultivation. And the frightful sadness that one felt arose from the fact that so creative and great a past had culminated in such present-day impotency—Rome, who had covered the world with indestructible monuments, now so reduced that she could only generate ruins.

'Oh, they'll be finished some day!' said Pierre.

Narcisse gazed at him in astonishment: 'For whom?'

That was the cruel question! Only by dint of patriotic enthusiasm on the morrow of the conquest had one been able to indulge in the hope of a mighty influx of population, and now singular blindness was needed for the belief that such an influx would ever take place. The past experiment seemed decisive; moreover, there was no reason why the population should double: Rome offered neither the attraction of pleasure nor

that of gain to be amassed in commerce and industry for those
she had not, nor of intensity of social and intellectual life,
since of this she seemed no longer capable. In any case, years
and years would be requisite. And, meantime, how could one
people those houses which were finished; and for whom was
one to finish those which had remained mere skeletons, falling
to pieces under sun and rain? Must they all remain there in-
definitely, some gaunt and open to every blast and others closed
and silent like tombs, in the wretched hideousness of their
inutility and abandonment? What a terrible proof of error
they offered under the radiant sky! The new masters of Rome
had made a bad start, and even if they now knew what they
ought to have done would they have the courage to undo what
they had done? Since the milliard sunk there seemed to be
definitively lost and wasted, one actually hoped for the advent
of a Nero, endowed with mighty, sovereign will, who would
take torch and pick and burn and raze everything in the
avenging name of reason and beauty.

'Ah!' resumed Narcisse, 'here are the Contessina and the
Prince.'

Benedetta had told the coachman to pull up in one of the
open spaces intersecting the deserted streets, and now along
the broad, quiet, grassy road—well fitted for a lovers' stroll—
she was approaching on Dario's arm, both of them delighted
with their outing, and no longer thinking of the sad things
which they had come to see. 'What a nice day it is!' the
Contessina gaily exclaimed as she reached Pierre and Narcisse.
'How pleasant the sunshine is! It's quite a treat to be able
to walk about a little as if one were in the country!'

Dario was the first to cease smiling at the blue sky, all
the delight of his stroll with his cousin on his arm suddenly
departing. 'My dear,' said he, 'we must go to see those
people, since you are bent on it, though it will certainly spoil
our day. But first I must take my bearings. I'm not
particularly clever, you know, in finding my way in places
where I don't care to go. Besides, this district is idiotic with
all its dead streets and dead houses, and never a face or a shop
to serve as a reminder. Still I think the place is over
yonder. Follow me; at all events, we shall see.'

The four friends then wended their way towards the central
part of the district, the part facing the Tiber, where a small
nucleus of a population had collected. The landlords turned
the few completed houses to the best advantage they could,

letting the rooms at very low rentals, and waiting patiently enough for payment. Some needy employees, some poverty-stricken families had thus installed themselves there, and in the long run contrived to pay a trifle for their accommodation. In consequence, however, of the demolition of the ancient Ghetto and the opening of the new streets by which air had been let into the Trastevere district, perfect hordes of tatter-demalions, famished and homeless, and almost without garments, had swooped upon the unfinished houses, filling them with wretchedness and vermin; and it had been necessary to tolerate this lawless occupation lest all the frightful misery should remain displayed in the public thoroughfares. And so it was to those frightful tenants that had fallen the huge four and five storied palaces, entered by monumental doorways flanked by lofty statues and having carved balconies upheld by Caryatides all along their fronts. Each family had made its choice, often closing the frameless windows with boards and the gaping doorways with rags, and occupying now an entire princely flat and now a few small rooms, according to its taste. Horrid-looking linen hung drying from the carved balconies, foul stains already degraded the white walls, and from the magnificent porches, intended for sumptuous equipages, there poured a stream of filth which rotted in stagnant pools in the roads, where there was neither pavement nor footpath.

On two occasions already Dario had caused his companions to retrace their steps. He was losing his way and becoming more and more gloomy. 'I ought to have turned to the left,' said he, ' but how is one to know amidst such a set as that ! '

Parties of verminous children were now to be seen rolling in the dust; they were wondrously dirty, almost naked, with black skins and tangled locks as coarse as horsehair. There were also women in sordid skirts and with their loose jackets unhooked. Many stood talking together in yelping voices, whilst others, seated on old chairs, with their hands on their knees, remained like that idle for hours. Not many men were met; but a few lay on the scorched grass, sleeping heavily in the sunlight. However, the stench was becoming unbearable—a stench of misery as when the human animal eschews all cleanliness to wallow in filth. And matters were made worse by the smell from a small improvised market—the emanations of the rotting fruit, cooked and sour vegetables, and stale fried fish which a few poor women had set out on the ground amidst a throng of famished, covetous children.

'Ah! well, my dear, I really don't know where it is,' all at once exclaimed the Prince, addressing his cousin. 'Be reasonable; we've surely seen enough; let's go back to the carriage.'

He was really suffering, and, as Benedetta had said, he did not know how to suffer. It seemed to him monstrous that one should sadden one's life by such an excursion as this. Life ought to be buoyant and benign under the clear sky, brightened by pleasant sights, by dance and song. And he, with his naïve egotism, had a positive horror of ugliness, poverty, and suffering, the sight of which caused him both mental and physical pain.

Benedetta shuddered even as he did, but in presence of Pierre she desired to be brave. Glancing at him, and seeing how deeply interested and compassionate he looked, she desired to persevere in her effort to sympathise with the humble and the wretched. 'No, no, Dario, we must stay. These gentlemen wish to see everything—is it not so?'

'Oh, the Rome of to-day is here,' exclaimed Pierre; 'this tells one more about it than all the promenades among the ruins and the monuments.'

'You exaggerate, my dear Abbé,' declared Narcisse. 'Still, I will admit that it is very interesting. Some of the old women are particularly expressive.'

At this moment Benedetta, seeing a superbly beautiful girl in front of her, could not restrain a cry of enraptured admiration: '*O che bellezza!*'

And then Dario, having recognised the girl, exclaimed with the same delight: 'Why, it's La Pierina; she'll show us the way.'

The girl had been following the party for a moment already without daring to approach. Her eyes, glittering with the joy of a loving slave, had at first darted towards the Prince, and then had hastily scrutinised the Contessina—not, however, with any show of jealous anger, but with an expression of affectionate submission and resigned happiness at seeing that she also was very beautiful. And the girl fully answered to the Prince's description of her—tall, sturdy, with the bust of a goddess, a real antique, a Juno of twenty, her chin somewhat prominent, her mouth and nose perfect in contour, her eyes large and full like a heifer's, and her whole face quite dazzling—gilded, so to say, by a sunflash—beneath her casque of heavy jet black hair.

'So you will show us the way?' said Benedetta, familiar and smiling, already consoled for all the surrounding ugliness by the thought that there should be such beautiful creatures in the world.

'Oh yes, signora, yes, at once!' And thereupon Pierina ran off before them, her feet in shoes which at any rate had no holes, whilst the old brown woollen dress which she wore appeared to have been recently washed and mended. One seemed to divine in her a certain coquettish care, a desire for cleanliness, which none of the others displayed; unless, indeed, it were simply that her great beauty lent radiance to her humble garments and made her appear a goddess.

'*Che bellezza! che bellezza!*' the Contessina repeated without wearying. 'That girl, Dario *mio*, is a real feast for the eyes!'

'I knew she would please you,' he quietly replied, flattered at having discovered such a beauty, and no longer talking of departure, since he could at last rest his eyes on something pleasant.

Behind them came Pierre, likewise full of admiration, whilst Narcisse spoke to him of the scrupulosity of his own tastes, which were for the rare and the subtle. 'She's beautiful, no doubt,' said he; 'but at bottom nothing can be more gross than the Roman style of beauty; there's no soul, none of the infinite in it. These girls simply have blood under their skins without ever a glimpse of heaven.'

Meantime Pierina had stopped, and with a wave of the hand directed attention to her mother, who sat on a broken box beside the lofty doorway of an unfinished mansion. She also must have once been very beautiful, but at forty she was already a wreck, with dim eyes, drawn mouth, black teeth, broadly wrinkled countenance, and huge fallen bosom. And she was also fearfully dirty, her grey wavy hair dishevelled and her skirt and jacket soiled and slit, revealing glimpses of grimy flesh. On her knees she held a sleeping infant, her last born, at whom she gazed like one overwhelmed and courageless, like a beast of burden resigned to her fate.

'*Bene, bene,*' said she, raising her head, 'it's the gentleman who came to give me a crown because he saw you crying. And he's come back to see us with some friends. Well, well, there are some good hearts in the world after all.'

Then she related their story, but in a spiritless way, without seeking to move her visitors. She was called Giacinta, it appeared, and had married a mason, one Tomaso Gozzo, by whom she had had seven children, Pierina, then Tito, a big fellow of eighteen, then four more girls, each at an interval of two years, and finally the infant, a boy, whom she now had on her lap. They had long lived in the Trastevere district, in an old house which had lately been pulled down; and their existence seemed to have then been shattered, for since they had taken refuge in the Quartiere dei Prati the crisis in the building trade had reduced Tomaso and Tito to absolute idleness, and the bead factory where Pierina had earned as much as tenpence a day—just enough to prevent them from dying of hunger—had closed its doors. At present not one of them had any work; they lived purely by chance.

'If you like to go up,' the woman added, 'you'll find Tomaso there with his brother Ambrogio, whom we've taken to live with us. They'll know better than I what to say to you. Tomaso is resting; but what else can he do? It's like Tito—he's dozing over there.'

So saying she pointed towards the dry grass amidst which lay a tall young fellow with a pronounced nose, hard mouth, and eyes as admirable as Pierina's. He had raised his head to glance suspiciously at the visitors, a fierce frown gathering on his forehead when he remarked how rapturously his sister contemplated the Prince. Then he let his head fall again, but kept his eyes open, watching the pair stealthily.

'Take the lady and gentlemen upstairs, Pierina, since they would like to see the place,' said the mother.

Other women had now drawn near shuffling along with bare feet in old shoes; bands of children, too, were swarming around; little girls but half clad, amongst whom, no doubt, were Giacinta's four. However, with their black eyes under their tangled mops they were all so much alike that only their mothers could identify them. And the whole resembled a teeming camp of misery pitched on that spot of majestic disaster, that street of palaces, unfinished yet already in ruins.

With a soft, loving smile, Benedetta turned to her cousin. 'Don't you come up,' she gently said; 'I don't desire your death, Dario *mio*. It was very good of you to come so far. Wait for me here in the pleasant sunshine: Monsieur l'Abbé and Monsieur Habert will go up with me.'

Dario began to laugh, and willingly acquiesced. Then lighting a cigarette, he walked slowly up and down, well pleased with the mildness of the atmosphere.

La Pierina had already darted into the spacious porch whose lofty, vaulted ceiling was adorned with panels displaying a rosaceous pattern. However, a veritable manure heap covered such marble slabs as had already been laid in the vestibule, whilst the steps of the monumental stone staircase with sculptured balustrade were already cracked and so grimy that they seemed almost black. On all sides appeared the greasy stains of hands ; the walls, whilst awaiting the painter and gilder, had been smeared with repulsive filth.

On reaching the spacious first floor landing, Pierina paused, and contented herself with calling through a gaping portal which lacked both door and framework : ' Father, here's a lady and two gentlemen to see you.' Then to the Contessina she added : ' It's the third room at the end.' And forthwith she herself rapidly descended the stairs, hastening back to her passion.

Benedetta and her companions passed through two large rooms, bossy with plaster under foot and having frameless windows wide open upon space ; and at last they reached a third room, where the whole Gozzo family had installed itself with the remnants it used as furniture. On the floor, where the bare iron girders showed, no boards having been laid down, were five or six leprous-looking palliasses. A long table, which was still strong, occupied the centre of the room, and here and there were a few old, damaged, straw-seated chairs mended with bits of rope. The great business had been to close two of the three windows with boards, whilst the third one and the door were screened with some old mattrass ticking studded with stains and holes.

Tomaso's face expressed the surprise of a man who is unaccustomed to visits of charity. Seated at the table, with his elbows resting on it and his chin supported by his hands, he was taking repose, as his wife Giacinta had said. He was a sturdy fellow of five and forty, bearded and long-haired ; and, in spite of all his misery and idleness, his large face had remained as serene as that of a Roman senator. However, the sight of the two foreigners—for such he at once judged Pierre and Narcisse to be, made him rise to his feet with sudden distrust. But he smiled on recognising Benedetta, and as she began to speak of Dario, and to explain the chari-

table purpose of their visit, he interrupted her: ' Yes, yes, I
know, Contessina. Oh! I well know who you are, for in my
father's time I once walled up a window at the Palazzo
Boccanera.'

Then he complaisantly allowed himself to be questioned,
telling Pierre, who was surprised, that although they were
certainly not happy, they would have found life tolerable had
they been able to work two days a week. And one could
divine that he was, at heart, fairly well content to go on short
commons, provided that he could live as he listed without
fatigue. His narrative and his manner suggested the familiar
locksmith who, on being summoned by a traveller to open
his trunk, the key of which was lost, sent word that he could
not possibly disturb himself during the hour of the siesta.
In short, there was no rent to pay, as there were plenty of
empty mansions open to the poor, and a few coppers would
have sufficed for food, easily contented and sober as one was.

' But oh, sir,' Tomaso continued, ' things were ever so
much better under the Pope. My father, a mason like myself, worked at the Vatican all his life, and even now, when I
myself get a job or two, it's always there. We were spoilt,
you see, by those ten years of busy work, when we never left
our ladders and earned as much as we pleased. Of course,
we fed ourselves better, and bought ourselves clothes, and
took such pleasure as we cared for; so that it's all the harder
nowadays to have to stint ourselves. But if you'd only
come to see us in the Pope's time! No taxes, everything to
be had for nothing, so to say—why, one merely had to let
oneself live.'

At this moment a growl arose from one of the palliasses
lying in the shade of the boarded windows, and the mason,
in his slow, quiet way, resumed: ' It's my brother Ambrogio,
who isn't of my opinion. He was with the Republicans in
'49, when he was fourteen. But it doesn't matter; we took
him with us when we heard that he was dying of hunger and
sickness in a cellar.'

The visitors could not help quivering with pity. Ambrogio
was the elder by some fifteen years; and now, though
scarcely sixty, he was already a ruin, consumed by fever, his
legs so wasted that he spent his days on his palliasse without
ever going out. Shorter and slighter, but more turbulent
than his brother, he had been a carpenter by trade. And,
despite his physical decay, he retained an extraordinary head

—the head of an apostle and martyr, at once noble and tragic in its expression, and encompassed by bristling snowy hair and beard.

'The Pope,' he growled; 'I've never spoken badly of the Pope. Yet it's his fault if tyranny continues. He alone in '49 could have given us the Republic, and then we shouldn't have been as we are now.'

Ambrogio had known Mazzini, whose vague religiosity remained in him—the dream of a Republican pope at last establishing the reign of liberty and fraternity. But later on his passion for Garibaldi had disturbed these views, and led him to regard the Papacy as worthless, incapable of achieving human freedom. And so, between the dream of his youth and the stern experience of his life, he now hardly knew in which direction the truth lay. Moreover, he had never acted save under the impulse of violent emotion, but contented himself with fine words—vague, indeterminate wishes.

'Brother Ambrogio,' replied Tomaso, all tranquillity, 'the Pope is the Pope, and wisdom lies in putting oneself on his side, because he will always be the Pope—that is to say, the stronger. For my part, if we had to vote to-morrow I'd vote for him.'

Calmed by the shrewd prudence characteristic of his race, the old carpenter made no haste to reply. At last he said, 'Well, as for me, brother Tomaso, I should vote against him— always against him. And you know very well that we should have the majority. The Pope-King indeed! That's all over. The very Borgo would revolt. Still, I won't say that we oughtn't to come to an understanding with him, so that everybody's religion may be respected.'

Pierre listened, deeply interested, and at last ventured to ask: 'Are there many socialists among the Roman working classes?'

This time the answer came after a yet longer pause. 'Socialists? Yes, there are some, no doubt, but much fewer than in other places. All those things are novelties which impatient fellows go in for without understanding much about them. We old men, we were for liberty; we don't believe in fire and massacre.'

Then, fearing to say too much in presence of that lady and those gentlemen, Ambrogio began to moan on his pallet, whilst the Contessina, somewhat upset by the smell of the place, took her departure, after telling the young priest that it would be best for them to leave their alms with the wife downstairs. Meantime Tomaso resumed his seat at the table, again letting his chin rest on his hands as he nodded to his visitors, no more impressed by their departure than he had been by their arrival : ' To the pleasure of seeing you again, and am happy to have been able to oblige you.'

On the threshold, however, Narcisse's enthusiasm burst forth ; he turned to cast a final admiring glance at old Ambrogio's head, ' a perfect masterpiece,' which he continued praising whilst he descended the stairs.

Down below Giacinta was still sitting on the broken box with her infant across her lap, and a few steps away Pierina stood in front of Dario, watching him with an enchanted air whilst he finished his cigarette. Tito, lying low in the grass like an animal on the watch for prey, did not for a moment cease to gaze at them.

' Ah, signora ! ' resumed the woman, in her resigned, doleful voice, ' the place is hardly inhabitable, as you must have seen. The only good thing is that one gets plenty of room. But there are draughts enough to kill me, and I'm always so afraid of the children falling down some of the holes.'

Thereupon she related a story of a woman who had lost her life through mistaking a window for a door one evening and falling headlong into the street. Then, too, a little girl had broken both arms by tumbling from a staircase which had no banisters. And you could die there without anybody knowing how bad you were and coming to help you. Only the previous day the corpse of an old man had been found lying on the plaster in a lonely room. Starvation must have killed him quite a week previously, yet he would still have been stretched there if the odour of his remains had not attracted the attention of neighbours.

' If one only had something to eat, things wouldn't be so bad ! ' continued Giacinta. ' But it's dreadful when there's a baby to suckle and one gets no food, for after a while one has no milk. This little fellow wants his titty and gets angry with me because I can't give him any. But it isn't my fault. He has sucked me till the blood came, and all I can do is to cry.'

As she spoke, tears welled into her poor dim eyes. But all at once she flew into a tantrum with Tito, who was still wallowing in the grass like an animal instead of rising by

way of civility towards those fine people, who would surely
leave her some alms. 'Eh! Tito, you lazy fellow, can't you
get up when people come to see you?' she called.

After some pretence of not hearing, the young fellow at
last rose with an air of great ill-humour; and Pierre, feeling
interested in him, tried to draw him out as he had done with
the father and uncle upstairs. But Tito only returned curt
answers, as if both bored and suspicious. Since there was no
work to be had, said he, the only thing was to sleep. It was
of no use to get angry; that wouldn't alter matters. So the
best was to live as one could without increasing one's worry.
As for socialists—well, yes, perhaps there were a few, but he
didn't know any. And his weary, indifferent manner made
it quite clear that, if his father was for the Pope and his uncle
for the Republic, he himself was for nothing at all. In this
Pierre divined the end of a nation, or rather the slumber of a
nation in which democracy has not yet awakened. However,
as the priest continued, asking Tito his age, what school he
had attended, and in what district he had been born, the
young man suddenly cut the questions short by pointing with
one finger to his breast and saying gravely, '*Io son' Romano
di Roma.*'

And, indeed, did not that answer everything? 'I am a
Roman of Rome.' Pierre smiled sadly and spoke no further.
Never had he more fully realised the pride of that race, the
long descending inheritance of glory which was so heavy to
bear. The sovereign vanity of the Cæsars lived anew in that
degenerate young fellow who was scarcely able to read and
write. Starveling though he was, he knew his city, and could
instinctively have recounted the grand pages of its history.
The names of the great emperors and great popes were familiar
to him. And why should men toil and moil when they had been
the masters of the world? Why not live nobly and idly in
the most beautiful of cities, under the most beautiful of skies?
'*Io son' Romano di Roma!*'

Benedetta had slipped her alms into the mother's hand,
and Pierre and Narcisse were following her example when
Dario, who had already done so, thought of Pierina. He did
not like to offer her money, but a pretty, fanciful idea occurred
to him. Lightly touching his lips with his finger-tips, he said,
with a faint laugh, 'For beauty!'

There was something really pretty and pleasing in the kiss
thus wafted with a slightly mocking laugh by that familiar,

good-natured young Prince who, as in some love story of the olden time, was touched by the beautiful bead-worker's mute adoration. Pierina flushed with pleasure, and, losing her head, darted upon Dario's hand and pressed her warm lips to it with unthinking impulsiveness, in which there was as much divine gratitude as tender passion. But Tito's eyes flashed with anger at the sight, and, brutally seizing his sister by the skirt, he threw her back, growling between his teeth, ' None of that, you know, or I'll kill you, and him too ! '

It was high time for the visitors to depart, for other women, scenting the presence of money, were now coming forward with outstretched hands, or despatching tearful children in their stead. The whole wretched, abandoned district was in a flutter, a distressful wail ascended from those lifeless streets with high resounding names. But what was to be done ? One could not give to all. So the only course lay in flight— amidst deep sadness as one realised how powerless was charity in presence of such appalling want.

When Benedetta and Dario had reached their carriage they hastened to take their seats and nestle side by side, glad to escape from all such horrors. Still the Contessina was well pleased with her bravery in the presence of Pierre, whose hand she pressed with the emotion of a pupil touched by the master's lesson, after Narcisse had told her that he meant to take the young priest to lunch at the little restaurant on the Piazza of St. Peter's, whence one obtained such an interesting view of the Vatican.

' Try some of the light white wine of Genzano,' said Dario, who had become quite gay again. ' There's nothing better to drive away the blues.'

However, Pierre's curiosity was insatiable, and on the way he again questioned Narcisse about the people of modern Rome, their life, habits, and manners. There was little or no education, he learnt; no large manufactures and no export trade existed. The men carried on the few trades that were current, all consumption being virtually limited to the city itself. Among the women there were bead-workers and embroiderers ; and the manufacture of religious articles, such as medals and chaplets, and of certain popular jewellery had always occupied a fair number of hands. But after marriage the women, invariably burdened with numerous offspring, attempted little beyond household work. Briefly, the population took life as it came, working just sufficiently to secure

food, contenting itself with vegetables, pastes, and scraggy
mutton, without thought of rebellion or ambition. The only
vices were gambling and a partiality for the red and white
wines of the Roman province—wines which excited to quarrel
and murder, and on the evenings of feast days, when the
taverns emptied, strewed the streets with groaning men,
slashed and stabbed with knives. The girls, however, but
seldom went wrong; one could count those who allowed themselves to be seduced; and this arose from the great union
prevailing in each family, every member of which bowed
submissively to the father's absolute authority. Moreover,
the brothers watched over their sisters even as Tito did over
Pierina, guarding them fiercely for the sake of the family
honour. And amidst all this there was no real religion, but
simply a childish idolatry, all hearts going forth to the Madonna
and the Saints, who alone were entreated and regarded
as having being: for it never occurred to anybody to think of
God.

Thus the stagnation of the lower orders could easily be
understood. Behind them were the many centuries during
which idleness had been encouraged, vanity flattered, and
nerveless life willingly accepted. When they were neither
masons, nor carpenters, nor bakers, they were servants
serving the priests, and more or less directly in the pay of
the Vatican. Thence sprang the two antagonistic parties, on
the one hand the more numerous party composed of the old
Carbonari, Mazzinians, and Garibaldians, the *élite* of the
Trastevere; and on the other the 'clients' of the Vatican,
all who lived on or by the Church and regretted the Pope-
King. But, after all, the antagonism was confined to opinions;
there was no thought of making an effort or incurring a risk.
For that, some sudden flare of passion, strong enough to
overcome the sturdy calmness of the race, would have been
needed. But what would have been the use of it? The
wretchedness had lasted for so many centuries, the sky was
so blue, the siesta preferable to aught else during the hot
hours! And only one thing seemed positive—that the majority
was certainly in favour of Rome remaining the capital of
Italy. Indeed, rebellion had almost broken out in the Leonine
City when the cession of the latter to the Holy See was
rumoured. As for the increase of want and poverty, this was
largely due to the circumstance that the Roman workman
had really gained nothing by the many works carried on in

his city during fifteen years. First of all, over 40,000 provincials, mostly from the North, more spirited and resistant than himself, and working at cheaper rates, had invaded Rome; and when he, the Roman, had secured his share of the labour, he had lived in better style, without thought of economy; so that after the crisis, when the 40,000 men from the provinces were sent home again, he had found himself once more in a dead city where trade was always slack. And thus he had relapsed into his antique indolence, at heart well pleased at no longer being hustled by press of work, and again accommodating himself as best he could to his old mistress, want, empty in pocket yet always a *grand seigneur*.

However, Pierre was struck by the great difference between the want and wretchedness of Rome and Paris. In Rome the destitution was certainly more complete, the food more loathsome, the dirt more repulsive. Yet at the same time the Roman poor retained more ease of manner and more real gaiety. The young priest thought of the fireless, breadless poor of Paris, shivering in their hovels at winter time; and suddenly he understood. The destitution of Rome did not know cold. What a sweet and eternal consolation; a sun for ever bright, a sky for ever blue and benign out of charity to the wretched! And what mattered the vileness of the dwelling if one could sleep under the sky, fanned by the warm breeze? What mattered even hunger if the family could await the windfall of chance in sunlit streets or on the scorched grass? The climate induced sobriety; there was no need of alcohol or red meat to enable one to face treacherous fogs. Blissful idleness smiled on the golden evenings, poverty became like the enjoyment of liberty in that delightful atmosphere where the happiness of living seemed to be all sufficient. Narcisse told Pierre that at Naples, in the narrow odoriferous streets of the port and Santa Lucia districts, the people spent virtually their whole lives out of doors, gay, childish, and ignorant, seeking nothing beyond the few pence that were needed to buy food. And it was certainly the climate which fostered the prolonged infancy of the nation, which explained why such a democracy did not awaken to social ambition and consciousness of itself. No doubt the poor of Naples and Rome suffered from want; but they did not know the rancour which cruel winter implants in men's hearts, the dark rancour which one feels on shivering with cold while rich people are warming themselves before blazing fires.

They did not know the infuriated reveries in snow-swept hovels, when the guttering dip burns low, the passionate need which then comes upon one to wreak justice, to revolt, as from a sense of duty, in order that one may save wife and children from consumption, in order that they also may have a warm nest where life shall be a possibility! Ah! the want that shivers with the bitter cold—therein lies the excess of social injustice, the most terrible of schools, where the poor learn to realise their sufferings, where they are roused to indignation, and swear to make those sufferings cease, even if in doing so they annihilate all olden society!

And in that same clemency of the southern heavens Pierre also found an explanation of the life of St. Francis,[1] that divine mendicant of love who roamed the highroads extolling the charms of poverty. Doubtless he was an unconscious revolutionary, protesting against the overflowing luxury of the Roman Court by his return to the love of the humble, the simplicity of the primitive Church. But such a revival of innocence and sobriety would never have been possible in a northern land. The enchantment of nature, the frugality of a people whom the sunlight nourished, the benignity of mendicancy on roads for ever warm, were needed to effect it. And yet how was it possible that a St. Francis, glowing with brotherly love, could have appeared in a land which nowadays so seldom practises charity, which treats the lowly so harshly and contemptuously, and cannot even bestow alms on its own Pope? Is it because ancient pride ends by hardening all hearts, or because the experience of very old races leads finally to egotism, that one now beholds Italy seemingly benumbed amidst dogmatic and pompous Catholicism, whilst the return to the ideals of the gospel, the passionate interest in the poor and the suffering comes from the woeful plains of the North, from the nations whose sunlight is so limited? Yes, doubtless all that has much to do with the change, and the success of St. Francis was in particular due to the circumstance that, after so gaily espousing his lady, Poverty, he was able to lead her, barefooted and scarcely clad, during endless and delightful springtides, among communities whom an ardent need of love and compassion then consumed.

While conversing, Pierre and Narcisse had reached the

---

[1] St. Francis of Assisi, the founder of the famous order of mendicant friars.—*Trans.*

Piazza of St. Peter's, and they sat down at one of the little
tables skirting the pavement outside the restaurant where
they had lunched once before. The linen was none too clean,
but the view was splendid. The basilica rose up in front of
them, and the Vatican on the right, above the majestic curve
of the colonnade. Just as the waiter was bringing the *hors-
d'œuvre*, some *finocchio* [1] and anchovies, the young priest,
who had fixed his eyes on the Vatican, raised an exclamation
to attract Narcisse's attention: 'Look, my friend, at that
window, which I am told is the Holy Father's. Can't you
distinguish a pale figure standing there, quite motionless?'

The young man began to laugh. 'Oh! well,' said he,
'it must be the Holy Father in person. You are so anxious
to see him that your very anxiety conjures him into your
presence.'

'But I assure you,' repeated Pierre, 'that he is over there
behind the window-pane. There is a white figure looking this
way.'

Narcisse, who was very hungry, began to eat whilst still
indulging in banter. All at once, however, he exclaimed:
'Well, my dear Abbé, as the Pope is looking at us, this is the
moment to speak of him. I promised to tell you how he sank
several millions of St. Peter's Patrimony in the frightful
financial crisis of which you have just seen the ruins; and,
indeed, your visit to the new district of the castle fields would
not be complete without this story by way of appendix.'

Thereupon, without losing a mouthful, Narcisse spoke at
considerable length. At the death of Pius IX. the Patrimony
of St. Peter, it seemed, had exceeded twenty millions of francs.
Cardinal Antonelli, who speculated, and whose ventures were
usually successful, had for a long time left a part of this money
with the Rothschilds and a part in the hands of different
nuncios, who turned it to profit abroad. After Antonelli's
death, however, his successor, Cardinal Simeoni, withdrew the
money from the nuncios to invest it at Rome; and Leo XIII
on his accession entrusted the administration of the Patrimony
to a commission of cardinals, of which Monsignor Folchi was
appointed secretary. This prelate, who for twelve years
played such an important *rôle*, was the son of an employee of
the Dataria, who, thanks to skilful financial operations, had

[1] Fennel-root, eaten raw; a favourite 'appetiser' in Rome during the
spring and autumn.—*Trans.*

left a fortune of a million francs. Monsignor Folchi inherited
his father's cleverness, and revealed himself to be a financier
of the first rank in such wise that the commission gradually
relinquished its powers to him, letting him act exactly as he
pleased and contenting itself with approving the reports which
he laid before it at each meeting. The Patrimony, however,
yielded scarcely more than a million francs per annum, and,
as the expenditure amounted to seven millions, six had to be
found. Accordingly, from that other source of income, the
Peter's Pence, the Pope annually gave three million francs to
Monsignor Folchi, who, by skilful speculations and investments,
was able to double them every year, and thus provide for all
disbursements without ever breaking into the capital of the
Patrimony.

In the earlier times he realised considerable profit by
gambling in land in and about Rome. He took shares also in
many new enterprises, speculated in mills, omnibuses, and
water-services, without mentioning all the gambling in which
he participated with the Banca di Roma, a Catholic institution. Wonderstruck by his skill, the Pope, who, on his own
side, had hitherto speculated through the medium of a confidential employee named Sterbini, dismissed the latter, and
entrusted Monsignor Folchi with the duty of turning his money
to profit in the same way as he turned that of the Holy See.
This was the climax of the prelate's favour, the apogee of his
power. Bad days were dawning, things were tottering already,
and the great collapse was soon to come, sudden and swift like
lightning. One of Leo XIII's practices was to lend large sums
to the Roman princes who, seized with the gambling frenzy,
and mixed up in land and building speculations, were at a loss
for money. To guarantee the Pope's advances they deposited
shares with him, and thus, when the downfall came, he was
left with heaps of worthless paper on his hands. Then
another disastrous affair was an attempt to found a house of
credit in Paris in view of working off the shares which could
not be disposed of in Italy among the French aristocracy and
religious people. To egg these on it was said that the Pope
was interested in the venture ; and the worst was that he
dropped three millions of francs in it.[1] The situation then

[1] The allusion is evidently to the famous Union Générale, on which
the Pope bestowed his apostolic benediction, and with which M. Zola
deals at length in his novel *Money*. Certainly a very brilliant idea was
embodied in the Union Générale, that of establishing a great inter-

became the more critical as he had gradually risked all the
money he disposed of in the terrible agiotage going on in
Rome, tempted thereto by the prospect of huge profits and
perhaps indulging in the hope that he might win back by
money the city which had been torn from him by force. His
own responsibility remained complete, for Monsignor Folchi
never made an important venture without consulting him;
and he must have been therefore the real artisan of the
disaster, mastered by his passion for gain, his desire to endow
the Church with a huge capital, that great source of power in
modern times. As always happens, however, the prelate was
the only victim. He had become imperious and difficult to
deal with; and was no longer liked by the cardinals of the
commission, who were merely called together to approve such
transactions as he chose to entrust to them. So, when the
crisis came, a plot was laid; the cardinals terrified the Pope
by telling him of all the evil rumours which were current, and
then forced Monsignor Folchi to render a full account of his
speculations. The situation proved to be very bad; it was no
longer possible to avoid heavy losses. And so Monsignor
Folchi was disgraced, and since then has vainly solicited an
audience of Leo XIII, who has always refused to receive him,
as if determined to punish him for their common fault—that
passion for lucre which blinded them both. Very pious and
submissive, however, Monsignor Folchi has never complained,
but has kept his secrets and bowed to fate. Nobody can say
exactly how many millions the Patrimony of St. Peter lost
when Rome was changed into a gambling-hell, but if some
prelates only admit ten, others go as far as thirty. The probability is that the loss was about fifteen millions.[1]

Whilst Narcisse was giving this account he and Pierre
had despatched their cutlets and tomatoes, and the waiter was
now serving them some fried chicken. 'At the present time,'
said Narcisse by way of conclusion, 'the gap has been filled
up; I told you of the large sums yielded by the Peter's Pence
fund, the amount of which is only known by the Pope, who

national Catholic bank which would destroy the Jewish financial auto-
cracy throughout Europe, and provide both the papacy and the Legitimist
cause in several countries with the sinews of war. But in the battle
which ensued the great Jew financial houses proved the stronger, and
the disaster which overtook the Catholic speculators was a terrible one.—
Trans.

[1] That is 600,000l.

alone fixes its employment. And, by the way, he isn't cured of speculating : I know from a good source that he still gambles, though with more prudence. Moreover, his confidential assistant is still a prelate. And, when all is said, my dear Abbé, he's in the right : a man must belong to his times—dash it all ! '

Pierre had listened with growing surprise, in which terror and sadness mingled. Doubtless such things were natural, even legitimate ; yet he, in his dream of a pastor of souls free from all terrestrial cares, had never imagined that they existed. What ! the Pope—the spiritual father of the lowly and the suffering—had speculated in land and in stocks and shares ! He had gambled, placed funds in the hands of Jew bankers, practised usury, extracted hard interest from money—he, the successor of the Apostle, the Pontiff of Christ, the representative of Jesus of the Gospel, that divine friend of the poor ! And, besides, what a painful contrast : so many millions stored away in those rooms of the Vatican, and so many millions working and fructifying, constantly being diverted from one speculation to another in order that they might yield the more gain ; and then down below, near at hand, so much want and misery in those abominable unfinished buildings of the new districts, so many poor folks dying of hunger amidst filth, mothers without milk for their babes, men reduced to idleness by lack of work, old ones at the last gasp like beasts of burden who are pole-axed when they are of no more use ! Ah ! God of Charity, God of Love, was it possible ! The Church doubtless had material wants ; she could not live without money ; prudence and policy had dictated the thought of gaining for her such a treasure as would enable her to fight her adversaries victoriously. But how grievously this wounded one's feelings, how it soiled the Church, how she descended from her divine throne to become nothing but a party, a vast international association organised for the purpose of conquering and possessing the world !

And the more Pierre thought of the extraordinary adventure the greater was his astonishment. Could a more unexpected, startling drama be imagined ? That Pope shutting himself up in his palace—a prison, no doubt, but one whose hundred windows overlooked immensity ; that Pope who, at all hours of the day and night, in every season, could from his window see his capital, the city which had been stolen from him, and the restitution of which he never ceased

to demand; that Pope who, day by day, beheld the changes
effected in the city—the opening of new streets, the demolition
of ancient districts, the sale of land, and the gradual erection
of new buildings which ended by forming a white girdle
around the old ruddy roofs; that Pope who, in presence of this
daily spectacle, this building frenzy, which he could follow
from morn till eve, was himself finally overcome by the
gambling passion, and, secluded in his closed chamber, began
to speculate on the embellishments of his old capital, seeking
wealth in the spurt of work and trade brought about by that
very Italian Government which he reproached with spoliation;
and finally that Pope losing millions in a catastrophe which
he ought to have desired, but had been unable to foresee! No,
never had dethroned monarch yielded to a stranger idea,
compromised himself in a more tragical venture, the result of
which fell upon him like divine punishment. And it was no
mere king who had done this, but the delegate of God, the
man who, in the eyes of idolatrous Christendom, was the
living manifestation of the Deity!

Dessert had now been served—a goat's cheese and some
fruit—and Narcisse was just finishing some grapes when, on
raising his eyes, he in turn exclaimed: 'Well, you are quite
right, my dear Abbé, I myself can see a pale figure at the
window of the Holy Father's room.'

Pierre, who scarcely took his eyes from the window,
answered slowly: 'Yes, yes, it went away, but has just come
back, and stands there white and motionless.'

'Well, after all, what would you have the Pope do?'
resumed Narcisse with his languid air. 'He's like everybody
else; he looks out of the window when he wants a little distraction, and certainly there's plenty for him to look at.'

The same idea had occurred to Pierre, and was filling him
with emotion. People talked of the Vatican being closed, and
pictured a dark, gloomy palace, encompassed by high walls,
whereas this palace overlooked all Rome, and the Pope from
his window could see the world. Pierre himself had viewed
the panorama from the summit of the Janiculum, the *loggie*
of Raffaelle, and the dome of St. Peter's, and so he well knew
what it was that Leo XIII was able to behold. In the centre
of the vast desert of the Campagna, bounded by the Sabine
and Alban mountains, the seven illustrious hills appeared to
him with their trees and edifices. His eyes ranged also over
all the basilicas, Santa Maria Maggiore, San Giovanni in

Laterano, the cradle of the papacy, San Paolo fuori-le-Mura, Santa Croce in Gerusalemme, Sant' Agnese, and the others; they beheld, too, the domes of the Gesù, of Sant' Andrea della Valle, San Carlo and San Giovanni dei Fiorentini, and indeed all those four hundred churches of Rome which make the city like a *campo santo* studded with crosses. And Leo XIII could moreover see the famous monuments testifying to the pride of successive centuries—the castle of Sant' Angelo, that imperial mausoleum which was transformed into a papal fortress, the distant white line of the tombs of the Appian Way, the scattered ruins of the baths of Caracalla and the abode of Septimius Severus; and then, after the innumerable columns, porticoes, and triumphal arches, there were the palaces and villas of the sumptuous cardinals of the Renascence, the Palazzo Farnese, the Palazzo Borghese, the Villa Medici, and others, amidst a swarming of façades and roofs. But, in particular, just under his window, on the left, the Pope was able to see the abominations of the unfinished district of the castle fields. In the afternoon, when he strolled through his gardens, bastioned by the wall of the fourth Leo like the plateau of a citadel, his view stretched over the ravaged valley at the foot of Monte Mario, where so many brickworks were established during the building frenzy. The green slopes are still ripped up, yellow trenches intersect them in all directions, and the closed works and factories have become wretched ruins with lofty, black, and smokeless chimneys. And at any other hour of the day Leo XIII could not approach his window without beholding the abandoned houses for which all those brickfields had worked, those houses which had died before they even lived, and where there was now nought but the swarming misery of Rome, rotting there like some decomposition of olden society.

However, Pierre more particularly thought of Leo XIII forgetting the rest of the city to let his thoughts dwell on the Palatine, now bereft of its crown of palaces and rearing only its black cypresses towards the blue heavens. Doubtless in his mind he rebuilt the palaces of the Cæsars, whilst before him rose great shadowy forms arrayed in purple, visions of his real ancestors, those emperors and supreme pontiffs who alone could tell him how one might reign over every nation and be the absolute master of the world. Then, however, his glances strayed to the Quirinal, and there he could contemplate the new and neighbouring royalty. How strange the meeting of those two palaces, the Quirinal and the Vatican, which rise up and gaze at one another across the Rome of the Middle Ages and the Renascence, whose roofs, baked and gilded by the burning sun, are jumbled in confusion alongside the Tiber. When the Pope and the King go to their windows they can with a mere opera-glass see each other quite distinctly. True, they are but specks in the boundless immensity, and what a gulf there is between them—how many centuries of history, how many generations that battled and suffered, how much departed greatness, and how much new seed for the mysterious future! Still, they can see one another, and they are yet waging the eternal fight, the fight as to which of them—the pontiff and shepherd of the soul or the monarch and master of the body—shall possess the people whose stream rolls beneath them, and in the result remain the absolute sovereign. And Pierre wondered also what might be the thoughts and dreams of Leo XIII behind those window panes where he still fancied he could distinguish his pale, ghostly figure. On surveying new Rome, the ravaged olden districts and the new ones laid waste by the blast of disaster, the Pope must certainly rejoice at the colossal failure of the Italian Government. His city had been stolen from him; the new comers had virtually declared that they would show him how a great capital was created, and their boast had ended in that catastrophe—a multitude of hideous and useless buildings which they did not even know how to finish! He, the Pope, could moreover only be delighted with the terrible worries into which the usurping *régime* had fallen, the political crisis and the financial crisis, the whole growing national unrest amidst which that *régime* seemed likely to sink some day; and yet did not he himself possess a patriotic soul, was he not a loving son of that Italy whose genius and ancient ambition coursed in the blood of his veins? Ah! no, nothing against Italy; rather everything that would enable her to become once more the mistress of the world. And so, even amidst the joy of hope, he must have been grieved to see her thus ruined, threatened with bankruptcy, displaying like a sore that overturned, unfinished Rome which was a confession of her impotency. But, on the other hand, if the House of Savoy were to be swept away, would he not be there to take its place, and at last resume possession of his capital, which, from his window, for fifteen years past, he had beheld in the grip of masons and demolishers? And then he would again

be the master and reign over the world, enthroned in the predestined city to which prophecy has ensured eternity and universal dominion.

But the horizon spread out, and Pierre wondered what
Leo XIII beheld beyond Rome, beyond the Campagna and the
Sabine and Alban mountains. What had he seen for eighteen
years past from that window whence he obtained his only
view of the world ? What echoes of modern society, its
truths and certainties, had reached his ears ? From the heights
of the Viminal, where the railway terminus stands, the prolonged
whistling of engines must have occasionally been carried
towards him, suggesting our scientific civilisation, the nations
brought nearer together, free humanity marching on towards
the future. Did he himself ever dream of liberty when, on
turning to the right, he pictured the sea over yonder, past the
tombs of the Appian Way ? Had he ever desired to go off,
quit Rome and her traditions and found the Papacy of the
new democracies elsewhere ? As he was said to possess so
clear and penetrating a mind he ought to have understood and
trembled at the far-away stir and noise that came from certain
lands of battle, from those United States of America, for
instance, where revolutionary bishops were conquering, winning over the people. Were they working for him or for
themselves ? If he could not follow them, if he remained
stubborn within his Vatican, bound on every side by dogma
and tradition, might not rupture some day become unavoidable ?
And, indeed, the fear of a blast of schism, coming from afar,
must have filled him with growing anguish. It was assuredly
on that account that he had practised the diplomacy of conciliation, seeking to unite in his hands all the scattered forces
of the Church, overlooking the audacious proceedings of
certain bishops as far as possible, and himself striving to gain
the support of the people by putting himself on its side
against the fallen monarchies. But would he ever go any
farther ? Shut up in that Vatican, behind that bronze
portal, was he not bound to the strict formulas of Catholicism,
chained to them by the force of centuries ? There obstinacy
was fated ; it was impossible for him to resign himself to that
which was his real and surpassing power, the purely spiritual
power, the moral authority which brought mankind to his
feet, made thousands of pilgrims kneel and women swoon.
Departure from Rome and the renunciation of the temporal
power would not displace the centre of the Catholic world,

but would transform him, the head of the Catholic Church, into the head of something else. And how anxious must have been his thoughts if the evening breeze ever brought him a vague presentiment of that something else, a fear of the new religion which was yet dimly, confusedly dawning amidst the tramp of the nations on the march, and the sound of which must have reached him at one and the same time from every point of the compass.

At this precise moment, however, Pierre felt that the white and motionless shadow behind those window panes was held erect by pride, by the ever present conviction of victory. If man could not achieve it, a miracle would intervene. He, the Pope, was absolutely convinced that he or some successor would recover possession of Rome. Had not the Church all eternity before it ? And, moreover, why should not the victor be himself ? Could not God accomplish the impossible ? Why, if it so pleased God, on the very morrow his city would be restored to him, in spite of all the objections of human reason, all the apparent logic of facts. Ah ! how he would welcome the return of that prodigal daughter whose equivocal adventures he had ever watched with tears bedewing his paternal eyes ! He would soon forget the excesses which he had beheld during eighteen years at all hours and in all seasons. Perhaps he dreamt of what he would do with those new districts with which the city had been soiled. Should they be razed, or left as evidence of the insanity of the usurpers ? At all events, Rome would again become the august and lifeless city, disdainful of such vain matters as material cleanliness and comfort, and shining forth upon the world like a pure soul encompassed by the traditional glory of the centuries. And his dream continued, picturing the course which events would take on the very morrow, no doubt. Anything, even a republic was preferable to that House of Savoy. Why not a federal republic, reviving the old political divisions of Italy, restoring Rome to the Church, and choosing him, the Pope, as the natural protector of the country thus re-organised ? But his eyes travelled beyond Rome and Italy, and his dream expanded, embracing republican France, Spain which might become republican again, Austria which would some day be won, and indeed all the Catholic nations welded into the United States of Europe, and fraternising in peace under his high presidency as Sovereign Pontiff. And then would follow the supreme triumph, all the other Churches at last vanishing, and all the dissident communities coming to him as to the one and only pastor, who would reign in the name of Jesus over the universal democracy.

However, whilst Pierre was immersed in this dream which he attributed to Leo XIII, he was all at once interrupted by Narcisse, who exclaimed: 'Oh! my dear Abbé, just look at those statues on the colonnade.' The young fellow had ordered a cup of coffee and was languidly smoking a cigar, deep once more in the subtle æsthetics which were his only preoccupation. 'They are rosy, are they not?' he continued; 'rosy, with a touch of mauve, as if the blue blood of angels circulated in their stone veins. It is the sun of Rome which gives them that supra-terrestrial life; for they live, my friend; I have seen them smile and hold out their arms to me during certain fine sunsets. Ah! Rome, marvellous, delicious Rome! One could live here as poor as Job, content with the very atmosphere, and in everlasting delight at breathing it!'

This time Pierre could not help feeling surprised at Narcisse's language, for he remembered his incisive voice and clear, precise, financial acumen when speaking of money matters. And, at this recollection, the young priest's mind reverted to the castle fields, and intense sadness filled his heart as for the last time all the want and suffering rose before him. Again he beheld the horrible filth which was tainting so many human beings, that shocking proof of the abominable social injustice which condemns the greater number to lead the joyless, breadless lives of accursed beasts. And as his glance returned yet once more to the window of the Vatican, and he fancied he could see a pale hand uplifted behind the glass-panes, he thought of that papal benediction which Leo XIII gave from that height, over Rome, and over the plain and the hills, to the faithful of all Christendom. And that papal benediction suddenly seemed to him a mockery, destitute of all power, since throughout such a multitude of centuries it had not once been able to stay a single one of the sufferings of mankind, and could not even bring a little justice for those poor wretches who were agonising yonder beneath the very window.

IX

THAT evening at dusk, as Benedetta had sent Pierre word that she desired to see him, he went down to her little *salon*, and there found her chatting with Celia.

'I've seen your Pierina, you know,' exclaimed the latter, just as the young priest came in. 'And with Dario, too. Or rather, she must have been watching for him; he found her waiting in a path on the Pincio and smiled at her. I understood at once. What a beauty she is!'

Benedetta smiled at her friend's enthusiasm; but her lips twitched somewhat painfully, for, however sensible she might be, this passion, which she realised to be so naïve and so strong, was beginning to make her suffer. She certainly made allowances for Dario, but the girl was too much in love with him, and she feared the consequences. Even in turning the conversation she allowed the secret of her heart to escape her. 'Pray sit down, Monsieur l'Abbé,' she said, 'we are talking scandal, you see. My poor Dario is accused of making love to every pretty woman in Rome. People say that it's he who gives La Tonietta those white roses which she has been exhibiting at the Corso every afternoon for a fortnight past.'

'That's certain, my dear,' retorted Celia impetuously. 'At first people were in doubt, and talked of little Pontecorvo and Lieutenant Moretta. But everyone now knows that La Tonietta's caprice is Dario. Besides, he joined her in her box at the Costanzi the other evening.'

Pierre remembered that the young Prince had pointed out La Tonietta at the Pincio one afternoon. She was one of the few *demi-mondaines* that the higher class society of Rome took an interest in. For a month or so the rich Englishman to whom she owed her means had been absent, travelling.

'Ah!' resumed Benedetta, whose budding jealousy was entirely confined to La Pierina, 'so my poor Dario is ruining himself in white roses! Well, I shall have to twit him about it. But one or another of these beauties will end by robbing me of him if our affairs are not soon settled. Fortunately, I have had some better news. Yes, my suit is to be taken in hand again, and my aunt has gone out to-day on that very account.'

Then, as Victorine came in with a lamp, and Celia rose to depart, Benedetta turned towards Pierre, who also was rising from his chair: 'Please stay,' said she; 'I wish to speak to you.'

However, Celia still lingered, interested by the mention of the divorce suit, and eager to know if the cousins would soon be able to marry. And at last, throwing her arms round Benedetta, she kissed her passionately. 'So you are hopeful,

my dear,' she exclaimed. 'You think that the Holy Father
will give you back your liberty? Oh! I am so pleased; it
will be so nice for you to marry Dario! And I'm well pleased
on my own account, for my father and mother are beginning
to yield. Only yesterday I said to them with that quiet little
air of mine, "I want Attilio, and you must give him me." And
then my father flew into a furious passion and upbraided me,
and shook his fist at me, saying that if he'd made my head as
hard as his own he would know how to break it. My mother
was there quite silent and vexed, and all at once he turned to
her and said: "Here, give her that Attilio she wants, and
then perhaps we shall have some peace!" Oh yes! I'm well
pleased, very well pleased indeed!'

As she spoke her pure virginal face beamed with so much
innocent, celestial joy that Pierre and Benedetta could not
help laughing. And at last she went off attended by a maid
who had waited for her in the first *salon*.

When they were alone Benedetta made the priest sit down
again: 'I have been asked to give you some important advice,
my friend,' she said. 'It seems that the news of your
presence in Rome is spreading, and that bad reports of you are
circulated. Your book is said to be a fierce appeal to schism,
and you are spoken of as a mere ambitious, turbulent schismatic.
After publishing your book in Paris you have come to Rome,
it is said, to raise a fearful scandal over it in order to make it
sell. Now, if you still desire to see his Holiness, so as to
plead your cause before him, you are advised to make people
forget you, to disappear altogether for a fortnight or three
weeks.'

Pierre was stupefied. Why, they would end by maddening
him with all the obstacles they raised to exhaust his patience;
they would actually implant in him an idea of schism, of an
avenging, liberating scandal! He wished to protest and refuse
the advice, but all at once he made a gesture of weariness.
What would be the good of it, especially with that young
woman, who was certainly sincere and affectionate? 'Who
asked you to give me this advice?' he inquired. She did not
answer, but smiled, and with sudden intuition he resumed:
'It was Monsignor Nani, was it not?'

Thereupon, still unwilling to give a direct reply, she began
to praise the prelate. He had at last consented to guide her
in her divorce affair; and Donna Serafina had gone to the
Palace of the Inquisition that very afternoon in order to

acquaint him with the result of certain steps she had taken. Father Lorenza, the confessor of both the Boccanera ladies, was to be present at the interview, for the idea of the divorce was in reality his own. He had urged the two women to it in his eagerness to sever the bond which the patriotic priest Pisoni had tied full of such fine illusions. Benedetta became quite animated as she explained the reasons of her hopefulness. 'Monsignor Nani can do everything,' she said, 'and I am very happy that my affair should be in his hands. You must be reasonable also, my friend; do as you are requested. I'm sure you will some day be well pleased at having taken this advice.'

Pierre had bowed his head and remained thoughtful. There was nothing unpleasant in the idea of remaining for a few more weeks in Rome, where day by day his curiosity found so much fresh food. Of course, all these delays were calculated to discourage him and bend his will. Yet what did he fear, since he was still determined to relinquish nothing of his book, and to see the Holy Father for the sole purpose of proclaiming his new faith? Once more, in silence, he took that oath, then yielded to Benedetta's entreaties. And as he apologised for being a source of embarrassment in the house she exclaimed: 'No, no, I am delighted to have you here. I fancy that your presence will bring us good fortune now that luck seems to be changing in our favour.'

It was then agreed that he would no longer prowl around St. Peter's and the Vatican, where his constant presence must have attracted attention. He even promised that he would virtually spend a week indoors, desirous as he was of reperusing certain books, certain pages of Rome's history. Then he went on chatting for a moment, lulled by the peacefulness which reigned around him, since the lamp had illumined the *salon* with its sleepy radiance. Six o'clock had just struck, and outside all was dark.

'Wasn't his Eminence indisposed to-day?' the young man asked.

'Yes,' replied the Contessina. 'But we are not anxious: it is only a little fatigue. He sent Don Vigilio to tell me that he intended to shut himself up in his room and dictate some letters. So there can be nothing much the matter, you see.'

Silence fell again. For a while not a sound came from the deserted street or the old empty mansion, mute and dreamy

like a tomb. But all at once the soft somnolence, instinct
with all the sweetness of a dream of hope, was disturbed by a
tempestuous entry, a whirl of skirts, a gasp of terror. It was
Victorine, who had gone off after bringing the lamp, but now
returned, scared and breathless : 'Contessina! Contessina!'

Benedetta had risen, suddenly quite white and cold, as at
the advent of a blast of misfortune. 'What, what is it? Why
do you run and tremble?' she asked.

'Dario, Monsieur Dario—down below. I went down to
see if the lantern in the porch were alight, as it is so often forgotten. And in the dark, in the porch, I stumbled against
Monsieur Dario. He is on the ground; he has a knife-thrust
somewhere.'

A cry leapt from the *amorosa's* heart : 'Dead!'

'No, no, wounded.'

But Benedetta did not hear; in a louder and louder voice
she cried : 'Dead! dead!'

'No, no, I tell you, he spoke to me. And for heaven's
sake, be quiet. He silenced me because he did not want anyone to know; he told me to come and fetch you—only you.
However, as Monsieur l'Abbé is here, he had better help us.
We shall be none too many.'

Pierre listened, also quite aghast. And when Victorine
wished to take the lamp her trembling hand, with which she
had no doubt felt the prostrate body, was seen to be quite
bloody. The sight filled Benedetta with so much horror that
she again began to moan wildly.

'Be quiet, be quiet!' repeated Victorine. 'We ought not
to make any noise in going down. I shall take the lamp,
because we must at all events be able to see. Now, quick,
quick!'

Across the porch, just at the entrance of the vestibule,
Dario lay prone upon the slabs, as if, after being stabbed in
the street, he had only had sufficient strength to take a few
steps before falling. And he had just fainted, and lay there
with his face very pale, his lips compressed, and his eyes
closed. Benedetta, recovering the energy of her race amidst
her excessive grief, no longer lamented or cried out, but gazed
at him with wild, tearless, dilated eyes, as though unable to
understand. The horror of it all was the suddenness and
mysteriousness of the catastrophe, the why and wherefore of
this murderous attempt amidst the silence of the old deserted
palace, black with the shades of night. The wound had as

yet bled but little, for only the Prince's clothes were
stained.

'Quick, quick!' repeated Victorine in an undertone after
lowering the lamp and moving it around. 'The porter isn't
there—he's always at the carpenter's next door—and you see
that he hasn't yet lighted the lantern. Still he may come
back at any moment. So the Abbé and I will carry the Prince
into his room at once.' She alone retained her head, like a
woman of well balanced mind and quiet activity. The two
others, whose stupor continued, listened to her and obeyed
her with the docility of children. 'Contessina,' she continued,
'you must light us. Here, take the lamp and lower it a little
so that we may see the steps. You, Abbé, take the feet; I'll
take hold of him under the armpits. And don't be alarmed,
the poor dear fellow isn't heavy.'

Ah! that ascent of the monumental staircase with its
low steps and its landings as spacious as guard rooms. They
facilitated the cruel journey, but how lugubrious looked the
little *cortège* under the flickering glimmer of the lamp which
Benedetta held with arm outstretched, stiffened by determination! And still not a sound came from the old lifeless dwelling, nothing but the silent crumbling of the walls, the slow
decay which was making the ceilings crack. Victorine continued to whisper words of advice whilst Pierre, afraid of
slipping on the shiny slabs, put forth an excess of strength
which made his breath come short. Huge, wild shadows
danced over the big expanse of bare wall up to the very
vaults decorated with sunken panels. So endless seemed the
ascent that at last a halt became necessary; but the slow
march was soon resumed. Fortunately Dario's apartments—
bed chamber, dressing-room, and sitting-room—were on the
first floor adjoining those of the cardinal in the wing facing
the Tiber, so, on reaching the landing, they only had to walk
softly along the corridor, and at last, to their great relief, laid
the wounded man upon his bed.

Victorine vented her satisfaction in a light laugh. 'That's
done,' said she; 'put the lamp on that table, Contessina. I'm
sure nobody heard us. It's lucky that Donna Serafina should
have gone out, and that his Eminence should have shut himself up with Don Vigilio. I wrapped my skirt round Monsieur
Dario's shoulders, you know, so I don't think any blood fell
on the stairs. By and by, too, I'll go down with a sponge and
wipe the slabs in the porch'——— She stopped short, looked at

Dario, and then quickly added: 'He's breathing—now I'll leave you both to watch over him while I go for good Doctor Giordano, who saw you come into the world, Contessina. He's a man to be trusted.'

Alone with the unconscious sufferer in that dim chamber, which seemed to quiver with the frightful horror that filled their hearts, Benedetta and Pierre remained on either side of the bed, as yet unable to exchange a word. The young woman first opened her arms and wrung her hands whilst giving vent to a hollow moan, as if to relieve and exhale her grief; and then, leaning forward, she watched for some sign of life on that pale face whose eyes were closed. Dario was certainly breathing, but his respiration was slow and very faint, and some time went by before a touch of colour returned to his cheeks. At last, however, he opened his eyes, and then she at once took hold of his hand and pressed it, instilling into the pressure all the anguish of her heart. Great was her happiness on feeling that he feebly returned the clasp.

'Tell me,' she said, 'you can see me and hear me, can't you? What has happened, good God?'

He did not at first answer, being worried by the presence of Pierre. On recognising the young priest, however, he seemed content that he should be there, and then glanced apprehensively round the room to see if there were anybody else. And at last he murmured: 'No one saw me, no one knows.'

'No, no; be easy. We carried you up with Victorine without meeting a soul. Aunt has just gone out, uncle is shut up in his rooms.'

At this Dario seemed relieved, and he even smiled. 'I don't want anybody to know, it is so stupid,' he murmured.

'But in God's name what has happened?' she again asked him.

'Ah! I don't know, I don't know,' was his response as he lowered his eyelids with a weary air as if to escape the question. But he must have realised that it was best for him to confess some portion of the truth at once, for he resumed: 'A man was hidden in the shadow of the porch—he must have been waiting for me. And so, when I came in, he dug his knife into my shoulder, there.'

Forthwith she again leant over him, quivering, and gazing into the depths of his eyes: 'But who was the man? who was he?' she asked. Then, as he, in a yet more weary way, began

to stammer that he didn't know, that the man had fled into
the darkness before he could recognise him, she raised a terrible
cry: 'It was Prada! it was Prada; confess it, I know it
already!' And, quite delirious, she went on: 'I tell you that
I know it! Ah! I would not be his, and he is determined
that we shall never belong to one another. Rather than
have that he will kill you on the day when I am free to be
your wife! Oh! I know him well; I shall never, never be
happy. Yes, I know it well, it was Prada, Prada!'

But sudden energy upbuoyed the wounded man, and he
loyally protested: 'No, no, it was not Prada, nor was it anyone working for him. That I swear to you. I did not recognise the man, but it wasn't Prada—no, no!'

There was such a ring of truth in Dario's words that
Benedetta must have been convinced by them. But terror
once more overpowered her, for the hand she held was suddenly
growing soft, moist, and powerless. Exhausted by his effort,
Dario had fallen back, again fainting, his face quite white and
his eyes closed. And it seemed to her that he was dying.
Distracted by her anguish, she felt him with trembling, groping
hands: 'Look, look, Monsieur l'Abbé!' she exclaimed. 'But
he is dying, he is dying; he is already quite cold. Ah! God
of Heaven, he is dying!'

Pierre, terribly upset by her cries, sought to reassure her,
saying: 'He spoke too much; he has lost consciousness, as he
did before. But I assure you that I can feel his heart beating.
Here, put your hand here, Contessina. For mercy's sake don't
distress yourself like that; the doctor will soon be here, and
everything will be all right.'

But she did not listen to him, and all at once he was lost
in amazement, for she flung herself upon the body of the man
she adored, caught it in a frantic embrace, bathed it with tears
and covered it with kisses whilst stammering words of fire:
'Ah! if I were to lose you, if I were to lose you! And to
think that I repulsed you, that I would not accept happiness
when it was yet possible! Yes, that idea of mine, that vow I
made to the Madonna! Yet how could she be offended by
our happiness? And then, and then, if she has deceived me,
if she takes you from me, ah! then I can have but one regret
—that I did not damn myself with you—yes, yes, damnation
rather than that we should never, never be each other's!'

Was this the woman who had shown herself so calm, so
sensible, so patient the better to ensure her happiness?

Pierre was terrified, and no longer recognised her. He had hitherto seen her so reserved, so modest, with a childish charm that seemed to come from her very nature! But under the threatening blow she feared, the terrible blood of the Boccaneras had awoke within her with a long heredity of violence, pride, frantic and exasperated longings. She wished for her share of life, her share of love! And she moaned and she clamoured, as if death, in taking her lover from her, were tearing away some of her own flesh.

'Calm yourself, I entreat you, madame,' repeated the priest. 'He is alive, his heart beats. You are doing yourself great harm.'

But she wished to die with her lover: 'O my darling! if you must go, take me, take me with you. I will lay myself on your heart, I will clasp you so tightly with my arms that they shall be joined to yours, and then we must needs be buried together. Yes, yes, we shall be dead, and we shall be wedded all the same—wedded in death! I promised that I would belong to none but you, and I will be yours in spite of everything, even in the grave. O my darling, open your eyes, open your mouth, kiss me if you don't want me to die as soon as you are dead!'

A blaze of wild passion, full of blood and fire, had passed through that mournful chamber with old, sleepy walls. But tears were now overcoming Benedetta, and big gasping sobs at last threw her, blinded and strengthless, on the edge of the bed. And fortunately an end was put to the terrible scene by the arrival of the doctor whom Victorine had fetched.

Doctor Giordano was a little old man of over sixty, with white curly hair, and fresh-looking, clean-shaven countenance. By long practice among Churchmen he had acquired the paternal appearance and manner of an amiable prelate. And he was said to be a very worthy man, tending the poor for nothing, and displaying ecclesiastical reserve and discretion in all delicate cases. For thirty years past the whole Boccanera family, children, women, and even the most eminent Cardinal himself, had in all cases of sickness been placed in the hands of this prudent practitioner. Lighted by Victorine and helped by Pierre, he undressed Dario, who was roused from his swoon by pain; and after examining the wound he declared with a smile that it was not at all dangerous. The young Prince would at the utmost have to spend three weeks in bed, and no complications were to be feared. Then, like all the doctors of

Rome, enamoured of the fine thrusts and cuts which day by day they have to dress among chance patients of the lower classes, he complacently lingered over the wound, doubtless regarding it as a clever piece of work, for he ended by saying to the Prince in an undertone: 'That's what we call a warning. The man didn't want to kill, the blow was dealt downwards so that the knife might slip through the flesh without touching the bone. Ah! a man really needs to be skilful to deal such a stab; it was very neatly done.'

'Yes, yes,' murmured Dario, 'he spared me; had he chosen he could have pierced me through.'

Benedetta did not hear. Since the doctor had declared the case to be free from danger, and had explained that the fainting fits were due to nervous shock, she had fallen in a chair, quite prostrated. Gradually, however, some gentle tears coursed from her eyes, bringing relief after her frightful despair, and then, rising to her feet, she came and kissed Dario with mute and passionate delight.

'I say, my dear doctor,' resumed the Prince, 'it's useless for people to know of this. It's so ridiculous. Nobody has seen anything, it seems, excepting Monsieur l'Abbé, whom I ask to keep the matter secret. And in particular I don't want anybody to alarm the Cardinal or my aunt, or indeed any of our friends.'

Doctor Giordano indulged in one of his placid smiles. 'Very good,' said he, 'that's natural; don't worry yourself. We will say that you have had a fall on the stairs and have dislocated your shoulder. And now that the wound is dressed you must try to sleep, and don't get feverish. I will come back to-morrow morning.'

That evening of excitement was followed by some very tranquil days, and a new life began for Pierre, who at first remained indoors, reading and writing, with no other recreation than that of spending his afternoons in Dario's room, where he was certain to find Benedetta. After a somewhat intense fever lasting for eight and forty hours, cure took its usual course, and the story of the dislocated shoulder was so generally believed, that the Cardinal insisted on Donna Serafina departing from her habits of strict economy, to have a second lantern lighted on the landing in order that no such accident might occur again. And then the monotonous peacefulness was only disturbed by a final incident, a threat of trouble, as it

were, with which Pierre found himself mixed up one evening
when he was lingering beside the convalescent patient.

Benedetta had absented herself for a few minutes, and as
Victorine, who had brought up some broth, was leaning towards the Prince to take the empty cup from him, she said in
a low voice: 'There's a girl, Monsieur, La Pierina, who
comes here every day, crying and asking for news of you. I
can't get rid of her, she's always prowling about the place, so
I thought it best to tell you of it.'

Unintentionally, Pierre heard her and understood everything. Dario, who was looking at him, at once guessed his
thoughts, and, without answering Victorine, exclaimed: 'Yes,
Abbé, it was that brute Tito! How idiotic, eh?' At the
same time, although the young man protested that he had
done nothing whatever for the girl's brother to give him such
a 'warning,' he smiled in an embarrassed way, as if vexed and
even somewhat ashamed of being mixed up in an affair of the
kind. And he was evidently relieved when the priest promised that he would see the girl, should she come back, and
make her understand that she ought to remain at home.

'It was such a stupid affair!' the Prince repeated with
an exaggerated show of anger. 'Such things are not of our
times.'

But all at once he ceased speaking, for Benedetta entered
the room. She sat down again beside her dear patient, and
the sweet, peaceful evening then took its course in the old
sleepy chamber, the old, lifeless palace, whence never a sound
arose.

When Pierre began to go out again he at first merely took
a brief airing in the district. The Via Giulia interested him,
for he knew how splendid it had been in the time of Julius
II who had dreamt of lining it with sumptuous palaces.
Horse and foot races then took place there during the carnival,
the Palazzo Farnese being the starting-point, and the Piazza
of St. Peter's the goal. Pierre had also lately read that a
French ambassador, D'Estrée, Marquis de Couré, had resided
at the Palazzo Sacchetti, and in 1638 had given some magnificent entertainments in honour of the birth of the Dauphin,[1]
when on three successive days there had been racing from the
Ponte Sisto to San Giovanni dei Fiorentini amidst an extraordinary display of sumptuosity: the street being strewn with

---

[1] Afterwards Louis XIV.—*Trans.*

flowers, and rich hangings adorning every window. On the second evening there had been fireworks on the Tiber, with a machine representing the ship Argo carrying Jason and his companions to the recovery of the Golden Fleece ; and, on another occasion, the Farnese fountain, the Mascherone, had flowed with wine. Nowadays, however, all was changed. The street, bright with sunshine or steeped in shadow according to the hour, was ever silent and deserted. The heavy, ancient palatial houses, their old doors studded with plates and nails, their windows barred with huge iron gratings, always seemed to be asleep, whole storeys showing nothing but closed shutters as if to keep out the daylight for evermore. Now and again, when a door was open, you espied deep vaults, damp, cold courts, green with mildew, and encompassed by colonnades like cloisters. Then, in the outbuildings of the mansions, the low structures which had collected more particularly on the side of the Tiber, various small silent shops had installed themselves. There was a baker's, a tailor's and a bookbinder's, some fruiterers' shops with a few tomatoes and salad plants set out on boards, and some wine-shops which claimed to sell the vintages of Frascati and Genzano, but whose customers seemed to be dead. Midway along the street was a modern prison, whose horrid yellow wall in no wise enlivened the scene, whilst, overhead, a flight of telegraph wires stretched from the arcades of the Farnese Palace to the distant vista of trees beyond the river. With its infrequent traffic the street, even in the daytime, was like some sepulchral corridor where the past was crumbling into dust, and when night fell its desolation quite appalled Pierre. You did not meet a soul, you did not see a light in any window, and the glimmering gas lamps, few and far between, seemed powerless to pierce the gloom. On either hand the doors were barred and bolted, and not a sound, not a breath came from within. Even when, after a long interval, you passed a lighted wine-shop, behind whose panes of frosted glass a lamp gleamed dim and motionless, not an exclamation, not a suspicion of a laugh ever reached your ear. There was nothing alive save the two sentries placed outside the prison, one before the entrance and the other at the corner of the right-hand lane, and they remained erect and still, coagulated, as it were, in that dead street.

Pierre's interest, however, was not merely confined to the Via Giulia ; it extended to the whole district, once so fine and fashionable, but now fallen into sad decay, far removed from

modern life, and exhaling a faint musty odour of monasticism.
Towards San Giovanni dei Fiorentini, where the new Corso
Vittorio Emanuele has ripped up every olden district, the
lofty five-storeyed houses with their dazzling sculptured fronts
contrasted violently with the black sunken dwellings of the
neighbouring lanes. In the evening the globes of the electric
lamps on the Corso shone out with such dazzling whiteness
that the gas lamps of the Via Giulia and other streets
looked like smoky lanterns. There were several old and
famous thoroughfares, the Via Banchi Vecchi, the Via del
Pellegrino, the Via di Monserrato, and an infinity of cross-
streets which intersected and connected the others, all going
towards the Tiber, and for the most part so narrow that
vehicles scarcely had room to pass. And each street had its
church, a multitude of churches all more or less alike,
highly decorated, gilded, and painted, and open only at
service time when they were full of sunlight and incense.
In the Via Giulia, in addition to San Giovanni dei Fiorentini,
San Biagio della Pagnotta, San Eligio degli Orefici, and
three or four others, there was the so-called Church of the
Dead, Santa Maria dell' Orazione ; and this church, which
is at the lower end behind the Farnese palace, was often
visited by Pierre, who liked to dream there of the wild life
of Rome, and of the pious brothers of the Confraternità
della Morte, who officiate there, and whose mission is to
search for and bury such poor outcasts as die in the Campagna.
One evening he was present at the funeral of two unknown
men, whose bodies, after remaining unburied for quite a
fortnight, had been discovered in a field near the Appian
Way.

However, Pierre's favourite promenade soon became the
new quay of the Tiber beyond the Palazzo Boccanera. He
had merely to take the narrow lane skirting the mansion
to reach a spot where he found much food for reflection.
Although the quay was not yet finished, the work seemed to
be quite abandoned. There were heaps of rubbish, blocks
of stone, broken fences, and dilapidated tool-sheds all around.
To such a height had it been necessary to carry the quay
walls—designed to protect the city from floods, for the
river bed has been rising for centuries past—that the old
terrace of the Boccanera gardens, with its double flight of
steps to which pleasure boats had once been moored, now lay
in a hollow, threatened with annihilation whenever the works

should be finished. But nothing had yet been levelled; the
soil, brought thither for making up the bank, lay as it
had fallen from the carts, and on all sides were pits and
mounds interspersed with the abandoned building materials.
Wretched urchins came to play there, workmen without work
slept in the sunshine, and women after washing ragged linen
spread it out to dry upon the stones. Nevertheless the spot
proved a happy, peaceful refuge for Pierre, one fruitful in inexhaustible reveries when for hours at a time he lingered gazing
at the river, the quays, and the city, stretching in front of him
and on either hand.

At eight in the morning the sun already gilded the vast
opening. On turning to the left he perceived the roofs of the
Trastevere, of a misty, bluish grey against the dazzling sky.
Then, just beyond the apse of San Giovanni, on the right,
the river curved, and on its other bank the poplars of the
Ospedale di Santo Spirito formed a green curtain, while the
castle of Sant' Angelo showed brightly in the distance. But
Pierre's eyes dwelt more particularly on the bank just in front
of him, for there he found some lingering vestiges of old Rome.
On that side indeed between the Ponte Sisto and the Ponte
Sant' Angelo, the quays, which were to imprison the river
within high, white, fortress-like walls, had not yet been raised,
and the bank with its remnants of the old papal city conjured up
an extraordinary vision of the middle ages. The houses, descending to the river brink, were cracked, scorched, rusted by innumerable burning summers, like so many antique bronzes. Down
below there were black vaults into which the water flowed, piles
upholding walls, and fragments of Roman stonework plunging
into the river-bed; then, rising from the shore, came steep,
broken stairways, green with moisture, tiers of terraces, storeys
with tiny windows pierced here and there in hap-hazard
fashion, houses perched atop of other houses, and the whole
jumbled together with a fantastic commingling of balconies
and wooden galleries, footbridges spanning courtyards, clumps
of trees growing apparently on the very roofs, and attics
rising from amidst pinky tiles. The contents of a drain fell
noisily into the river from a worn and soiled gorge of stone ;
and wherever the houses stood back and the bank appeared
it was covered with wild vegetation, weeds, shrubs, and
mantling ivy, which trailed like a kingly robe of state. And
in the glory of the sun the wretchedness and dirt vanished ;
the crooked, jumbled houses seemed to be of gold, draped

with the purple of the red petticoats and the dazzling white
of the shifts which hung drying from their windows ; while
higher still, above the district, the Janiculum rose into all the
luminary's dazzlement, uprearing the slender profile of Sant'
Onofrio amidst cypresses and pines.

Leaning on the parapet of the quay wall, Pierre sadly
gazed at the Tiber for hours at a time. Nothing could convey
an idea of the weariness of those old waters, the mournful
slowness of their flow along that Babylonian trench where
they were confined within huge, bare, livid prison-like walls.
In the sunlight their yellowness was gilded, and the faint
quiver of the current brought ripples of green and blue ; but
as soon as the shade spread over it the stream became opaque
like mud, so turbid in its venerable old age that it no longer
even gave back a reflection of the houses lining it. And how
desolate was its abandonment, what a stream of silence and
solitude it was ! After the winter rains it might roll furiously
and threateningly, but during the long months of bright
weather it traversed Rome without a sound, and Pierre could
remain there all day long without seeing either a skiff or a
sail. The two or three little steam-boats which arrived from
the coast, the few tartanes which brought wine from Sicily,
never came higher than the Aventine, beyond which there was
only a watery desert in which here and there, at long intervals,
a motionless angler let his line dangle. All that Pierre ever
saw in the way of shipping was a sort of ancient, covered
pinnace, a rotting Noah's ark, moored on the right beside the
old bank, and he fancied that it might be used as a washhouse,
though on no occasion did he see anyone in it. And on a neck
of mud there also lay a stranded boat with one side broken in,
a lamentable symbol of the impossibility and the relinquishment of navigation. Ah ! that decay of the river, that decay
of father Tiber, as dead as the famous ruins whose dust he is
weary of laving ! And what an evocation ! all the centuries
of history, so many things, so many men, that those yellow
waters have reflected till, full of lassitude and disgust, they
have grown heavy, silent and deserted, longing only for annihilation.

One morning on the river bank Pierre found La Pierina
standing behind an abandoned tool-shed. With her neck
extended, she was looking fixedly at the window of Dario's
room, at the corner of the quay and the lane. Doubtless she
had been frightened by Victorine's severe reception, and had

not dared to return to the mansion; but some servant, possibly, had told her which was the young Prince's window, and so she now came to this spot, where without wearying she waited for a glimpse of the man she loved, for some sign of life and salvation, the mere hope of which made her heart leap. Deeply touched by the way in which she hid herself, all humility and quivering with adoration, the priest approached her, and instead of scolding her and driving her away as he had been asked to do, spoke to her in a gentle, cheerful manner, asking her for news of her people as though nothing had happened, and at last contriving to mention Dario's name in order that she might understand that he would be up and about again within a fortnight. On perceiving Pierre, La Pierina had started with timidity and distrust as if anxious to flee; but when she understood him, tears of happiness gushed from her eyes, and with a bright smile she kissed her hand to him, calling: '*Grazie, grazie*, thanks, thanks!' And thereupon she darted away, and he never saw her again.

On another morning at an early hour, as Pierre was going to say mass at Santa Brigida on the Piazza Farnese, he was surprised to meet Benedetta coming out of the church and carrying a small phial of oil. She evinced no embarrassment, but frankly told him that every two or three days she went thither to obtain from the beadle a few drops of the oil used for the lamp that burnt before an antique wooden statue of the Madonna, in which she had perfect confidence. She even confessed that she had never had confidence in any other Madonna, having never obtained anything from any other, though she had prayed to several of high repute, Madonnas of marble and even of silver. And so her heart was full of ardent devotion for the holy image which refused her nothing. And she declared in all simplicity, as though the matter were quite natural and above discussion, that the few drops of oil which she applied, morning and evening, to Dario's wound, were alone working his cure, so speedy a cure as to be quite miraculous. Pierre, fairly aghast, distressed indeed to find such childish, superstitious notions in one so full of sense and grace and passion, did not even venture to smile.

In the evenings, when he came back from his strolls and spent an hour or so in Dario's room, he would for a time divert the patient by relating what he had done and seen and thought of during the day. And when he again ventured to stray beyond the district, and became enamoured of the lovely gardens of Rome, which he visited as soon as they opened in the morning in order that he might be virtually alone, he delighted the young prince and Benedetta with his enthusiasm, his rapturous passion for the splendid trees, the plashing water, and the spreading terraces whence the views were so sublime. It was not the most extensive of these gardens which the more deeply impressed his heart. In the grounds of the Villa Borghese, the little Roman Bois de Boulogne, there were certainly some majestic clumps of greenery, some regal avenues where carriages took a turn in the afternoon before the obligatory drive to the Pincio; but Pierre was more touched by the reserved garden of the villa—that villa dazzling with marble and now containing one of the finest museums in the world. There was a simple lawn of fine grass with a vast central basin surmounted by a figure of Venus, nude and white; and antique fragments, vases, statues, columns and sarcophagi were ranged symmetrically all around the deserted, sunlit yet melancholy sward. On returning on one occasion to the Pincio Pierre spent a delightful morning there, penetrated by the charm of this little nook with its scanty evergreens, and its admirable vista of all Rome and St. Peter's rising up afar off in the soft limpid radiance. At the Villa Albani and the Villa Pamphili he again came upon superb parasol pines, tall, stately and graceful, and powerful elm-trees with twisted limbs and dusky foliage. In the Pamphili grounds, the elm-trees steeped the paths in a delicious half light, the lake with its weeping willows and tufts of reeds had a dreamy aspect, while down below the *parterre* displayed a fantastic floral mosaic bright with the various hues of flowers and foliage. That which most particularly struck Pierre, however, in this, the noblest, most spacious, and most carefully tended garden of Rome, was the novel and unexpected view that he suddenly obtained of St. Peter's whilst skirting a low wall: a view whose symbolism for ever clung to him. Rome had completely vanished, and between the slopes of Monte Mario and another wooded height which hid the city, there only appeared the colossal dome which seemed to be poised on an infinity of scattered blocks, now white, now red. These were the houses of the Borgo, the jumbled piles of the Vatican and the basilica which the huge dome surmounted and annihilated, showing greyly blue in the light blue of the heavens, whilst far away stretched a delicate, boundless vista of the Campagna, likewise of a bluish tint.

It was, however, more particularly in the less sumptuous
gardens, those of a more homely grace, that Pierre realised
that even things have souls. Ah! that Villa Mattei on one
side of the Cœlius with its terraced grounds, its sloping alleys
edged with laurel, aloe and spindle-tree, its box-plants forming
arbours, its oranges, its roses and its fountains! Pierre spent
some delicious hours there, and only found a similar charm on
visiting the Aventine, where three churches are embowered in
verdure. The little garden of Santa Sabina, the birthplace
of the Dominican order, is closed on all sides and affords no
view: it slumbers in quiescence, warm and perfumed by its
orange trees, amongst which that planted by St. Dominic
stands huge and gnarled but still laden with ripe fruit. At
the adjoining Priorato, however, the garden, perched high
above the Tiber, overlooks a vast expanse, with the river and
the buildings on either bank as far as the summit of the
Janiculum. And in these gardens of Rome Pierre ever found
the same clipped box-shrubs, the same eucalypti with white
trunks and pale leaves long like hair, the same ilex-trees squat
and dusky, the same giant pines, the same black cypresses,
the same marbles whitening amidst tufts of roses, and the
same fountains gurgling under mantling ivy. Never did he
enjoy more gentle, sorrow-tinged delight than at the Villa of
Pope Julius, where all the life of a gay and sensual period is
suggested by the semi-circular porticus opening on the gardens,
a porticus decorated with paintings, golden trellis-work laden
with flowers, amidst which flutter flights of smiling Cupids.
Then, on the evening when he returned from the Farnesina,
he declared that he had brought all the dead soul of ancient
Rome away with him, and it was not the paintings executed
after Raffaelle's designs that had touched him, it was rather
the pretty hall on the river side decorated in soft blue and
pink and lilac, with an art devoid of genius yet so charming
and so Roman; and in particular it was the abandoned garden
once stretching down to the Tiber, and now shut off from it
by the new quay, and presenting an aspect of woful desolation, ravaged, bossy and weedy like a cemetery, albeit the
golden fruit of orange and citron tree still ripened there.

And for the last time a shock came to Pierre's heart on
the lovely evening when he visited the Villa Medici. There
he was on French soil.[1] And again what a marvellous garden

[1] Here is the French Academy, where winners of the 'Prix de Rome'
in painting, sculpture, architecture, engraving and music are maintained

he found with box-plants, and pines, and avenues full of magnificence and charm ! What a refuge for antique reverie was that wood of ilex-trees, so old and so sombre, where the sun in declining cast fiery gleams of red gold amidst the sheeny bronze of the foliage. You ascend by endless steps, and from the crowning belvedere on high you embrace all Rome at a glance, as though by opening your arms you could seize it in its entirety. From the villa's dining-room, decorated with portraits of all the artists who have successively sojourned there, and from the spacious peaceful library one beholds the same splendid, broad, all-conquering panorama, a panorama of unlimited ambition, whose infinite ought to set in the hearts of the young men dwelling there a determination to subjugate the world. Pierre, who came thither opposed to the principle of the 'Prix de Rome,' that traditional, uniform education so dangerous for originality, was for a moment charmed by the warm peacefulness, the limpid solitude of the garden, and the sublime horizon where the wings of genius seemed to flutter. Ah ! how delightful, to be only twenty and to live for three years amidst such infinite sweetness, encompassed by the finest works of man ; to say to oneself that one is as yet too young to produce, and to reflect, and seek, and learn how to enjoy, suffer and love ! But Pierre afterwards reflected that this was not a fit task for youth, and that to appreciate the divine enjoyment of such a retreat, all art and blue sky, ripe age was needed, age with victories already gained and weariness following upon the accomplishment of work. He chatted with some of the young pensioners, and remarked that if those who were inclined to dreaminess and contemplation, like those who could merely claim mediocrity, accommodated themselves to this life cloistered in the art of the past, on the other hand artists of active bent and personal temperament pined with impatience, their eyes ever turned towards Paris, their souls eager to plunge into the furnace of battle and production.

All those gardens of which Pierre spoke to Dario and Benedetta with so much rapture, awoke within them the memory of the garden of the Villa Montefiori now a waste, but once so green, planted with the finest orange-trees of Rome, a grove of centenarian orange-trees where they had learnt to love one another. And the memory of their early love brought

by the French Government for three years. The creation dates from Louis XIV.—*Trans.*

thoughts of their present situation and their future prospects.
To these the conversation always reverted, and evening after
evening Pierre witnessed their delight, and heard them talk
of coming happiness like lovers transported to the seventh
heaven. The suit for the dissolution of Benedetta's marriage
was now assuming a more and more favourable aspect.
Guided by a powerful hand, Donna Serafina was apparently
acting very vigorously, for almost every day she had some
further good news to report. She was indeed anxious to
finish the affair both for the continuity and for the honour of
the name, for on the one hand Dario refused to marry anyone but his cousin, and on the other this marriage would
explain everything and put an end to an intolerable situation.
The scandalous rumours which circulated both in the white
and the black world quite incensed her, and a victory was the
more necessary as Leo XIII, already so aged, might be
snatched away at any moment, and in the Conclave which would
follow she desired that her brother's name should shine forth
with untarnished, sovereign radiance. Never had the secret
ambition of her life, the hope that her race might give a
third pope to the Church, filled her with so much passion.
It was as if she therein sought a consolation for the harsh
abandonment of Advocate Morano. Invariably clad in sombre
garb, ever active and slim, so tightly laced that from behind
one might have taken her for a young girl, she was so to
say the black soul of that old palace; and Pierre who met
her everywhere, prowling and inspecting like a careful housekeeper, and jealously watching over her brother the Cardinal,
bowed to her in silence, chilled to the heart by the stern look
of her withered wrinkled face in which was set the large,
opiniative nose of her family. However she barely returned
his bows, for she still disdained that paltry foreign priest, and
only tolerated him in order to please Monsignor Nani and
Viscount Philibert de la Choue.

A witness every evening of the anxious delight and impatience of Benedetta and Dario, Pierre by degrees became
almost as impassioned as themselves, as desirous for an early
solution. Benedetta's suit was about to come before the Congregation of the Council once more. Monsignor Palma, the
defender of the marriage, had demanded a supplementary
inquiry after the favourable decision arrived at in the first
instance by a bare majority of one vote—a majority which
the Pope would certainly not have thought sufficient had he

been asked for his ratification. So the question now was to gain votes among the ten Cardinals who formed the Congregation, to persuade and convince them, and if possible ensure an almost unanimous pronouncement. The task was arduous, for, instead of facilitating matters, Benedetta's relationship to Cardinal Boccanera raised many difficulties, owing to the intriguing spirit rife at the Vatican, the spite of rivals who, by perpetuating the scandal, hoped to destroy Boccanera's chance of ever attaining to the papacy. Every afternoon, however, Donna Serafina devoted herself to the task of winning votes under the direction of her confessor, Father Lorenza, whom she saw daily at the Collegio Germanico, now the last refuge of the Jesuits in Rome, for they have ceased to be masters of the Gesù. The chief hope of success lay in Prada's formal declaration that he would not put in an appearance. The whole affair wearied and irritated him; the imputations levelled against him as a man seemed to him supremely odious and ridiculous; and he no longer even took the trouble to reply to the assignations which were sent to him. He acted indeed as if he had never been married, though deep in his heart the wound dealt to his passion and his pride still lingered, bleeding afresh whenever one or another of the scandalous rumours in circulation reached his ears. However, as their adversary desisted from all action, one can understand that the hopes of Benedetta and Dario increased, the more so as hardly an evening passed without Donna Serafina telling them that she believed she had gained the support of another cardinal.

But the man who terrified them all was Monsignor Palma, whom the congregation had appointed to defend the sacred ties of matrimony. His rights and privileges were almost unlimited, he could appeal yet again, and in any case would make the affair drag on as long as it pleased him. His first report, in reply to Morano's memoir, had been a terrible blow, and it was now said that a second one which he was preparing would prove yet more pitiless, establishing as a fundamental principle of the Church that it could not annul a marriage whose nonconsummation was purely and simply due to the action of the wife in refusing obedience to her husband. In presence of such energy and logic, it was unlikely that the cardinals, even if sympathetic, would dare to advise the Holy Father to dissolve the marriage. And so discouragement was once more overcoming Benedetta when Donna Serafina, on

returning from a visit to Monsignor Nani, calmed her somewhat by telling her that a mutual friend had undertaken to
deal with Monsignor Palma. However, said she, even if they
succeeded, it would doubtless cost them a large sum.

Monsignor Palma, a theologist expert in all canonical
affairs, and a perfectly honest man in pecuniary matters, had
met with a great misfortune in his life. He had a niece, a
poor and lovely girl, for whom, unhappily, in his declining
years he conceived an insensate passion, with the result that
to avoid a scandal he was compelled to marry her to a rascal
who now preyed upon her and even beat her. And the prelate
was now passing through a fearful crisis, weary of reducing
himself to beggary, and indeed no longer having the money
necessary to extricate his nephew by marriage from a very
nasty predicament, the result of cheating at cards. So the
idea was to save the young man by a considerable pecuniary
payment, and then to procure him employment without asking
aught of his uncle, who, as if offering complicity, came in tears
one evening, when night had fallen, to thank Donna Serafina
for her exceeding goodness.

Pierre was with Dario that evening when Benedetta entered
the room laughing, and joyfully clapping her hands. 'It's
done, it's done!' she said, 'he has just left aunt, and vowed
eternal gratitude to her. He will now be obliged to show
himself amiable.'

However Dario distrustfully inquired : 'But was he made
to sign anything? did he enter into a formal engagement?

'Oh! no ; how could one do that? It's such a delicate
matter,' replied Benedetta. 'But people say that he is a very
honest man.' Nevertheless, in spite of these words, she herself became uneasy. What if Monsignor Palma should remain
incorruptible in spite of the great service which had been
rendered him? Thenceforth this idea haunted them, and
their suspense began once more.

Dario, eager to divert his mind, was imprudent enough to
get up before he was perfectly cured, and, his wound reopen-
ing, he was obliged to take to his bed again for a few days.
Every evening, as previously, Pierre strove to enliven him with
an account of his strolls. The young priest was now getting
bolder, rambling in turn through all the districts of Rome,
and discovering the many 'classical' curiosities catalogued in
the guide-books. One evening he spoke with a kind of affection of the principal squares of the city which he had first

thought commonplace, but which now seemed to him very varied,
each with original features of its own. There was the noble
Piazza del Popolo of such monumental symmetry and so full
of sunlight; there was the Piazza di Spagna, the lively meet-
ing-place of foreigners, with its double flight of a hundred and
thirty steps gilded by the sun; there was the vast Piazza
Colonna, always swarming with people, and the most Italian
of all the Roman squares from the presence of the idle, careless crowd which ever lounged round the column of Marcus
Aurelius as if waiting for fortune to fall from heaven; there
was also the long and regular Piazza Navona, deserted since
the market was no longer held there, and retaining a melancholy recollection of its former bustling life; and there was
the Campo dei Fiori, which was invaded each morning by the
tumultuous fruit and vegetable markets, quite a plantation of
huge umbrellas sheltering heaps of tomatoes, pimentoes, and
grapes amidst a noisy stream of dealers and housewives.
Pierre's great surprise, however, was the Piazza del Campidoglio—the 'Square of the Capitol'—which to him suggested
a summit, an open spot overlooking the city and the world,
but which he found to be small and square, and on three sides
enclosed by palaces, whilst on the fourth side the view was of
little extent.[1] There are no passers-by there; visitors usually
come up by a flight of steps bordered by a few palm-trees,
only foreigners making use of the winding carriage-ascent.
The vehicles wait, and the tourists loiter for a while with their
eyes raised to the admirable equestrian statue of Marcus
Aurelius, in antique bronze, which occupies the centre of the
piazza. Towards four o'clock, when the sun gilds the left-hand
palace, and the slender statues of its entablature show vividly
against the blue sky, you might think yourself in some warm,
cosy square of a little provincial town, what with the women
of the neighbourhood who sit knitting under the arcade, and
the bands of ragged urchins who disport themselves on all
sides like schoolboys in a playground.

Then, on another evening Pierre told Benedetta and Dario
of his admiration for the Roman fountains, for in no other
city of the world does water flow so abundantly and magnificently in fountains of bronze and marble, from the boat-shaped

---

[1] The Piazza del Campidoglio is really a depression between the
Capitolium proper and the northern height called the Arx. It is sup-
posed to have been the exact site of Romulus's traditional Asylum.—
Trans.

Fontana della Barcaccia on the Piazza di Spagna, the Triton
on the Piazza Barberini, and the Tortoises which give their
name to the Piazza delle Tartarughe, to the three fountains
of the Piazza Navona where Bernini's vast central composition
of rock and river-gods rises so triumphantly, and to the colossal
and pompous fountain of Trevi, where King Neptune stands
on high attended by lofty figures of Health and Fruitfulness.
And on yet another evening Pierre came home quite pleased,
relating that he had at last discovered why it was that the old
streets around the Capitol and along the Tiber seemed to him
so strange : it was because they had no footways, and pedestrians, instead of skirting the walls, invariably took the middle
of the road, leisurely wending their way among the vehicles.
Pierre was very fond of those old districts with their winding
lanes, their tiny squares so irregular in shape, and their huge
square mansions swamped by a multitudinous jumble of little
houses. He found a charm, too, in the district of the Esquiline,
where, besides innumerable flights of ascending steps, each of
grey pebbles edged with white stone, there were sudden sinuous
slopes, tiers of terraces, seminaries and convents, lifeless, with
their windows ever closed, and lofty, blank walls above which
a superb palm tree would now and again soar into the spotless
blue of the sky. And on yet another evening, having strolled
into the Campagna beside the Tiber and above the Ponte
Molle, he came back full of enthusiasm for a form of classical
art which hitherto he had scarcely appreciated. Along the
river bank, however, he had found the very scenery that
Poussin so faithfully depicted : the sluggish, yellow stream
fringed with reeds ; low riven cliffs, whose chalky whiteness
showed against the ruddy background of a far-stretching, undulating plain, bounded by blue hills ; a few spare trees with
a ruined porticus opening on to space atop of the bank, and a
line of pale-hued sheep descending to drink, whilst the shepherd, with an elbow resting on the trunk of an ilex-tree, stood
looking on. It was a special kind of beauty, broad and ruddy,
made up of nothing, sometimes simplified into a series of
low, horizontal lines, but ever ennobled by the great memories
it evoked : the Roman legions marching along the paved highways across the bare Campagna ; the long slumber of the
middle ages ; and then the awakening of antique nature in
the midst of Catholicism, whereby, for the second time, Rome
became ruler of the world.

One day when Pierre came back from seeing the great

modern cemetery, the Campo Verano, he found Celia, as well
as Benedetta, by the side of Dario's bed. 'What, Monsieur
l'Abbé!' exclaimed the little Princess when she learnt where
he had been; 'it amuses you to visit the dead?'

'Oh those Frenchmen,' remarked Dario, to whom the
mere idea of a cemetery was repulsive; 'those Frenchmen
seem to take a pleasure in making their lives wretched with
their partiality for gloomy scenes.'

'But there is no escaping the reality of death,' gently
replied Pierre; 'the best course is to look it in the face.'

This made the Prince quite angry. 'Reality, reality,' said
he, 'when reality isn't pleasant I don't look at it; I try never
to think of it even.'

In spite of this rejoinder, Pierre, with his smiling, placid
air, went on enumerating the things which had struck him:
first, the admirable manner in which the cemetery was kept,
then the festive appearance which it derived from the bright
autumn sun, and the wonderful profusion in which marble was
lavished in slabs, statues, and chapels. The ancient atavism
had surely been at work, the sumptuous mausoleums of the
Appian Way had here sprung up afresh, making death a pretext for the display of pomp and pride. In the upper part of
the cemetery the Roman nobility had a district of its own,
crowded with veritable temples, colossal statues, groups of
several figures; and if at times the taste shown in these
monuments was deplorable, it was none the less certain that
millions had been expended on them. One charming feature
of the place, said Pierre, was that the marbles, standing among
yews and cypresses, were remarkably well preserved, white and
spotless; for, if the summer sun slowly gilded them, there
were none of those stains of moss and rain which impart an
aspect of melancholy decay to the statues of northern climes.

Touched by the discomfort of Dario, Benedetta, hitherto
silent, ended by interrupting Pierre. 'And was the hunt interesting?' she asked, turning to Celia.

The little Princess had been taken by her mother to see a
fox-hunt, and had been speaking of it when the priest entered
the room.

'Yes, it was very interesting, my dear,' she replied;
'the meet was at noon near the tomb of Cecilia Metella, where
a buffet had been arranged under a tent. And there was such
a number of people—the foreign colony, the young men of the
embassies, and some officers, not to mention ourselves—all the

men in scarlet and a great many ladies in habits. The
" throw-off " was at one o'clock, and the gallop lasted more
than two hours and a half, so that the fox had a very long run.
I wasn't able to follow, but all the same I saw some extraordinary things—a great wall which the whole hunt had to leap,
and then ditches and hedges—a mad race indeed in the rear
of the hounds. There were two accidents, but nothing serious ;
one gentleman, who was unseated, sprained his wrist badly,
and another broke his leg.' [1]

Dario had listened to Celia with passionate interest, for
fox hunting is one of the great pleasures of Rome, and the
Campagna, flat and yet bristling with obstacles, is certainly
well adapted to the sport. ' Ah ! ' said the young Prince in a
despairing tone, ' how idiotic it is to be riveted to this room !
I shall end by dying of *ennui !* '

Benedetta contented herself with smiling ; neither reproach
nor expression of sadness came from her at this candid display
of egotism. Her own happiness at having him all to herself
in the room where she nursed him was great indeed ; still her
love, at once full of youth and good sense, included a maternal
element, and she well understood that he hardly amused himself, deprived as he was of his customary pleasures and severed
from his friends, few of whom he was willing to receive, for
he feared that they might think the story of the dislocated
shoulder suspicious. Of course there were no more *fêtes,* no
more evenings at the theatre, no more flirtations. But above
everything else Dario missed the Corso, and suffered despairingly at no longer seeing or learning anything by watching
the procession of Roman society from four to five each afternoon. Accordingly, as soon as an intimate called, there were
endless questions : Had the visitor seen so and so ? Had such a
one reappeared ? How had a certain friend's love affair ended ?
Was any new adventure setting the city agog ? And so forth ;
all the petty frivolities, nine days' wonders, and puerile intrigues in which the young Prince had hitherto expended his
manly energy.

After a pause Celia, who was fond of coming to him with
innocent gossip, fixed her candid eyes on him—the fathomless
eyes of an enigmatical virgin, and resumed : ' How long it
takes to set a shoulder right ! '

Had she, child as she was, with love her only business,

[1] The Roman Hunt, which counts about one hundred subscribers, has
flourished since 1840.   There is a kennel of English hounds, an English
huntsman and whip, and a stable of English hunters.—*Trans.*

divined the truth ? Dario in his embarrassment glanced at Benedetta, who still smiled. However, the little Princess was already darting to another subject : 'Ah ! you know, Dario, at the Corso yesterday I saw a lady——' Then she stopped short, surprised and embarrassed that these words should have escaped her. However, in all bravery she resumed like one who had been a friend since childhood, sharing many a little love secret : 'Yes, a very pretty person whom you know. Well, she had a bouquet of white roses with her all the same.'

At this Benedetta indulged in a burst of frank merriment, and Dario, still looking at her, also laughed. She had twitted him during the early days because no young woman ever sent to make inquiries about him. For his part, he was not displeased with the rupture, for the continuance of the connection might have proved embarrassing ; and so, although his vanity may have been slightly hurt, the news that he was already replaced in La Tonietta's affections was welcome rather than otherwise. 'Ah !' he contented himself with saying, 'the absent are always in the wrong.'

'The man one loves is never absent,' declared Celia with her grave, candid air.

However, Benedetta had stepped up to the bed to raise the young man's pillows : 'Never mind, Dario *mio*,' said she, 'all those things are over ; I mean to keep you, and you will only have me to love.'

He gave her a passionate glance and kissed her hair. She spoke the truth : he had never loved anyone but her, and she was not mistaken in her anticipation of keeping him always to herself alone as soon as they should be wedded. To her great delight, since she had been nursing him he had become quite childish again, such as he had been when she had learnt to love him under the orange trees of the Villa Montefiori. He retained a sort of puerility, doubtless the outcome of impoverished blood, that return to childhood which one remarks amongst very ancient races ; and he toyed on his bed with pictures, gazed for hours at photographs, which made him laugh. Moreover, his inability to endure suffering had yet increased ; he wished Benedetta to be gay and sing, and amused her with his pretty egotism which led him to dream of a life of continual joy with her. Ah ! how pleasant it would be to live together and for ever in the sunlight, to do nothing and care for nothing, and even if the world should crumble somewhere to heed it not !

'One thing which greatly pleases me,' suddenly said the young Prince, ' is that Monsieur l'Abbé has ended by falling in love with Rome.'

Pierre admitted it with a good grace.

' We told you so,' remarked Benedetta. ' A great deal of time is needed for one to understand and love Rome. If you had only stayed here for a fortnight you would have gone off with a deplorable idea of us, but now that you have been here for two full months we are quite at ease, for you will never think of us without affection.'

She looked exceedingly charming as she spoke these words, and Pierre again bowed. However, he had already given thought to the phenomenon, and fancied he could explain it. When a stranger comes to Rome he brings with him a Rome of his own, a Rome such as he dreams of, so ennobled by imagination that the real Rome proves a terrible disenchantment. And so it is necessary to wait for habituation, for the mediocrity of the reality to soften, and for the imagination to have time to kindle again, and only behold things such as they are athwart the prodigious splendour of the past.

However, Celia had risen and was taking leave. ' Goodbye, dear,' she said ; ' I hope the wedding will soon take place. You know, Dario, that I mean to be betrothed before the end of the month. Oh yes, I intend to make my father give a grand entertainment. And how nice it would be if the two weddings could take place at the same time ! '

Two days later, after a long ramble through the Trastevere district, followed by a visit to the Palazzo Farnese, Pierre felt that he could at last understand the terrible, melancholy truth about Rome. He had several times already strolled through the Trastevere, attracted towards its wretched denizens by his compassion for all who suffered. Ah ! that quagmire of wretchedness and ignorance ! He knew of abominable nooks in the faubourgs of Paris, frightful ' rents ' and ' courts ' where people rotted in heaps, but there was nothing in France to equal the listless, filthy stagnation of the Trastevere. On the brightest days a dank gloom chilled the sinuous, cellar-like lanes, and the smell of rotting vegetables, rank oil, and human animality brought on fits of nausea. Jumbled together in a confusion which artists of romantic turn would admire, the antique, irregular houses had black, gaping entrances diving below ground, outdoor stairways conducting to upper floors, and wooden balconies which only a miracle upheld. There were crumbling fronts, shored up with beams; sordid lodgings whose filth and bareness could be seen through shattered windows; and numerous petty shops, all the open-air cookstalls of a lazy race which never lighted a fire at home: you saw frying-shops with heaps of polenta, and fish swimming in stinking oil, and dealers in cooked vegetables displaying huge turnips, celery, cauliflowers, and spinach, all cold and sticky. The butcher's meat was black and clumsily cut up; the necks of the animals bristled with bloody clots, as though the heads had simply been torn away. The bakers' loaves, piled on planks, looked like little round paving-stones; at the beggarly greengrocers' merely a few pimentoes and fir-apples were shown under the strings of dry tomatoes which festooned the doorways; and the only shops which were at all attractive were those of the pork butchers with their salted provisions and their cheese, whose pungent smell slightly attenuated the pestilential reek of the gutters. Lottery offices, displaying lists of winning numbers, alternated with wine shops, of which latter there was a fresh one every thirty yards with large inscriptions setting forth that the best wines of Genzano, Marino, and Frascati were to be found within. And the whole district teemed with ragged, grimy denizens, children halfnaked and devoured by vermin, bare-headed, gesticulating and shouting women, whose skirts were stiff with grease, old men who remained motionless on benches amidst swarms of hungry flies; idleness and agitation appearing on all sides, whilst cobblers sat on the sidewalks quietly plying their trade, and little donkeys pulled carts hither and thither, and men drove turkeys along, whip in hand, and bands of beggars rushed upon the few anxious tourists who had timorously ventured into the district. At the door of a little tailor's shop an old house-pail dangled full of earth, in which a succulent plant was flowering. And from every window and balcony, as from the many cords which stretched across the street from house to house, all the household washing hung like bunting, nameless drooping rags, the symbolical banners of abominable misery.

Pierre's fraternal soul filled with pity at the sight. Ah! yes, it was necessary to demolish all those pestilential districts where the populace had wallowed for centuries as in a poisonous gaol! He was for demolition and sanitary improvement, even if old Rome were killed and artists scandalised.

Doubtless the Trastevere was already greatly changed, pierced
with several new thoroughfares which let the sun stream in.
And amidst the *abattis* of rubbish and the spacious clearings,
where nothing new had yet been erected, the remaining
portions of the old district seemed even blacker and more
loathsome.   Some day, no doubt, it would all be rebuilt, but
how interesting was this phase of the city's evolution : old
Rome expiring and new Rome just dawning amidst countless
difficulties !   To appreciate the change it was necessary to
have known the filthy Rome of the past, swamped by sewage
in every form.   The recently levelled Ghetto had, over a
course of centuries, so rotted the soil on which it stood that
an awful, pestilential odour yet arose from its bare site.   It
was only fitting it should long remain waste, so that it might
dry and become purified in the sun.   In all the districts on
either side of the Tiber where extensive improvements have
been undertaken you find the same scenes.   You follow some
narrow, damp, evil-smelling street with black house fronts
and overhanging roofs, and suddenly come upon a clearing
as in a forest of ancient leprous hovels.   There are squares,
broad footways ; lofty white carved buildings yet in the
rough, littered with rubbish and fenced off.   On every side
you find as it were a huge building yard, which the financial
crisis perpetuates ; the city of to-morrow arrested in its
growth, stranded there in its monstrous, precocious, surprising infancy.   Nevertheless, therein lies good and healthful
work, such as was and is absolutely necessary if Rome is to
become a great modern city, instead of being left to rot, to
dwindle into a mere ancient curiosity, a museum show-piece.

   That day, as Pierre went from the Trastevere to the
Palazzo Farnese, where he was expected, he chose a round-
about route, following the Via di Pettinari and the Via dei
Giubbonari, the former so dark and narrow with a great
hospital wall on one side and a row of wretched houses on the
other, and the latter animated by a constant stream of people
and enlivened by the jewellers' windows, full of big gold
chains, and the displays of the drapers' shops, where stuffs
hung in bright red, blue, green and yellow lengths.   And the
popular district through which he had roamed and the trad-
ing district which he was now crossing reminded him of the
castle-fields with their mass of workpeople reduced to
mendicity by lack of employment and forced to camp in the
superb, unfinished, abandoned mansions.   Ah ! the poor, sad

people, who were yet so childish, kept in the ignorance and
credulity of a savage race by centuries of theocracy, so
habituated to mental night and bodily suffering that even to-
day they remained apart from the social awakening, simply
desirous of enjoying their pride, indolence, and sunlight in
peace! They seemed both blind and deaf in their decadence,
and whilst Rome was being overturned they continued to
lead the stagnant life of former times, realising naught but
the worries of the improvements, the demolition of the old
favourite districts, the consequent change in habits, and the
rise in the cost of food, as if indeed they would rather have
gone without light, cleanliness, and health, since these could
only be secured by a great financial and labour crisis. And
yet, at bottom, it was solely for the people, the populace, that
Rome was being cleansed and rebuilt with the idea of making
it a great modern capital, for democracy lies at the end of
these present day transformations; it is the people who will
inherit the cities whence dirt and disease are being expelled,
and where the law of labour will end by prevailing and killing
want. And so, though one may curse the dusting and repairing of the ruins and the stripping of all the wild flora from
the Colosseum, though one may wax indignant at sight of the
hideous fortress-like ramparts which imprison the Tiber, and
bewail the old romantic banks with their greenery and their
antique dwellings dipping into the stream, one must at the
same time acknowledge that life springs from death, and that
to-morrow must perforce blossom in the dust of the past.

While thinking of all these things Pierre had reached the
deserted, stern-looking Piazza Farnese, and for a moment he
looked up at the bare monumental façade of the heavy square
Palazzo, its lofty entrance where hung the tricolour, its rows
of windows and its famous cornice sculptured with such marvellous art. Then he went in. A friend of Narcisse Habert,
one of the *attachés* of the embassy to the King of Italy, was
waiting for him, having offered to show him over the huge
pile, the finest palace in Rome, which France had leased as a
lodging for her ambassador.[1] Ah! that colossal, sumptuous,
deadly dwelling, with its vast court whose porticus is so dark
and damp, its giant staircase with low steps, its endless
corridors, its immense galleries and halls. All was sovereign

[1] The French have two embassies at Rome: one at the Palazzo
Farnese, to the Italian Court, and the other at the Palazzo Rospigliosi,
to the Vatican.—*Trans.*

pomp blended with death. An icy, penetrating chill fell from the walls. With a discreet smile the *attaché* owned that the embassy was frozen in winter and baked in summer. The only part of the building which was at all lively and pleasant was the first storey, overlooking the Tiber, which the ambassador himself occupied. From the gallery there, containing the famous frescoes of Annibale Caracci, one can see the Janiculum, the Corsini gardens, and the Acqua Paola above San Pietro in Montorio. Then, after a vast drawing-room comes the study, peaceful and pleasant, and enlivened by sunshine. But the dining-room, the bed-chambers, and other apartments occupied by the *personnel* look out on to the mournful gloom of a side street. All these vast rooms, twenty and four-and-twenty feet high, have admirable carved or painted ceilings, bare walls, a few of them decorated with frescoes, and incongruous furniture, superb pier-tables mingling with modern *bric-à-brac*. And things become abominable when you enter the gala reception rooms overlooking the piazza, for there you no longer find an article of furniture, no longer a hanging, nothing but disaster, a series of magnificent deserted halls given over to rats and spiders. The embassy occupies but one of them, where it heaps up its dusty archives. Near by is a huge hall occupying the height of two floors, and thus sixty feet in elevation. Reserved by the owner of the palace, the ex-King of Naples, it has become a mere lumber-room where *maquettes*, unfinished statues and a very fine sarcophagus are stowed away amidst all kinds of remnants. And this is but a part of the palace. The ground floor is altogether uninhabited; the French 'École de Rome' occupies a corner of the second floor; while the embassy huddles in chilly fashion in the most habitable corner of the first floor, compelled to abandon everything else and lock the doors to spare itself the useless trouble of sweeping. No doubt it is grand to live in the Palazzo Farnese, built by Pope Paul III and for more than a century inhabited by cardinals; but how cruel the discomfort and how frightful the melancholy of this huge ruin, three-fourths of whose rooms are dead, useless, impossible, cut off from life. And the evenings, oh! the evenings, when porch, court, stairs and corridors are invaded by dense gloom, against which a few smoky gas lamps struggle in vain, when a long, long journey lies before one through the lugubrious desert of stone, before one reaches the ambassador's warm and cheerful drawing-room!

Pierre came away quite aghast. And, as he walked along, the many other grand palaces which he had seen during his strolls rose before him, one and all of them stripped of their splendour, shorn of their princely establishments, let out in uncomfortable flats! What could be done with those grandiose galleries and halls now that no fortune could defray the cost of the pompous life for which they had been built, or even feed the retinue needed to keep them up? Few indeed were the nobles who, like Prince Aldobrandini, with his numerous progeny, still occupied their entire mansions. Almost all of them let the antique dwellings of their forefathers to companies or individual tenants, reserving only a storey, and at times a mere lodging in some dark corner, for themselves. The Palazzo Chigi was let: the ground floor to bankers and the first floor to the Austrian ambassador, while the Prince and his family divided the second floor with a cardinal. The Palazzo Sciarra was let: the first floor to the Minister of Foreign Affairs and the second to a senator, while the Prince and his mother merely occupied the ground floor. The Palazzo Barberini was let: its ground floor, first floor, and second floor to various families, whilst the Prince found a refuge on the third floor in the rooms which had been occupied by his ancestors' lacqueys. The Palazzo Borghese was let: the ground floor to a dealer in antiquities, the first floor to a Lodge of Freemasons, and the rest to various households, whilst the Prince only retained the use of a small suite of apartments. And the Palazzo Odescalchi, the Palazzo Colonna, the Palazzo Doria were let: their Princes reduced to the position of needy landlords eager to derive as much profit as possible from their property in order to make both ends meet. A blast of ruin was sweeping over the Roman *patriziato*, the greatest fortunes had crumbled in the financial crisis, very few remained wealthy, and what a wealth it was, stagnant and dead, which neither commerce nor industry could renew. The numerous princes who had tried speculation were stripped of their fortunes. The others, terrified, called upon to pay enormous taxes, amounting to nearly one-third of their incomes, could henceforth only wait and behold their last stagnant millions dwindle away till they were exhausted or distributed according to the succession laws. Such wealth as remained to these nobles must perish, for, like everything else, wealth perishes when it lacks a soil in which it may fructify. In all this there was solely a question of time : eventual ruin was a foregone and irremediable conclusion, of absolute, historical certainty. Those who resigned themselves to the course of letting their deserted mansions still struggled for life, seeking to accommodate themselves to present day exigencies; whilst death already dwelt among the others, those stubborn, proud ones who immured themselves in the tombs of their race, like that appalling Palazzo Boccanera, which was falling into dust amidst such chilly gloom and silence, the latter only broken at long intervals when the Cardinal's old coach rumbled over the grassy court.

The point which most struck Pierre, however, was that his visits to the Trastevere and the Palazzo Farnese shed light one on the other, and led him to a conclusion which had never previously seemed so manifest. As yet no ' people,' and soon no aristocracy. He had found the people so wretched, ignorant, and resigned in its long infancy induced by historic and climatic causes that many years of instruction and culture were necessary for it to become a strong, healthy, and laborious democracy, conscious of both its rights and its duties. As for the aristocracy, it was dwindling to death in its crumbling palaces, no longer aught than a finished, degenerate race, with such an admixture also of American, Austrian, Polish and Spanish blood that pure Roman blood became a rare exception ; and, moreover, it had ceased to belong either to sword or gown, unwilling to serve constitutional Italy and forsaking the Sacred College, where only *parvenus* now donned the purple. And between the lowly and the aristocracy there was as yet no firmly seated middle class, with the vigour of fresh sap and sufficient knowledge and good sense to act as the transitional educator of the nation. The middle class was made up in part of the old servants and clients of the princes, the farmers who rented their lands, the stewards, notaries, and solicitors who managed their fortunes ; in part, too, of all the employees, the functionaries of every rank and class, the deputies and senators, whom the new government had brought from the provinces ; and, in particular, of the voracious hawks who had swooped down upon Rome, the Pradas, the men of prey from all parts of the kingdom, who with beak and talon devoured both people and aristocracy. For whom, then, had one laboured ? For whom had those gigantic works of new Rome been undertaken ? A shudder of fear sped by, a crack as of doom was heard, arousing pitiful disquietude in every fraternal heart. Yes, a threat of doom and annihilation : as yet no people, soon no aristocracy, and only a ravenous middle class, quarrying, vulture-like, among the ruins.

On the evening of that day, when all was dark, Pierre went to spend an hour on the river quay beyond the Boccanera mansion. He was very fond of meditating on that deserted spot in spite of the warnings of Victorine, who asserted that it was not safe. And, indeed, on such inky nights as that one no cut-throat place ever presented a more tragic aspect. Not a soul, not a passer-by; a dense gloom, a void in front and on either hand. At a corner of the mansion, now steeped in darkness, there was a gas lamp which stood in a hollow since the river margin had been banked up, and this lamp cast an uncertain glimmer upon the quay, level with the latter's bossy soil. Thus long vague shadows stretched from the various materials, piles of bricks and piles of stone, which were strewn around. On the right a few lights shone upon the bridge near San Giovanni and in the windows of the hospital of the Santo Spirito. On the left, amidst the dim recession of the river, the distant districts were blotted out. Then yonder, across the stream, was the Trastevere, the houses on the bank looking like vague, pale phantoms, with infrequent window-panes showing a blurred yellow glimmer, whilst on high only a dark band shadowed the Janiculum, near whose summit the lamps of some promenade scintillated like a triangle of stars. But it was the Tiber which impassioned Pierre; such was its melancholy majesty during those nocturnal hours. Leaning over the parapet, he watched it gliding between the new walls, which looked like those of some black and monstrous prison built for a giant. So long as lights gleamed in the windows of the houses opposite he saw the sluggish water flow by, showing slow, moire-like ripples there where the quivering reflections endowed it with a mysterious life. And he often mused on the river's famous past and evoked the legends which assert that fabulous wealth lies buried in its muddy bed. At each fresh invasion of the Barbarians, and particularly when Rome was sacked, the treasures of palaces and temples are said to have been cast into the water to prevent them from falling into the hands of the conquerors. Might not those golden bars trembling yonder in the glaucous stream be the branches of the famous candelabrum which Titus brought from Jerusalem? Might not those pale patches whose shape remained uncertain amidst the frequent eddies indicate the

white marble of statues and columns ?   And those deep moires
glittering with little flamelets, were they not promiscuous
heaps of precious metal, cups, vases, ornaments enriched with
gems ?   What a dream was that of the swarming riches
espied athwart the old river's bosom, of the hidden life of the
treasures which were said to have slumbered there for centuries;
and what a hope for the nation's pride and enrichment centred
in the miraculous finds which might be made in the Tiber if
one could some day dry it up and search its bed, as had already
been suggested !   Therein, perchance, lay Rome's new fortune.

However, on that black night, whilst Pierre leant over the
parapet, it was stern reality alone which occupied his mind.
He was still pursuing the train of thought suggested by his
visits to the Trastevere and the Farnese palace, and in presence
of that lifeless water was coming to the conclusion that the
selection of Rome for transformation into a modern capital
was the great misfortune to which the sufferings of young
Italy were due.   He knew right well that the selection had
been inevitable : Rome being the queen of glory, the antique
ruler of the world to whom eternity had been promised, and
without whom the national unity had always seemed an impossibility.   And so the problem was a terrible one, since
without Rome Italy could not exist, and with Rome it seemed
difficult for it to exist.   Ah ! that dead river, how it symbolised disaster !   Not a boat upon its surface, not a quiver of
the commercial and industrial activity of those waters which
bear life to the very hearts of great modern cities !   There
had been fine schemes, no doubt—Rome a seaport, gigantic
works, canalisation to enable vessels of heavy tonnage to come
up to the Aventine ; but these were mere delusions ; the
authorities would scarcely be able to clear the river mouth,
which deposits were continually choking.   And there was that
other cause of mortal languishment, the Campagna—the desert
of death which the dead river crossed and which girdled Rome
with sterility.   There was talk of draining and planting it ;
much futile discussion on the question whether it had been
fertile in the days of the old Romans ; and even a few experiments were made ; but, all the same, Rome remained in the
midst of a vast cemetery like a city of other times, for ever
separated from the modern world by that *lande* or moor where
the dust of centuries had accumulated.   The geographical
considerations which once gave the city the empire of the
world no longer exist.   The centre of civilisation has been dis-

placed. The basin of the Mediterranean has been divided among powerful nations. In Italy all roads now lead to Milan, the city of industry and commerce, and Rome is but a town of passage. And so the most valiant efforts have failed to rouse it from its invincible slumber. The capital which the new-comers sought to improvise with such extreme haste has remained unfinished, and has almost ruined the nation. The Government, legislators, and functionaries only camp there, fleeing directly the warm weather sets in so as to escape the pernicious climate. The hotels and shops even put up their shutters, and the streets and promenades become deserts, the city having failed to acquire any life of its own, and relapsing into death as soon as the artificial life instilled into it is withdrawn. So all remains in suspense in this purely decorative capital, where only a fresh growth of men and money can finish and people the huge useless piles of the new districts. If it be true that to-morrow always blooms in the dust of the past, one ought to force oneself to hope; but Pierre asked himself if the soil were not exhausted, and since mere buildings could no longer grow on it, if it were not for ever drained of the sap which makes a race healthy, a nation powerful.

As the night advanced the lights in the houses of the Trastevere went out one by one: yet Pierre for a long time lingered on the quay, leaning over the blackened river and yielding to hopelessness. There was now no distance to the gloom; all had become dense; no longer did any reflections set a moire-like, golden quiver in the water, or reveal beneath its mystery-concealing current a fantastic, dancing vision of fabulous wealth. Gone was the legend, gone the seven-branched golden candelabrum, gone the golden vases, gone the golden jewellery, the whole dream of antique treasure that had vanished into night, even like the antique glory of Rome. Not a glimmer, nothing but slumber, disturbed solely by the heavy fall of sewage from the drain on the right hand, which could not be seen. The very water had disappeared, and Pierre no longer espied its leaden flow through the darkness, no longer had any perception of the sluggish senility, the long-dating weariness, the intense sadness of that ancient and glorious Tiber, whose waters now rolled nought but death. Only the vast, opulent sky, the eternal, pompous sky displayed the dazzling life of its milliards of planets above that river of darkness, bearing away the ruins of well-nigh three thousand years.

Before returning to his own chamber that evening Pierre
entered Dario's room, and found Victorine there preparing
things for the night. And as soon as she heard where he
had been she raised her voice in protest : 'What! you have
again been to the quay at this time of night, Monsieur
l'Abbé? You want to get a good knife-thrust yourself, it
seems. Well, for my part, I certainly wouldn't take the air
at such a late hour in this dangerous city.' Then, with her
wonted familiarity, she turned and spoke to the Prince, who
was lying back in an arm-chair and smiling : 'That girl, La
Pierina,' she said, 'hasn't been back here, but all the same
I've lately seen her prowling about among the building
materials.'

Dario raised his hand to silence her, and, addressing Pierre,
exclaimed : 'But you spoke to her, didn't you? It's becoming
idiotic! Just fancy that brute Tito coming back to dig his
knife into my other shoulder——'

All at once he paused, for he had just perceived Benedetta
standing there and listening to him ; she had slipped into the
room a moment previously in order to wish him good night.
At sight of her his embarrassment was great indeed ; he wished
to speak, explain his words, and swear that he was wholly
innocent in the affair. But she, with a smiling face, contented herself with saying, 'I knew all about it, Dario *mio*. I
am not so foolish as not to have thought it all over and understood the truth. If I ceased questioning you it was because I
knew, and loved you all the same.'

The young woman looked very happy as she spoke, and
for this she had good cause, for that very evening she had
learnt that Monsignor Palma had shown himself grateful for
the service rendered to his nephew by laying a fresh and
favourable memoir on the marriage affair before the Congregation of the Council. He had been unwilling to recall his
previous opinions so far as to range himself completely on the
Contessina's side, but the certificates of two doctors whom she
had recently seen had enabled him to conclude that her own
declarations were accurate. And gliding over the question of
wifely obedience, on which he had previously laid stress, he
had skilfully set forth the reasons which made a dissolution
of the marriage desirable. No hope of reconciliation could be
entertained, so it was certain that both parties were constantly
exposed to temptation and sin. He discreetly alluded to the
fact that the husband had already succumbed to this danger,

and praised the wife's lofty morality and piety, all the virtues which she displayed, and which guaranteed her veracity. Then, without formulating any conclusion of his own, he left the decision to the wisdom of the Congregation. And as he virtually repeated Advocate Morano's arguments, and Prada stubbornly refused to enter an appearance, it now seemed certain that the Congregation would by a great majority pronounce itself in favour of dissolution, a result which would enable the Holy Father to act benevolently.

'Ah! Dario *mio!*' said Benedetta, 'we are at the end of our worries. But what a lot of money, what a lot of money it all costs! Aunt says that they will scarcely leave us water to drink.'

So speaking she laughed with the happy heedlessness of an impassioned *amorosa*. It was not that the jurisdiction of the Congregations was in itself ruinous; indeed, in principle, it was gratuitous. Still there was a multitude of petty expenses, payments to subaltern employees, payments for medical consultations and certificates, copies of documents, and the memoirs and addresses of counsel. And although the votes of the cardinals were certainly not bought direct, some of them ended by costing considerable sums, for it often became necessary to win over dependants, to induce quite a little world to bring influence to bear upon their Eminences; without mentioning that large pecuniary gifts, when made with tact, have a decisive effect in clearing away the greatest difficulties in that sphere of the Vatican. And, briefly, Monsignor Palma's nephew by marriage had cost the Boccaneras a large sum.

'But it doesn't matter, does it, Dario *mio?*' continued Benedetta. 'Since you are now cured, they must make haste to give us permission to marry. That's all we ask of them. And if they want more, well, I'll give them my pearls, which will be all I shall have left me.'

He also laughed, for money had never held any place in his life. He had never had it at his pleasure, and simply hoped that he would always live with his uncle the cardinal, who would certainly not leave him and his young wife in the streets. Ruined as the family was, one or two hundred thousand francs represented nothing to his mind, and he had heard that certain dissolutions of marriage had cost as much as half a million. So, by way of response, he could only find a jest: 'Give them my ring as well,' said he; 'give them everything, my dear, and we shall still be happy in this old palace even if we have to sell the furniture ! '

His words filled her with enthusiasm ; she took his head between both hands and kissed him madly on the eyes in an extraordinary transport of passion. Then, suddenly turning to Pierre, she said : ' Oh ! excuse me, Monsieur l'Abbé. I was forgetting that I have a commission for you. Yes, Monsignor Nani, who brought us that good news, bade me tell you that you are making people forget you too much, and that you ought to set to work to defend your book.'

The priest listened in astonishment ; then replied : ' But it was he who advised me to disappear.'

' No doubt—only it seems that the time has now come for you to see people and plead your cause. And Monsignor Nani has been able to learn that the reporter appointed to examine your book is Monsignor Fornaro, who lives on the Piazza Navona.'

Pierre's stupefaction was increasing, for a reporter's name is never divulged, but kept quite secret, in order to ensure a free exercise of judgment. Was a new phase of his sojourn in Rome about to begin then ? His mind was all wonderment. However, he simply answered : ' Very good, I will set to work and see everybody.'

X

IN his anxiety to bring things to a finish, Pierre wished to begin his campaign on the very next day. But on whom should he first call if he were to steer clear of blunders in that intricate and conceited ecclesiastical world ? The question greatly perplexed him ; however, on opening his door that morning he luckily perceived Don Vigilio in the passage, and with a sudden inspiration asked him to step inside. He realised that this thin little man with the saffron face, who always trembled with fever and displayed such exaggerated, timorous discretion, was in reality well informed, mixed up in everything. At one period it had seemed to Pierre that the secretary purposely avoided him, doubtless for fear of compromising himself ; but recently Don Vigilio had proved less unsociable, as though he were not far from sharing the impatience which must be consuming the young Frenchman amidst his long enforced inactivity. And so, on this occasion, he did not seek to avoid the chat on which Pierre was bent.

'I must apologise,' said the latter, 'for asking you in here when things are in such disorder. But I have just received some more linen and some winter clothing from Paris. I came, you know, with just a little valise, meaning to stay for a fortnight, and yet I've now been here for nearly three months, and am no more advanced than I was on the morning of my arrival.'

Don Vigilio nodded. 'Yes, yes, I know,' said he.

Thereupon Pierre explained to him that Monsignor Nani had informed him, through the Contessina, that he now ought to act and see everybody for the defence of his book. But he was much embarrassed, as he did not know in what order to make his visits so that they might benefit him. For instance, ought he call in the first place on Monsignor Fornaro, the *consultore* selected to report on his book, and whose name had been given him?

'Ah!' exclaimed Don Vigilio, quivering; 'has Monsignor Nani gone as far as that—given you the reporter's name? That's even more than I expected.' Then, forgetting his prudence, yielding to his secret interest in the affair, he resumed: 'No, no; don't begin with Monsignor Fornaro. Your first visit should be a very humble one to the Prefect of the Congregation of the Index—his Eminence Cardinal Sanguinetti; for he would never forgive you for having offered your first homage to another should he some day hear of it.' And, after a pause, Don Vigilio added, in a low voice, amidst a faint feverish shiver: 'And he *would* hear of it; everything becomes known.'

Again he hesitated, and then, as if yielding to sudden, sympathetic courage, he took hold of the young Frenchman's hands. 'I swear to you, my dear Monsieur Froment,' he said, 'that I should be very happy to help you, for you are a man of simple soul, and I really begin to feel worried for you. But you must not ask me for impossibilities. Ah! if you only knew—if I could only tell you of all the perils which surround us! However, I think I can repeat to you that you must in no wise rely on my patron, his Eminence Cardinal Boccanera. He has expressed absolute disapproval of your book in my presence on several occasions. Only he is a saint, a most worthy, honourable man; and, though he won't defend you, he won't attack you—he will remain neutral out of regard for his niece, whom he loves so dearly, and who protects you. So, when you see him, don't plead your cause; it would be of no avail, and might even irritate him.'

Pierre was not particularly distressed by this news, for at his first interview with the Cardinal, and on the few subsequent occasions when he had respectfully visited him, he had fully understood that his Eminence would never be other than an adversary. 'Well,' said he, 'I will wait on him to thank him for his neutrality.'

But at this all Don Vigilio's terrors returned. 'No, no, don't do that; he would perhaps realise that I have spoken to you, and then what a disaster—my position would be compromised. I've said nothing, nothing! See the cardinals to begin with, see all the cardinals. Let it be understood between us that I've said nothing more.' And, on that occasion at any rate, Don Vigilio would speak no further, but left the room shuddering and darting fiery, suspicious glances on either side of the corridor.

Pierre at once went out to call on Cardinal Sanguinetti. It was ten o'clock, and there was a chance that he might find him at home. This cardinal resided on the first floor of a little palazzo in a dark, narrow street near San Luigi dei Francesi.[1] There was here none of the giant ruin full of princely and melancholy grandeur amidst which Cardinal Boccanera so stubbornly remained. The old regulation gala suite of rooms had been cut down just like the number of servants. There was no throne room, no red hat hanging under a *baldacchino*, no arm-chair turned to the wall pending a visit from the Pope. A couple of apartments served as anterooms, and then came a *salon* where the Cardinal received; and there was no luxury, indeed scarcely any comfort; the furniture was of mahogany, dating from the Empire period, and the hangings and carpets were dusty and faded by long use. Moreover, Pierre had to wait a long time for admittance, and when a servant, leisurely putting on his jacket, at last set the door ajar, it was only to say that his Eminence had been away at Frascati since the previous day.

Pierre then remembered that Cardinal Sanguinetti was one of the suburban bishops. At his see of Frascati he had a villa where he occasionally spent a few days whenever a desire for rest or some political motive impelled him to do so.

[1] This is the French church of Rome, and is under the protection of the French government.—*Trans.*

'And will his Eminence soon return?' Pierre inquired.

'Ah! we don't know. His Eminence is poorly, and expressly desired us to send nobody to worry him.'

When Pierre reached the street again he felt quite bewildered by this disappointment. At first he wondered whether he had not better call on Monsignor Fornaro without more ado, but he recollected Don Vigilio's advice to see the cardinals first of all, and, an inspiration coming to him, he resolved that his next visit should be for Cardinal Sarno, whose acquaintance he had eventually made at Donna Serafina's Mondays. In spite of Cardinal Sarno's voluntary self-effacement, people looked upon him as one of the most powerful and redoubtable members of the Sacred College, albeit his nephew Narcisse Habert declared that he knew no man who showed more obtuseness in matters which did not pertain to his habitual occupations. At all events, Pierre thought that the Cardinal, although not a member of the Congregation of the Index, might well give him some good advice, and possibly bring his great influence to bear on his colleagues.

The young man straightway betook himself to the Palace of the Propaganda, where he knew he would find the Cardinal. This palace, which is seen from the Piazza di Spagna, is a bare, massive corner pile between two streets. And Pierre, hampered by his faulty Italian, quite lost himself in it, climbing to floors whence he had to descend again, and finding himself in a perfect labyrinth of stairs, passages, and halls. At last he luckily came across the Cardinal's secretary, an amiable young priest, whom he had already seen at the Boccanera mansion. 'Why, yes,' said the secretary, 'I think that his Eminence will receive you. You did well to come at this hour, for he is always here of a morning. Kindly follow me, if you please.'

Then came a fresh journey. Cardinal Sarno, long a secretary of the Propaganda, now presided over the commission which controlled the organisation of worship in those countries of Europe, Africa, America, and Oceania where Catholicism had lately gained a footing; and he thus had a private room of his own with special offices and assistants, reigning there with the ultra-methodical habits of a functionary who had grown old in his arm-chair, closely surrounded by nests of drawers, and knowing nothing of the world save the usual sights of the street below his window.

The secretary left Pierre on a bench at the end of a dark passage, which was lighted by gas even in full daylight. And quite a quarter of an hour went by before he returned with his eager, affable air. 'His Eminence is conferring with some missionaries who are about to leave Rome,' he said; 'but it will soon be over, and he told me to take you to his room, where you can wait for him.'

As soon as Pierre was alone in the Cardinal's sanctum he examined it with curiosity. Fairly spacious, but in no wise luxurious, it had green paper on its walls, and its furniture was of black wood and green damask. From two windows overlooking a narrow side-street a mournful light reached the dark wall-paper and faded carpets. There were a couple of pier tables and a plain black writing-table, which stood near one window, its worn moleskin covering littered with all sorts of papers. Pierre drew near to it for a moment, and glanced at the arm-chair with damaged, sunken seat, the screen which sheltered it from draughts, and the old inkstand splotched with ink. And then, in the lifeless and oppressive atmosphere, the disquieting silence, which only the low rumbles from the street disturbed, he began to grow impatient.

However, whilst he was softly walking up and down he suddenly espied a map affixed to one wall, and the sight of it filled him with such absorbing thoughts that he soon forgot everything else. It was a coloured map of the world, the different tints indicating whether the territories belonged to victorious Catholicism or whether Catholicism was still warring there against unbelief; these last countries being classified as vicariates or prefectures, according to the general principles of organisation. And the whole was a graphic presentment of the long efforts of Catholicism in striving for the universal dominion which it has sought so unremittingly since its earliest hour. God has given the world to His Church, but it is needful that she should secure possession of it since error so stubbornly abides. From this has sprung the eternal battle, the fight which is carried on, even in our days, to win nations over from other religions, as it was in the days when the Apostles quitted Judæa to spread abroad the tidings of the Gospel. During the middle ages the great task was to organise conquered Europe, and this was too absorbing an enterprise to allow of any attempt at reconciliation with the dissident churches of the East. Then the Reformation burst forth, schism was added to schism, and the Protestant half of Europe had to be reconquered as well as all the orthodox East.

Warlike ardour, however, awoke at the discovery of the New World. Rome was ambitious of securing that other side of the earth, and missions were organised for the subjection of races of which nobody had known anything the day before, but which God had, nevertheless, given to His Church, like all the others. And by degrees the two great divisions of Christianity were formed, on one hand the Catholic nations, those where the faith simply had to be kept up, and which the Secretariate of State installed at the Vatican guided with sovereign authority, and on the other the schismatical or pagan nations which were to be brought back to the fold or converted, and over which the Congregation of the Propaganda sought to reign. Then this Congregation had been obliged to divide itself into two branches in order to facilitate its work— the Oriental branch, which dealt with the dissident sects of the East, and the Latin branch, whose authority extended over all the other lands of mission : the two forming a vast organisation—a huge, strong, closely-meshed net cast over the whole world in order that not a single soul might escape.

It was in presence of that map that Pierre for the first time became clearly conscious of the mechanism which for centuries had been working to bring about the absorption of humanity. The Propaganda, richly dowered by the popes and disposing of a considerable revenue, appeared to him like a separate force, a papacy within the papacy, and he well understood that the Prefect of the Congregation should be called the ' Red Pope,' for how limitless were the powers of that man of conquest and domination, whose hands stretched from one to the other end of the earth. Allowing that the Cardinal Secretary held Europe, that diminutive portion of the globe, did not he, the Prefect, hold all the rest—the infinity of space, the distant countries as yet almost unknown ? Besides, statistics showed that Rome's uncontested dominion was limited to 200 millions of Apostolic and Roman Catholics ; whereas the schismatics of the East and the Reformation, if added together, already exceeded that number, and how small became the minority of the true believers when, besides the schismatics, one brought into line the 1,000 millions of infidels who yet remained to be converted. The figures struck Pierre with a force which made him shudder. What ! there were 5 million Jews, nearly 200 million Mahommedans, more than 700 million Brahmanists and Buddhists, without counting another 100 million pagans of divers creeds, the whole making 1,000 millions, and against these the Christians could marshal barely more than 400 millions, who were divided among themselves, ever in conflict, one half with Rome and the other half against her?[1] Was it possible that in 1,800 years Christianity had not proved victorious over even one-third of mankind, and that Rome, the eternal and all-powerful, only counted a sixth part of the nations among her subjects? Only one soul saved out of every six—how fearful was the disproportion! However, the map spoke with brutal eloquence: the red-tinted empire of Rome was but a speck when compared with the yellow-hued empire of the other gods —the endless countries which the Propaganda still had to conquer. And the question arose: How many centuries must elapse before the promises of the Christ were realised, before the whole world were gained to Christianity, before religious society spread over secular society, and there remained but one kingdom and one belief? And in presence of this question, in presence of the prodigious labour yet to be accomplished, how great was one's astonishment when one thought of Rome's tranquil serenity, her patient stubbornness, which has never known doubt or weariness, her bishops and ministers toiling without cessation in the conviction that she alone will some day be the mistress of the world!

Narcisse had told Pierre how carefully the embassies at Rome watched the doings of the Propaganda, for the missions were often the instruments of one or another nation, and exercised decisive influence in far-away lands. And so there was a continual struggle, in which the Congregation did all it could to favour the missionaries of Italy and her allies. It had always been jealous of its French rival, 'L'Œuvre de la Propagation de la Foi,' installed at Lyons, which is as wealthy in money as itself, and richer in men of energy and courage.

---

[1] Some readers may question certain of the figures given by M. Zola, but it must be remembered that all such calculations (even those of the best 'authorities') are largely guesswork. I myself think that there are more than 5 million Jews, and more than 200 millions of Mahommedans, but I regard the alleged number of Brahmanists and Buddhists as exaggerated. On the other hand, some statistical tables specify 80 millions of Confucianists, of whom M. Zola makes no separate mention. However, as regards the number of Christians in the world, the figures given above are, within a few millions, probably accurate.—*Trans.*

However, not content with levelling tribute on this French association, the Propaganda thwarted it, sacrificed it on every occasion when it had reason to think it might achieve a victory. Not once or twice, but over and over again had the French missionaries, the French orders, been driven from the scenes of their labours to make way for Italians or Germans. And Pierre, standing in that mournful, dusty room, which the sunlight never brightened, pictured the secret hot-bed of political intrigue masked by the civilising ardour of faith. Again he shuddered as one shudders when monstrous, terrifying things are brought home to one. And might not the most sensible be overcome ? Might not the bravest be dismayed by the thought of that universal engine of conquest and domination, which worked with the stubbornness of eternity, not merely content with the gain of souls, but ever seeking to ensure its future sovereignty over the whole of corporeal humanity, and—pending the time when it might rule the nations itself—disposing of them, handing them over to the charge of this or that temporary master, in accordance with its good pleasure. And then, too, what a prodigious dream ! Rome smiling and tranquilly awaiting the day when she will have united Christians, Mahommedans, Brahmanists, and Buddhists into one sole nation, of whom she will be both the spiritual and the temporal queen !

However, a sound of coughing made Pierre turn, and he started on perceiving Cardinal Sarno, whom he had not heard enter. Standing in front of that map, he felt like one caught in the act of prying into a secret, and a deep flush overspread his face. The Cardinal, however, after looking at him fixedly with his dim eyes, went to his writing-table, and let himself drop into the arm-chair without saying a word. With a gesture he dispensed Pierre of the duty of kissing his ring.

' I desired to offer my homage to your Eminence,' said the young man. ' Is your Eminence unwell ? '

' No, no, it's nothing but a dreadful cold which I can't get rid of. And then, too, I have so many things to attend to just now.'

Pierre looked at the Cardinal as he appeared in the livid light from the window, puny, lopsided, with the left shoulder higher than the right, and not a sign of life on his worn and ashen countenance. The young priest was reminded of one of his uncles, who, after thirty years spent in the offices of a French public department, displayed the same lifeless glance, parchment-like skin, and weary hebetation. Was it possible that this withered old man, so lost in his black cassock with red edging, was really one of the masters of the world, with the map of Christendom so deeply stamped on his mind, albeit he had never left Rome, that the Prefect of the Propaganda did not take a decision without asking his opinion?

'Sit down, Monsieur l'Abbé,' said the Cardinal. 'So you have come to see me—you have something to ask of me!' And, whilst disposing himself to listen, he stretched out his thin bony hands to finger the documents heaped up before him, glancing at each of them like some general, some strategist, profoundly versed in the science of his profession, who, although his army is far away, nevertheless directs it to victory from his private room, never for a moment allowing it to escape his mind.

Pierre was somewhat embarrassed by such a plain enunciation of the interested object of his visit; still, he decided to go to the point. 'Yes, indeed,' he answered, 'it is a liberty I have taken to come and appeal to your Eminence's wisdom for advice. Your Eminence is aware that I am in Rome for the purpose of defending a book of mine, and I should be grateful if your Eminence would help and guide me.' Then he gave a brief account of the present position of the affair, and began to plead his cause; but as he continued speaking he noticed that the Cardinal gave him very little attention, as though indeed he were thinking of something else, and failed to understand.

'Ah! yes,' the great man at last muttered, 'you have written a book. There was some question of it at Donna Serafina's one evening. But a priest ought not to write; it is a mistake for him to do so. What is the good of it? And the Congregation of the Index must certainly be in the right if it is prosecuting your book. At all events, what can I do? I don't belong to the Congregation, and I know nothing, nothing about the matter.'

Pierre, pained at finding him so listless and indifferent, went on trying to enlighten and move him. But he realised that this man's mind, so far-reaching and penetrating in the field in which it had worked for forty years, closed up as soon as one sought to divert it from its speciality. It was neither an inquisitive nor a supple mind. All trace of life faded from the Cardinal's eyes, and his entire countenance assumed an expression of mournful imbecility. 'I know nothing, nothing,' he repeated, 'and I never recommend anybody.' However,

at last he made an effort : ' But Nani is mixed up in this,'
said he. ' What does Nani advise you to do ? '

' Monsignor Nani has been kind enough to reveal to me
that the reporter is Monsignor Fornaro, and advises me to see
him.'

At this Cardinal Sarno seemed surprised and somewhat
roused. A little light returned to his eyes. ' Ah ! really,' he
rejoined, ' ah ! really—— Well, if Nani has done that he must
have some idea. Go and see Monsignor Fornaro.' Then,
after rising and dismissing his visitor, who was compelled to
thank him, bowing deeply, he resumed his seat, and a moment
later the only sound in the lifeless room was that of his bony
fingers turning over the documents before him.

Pierre, in all docility, followed the advice given him, and
immediately betook himself to the Piazza Navona, where,
however, he learnt from one of Monsignor Fornaro's servants
that the prelate had just gone out, and that to find him at home
it was necessary to call in the morning at ten o'clock. Accordingly it was only on the following day that Pierre was able to
obtain an interview. He had previously made inquiries and
knew what was necessary concerning Monsignor Fornaro.
Born at Naples, he had there begun his studies under the
Barnabites, had finished them at the Seminario Romano, and
had subsequently, for many years, been a professor at the
Università Gregoriana. Nowadays Consultor to several congregations and a Canon of Santa Maria Maggiore, he placed
his immediate ambition in a Canonry at St. Peter's, and harboured the dream of some day becoming secretary of the
Consistorial Congregation, a post conducting to the cardinalate.
A theologian of remarkable ability, Monsignor Fornaro incurred
no other reproach than that of occasionally sacrificing to literature by contributing articles, which he carefully abstained
from signing, to certain religious reviews. He was also said
to be very worldly.

Pierre was received as soon as he had sent in his card, and
perhaps he would have fancied that his visit was expected had
not an appearance of sincere surprise, blended with a little
anxiety, marked his reception.

' Monsieur l'Abbé Froment, Monsieur l'Abbé Froment,'
repeated the prelate, looking at the card which he still held.
' Kindly step in—I was about to forbid my door, for I have
some urgent work to attend to. But no matter, sit down.'

Pierre, however, remained standing, quite charmed by the

blooming appearance of this tall, strong, handsome man who, although five and forty years of age, was quite fresh and rosy, with moist lips, caressing eyes, and scarcely a grey hair among his curly locks. Nobody more fascinating and decorative could be found among the whole Roman prelacy. Careful of his person undoubtedly, and aiming at a simple elegance, he looked really superb in his black cassock with violet collar. And around him the spacious room where he received his visitors, gaily lighted as it was by two large windows facing the Piazza Navona, and furnished with a taste nowadays seldom met with among the Roman clergy, diffused a pleasant odour and formed a setting instinct with kindly cheerfulness.

'Pray sit down, Monsieur l'Abbé Froment,' he resumed, 'and tell me to what I am indebted for the honour of your visit.'

He had already recovered his self-possession and assumed a *naïf*, purely obliging air; and Pierre, though the question was only natural, and he ought to have foreseen it, suddenly felt greatly embarrassed, more embarrassed indeed than in Cardinal Sarno's presence. Should he go to the point at once, confess the delicate motive of his visit? A moment's reflection showed him that this would be the best and worthier course. 'Dear me, Monseigneur,' he replied, 'I know very well that the step I have taken in calling on you is not usually taken, but it has been advised me, and it has seemed to me that among honest folks there can never be any harm in seeking in all good faith to elucidate the truth.'

'What is it, what is it, then?' asked the prelate with an expression of perfect candour, and still continuing to smile.

'Well, simply this. I have learnt that the Congregation of the Index has handed you my book "New Rome," and appointed you to examine it; and I have ventured to present myself before you in case you should have any explanations to ask of me.'

But Monsignor Fornaro seemed unwilling to hear any more. He had carried both hands to his head and drawn back, albeit still courteous. 'No, no,' said he, 'don't tell me that, don't continue, you would grieve me dreadfully. Let us say, if you like, that you have been deceived, for nothing ought to be known, in fact nothing is known, either by others or myself. I pray you, do not let us talk of such matters.'

Pierre, however, had fortunately remarked what a decisive

effect was produced when he had occasion to mention the name of the Assessor of the Holy Office. So it occurred to him to reply: 'I most certainly do not desire to give you the slightest cause for embarrassment, Monseigneur, and I repeat to you that I would never have ventured to importune you if Monsignor Nani himself had not acquainted me with your name and address.'

This time the effect was immediate, though Monsignor Fornaro, with that easy grace which he introduced into all things, made some ceremony about surrendering. He began by a demurrer, speaking archly with subtle shades of expression. 'What! is Monsignor Nani the tattler! But I shall scold him, I shall get angry with him! And what does he know? He doesn't belong to the Congregation; he may have been led into error. You must tell him that he has made a mistake, and that I have nothing at all to do with your affair. That will teach him not to reveal needful secrets which everybody respects!' Then, in a pleasant way, with winning glance and flowery lips, he went on: 'Come, since Monsignor Nani desires it, I am willing to chat with you for a moment, my dear Monsieur Froment, but on condition that you shall know nothing of my report or of what may have been said or done at the Congregation.'

Pierre in his turn smiled, admiring how easy things became when forms were respected and appearances saved. And once again he began to explain his case, the profound astonishment into which the prosecution of his book had thrown him, and his ignorance of the objections which were taken to it, and for which he had vainly sought a cause.

'Really, really,' repeated the prelate, quite amazed at so much innocence. 'The Congregation is a tribunal, and can only act when a case is brought before it. Proceedings have been taken against your book simply because it has been denounced.'

'Yes, I know, denounced.'

'Of course. Complaint was laid by three French bishops, whose names you will allow me to keep secret, and it consequently became necessary for the Congregation to examine the incriminated work.'

Pierre looked at him quite scared. Denounced by three bishops? Why? With what object? Then he thought of his protector. 'But Cardinal Bergerot,' said he, 'wrote me a letter of approval, which I placed at the beginning of my work as a preface. Ought not a guarantee like that to have been sufficient for the French episcopacy?'

Monsignor Fornaro wagged his head in a knowing way before making up his mind to reply: 'Ah! yes, no doubt, his Eminence's letter, a very beautiful letter. I think, however, that it would have been much better if he had not written it, both for himself and for you especially.' Then as the priest, whose surprise was increasing, opened his mouth to urge him to explain himself, he went on: 'No, no, I know nothing, I say nothing. His Eminence Cardinal Bergerot is a saintly man whom everybody venerates, and if it were possible for him to sin it would only be through pure goodness of heart.'

Silence fell. Pierre could divine that an abyss was opening, and dared not insist. However, he at last resumed with some violence: 'But, after all, why should my book be prosecuted, and the books of others be left untouched? I have no intention of acting as a denouncer myself, but how many books there are to which Rome closes her eyes, and which are far more dangerous than mine can be!'

This time Monsignor Fornaro seemed glad to be able to support Pierre's view. 'You are right,' said he, 'we cannot deal with every bad book, and it greatly distresses us. But you must remember what an incalculable number of works we should be compelled to read. And so we have to content ourselves with condemning the worst *en bloc*.'

Then he complacently entered into explanations. In principle, no printer ought to send any work to press without having previously submitted the manuscript to the approval of the bishop of the diocese. Nowadays, however, with the enormous output of the printing trade, one could understand how terribly embarrassed the bishops would be if the printers were suddenly to conform to the Church's regulation. There was neither the time nor the money, nor were there the men necessary for such colossal labour. And so the Congregation of the Index condemned *en masse*, without examination, all works of certain categories: first, books which were dangerous for morals, all erotic writings, and all novels; next the various bibles in the vulgar tongue, for the perusal of Holy Writ without discretion was not allowable; then the books on magic and sorcery, and all works on science, history, or philosophy that were in any way contrary to dogma, as well as the writings of heresiarchs or more ecclesiastics discussing

ROME   333

religion, which should never be discussed. All these were
wise laws made by different popes, and were set forth in the
preface to the catalogue of forbidden books which the Congregation published, and without them this catalogue to
have been complete would in itself have formed a large
library.   On turning it over one found that the works
singled out for interdiction were chiefly those of priests, the
task being so vast and difficult that Rome's concern extended
but little beyond the observance of good order within the
Church.   And Pierre and his book came within the limit.
    'You will understand,' continued Monsignor Fornaro,
' that we have no desire to advertise a heap of unwholesome
writings by honouring them with special condemnation.
Their name is legion in every country, and we should have
neither enough paper nor enough ink to deal with them all.
So we content ourselves with condemning one from time to
time, when it bears a famous name and makes too much noise,
or contains disquieting attacks on the faith.   This suffices to
remind the world that we exist and defend ourselves without
abandoning aught of our rights or duties.'
    'But my book, my book,' exclaimed Pierre, 'why these
proceedings against my book?'
    'I am explaining that to you as far as it is allowable for
me to do, my dear Monsieur Froment.   You are a priest, your
book is a success, you have published a cheap edition of it
which sells very readily; and I don't speak of its literary merit,
which is remarkable, for it contains a breath of real poetry
which transported me, and on which I must really compliment you.   However, under the circumstances which I have
enumerated, how could we close our eyes to such a work as
yours, in which the conclusion arrived at is the annihilation of
our holy religion and the destruction of Rome?'
    Pierre remained open-mouthed, suffocating with surprise.
'The destruction of Rome!' he at last exclaimed; 'but I
desire to see Rome rejuvenated, eternal, again the queen of
the world.'   And, once more mastered by his glowing enthusiasm, he defended himself and confessed his faith : Catholicism reverting to the principles and practices of the primitive
church, drawing the blood of regeneration from the fraternal
Christianity of Jesus; the Pope, freed from all terrestrial
royalty, governing the whole of humanity with charity and
love, and saving the world from the frightful social cataclysm
that threatens it by leading it to the real Kingdom of God :

the Christian communion of all nations united in one nation
only. 'And can the Holy Father disavow me ?' he continued.
'Are not these his secret ideas, which people are beginning to
divine, and does not my only offence lie in having expressed
them perhaps too soon and too freely ?   And if I were allowed
to see him should I not at once obtain from him an order to
stop these proceedings ?'

Monsignor Fornaro no longer spoke, but wagged his head
without appearing offended by the priest's juvenile ardour.
On the contrary, he smiled with increasing amiability, as
though highly amused by so much innocence and imagination.
At last he gaily responded, 'Oh ! speak on, speak on ; it isn't I
who will stop you. I'm forbidden to say anything. But the
temporal power, the temporal power.'

'Well, what of the temporal power ?' asked Pierre.

The prelate had again become silent, raising his amiable
face to heaven and waving his white hands with a pretty gesture. And when he once more opened his mouth it was
to say : 'Then there's your new religion—for the expression occurs twice : the new religion, the new religion—Ah,
Dio !'

Again he became restless, going off into an ecstasy of
wonderment, at sight of which Pierre impatiently exclaimed :
'I do not know what your report will be, Monseigneur, but I
declare to you that I have had no desire to attack dogma.
And, candidly now, my whole book shows that I only sought
to write a work of pity and salvation. It is only justice that
some account should be taken of one's intentions.'

Monsignor Fornaro had become very calm and paternal
again. 'Oh ! intentions ! intentions !' he said as he rose to
dismiss his visitor. 'You may be sure, my dear Monsieur
Froment, that I feel much honoured by your visit. Naturally
I cannot tell you what my report will be ; as it is, we have
talked too much about it, and, in fact, I ought to have refused
to listen to your defence. At the same time, you will always
find me ready to be of service to you in anything that does
not go against my duty. But I greatly fear that your book
will be condemned.' And then, as Pierre again started, he
added : 'Well, yes. It is facts that are judged, you know, not
intentions. So all defence is useless ; the book is there, and
we take it such as it is. However much you may try to explain it, you cannot alter it. And this is why the Congregation
never calls the accused parties before it, and never accepts from

them aught but retraction pure and simple. And, indeed, the wisest course would be for you to withdraw your book and make your submission. No? You won't? Ah! how young you are, my friend!'

He laughed yet more loudly at the gesture of revolt, of indomitable pride which had just escaped his young friend, as he called him. Then, on reaching the door, he again threw off some of his reserve, and said in a low voice, 'Come, my dear Abbé, there is something I will do for you. I will give you some good advice. At bottom, I myself am nothing. I deliver my report, and it is printed, and the members of the Congregation read it, but are quite free to pay no attention to it. However, the Secretary of the Congregation, Father Dangelis, can accomplish everything, even impossibilities. Go to see him; you will find him at the Dominican convent behind the Piazza di Spagna. Don't name me. And for the present good-bye, my dear fellow, good-bye.'

Pierre once more found himself on the Piazza Navona, quite dazed, no longer knowing what to believe or hope. A cowardly idea was coming over him; why should he continue this struggle, in which his adversaries remained unknown and indiscernible? Why carry obstinacy any further, why linger any longer in that impassionating but deceptive Rome? He would flee that very evening, return to Paris, disappear there, and forget his bitter disillusion in the practice of humble charity. He was traversing one of those hours of weakness when the long-dreamt-of task suddenly seems to be an impossibility. However, amidst his great confusion he was nevertheless walking on, going towards his destination. And when he found himself in the Corso, then in the Via dei Condotti, and finally in the Piazza di Spagna, he resolved that he would at any rate see Father Dangelis. The Dominican convent is there, just below the Trinità de' Monti.

Ah! those Dominicans! Pierre had never thought of them without a feeling of respect with which mingled a little fear. What vigorous pillars of the principle of authority and theocracy they had for centuries proved themselves to be! To them the Church had been indebted for its greatest measure of authority; they were the glorious soldiers of its triumph. Whilst St. Francis won the souls of the humble over to Rome, St. Dominic, on Rome's behalf, subjected all the superior souls— those of the intelligent and powerful. And this he did with passion, amidst a blaze of faith and determination, making use of all possible means, preachings, writings, and police and judicial pressure. Though he did not found the Inquisition, its principles were his, and it was with fire and sword that his fraternal, loving heart waged war on schism. Living like his monks, in poverty, chastity, and obedience—the great virtues of those times of pride and licentiousness—he went from city to city, exhorting the impious, striving to bring them back to the Church and arraigning them before the ecclesiastical courts when his preachings did not suffice. He also laid siege to science, sought to make it his own, dreamt of defending God with the weapons of reason and human knowledge like a true forerunner of the angelic St. Thomas, that light of the middle ages, who joined the Dominican order and set every-thing in his 'Summa Theologiæ,' psychology, logic, policy, and morals. And thus it was that the Dominicans filled the world, upholding the doctrines of Rome in the most famous pulpits of every nation, and contending almost everywhere against the free spirit of the Universities, like the vigilant guardians of dogma that they were, the unwearying artisans of the fortunes of the popes, the most powerful amongst all the artistic, scientific, and literary workers who raised the huge edifice of Catholicism such as it exists to-day.

However, Pierre, who could feel that this edifice was even now tottering, though it had been built, people fancied, so substantially as to last through all eternity, asked himself what could be the present use of the Dominicans, those toilers of another age, whose police system and whose tribunals had perished beneath universal execration, whose voices were no longer listened to, whose books were but seldom read, and whose *rôle* as *savants* and civilisers had come to an end in presence of latter day science, the truths of which were rending dogma on all sides. Certainly the Dominicans still form an influential and prosperous order; but how far one is from the times when their general reigned in Rome, Master of the Holy Palace, with convents and schools, and subjects throughout Europe. Of all their vast inheritance, so far as the Roman curia is concerned, only a few posts now remain to them, and among others the secretaryship of the Congregation of the Index, a former dependency of the Holy Office where they once despotically ruled.

Pierre was immediately ushered into the presence of Father Dangelis. The convent parlour was vast, bare, and white, flooded with bright sunshine. The only furniture was a table and some stools; and a large brass crucifix hung from the wall. Near the table stood the Father, a very thin man of about fifty, severely draped in his ample white habit and black mantle. From his long ascetic face, with thin lips, thin nose, and pointed, obstinate chin, his grey eyes shone out with a fixity that embarrassed one. And, moreover, he showed himself very plain and simple of speech, and frigidly polite in manner.

'Monsieur l'Abbé Froment—the author of "New Rome," I suppose?' Then seating himself on one stool and pointing to another, he added: 'Pray acquaint me with the object of your visit, Monsieur l'Abbé.'

Thereupon Pierre had to begin his explanations, his defence, all over again; and the task soon became the more painful as his words fell from his lips amidst death-like silence and frigidity. Father Dangelis did not stir; with his hands crossed upon his knees he kept his sharp, penetrating eyes fixed upon those of the priest. And when the latter had at last ceased speaking, he slowly said: 'I did not like to interrupt you, Monsieur l'Abbé, but it was not for me to hear all this. Process against your book has begun, and no power in the world can stay or impede its course. I do not therefore realise what it is that you apparently expect of me.'

In a quivering voice Pierre was bold enough to answer: 'I look for some kindness and justice.'

A pale smile, instinct with proud humility, arose to the Dominican's lips. 'Be without fear,' he replied, 'God has ever deigned to enlighten me in the discharge of my modest duties. Personally, be it said, I have no justice to render; I am but an employee whose duty is to classify matters and draw up documents concerning them. Their Eminences, the members of the Congregation, will alone pronounce judgment on your book. And assuredly they will do so with the help of the Holy Spirit. You will only have to bow to their sentence when it shall have been ratified by His Holiness.'

Then he broke off the interview by rising, and Pierre was obliged to do the same. The Dominican's words were virtually identical with those that had fallen from Monsignor Fornaro, but they were spoken with cutting frankness, a sort of tranquil bravery. On all sides Pierre came into collision with the same anonymous force, the same powerful engine whose component parts sought to ignore one another.

For a long time yet, no doubt, he would be sent from one to the other, without ever finding the volitional element which reasoned and acted. And the only thing that he could do was to bow to it all.

However, before going off, it occurred to him once more to mention the name of Monsignor Nani, the powerful effect of which he had begun to realise. 'I ask your pardon,' he said, 'for having disturbed you to no purpose, but I simply deferred to the kind advice of Monsignor Nani, who has condescended to show me some interest.'

The effect of these words was unexpected. Again did Father Dangelis's thin face brighten into a smile, but with a twist of the lips, sharp with ironical contempt. He had become yet paler than before, and his keen intelligent eyes were flaming.

'Ah! it was Monsignor Nani who sent you!' he said. 'Well, if you think you need a protector, it is useless for you to apply to any other than himself. He is all-powerful. Go to see him; go to see him!'

And that was the only encouragement Pierre derived from his visit: the advice to go back to the man who had sent him. At this he felt that he was losing ground, and he resolved to return home in order to reflect on things and try to understand them before taking any further steps. The idea of questioning Don Vigilio at once occurred to him, and that same evening after supper he luckily met the secretary in the corridor, just as, candle in hand, he was on his way to bed.

'I have so many things that I should like to say to you,' Pierre said to him. 'Can you kindly come to my rooms for a moment?'

But the other promptly silenced him with a gesture, and then whispered: 'Didn't you see Abbé Paparelli on the first floor? He was following us, I'm sure.'

Pierre often saw the train-bearer roaming about the house, and greatly disliked his stealthy, prying ways. However, he had hitherto attached no importance to him, and was therefore much surprised by Don Vigilio's question. The other, without awaiting his reply, had returned to the end of the corridor, where for a long while he remained listening. Then he came back on tiptoe, blew out his candle, and darted into Pierre's sitting-room. 'There—that's done,' he murmured directly the door was shut. 'But if it is all the same to you, we won't stop in this sitting-room. Let us go into your bedroom. Two walls are better than one.'

When the lamp had been placed on the table and they found themselves seated face to face in that bare, faded bedchamber, Pierre noticed that the secretary was suffering from a more violent attack of fever than usual. His thin puny figure was shivering from head to foot, and his ardent eyes had never before blazed so blackly in his ravaged, yellow face. 'Are you poorly?' asked Pierre. 'I don't want to tire you.'

'Poorly, yes, I am on fire—but I want to talk. I can't bear it any longer. One always has to relieve oneself some day or other.'

Was it his complaint that he desired to relieve; or was he anxious to break his long silence in order that it might not stifle him? This at first remained uncertain. He immediately asked for an account of the steps that Pierre had lately taken, and became yet more restless when he heard how the other had been received by Cardinal Sarno, Monsignor Fornaro, and Father Dangelis. 'Yes, that's quite it,' he repeated, 'nothing astonishes me nowadays, and yet I feel indignant on your account. Yes, it doesn't concern me, but all the same it makes me ill, for it reminds me of all my own troubles. You must not rely on Cardinal Sarno, remember, for he is always elsewhere, with his mind far away, and has never helped anybody. But that Fornaro, that Fornaro!'

'He seemed to me very amiable, even kindly disposed,' replied Pierre; ' and I really think that after our interview, he will considerably soften his report.'

'He! Why, the gentler he was with you the more grievously he will saddle you! He will devour you, fatten himself with such easy prey. Ah! you don't know him, *dilizioso* that he is, ever on the watch to rear his own fortune on the troubles of poor devils whose defeat is bound to please the powerful. I prefer the other one, Father Dangelis, a terrible man, no doubt, but frank and brave and of superior mind. I must admit, however, that he would burn you like a handful of straw if he were the master. And ah! if I could tell you everything, if I could show you the frightful underside of this world of ours, the monstrous, ravenous ambition, the abominable network of intrigues, venality, cowardice, treachery, and even crime!'

On seeing Don Vigilio so excited, in such a blaze of spite, Pierre thought of extracting from him some of the many items of information which he had hitherto sought in vain. 'Well, tell me merely what is the position of my affair,' he responded. 'When I questioned you on my arrival here you said that nothing had yet reached Cardinal Boccanera. But all information must now have been collected, and you must know of it. And, by the way, Monsignor Fornaro told me that three French bishops had asked that my book should be prosecuted. Three bishops, is it possible?'

Don Vigilio shrugged his shoulders. 'Ah!' said he, 'yours is an innocent soul! I'm surprised that there were *only* three! Yes, several documents relating to your affair are in our hands; and, moreover, things have turned out much as I suspected. The three bishops are first the Bishop of Tarbes, who evidently carries out the vengeance of the Fathers of Lourdes; and then the Bishops of Poitiers and Evreux, who are both known as uncompromising Ultramontanists and passionate adversaries of Cardinal Bergerot. The Cardinal, you know, is regarded with disfavour at the Vatican, where his Gallican ideas and broad liberal mind provoke perfect anger. And don't seek for anything else. The whole affair lies in that: an execution which the powerful Fathers of Lourdes demand of his Holiness, and a desire to reach and strike Cardinal Bergerot through your book, by means of the letter of approval which he imprudently wrote to you and which you published by way of preface. For a long time past the condemnations of the Index have largely been secret knock-down blows levelled at Churchmen. Denunciation reigns supreme, and the law applied is that of good pleasure. I could tell you some almost incredible things, how perfectly innocent books have been selected among a hundred for the sole object of killing an idea or a man; for the blow is almost always levelled at someone behind the author, someone higher than he is. And there is such a hotbed of intrigue, such a source of abuses in this institution of the Index, that it is tottering, and even among those who surround the Pope it is felt that it must soon be freshly regulated if it is not to fall into complete discredit. I well understand that the Church should endeavour to retain universal power, and govern by every fit weapon, but the weapons must be such as one can use without their injustice leading to revolt, or their antique childishness provoking merriment!'

Pierre listened with dolorous astonishment in his heart. Since he had been at Rome and had seen the Fathers of the

Grotto saluted and feared there, holding an authoritative position, thanks to the large alms which they contributed to the Peter's Pence, he had felt that they were behind the proceedings instituted against him, and realised that he would have to pay for a certain page of his book in which he had called attention to an iniquitous displacement of fortune at Lourdes, a frightful spectacle which made one doubt the very existence of the Divinity, a continual cause of battle and conflict which would disappear in the truly Christian society of to-morrow. And he could also now understand that his delight at the loss of the temporal power must have caused a scandal, and especially that the unfortunate expression 'a new religion' had alone been sufficient to arm *delatores* against him. But that which amazed and grieved him was to learn that Cardinal Bergerot's letter was looked upon as a crime, and that his (Pierre's) book was denounced and condemned in order that adversaries who dared not attack the venerable pastor face to face might deal him a cowardly blow from behind. The thought of afflicting that saintly man, of serving as the implement to strike him in his ardent charity, cruelly grieved Pierre. And how bitter and disheartening it was to find the most hideous questions of pride and money, ambition and appetite, running riot with the most ferocious egotism, beneath the quarrels of those leaders of the Church who ought only to have contended together in love for the poor !

And then Pierre's mind revolted against that supremely odious and idiotic Index. He now understood how it worked, from the arrival of the denunciations to the public posting of the titles of the condemned works. He had just seen the secretary of the Congregation, Father Dangelis, to whom the denunciations came, and who then investigated the affair, collecting all documents and information concerning it with the passion of a cultivated authoritarian monk, who dreamt of ruling minds and consciences as in the heroic days of the Inquisition. Then, too, Pierre had visited one of the consultive prelates, Monsignor Fornaro, who was so ambitious and affable, and so subtle a theologian that he would have discovered attacks against the faith in a treatise on algebra, had his interests required it. Next there were the infrequent meetings of the cardinals, who at long intervals voted for the interdiction of some hostile book, deeply regretting that they could not suppress them all ; and finally came the Pope, approving and signing the decrees, which was a mere formality,

for were not all books guilty? But what an extraordinary
wretched Bastille of the past was that aged Index, that senile
institution now sunk into second childhood. One realised
that it must have been a formidable power when books were
rare and the Church had tribunals of blood and fire to
enforce her edicts. But books had so greatly multiplied, the
written, printed thoughts of mankind had swollen into such
a deep broad river, that they had swept all opposition away,
and now the Index was swamped and reduced to powerless-
ness, compelled more and more to limit its field of action, to
confine itself to the examination of the writings of ecclesiastics, and even in this respect it was becoming corrupt,
fouled by the worst passions and changed into an instrument
of intrigue, hatred and vengeance. Ah! that confession of
decay, of paralysis which grew more and more complete
amidst the scornful indifference of the nations. To think
that Catholicism, the once glorious agent of civilisation, had
come to such a pass that it cast books into hell-fire by the
heap; and what books they were, almost the entire literature,
history, philosophy and science of the past and the present!
Few works, indeed, are published nowadays that would not
fall under the ban of the Church. If she seems to close her
eyes, it is in order to avoid the impossible task of hunting out
and destroying everything. Yet she stubbornly insists on
retaining a semblance of sovereign authority over human
intelligence, just as some very aged queen, dispossessed of
her states and henceforth without judges or executioners,
might continue to deliver vain sentences to which only an
infinitesimal minority would pay heed. But imagine the
Church momentarily victorious, miraculously mastering the
modern world, and ask yourself what she, with her tribunals
to condemn and her gendarmes to enforce, would do with
human thought. Imagine a strict application of the Index
regulations: no printer able to put anything whatever to
press without the approval of his bishop, and even then
every book laid before the Congregation, the past expunged,
the present throttled, subjected to an intellectual Reign of
Terror! Would not the closing of every library perforce
ensue, would not the long heritage of written thought
be cast into prison, would not the future be barred,
would not all progress, all conquest of knowledge, be
totally arrested? Rome herself is nowadays a terrible
example of such a disastrous experiment—Rome with her

congealed soil, her dead sap, killed by centuries of papal government, Rome which has become so barren that not a man, not a work has sprung from her midst even after five and twenty years of awakening and liberty! And who would accept such a state of things, not among people of revolutionary mind, but among those of religious mind that might possess any culture and breadth of view? Plainly enough it was all mere childishness and absurdity.

Deep silence reigned, and Pierre, quite upset by his reflections, made a gesture of despair whilst glancing at Don Vigilio, who sat speechless in front of him. For a moment longer, amidst the death-like quiescence of that old sleeping mansion, both continued silent, seated face to face in the closed chamber which the lamp illumined with a peaceful glow. But at last Don Vigilio leant forward, his eyes sparkling, and with a feverish shiver murmured: 'It is they, you know, always they, at the bottom of everything.'

Pierre, who did not understand, felt astonished, indeed somewhat anxious at such a strange remark coming without any apparent transition. 'Who are *they*?' he asked.

'The Jesuits!'

In this reply the little, withered, yellow priest had set all the concentrated rage of his exploding passion. Ah! so much the worse if he had perpetrated a fresh act of folly. The cat was out of the bag at last! Nevertheless, he cast a final suspicious glance around the walls. And then he relieved his mind at length, with a flow of words which gushed forth the more irresistibly since he had so long held them in check. 'Ah! the Jesuits, the Jesuits! You fancy that you know them, but you haven't even an idea of their abominable actions and incalculable power. They it is whom one always comes upon, everywhere, in every circumstance. Remember *that* whenever you fail to understand anything, if you wish to understand it. Whenever grief or trouble comes upon you, whenever you suffer, whenever you weep, say to yourself at once: "It is they; they are there!" Why, for all I know, there may be one of them under that bed, inside that cupboard—Ah! the Jesuits, the Jesuits! They have devoured me, they are devouring me still, they will leave nothing of me at last, neither flesh nor bone.'

Then, in a halting voice, he related the story of his life, beginning with his youth, which had opened so hopefully. He belonged to the petty provincial nobility, and had been dowered with a fairly large income, besides a keen, supple intelligence, which looked smilingly towards the future. Nowadays, he would assuredly have been a prelate, on the road to high dignities, but he had been foolish enough to speak ill of the Jesuits and to thwart them in two or three circumstances. And from that moment, if he were to be believed, they had caused every imaginable misfortune to rain upon him: his father and mother had died, his banker had robbed him and fled, good positions had escaped him at the very moment when he was about to occupy them, the most awful misadventures had pursued him amidst the duties of his ministry to such a point indeed, that he had narrowly escaped interdiction. It was only since Cardinal Boccanera, compassionating his bad luck, had taken him into his house and attached him to his person, that he had enjoyed a little repose. 'Here I have a refuge, an asylum,' he continued. 'They execrate his Eminence, who has never been on their side, but they haven't yet dared to attack him or his servants. Oh! I have no illusions, they will end by catching me again, all the same. Perhaps they will even hear of our conversation this evening, and make me pay dearly for it; for I do wrong to speak, I speak in spite of myself. They have stolen all my happiness, and brought all possible misfortune on me, everything that was possible, everything—you hear me!'

Increasing discomfort was taking possession of Pierre, who, seeking to relieve himself by a jest, exclaimed: 'Come, come, at any rate it wasn't the Jesuits who gave you the fever.'

'Yes, yes, it was!' Don Vigilio violently declared. 'I caught it on the bank of the Tiber one evening, when I went to weep there in my grief at having been driven from the little church where I officiated.'

Pierre, hitherto, had never believed in the terrible legend of the Jesuits. He belonged to a generation which laughed at the idea of wehr-wolves, and considered the *bourgeoise* fear of the famous black men, who hid themselves in walls and terrorised families, to be a trifle ridiculous. To him all such things seemed to be nursery tales, exaggerated by religious and political passion. And so it was with amazement that he examined Don Vigilio, suddenly fearing that he might have to deal with a maniac.

Nevertheless he could not help recalling the extraordinary story of the Jesuits. If St. Francis of Assisi and St. Dominic are the very soul and spirit of the middle ages, its masters and teachers, the former a living expression of all the ardent, charitable faith of the humble, and the other defending dogma and fixing doctrines for the intelligent and the powerful, on the other hand Ignatius de Loyola appeared on the threshold of modern times to save the tottering heritage by accommodating religion to the new developments of society, thereby ensuring it the empire of the world which was about to appear.

At the advent of the modern era it seemed as if the Deity were to be vanquished in the uncompromising struggle with sin, for it was certain that the old determination to suppress nature, to kill the man within man, with his appetites, passions, heart and blood, could only result in a disastrous defeat, in which, indeed, the Church found herself on the very eve of sinking; and it was the Jesuits who came to extricate her from this peril and reinvigorate her by deciding that it was she who now ought to go to the world, since the world seemed unwilling to go any longer to her. All lay in that; you find the Jesuits declaring that one can enter into arrangements with heaven; they bend and adjust themselves to the customs, prejudices and even vices of the times; they smile, all condescension, cast rigorism aside, and practice the diplomacy of amiability, ever ready to turn the most awful abominations ' to the greater glory of God.' That is their motto, their battle-cry, and thence springs the moral principle which many regard as their crime: that all means are good to attain one's end, especially when that end is the furtherance of the Deity's interests as represented by those of the Church. And what overwhelming success attends the efforts of the Jesuits! they swarm and before long cover the earth, on all sides becoming uncontested masters. They shrive kings, they acquire immense wealth, they display such victorious power of invasion that, however humbly they may set foot in any country, they soon wholly possess it: souls, bodies, power and fortune alike falling to them. And they are particularly zealous in founding schools, they show themselves to be incomparable moulders of the human brain, well understanding that power always belongs to the morrow, to the generations which are growing up and whose master one must be if one desire to reign eternally. So great is their power, based on the necessity of compromise with sin, that, on the morrow of the Council of Trent, they transform the very spirit of Catholicism, penetrate it, identify it with themselves and become the indispensable soldiers of the papacy which lives by them and for them. And from that moment Rome is theirs, Rome where their general so long commands, whence so long go forth the directions for the obscure tactics which are blindly followed by their innumerable army, whose skilful organisation covers the globe as with an iron network hidden by the velvet of hands expert in dealing gently with poor suffering humanity. But, after all, the most prodigious feature is the stupefying vitality of the Jesuits who are incessantly tracked, condemned, executed, and yet still and ever erect. As soon as their power asserts itself, their unpopularity begins and gradually becomes universal. Hoots of execration arise around them, abominable accusations, scandalous law cases in which they appear as corruptors and felons. Pascal devotes them to public contempt, parliaments condemn their books to be burnt, universities denounce their system of morals and their teaching as poisonous. They foment such disturbances, such struggles in every kingdom, that organised persecution sets in, and they are soon driven from everywhere. During more than a century they become wanderers, expelled, then recalled, passing and repassing frontiers, leaving a country amidst cries of hatred to return to it as soon as quiet has been restored. Finally, for supreme disaster, they are suppressed by one pope, but another re-establishes them, and since then they have been virtually tolerated everywhere. And in the diplomatic self-effacement, the shade in which they have the prudence to sequester themselves, they are none the less triumphant, quietly confident of their victory like soldiers who have once and for ever subdued the earth.

Pierre was aware that, judging by mere appearances, the Jesuits were nowadays dispossessed of all influence in Rome. They no longer officiated at the Gesù, they no longer directed the Collegio Romano, where they formerly fashioned so many souls ; and with no abode of their own, reduced to accept foreign hospitality, they had modestly sought a refuge at the Collegio Germanico, where there is a little chapel. There they taught and there they still confessed, but without the slightest bustle or display. Was one to believe, however, that this effacement was but masterly cunning, a feigned disappearance in order that they might really remain secret, all-powerful masters, the hidden hand which directs and guides everything ? People certainly said that the proclamation of papal Infallibility had been their work, a weapon with which they had armed

themselves whilst feigning to bestow it on the papacy, in
readiness for the coming decisive task which their genius foresaw in the approaching social upheavals. And thus there
might perhaps be some truth in what Don Vigilio, with a
shiver of mystery, related about their occult sovereignty, a
seizin, as it were, of the government of the Church, a royalty
ignored but nevertheless complete.

As this idea occurred to Pierre, a dim connection between
certain of his experiences arose in his mind and he all at once
inquired : ' Is Monsignor Nani a Jesuit, then ? '

These words seemed to revive all Don Vigilio's anxious
passion. He waved his trembling hand, and replied : ' He ?
Oh, he's too clever, too skilful by far to have taken the robe.
But he comes from that Collegio Romano where his generation
grew up, and he there imbibed that Jesuit genius which
adapted itself so well to his own. Whilst fully realising the
danger of wearing an unpopular and embarrassing livery, and
wishing to be free, he is none the less a Jesuit in his flesh, in
his bones, in his very soul. He is evidently convinced that
the Church can only triumph by utilising the passions of mankind, and withal he is very fond of the Church, very pious at
bottom, a very good priest, serving God without weakness in
gratitude for the absolute power which God gives to His
ministers. And besides, he is so charming, incapable of any
brutal action, full of the good breeding of his noble Venetian
ancestors, and deeply versed in knowledge of the world, thanks
to his experiences at the nunciatures of Paris, Vienna and
other places, without mentioning that he knows everything
that goes on by reason of the delicate functions which he has
discharged for ten years past as Assessor of the Holy Office.
Yes, he is powerful, all-powerful, and in him you do not
have the furtive Jesuit whose robe glides past amidst suspicion, but the head, the brain, the leader whom no uniform
designates.'

This reply made Pierre grave, for he was quite willing to
admit that an opportunist code of morals, like that of the
Jesuits, was inoculable and now predominated throughout the
Church. Indeed, the Jesuits might disappear, but their doctrine
would survive them, since it was the one weapon of combat,
the one system of strategy which might again place the nations
under the dominion of Rome. And in reality the struggle
which continued lay precisely in the attempts to accommodate
religion to the century, and the century to religion. Such

being the case, Pierre realised that men like Monsignor Nani might acquire vast and even decisive importance.

'Ah! if you knew, if you knew,' continued Don Vigilio, 'he's everywhere, he has his hand in everything. For instance, nothing has ever happened here, among the Boccaneras, but I've found him at the bottom of it, tangling or untangling the threads according to necessities with which he alone is acquainted.'

Then, in the unquenchable fever for confiding things which was now consuming him, the secretary related how Monsignor Nani had most certainly brought on Benedetta's divorce case. The Jesuits, in spite of their conciliatory spirit, have always taken up a hostile position with regard to Italy, either because they do not despair of reconquering Rome, or because they wait to treat in due season with the ultimate and real victor, whether King or Pope. And so Nani, who had long been one of Donna Serafina's intimates, had helped to precipitate the rupture with Prada as soon as Benedetta's mother was dead. Again, it was he who, to prevent any interference on the part of the patriotic Abbé Pisoni, the young woman's confessor and the artisan of her marriage, had urged her to take the same spiritual director as her aunt, Father Lorenza, a handsome Jesuit with clear and kindly eyes, whose confessional in the chapel of the Collegio Germanico was incessantly besieged by penitents. And it seemed certain that this manœuvre had brought about everything; what one cleric working for Italy had done, was to be undone by another cleric working against Italy.

Why was it, however, that Nani, after bringing about the rupture, had momentarily ceased to show all interest in the affair to the point even of jeopardising the suit for the dissolution of the marriage? And why was he now again busying himself with it, setting Donna Serafina in action, prompting her to buy Monsignor Palma's support, and bringing his own influence to bear on the cardinals of the Congregation? There was mystery in all this, as there was in everything he did, for his schemes were always complicated and distant in their effects. However, one might suppose that he now wished to hasten the marriage of Benedetta and Dario, in order to stop all the abominable rumours which were circulating in the white world; unless, indeed, this divorce secured by pecuniary payments and the pressure of notorious influences were an intentional scandal at first spun out and now hastened, in order to harm Cardinal Boccanera, whom the Jesuits might desire to brush aside in certain eventualities which were possibly near at hand.

'To tell the truth, I rather incline to the latter view,' said Don Vigilio, 'the more so indeed as I learnt this evening that the Pope is not well. With an old man of eighty-four the end may come at any moment, and so the Pope can never catch cold but what the Sacred College and the prelacies are all agog, stirred by sudden ambitious rivalries. Now, the Jesuits have always opposed Cardinal Boccanera's candidature. They ought to be on his side, on account of his rank, and his uncompromising attitude towards Italy, but the idea of giving themselves such a master disquiets them, for they consider him unseasonably rough and stern, too violent in his faith, which unbending as it is would prove dangerous in these diplomatic times through which the Church is passing. And so I should in no wise be astonished if there were an attempt to discredit him and render his candidature impossible, by employing the most underhand and shameful means.'

A little quiver of fear was coming over Pierre. The contagion of the unknown, of the black intrigues plotted in the dark, was spreading amidst the silence of the night in the depths of that palace, near that Tiber, in that Rome so full of legendary tragedies. But all at once the young man's mind reverted to himself, to his own affair. 'But what is my part in all this?' he asked: 'why does Monsignor Nani seem to take an interest in me? Why is he mixed up in the proceedings against my book?'

'Oh! one never knows, one never knows exactly!' replied Don Vigilio, waving his arms. 'One thing I can say, that he only knew of the affair when the denunciations of the three bishops were already in the hands of Father Dangelis; and I have also learnt that he then tried to stop the proceedings, which he no doubt thought both useless and impolitic. But when a matter is once before the Congregation it is almost impossible for it to be withdrawn, and Monsignor Nani must also have come into collision with Father Dangelis who, like a faithful Dominican, is the passionate adversary of the Jesuits. It was then that he caused the Contessina to write to Monsieur de la Choue, requesting him to tell you to hasten here in order to defend yourself, and to arrange for your acceptance of hospitality in this mansion, during your stay.'

This revelation brought Pierre's emotion to a climax. 'You are sure of that?' he asked.

'Oh! quite sure. I heard Nani speak of you one Monday, and some time ago I told you that he seemed to know all about you, as if he had made most minute inquiries. My belief is that he had already read your book, and was extremely preoccupied about it.'

'Do you think that he shares my ideas, then? Is he sincere, is he defending himself while striving to defend me?'

'Oh! no, no, not at all. Your ideas, why he certainly hates them, and your book and yourself as well. You have no idea what contempt for the weak, what hatred of the poor and love of authority and domination he conceals under his caressing amiability. Lourdes he might abandon to you, though it embodies a marvellous weapon of government; but he will never forgive you for being on the side of the little ones of the world, and for pronouncing against the temporal power. If you only heard with what gentle ferocity he derides Monsieur de la Choue, whom he calls the weeping willow of neo-Catholicism!'

Pierre carried his hands to his temples and pressed his head despairingly. 'Then why, why, tell me I beg of you, why has he brought me here and kept me here in this house at his disposal? Why has he promenaded me up and down Rome for three long months, throwing me against obstacles and wearying me, when it was so easy for him to let the Index condemn my book if it embarrassed him? It's true, of course, that things would not have gone quietly, for I was disposed to refuse submission and openly confess my new faith, even against the decisions of Rome.'

Don Vigilio's black eyes flared in his yellow face: 'Perhaps it was that which he wished to prevent. He knows you to be very intelligent and enthusiastic, and I have often heard him say that intelligence and enthusiasm should not be fought openly.'

Pierre, however, had risen to his feet, and, instead of listening, was striding up and down the room as though carried away by the whirlwind of his thoughts. 'Come, come,' he said at last, 'it is necessary that I should know and understand things if I am to continue the struggle. You must be kind enough to give me some detailed particulars about each of the persons mixed up in my affair. Jesuits, Jesuits everywhere? *Mon Dieu!* it may be so, you are perhaps right! But all the same you must point out the different shades to me. Now, for instance, what of that Fornaro?'

'Monsignor Fornaro, oh! he's whatever you like. Still he also was brought up at the Collegio Romano, so you may be certain that he is a Jesuit, a Jesuit by education, position and ambition. He is longing to become a cardinal, and if he some day becomes one, he'll long to be the next pope. Besides, you know, everyone here is a candidate to the papacy as soon as he enters the seminary.'

'And Cardinal Sanguinetti?'

'A Jesuit, a Jesuit! To speak plainly, he was one, then ceased to be one, and is now undoubtedly one again. Sanguinetti has flirted with every influence. It was long thought that he was in favour of conciliation between the Holy See and Italy; but things drifted into a bad way, and he violently took part against the usurpers. In the same style he has frequently fallen out with Leo XIII and then made his peace. To-day at the Vatican, he keeps on a footing of diplomatic reserve. Briefly he only has one object, the tiara, and even shows it too plainly, which is a mistake, for it uses up a candidate. Still, just at present the struggle seems to be between him and Cardinal Boccanera. And that's why he has gone over to the Jesuits again, utilising their hatred of his rival, and anticipating that they will be forced to support *him* in order to defeat the other. But I doubt it, they are too shrewd, they will hesitate to patronise a candidate who is already so compromised. He, blunderhead, passionate and proud as he is, doubts nothing, and since you say that he is now at Frascati, I'm certain that he made all haste to shut himself up there with some grand strategical object in view, as soon as he heard of the Pope's illness.'

'Well, and the Pope himself, Leo XIII?' asked Pierre.

This time Don Vigilio slightly hesitated, his eyes blinking, Then he said: 'Leo XIII? He is a Jesuit, a Jesuit! Oh! I know it is said that he sides with the Dominicans, and this is in a measure true, for he fancies that he is animated with their spirit and he has brought St. Thomas into favour again, and has restored all the ecclesiastical teaching of doctrine. But there is also the Jesuit, remember, who is one involuntarily and without knowing it, and of this category the present Pope will prove the most famous example. Study his acts, investigate his policy, and you will find that everything in it emanates from the Jesuit spirit. The fact is that he has unwittingly become impregnated with that spirit, and that all the influence, directly or indirectly brought to bear on him comes from a Jesuit centre. Ah! why don't you believe me? I repeat that the Jesuits have conquered and absorbed everything, that all Rome belongs to them from the most insignificant cleric to his Holiness in person.'

Then he continued, replying to each fresh name that Pierre gave with the same obstinate, maniacal cry: 'Jesuit, Jesuit!' It seemed as if a Churchman could be nothing else, as if each answer were a confirmation of the proposition that the clergy must compound with the modern world if it desired to preserve its Deity. The heroic age of Catholicism was accomplished, henceforth it could only live by dint of diplomacy and ruses, concessions and arrangements. 'And that Paparelli, he's a Jesuit too, a Jesuit!' Don Vigilio went on, instinctively lowering his voice. 'Yes, the humble but terrible Jesuit, the Jesuit in his most abominable *rôle* as a spy and a perverter! I could swear that he has merely been placed here in order to keep watch on his Eminence! And you should see with what supple talent and craft he has performed his task, to such a point indeed that it is now he alone who wills and orders things. He opens the door to whomsoever he pleases, uses his master like something belonging to him, weighs on each of his resolutions, and holds him in his power by dint of his stealthy unremitting efforts. Yes! it's the lion conquered by the insect; the infinitesimally small disposing of the infinitely great; the train-bearer—whose proper part is to sit at his cardinal's feet like a faithful hound—in reality reigning over him, and impelling him in whatsoever direction he chooses— Ah! the Jesuit! the Jesuit! Mistrust him when you see him gliding by in his shabby old cassock, with the flabby wrinkled face of a devout old maid. And make sure that he isn't behind the doors, or in the cupboards, or under the beds. Ah! I tell you that they'll devour you as they've devoured me; and they'll give you the fever too, perhaps even the plague if you are not careful!'

Pierre suddenly halted in front of his companion. He was losing all assurance, both fear and rage were penetrating him.

And, after all, why not? These extraordinary stories must be true. 'But in that case give me some advice,' he exclaimed, 'I asked you to come in here this evening precisely because I no longer know what to do, and need to be set in the right path——' Then he broke off and again paced to and fro, as if urged into motion by his exploding passion. 'Or rather no, tell me nothing!' he abruptly resumed. 'It's all over; I prefer to go away. The thought occurred to me before, but it was in a moment of cowardice and with the idea of disappearing and of returning to live in peace in my little nook: whereas now, if I go off, it will be as an avenger, a judge, to cry aloud to all the world from Paris, to proclaim what I have seen in Rome, what men have done there with the Christianity of Jesus, the Vatican falling into dust, the corpse-like odour which comes from it, the idiotic illusions of those who hope that they will one day see a renascence of the modern soul arise from a sepulchre where the remnants of dead centuries rot and slumber. Oh! I will not yield, I will not make my submission, I will defend my book by a fresh one. And that book, I promise you, will make some noise in the world, for it will sound the last agony of a dying religion, which one must make all haste to bury lest its remains should poison the nations!'

All this was beyond Don Vigilio's mind. The Italian priest, with narrow belief and ignorant terror of the new ideas, awoke within him. He clasped his hands, affrighted. 'Be quiet, be quiet! You are blaspheming! And, besides, you cannot go off like that without again trying to see his Holiness. He alone is sovereign. And I know that I shall surprise you; but Father Dangelis has given you in jest the only good advice that can be given: Go back to see Monsignor Nani, for he alone will open the door of the Vatican for you.'

Again did Pierre give a start of anger: 'What! It was with Monsignor Nani that I began, from him that I set out; and I am to go back to him? What game is that? Can I consent to be a shuttlecock sent flying hither and thither by every battledore? People are having a game with me!'

Then, harassed and distracted, the young man fell on his chair in front of Don Vigilio, who with his face drawn by his prolonged vigil, and his hands still and ever faintly trembling, remained for some time silent. At last he explained that he had another idea. He was slightly acquainted with the Pope's confessor, a Franciscan Father, a man of great simplicity, to whom he might recommend Pierre. This Franciscan, despite his self-effacement, would perhaps prove of service to him. At all events he might be tried. Then, once more, silence fell, and Pierre, whose dreamy eyes were turned towards the wall, ended by distinguishing the old picture which had touched him so deeply on the day of his arrival. In the pale glow of the lamp it gradually showed forth and lived, like an incarnation of his own case, his own futile despair before the sternly-closed portal of truth and justice. Ah! that outcast woman, that stubborn victim of love, weeping amidst her streaming hair, her visage hidden whilst with pain and grief she sank upon the steps of that palace whose door was so pitilessly shut—how she resembled him! Draped with a mere strip of linen, she was shivering, and amidst the overpowering distress of her abandonment she did not reveal her secret, misfortune or transgression, whichever it might be. But he, behind her close-pressed hands, endowed her with a face akin to his own: she became his sister, as were all the poor creatures without roof or certainty who weep because they are naked and alone, and wear out their strength in seeking to force the wicked thresholds of men. He could never gaze at her without pitying her, and it stirred him so much that evening to find her ever so unknown, nameless and visageless, yet steeped in the most bitter tears, that he suddenly began to question his companion.

'Tell me,' said he, 'do you know who painted that old picture? It stirs me to the soul like a masterpiece.'

Stupefied by this unexpected question, the secretary raised his head and looked, feeling yet more astonished when he had examined the blacken, forsaken panel in its sorry frame.

'Where did it come from?' resumed Pierre, 'why has it been stowed away in this room?'

'Oh!' replied Don Vigilio, with a gesture of indifference, 'it's nothing. There are heaps of valueless old paintings everywhere. That one, no doubt, has always been here. But I don't know; I never noticed it before.'

Whilst speaking he had at last risen to his feet, and this simple action had brought on such a fit of shivering that he could scarcely take leave, so violently did his teeth chatter with fever. 'No, no, don't show me out,' he stammered, 'keep the lamp here. And to conclude: the best course is for you to leave yourself in the hands of Monsignor Nani, for

he, at all events, is a superior man. I told you on your arrival
that, whether you would or not, you would end by doing as
he desired. And so what's the use of struggling ? And mind,
not a word of our conversation to-night; it would mean my
death.'

Then he noiselessly opened the doors, glanced distrustfully
into the darkness of the passage, and at last ventured out and
disappeared, regaining his own room with such soft steps that
not the faintest footfall was heard amidst the tomb-like slumber
of the old mansion.

On the morrow, Pierre, again mastered by a desire to fight
on to the very end, got Don Vigilio to recommend him to the
Pope's confessor, the Franciscan Friar with whom the secretary was slightly acquainted. However, this friar proved to
be an extremely timid if worthy man, selected precisely on
account of his great modesty, simplicity, and absolute lack of
influence in order that he might not abuse his position with
respect to the Holy Father. And doubtless there was an
affectation of humility on the latter's part in taking for confessor a member of the humblest of the regular orders, a friend
of the poor, a holy beggar of the roads. At the same time the
friar certainly enjoyed a reputation for oratory ; and hidden
by a veil the Pope at times listened to his sermons ; for although
as infallible Sovereign Pontiff Leo XIII could not receive
lessons from any priest, it was admitted that as a man he
might reap profit by listening to good discourse. Nevertheless
apart from his natural eloquence, the worthy friar was really
a mere washer of souls, a confessor who listens and absolves
without even remembering the impurities which he removes
in the waters of penitence. And Pierre, finding him really so
poor and such a cipher, did not insist on an intervention which
he realised would be futile.

All that day the young priest was haunted by the figure of
that ingenuous lover of poverty, that delicious St. Francis, as
Narcisse Habert was wont to say. Pierre had often wondered
how such an apostle, so gentle towards both animate and
inanimate creation, and so full of ardent charity for the
wretched, could have arisen in a country of egotism and enjoyment like Italy, where the love of beauty alone has remained
queen. Doubtless the times have changed ; yet what a strong
sap of love must have been needed in the old days, during the
great sufferings of the middle ages, for such a consoler of the
humble to spring from the popular soil and preach the gift of

self to others, the renunciation of wealth, the horror of brutal force, the equality and obedience which would ensure the peace of the world. St. Francis trod the roads clad as one of the poorest, a rope girdling his grey gown and his bare feet shod with sandals, and he carried with him neither purse nor staff. And he and his brethren spoke aloud and freely, with sovereign florescence of poetry and boldness of truth, attacking the rich and the powerful, and daring even to denounce the priests of evil life, the debauched, simoniacal and perjured bishops. A long cry of relief greeted the Franciscans, the people followed them in crowds—they were the friends, the liberators of all the humble ones who suffered. And thus, like revolutionaries, they at first so alarmed Rome, that the popes hesitated to authorise their Order. When they at last gave way it was assuredly with the hope of using this new force for their own profit, by conquering the whole vague mass of the lowly whose covert threats have ever growled through the ages, even in the most despotic times. And thenceforward in the sons of St. Francis the Church possessed an ever-victorious army—a wandering army which spread over the roads, in the villages and through the towns, penetrating to the firesides of artisan and peasant, and gaining possession of all simple hearts. How great the democratic power of such an Order which had sprung from the very entrails of the people! And thence its rapid prosperity, its teeming growth in a few years, friaries arising upon all sides, and the third Order [1] so invading the secular population as to impregnate and absorb it. And that there was here a genuine growth of the soil, a vigorous vegetation of the plebeian stock was shown by an entire national art arising from it—the precursors of the Renascence in painting and even Dante himself, the soul of Italia's genius.

For some days now, in the Rome of the present time, Pierre had been coming into contact with those great Orders of the past. The Franciscans and the Dominicans were there face to face in their vast convents of prosperous aspect. But it seemed as if the humility of the Franciscans had in the long

---

[1] The Franciscans, like the Dominicans and others, admit, in addition to the two Orders of friars and nuns, a third Order comprising devout persons of either sex who have neither the vocation nor the opportunity for cloistered life, but live in the world, privately observing the chief principles of the fraternity with which they are connected. In central and southern Europe members of these third Orders are still numerous. —*Trans.*

run deprived them of influence. Perhaps, too, their *rôle* as friends and liberators of the people was ended since the people now undertook to liberate itself. And so the only real remaining battle was between the Dominicans and the Jesuits, both of whom still claimed to mould the world according to their particular views. Warfare between them was incessant, and Rome—the supreme power at the Vatican—was ever the prize for which they contended. But, although the Dominicans had St. Thomas on their side, they must have felt that their old dogmatic science was crumbling, compelled as they were each day to surrender a little ground to the Jesuits whose principles accorded better with the spirit of the century. And, in addition to these, there were the white-robed Carthusians, those very holy, pure and silent meditators who fled from the world into quiet cells and cloisters, those despairing and consoled ones whose numbers may decrease but whose Order will live for ever, even as grief and desire for solitude will live. And then there were the Benedictines whose admirable rules have sanctified labour, passionate toilers in literature and science, once powerful instruments of civilisation, enlarging universal knowledge by their immense historical and critical works. These Pierre loved, and with them would have sought a refuge two centuries earlier, yet he was astonished to find them building on the Aventine a huge dwelling, for which Leo XIII has already given millions, as if the science of to-day and to-morrow were yet a field where they might garner harvests. But *cui bono*, when the workmen have changed, and dogmas are there to bar the road—dogmas which totter, no doubt, but which believers may not fling aside in order to pass onward? And finally came the swarm of less important Orders, hundreds in number; there were the Carmelites, the Trappists, the Minims, the Barnabites, the Lazarists, the Eudists, the Mission Fathers, the Servites, the Brothers of the Christian Doctrine; there were the Bernadines, the Augustinians, the Theatines, the Observants, the Passionists, the Celestines, and the Capuchins, without counting the corresponding Orders of women or the Poor Clares, or the innumerable nuns like those of the Visitation and the Calvary. Each community had its modest or sumptuous dwelling, certain districts of Rome were entirely composed of convents, and behind the silent lifeless façades all those people buzzed, intrigued, and waged the everlasting warfare of rival interests and passions. The social evolution which produced them had long since ceased, still

they obstinately sought to prolong their life, growing weaker
and more useless day by day, destined to a slow agony until
the time shall come when the new development of society will
leave them neither foothold nor breathing space.

And it was not only with the regulars that Pierre came in
contact during his peregrinations through Rome; indeed, he
more particularly had to deal with the secular clergy, and
learnt to know them well. A hierarchical system which was
still vigorously enforced maintained them in various ranks and
classes. Up above, around the Pope, reigned the pontifical
family, the high and noble cardinals and prelates whose
conceit was great in spite of their apparent familiarity.
Below them the parish clergy formed a very worthy middle
class of wise and moderate minds; and here patriot priests
were not rare. Moreover, the Italian occupation of a quarter
of a century, by installing in the city a world of functionaries
who saw everything that went on, had, curiously enough,
greatly purified the private life of the Roman priesthood, in
which under the popes women, beyond all question, played a
supreme part. And finally one came to the plebeian clergy
whom Pierre studied with curiosity, a collection of wretched,
grimy, half-naked priests who like famished animals prowled
around in search of masses, and drifted into disreputable
taverns in the company of beggars and thieves. However, he
was more interested by the floating population of foreign
priests from all parts of Christendom—the adventurers, the
ambitious ones, the believers, the madmen whom Rome
attracted just as a lamp at night-time attracts the insects of
the gloom. Among these were men of every nationality,
position and age, all lashed on by their appetites and scram-
bling from morn till eve around the Vatican, in order to snap
at the prey which they hoped to secure. He found them
everywhere, and told himself with some shame that he was
one of them, that the unit of his own personality served to
increase the incredible number of cassocks that one
encountered in the streets. Ah! that ebb and flow, that
ceaseless tide of black gowns and frocks of every hue ! With
their processions of students ever walking abroad, the
seminaries of the different nations would alone have sufficed
to drape and decorate the streets, for there were the French
and the English all in black, the South Americans in black
with blue sashes, the North Americans in black with red
sashes, the Poles in black with green sashes, the Greeks in

blue, the Germans in red, the Scots in violet, the Romans in
black or violet or purple, the Bohemians with chocolate sashes,
the Irish with red lappets, the Spaniards with blue cords, to
say nothing of all the others with broidery and bindings and
buttons in a hundred different styles. And in addition there
were the confraternities, the penitents, white, black, blue and
grey, with sleeveless frocks and capes of different hue, grey,
blue, black, or white. And thus even nowadays Papal Rome
at times seemed to resuscitate, and one could realise how
tenaciously and vivaciously she struggled on in order that she
might not disappear in the cosmopolitan Rome of the new
era.

However, Pierre, whilst running about from one prelate
to another, frequenting priests and crossing churches, could
not accustom himself to the worship, the Roman piety which
astonished him when it did not wound him. One rainy
Sunday morning, on entering Santa Maria Maggiore, he
fancied himself in some waiting-room, a very splendid one, no
doubt, but where God seemed to have no habitation. There
was not a bench, not a chair in the nave, across which people
passed, as they might pass through a railway station, wetting
and soiling the precious mosaic pavement with their muddy
shoes; and tired women and children sat round the bases of
the columns, even as in railway stations one sees people sitting
and waiting for their trains during the great crushes of the
holiday season. And for this tramping throng of folks of
small degree, who had looked in *en passant*, a priest was saying a low mass in a side chapel, before which a narrow file of
standing people had gathered, extending across the nave, and
recalling the crowds which wait in front of theatres for the
opening of the doors. At the elevation of the Host one and
all inclined themselves devoutly, but almost immediately
afterwards the gathering dispersed. And indeed why linger?
The mass was said. Pierre everywhere found the same form
of attendance, peculiar to the countries of the sun; the
worshippers were in a hurry and only favoured the Deity with
short familiar visits, unless it were a question of some gala
scene at San Paolo or San Giovanni in Laterano or some
other of the old basilicas. It was only at the Gesù, on
another Sunday morning, that the young priest came upon a
high mass congregation, which reminded him of the devout
throngs of the North. Here there were benches and women
seated, a worldly warmth and cosiness under the luxurious,

gilded, carved, and painted roof, whose tawny splendour is very fine now that time has toned down the eccentricities of the decoration. But how many of the churches were empty, among them some of the most ancient and venerable, San Clemente, Sant' Agnese, Santa Croce in Gerusalemme, where during the offices one saw but a few believers of the neighbourhood. Four hundred churches were a good many for even Rome to people ; and, indeed, some were merely attended on fixed ceremonial occasions, and a good many merely opened their doors once every year—on the feast day, that is, of their patron saint. Some also subsisted on the lucky possession of a fetish, an idol compassionate to human sufferings. Santa Maria in Ara Cœli possessed the miraculous little Jesus, the 'Bambino,' who healed sick children, and Sant' Agostino had the 'Madonna del Parto,' who grants a happy delivery to mothers. Then others were renowned for the holy water of their fonts, the oil of their lamps, the power of some wooden saint or marble virgin. Others again seemed forsaken, given up to tourists and the perquisites of beadles, like mere museums peopled with dead gods. Finally, others disturbed one's faith by the suggestiveness of their aspect, as, for instance, that Santa Maria Rotonda, which is located in the Pantheon, a circular hall recalling a circus, where the Virgin remains the evident tenant of the Olympian deities.

Pierre took no little interest in the churches of the poor districts, but did not find there the keen faith and the throngs he had hoped for. One afternoon, at Santa Maria in Trastevere, he heard the choir in full song, but the church was quite empty, and the chant had a most lugubrious sound in such a desert. Then, another day, on entering San Crisogono, he found it draped, probably in readiness for some festival on the morrow. The columns were cased with red damask, and between them were hangings and curtains alternately yellow and blue, white and red ; and the young man fled from such a fearful decoration as gaudy as that of a fair booth. Ah ! how far he was from the cathedrals where in childhood he had believed and prayed ! On all sides he found the same type of church, the antique basilica accommodated to the taste of eighteenth century Rome. Though the style of San Luigi dei Francesi is better, more soberly elegant, the only thing that touched him even there was the thought of the heroic or saintly Frenchmen, who sleep in foreign soil beneath the flags. And as he sought for something Gothic, he ended by going to see Santa Maria sopra Minerva,[1] which, he was told, was the only example of the Gothic style in Rome. Here his stupefaction attained a climax at sight of the clustering columns cased in stucco imitating marble, the ogives which dared not soar, the rounded vaults condemned to the heavy majesty of the dome style. No, no, thought he, the faith whose cooling cinders lingered there was no longer that whose brazier had invaded and set all Christendom aglow! However, Monsignor Fornaro whom he chanced to meet as he was leaving the church, inveighed against the Gothic style as rank heresy. The first Christian Church said the prelate had been the basilica which had sprung from the temple, and it was blasphemy to assert that the Gothic cathedral was the real Christian house of prayer, for Gothic embodied the hateful Anglo-Saxon spirit, the rebellious genius of Luther. At this a passionate reply rose to Pierre's lips, but he said nothing for fear that he might say too much. However, he asked himself whether in all this, there were not a decisive proof that Catholicism was the very vegetation of Rome, Paganism modified by Christianity. Elsewhere Christianity has grown up in quite a different spirit, to such a point that it has risen in rebellion and schismatically turned against the mother-city. And the breach has ever gone on widening, the dissemblance has become more and more marked; and amidst the evolution of new societies yet a fresh schism appears inevitable and proximate in spite of all the despairing efforts to maintain union.

While Pierre thus visited the Roman churches, he also continued his efforts to gain support in the matter of his book, his irritation tending to such stubbornness, that if in the first instance he failed to obtain an interview, he went back again and again to secure one, steadfastly keeping his promise to call in turn upon each cardinal of the Congregation of the Index. And as a cardinal may belong to several congregations, it resulted that he gradually found himself roaming through those former ministries of the old pontifical government which, if less numerous than formerly, are still very intricate institutions, each with its cardinal-prefect, its cardinal-members, its consultative prelates and its numerous employees. Pierre repeatedly had to return to the Cancelleria, where the

---

[1] So called because it occupies the site of a temple to Minerva.— *Trans.*

Congregation of the Index meets, and lost himself in its world of staircases, corridors and halls. From the moment he passed under the porticus he was overcome by the icy shiver which fell from the old walls, and was quite unable to appreciate the bare, frigid beauty of the palace, Bramante's masterpiece though it be, so purely typical of the Roman Renascence. He also knew the Propaganda where he had seen Cardinal Sarno ; and, sent as he was hither and thither, in his efforts to gain over influential prelates, chance made him acquainted with the other Congregations, that of the Bishops and Regulars, that of the Rites and that of the Council. He even obtained a glimpse of the Consistorial, the Dataria,[1] and the sacred Penitentiary. All these formed part of the administrative mechanism of the Church under its several aspects—the government of the Catholic world, the enlargement of the Church's conquests, the administration of its affairs in conquered countries, the decision of all questions touching faith, morals and individuals, the investigation and punishment of offences, the grant of dispensations and the sale of favours. One can scarcely imagine what a fearful number of affairs are each morning submitted to the Vatican, questions of the greatest gravity, delicacy and intricacy, the solution of which gives rise to endless study and research. It is necessary to reply to the innumerable visitors who flock to Rome from all parts, and to the letters, the petitions and the batches of documents which are submitted and require to be distributed among the various offices. And Pierre was struck by the deep and discreet silence in which all this colossal labour was accomplished ; not a sound reaching the streets from the tribunals, parliaments and factories for the manufacture of saints and nobles, whose mechanism was so well greased, that in spite of the rust of centuries and the deep and irremediable wear and tear, the whole continued working without clank or creak to denote its presence behind the walls. And did not that silence embody the whole policy of the Church, which is to remain mute and await developments ? Nevertheless what a prodigious mechanism it was, antiquated no doubt, but still so powerful ! And amidst those Congregations how keenly Pierre felt himself to be in the grip of the most absolute power ever devised for the

[1] It is from the Dataria that bulls, rescripts, letters of appointment to benefices and dispensations of marriage, are issued, after the affixture of the date and formula *Datum Romæ*, ' Given at Rome.'—*Trans.*

domination of mankind. However much he might notice
signs of decay and coming ruin he was none the less seized,
crushed and carried off by that huge engine made up of vanity
and venality, corruption and ambition, meanness and greatness.
And how far, too, he now was from the Rome that he had
dreamt of, and what anger at times filled him amidst his
weariness, as he persevered in his resolve to defend himself!

All at once certain things which he had never understood
were explained to him. One day, when he returned to the
Propaganda, Cardinal Sarno spoke to him of Freemasonry
with such icy rage that he was abruptly enlightened. Freemasonry had hitherto made him smile; he had believed in it
no more than he had believed in the Jesuits. Indeed, he had
looked upon the ridiculous stories which were current—the
stories of mysterious, shadowy men who governed the world
with secret incalculable power—as mere childish legends.
In particular he had been amazed by the blind hatred which
maddened certain people as soon as Freemasonry was mentioned. However, a very distinguished and intelligent prelate
had declared to him, with an air of profound conviction, that
at least on one occasion every year each masonic Lodge was
presided over by the Devil in person, incarnate in a visible
shape! And now, by Cardinal Sarno's remarks, he understood
the rivalry, the furious struggle of the Roman Catholic Church
against that other Church, the Church of over the way.[1]
Although the former counted on her own triumph, she none
the less felt that the other, the Church of Freemasonry, was
a competitor, a very ancient enemy, who indeed claimed to be
more ancient than herself, and whose victory always remained
a possibility. And the friction between them was largely due to
the circumstance that they both aimed at universal sovereignty,
and had a similar international organisation, a similar net
thrown over the nations, and in a like way mysteries, dogmas,
and rites. It was deity against deity, faith against faith,

[1] Some readers may think the above passages an exaggeration, but
such is not the case. The hatred with which the Catholic priesthood,
especially in Italy, Spain, and France, regards Freemasonry is remarkable. At the moment of writing these lines I have before me several
French clerical newspapers, which contain the most abusive articles
levelled against President Faure solely because he is a Freemason. One
of these prints, a leading journal of Lyons, tells the French President
that he cannot serve both God and the Devil; and that if he cannot
give up Freemasonry he would do well to cease desecrating the abode of
the Deity by his attendance at divine service.—*Trans.*

conquest against conquest : and so, like competing tradesmen in the same street, they were a source of mutual embarrassment, and one of them was bound to kill the other. But if Roman Catholicism seemed to Pierre to be worn out and threatened with ruin, he remained quite as sceptical with regard to the power of Freemasonry. He had made inquiries as to the reality of that power in Rome, where both Grand Master and Pope were enthroned, one in front of the other. He was certainly told that the last Roman princes had thought themselves compelled to become Freemasons in order to render their own difficult position somewhat easier and facilitate the future of their sons. But was this true ? had they not simply yielded to the force of the present social evolution ? And would not Freemasonry eventually be submerged by its own triumph—that of the ideas of justice, reason, and truth, which it had defended through the dark and violent ages of history ? It is a thing which constantly happens ; the victory of an idea kills the sect which has propagated it, and renders the apparatus with which the members of the sect surrounded themselves, in order to fire imaginations, both useless and somewhat ridiculous. Carbonarism did not survive the conquest of the political liberties which it demanded ; and on the day when the Catholic Church crumbles, having accomplished its work of civilisation, the other Church, the Freemasons' Church of across the road, will in a like way disappear, its task of liberation ended. Nowadays the famous power of the Lodges, hampered by traditions, weakened by a ceremonial which provokes laughter, and reduced to a simple bond of brotherly agreement and mutual assistance, would be but a sorry weapon of conquest for humanity, were it not that the vigorous breath of science impels the nations onwards and helps to destroy the old religions.

However, all Pierre's journeyings and applications brought him no certainty ; and, while stubbornly clinging to Rome, intent on fighting to the very end, like a soldier who will not believe in the possibility of defeat, he remained as anxious as ever. He had seen all the cardinals whose influence could be of use to him. He had seen the Cardinal Vicar, entrusted with the diocese of Rome, who, like the man of letters he was, had spoken to him of Horace, and, like a somewhat blundering politician, had questioned him about France, the Republic, the Army and the Navy Estimates, without dealing in the slightest degree with the incriminated book. He had also seen the Grand Penitentiary, that tall old man, with fleshless, ascetic face, of whom he had previously caught a glimpse at the Boccanera mansion, and from whom he now only drew a long and severe sermon on the wickedness of young priests, whom the century had perverted and who wrote most abominable books. Finally, at the Vatican, he had seen the Cardinal Secretary, in some wise His Holiness's minister of foreign affairs, the great power of the Holy See, whom he had hitherto been prevented from approaching by terrifying warnings as to the possible result of an unfavourable reception. However, whilst apologising for calling at such a late stage, he had found himself in presence of a most amiable man, whose somewhat rough appearance was softened by diplomatic affability, and who, after making him sit down, questioned him with an air of interest, listened to him, and even spoke some words of comfort. Nevertheless, on again reaching the Piazza of St. Peter's, Pierre well understood that his affair had not made the slightest progress, and that if he ever managed to force the Pope's door, it would not be by way of the Secretariate of State. And that evening he returned home quite exhausted by so many visits, in such distraction at feeling that little by little he had been wholly caught in that huge mechanism with its hundred wheels, that he asked himself in terror what he should do on the morrow now that there remained nothing for him to do—unless, indeed, it were to go mad.

However, meeting Don Vigilio in a passage of the house, he again wished to ask him for some good advice. But the secretary, who had a gleam of terror in his eyes, silenced him, he knew not why, with an anxious gesture. And then in a whisper, in Pierre's ear, he said : ' Have you seen Monsignor Nani ? No ! Well, go to see him, go to see him. I repeat that you have nothing else to do ! '

Pierre yielded. And indeed why should he have resisted ? Apart from the motives of ardent charity which had brought him to Rome to defend his book, was he not there for a self-educating, experimental purpose ? It was necessary that he should carry his attempts to the very end.

On the morrow, when he reached the colonnade of St. Peter's, the hour was so early that he had to wait there awhile. He had never better realised the enormity of those four curving rows of columns, forming a forest of gigantic stone trunks, among which nobody ever promenades. In fact, the spot is a

grandiose and dreary desert, and one asks oneself the why and
wherefore of such a majestic porticus.   Doubtless, however, it
was for its sole majesty, for the mere pomp of decoration, that
this colonnade was reared ; and therein, again, one finds the
whole Roman spirit.   However, Pierre at last turned into the
Via di Sant' Offizio, and, passing the sacristry of St. Peter's,
found himself before the Palace of the Holy Office in a solitary
silent district, which the footfall of pedestrians or the rumble
of wheels but seldom disturbs.   The sun alone lives there, in
sheets of light which spread slowly over the small, white
paving.   You divine the vicinity of the basilica, for there is a
smell as of incense, a cloisteral quiescence as of the slumber
of centuries.   And at one corner the Palace of the Holy Office
rises up with heavy, disquieting bareness, only a single row of
windows piercing its lofty, yellow front.   The wall which skirts
a side street looks yet more suspicious with its row of even
smaller casements, mere peep-holes with glaucous panes.   In
the bright sunlight this huge cube of mud-coloured masonry
ever seems to be asleep, mysterious, and closed like a prison,
with scarcely an aperture for communication with the outer
world.

Pierre shivered, but then smiled as at an act of childishness, for he reflected that the Holy Roman and Universal
Inquisition, nowadays the Sacred Congregation of the Holy
Office, was no longer the institution it had been, the purveyor
of heretics for the stake, the occult tribunal beyond appeal
which had right of life and death over all mankind.   True, it
still laboured in secrecy, meeting every Wednesday, and judging and condemning without a sound issuing from within its
walls.   But on the other hand if it still continued to strike at
the crime of heresy, if it smote men as well as their works, it
no longer possessed either weapons or dungeons, steel or fire
to do its bidding, but was reduced to a mere *rôle* of protest,
unable to inflict aught but disciplinary penalties even upon the
ecclesiastics of its own Church.

When Pierre on entering was ushered into the reception
room of Monsignor Nani, who, as assessor, lived in the palace,
he experienced an agreeable surprise.   The apartment faced
the south, and was spacious and flooded with sunshine.   And
stiff as was the furniture, dark as were the hangings, an exquisite sweetness pervaded the room, as though a woman had lived
in it and accomplished the prodigy of imparting some of her
own grace to all those stern-looking things.   There were no

flowers, yet there was a pleasant smell. A charm expanded and conquered every heart from the very threshold.

Monsignor Nani at once came forward, with a smile on his rosy face, his blue eyes keenly glittering, and his fine light hair powdered by age. With hands outstretched, he exclaimed : ' Ah ! how kind of you to have come to see me, my dear son ! Come, sit down, let us have a friendly chat.' Then with an extraordinary display of affection, he began to question Pierre : ' How are you getting on ?   Tell me all about it, exactly what you have done.'

Touched in spite of Don Vigilio's revelations, won over by the sympathy which he fancied he could detect, Pierre there-upon confessed himself, relating his visits to Cardinal Sarno, Monsignor Fornaro and Father Dangelis, his applications to all the influential cardinals, those of the Index, the Grand Penitentiary, the Cardinal Vicar and the Cardinal Secretary ; and dwelling on his endless journeys from door to door through all the congregations and all the clergy, that huge active, silent bee-hive amidst which he had wearied his feet, exhausted his limbs, and bewildered his poor brain.   And at each suc-cessive Station of this Calvary of entreaty, Monsignor Nani, who seemed to listen with an air of rapture, exclaimed : ' But that's very good, that's capital !   Oh ! your affair is progress-ing.   Yes, yes, it's progressing marvellously well.'

He was exultant, though he allowed no unseemly irony to appear, while his pleasant, penetrating eyes fathomed the young priest, to ascertain if he had been brought to the requi-site degree of obedience.   Had he been sufficiently wearied, disillusioned and instructed in the reality of things, for one to finish with him ?   Had three months' sojourn in Rome sufficed to turn the somewhat mad enthusiast of the first days into an unimpassioned or at least resigned being ?

However, all at once Monsignor Nani remarked : ' But, my dear son, you tell me nothing of his Eminence Cardinal Sanguinetti.'

' The fact is, Monseigneur, that his Eminence is at Frascati, so I have been unable to see him.'

Thereupon the prelate, as if once more postponing the *dénouement* with the secret enjoyment of an artistic *diplomate*, began to protest, raising his little plump hands with the anxious air of a man who considers everything lost : ' Oh ! but you must see his Eminence ; it is absolutely necessary !   Think of it !   The Prefect of the Index !   We can only act after your

visit to him, for as you have not seen *him* it is as if you
had seen nobody. Go, go to Frascati, my dear son.'

And thereupon Pierre could only bow and reply : 'I will
go, Monseigneur.'

<h1 style="text-align:center">XI</h1>

ALTHOUGH Pierre knew that he would be unable to see Cardinal
Sanguinetti before eleven o'clock, he nevertheless availed himself of an early train, so that it was barely nine when he
alighted at the little station of Frascati. He had already
visited the place during his enforced idleness, when he had
made the classical excursion to the Roman castles which
extend from Frascati to Rocco di Papa, and from Rocco di
Papa to Monte Cavo, and he was now delighted with the prospect of strolling for a couple of hours along those first slopes
of the Alban hills, where, amidst rushes, olives, and vines,
Frascati, like a promontory, overlooks the immense ruddy sea
of the Campagna even as far as Rome, which, six full leagues
away, wears the whitish aspect of a marble isle.

Ah ! that charming Frascati, on its greeny knoll at the foot
of the wooded Tusculan heights, with its famous terrace
whence one enjoys the finest view in the world, its old patrician villas with proud and elegant renascence façades and
magnificent parks, which, planted with cypress, pine, and ilex,
are for ever green ! There was a sweetness, a delight, a
fascination about the spot, of which Pierre would have never
wearied. And for more than an hour he had wandered
blissfully along roads edged with ancient, knotty olive
trees, along dingle ways shaded by the spreading foliage
of neighbouring estates, and along perfumed paths, at each
turn of which the Campagna was seen stretching far away,
when all at once he was accosted by a person whom he was
both surprised and annoyed to meet. He had strolled down
to some low ground near the railway station, some old vineyards where a number of new houses had been built of recent
years, and suddenly saw a stylish pair-horse victoria, coming
from the direction of Rome, draw up close by, whilst its
occupant called to him : ' What ! Monsieur l'Abbé Froment,
are you taking a walk here, at this early hour ? '

Thereupon Pierre recognised Count Luigi Prada, who
alighted, shook hands with him and began to walk beside him,
whilst the empty carriage went on in advance. And forth-

with the Count explained his tastes: 'I seldom take the train,' he said, 'I drive over. It gives my horses an outing. I have interests over here as you may know, a big building enterprise which is unfortunately not progressing very well. And so, although the season is advanced, I'm obliged to come rather more frequently that I care to do.'

As Prada suggested, Pierre was acquainted with the story. The Boccaneras had been obliged to sell a sumptuous villa which a cardinal of their family had built at Frascati in accordance with the plans of Giacomo della Porta, during the latter part of the sixteenth century : a regal summer residence it had been, finely wooded, with groves and basins and cascades, and in particular a famous terrace projecting like a cape above the Roman Campagna whose expanse stretches from the Sabine mountains to the Mediterranean sands. Through the division of the property, Benedetta had inherited from her mother some very extensive vineyards below Frascati, and these she had brought as dowry to Prada at the very moment when the building mania was extending from Rome into the provinces. And thereupon Prada had conceived the idea of erecting on the spot a number of middle-class villas like those which litter the suburbs of Paris. Few purchasers, however, had come forward, the financial crash had supervened, and he was now with difficulty liquidating this unlucky business, having indemnified his wife at the time of their separation.

'And then,' he continued, addressing Pierre, 'one can come and go as one likes with a carriage, whereas, on taking the train, one is at the mercy of the time table. This morning, for instance, I have appointments with contractors, experts, and lawyers, and I have no notion how long they will keep me. It's a wonderful country, isn't it ? And we are quite right to be proud of it in Rome. Although I may have some worries just now, I can never set foot here without my heart beating with delight.'

A circumstance which he did not mention, was that his *amica*, Lisbeth Kauffmann, had spent the summer in one of the newly erected villas, where she had installed her studio and had been visited by all the foreign colony which tolerated her irregular position on account of her gay spirits and artistic talent. Indeed, people had even ended by accepting the outcome of her connection with Prada, and a fortnight previously she had returned to Rome, and there given birth to a son—

an event which had again revived all the scandalous tittle-
tattle respecting Benedetta's divorce suit. And Prada's
attachment to Frascati doubtless sprang from the recollection
of the happy hours he had spent there, and the joyful pride
with which the birth of the boy inspired him.

Pierre, for his part, felt ill at ease in the young Count's
presence, for he had an instinctive hatred of money-mongers
and men of prey. Nevertheless, he desired to respond to his
amiability, and so inquired after his father, old Orlando, the
hero of the Liberation.

'Oh!' replied Prada, 'excepting for his legs he's in
wonderfully good health. He'll live a hundred years. Poor
father! I should so much have liked to install him in one of
these little houses, last summer. But I could not get him to
consent; he's determined not to leave Rome; he's afraid,
perhaps, that it might be taken away from him during his
absence.' Then the young Count burst into a laugh, quite
merry at the thought of jeering at the heroic but no longer
fashionable age of independence. And afterwards he said,
'My father was speaking of you again only yesterday,
Monsieur l'Abbé. He is astonished that he has not seen you
lately.'

This distressed Pierre, for he had begun to regard Orlando
with respectful affection. Since his first visit, he had twice
called on the old hero, but the latter had refused to broach
the subject of Rome so long as his young friend should not
have seen, felt, and understood everything. There would be
time for a talk later on, said he, when they were both in a
position to formulate their conclusions.

'Pray tell Count Orlando,' responded Pierre, 'that I have
not forgotten him, and that, if I have deferred a fresh visit,
it is because I desire to satisfy him. However, I certainly
will not leave Rome without going to tell him how deeply his
kind greeting has touched me.'

Whilst talking, the two men slowly followed the ascending road past the newly erected villas, several of which were
not yet finished. And when Prada learned that the priest
had come to call on Cardinal Sanguinetti, he again laughed,
with the laugh of a good-natured wolf, showing his white
fangs. 'True,' he exclaimed, 'the Cardinal has been here
since the Pope has been laid up. Ah! you'll find him in a
pretty fever.'

'Why?'

'Why, because there's bad news about the Holy Father this morning. When I left Rome it was rumoured that he had spent a fearful night.'

So speaking, Prada halted at a bend of the road, not far from an antique chapel, a little church of solitary, mournful grace of aspect, on the verge of an olive grove. Beside it stood a ruinous building, the old parsonage, no doubt, whence there suddenly emerged a tall, knotty priest with coarse and earthy face, who, after roughly locking the door, went off in the direction of the town.

'Ah!' resumed the Count in a tone of raillery, 'that fellow's heart also must be beating violently; he's surely gone to your Cardinal in search of news.'

Pierre had looked at the priest. 'I know him,' he replied, 'I saw him, I remember, on the day after my arrival at Cardinal Boccanera's. He brought the Cardinal a basket of figs and asked him for a certificate in favour of his young brother, who had been sent to prison for some deed of violence —a knife-thrust if I recollect rightly. However, the Cardina absolutely refused him the certificate.'

'It's the same man,' said Prada, 'you may depend on it. He was often at the Villa Boccanera formerly; for his young brother was gardener there. But he's now the client, the creature of Cardinal Sanguinetti. Santobono his name is, and he's a curious character, such as you wouldn't find in France, I fancy. He lives all alone in that falling hovel, and officiates at that old chapel of St. Mary in the Fields, where people don't go to hear mass three times in a year. Yes, it's a perfect sinecure, which with its stipend of a thousand francs enables him to live there like a peasant philosopher, cultivating the somewhat extensive garden whose big walls you see yonder.'

The close to which he called attention stretched down the slope behind the parsonage, without an aperture, like some savage place of refuge into which not even the eye could penetrate. And all that could be seen above the left-hand wall was a superb, gigantic fig tree, whose big leaves showed blackly against the clear sky. Prada had moved on again, and continued to speak of Santobono, who evidently interested him. Fancy, a patriot priest, a Garibaldian! Born at Nemi, in that yet savage nook among the Alban hills, he belonged to the people and was still near to the soil. However, he had studied, and knew sufficient history to realise the past greatness of

Rome, and dream of the re-establishment of Roman dominion as represented by young Italy. And he had come to believe, with passionate fervour, that only a great pope could realise his dream by seizing upon power, and then conquering all the other nations. And what could be easier, since the Pope commanded millions of Catholics? Did not half Europe belong to him? France, Spain, and Austria would give way as soon as they should see him powerful, dictating laws to the world. Germany and Great Britain, indeed all the Protestant countries, would also inevitably be conquered, for the papacy was the only dike that could be opposed to error, which must some day fatally succumb in its efforts against such a barrier. Politically, however, Santobono had declared himself for Germany, for he considered that France needed to be crushed before she would throw herself into the arms of the Holy Father. And thus contradictions and fancies clashed in his foggy brain, whose burning ideas swiftly turned to violence under the influence of primitive, racial fierceness. Briefly, the priest was a barbarian upholder of the Gospel, a friend of the humble and woeful, a sectarian of that school which is capable alike of great virtues and great crimes.

'Yes,' concluded Prada, 'he is now devoted to Cardinal Sanguinetti because he believes that the latter will prove the great pope of to-morrow, who is to make Rome the one capital of the nations. At the same time he doubtless harbours a lower personal ambition, that of attaining to a canonry or of gaining assistance in the little worries of life, as when he wished to extricate his brother from trouble. Here, you know, people stake their luck on a cardinal just as they nurse a " trey " in the lottery, and if their cardinal proves the winning number and becomes pope they gain a fortune. And that's why you now see Santobono striding along yonder, all anxiety to know if Leo XIII will die and Sanguinetti don the tiara.'

'Do you think the Pope so very ill, then?' asked Pierre, both anxious and interested.

The Count smiled and raised both arms: 'Ah!' said he, 'can one ever tell? They all get ill when their interest lies that way. However, I believe that the Pope is this time really indisposed; a complaint of the bowels, it is said; and at his age, you know, the slightest indisposition may prove fatal.'

The two men took a few steps in silence, then the priest again asked a question: 'Would Cardinal Sanguinetti have a great chance if the Holy See were vacant?'

'A great chance! Ah! that's another of those things
which one never knows. The truth is people class Sanguinetti
among the acceptable candidates, and if personal desire sufficed
he would certainly be the next pope, for ambition consumes
him to the marrow, and he displays extraordinary passion and
determination in his efforts to succeed. But therein lies his
very weakness; he is using himself up, and he knows it. And
so he must be resolved to every step during the last days of
battle. You may be quite sure that if he has shut himself up
here at this critical time, it is in order that he may the better
direct his operations from a distance, whilst at the same time
feigning a retreat, a disinterestedness which is bound to have
a good effect.'

Then Prada began to expatiate on Sanguinetti with no
little complacency, for he liked the man's spirit of intrigue,
his keen, conquering appetite, his excessive, and even somewhat blundering activity. He had become acquainted with
him on his return from the nunciature at Vienna, when he
had already resolved to win the tiara. That ambition explained everything, his quarrels and reconciliations with the
reigning Pope, his affection for Germany, followed by a sudden
evolution in the direction of France, his varying attitude with
regard to Italy, at first a desire for agreement, and then
absolute rejection of all compromises, a refusal to grant any
concession, so long as Rome should not be evacuated. This,
indeed, seemed to be Sanguinetti's definite position; he made
a show of disliking the wavering sway of Leo XIII, and of
retaining a fervent admiration for Pius IX, the great, heroic
pope of the days of resistance, whose goodness of heart had
proved no impediment to unshakable firmness. And all this
was equivalent to a promise that he, Sanguinetti, would again
make kindliness exempt from weakness, the rule of the
Church, and steer clear of the dangerous compoundings of
politics. Nevertheless, at bottom, politics were his only
dream, and he had even formulated a complete programme of
intentional vagueness, which his clients and creatures spread
abroad with an air of rapturous mystery. However, since a
previous indisposition of the Pope's, during the spring, he had
been living in mortal disquietude, for it had then been
rumoured that the Jesuits would resign themselves to support
Cardinal Pio Boccanera, although the latter scarcely favoured
them. He was rough and stern, no doubt, and his extreme
bigotry might be a source of danger in this tolerant age; but,

on the other hand, was he not a patrician, and would not his
election imply that the papacy would never cease to claim the
temporal power? From that moment Boccanera had been
the one man whom Sanguinetti feared, for he beheld himself
despoiled of his prize, and spent his time in devising plans to
rid himself of such a powerful rival, repeating abominable
stories of Cardinal Pio's alleged complaisance with regard to
Benedetta and Dario, and incessantly representing him as Antichrist, the man of sin, whose reign would consummate the
ruin of the papacy. Finally, to regain the support of the
Jesuits, Sanguinetti's last idea was to repeat through his
familiars that for his part he would not merely maintain
the principle of the temporal power intact, but would even
undertake to regain that power. And he had a full plan on
the subject, which folks confided to one another in whispers,
a plan which, in spite of its apparent concessions, would lead
to the overwhelming victory of the Church. It was to raise
the prohibition which prevented Catholics from voting or
becoming candidates at the Italian elections; to send a
hundred, then two hundred, and then three hundred deputies
to the Chamber, and in that wise to overthrow the House of
Savoy, and establish a Federation of the Italian provinces,
whereof the Holy Father, once more placed in possession of
Rome, would become the august and sovereign President.

As Prada finished he again laughed, showing his white
teeth—teeth which would never readily relinquish the prey
they held. ' So you see,' he added, ' we need to defend ourselves, since it's a question of turning us out. Fortunately
there are some little obstacles in the way of that. Nevertheless, such dreams naturally have great influence on excited
minds, such as that of Santobono, for instance. He's a man
whom one word from Sanguinetti would lead far indeed.
Ah! he has good legs. Look at him up yonder, he has
already reached the Cardinal's little palace—that white villa
with the sculptured balconies.'

Pierre raised his eyes and perceived the episcopal residence
which was one of the first houses of Frascati. Of modern
construction and Renascence style, it overlooked the immensity
of the Roman Campagna.

It was now eleven o'clock, and as the young priest, before
going up to pay his own visit, bade the Count good-bye, the
latter for a moment kept hold of his hand. ' Do you know,'
said he, ' it would be very kind of you to lunch with me—will

you? Come and join me at that restaurant yonder with the
pink front as soon as you are at liberty. I shall have settled
my own business in an hour's time, and I shall be delighted
to have your company at table.'

Pierre began by declining, but he could offer no possible
excuse, and at last surrendered, won over, despite himself, by
Prada's real charm of manner. When they had parted, the
young priest only had to climb a street in order to reach the
Cardinal's door. With his natural expansiveness and craving
for popularity, Sanguinetti was easy of access, and at Frascati
in particular his doors were flung open even to the most
humble cassocks. So Pierre was at once ushered in, a circumstance which somewhat surprised him, for he remembered
the bad humour of the servant whom he had seen on calling
at the Cardinal's residence in Rome, when he had been
advised to forego the journey, as his Eminence did not like
to be disturbed when he was ill. However, nothing spoke of
illness in that pleasant villa, flooded with sunshine. True,
the waiting room, where he was momentarily left alone, displayed neither luxury nor comfort; but it was brightened by
the finest light in the world, and overlooked that extraordinary Campagna, so flat, so bare, and so unique in its
beauty, for in front of it one ever dreams and sees the Past
arise. And so, whilst waiting, Pierre stationed himself at an
open window, conducting on to a balcony, and his eyes roamed
over the endless sea of herbage to the far away whiteness of
Rome, above which rose the dome of St. Peter's, at that
distance a mere sparkling speck, barely as large as the nail of
one's little finger.

However, the young man had scarcely taken up this
position when he was surprised to hear some people talking,
their words reaching him with great distinctness. And on
leaning forward he realised that his Eminence in person was
standing on another balcony close by, and conversing with a
priest, only a portion of whose cassock could be seen. Still,
this sufficed for Pierre to recognise Santobono. His first impulse, dictated by natural discretion, was to withdraw from
the window, but the words he next heard riveted him to the
spot.

'We shall know in a moment,' his Eminence was saying
in his full voice. 'I sent Eufemio to Rome, for he is the only
person in whom I've any confidence. And see, there is the
train bringing him back.'

A train, still as small as a plaything, could in fact be seen approaching over the vast plain, and doubtless it was to watch for its arrival that Sanguinetti had stationed himself on the balcony. And there he lingered, with his eyes fixed on distant Rome. Then Santobono, in a passionate voice, spoke some words which Pierre imperfectly understood, but the Cardinal with clear articulation rejoined, 'Yes, yes, my dear fellow, a catastrophe would be a great misfortune. Ah! may his Holiness long be preserved to us.' Then he paused, and as he was no hypocrite, gave full expression to the thoughts which were in his mind: 'At least, I hope that he will be preserved just now, for the times are bad, and I am in frightful anguish. The partisans of Antichrist have lately gained much ground.'

A cry escaped Santobono: 'Oh! your Eminence will act and triumph.'

'I, my dear fellow? What would you have *me* do? I am simply at the disposal of my friends, those who are willing to believe in me, with the sole object of ensuring the victory of the Holy See. It is they who ought to act, it is they—each according to the measure of his means—who ought to bar the road to the wicked in order that the righteous may succeed. Ah! if Antichrist should reign——'

The recurrence of this word Antichrist greatly disturbed Pierre; but he suddenly remembered what the Count had told him: Antichrist was Cardinal Boccanera.

'Think of that, my dear fellow,' continued Sanguinetti. 'Picture Antichrist at the Vatican, consummating the ruin of religion by his implacable pride, his iron will, his gloomy passion for nihility; for there can be no doubt of it, he is the Beast of Death announced by the prophecies, the Beast who will expose one and all to the danger of being swallowed up with him in his furious rush into abysmal darkness. I know him; he only dreams of obstinacy and destruction, he will seize the pillars of the temple and shake them in order that he may sink beneath the ruins, he and the whole Catholic world! In less than six months he will be driven from Rome, at strife with all the nations, execrated by Italy, and roaming the world like the phantom of the last pope!'

It was with a low growl, suggestive of a stifled oath, that Santobono responded to this frightful prediction. But the train had now reached the station, and among the few passengers who had alighted, Pierre could distinguish a little

Abbé, who was walking so fast that his cassock flapped against his hips. It was Abbé Eufemio, the Cardinal's secretary, and when he had perceived his Eminence on the balcony he lost all self-respect, and broke into a run, in order that he might the sooner ascend the sloping street. 'Ah! here's Eufemio,' exclaimed the Cardinal, quivering with anxiety. 'We shall know now, we shall know now.'

The secretary had plunged into the doorway below, and he climbed the stairs with such rapidity that almost immediately afterwards Pierre saw him rush breathlessly across the waiting-room, and vanish into the Cardinal's sanctum. Sanguinetti had quitted the balcony to meet his messenger, but soon afterwards he returned to it asking questions, venting exclamations, raising, in fact, quite a tumult over the news which he had received. 'And so it's really true, the night was a bad one. His Holiness scarcely slept! Colic, you were told? But nothing could be worse at his age; it might carry him off in a couple of hours. And the doctors, what do they say?'

The answer did not reach Pierre, but he understood its purport as the Cardinal in his naturally loud voice resumed: 'Oh! the doctors never know. Besides, when they refuse to speak death is never far off. Ah! what a misfortune if the catastrophe cannot be deferred for a few days!'

Then he became silent, and Pierre realised that his eyes were once more travelling towards Rome, gazing with ambitious anguish at the dome of St. Peter's, that little, sparkling speck above the vast, ruddy plain. What a commotion, what agitation if the Pope were dead! And he wished that it had merely been necessary for him to stretch forth his arm in order to take and hold the Eternal City, the Holy City, which, yonder on the horizon, occupied no more space than a heap of gravel cast there by a child's spade. And he was already dreaming of the coming Conclave, when the canopy of each other cardinal would fall, and his own, motionless and sovereign, would crown him with purple.

'But you are right, my friend!' he suddenly exclaimed, addressing Santobono, 'one must act, the salvation of the Church is at stake. And, besides, it is impossible that heaven should not be with us, since our sole desire is its triumph. If necessary, at the supreme moment, heaven will know how to crush Antichrist.'

Then, for the first time, Pierre distinctly heard the voice

of Santobono, who, gruffly, with a sort of savage decision, responded : ' Oh! if heaven is tardy it shall be helped.'

That was all ; the young man heard nothing further save a confused murmur of voices. The speakers quitted the balcony, and his spell of waiting began afresh in the sunlit *salon* so peaceful and delightful in its brightness. But all at once the door of his Eminence's private room was thrown wide open and a servant ushered him in ; and he was surprised to find the cardinal alone, for he had not witnessed the departure of the two priests who had gone off by another door. The Cardinal, with his highly coloured face, big nose, thick lips, square-set, vigorous figure, which still looked young despite his sixty years, was standing near a window in the bright golden light. He had put on the paternal smile with which he greeted even the humblest from motives of good policy, and as soon as Pierre had knelt and kissed his ring, he motioned him to a chair. ' Sit down, dear son, sit down. You have come of course about that unfortunate affair of your book. I am very pleased indeed to be able to speak with you about it.'

He himself then took a chair in front of that window overlooking Rome whence he seemed unable to drag himself. And the young priest, whilst apologising for coming to disturb his rest, perceived that he scarcely listened, for his eyes again sought the prey which he so ardently coveted. Yet the semblance of good-natured attention was perfect, and Pierre marvelled at the force of will which this man must possess to appear so calm, so interested in the affairs of others, when such a tempest was raging in him.

' Your Eminence will, I hope, kindly forgive me,' continued the young priest.

' But you have done right to come, since I am kept here by my failing health,' said the Cardinal. ' Besides, I am somewhat better, and it is only natural that you should wish to give me some explanations and defend your work and enlighten my judgment. In fact, I was astonished at not yet having seen you, for I know that your faith in your cause is great and that you spare no steps to convert your judges. So speak, my dear son, I am listening and shall be pleased indeed if I can absolve you.'

Pierre was caught by these kind words, and a hope returned to him, that of winning the support of the all-powerful Prefect of the Index. He already regarded this ex-nuncio— who at Brussels and Vienna had acquired the worldly art of sending people away satisfied with indefinite promises though he meant to grant them nothing—as a man of rare intelligence and exquisite cordiality. And so once more he regained the fervour of his apostolate to express his views respecting the future Rome, the Rome he dreamt of, which was destined yet again to become the mistress of the world if she would return to the Christianity of Jesus, to an ardent love for the weak and the humble.

Sanguinetti smiled, wagged his head, and raised exclamations of rapture : ' Very good, very good indeed, perfect ! Oh ! I agree with you, dear son. One cannot put things better. It is quite evident ; all good minds must agree with you.' And then, said he, the poetic side deeply touched him. Like Leo XIII—and doubtless in a spirit of rivalry—he courted the reputation of being a very distinguished Latinist, and professed a special and boundless affection for Virgil. ' I know, I know,' he exclaimed, ' I remember your page on the return of spring, which consoles the poor whom winter has frozen. Oh ! I read it three times over ! And are you aware that your writing is full of Latin turns of style. I noticed more than fifty expressions which could be found in the " Bucolics." Your book is a charm, a perfect charm ! '

As he was no fool, and realised that the little priest before him was a man of high intelligence, he ended by interesting himself, not in Pierre personally, but in the profit which he might possibly derive from him. Amidst his feverish intrigues, he unceasingly sought to utilise all the qualities possessed by those whom God sent to him that might in any way be conducive to his own triumph. So, for a moment, he turned away from Rome and looked his companion in the face, listening to him and asking himself in what way he might employ him—either at once in the crisis through which he was passing, or later on when he should be pope. But the young priest again made the mistake of attacking the temporal power, and of employing that unfortunate expression, ' a new religion.' Thereupon the Cardinal stopped him with a gesture, still smiling, still retaining all his amiability, although the resolution which he had long since formed became from that moment definitive. ' You are certainly in the right on many points, my dear son,' he said, ' and I often share your views— share them completely. But come, you are doubtless not aware that I am the protector of Lourdes here at Rome. And so, after the page which you have written about the Grotto, how can I possibly pronounce in your favour and against the Fathers ? '

Pierre was utterly overcome by this announcement, for he was indeed unaware of the Cardinal's position with respect to Lourdes, nobody having taken the precaution to warn him. However, each of the Catholic enterprises distributed throughout the world has a protector at Rome, a cardinal who is designated by the Pope to represent it and, if need be, to defend it.

' Those good Fathers ! ' Sanguinetti continued in a gentle voice, ' you have caused them great grief, and really our hands are tied, we cannot add to their sorrow. If you only knew what a number of masses they send us ! I know more than one of our poor priests who would die of hunger if it were not for them.'

Pierre could only bow beneath the blow. Once more he found himself in presence of the pecuniary question, the necessity in which the Holy See is placed to secure the revenue it requires one year with another. And thus the Pope was ever in servitude, for if the loss of Rome had freed him of the cares of state, his enforced gratitude for the alms he received still riveted him to earth. So great, indeed, were the requirements, that money was the ruler, the sovereign power, before which all bowed at the Court of Rome.

And now Sanguinetti rose to dismiss his visitor. ' You must not despair, dear son,' he said effusively. ' I have only my own vote, you know, and I promise you that I will take into account the excellent explanations which you have just given me. And who can tell ? If God be with you, He will save you even in spite of all ! ' This speech formed part of the Cardinal's usual tactics ; for one of his principles was never to drive people to extremes by sending them away hopeless. What good, indeed, would it do to tell this one that the condemnation of his book was a foregone conclusion, and that his only prudent course would be to disavow it ? Only a savage like Boccanera breathed anger upon fiery souls and plunged them into rebellion. ' You must hope, hope ! ' repeated Sanguinetti with a smile, as if implying a multitude of fortunate things which he could not plainly express.

Thereupon Pierre, who was deeply touched, felt born anew. He even forgot the conversation he had surprised, the Cardinal's keen ambition and covert rage with his redoubtable rival. Besides, might not intelligence take the place of heart among the powerful? If this man should some day become pope, and had understood him, might he not prove the pope who was awaited, the pope who would accept the task of reorganising the Church of the united States of Europe, and making it the spiritual sovereign of the world? So he thanked him with emotion, bowed, and left him to his dream, standing before that widely open window whence Rome appeared to him, glittering like a jewel, even indeed as the tiara of gold and gems, in the splendour of the autumn sun.

It was nearly one o'clock when Pierre and Count Prada were at last able to sit down to *déjeuner* in the little restaurant where they had agreed to meet. They had both been delayed by their affairs. However, the Count, having settled some worrying matters to his own advantage, was very lively, whilst the priest on his side was again hopeful, and yielded to the delightful charm of that last fine day. And so the meal proved a very pleasant one in the large, bright room, which, as usual at that season of the year, was quite deserted. Pink and blue predominated in the decoration, but Cupids fluttered on the ceiling, and landscapes, vaguely recalling the Roman castles, adorned the walls. The things they ate were fresh, and they drank the wine of Frascati, to which the soil imparts a kind of burnt flavour as if the old volcanoes of the region had left some little of their fire behind.

For a long while the conversation ranged over those wild and graceful Alban hills, which, fortunately for the pleasure of the eye, overlook the flat Roman Campagna. Pierre, who had made the customary carriage excursion from Frascati to Nemi, still felt its charm and spoke of it in glowing language. First came the lovely road from Frascati to Albano, ascending and descending hillsides planted with reeds, vines and olive trees, amongst which one obtained frequent glimpses of the Campagna's wavy immensity. On the right hand the village of Rocca di Papa arose in amphitheatrical fashion, showing whitely on a knoll below Monte Cavo, which was crowned by lofty and ancient trees. And from this point of the road, on looking back towards Frascati, one saw high up, on the verge of a pine wood, the ruins of Tusculum, large ruddy ruins, baked by centuries of sunshine, and whence the boundless panorama must have been superb. Next one passed through Marino, with its sloping streets, its large cathedral, and its black decaying palace belonging to the Colonnas. Then, beyond a wood of ilex-trees, the lake of Albano was skirted with scenery which has no parallel in the world. In front, beyond the clear mirror of motionless water, were the ruins of Alba Longa ; on the left rose Monte Cavo with Rocca di Papa and Palazzuolo ; whilst on the right Castel Gandolfo overlooked the lake as from the summit of a cliff. Down below in the extinct crater, as in the depths of a gigantic cup of verdure, the lake slept heavy and lifeless: a sheet of molten metal, which the sun on one side streaked with gold, whilst the other was black with shade. And the road then ascended all the way to Castel Gandolfo, which was perched on its rock, like a white bird betwixt the lake and the sea. Ever refreshed by breezes, even in the most burning hours of summer, the little place was once famous for its papal villa, where Pius IX loved to spend hours of indolence, and whither Leo XIII has never come. And next the road dipped down, and the ilex-trees appeared again, ilex-trees famous for their size, a double row of monsters with twisted limbs, two and three hundred years old. Then one at last reached Albano, a small town less modernised and less cleansed than Frascati, a patch of the old land which has retained some of its ancient wildness ; and afterwards there was Ariccia with the Palazzo Chigi, and hills covered with forests and viaducts spanning ravines which overflowed with foliage ; and there was yet Genzano, and yet Nemi, growing still wilder and more remote, lost in the midst of rocks and trees.

Ah ! how ineffaceable was the recollection which Pierre had retained of Nemi, Nemi on the shore of its lake, Nemi so delicious and fascinating from afar, conjuring up all the ancient legends of fairy towns springing from amidst the greenery of mysterious waters, but so repulsively filthy when one at last reaches it, crumbling on all sides but yet dominated by the Orsini tower, as by the evil genius of the middle ages, which there seems to perpetuate the ferocious habits, the violent passions, the knife-thrusts of the past ! Thence came that Santobono whose brother had killed, and who himself, with his eyes of crime glittering like live embers, seemed to be consumed by a murderous flame. And the lake, that lake round like an extinguished moon fallen into the depths of a former crater, a deeper and less open cup than that of the lake of Albano, a cup rimmed with trees of wondrous vigour and density ! Pines, elms and willows descend to the very margin, with a green mass of tangled branches which weigh each other down. This formidable fecundity springs from the

vapour which constantly arises from the water under the
parching action of the sun whose rays accumulate in this
hollow till it becomes like a furnace. There is a warm,
heavy dampness, the paths of the adjacent gardens grow
green with moss, and in the morning dense mists often fill
the large cup with white vapour, as with the steaming milk
of some sorceress of malevolent craft.   And Pierre well
remembered how uncomfortable he had felt before that lake
where ancient atrocities, a mysterious religion with abominable rites, seemed to slumber amidst the superb scenery. He
had seen it at the approach of evening, looking, in the shade
of its forest girdle, like a plate of dull metal, black and silver,
motionless by reason of its weight. And that water, clear
and yet so deep, that water deserted, without a bark upon
its surface, that water august, lifeless and sepulchral had
left him a feeling of inexpressible sadness, of mortal melancholy, the hopelessness of great solitary passion, earth and
water alike swollen by the mute spasms of germs, troublous
in their fecundity. Ah! those black and plunging banks, and
that black mournful lake prone at the bottom ! [1]

Count Prada began to laugh when Pierre told him of these
impressions. 'Yes, yes,' said he, 'it's true, Nemi isn't always
gay. In dull weather I have seen the lake looking like lead,
and even the full sunshine scarcely animates it.   For my
part, I know I should die of ennui if I had to live face to face
with that bare water. But it is admired by poets and romantic
women, those who adore great tragedies of passion.'

Then, as he and Pierre rose from table to go and take
coffee on the terrace of the restaurant, the conversation changed :
'Do you mean to attend Prince Buongiovanni's reception this
evening ?' the Count inquired. 'It will be a curious sight
especially for a foreigner, and I advise you not to miss it.'

'Yes, I have an invitation,' Pierre replied. 'A friend of
mine, Monsieur Narcisse Habert, an *attaché* at our embassy,
procured it for me, and I am going with him.'

[1] Some literary interest attaches to M. Zola's account of Nemi,
whose praises have been sung by a hundred poets. It will be observed
that he makes no mention of Egeria. The religion, distinguished by
abominable practices to which he alludes, may perhaps be the worship
of the Egyptian Diana, who had a famous temple near Nemi, which was
excavated by Lord Savile some ten years ago, when all the smaller objects
discovered were presented to the town of Nottingham. At this temple,
according to some classical writers, the chief priest was required to
murder his predecessor, and there were other abominable usages.—*Trans.*

That evening, indeed, there was to be a *fête* at the Palazzo
Buongiovanni on the Corso, one of the few *galas* that take
place in Rome each winter. People said that this one would
surpass all others in magnificence, for it was to be given in
honour of the betrothal of little Princess Celia. The Prince,
her father, after boxing her ears, it was rumoured, and
narrowly escaping an attack of apoplexy as the result of a
frightful fit of anger, had, all at once, yielded to her quiet,
gentle stubbornness, and consented to her marriage with
Lieutenant Attilio, the son of Minister Sacco. And all the
drawing-rooms of Rome, those of the white world quite as
much as those of the black, were thoroughly upset by the
tidings.

Count Prada made merry over the affair. 'Ah! you'll
see a fine sight!' he exclaimed. 'Personally, I'm delighted
with it all for the sake of my good cousin Attilio, who is really
a very nice and worthy fellow. And nothing in the world
would keep me from going to see my dear uncle Sacco make
his entry into the ancient *salons* of the Buongiovanni. It will
be something extraordinary and superb. He has at last
become Minister of Agriculture, you know. My father, who
always takes things so seriously, told me this morning that the
affair so worried him he hadn't closed his eyes all night.'

The Count paused, but almost immediately added : 'I say,
it is half-past two and you won't have a train before five o'clock.
Do you know what you ought to do? Why, drive back to
Rome with me in my carriage.'

'No, no,' rejoined Pierre, 'I'm deeply obliged to you but
I'm to dine with my friend Narcisse this evening, and I
mustn't be late.'

'But you won't be late—on the contrary! We shall start
at three and reach Rome before five o'clock. There can't be
a more pleasant promenade when the light falls; and, come,
I promise you a splendid sunset.'

He was so pressing that the young priest had to accept,
quite subjugated by so much amiability and good humour.
They spent another half-hour very pleasantly in chatting about
Rome, Italy, and France. Then, for a moment, they went up
into Frascati where the Count wished to say a few words to a
contractor, and just as three o'clock was striking they started
off, seated side by side on the soft cushions and gently rocked
by the motion of the victoria as the two horses broke into a
light trot. As Prada had predicted, that return to Rome across

the bare Campagna under the vast limpid heavens at the close
of such a mild autumn day, proved most delightful. First of
all, however, the victoria had to descend the slopes of Frascati
between vineyards and olive trees. The paved road snaked,
and was but little frequented; they merely saw a few peasants
in old felt hats, a white mule and a cart drawn by a donkey,
for it is only upon Sundays that the *osterie* or wine-shops are
filled and that artisans in easy circumstances come to eat a
dish of kid at the surrounding *bastides*. However, at one
turn of the road they passed a monumental fountain. Then a
flock of sheep momentarily barred the way before defiling past.
And beyond the gentle undulations of the ruddy Campagna
Rome appeared amidst the violet vapours of evening, sinking
by degrees as the carriage itself descended to a lower and
lower level. There came a moment when the city was a
mere thin grey streak, speckled whitely here and there by a
few sunlit house-fronts. And then it seemed to plunge below
the ground—to be submerged by the swell of the far-spreading
fields.

The victoria was now rolling over the plain, leaving the
Alban hills behind, whilst before it and on either hand came
the expanse of meadows and stubbles. And then it was that
the Count, after leaning forward, exclaimed: 'Just look
ahead, yonder, there's our man of this morning, Santobono in
person—what a strapping fellow he is, and how fast he
walks! My horses can scarcely overtake him.'

Pierre in his turn leant forward and likewise perceived the
priest of St. Mary in the Fields, looking tall and knotty,
fashioned as it were with a bill-hook. Robed in a long black
cassock, he showed like a vigorous splotch of ink amidst the
bright sunshine streaming around him; and he was walking
on at such a fast, stern, regular pace that he suggested
Destiny on the march. Something, which could not be well
distinguished, was hanging from his right arm.

When the carriage had at last overtaken him Prada told
the coachman to slacken speed, and then entered into conversation.

'Good day, Abbé; you are well, I hope?' he asked.

'Very well, Signor Conte, I thank you.'

'And where are you going so bravely?'

'Signor Conte, I am going to Rome.'

'What! to Rome, at this late hour?'

'Oh! I shall be there nearly as soon as yourself. The

distance doesn't frighten me, and money's quickly earned by
walking.'

Scarcely turning his head to reply, stepping out beside the
wheels, Santobono did not miss a stride. And Prada, diverted
by the meeting, whispered to Pierre: 'Wait a bit, he'll
amuse us.' Then he added aloud: 'Since you are going to
Rome, Abbé, you had better get in here; there's room for
you.'

Santobono required no pressing, but at once accepted the
offer. 'Willingly; a thousand thanks,' he said. 'It's still
better to save one's shoe leather.'

Then he got in and installed himself on the bracket-seat,
declining with abrupt humility the place which Pierre politely
offered him beside the Count. The young priest and the
latter now saw that the object he was carrying was a little
basket of fresh figs, nicely arranged and covered with leaves.

The horses set off again at a faster trot, and the carriage
rolled on and on over the superb, flat plain. 'So you are
going to Rome?' the Count resumed in order to make Santobono talk.

'Yes,' the other replied, 'I am taking his Eminence Cardinal Boccanera these few figs, the last of the season: a little
present which I had promised him.' He had placed the basket
on his knees and was holding it between his big knotty hands
as if it were something rare and fragile.

'Ah! some of the famous figs of your garden,' said Prada.
'It's quite true, they are like honey. But why don't you rid
yourself of them? You surely don't mean to keep them on
your knees all the way to Rome. Give them to me, I'll put
them in the hood.'

However, Santobono became quite agitated, and vigorously
declined the offer. 'No, no, a thousand thanks! They don't
embarrass me in the least; they are very well here; and in
this way I shall be sure that no accident will befall them.'

His passion for the fruit he grew quite amused Prada, who
nudged Pierre, and then inquired: 'Is the Cardinal fond of
your figs?'

'Oh! his Eminence condescends to adore them. In former
years, when he spent the summer at the villa, he would never
touch the figs from other trees. And so, you see, knowing his
tastes, it costs me very little to gratify him.'

Whilst making this reply Santobono had shot such a keen
glance in the direction of Pierre that the Count felt it necessary

to introduce them to one another. This he did saying: 'As
it happens, Monsieur l'Abbé Froment is stopping at the
Palazzo Boccanera; he has been there for three months or
so.'

'Yes, I'm aware of it,' Santobono quietly replied; 'I found
Monsieur l'Abbé with his Eminence one day when I took
some figs to the Palazzo. Those were less ripe, but these are
perfect.' So speaking he gave the little basket a complacent
glance, and seemed to press it yet more closely between his
huge and hairy fingers.

Then came a spell of silence, whilst on either hand the
Campagna spread out as far as the eye could reach. All
houses had long since disappeared; there was not a wall, not
a tree, nothing but the undulating expanse whose sparse,
short herbage was, with the approach of winter, beginning to
turn green once more. A tower, a half-fallen ruin which
came into sight on the left, rising in solitude into the
limpid sky above the flat, boundless line of the horizon,
suddenly assumed extraordinary importance. Then, on the
right, the distant silhouettes of cattle and horses were seen in
a large enclosure with wooden rails. Urged on by the goad,
oxen, still yoked, were slowly coming back from ploughing;
whilst a farmer, cantering beside the ploughed land on a little
sorrel nag, gave a final look round for the night. Now and
again the road became peopled. A *biroccino*, an extremely
light vehicle with two huge wheels and a small seat perched
upon the springs, whisked by like a gust of wind. From time
to time also the victoria passed a *carrotino*, one of the low
carts in which peasants, sheltered by a kind of bright-hued
tent, bring the wine, vegetables, and fruit of the castle-lands
to Rome. The shrill tinkling of horses' bells was heard afar
off as the animals followed the well-known road of their own
accord, their peasant drivers usually being sound asleep.
Women with bare, black hair, scarlet neckerchiefs, and skirts
caught up, were seen going home in groups of three and four.
And then the road again emptied, and the solitude became
more and more complete, without a wayfarer or an animal
appearing for miles and miles, whilst yonder, at the far end of
the lifeless sea, so grandiose and mournful in its monotony,
the sun continued to descend from the infinite vault of
heaven.

'And the Pope, Abbé, is he dead?' Prada suddenly inquired.

Santobono did not even start. 'I trust,' he replied in all simplicity, 'that his Holiness still has many long years to live for the triumph of the Church.'

'So you had good news this morning when you called on your bishop, Cardinal Sanguinetti?'

This time the priest was unable to restrain a slight start. Had he been seen, then? In his haste he had failed to notice the two men following the road behind him. However, he at once regained self-possession, and replied: 'Oh! one can never tell exactly whether news is good or bad. It seems that his Holiness passed a somewhat painful night, but I devoutly hope that the next will be a better one.' Then he seemed to meditate for a moment, and added: 'Moreover, if God should have deemed it time to call his Holiness to Himself, He would not leave His flock without a shepherd. He would have already chosen and designated the Sovereign Pontiff of to-morrow.'

This superb answer increased Prada's gaiety. 'You are really extraordinary, Abbé,' he said. 'So you think that popes are solely created by the grace of the Divinity! The pope of to-morrow is chosen up in heaven, eh, and simply waits? Well, I fancied that men had something to do with the matter. But perhaps you already know which cardinal it is that the Divine favour has thus elected in advance?'

Then, like the unbeliever he was, he went on with his facile jests, which left the priest unruffled. In fact, the latter also ended by laughing when the Count, after alluding to the gambling passion which at each fresh conclave sets well-nigh the whole population of Rome betting for or against this or that candidate, told him that he might easily make his fortune if he were in the Divine secret. Next the talk turned on the three white cassocks of different sizes which are always kept in readiness in a cupboard at the Vatican. Which of them would be required on this occasion?—the short one, the long one, or the one of medium size? Each time that the reigning pope falls somewhat seriously ill there is in this wise an extraordinary outburst of emotion, a keen awakening of all ambitions and intrigues, to such a point that not merely in the black world, but throughout the city, people have no other subject of curiosity, conversation, and occupation than that of discussing the relative claims of the cardinals and predicting which of them will be elected.

'Come, come,' Prada resumed, 'since you know the truth,

I'm determined that you shall tell me. Will it be Cardinal Moretta ? '

Santobono, in spite of his evident desire to remain dignified and disinterested, like a good, pious priest, was gradually growing impassioned, yielding to the hidden fire which consumed him. And this interrogatory finished him off; he could no longer restrain himself, but replied : 'Moretta ! What an idea ! Why, he is sold to all Europe ! '

'Well, will it be Cardinal Bartolini ? '

'Oh ! you can't think that. Bartolini has used himself up in striving for everything and getting nothing.'

'Will it be Cardinal Dozio, then ?'

'Dozio, Dozio ! Why, if Dozio were to win one might altogether despair of our Holy Church, for no man can have a baser mind than he ! '

Prada raised his hands, as if he had exhausted the serious candidates. In order to increase the priest's exasperation he maliciously refrained from naming Cardinal Sanguinetti, who was certainly Santobono's nominee. All at once, however, he pretended to make a good guess, and gaily exclaimed : 'Ah ! I have it ; I know your man—Cardinal Boccanera ! '

The blow struck Santobono full in the heart, wounding him both in his rancour and his patriotic faith. His terrible mouth was already opening, and he was about to shout 'No !' no !' with all his strength, but he managed to restrain the cry, compelled as he was to silence by the present on his knees—that little basket of figs which he pressed so convulsively with both hands ; and the effort which he was obliged to make left him quivering to such a point that he had to wait some time before he could reply in a calm voice : 'His most reverend Eminence Cardinal Boccanera is a saintly man, well worthy of the throne, and my only fear is that, with his hatred of new Italy, he might bring us warfare.'

Prada, however, desired to enlarge the wound. 'At all events,' said he, 'you accept him and love him too much not to rejoice over his chances of success. And I really think that we have arrived at the truth, for everybody is convinced that the Conclave's choice cannot fall elsewhere. Come, come ; Boccanera is a very tall man, so it's the long white cassock which will be required.'

'The long cassock, the long cassock,' growled Santobono, despite himself ; 'that's all very well, but——'

Then he stopped short, and, again overcoming his passion,

left his sentence unfinished. Pierre, listening in silence, marvelled at the man's self-restraint, for he remembered the conversation which he had overheard at Cardinal Sanguinetti's. Those figs were evidently a mere pretext for gaining admission to the Boccanera mansion, where some friend—Abbé Paparelli, no doubt—could alone supply certain positive information which was needed. But how great was the command which that hot-blooded priest exercised over himself amidst the riotous impulses of his soul!

On either side of the road the Campagna still and ever spread its expanse of verdure, and Prada, who had become grave and dreamy, gazed before him without seeing anything. At last, however, he gave expression to his thoughts : 'You know, Abbé, what will be said if the Pope should die this time. That sudden illness, those colics, those refusals to make any information public, mean nothing good—— Yes, yes, poison, just as for the others!'

Pierre gave a start of stupefaction. The Pope poisoned! 'What! Poison? Again?' he exclaimed, as he gazed at his companions with dilated eyes. Poison at the end of the nineteenth century, as in the days of the Borgias, as on the stage in a romanticist melodrama! To him the idea appeared both monstrous and ridiculous.

Santobono, whose features had become motionless and impenetrable, made no reply. But Prada nodded, and the conversation was henceforth confined to him and the young priest. 'Why, yes, poison,' he replied. 'The fear of it has remained very great in Rome. Whenever a death seems inexplicable, either by reason of its suddenness or the tragic circumstances which attend it, the unanimous thought is poison. And remark this : in no city, I believe, are sudden deaths so frequent. The causes I don't exactly know, but some doctors put everything down to the fevers. Among the people, however, the one thought is poison, poison with all its legends, poison which kills like lightning and leaves no trace, the famous recipe bequeathed from age to age, through the emperors and the popes, down to these present times of middle-class democracy.'

As he spoke he ended by smiling, for he was inclined to be somewhat sceptical on the point, despite the covert terror with which he was inspired by racial and educational causes. However, he quoted instances. The Roman matrons had rid themselves of their husbands and lovers by employing the venom of red toads. Locusta, in a more practical spirit, sought poison in plants, one of which, probably aconite, she was wont to boil. Then, long afterwards, came the age of the Borgias, and subsequently, at Naples, La Toffana sold a famous water, doubtless some preparation of arsenic, in phials decorated with a representation of St Nicholas of Bari. There were also extraordinary stories of pins, a prick from which killed one like lightning, of cups of wine poisoned by the infusion of rose petals, of wood-cocks cut in half with prepared knives, which poisoned but one half of the bird, so that he who partook of that half was killed. 'I myself, in my younger days,' continued Prada, ' had a friend whose bride fell dead in church during the marriage service through simply inhaling a bouquet of flowers. And so isn't it possible that the famous recipe may really have been handed down, and have remained known to a few adepts ? '

'But chemistry has made too much progress,' Pierre replied. 'If mysterious poisons were believed in by the ancients and remained undetected in their time it was because there were no means of analysis. But the drug of the Borgias would now lead the simpleton who might employ it straight to the Assizes. Such stories are mere nonsense, and at the present day people scarcely tolerate them in newspaper serials and shockers.'

'Perhaps so,' resumed the Count with his uneasy smile. ' You are right, no doubt—only go and tell that to your host, for instance, Cardinal Boccanera, who last summer held in his arms an old and deeply loved friend, Monsignor Gallo, who died after a seizure of a couple of hours.'

' But apoplexy may kill one in two hours, and aneurism only takes two minutes.'

' True, but ask the Cardinal what he thought of his friend's prolonged shudders, the leaden hue which overcame his face, the sinking of his eyes and the expression of terror which made him quite unrecognisable. The Cardinal is convinced that Monsignor Gallo was poisoned, because he was his dearest confidant, the counsellor to whom he always listened, and whose wise advice was a guarantee of success.'

Pierre's bewilderment was increasing, and, irritated by the impassibility of Santobono, he addressed him direct. 'It's idiotic, it's awful! Does your reverence also believe in these frightful stories ? '

But the priest of Frascati gave no sign. His thick,

passionate lips remained closed while his black glowing eyes
never ceased to gaze at Prada. The latter, moreover, was
quoting other instances. There was the case of Monsignor
Nazzarelli, who had been found in bed, shrunken and calcined
like carbon. And there was that of Monsignor Brando, struck
down in his sacerdotal vestments at St. Peter's itself, in the
very sacristy, during vespers !

'Ah ! *Mon Dieu !*' sighed Pierre, 'you will tell me so
much that I myself shall end by trembling, and sha'n't dare
to eat anything but boiled eggs as long as I stay in this
terrible Rome of yours.'

For a moment this whimsical reply enlivened both the
Count and Pierre. But it was quite true that their conversation showed Rome under a terrible aspect, for it conjured up
the Eternal City of Crime, the city of poison and the knife,
where for more than two thousand years, ever since the raising of the first bit of wall, the lust of power, the frantic
hunger for possession and enjoyment, had armed men's hands,
ensanguined the pavements, and cast victims into the river
and the ground. Assassinations and poisonings under the
emperors, poisonings and assassinations under the popes, ever
did the same torrent of abominations strew that tragic soil
with death amidst the sovereign glory of the sun.

'All the same,' said the Count, 'those who take precau-
tions are perhaps not ill advised. It is said that more than
one cardinal shudders and mistrusts people. One whom I
know will never eat anything that has not been bought and
prepared by his own cook. And as for the Pope, if he is
anxious——'

Pierre again raised a cry of stupefaction. ' What, the Pope
himself ! The Pope afraid of being poisoned ! '

'Well, my dear Abbé, people commonly assert it. There
are certainly days when he considers himself more menaced
than anybody else. And are you not aware of the old Roman
view that a pope ought never to live till too great an age, and
that when he is so obstinate as not to die at the right time he
ought to be assisted? As soon as a pope begins to fall into
second childhood, and by reason of his senility becomes a
source of embarrassment, and possibly even danger, to the
Church, his right place is Heaven. Moreover, matters are
managed in a discreet manner ; a slight cold becomes a decent
pretext to prevent him from tarrying any longer on the throne
of St. Peter.'

Prada then gave some curious details. One prelate, it was said, wishing to dispel his Holiness's fears, had devised an elaborate precautionary system which, among other things, was to comprise a little padlocked vehicle, in which the food destined for the frugal pontifical table was to be securely placed before leaving the kitchen, so that it might not be tampered with on its way to the Pope's apartments. However, this project had not yet been carried into effect.

'After all,' the Count concluded with a laugh, 'every pope has to die some day, especially when his death is needful for the welfare of the Church. Isn't that so, Abbé?'

Santobono, whom he addressed, had a moment previously lowered his eyes as if to contemplate the little basket of figs which he held on his lap with as much care as if it had been the Blessed Sacrament. On being questioned in such a direct, sharp fashion he could not do otherwise than look up. However, he did not depart from his prolonged silence, but limited his answer to a slow nod.

'And it is God alone, and not poison, Who causes one to die. Is that not so, Abbé?' repeated Prada. 'It is said that those were the last words of poor Monsignor Gallo before he expired in the arms of his friend Cardinal Boccanera.'

For the second time Santobono nodded without speaking. And then silence fell, all three sinking into a dreamy mood.

Meantime, without a pause, the carriage rolled on across the immensity of the Campagna. The road, straight as an arrow, seemed to extend into the infinite. As the sun descended towards the horizon the play of light and shade became more marked on the broad undulations of the ground which stretched away, alternately of a pinky green and a violet grey, till they reached the distant fringe of the sky. At the roadside on either hand there were still and ever tall withered thistles and giant fennel with yellow umbels. Then, after a time, came a team of four oxen, that had been kept ploughing until late, and stood forth black and huge in the pale atmosphere and mournful solitude. Farther on some flocks of sheep, whence the breeze wafted a tallowy odour, set patches of brown amidst the herbage, which once more was becoming verdant; whilst at intervals a dog was heard to bark, his voice the only distinct sound amidst the low quivering of that silent desert where the sovereign peacefulness of death seemed to reign. But all at once a light melody arose and some larks flew up, one of them soaring into the limpid golden heavens. And

ahead, at the far extremity of the pure sky, Rome, with her
towers and domes, grew larger and larger, like a city of white
marble springing from a mirage amidst the greenery of some
enchanted garden.

'Matteo!' Prada called to his coachman, 'pull up at the
Osteria Romana.' And to his companions he added : ' Pray
excuse me, but I want to see if I can get some new-laid eggs
for my father. He is so fond of them.'

A few minutes afterwards the carriage stopped. At the
very edge of the road stood a primitive sort of inn, bearing the
proud and sonorous name of ' Antica Osteria Romana.' It had
now become a mere house of call for carters and chance
sportsmen, who ventured to drink a flagon of white wine whilst
eating an omelet and a slice of ham. Occasionally, on Sundays, some of the humble classes would walk over from Rome
and make merry there; but the week days often went by without a soul entering the place, such was its isolation amidst
the bare Campagna.

The Count was already springing from the carriage. 'I
shall only be a minute,' said he as he turned away.

The *osteria* was a long, low pile with a ground floor and
one upper story, the last being reached by an out-door stairway
built of large blocks of stone which had been scorched by the
hot suns. The entire place, indeed, was corroded, tinged with
the hue of old gold. On the ground floor one found a common
room, a carthouse, and a stable with adjoining sheds. At one
side, near a cluster of parasol pines—the only trees that could
grow in that ungrateful soil—there was an arbour of reeds
where five or six rough wooden tables were set out. And, as
a background to this sorry, mournful nook of life, there arose
a fragment of an ancient aqueduct whose arches, half fallen
and opening on to space, alone interrupted the flat line of the
horizon.

All at once, however, the Count retraced his steps, and,
addressing Santobono, exclaimed : ' I say, Abbé, you'll surely
accept a glass of white wine. I know that you are a bit of a vine
grower, and they have a little white wine here which you ought
to make acquaintance with.'

Santobono again required no pressing, but quietly alighted.
' Oh! I know it,' said he; ' it's a wine from Marino ; it's grown
in a lighter soil than ours at Frascati.'

Then, as he would not relax his hold on his basket of figs,
but even now carried it along with him, the Count lost patience,

' Come, you don't want that basket,' said he; ' leave it in the carriage.'

The priest gave no reply, but walked ahead, whilst Pierre also made up his mind to descend from the carriage in order to see what a suburban *osteria* was like. Prada was known at this place, and an old woman, tall, withered, but looking quite queenly in her wretched garments, had at once presented herself. On the last occasion when the Count had called she had managed to find half-a-dozen eggs. This time she said she would go to see, but could promise nothing, for the hens laid here and there all over the place, and she could never tell what eggs there might be.

' All right ! ' Prada answered, ' go and look; and meantime we will have a *caraffa* of white wine.'

The three men entered the common room, which was already quite dark. Although the hot weather was now over, one heard the buzzing of innumerable flies immediately one reached the threshold, and a pungent odour of acidulous wine and rancid oil caught one at the throat. As soon as their eyes became accustomed to the dimness they were able to distinguish the spacious, blackened, malodorous chamber, whose only furniture consisted of some roughly made tables and benches. It seemed to be quite empty, so complete was the silence, apart from the buzz of the flies. However, two men were seated there, two wayfarers who remained mute and motionless before their untouched, brimming glasses. Moreover, on a low chair near the door, in the little light which penetrated from without, a thin, sallow girl, the daughter of the house, sat idle, trembling with fever, her hands close pressed between her knees.

Realising that Pierre felt uncomfortable there, the Count proposed that they should drink their wine outside. ' We shall be better out of doors,' said he, ' it's so very mild this evening.'

Accordingly, whilst the mother looked for the eggs, and the father mended a wheel in an adjacent shed, the daughter was obliged to get up shivering to carry the flagon of wine and the three glasses to the arbour, where she placed them on one of the tables. And, having pocketed the price of the wine— three pence—in silence, she went back to her seat with a sullen look, as if annoyed at having been compelled to make such a long journey. Meanwhile the three men had sat down, and Prada gaily filled each of the glasses, although Pierre declared

that he was quite unable to drink wine between his meals.
'Pooh, pooh,' said the Count, 'you can always chink glasses
with us. And now, Abbé, isn't this little wine droll? Come,
here's to the Pope's better health, since he's unwell!'

Santobono at one gulp emptied his glass and clacked his
tongue. With gentle, paternal care he had deposited his
basket on the ground beside him : and, taking off his hat, he
drew a long breath. The evening was really delightful. A
superb sky of a soft golden hue stretched over that endless sea
of the Campagna which was soon to fall asleep with sovereign
quiescence. And the light breeze which went by amidst the
deep silence brought with it an exquisite odour of wild herbs
and flowers.

'How pleasant it is!' muttered Pierre, affected by the
surrounding charm. 'And what a desert for eternal rest, for
forgetfulness of all the world!'

Prada, who had emptied the flagon by filling Santobono's
glass a second time, made no reply ; he was silently amusing
himself with an occurrence which at first he was the only one
to observe. However, with a merry expression of complicity,
he gave the young priest a wink, and then they both watched
the dramatic incidents of the affair. Some scraggy fowls were
wandering round them searching the yellow turf for grasshoppers; and one of these birds, a little shiny black hen with
an impudent manner, had caught sight of the basket of figs
and was boldly approaching it. When she got near, however,
she took fright, and retreated somewhat, with neck stiffened
and head turned, so as to cast suspicious glances at the basket
with her round sparkling eye. But at last covetousness gained
the victory, for she could see one of the figs between the leaves,
and so she slowly advanced, lifting her feet very high at each
step, and, all at once, stretching out her neck, she gave the
fig a formidable peck, which ripped it open and made the juice
exude.

Prada, who felt as happy as a child, was then able to give
vent to the laughter which he had scarcely been able to restrain : 'Look out, Abbé,' he called, 'mind your figs!'

At that very moment Santobono was finishing his second
glass of wine with his head thrown back and his eyes blissfully raised to heaven. He gave a start, looked round, and
on seeing the hen at once understood the position. And then
came a terrible outburst of anger, with sweeping gestures and
terrible invectives. But the hen, who was again pecking,

would not be denied; she dug her beak into the fig and carried it off, flapping her wings, so quick and so comical that Prada, and Pierre as well, laughed till tears came into their eyes, their merriment increasing at sight of the impotent fury of Santobono, who, for a moment, pursued the thief, threatening her with his fist.

'Ah!' said the Count, 'that's what comes of not leaving the basket in the carriage. If I hadn't warned you the hen would have eaten all the figs.'

The priest did not reply, but, growling out vague imprecations, placed the basket on the table, where he raised the leaves and artistically rearranged the fruit so as to fill up the void. Then, the harm having been repaired as far as was possible, he at last calmed down.

It was now time for them to resume their journey, for the sun was sinking towards the horizon, and night would soon fall. Thus the Count ended by getting impatient. 'Well, and those eggs?' he called.

Then, as the woman did not return, he went to seek her. He entered the stable, and afterwards the cart-house, but she was neither here nor there. Next he went towards the rear of the *osteria* in order to look in the sheds. But all at once an unexpected spectacle made him stop short. The little black hen was lying on the ground, dead, killed as by lightning. She showed no sign of hurt; there was nothing but a little streamlet of violet blood still trickling from her beak. Prada was at first merely astonished. He stooped and touched the hen. She was still warm and soft like a rag. Doubtless some apoplectic stroke had killed her. But immediately afterwards he became fearfully pale; the truth appeared to him, and turned him as cold as ice. In a moment he conjured up everything: Leo XIII attacked by illness, Santobono hurrying to Cardinal Sanguinetti for tidings, and then starting for Rome to present a basket of figs to Cardinal Boccanera. And Prada also remembered the conversation in the carriage: the possibility of the Pope's demise, the candidates for the tiara, the legendary stories of poison which still fostered terror in and around the Vatican; and he once more saw the priest, with his little basket on his knees, lavishing paternal attention on it, and he saw the little black hen pecking at the fruit and fleeing with a fig on her beak. And now that little black hen lay there, suddenly struck down, dead!

His conviction was immediate and absolute. But he did

not have time to decide what course he should take, for a voice
behind him exclaimed : ' Why, it's the little hen ; what's the
matter with her ? '

The voice was that of Pierre, who, letting Santobono climb
into the carriage alone, had in his turn come round to the
rear of the house in order to obtain a better view of the ruined
aqueduct among the parasol pines.

Prada, who shuddered as if he himself were the culprit,
answered him with a lie, a lie which he did not premeditate,
but to which he was impelled by a sort of instinct. ' But she's
dead,' he said. . . . ' Just fancy, there was a fight. At the
moment when I got here that other hen, which you see yonder,
sprang on this one to get the fig, which she was still holding,
and with a thrust of the beak split her head open. . . . The
blood's flowing, as you can see yourself.'

Why did he say these things ?   He himself was astonished
at them whilst he went on inventing them. Was it then that he
wished to remain master of the situation, keep the abominable
secret entirely to himself, in order that he might afterwards
act in accordance with his own desires ? Certainly his feelings partook of shame and embarrassment in presence of that
foreigner, whilst his personal inclination for violence set some
admiration amidst the revolt of his conscience, and a covert
desire arose within him to examine the matter from the
standpoint of his interests before he came to a decision. But,
on the other hand, he claimed to be a man of integrity, and
would assuredly not allow people to be poisoned.

Pierre, who was compassionately inclined towards all
creation, looked at the hen with the emotion which he
always felt at the sudden severance of life. However, he at
once accepted Prada's story. ' Ah ! those fowls ! ' said he.
' They treat one another with an idiotic ferocity which even
men can scarcely equal. I kept fowls at home at one time,
and one of the hens no sooner hurt her leg than all the others,
on seeing the blood oozing, would flock round and peck at the
limb till they stripped it to the bone.'

Prada, however, did not listen, but at once went off ; and
it so happened that the woman was, on her side, looking for
him in order to hand him four eggs which, after a deal of
searching, she had discovered in odd corners about the house.
The Count made haste to pay for them, and called to Pierre,
who was lingering behind : ' We must look sharp ! We shan't
reach Rome now until it is quite dark.'

They found Santobono quietly waiting in the carriage, where he had again installed himself on the bracket with his spine resting against the box-seat and his long legs drawn back under him, and he again had the little basket of figs on his knees, and clasped it with his big knotty hands as though it was something fragile and rare which the slightest jolting might damage. His cassock showed like a huge blot, and in his coarse ashen face, that of a peasant yet near to the wild soil and but slightly polished by a few years of theological studies, his eyes alone seemed to live, glowing with the dark flame of a devouring passion. On seeing him seated there in such composure Prada could not restrain a slight shudder. Then, as soon as the victoria was again rolling along the road, he exclaimed : ' Well, Abbé, that glass of wine will guarantee us against the malaria. The Pope would soon be cured if he could imitate our example.'

Santobono's only reply was a growl. He was in no mood for conversation, but wrapped himself in perfect silence, as in the night which was slowly falling. And Prada in his turn ceased to speak, and, with his eyes still fixed upon the other, reflected on the course that he should follow.

The road turned, and then the carriage rolled on and on over another interminable straight highway with white paving, whose brilliancy made the road look like a ribbon of snow stretching across the Campagna, where delicate shadows were slowly falling. Gloom gathered in the hollows of the broad undulations whence a tide of violet hue seemed to spread over the short herbage until all mingled and the expanse became an indistinct swell of neutral hue from one to the other horizon. And the solitude was now yet more complete ; a last indolent cart had gone by and a last tinkling of horses' bells had subsided in the distance. There was no longer a passer-by, no longer a beast of the fields to be seen, colour and sound died away, all forms of life sank into slumber, into the serene stillness of nihility. Some fragments of an aqueduct were still to be seen at intervals on the right hand, where they looked like portions of gigantic millepedes severed by the scythe of time ; next, on the left, came another tower, whose dark and ruined pile barred the sky as with a huge black stake ; and then the remains of another aqueduct spanned the road assuming yet greater dimensions against the sunset glow. Ah ! that unique hour, the hour of twilight in the Campagna, when all is blotted out and simplified, the hour of

bare immensity, of the infinite in its simplest expression!
There is nothing, nothing all around you, but the flat line of
the horizon with the one splotch of an isolated tower, and
yet that nothing is instinct with sovereign majesty.

However, on the left, towards the sea, the sun was setting,
descending in the limpid sky like a globe of fire of blinding
redness. It slowly plunged beneath the horizon, and the
only sign of cloud was some fiery vapour, as if indeed the
distant sea had seethed at contact with that royal and flaming
visit. And directly the sun had disappeared the heavens
above it purpled and became a lake of blood, whilst the
Campagna turned to grey. At the far end of the fading
plain there was only left that purple lake whose brasier
slowly died out behind the black arches of the aqueduct,
while in the opposite direction the scattered arches remained
bright and rosy against a pewter-like sky. Then the fiery
vapour was dissipated, and the sunset ended by fading away.
One by one the stars came out in the pacified vault, now of
an ashen blue, while the lights of Rome, still far away on the
verge of the horizon, scintillated like the lamps of light-
houses.

And Prada, amidst the dreamy silence of his companions
and the infinite melancholy of the evening and the inexpressible distress which even he experienced, continued to ask
himself what course he should adopt. Again and again he
mentally repeated that he could not allow people to be
poisoned. The figs were certainly intended for Cardinal
Boccanera, and on the whole it mattered little to him whether
there were a cardinal the more or the fewer in the world.
Moreover, it had always seemed to him best to let destiny
follow its course; and, infidel that he was, he saw no harm
in one priest devouring another. Again, it might be dangerous for him to intervene in that abominable affair, to mix
himself up in the base, fathomless intrigues of the black
world. But on the other hand the Cardinal was not the
only person who lived in the Boccanera mansion, and might
not the figs go to others, might they not be eaten by people
to whom no harm was intended? This idea of a treacherous
chance haunted him, and in spite of every effort the figures of
Benedetta and Dario rose up before him, returned and imposed themselves on him though he again and again sought
to banish them from his mind. What if Benedetta, what if
Dario should partake of that fruit? For Benedetta he felt

no fear, for he knew that she and her aunt ate their meals by themselves, and that their *cuisine* and the Cardinal's had nothing in common. But Dario sat at his uncle's table every day, and for a moment Prada pictured the young Prince suddenly seized with a spasm, then falling, like poor Monsignor Gallo, into the Cardinal's arms with livid face and receding eyes, and dying within two hours.

But no, no! That would be frightful, he could not suffer such an abomination. And thereupon he made up his mind. He would wait till the night had completely gathered round and would then simply take the basket from Santobono's lap and fling it into some dark hollow without saying a word. The priest would understand him. The other one, the young Frenchman, would perhaps not even notice the incident. Besides, that mattered little, for he would not even attempt to explain his action. And he felt quite calm again when the idea occurred to him to throw the basket away while the carriage passed through the Porta Furba, a couple of miles or so before reaching Rome. That would suit him exactly; in the darkness of the gateway nothing whatever would be seen.

'We stopped too long at that *osteria*,' he suddenly exclaimed aloud, turning towards Pierre. 'We sha'n't reach Rome much before six o'clock. Still you will have time to dress and join your friend.' And then, without awaiting the young man's reply, he said to Santobono: 'Your figs will arrive very late, Abbé.'

'Oh!' answered the priest, 'His Eminence receives until eight o'clock. And, besides, the figs are not for this evening. People don't eat figs in the evening. They will be for to-morrow morning.' And thereupon he again relapsed into silence.

'For to-morrow morning—yes, yes, no doubt,' repeated Prada. 'And the Cardinal will be able to thoroughly regale himself if nobody helps him to eat the fruit.'

Thereupon Pierre, without pausing to reflect, exclaimed: 'He will no doubt eat it by himself, for his nephew, Prince Dario, must have started to-day for Naples on a little convalescence trip to rid himself of the effects of the accident which laid him up during the last month.' Then, having got so far, the young priest remembered to whom he was speaking, and abruptly stopped short.

The Count noticed his embarrassment. 'Oh! speak on,

my dear Monsieur Froment,' said he, 'you don't offend me.
It's an old affair now. So that young man has left, you say ?'

'Yes, unless he has postponed his departure. However,
I don't expect to find him at the *palazzo* when I get there.'

For a moment the only sound was that of the continuous
rumble of the wheels. Prada again felt worried, a prey to the
discomfort of uncertainty. Why should he mix himself up in
the affair if Dario were really absent? All the ideas which
came to him tired his brain, and he ended by thinking aloud:
'If he has gone away it must be for propriety's sake, so as to
avoid attending the Buongiovanni reception, for the Congregation of the Council met this morning to give its decision in
the suit which the Countess has brought against me. Yes, I
shall know by-and-by whether our marriage is to be dissolved.'

It was in a somewhat hoarse voice that he spoke these
words, and one could realise that the old wound was again
bleeding within him. Although Lisbeth had borne him a son,
the charge levelled against him in his wife's petition for divorce
still filled him with blind fury each time that he thought of it.
And all at once he shuddered violently, as if an icy blast had
darted through his frame. Then, turning the conversation,
he added: 'It's not at all warm this evening. This is the
dangerous hour of the Roman climate, the twilight hour, when
it's easy to catch a terrible fever if one isn't prudent. Here,
pull the rug over your legs, wrap it round you as carefully as
you can.'

Then, as they drew near to the Porta Furba, silence again
fell, more profound, like the slumber which was invincibly
spreading over the Campagna, now steeped in night. And at
last, in the bright starlight, appeared the gate, an arch of the
Acqua Felice, under which the road passed. From a distance,
this fragment seemed to bar the way with its mass of ancient
half-fallen walls. But afterwards the gigantic arch where
all was black opened like a gaping porch. And the carriage
passed under it in darkness whilst the wheels rumbled with
increased sonority.

When the victoria emerged on the other side, Santobono
still had the little basket of figs upon his knees and Prada
looked at it, quite overcome, asking himself what sudden
paralysis of the hands had prevented him from seizing it and
throwing it into the darkness. Such had still been his intention but a few seconds before they passed under the arch. He
had even given the basket a final glance in order that he might

the better realise what movements he should make. What
had taken place within him then? At present he was yielding
to increasing irresolution, henceforth incapable of decisive
action, feeling a need of delay in order that he might, before
everything else, fully satisfy himself as to what was likely to
happen. And as Dario had doubtless gone away and the figs
would certainly not be eaten until the following morning,
what reason was there for him to hurry? He would know
that evening if the Congregation of the Council had annulled
his marriage, he would know how far the so-called 'Justice of
God' was venal and mendacious! Certainly he would suffer
nobody to be poisoned, not even Cardinal Boccanera, though
the latter's life was of little account to him personally. But
had not that little basket, ever since leaving Frascati, been
like Destiny on the march? And was it not enjoyment, the
enjoyment of omnipotence, to be able to say to himself that he
was the master who could stay that basket's course, or allow
it to go onward and accomplish its deadly purpose? Moreover,
he yielded to the dimmest of mental struggles, ceasing to
reason, unable to raise his hand, and yet convinced that he
would drop a warning note into the letter-box at the *palazzo*
before he went to bed, though at the same time he felt happy
in the thought that if his interest directed otherwise he would
not do so.

And the remainder of the journey was accomplished in silent
weariness, amidst the shiver of evening which seemed to have
chilled all three men. In vain did the Count endeavour to
escape from the battle of his thoughts, by reverting to the
Buongiovanni reception, and giving particulars of the splendours which would be witnessed at it, his words fell sparsely
in an embarrassed and absent-minded way. Then he sought
to inspirit Pierre by speaking to him of Cardinal Sanguinetti's
amiable manner and fair words, but although the young priest
was returning home well pleased with his journey, in the idea
that with a little help he might yet triumph, he scarcely
answered the Count, so wrapt he was in his reverie. And,
Santobono, on his side, neither spoke nor moved. Black like
the night itself, he seemed to have vanished. However,
the lights of Rome were increasing in number, and houses
again appeared on either hand, at first at long intervals, and
then in close succession. They were suburban houses, and
there were yet more fields of reeds, quickset hedges, olive
trees overtopping long walls, and big gateways with vase-

surmounted pillars; but at last came the city with its rows of small grey houses, its petty shops and its dingy taverns, whence at times came shouts and rumours of battle.

Prada insisted on setting his companions down in the Via Giulia, at fifty paces from the palazzo. 'It doesn't inconvenience me at all,' said he to Pierre. 'Besides, with the little time you have before you, it would never do for you to go on foot.'

The Via Giulia was already steeped in slumber, and wore a melancholy aspect of abandonment in the dreary light of the gas lamps standing on either hand. And as soon as Santobono had alighted from the carriage, he took himself off without waiting for Pierre, who, moreover, always went in by the little door in the side-lane.

'Good-bye, Abbé,' exclaimed Prada.

'Good-bye, Count, a thousand thanks,' was Santobono's response.

Then the two others stood watching him as he went towards the Boccanera mansion, whose old, monumental entrance, full of gloom, was still wide open. For a moment they saw his tall, rugged figure erect against that gloom. Then in he plunged, he and his little basket, bearing Destiny.

XII

It was ten o'clock when Pierre and Narcisse, after dining at the Caffè di Roma, where they had long lingered chatting, at last walked down the Corso towards the Palazzo Buongiovanni. They had the greatest difficulty to reach its entrance, for carriages were coming up in serried files, and the inquisitive crowd of on-lookers, who pressed even into the roadway, in spite of the injunctions of the police, was growing so compact that even the horses could no longer approach. The ten lofty windows on the first floor of the long monumental façade shone with an intense white radiance, the radiance of electric lamps, which illumined the street like sunshine, spreading over the equipages aground in that human sea, whose billows of eager, excited faces rolled to and fro amidst an extraordinary tumult.

And in all this there was not merely the usual curiosity to see uniforms go by, and ladies in rich attire alight from their carriages, for Pierre soon gathered from what he heard that

the crowd had come to witness the arrival of the King and
Queen, who had promised to appear at the ball given by
Prince Buongiovanni, in celebration of the betrothal of his
daughter Celia to Lieutenant Attilio Sacco, the son of one of
His Majesty's ministers. Moreover, people were enraptured
with this marriage, the happy ending of a love story which
had impassioned the whole city : to begin with, love at first
sight, with the suddenness of a lightning-flash, and then
stubborn fidelity triumphing over all obstacles, amidst romantic
circumstances whose story sped from lip to lip, moistening
every eye and stirring every heart.

It was this story that Narcisse had related at dessert to
Pierre, who already knew some portion of it. People asserted
that if the Prince had ended by yielding after a final
terrible scene, it was only from fear of seeing Celia elope from
the palace with her lover. She did not threaten to do so, but,
amidst her virginal calmness, there was so much contempt
for everything foreign to her love, that her father felt her to
be capable of acting with the greatest folly in all ingenuous-
ness. Only indifference was manifested by the Prince's wife,
a phlegmatic and still beautiful Englishwoman, who considered that she had done quite enough for the household by
bringing her husband a dowry of five millions, and bearing
him five children. The Prince, anxious and weak despite his
violence, in which one found a trace of the old Roman blood,
already spoilt by mixture with that of a foreign race, was
nowadays ever influenced in his actions by the fear that his
house and fortune—which hitherto had remained intact
amidst the accumulated ruins of the *patriziato*—might
suddenly collapse. And in finally yielding to Celia, he must
have been guided by the idea of rallying to the new *régime*
through his daughter, so as to have one foot firmly set at the
Quirinal, without withdrawing the other from the Vatican.
It was galling, no doubt ; his pride must have bled at the idea
of allying his name with that of such low folks as the Saccos.
But then Sacco was a minister, and had sped so quickly from
success to success that it seemed likely he would rise yet higher,
and, after the portfolio of Agriculture, secure that of Finances,
which he had long coveted. And an alliance with Sacco
meant the certain favour of the King, an assured retreat in
that direction should the papacy some day collapse. Then,
too, the Prince had made inquiries respecting the son, and
was somewhat disarmed by the good looks, bravery, and

rectitude of young Attilio, who represented the future, and
possibly the glorious Italy of to-morrow. He was a soldier,
and could be helped forward to the highest rank. And
people spitefully added that the last reason which had influenced the Prince, who was very avaricious, and greatly
worried by the thought that his fortune must be divided
among his five children,[1] was that an opportunity presented
itself for him to bestow a ridiculously small dowry on Celia.
However, having consented to the marriage, he resolved to
give a splendid *fête*, such as was now seldom witnessed in
Rome, throwing his doors open to all the rival sections of
society, inviting the sovereigns, and setting the *palazzo* ablaze
as in the grand days of old. In doing this he would necessarily have to expend some of the money to which he clung,
but a boastful spirit incited him to show the world that
he at any rate had not been vanquished by the financial
crisis, and that the Buongiovannis had nothing to hide and
nothing to blush for. To tell the truth, some people asserted
that this bravado had not originated with himself, but had
been instilled into him without his knowledge by the quiet
and innocent Celia, who wished to exhibit her happiness to all
applauding Rome.

'Dear me!' said Narcisse, whom the throng prevented
from advancing. 'We shall never get in. Why, they seem
to have invited the whole city.' And then, as Pierre seemed
surprised to see a prelate drive up in his carriage, the *attaché*
added: 'Oh! you will elbow more than one of them upstairs.
The cardinals won't like to come on account of the presence
of the King and Queen, but the prelates are sure to be here.
This, you know, is a neutral drawing-room where the black
and the white worlds can fraternise. And then too, there are
so few *fêtes* that people rush on them.'

He went on to explain that there were two grand balls at
Court every winter, but that it was only under exceptional
circumstances that the *patriziato* gave similar galas. Two
or three of the black *salons* were opened once in a way
towards the close of the Carnival, but little dances among
intimates replaced the pompous entertainments of former
times. Some princesses, moreover, merely had their day.
And as for the few white *salons* that existed, these likewise

---

[1] The Italian succession law is similar to the French. Children
cannot be disinherited. All property is divided among them, and thus
the piling up of large hereditary fortunes is prevented.—*Trans.*

retained the same character of intimacy, more or less mixed, for no lady had yet become the undisputed queen of the new society.

'Well, here we are at last,' resumed Narcisse as they eventually climbed the stairs.

'Let us keep together,' Pierre somewhat anxiously replied. 'My only acquaintance is with the *fiancée*, and I want you to introduce me.'

However, a considerable effort was needed even to climb the monumental staircase, so great was the crush of arriving guests. Never, in the old days of wax candles and oil lamps, had this staircase offered such a blaze of light. Electric lamps, burning in clusters in superb bronze candelabra on the landings, steeped everything in a white radiance. The cold stucco of the walls was hidden by a series of lofty tapestries depicting the story of Cupid and Psyche, marvels which had remained in the family since the days of the Renascence. And a thick carpet covered the worn marble steps, whilst clumps of evergreens and tall spreading palms decorated every corner. An affluence of new blood warmed the antique mansion that evening; there was a resurrection of life, so to say, as the women surged up the staircase, smiling and perfumed, bare-shouldered and sparkling with diamonds.

At the entrance of the first reception-room Pierre at once perceived Prince and Princess Buongiovanni, standing side by side and receiving their guests. The Prince, a tall, slim man with fair complexion and hair turning grey, had the pale northern eyes of his American mother in an energetic face such as became a former captain of the popes. The Princess, with small, delicate and rounded features, looked barely thirty, though she had really passed her fortieth year. And still pretty, displaying a smiling serenity which nothing could disconcert, she purely and simply basked in self-adoration. Her gown was of pink satin, and a marvellous parure of large rubies set flamelets about her dainty neck and in her fine, fair hair. Of her five children, her son, the eldest, was travelling, and three of the girls, mere children, were still at school, so that only Celia was present, Celia in a modest gown of white muslin, fair like her mother, quite bewitching with her large innocent eyes and her candid lips, and retaining to the very end of her love-story the semblance of a closed lily of impenetrable, virginal mysteriousness. The Saccos had but just arrived, and Attilio, in his simple lieutenant's

uniform, had remained near his betrothed, so naïvely and
openly delighted with his great happiness that his handsome
face, with its caressing mouth and brave eyes, was quite
resplendent with youth and strength. Standing there, near
one another, in the triumph of their passion they appeared
like life's very joy and health, like the personification of hope
in the morrow's promises; and the entering guests who saw
them could not refrain from smiling and feeling moved,
momentarily forgetting their loquacious and malicious curiosity to give their hearts to those chosen ones of love who
looked so handsome and so enraptured.

Narcisse stepped forward in order to present Pierre, but
Celia anticipated him. Going to meet the young priest she
led him to her father and mother, saying: ‘ Monsieur l'Abbé
Pierre Froment, a friend of my dear Benedetta.' Ceremonious
salutations followed. Then the young girl, whose graciousness greatly touched Pierre, said to him: ‘ Benedetta is
coming with her aunt and Dario. She must be very happy
this evening! And you will also see how beautiful she will
be.'

Pierre and Narcisse next began to congratulate her, but
they could not remain there, the throng was ever jostling them;
and the Prince and Princess, quite lost in the crush, had
barely time to answer the many salutations with amiable,
continuous nods. And Celia, after conducting the two friends
to Attilio, was obliged to return to her parents so as to take
her place beside them as the little queen of the *fête*.

Narcisse was already slightly acquainted with Attilio,
and so fresh congratulations ensued. Then the two friends
manœuvred to find a spot where they might momentarily
tarry and contemplate the spectacle which this first *salon* presented. It was a vast hall, hung with green velvet broidered
with golden flowers, and contained a very remarkable collection of weapons and armour, breast-plates, battle-axes and
swords, almost all of which had belonged to the Buongiovannis
of the fifteenth and sixteenth centuries. And amidst those
stern implements of war there was a lovely sedan chair of the
last century, gilded and decorated with delicate paintings. It
was in this chair that the Prince's great-grandmother, the
celebrated Bettina, whose beauty was historical, had usually
been carried to mass. On the walls, moreover, there were
numerous historical paintings: battles, peace congresses, and
royal receptions in which the Buongiovannis had taken part,

without counting the many family portraits, tall and proud
figures of sea-captains, commanders in the field, great dignitaries of the Church, prelates and cardinals, amongst whom,
in the place of honour, appeared the family pope, the white-
robed Buongiovanni whose accession to the pontifical throne
had enriched a long line of descendants. And it was among
those armours, near that coquettish sedan, and below those
antique portraits, that the Saccos, husband and wife, had in
their turn just halted, at a few steps from the master and
mistress of the house, in order to secure their share of congratulations and bows.

'Look over there!' Narcisse whispered to Pierre, 'those
are the Saccos in front of us, that dark little fellow and the
lady in mauve silk.'

Pierre promptly recognised the bright face and pleasant
smile of Stefana, whom he had already met at old Orlando's.
But he was more interested in her husband, a dark dry man,
with big eyes, sallow complexion, prominent chin and vulturine
nose. Like some gay Neapolitan 'Pulcinello,' he was dancing,
shouting, and displaying such infectious good humour that it
spread to all around him. He possessed a wonderful gift of
speech, with a voice that was unrivalled as an instrument of
fascination and conquest; and on seeing how easily he in-
gratiated himself with the people in that drawing-room, one
could understand his lightning-like successes in the political
world. He had manœuvred with rare skill in the matter of
his son's marriage, affecting such exaggerated delicacy of feeling as to set himself against the lovers, and declare that he
would never consent to their union, as he had no desire to be
accused of stealing a dowry and a title. As a matter of fact,
he had only yielded after the Buongiovannis had given their
consent, and even then he had desired to take the opinion of
old Orlando, whose lofty integrity was proverbial. However,
he knew right well that he would secure the old hero's approval
in this particular affair, for Orlando made no secret of his
opinion that the Buongiovannis ought to be glad to admit his
grand-nephew into their family, as that handsome young fellow,
with brave and healthy heart, would help to regenerate their
impoverished blood. And throughout the whole affair, Sacco
had shrewdly availed himself of Orlando's famous name, for
ever talking of the relationship between them, and displaying
filial veneration for this glorious founder of the country, as
if indeed he had no suspicion that the latter despised and

execrated him and mourned his accession to power in the conviction that he would lead Italy to shame and ruin.

'Ah!' resumed Narcisse addressing Pierre, 'he's one of those supple, practical men who care nothing for a smack in the face. It seems that unscrupulous individuals like himself become necessary when States get into trouble and have to pass through political, financial and moral crises. It is said that Sacco with his imperturbable assurance and ingenious and resourceful mind has quite won the King's favour. Just look at him! Why, with that crowd of courtiers round him, one might think him the master of this palace!'

And indeed the guests, after passing the Prince and Princess with a bow, at once congregated around Sacco, for he represented power, emoluments, pensions and crosses; and if folks still smiled at seeing his dark, turbulent and scraggy figure amidst that framework of family portraits which proclaimed the mighty ancestry of the Buongiovannis, they none the less worshipped him as the personification of the new power, the democratic force which was confusedly rising even from the old Roman soil where the *patriziato* lay in ruins.

'What a crowd!' muttered Pierre. 'Who are all these people?'

'Oh!' replied Narcisse, 'it is a regular mixture. These people belong neither to the black nor the white world; they form a grey world as it were. The evolution was certain; a man like Cardinal Boccanera may retain an uncompromising attitude, but a whole city, a nation can't. The Pope alone will always say no and remain immutable. But everything around him progresses and undergoes transformation, so that in spite of all resistance, Rome will become Italian in a few years' time. Even now, whenever a prince has two sons only one of them remains on the side of the Vatican, the other goes over to the Quirinal. People must live, you see; and the great families threatened with annihilation have not sufficient heroism to carry obstinacy to the point of suicide. And I have already told you that we are here on neutral ground, for Prince Buongiovanni was one of the first to realise the necessity of conciliation. He feels that his fortune is perishing, he does not dare to risk it either in industry or in speculation, and already sees it portioned out among his five children, by whose descendants it will be yet further divided; and this is why he prudently makes advances to the King without, however, breaking with the Pope. In this *salon*, therefore, you see a perfect picture of the *débâcle*, the confusion which reigns in the Prince's ideas and opinions.' Narcisse paused, and then began to name some of the persons who were coming in. 'There's a general,' said he, 'who has become very popular since his last campaign in Africa. There will be a great many military men here this evening, for all Attilio's superiors have been invited, so as to give the young man an *entourage* of glory. Ah! and there's the German Ambassador. I fancy that nearly all the Corps Diplomatique will come on account of their Majesties' presence. But, by way of contrast, just look at that stout fellow yonder. He's a very influential deputy, a *parvenu* of the new middle class. Thirty years ago he was merely one of Prince Albertini's farmers, one of those *mercanti di campagna* who go about the environs of Rome in stout boots and a soft felt hat. And now look at that prelate coming in——'

'Oh! I know him,' Pierre interrupted. 'He's Monsignor Fornaro.'

'Exactly, Monsignor Fornaro, a personage of some importance. You told me, I remember, that he is the reporter of the Congregation in that affair of your book. A most delightful man! Did you see how he bowed to the Princess? And what a noble and graceful bearing he has in his little mantle of violet silk!'

Then Narcisse went on enumerating the princes and princesses, the dukes and duchesses, the politicians and functionaries, the diplomatists and ministers, and the officers and well-to-do middle-class people, who of themselves made up a most wonderful medley of guests, to say nothing of the representatives of the various foreign colonies, English people, Americans, Germans, Spaniards, and Russians, in a word, all ancient Europe, and both Americas. And afterwards the young man reverted to the Saccos, to the little Signora Sacco in particular, in order to tell Pierre of the heroic efforts which she had made to open a *salon* for the purpose of assisting her husband's ambition. Gentle and modest as she seemed, she was also very shrewd, endowed with genuine qualities, Piedmontese patience and strength of resistance, orderly habits and thriftiness. And thus it was she who re-established the equilibrium in household affairs which her husband by his exuberance so often disturbed. He was indeed greatly indebted to her, though nobody suspected it. At the same time, however, she had so far failed in her attempts to

establish a white *salon* which should take the lead in in-
fluencing opinion. Only the people of her own set visited
her, not a single prince ever came, and her Monday dances
were the same as in a score of other middle-class homes,
having no brilliancy and no importance. In fact, the real
white *salon*, which should guide men and things and sway all
Rome, was still in dreamland.

'Just notice her keen smile as she examines everything
here,' resumed Narcisse. 'She's teaching herself and forming plans, I'm sure of it. Now that she is about to be
connected with a princely family she probably hopes to
receive some of the best society.'

Large as was the room, the crowd in it had by this time
grown so dense that the two friends were pressed back to a
wall, and felt almost stifled. The *attaché* therefore decided
to lead the priest elsewhere, and as they walked along he
gave him some particulars concerning the palace, which was
one of the most sumptuous in Rome, and renowned for the
magnificence of its reception rooms. Dancing took place in
the picture gallery, a superb apartment more than sixty feet
long, with eight windows overlooking the Corso ; while the
buffet was installed in the Hall of the Antiques, a marble hall,
which among other precious things contained a statue of
Venus, rivalling the one at the Capitol. Then there was a
suite of marvellous *salons*, still resplendent with ancient
luxury, hung with the rarest stuffs, and retaining some
unique specimens of old-time furniture, on which covetous
antiquaries kept their eyes fixed, whilst waiting and hoping
for the inevitable future ruin. And one of these apartments,
the little Saloon of the Mirrors, was particularly famous. Of
circular shape and Louis XV style, it was surrounded by
mirrors in *rococo* frames, extremely rich, and most exquisitely
carved.

'You will see all that by-and-by,' continued Narcisse.
'At present we had better go in here if we want to breathe a
little. It is here that the arm-chairs from the adjacent gallery
have been brought for the accommodation of the ladies who
desire to sit down and be seen and admired.'

The apartment they entered was a spacious one, draped
with the most superb Genoese velvet, that antique *jardinière*
velvet with pale satin ground, and flowers once of dazzling
brightness, whose greens and blues and reds had now become
exquisitely soft, with the subdued, faded tones of old floral

love-tokens. On the pier-tables and in the cabinets all around were some of the most precious curios in the palace, ivory caskets, gilt and painted wood carvings, pieces of antique plate—briefly a collection of marvels. And several ladies, fleeing the crush, had already taken refuge on the numerous seats, clustering in little groups, and laughing and chatting with the few gentlemen who had discovered this retreat of grace and *galanterie*. In the bright glow of the lamps nothing could be more delightful than the sight of all those bare, sheeny shoulders, and those supple necks, above whose napes were coiled tresses of fair or raven hair. Bare arms emerged like living flowers of flesh from amidst the mingling lace and silk of soft-hued bodices. The fans played slowly, as if to heighten the fires of the precious stones, and at each beat wafted around an *odore di femina* blended with a predominating perfume of violets.

'Hallo!' exclaimed Narcisse, 'there's our good friend Monsignor Nani bowing to the Austrian ambassadress.'

As soon as Nani perceived the young priest and his companion he came towards them, and the trio then withdrew into the embrasure of a window in order that they might chat for a moment at their ease. The prelate was smiling like one enchanted with the beauty of the *fête*, but at the same time he retained all the serenity of innocence, as if he had not even noticed the exhibition of bare shoulders by which he was surrounded. 'Ah, my dear son!' he said to Pierre, 'I am very pleased to see you! Well, and what do you think of our Rome when she makes up her mind to give *fêtes*?'

'Why, it is superb, Monseigneur.'

Then, in an emotional manner, Nani spoke of Celia's lofty piety; and, in order to give the Vatican the credit of this sumptuous gala, affected to regard the Prince and Princess as staunch adherents of the Church, as if he were altogether unaware that the King and Queen were presently coming. And afterwards he abruptly exclaimed: 'I have been thinking of you all day, my dear son. Yes, I heard that you had gone to see his Eminence Cardinal Sanguinetti. Well, and how did he receive you?'

'Oh! in a most paternal manner,' Pierre replied. 'At first he made me understand the embarrassment in which he was placed by his position as protector of Lourdes; but just as I was going off he showed himself charming, and promised me his help with a delicacy which deeply touched me.'

'Did he indeed, my dear son? But it doesn't surprise me, his Eminence is so good-hearted!'

'And I must add, Monseigneur, that I came back with a light and hopeful heart. It now seems to me as if my suit were half gained.'

'Naturally, I understand it,' replied Nani, who was still smiling with that keen, intelligent smile of his, sharpened by a touch of almost imperceptible irony. And after a short pause he added in a very simple way: 'The misfortune is that on the day before yesterday your book was condemned by the Congregation of the Index, which was convoked by its secretary expressly for that purpose. And the judgment will be laid before his Holiness, for him to sign it, on the day after to-morrow.'

Pierre looked at the prelate in bewilderment. Had the old mansion fallen on his head he would not have felt more overcome. What! was it all over? His journey to Rome, the experiment he had come to attempt there, had resulted in that defeat, of which he was thus suddenly apprised amidst that betrothal *fête*. And he had not even been able to defend himself, he had sacrificed his time without finding anyone to whom he might speak, before whom he might plead his cause! Anger was rising within him, and he could not prevent himself from muttering bitterly: 'Ah! how I have been duped! And that Cardinal who said to me only this morning: "If God be with you He will save you in spite of everything." Yes, yes, I now understand him; he was juggling with words, he only desired a disaster in order that submission might lead me to Heaven! Submit, indeed; ah! I cannot, I cannot yet! My heart is too full of indignation and grief.'

Nani examined and studied him with curiosity. 'But my dear son,' he said, 'nothing is final so long as the Holy Father has not signed the judgment. You have all to-morrow and even the morning of the day after before you. A miracle is always possible.' Then, lowering his voice and drawing Pierre on one side whilst Narcisse in an æsthetical spirit examined the ladies, he added: 'Listen, I have a communication to make to you in great secrecy. Come and join me in the little Saloon of the Mirrors by-and-by, during the Cotillon. We shall be able to talk there at our ease.'

Pierre nodded, and thereupon the prelate discreetly withdrew and disappeared in the crowd. However, the young man's ears were buzzing; he could no longer hope; what

indeed could he accomplish in one day since he had lost three
months without even being able to secure an audience with the
Pope ? And his bewilderment increased as he suddenly heard
Narcisse speaking to him of art. 'It's astonishing how the
feminine figure has deteriorated in these dreadful democratic
days. It's all fat and horribly common. Not one of those
women yonder shows the Florentine contour, with small bosom
and slender, elegant neck. Ah! that one yonder isn't so bad
perhaps, the fair one with her hair coiled up, whom Monsignor
Fornaro has just approached.'

For a few minutes indeed Monsignor Fornaro had been
fluttering from beauty to beauty, with an amiable air of conquest. He looked superb that evening with his lofty decorative
figure, blooming cheeks and victorious affability. No unpleasant scandal was associated with his name; he was simply
regarded as a prelate of gallant ways who took pleasure in the
society of ladies. And he paused and chatted, and leant over
their bare shoulders with laughing eyes and humid lips as if
experiencing a sort of devout rapture. However, on perceiving
Narcisse whom he occasionally met, he at once came forward
and the *attaché* had to bow to him. ' You have been in good
health I hope, Monseigneur, since I had the honour of seeing
you at the embassy.'

' Oh! yes, I am very well, very well indeed. What a
delightful *fête*, is it not ?'

Pierre also had bowed. This was the man whose report
had brought about the condemnation of his book; and it was
with resentment that he recalled his caressing air and charming
greeting, instinct with such lying promise. However, the
prelate who was very shrewd, must have guessed that the
young priest was already acquainted with the decision of the
Congregation, and have thought it more dignified to abstain
from open recognition; for on his side he merely nodded and
smiled at him. ' What a number of people!' he went on,
'and how many charming persons there are! It will soon be
impossible for one to move in this room.'

All the seats in fact were now occupied by ladies, and
what with the strong perfume of violets and the exhalations
of warm necks and shoulders the atmosphere was becoming
most oppressive. The fans flapped more briskly, and clear
laughter rang out amidst a growing hubbub of conversation
in which the same words constantly recurred. Some news,
doubtless, had just arrived, some rumour was being whispered

from group to group, throwing them all into feverish excitement. As it happened, Monsignor Fornaro, who was always
well informed, desired to be the proclaimer of this news, which
nobody as yet had ventured to announce aloud.

'Do you know what is exciting them all?' he inquired.

'Is it the Holy Father's illness?' asked Pierre in his
anxiety. 'Is he worse this evening?'

The prelate looked at him in astonishment, and then
somewhat impatiently replied: 'Oh, no, no. His Holiness is
much better, thank Heaven. A person belonging to the Vatican was telling me just now that he was able to get up this
afternoon and receive his intimates as usual.'

'All the same, people have been alarmed,' interrupted
Narcisse. 'I must confess that we did not feel easy at the
embassy, for a Conclave at the present time would be a great
worry for France. She would exercise no influence at it. It
is a great mistake on the part of our Republican Government
to treat the Holy See as of no importance! However, can
one ever tell whether the Pope is ill or not? I know for a
certainty that he was nearly carried off last winter when
nobody breathed a word about any illness, whereas on the last
occasion when the newspapers killed him and talked about a
dreadful attack of bronchitis, I myself saw him quite strong
and in the best of spirits! His reported illnesses are mere
matters of policy, I fancy.'[1]

With a hasty gesture, however, Monsignor Fornaro
brushed this importunate subject aside. 'No, no,' said he,
'people are tranquilised and no longer talk of it. What
excites all those ladies is that the Congregation of the Council
to-day voted the dissolution of the Prada marriage by a great
majority.'

Again did Pierre feel moved. However, not having had
time to see any members of the Boccanera family on his return
from Frascati he feared that the news might be false and said
so. Thereupon the prelate gave his word of honour that
things were as he stated. 'The news is certain,' he declared.
'I had it from a member of the Congregation.' And then,
all at once, he apologised and hurried off: 'Excuse me but I
see a lady whom I had not yet caught sight of, and I desire to
pay my respects to her.'

---

[1] There is much truth in this; but the reader must not imagine that
the Pope is never ill. At his great age, indispositions are only natural.—
Trans.

He at once hastened to the lady in question, and, being unable to sit down, inclined his lofty figure as if to envelop her with his gallant courtesy; whilst she, young, fresh, and bare-shouldered, laughed with a pearly laugh as his cape of violet silk lightly brushed her sheeny skin.

'You know that person, don't you?' Narcisse inquired of Pierre. 'No! Really? Why, that is Count Prada's *innamorata*, the charming Lisbeth Kauffmann, by whom he has just had a son. It's her first appearance in society since that event. She is a German, you know, and lost her husband here. She paints a little; in fact, rather nicely. A great deal is forgiven to the ladies of the foreign colony, and this one is particularly popular on account of the very affable manner in which she receives people at her little palazzo in the Via Principe Amedeo. As you may imagine, the news of the dissolution of that marriage must amuse her!'

She looked really exquisite, that Lisbeth, very fair, rosy, and gay, with satiny skin, soft blue eyes, and lips wreathed in an amiable smile, which was renowned for its grace. And that evening, in her gown of white silk spangled with gold, she showed herself so delighted with life, so securely happy in the thought that she was free, that she loved and was loved in return, that the whispered tidings, the malicious remarks exchanged behind the fans of those around her, seemed to turn to her personal triumph. For a moment all eyes had sought her, and people talked of the outcome of her connection with Prada, the man whose manhood the Church solemnly denied by its decision of that very day! And there came stifled laughter and whispered jests, whilst she, radiant in her insolent serenity, accepted with a rapturous air the gallantry of Monsignor Fornaro, who congratulated her on a painting of the Virgin with the lily, which she had lately sent to a fine art show.

Ah! that matrimonial nullity suit, which for a year had supplied Rome with scandal, what a final hubbub it occasioned as the tidings of its termination burst forth amidst that ball! The black and white worlds had long chosen it as a battle-field for the exchange of incredible slander, endless gossip, the most nonsensical tittle-tattle. And now it was over; the Vatican with imperturbable impudence had pronounced the marriage null and void on the ground that the husband was no man, and all Rome would laugh over the affair, with that free scepticism which it displayed as soon as the pecuniary affairs of the Church came into question. The incidents of the struggle were already common property : Prada's feelings revolting to such a point that he had withdrawn from the contest, the Boccaneras moving heaven and earth in their feverish anxiety, the money which they had distributed among the creatures of the various cardinals in order to gain their influence, and the large sum which they had indirectly paid for the second and favourable report of Monsignor Palma. People said that, altogether, more than a hundred thousand francs had been expended, but this was not thought over much, as a well-known French countess had been obliged to disburse nearly ten times that amount to secure the dissolution of her marriage. But then the Holy Father's need was so great ! And, moreover, nobody was angered by this venality ; it merely gave rise to malicious witticisms ; and the fans continued waving in the increasing heat, and the ladies quivered with contentment as the whispered pleasantries took wing and fluttered over their bare shoulders.

' Oh ! how pleased the Contessina must be ! ' Pierre resumed. ' I did not understand what her little friend, Princess Celia, meant by saying when we came in that she would be so happy and beautiful this evening. It is doubtless on that account that she is coming here, after cloistering herself all the time the affair lasted, as if she were in mourning.'

However, Lisbeth's eyes had chanced to meet those of Narcisse, and as she smiled at him he was, in his turn, obliged to pay his respects to her, for, like everybody else of the foreign colony, he knew her through having visited her studio. He was again returning to Pierre when a fresh outburst of emotion stirred the diamond aigrettes and the flowers adorning the ladies' hair. People turned to see what was the matter, and again did the hubbub increase. ' Ah ! it's Count Prada in person ! ' murmured Narcisse, with an admiring glance. ' He has a fine bearing, whatever folks may say. Dress him up in velvet and gold, and what a splendid, unscrupulous, fifteenth-century adventurer he would make ! '

Prada entered the room, looking quite gay, in fact, almost triumphant. And above his large, white shirt-front, edged by the black of his coat, he really had a commanding, predacious expression, with his frank, stern eyes, and his energetic features barred by a large black moustache. Never had a more rapturous smile of sensuality revealed the wolfish teeth

of his voracious mouth. With rapid glances he took stock of
the women, dived into their very souls. Then, on seeing
Lisbeth, who looked so pink, and fair, and girlish, his
expression softened, and he frankly went up to her, without
troubling in the slightest degree about the ardent, inquisitive
eyes which were turned upon him. As soon as Monsignor
Fornaro had made room, he stooped and conversed with the
young woman in a low tone. And she no doubt confirmed
the news which was circulating, for as he again drew himself
erect, he laughed a somewhat forced laugh, and made an involuntary gesture.

However, he then caught sight of Pierre, and joined him
in the embrasure of the window; and when he had also
shaken hands with Narcisse, he said to the young priest with
all his wonted *bravura* : ' You recollect what I told you as we
were coming back from Frascati ? Well, it's done, it seems,
they've annulled my marriage It's such an impudent, such
an imbecile decision, that I still doubted it a moment ago ! '

' Oh ! the news is certain,' Pierre made bold to reply.
' It has just been confirmed to us by Monsignor Fornaro, who
had it from a member of the Congregation. And it is said
that the majority was very large.'

Prada again shook with laughter. ' No, no,' said he,
' such a farce is beyond belief ! It's the finest smack given
to justice and common-sense that I know of. Ah ! if the
marriage can also be annulled by the civil courts, and if my
friend whom you see yonder be only willing, we shall amuse
ourselves in Rome ! Yes, indeed, I'd marry her at Santa
Maria Maggiore with all possible pomp. And there's a dear
little being in the world who would take part in the *fête* in his
nurse's arms ! '

He laughed too loud as he spoke, alluded in too brutal a
fashion to his child, that living proof of his manhood. Was
it suffering that made his lips curve upwards and reveal his
white teeth ? It could be divined that he was quivering, fighting against an awakening of covert, tumultuous passion, which
he would not acknowledge even to himself.

' And you, my dear Abbé ? ' he hastily resumed. ' Do you
know the other report ? Do you know that the Countess is
coming here ? ' It was thus, by force of habit, that he designated Benedetta, forgetting that she was no longer his wife.

' Yes, I have just been told so,' Pierre replied ; and then he
hesitated for a moment before adding, with a desire to prevent

any disagreeable surprise : ' And we shall no doubt see Prince
Dario also, for he has not started for Naples as I told you.
Something prevented his departure at the last moment, I
believe. At least so I gathered from a servant.'

Prada no longer laughed. His face suddenly became grave,
and he contented himself with murmuring : ' Ah ! so the
cousin is to be of the party. Well, we shall see them, we shall
see them both ! '

Then, whilst the two friends went on chatting, he became
silent as if serious considerations impelled him to reflect. And
suddenly making a gesture of apology he withdrew yet farther
into the embrasure in which he stood, pulled a note-book out
of his pocket, and tore from it a leaf on which, without modify-
ing his hand-writing otherwise than by slightly enlarging it,
he pencilled these four lines : ' A legend avers that the fig-tree
of Judas now grows at Frascati, and that its fruit is deadly for
him who may desire to become Pope. Eat not the poisoned
figs, nor give them either to your servants or your fowls.'
Then he folded the paper, fastened it with a postage stamp,
and wrote on it the address : ' To his most Reverend and most
Illustrious Eminence, Cardinal Boccanera.' And when he had
placed everything in his pocket again, he drew a long breath
and once more called back his laugh.

A kind of invincible discomfort, a far-away terror had
momentarily frozen him. Without being guided by any clear
train of reasoning, he had felt the need of protecting himself
against any cowardly temptation, any possible abomination.
He could not have told what course of ideas had induced him
to write those four lines without a moment's delay, on the very
spot where he stood, under penalty of contributing to a great
catastrophe. But one thought was firmly fixed in his brain,
that on leaving the ball he would go to the Via Giulia and
throw that note into the letter-box at the Palazzo Boccanera.
And that decided, he was once more easy in mind.

' Why, what is the matter with you, my dear Abbé ? ' he
inquired on again joining in the conversation of the two friends.
' You are quite gloomy.' And on Pierre telling him of the
bad news which he had received, the condemnation of his
book, and the single day which remained to him for action if
he did not wish his journey to Rome to result in defeat, he
began to protest as if he himself needed agitation and diversion
in order to continue hopeful and bear the ills of life. ' Never
mind, never mind, don't worry yourself,' said he, ' one loses

all one's strength by worrying. A day is a great deal, one can do ever so many things in a day. An hour, a minute suffices for destiny to intervene and turn defeat into victory!' He grew feverish as he spoke, and all at once added, 'Come, let's go to the ball-room. It seems that the scene there is something prodigious.'

Then he exchanged a last loving glance with Lisbeth whilst Pierre and Narcisse followed him, the three of them extricating themselves from their corner with the greatest difficulty, and then wending their way towards the adjoining gallery through a sea of serried skirts, a billowy expanse of necks and shoulders whence ascended the passion which makes life the odour alike of love and of death.

With its eight windows overlooking the Corso, their panes uncurtained and throwing a blaze of light upon the houses across the road, the picture gallery, sixty-five feet in length and more than thirty in breadth, spread out with incomparable splendour. The illumination was dazzling. Clusters of electric lamps had changed seven pairs of huge marble candelabra into gigantic *torchères*, akin to constellations ; and all along the cornice up above, other lamps set in bright-hued floral glasses formed a marvellous garland of flaming flowers : tulips, pæonies, and roses. The antique red velvet worked with gold, which draped the walls, glowed like a furnace fire. About the doors and windows there were hangings of old lace broidered with flowers in coloured silk whose hues had the very intensity of life. But the sight of sights beneath the sumptuous panelled ceiling adorned with golden roses, the unique spectacle of a richness not to be equalled, was the collection of masterpieces such as no museum could excel. There were works of Raffaelle and Titian, Rembrandt and Rubens, Velasquez and Ribera, famous works which in this unexpected illumination suddenly showed forth, triumphant with youth regained, as if awakened to the immortal life of genius. And, as their Majesties would not arrive before midnight, the ball had just been opened, and flights of soft-hued gowns were whirling in a waltz past all the pompous throng, the glittering jewels and decorations, the gold-broidered uniforms and the pearl-broidered robes, whilst silk and satin and velvet spread and overflowed upon every side.

'It is prodigious, really!' declared Prada with his excited air, ' let us go this way and place ourselves in a window recess again. There is no better spot for getting a good view without being too much jostled.'

They lost Narcisse somehow or other, and on reaching the desired recess found themselves but two, Pierre and the Count. The orchestra, installed on a little platform at the far end of the gallery, had just finished the waltz, and the dancers, with an air of giddy rapture, were slowly walking through the crowd when a fresh arrival caused every head to turn. Donna Serafina, arrayed in a robe of purple silk as if she had worn the colours of her brother the Cardinal, was making a royal entry on the arm of Consistorial Advocate Morano. And never before had she laced herself so tightly, never had her waist looked so slim and girlish ; and never had her stern, wrinkled face, which her white hair scarcely softened, expressed such stubborn and victorious domination. A discreet murmur of approval ran round, a murmur of public relief as it were, for all Roman society had condemned the unworthy conduct of Morano in severing a connection of thirty years to which the drawing-rooms had grown as accustomed as if it had been a legal marriage. The rupture had lasted for two months, to the great scandal of Rome where the cult of long and faithful affections still abides. And so the reconciliation touched every heart and was regarded as one of the happiest consequences of the victory which the Boccaneras had that day gained in the affair of Benedetta's marriage. Morano repentant and Donna Serafina reappearing on his arm, nothing could have been more satisfactory ; love had conquered, decorum was preserved and good order re-established.

But there was a deeper sensation as soon as Benedetta and Dario were seen to enter, side by side, behind the others. This tranquil indifference for the ordinary forms of propriety, on the very day when the marriage with Prada had been annulled, this victory of love, confessed and celebrated before one and all, seemed so charming in its audacity, so full of the bravery of youth and hope, that the pair were at once forgiven amidst a murmur of universal admiration. And as in the case of Celia and Attilio, all hearts flew to them, to their radiant beauty, to the wondrous happiness that made their faces so resplendent. Dario, still pale after his long convalescence, somewhat slight and delicate of build, with the fine clear eyes of a big child, and the dark curly beard of a young god, bore himself with a light pride, in which all the old princely blood of the Boccaneras could be traced. And Benedetta, she so white under her casque of jetty hair, she so calm and so sensible, wore her lovely smile, that smile so seldom

seen on her face but which was irresistibly fascinating, trans-
figuring her, imparting the charm of a flower to her somewhat
full mouth, and filling the infinite of her dark and fathomless
eyes with a radiance as of heaven. And in this gay return of
youth and happiness, an exquisite instinct had prompted her
to put on a white gown, a plain girlish gown which symbolised
her maidenhood, which told that she had remained through
all a pure untarnished lily for the husband of her choice.
And nothing of her form was to be seen, not a glimpse of
bosom or shoulder. It was as if the impenetrable, redoubtable
mystery of love, the sovereign beauty of woman slumbered
there, all-powerful, but veiled with white. Again, not a jewel
appeared on her fingers or in her ears. There was simply a
necklace falling about her *corsage*, but a necklace fit for
royalty, the famous pearl necklace of the Boccaneras, which
she had inherited from her mother, and which was known to
all Rome—pearls of fabulous size cast negligently about her
neck, and sufficing, simply as she was gowned, to make her
queen of all.

'Oh !' murmured Pierre in ecstasy, 'how happy and how
beautiful she is ! '

But he at once regretted that he had expressed his thoughts
aloud, for beside him he heard a low plaint, an involuntary
growl which reminded him of the Count's presence. However,
Prada promptly stifled this cry of returning anguish, and
found strength enough to affect a brutish gaiety : ' The devil ! '
said he, ' they have plenty of impudence. I hope we shall
see them married and bedded at once ! ' Then regretting this
coarse jest which had been prompted by the revolt of passion,
he sought to appear indifferent : ' She looks very nice this
evening,' he said, ' she has the finest shoulders in the world,
you know, and it's a real success for her to hide them and yet
appear more beautiful than ever.'

He went on speaking, contriving to assume an easy tone,
and giving various little particulars about the Countess as he
still obstinately called the young woman. However, he had
drawn rather further into the recess, for fear, no doubt, that
people might remark his pallor, and the painful twitch which
contracted his mouth. He was in no state to fight, to show
himself gay and insolent in presence of the joy which the
lovers so openly and naïvely expressed. And he was glad of
the respite which the arrival of the King and Queen at this
moment offered him. ' Ah ! here are their Majesties ! ' he

exclaimed, turning towards the window. 'Look at the scramble in the street!'

Although the windows were closed, a tumult could be heard rising from the footways. And Pierre on looking down saw, by the light of the electric lamps, a sea of human heads pour over the road and encompass the carriages. He had several times already seen the King during the latter's daily drives to the grounds of the Villa Borghese, whither he came like any private gentleman—unguarded, unescorted, with merely an aide-de-camp accompanying him in his victoria. At other times he drove a light phaeton with only a footman in black livery to attend him. And on one occasion Pierre had seen him with the Queen, the pair of them seated side by side like worthy middle-class folks driving abroad for pleasure. And, as the royal couple went by, the busy people in the streets and the promenaders in the public gardens contented themselves with wafting them an affectionate wave of the hand, the most expansive simply approaching to smile at them, and no one importuning them with acclamations. Pierre, who harboured the traditional idea of kings closely guarded and passing processionally with all the accompaniment of military pomp, was therefore greatly surprised and touched by the amiable *bonhomie* of this royal pair, who went wherever they listed in full security amidst the smiling affection of their people. Everybody, moreover, had told him of the King's kindliness and simplicity, his desire for peace, and his passion for sport, solitude, and the open air, which, amidst the worries of power, must often have made him dream of a life of freedom far from the imperious duties of royalty for which he seemed unfitted.[1] But the Queen was yet more tenderly loved. So naturally and serenely virtuous that she alone remained ignorant of the scandals of Rome, she was also a woman of great culture and great refinement, conversant with every field of literature, and very happy in being so intelligent, so superior to those around her—a pre-eminence which she realised and which she was fond of showing, but in the most natural and most graceful of ways.

Like Pierre, Prada had remained with his face to the window, and suddenly pointing to the crowd he said: 'Now that they have seen the Queen they will go to bed well pleased.

[1] King Humbert inherited these tastes from his father Victor Emanuel, who was likewise a great sportsman and had a perfect horror of court life, pageantry, and the exigencies of politics.—*Trans.*

And there isn't a single police agent there, I'm sure. Ah! to be loved, to be loved!' Plainly enough his distress of spirit was coming back, and so, turning towards the gallery again, he tried to play the jester. 'Attention, my dear Abbé, we mustn't miss their Majesties' entry. That will be the finest part of the *fête !*'

A few minutes went by, and then, in the very midst of a polka, the orchestra suddenly ceased playing. But a moment afterwards, with all the blare of its brass instruments, it struck up the Royal March. The dancers fled in confusion, the centre of the gallery was cleared, and the King and Queen entered, escorted by the Prince and Princess Buongiovanni, who had received them at the foot of the staircase. The King was in ordinary evening dress, while the Queen wore a robe of straw-coloured satin, covered with superb white lace; and under the diadem of brilliants which encircled her beautiful fair hair, she looked still young, with a fresh and rounded face, whose expression was all amiability, gentleness, and wit. The music was still sounding with the enthusiastic violence of welcome. Behind her father and mother, Celia appeared amidst the press of people who were following to see the sight; and then came Attilio, the Saccos, and various relatives and official personages. And, pending the termination of the Royal March, only salutations, glances, and smiles were exchanged amidst the sonorous music and dazzling light; whilst all the guests crowded around on tip-toe, with outstretched necks and glittering eyes—a rising tide of heads and shoulders, flashing with the fires of precious stones.

At last the March ended and the presentations began. Their Majesties were already acquainted with Celia, and congratulated her with quite affectionate kindliness. However, Sacco, both as minister and father, was particularly desirous of presenting his son Attilio. He bent his supple spine, and summoned to his lips the fine words which were appropriate, in such wise that he contrived to make the young man bow to the King in the capacity of a lieutenant in his Majesty's army, whilst his homage as a handsome young man, so passionately loved by his betrothed, was reserved for Queen Margherita. Again did their Majesties show themselves very gracious, even towards the Signora Sacco, who, ever modest and prudent, had remained in the background. And then occurred an incident that was destined to give rise to endless gossip. Catching sight of Benedetta, whom Count Prada had presented to her after his marriage, the Queen, who greatly admired her beauty and charm of manner, addressed her a smile in such wise that the young woman was compelled to approach. A conversation of some minutes' duration ensued, and the Contessina was favoured with some extremely amiable expressions which were perfectly audible to all around. Most certainly the Queen was ignorant of the event of the day, the dissolution of Benedetta's marriage with Prada, and her coming union with Dario so publicly announced at this gala, which now seemed to have been given to celebrate a double betrothal. Nevertheless that conversation caused a deep impression ; the guests talked of nothing but the compliments which Benedetta had received from the most virtuous and intelligent of queens, and her triumph was increased by it all, she became yet more beautiful and more victorious amidst the happiness she felt at being at last able to bestow herself on the spouse of her choice, that happiness which made her look so radiant.

But, on the other hand, the torture which Prada experienced now became intense. Whilst the sovereigns continued conversing, the Queen with the ladies who came to pay her their respects, the King with the officers, diplomatists, and other important personages who approached him, Prada saw none but Benedetta—Benedetta congratulated, caressed, exalted by affection and glory. Dario was near her, flushing with pleasure, radiant like herself. It was for them that this ball had been given, for them that the lamps shone out, for them that the music played, for them that the most beautiful women of Rome had bared their bosoms and adorned them with precious stones. It was for them that their Majesties had entered to the strains of the Royal March, for them that the *fête* was becoming like an apotheosis, for them that a fondly-loved queen was smiling, appearing at that betrothal gala like the good fairy of the nursery tales, whose coming betokens lifelong happiness. And for Prada, this wondrously brilliant hour when good fortune and joyfulness attained their apogee, was one of defeat. It was fraught with the victory of that woman who had refused to be his wife in aught but name, and of that man who now was about to take her from him : such a public, ostentatious, insulting victory that it struck him like a buffet in the face. And not merely did his pride and passion bleed for that, he felt that the triumph of the Saccos dealt a blow to his fortune. Was it true, then, that the rough conquerors of the North were bound to deteriorate in the delightful climate of Rome, was that the reason why he already experienced such a sensation of weariness and exhaustion? That very morning at Frascati in connection with that disastrous building enterprise he had realised that his millions were menaced, albeit he refused to admit that things were going badly with him, as some people rumoured. And now, that evening, amidst that *fête* he beheld the South victorious, Sacco winning the day like one who feeds at his ease on the warm prey so gluttonously pounced upon under the flaming sun.

And the thought of Sacco being a minister, an intimate of the King, allying himself by marriage to one of the noblest families of the Roman aristocracy, and already laying hands on the people and the national funds with the prospect of some day becoming the master of Rome and Italy—that thought again was a blow for the vanity of this man of prey, for the ever-voracious appetite of this enjoyer, who felt as if he were being pushed away from table before the feast was over! All crumbled and escaped him, Sacco stole his millions, and Benedetta tortured his flesh, stirring up that awful wound of unsatisfied passion which never would be healed.

Again did Pierre hear that dull plaint, that involuntary despairing growl, which had upset him once before. And he looked at the Count, and asked him: 'Are you suffering?' But on seeing how livid was the face of Prada, who only retained his calmness by a superhuman effort, he regretted his indiscreet question, which, moreover, remained unanswered. And then to put the other more at ease, the young priest went on speaking, venting the thoughts which the sight before him inspired: 'Your father was right,' said he, 'we Frenchmen whose education is so full of the Catholic spirit, even in these days of universal doubt, we never think of Rome otherwise than as the old Rome of the popes. We scarcely know, we can scarcely understand the great changes which, year by year, have brought about the Italian Rome of the present day. Why, when I arrived here, the King and his government and the young nation working to make a great capital for itself, seemed to me of no account whatever! Yes, I dismissed all that, thought nothing of it, in my dream of resuscitating a Christian and evangelical Rome, which should assure the happiness of the world.'

He laughed as he spoke, pitying his own artlessness, and

then pointed towards the gallery where Prince Buongiovanni
was bowing to the King whilst the Princess listened to the
gallant remarks of Sacco : a scene full of symbolism, the old
papal aristocracy struck down, the *parvenus* accepted, the
black and white worlds so mixed together that one and all
were little else than subjects, on the eve of forming but one
united nation. That conciliation between the Quirinal and
the Vatican, which in principle was regarded as impossible, was
it not in practice fatal, in face of the evolution which went on
day by day ? People must go on living, loving and creating
life throughout the ages. And the marriage of Attilio and
Celia would be the symbol of the needful union : youth and
love triumphing over ancient hatred, all quarrels forgotten as
a handsome lad goes by, wins a lovely girl, and carries her off
in his arms in order that the world may last.

'Look at them!' resumed Pierre, 'how handsome and
young and gay both the *fiancés* are, all confidence in the future.
Ah ! I well understand that your King should have come here
to please his minister and win one of the old Roman families
over to his throne ; it is good, brave and fatherly policy. But
I like to think that he has also realised the touching significance of that marriage—old Rome, in the person of that
candid, loving child giving herself to young Italy, that upright,
enthusiastic young man who wears his uniform so jauntily.
And may their nuptials be definitive and fruitful ; from them
and from all the others may there arise the great nation which,
now that I begin to know you, I trust you will soon become !'

Amidst the tottering of his former dream of an evangelical
and universal Rome, Pierre expressed these good wishes for
the Eternal City's future fortune with such keen and deep
emotion that Prada could not help replying : 'I thank you ;
that wish of yours is in the heart of every good Italian.'

But his voice quavered, for even whilst he was looking at
Celia and Attilio, who stood smiling and talking together, he
saw Benedetta and Dario approach them, wearing the same
joyful expression of perfect happiness. And when the two
couples were united, so radiant and so triumphant, so full of
superb and happy life, he no longer had strength to stay there,
see them, and suffer.

'I am frightfully thirsty,' he coarsely exclaimed. 'Let's
go to the buffet to drink something.' And, thereupon, in order
to avoid notice, he so manœuvred as to glide behind the

throng, skirting the windows in the direction of the entrance
to the Hall of the Antiques which was beyond the gallery.

Whilst Pierre was following him they were parted by an
eddy of the crowd, and the young priest found himself carried
towards the two loving couples who still stood chatting
together. And Celia, on recognising him, beckoned to him in a
friendly way. With her passionate cult for beauty, she was
enraptured with the appearance of Benedetta, before whom she
joined her little lily hands as before the image of the Madonna.
'Oh! Monsieur l'Abbé,' said she, 'to please me now, do tell
her how beautiful she is, more beautiful than anything on
earth, more beautiful than even the sun, and the moon and
stars. If you only knew, my dear, it makes me quiver to see
you so beautiful as that, as beautiful as happiness, as beautiful
as love itself!'

Benedetta began to laugh, while the two young men made
merry. 'But you are as beautiful as I am, darling,' said the
Contessina.' 'And if we are beautiful it is because we are
happy.'

'Yes, yes, happy,' Celia gently responded. 'Do you
remember the evening when you told me that one didn't
succeed in marrying the Pope and the King? But Attilio and
I are marrying them, and yet we are very happy.'

'But we don't marry them, Dario and I! On the contrary!'
said Benedetta gaily. 'No matter; as you answered me that
same evening, it is sufficient that we should love one another,
love saves the world.'

When Pierre at last succeeded in reaching the door of the
Hall of the Antiques, where the buffet was installed, he found
Prada there, motionless, gazing despite himself on the
galling spectacle which he desired to flee. A power stronger
than his will had kept him there, forcing him to turn round
and look, and look again. And thus, with a bleeding heart,
he still lingered and witnessed the resumption of the dancing,
the first figure of a quadrille which the orchestra began to
play with a lively flourish of its brass instruments. Benedetta
and Dario, Celia and Attilio were *vis-à-vis*. And so charming
and delightful was the sight which the two couples presented
dancing in the white blaze, all youth and joy, that the King and
Queen drew near to them and became interested. And soon
bravos of admiration rang out, while from every heart spread
a feeling of infinite tenderness.

'I'm dying of thirst, let's go!' repeated Prada, at last managing to wrench himself away from the torturing sight.

He called for some iced lemonade and drank the glassful at one draught, gulping it down with the greedy eagerness of a man stricken with fever, who will never more be able to quench the burning fire within him.

The Hall of the Antiques was a spacious room with mosaic pavement, and decorations of stucco ; and a famous collection of vases, bas-reliefs, and statues, was disposed along its walls. The marbles predominated, but there were a few bronzes, and among them a dying gladiator of extreme beauty. The marvel, however, was the famous statue of Venus, a companion to that of the Capitol, but with a more elegant and supple figure and with the left arm falling loosely in a gesture of voluptuous surrender. That evening a powerful electric reflector threw a dazzling light upon the statue, which, in its divine and pure nudity, seemed to be endowed with super-human, immortal life. Against the end-wall was the buffet, a long table covered with an embroidered cloth and laden with fruit, pastry and cold meats. Sheaves of flowers rose up amidst bottles of champagne, hot punch and iced *sorbetto*, and here and there were marshalled armies of glasses, tea-cups, and broth-bowls, a perfect wealth of sparkling crystal, porcelain and silver. And a happy innovation had been to fill half of the hall with rows of little tables, at which the guests, in lieu of being obliged to refresh themselves standing, were able to sit down and order what they desired as in a café.

At one of these little tables, Pierre perceived Narcisse seated near a young woman, whom Prada, on approaching, recognised to be Lisbeth. 'You find me, you see, in delightful company,' gallantly exclaimed the *attaché*. 'As we lost one another, I could think of nothing better than of offering madame my arm to bring her here.'

'It was, in fact, a good idea,' said Lisbeth with her pretty laugh, ' for I was feeling very thirsty.'

They had ordered some iced coffee, which they were slowly sipping out of little silver-gilt spoons.

'I have a terrible thirst, too,' declared the Count, 'and I can't quench it. You will allow us to join you, will you not, my dear sir ? Some of that coffee will perhaps calm me.' And then to Lisbeth he added, 'Ah! my dear, allow me to introduce to you Monsieur l'Abbé Froment, a young French priest of great distinction.'

Then for a long time they all four remained seated at that table, chatting and making merry over certain of the guests who went by. Prada, however, in spite of his usual gallantry towards Lisbeth, frequently became absent-minded; at times he quite forgot her, being again mastered by his anguish, and, in spite of all his efforts, his eyes ever turned towards the neighbouring gallery whence the sound of music and dancing reached him.

'Why, what are you thinking of, *caro mio*?' Lisbeth asked in her pretty way, on seeing him at one moment so pale and lost. 'Are you indisposed?'

He did not reply, however, but suddenly exclaimed, 'Ah! look there, that's the real pair, there's real love and happiness for you!'

With a jerk of the hand he designated Dario's mother, the Marchioness Montefiori and her second husband, Jules Laporte —that ex-sergeant of the papal Swiss Guard, her junior by fifteen years, whom she had one day hooked at the Corso with her eyes of fire, which yet had remained superb, and whom she had afterwards triumphantly transformed into a Marquis Montefiori in order to have him entirely to herself. Such was her passion that she never relaxed her hold on him whether at ball or reception, but, despite all usages, kept him beside her, and even made him escort her to the buffet, so much did she delight in being able to exhibit him and say that this handsome man was her own exclusive property. And standing there side by side, the pair of them began to drink champagne and eat sandwiches, she yet a marvel of massive beauty although she was over fifty, and he with long wavy moustaches, and proud bearing, like a fortunate adventurer whose jovial impudence pleased the ladies.

'You know that she had to extricate him from a nasty affair,' resumed the Count in a lower tone. 'Yes, he travelled in relics; he picked up a living by supplying relics on commission to convents in France and Switzerland; and he had launched quite a business in false relics with the help of some Jews here who concocted little ancient reliquaries out of mutton bones, with everything sealed and signed by the most genuine authorities. The affair was hushed up, as three prelates were also compromised in it! Ah! the happy man! Do you see how she devours him with her eyes? And he, doesn't he look quite a *grand seigneur* by the mere way in

which he holds that plate for her whilst she eats the breast of
a fowl out of it ! '

Then, in a rough way and with biting irony, he went on
to speak of the *amours* of Rome. The Roman women, said
he, were ignorant, obstinate, and jealous. When a woman
had managed to win a man, she kept him for ever, he became
her property, and she disposed of him as she pleased. By
way of proof, he cited many interminable *liaisons*, such as
that of Donna Serafina and Morano, which in time became
virtual marriages ; and he sneered at such a lack of fancy,
such an excess of fidelity whose only ending, when it did end,
was some very disagreeable unpleasantness.

At this, Lisbeth interrupted him. 'But what is the
matter with you this evening, my dear ? ' she asked with a
laugh. ' What you speak of is, on the contrary, very nice and
pretty ! When a man and a woman love one another they
ought to do so for ever ! '

She looked delightful as she spoke, with her fine wavy
blond hair and delicate fair complexion ; and Narcisse with
a languorous expression in his half-closed eyes compared her
to a Botticelli which he had seen at Florence. However, the
night was now far advanced, and Pierre had once more sunk
into gloomy thoughtfulness when he heard a passing lady
remark that they had already begun to dance the Cotillon in
the gallery ; and thereupon he suddenly remembered that
Monsignor Nani had given him an appointment in the little
Saloon of the Mirrors.

' Are you leaving ? ' hastily inquired Prada on seeing him
rise and bow to Lisbeth.

' No, no, not yet,' Pierre answered.

' Oh ! all right. Don't go away without me. I want to
walk a little, and I'll see you home. It's agreed, eh ? You
will find me here.'

The young priest had to cross two rooms, one hung with
yellow and the other with blue, before he at last reached the
mirrored *salon*. This was really an exquisite example of the
rococo style, a rotunda as it were of pale mirrors framed with
superb gilded carvings. Even the ceiling was covered with
mirrors disposed slantwise so that on every side things multiplied, mingled and appeared under all possible aspects. Discreetly enough no electric lights had been placed in the room,
the only illumination being that of some pink tapers burning
in a pair of candelabra. The hangings and upholstery were

of soft blue silk, and the impression on entering was very sweet and charming, as if one had found oneself in the abode of some fairy queen of the rills, a palace of limpid water, illumined to its furthest depths by clusters of stars.

Pierre at once perceived Monsignor Nani, who was sitting on a low couch, and, as the prelate had hoped, he was quite alone, for the Cotillon had attracted almost everybody to the picture gallery. And the silence in the little *salon* was nearly perfect, for at that distance the blare of the orchestra subsided into a faint, flute-like murmur. The young priest at once apologised to the prelate for having kept him waiting.

'No, no, my dear son,' said Nani with his inexhaustible amiability. 'I was very comfortable in this retreat—when the press of the crowd became over-threatening I took refuge here.' He did not speak of the King and Queen, but he allowed it to be understood that he had politely avoided their company. If he had come to the *fête* it was on account of his sincere affection for Celia and also with a very delicate diplomatic object, for the Church wished to avoid any appearance of having entirely broken with the Buongiovanni family, that ancient house which was so famous in the annals of the papacy. Doubtless the Vatican was unable to subscribe to this marriage which seemed to unite old Rome with the young Kingdom of Italy, but on the other hand it did not desire people to think that it abandoned old and faithful supporters and took no interest in what befell them.

'But come, my dear son,' the prelate resumed, 'it is you who are now in question. I told you that although the Congregation of the Index had pronounced itself for the condemnation of your book, the sentence would only be submitted to the Holy Father and signed by him on the day after to-morrow. So you still have a whole day before you.'

At this Pierre could not refrain from a dolorous and vivacious interruption.

'Alas! monseigneur, what can I do?' said he; 'I have thought it all over, and I see no means, no opportunity of defending myself. How could I even see his Holiness now that he is so ill?'

'Oh! ill, ill!' muttered Nani with his shrewd expression. 'His Holiness is ever so much better, for this very day, like every other Wednesday, I had the honour to be received by him. When his Holiness is a little tired and people say that he is very ill, he often lets them do so, for it gives him a rest and enables him to judge certain ambitions and manifestations of impatience around him.'

Pierre, however, was too upset to listen attentively. ' No, it's all over,' he continued, ' I'm in despair. You spoke to me of the possibility of a miracle, but I am no great believer in miracles. Since I am defeated here at Rome, I shall go away, I shall return to Paris, and continue the struggle there. Oh! I cannot resign myself, my hope in salvation by the practice of love cannot die, and I shall answer my denouncers in a new book, in which I shall tell in what new soil the new religion will grow up!'

Silence fell. Nani looked at him with his clear eyes in which intelligence shone distinct and sharp like steel. And amidst the deep calm, the warm heavy atmosphere of the little *salon*, whose mirrors were starred with countless reflections of candles, a more sonorous burst of music was suddenly wafted from the gallery, a rhythmical waltz melody, which slowly expanded, then died away.

' My dear son,' said Nani, ' anger is always harmful. You remember that on your arrival here I promised that if your own efforts to obtain an interview with the Holy Father should prove unavailing, I would myself endeavour to secure an audience for you.' Then, seeing how agitated the young priest was getting, he went on: ' Listen to me and don't excite yourself. His Holiness, unfortunately, is not always prudently advised. Around him are persons whose devotion, however great, is at times deficient in intelligence. I told you that, and warned you against inconsiderate applications. And this is why, already three weeks ago, I myself handed your book to his Holiness in the hope that he would deign to glance at it. I rightly suspected that it had not been allowed to reach him. And this is what I am instructed to tell you: His Holiness, who has had the great kindness to read your book, expressly desires to see you.'

A cry of joy and gratitude died away in Pierre's throat: ' Ah! monseigneur. Ah! monseigneur!'

But Nani quickly silenced him and glanced around with an expression of keen anxiety as if he feared that someone might hear them. ' Hush! Hush!' said he, ' it is a secret. His Holiness wishes to see you privately, without taking anybody else into his confidence. Listen attentively. It is now two o'clock in the morning. Well, this very day, at nine in the evening precisely, you must present yourself at the Vatican and at every door ask for Signor Squadra. You will invariably be allowed to pass. Signor Squadra will be waiting for you upstairs, and will introduce you. And not a word, mind, not a soul must have the faintest suspicion of these things.'

Pierre's happiness and gratitude at last flowed forth. He had caught hold of the prelate's soft, plump hands, and stammered, 'Ah! monseigneur, how can I express my gratitude to you? If you only knew how full my soul was of night and rebellion since I realised that I had been a mere plaything in the hands of those powerful cardinals. But you have saved me, and again I feel sure that I shall win the victory, for I shall at last be able to fling myself at the feet of his Holiness, the father of all truth and all justice. He can but absolve me, I who love him, I who admire him, I who have never battled for aught but his own policy and most cherished ideas. No, no, it is impossible; he will not sign that judgment; he will not condemn my book!'

Releasing his hands, Nani sought to calm him with a fatherly gesture, whilst retaining a faint smile of contempt for such a useless expenditure of enthusiasm. At last he succeeded, and begged him to retire. The orchestra was again playing more loudly in the distance. And when the young priest at last withdrew, thanking him once more, he said very simply: 'Remember, my dear son, that only obedience is great.'

Pierre, whose one desire now was to take himself off, found Prada almost immediately afterwards in the first reception room. Their Majesties had just left the ball in grand ceremony, escorted to the threshold by the Buongiovannis and the Saccos. And before departing the Queen had maternally kissed Celia, whilst the King shook hands with Attilio—honours instinct with a charming good nature which made the members of both families quite radiant. However, a good many of the guests were following the example of the sovereigns and disappearing in small batches. And the Count, who seemed strangely nervous, and showed more sternness and bitterness than ever, was, on his side, also eager to be gone. 'Ah! it's you at last. I was waiting for you,' he said to Pierre. 'Well, let's get off at once, eh? Your compatriot Monsieur Narcisse Habert asked me to tell you not to look for him. The fact is, he has gone to see my friend Lisbeth to her carriage. I myself want a breath of fresh air, a stroll, and so I'll go with you as far as the Via Giulia.'

Then, as they took their things from the cloak-room, he could not help sneering and saying in his brutal way: ' I saw your good friends go off, all four together. It's lucky that you prefer to go home on foot, for there was no room for you in the carriage. What superb impudence it was on the part of that Donna Serafina to drag herself here, at her age, with that Morano of hers, so as to triumph over the return of the fickle one! And the two others, the two young ones—ah! I confess that I can hardly speak calmly of *them*, for in parading here together as they did this evening, they have shown an impudence and a cruelty such as is rarely seen!' Prada's hands trembled, and he murmured: 'A good journey, a good journey to the young man, since he is going to Naples. Yes, I heard Celia say that he was starting for Naples this evening at six o'clock. Well, my wishes go with him; a good journey!'

The two men found the change delightful when they at last emerged from the stifling heat of the reception rooms into the lovely, cool, and limpid night. It was a night illumined by a superb full moon, one of those matchless Roman nights when the city slumbers in Elysian radiance, steeped in a dream of the Infinite, under the vast vault of heaven. And they took the most agreeable route, going down the Corso proper and then turning into the Corso Vittorio Emmanuele.

Prada had grown somewhat calmer, but remained full of irony. To divert his mind, no doubt, he talked on in the most voluble manner, reverting to the women of Rome and to that *fête* which he had at first found splendid, but at which he now began to rail.

'Oh! of course they have very fine gowns,' said he, speaking of the women; 'but gowns which don't fit them, gowns which are sent them from Paris, and which, of course, they can't try on. It's just the same with their jewels; they still have diamonds and pearls, in particular, which are very fine, but they are so wretchedly, so heavily mounted that they look frightful. And if you only knew how ignorant and frivolous these women are, despite all their conceit! Everything is on the surface with them, even religion: there's nothing beneath. I looked at them eating at the buffet. Oh! they at least have fine appetites. This evening some decorum was observed, there wasn't too much gorging. But at one of the Court balls you would see a general pillage, the buffets besieged, and everything swallowed up amidst a scramble of amazing voracity!'

To all this talk Pierre only returned monosyllabic responses. He was wrapped in overflowing delight at the thought of that audience with the Pope, which, unable as he was to confide in any one, he strove to arrange and picture in his own mind, even in its pettiest details. And meantime the footsteps of the two men rang out on the dry pavement of the clear, broad, deserted thoroughfare, whose black shadows were sharply outlined by the moonlight.

All at once Prada himself became silent. His loquacious *bravura* was exhausted, the frightful struggle going on in his mind wholly possessed and paralysed him. Twice already he had dipped his hand into his coat pocket and felt the pencilled note whose four lines he mentally repeated : 'A legend avers that the fig tree of Judas now grows at Frascati, and that its fruit is deadly for him who may desire to become pope. Eat not the poisoned figs, nor give them either to your servants or your fowls.' The note was there ; he could feel it ; and if he had desired to accompany Pierre, it was in order that he might drop it into the letter-box at the Palazzo Boccanera. And he continued to step out briskly, so that within another ten minutes that note would surely be in the box, for no power in the world could prevent it, since such was his express determination. Never would he commit such a crime as to allow people to be poisoned.

But he was suffering such abominable torture. That Benedetta and that Dario had raised such a tempest of jealous hatred within him ! For them he forgot Lisbeth whom he loved, and even that flesh of his flesh, the child of whom he was so proud. All sex as he was, eager to conquer and subdue, he had never cared for facile loves. His passion was to overcome. And now there was a woman in the world who defied him, a woman forsooth whom he had bought, whom he had married, who had been handed over him, but who would never, never be his. Ah ! in the old days, to subdue her, he would if needful have fired Rome like a Nero ; but now he asked himself what he could possibly do to prevent her from belonging to another. That galling thought made the blood gush from his gaping wound. How that woman and her lover must deride him ! And to think that they had sought to turn him to ridicule by a baseless charge, an arrant lie which still and ever made him smart, all proof of its falsity to the contrary,

He, on his side, had accused them in the past without much belief in what he said, but now the charges he had imputed to them must come true, for they were free, freed at all events of the religious bond, and that no doubt was their only care. And then visions of their happiness passed before his eyes, infuriating him. Ah! no, ah! no, it was impossible, he would rather destroy the world!

Then, as he and Pierre turned out of the Corso Vittorio Emmanuele to thread the old narrow tortuous streets leading to the Via Giulia, he pictured himself dropping the note into the letter-box at the *palazzo*. And next he conjured up what would follow. The note would lie in the letter-box till morning. At an early hour Don Vigilio, the secretary, who by the Cardinal's express orders kept the key of the box, would come down, find the note and hand it to his Eminence, who never allowed another to open any communication addressed to him. And then the figs would be thrown away, there would be no further possibility of crime, the black world would in all prudence keep silent. But if the note should not be in the letter-box, what would happen then? And admitting that supposition he pictured the figs placed on the table at the one o'clock meal, in their pretty little, leaf-covered basket. Dario would be there as usual, alone with his uncle, since he was not to leave for Naples till the evening. And would both the uncle and the nephew eat the figs, or would only one of them partake of the fruit, and which of them would that be? At this point Prada's clearness of vision failed him; again he conjured up Destiny on the march, that Destiny which he had met on the road from Frascati, going on towards its unknown goal, athwart all obstacles without possibility of stoppage. Aye, the little basket of figs went ever on and on to accomplish its fateful purpose, which no hand in the world had power enough to prevent.

And at last, on either hand of Pierre and Prada, the Via Giulia stretched away in a long line white with moonlight, and the young priest emerged as if from a dream at sight of the Palazzo Boccanera rising blackly under the silver sky. Three o'clock struck at a neighbouring church. And he felt himself quivering slightly as once again he heard near him the dolorous moan of a lion wounded unto death, that low involuntary growl which the Count, amidst the frightful struggle of his feelings, had for the third time allowed to escape him. But immediately afterwards he burst into a sneering laugh, and pressing the priest's hands, exclaimed : ' No, no, I am not going farther. If I were seen here at this hour, people would think that I had fallen in love with my wife again.'

And thereupon he lighted a cigar, and retraced his steps in the clear night, without once looking round.

XIII

WHEN Pierre awoke he was much surprised to hear eleven o'clock striking. Fatigued as he was by that ball where he had lingered so long, he had slept like a child in delightful peacefulness, and as soon as he opened his eyes the radiant sunshine filled him with hope. His first thought was that he would see the Pope that evening at nine o'clock. Ten more hours to wait ! What would he be able to do with himself during that lovely day, whose radiant sky seemed to him of such happy augury ? He rose and opened the windows to admit the warm air which, as he had noticed on the day of his arrival, had a savour of fruit and flowers, a blending, as it were, of the perfume of rose and orange. Could this possibly be December ? What a delightful land, that the spring should seem to flower on the very threshold of winter ! Then, having dressed, he was leaning out of the window to glance across the golden Tiber at the evergreen slopes of the Janiculum, when he espied Benedetta seated in the abandoned garden of the mansion. And thereupon, unable to keep still, full of a desire for life, gaiety, and beauty, he went down to join her.

With radiant visage and outstretched hands, she at once vented the cry he had expected : 'Ah ! my dear Abbé, how happy I am ! '

They had often spent their mornings in that quiet, for-saken nook ; but what sad mornings those had been, hopeless as they both were ! To-day, however, the weed-grown paths, the box-plants growing in the old basin, the orange-trees which alone marked the outline of the beds—all seemed full of charm, instinct with a sweet and dreamy cosiness in which it was very pleasant to lull one's joy. And it was so warm, too, beside the big laurel bush, in the corner where the stream-let of water ever fell with flute-like music from the gaping, tragic mask.

'Ah!' repeated Benedetta, 'how happy I am! I was stifling upstairs, and my heart felt such a need of space, and air, and sunlight, that I came down here!'

She was seated on the fallen column beside the old marble sarcophagus, and desired the priest to place himself beside her. Never had he seen her looking so beautiful, with her black hair encompassing her pure face, which in the sunshine appeared pinky and delicate as a flower. Her large, fathomless eyes showed in the light like braziers rolling gold, and her childish mouth, all candour and good sense, laughed the laugh of one who was at last free to love as her heart listed, without offending either God or man. And, dreaming aloud, she built up plans for the future: 'It's all simple enough,' said she; 'I have already obtained a separation, and shall easily get that changed into civil divorce now that the Church has annulled my marriage. And I shall marry Dario next spring, perhaps sooner, if the formalities can be hastened. He is going to Naples this evening about the sale of some property which we still possessed there, but which must now be sold, for all this business has cost us a lot of money. Still, that doesn't matter since we now belong to one another. And when he comes back in a few days, what a happy time we shall have! I could not sleep when I got back from that splended ball last night, for my head was so full of plans—oh! splendid plans, as you shall see, for I mean to keep you in Rome until our marriage.'

Like herself, Pierre began to laugh, so gained upon by this explosion of youth and happiness that he had to make a great effort to refrain from speaking of his own delight, his hopefulness at the thought of his coming interview with the Pope. Of that, however, he had sworn to speak to nobody.

Every now and again, amidst the quivering silence of the sunlit garden, the cry of a bird persistently rang out; and Benedetta, raising her head and looking at a cage hanging beside one of the first-floor windows, jestingly exclaimed: 'Yes, yes, Tata, make a good noise, show that you are pleased, my dear. Everybody in the house must be pleased now.' Then, turning towards Pierre, she added gaily: 'You know Tata, don't you? What! No? Why, Tata is my uncle's parrot. I gave her to him last spring; he's very fond of her, and lets her help herself out of his plate. And he himself attends to her, puts her out and takes her in, and keeps her in his dining-room, for fear lest she should take cold, as that is the only room of his which is at all warm.'

Pierre in his turn looked up and saw the bird, one of those pretty little parrots with soft, silky, dull green plumage. It was hanging by the beak from a bar of its cage, swinging itself and flapping its wings, all mirth in the bright sunshine.

'Does the bird talk?' he asked.

'No, she only screams,' replied Benedetta, laughing. 'Still, my uncle pretends that he understands her.' And then the young woman abruptly darted to another subject, as if this mention of her uncle the Cardinal had made her think of the uncle by marriage whom she had in Paris. 'I suppose you have heard from Viscount de la Choue,' said she. 'I had a letter from him yesterday, in which he said how grieved he was that you were unable to see the Holy Father, as he had counted on you for the triumph of his ideas.'

Pierre indeed frequently heard from the Viscount, who was greatly distressed by the importance which his adversary, Baron de Fouras, had acquired since his success with the International Pilgrimage of the Peter's Pence. The old, uncompromising Catholic party would awaken, said the Viscount, and all the conquests of neo-Catholicism would be threatened, if one could not obtain the Holy Father's formal adhesion to the proposed system of free guilds, in order to overcome the demand for closed guilds which was brought forward by the Conservatives. And the Viscount overwhelmed Pierre with injunctions, and sent him all sorts of complicated plans in his eagerness to see him received at the Vatican. 'Yes, yes,' muttered the young priest in reply to Benedetta. 'I had a letter on Sunday, and found another waiting for me on my return from Frascati yesterday. Ah! it would make me very happy to be able to send the Viscount some good news.' Then again Pierre's joy overflowed at the thought that he would that evening see the Pope, and, on opening his loving heart to the pontiff, receive the supreme encouragement which would strengthen him in his mission to work social salvation in the name of the lowly and the poor. And he could not restrain himself any longer, but let his secret escape him: 'It's settled, you know,' said he. 'My audience is for this evening.'

Benedetta did not understand at first. 'What audience?' she asked.

'Oh! Monsignor Nani was good enough to tell me at the

ball this morning, that the Holy Father has read my book and desires to see me. I shall be received this evening at nine o'clock.'

At this the Contessina flushed with pleasure, participating in the delight of the young priest to whom she had grown much attached. And this success of his coming in the midst of her own felicity, acquired extraordinary importance in her eyes, as if it were an augury of complete success for one and all. Superstitious as she was, she raised a cry of rapture and excitement: 'Ah! *Dio*, that will bring us good luck. How happy I am, my friend, to see happiness coming to you at the same time as to me! You cannot think how pleased I am! And all will go well now, it's certain, for a house where there is anyone whom the Pope welcomes is blessed, the thunder of Heaven falls on it no more!'

She laughed yet more loudly as she spoke, and clapped her hands with such exuberant gaiety that Pierre became anxious. 'Hush! hush!' said he, 'it is a secret. Pray don't mention it to anyone, either your aunt or even his Eminence. Monsignor Nani would be much annoyed.'

She thereupon promised to say nothing, and in a kindly voice spoke of Nani as a benefactor, for was she not indebted to him for the dissolution of her marriage? Then, with a fresh explosion of gaiety, she went on: 'But come, my friend, is not happiness the only good thing? You don't ask me to weep over the suffering poor to-day! Ah! the happiness of life, that's everything. People don't suffer or feel cold or hungry when they are happy.'

He looked at her in stupefaction at the idea of that strange solution of the terrible question of human misery. And suddenly he realised that, with that daughter of the sun who had inherited so many centuries of sovereign aristocracy, all his endeavours at conversion were vain. He had wished to bring her to a Christian love for the lowly and the wretched, win her over to the new, enlightened and compassionate Italy that he had dreamt of; but if she had been moved by the sufferings of the multitude at the time when she herself had suffered, when grievous wounds had made her own heart bleed, she was no sooner healed than she proclaimed the doctrine of universal felicity like a true daughter of a clime of burning summers, and winters as mild as spring. 'But everybody is not happy!' said he.

'Yes, yes, they are!' she exclaimed. 'You don't know the

poor! Give a girl of the Trastevere the lad she loves, and she becomes as radiant as a queen, and finds her dry bread quite sweet. The mothers who save a child from sickness, the men who conquer in a battle, or who win at the lottery, one and all in fact are like that, people only ask for good fortune and pleasure. And despite all your striving to be just and to arrive at a more even distribution of fortune, the only satisfied ones will be those whose hearts sing—often without their knowing the cause—on a fine sunny day like this.'

Pierre made a gesture of surrender, not wishing to sadden her by again pleading the cause of all the poor ones who at that very moment were somewhere agonising with physical or mental pain. But, all at once, through the luminous mild atmosphere a shadow seemed to fall, tinging joy with sadness, the sunshine with despair. And the sight of the old sarcophagus, with its bacchanal of satyrs and nymphs, brought back the memory that death lurks even amidst the bliss of passion, the unsatiated kisses of love. For a moment the clear song of the water sounded in Pierre's ears like a long-drawn sob, and all seemed to crumble in the terrible shadow which had fallen from the invisible.

Benedetta, however, caught hold of his hands and roused him once more to the delight of being there beside her. ' Your pupil is rebellious, is she not, my friend ? ' said she. ' But what would you have ? There are ideas which can't enter into our heads. No, you will never get those things into the head of a Roman girl. So be content with loving us as we are, beautiful with all our strength, as beautiful as we can be.'

She herself, in her resplendent happiness, looked at that moment so beautiful that he trembled as in presence of a divinity whose all-powerfulness swayed the world. ' Yes, yes,' he stammered, ' beauty, beauty, still and ever sovereign. Ah! why can it not suffice to satisfy the eternal longings of poor suffering men ? '

' Never mind ! ' she gaily responded. ' Do not distress yourself ; it is pleasant to live. And now let us go upstairs, my aunt must be waiting.'

The midday meal was served at one o'clock, and on the few occasions when Pierre did not eat at one or another restaurant a cover was laid for him at the ladies' table in the little dining-room of the second floor, overlooking the courtyard. At the same hour, in the sunlit dining-room of the first floor, whose windows faced the Tiber, the Cardinal likewise

sat down to table, happy in the society of his nephew Dario,
for his secretary, Don Vigilio, who also was usually present,
never opened his mouth unless to reply to some question. And
the two services were quite distinct, each having its own kitchen
and servants, the only thing at all common to them both
being a large room downstairs which served as a pantry and
store place.

Although the second floor dining-room was so gloomy,
saddened by the greeny half-light of the courtyard, the meal
shared that day by the two ladies and the young priest proved
a very gay one. Even Donna Serafina, usually so rigid,
seemed to relax under the influence of great internal felicity.
She was no doubt still enjoying her triumph of the previous
evening, and it was she who first spoke of the ball and sung
its praises, though the presence of the King and Queen had
much embarrassed her, said she. According to her account,
she had only avoided presentation by skilful strategy; however
she hoped that her well-known affection for Celia, whose god-
mother she was, would explain her presence in that neutral
mansion where Vatican and Quirinal had met. At the same
time she must have retained certain scruples, for she declared
that directly after dinner she was going to the Vatican to see
the Cardinal Secretary, to whom she desired to speak about an
enterprise of which she was lady-patroness. This visit would
compensate for her attendance at the Buongiovanni entertainment. And on the other hand never had Donna Serafina
seemed so zealous and hopeful of her brother's speedy accession to the throne of St. Peter : therein lay a supreme triumph,
an elevation of her race, which her pride deemed both needful
and inevitable, and indeed during Leo XIII's last indisposition
she had actually concerned herself about the trousseau which
would be needed and which would require to be marked with
the new Pontiff's arms.

On her side, Benedetta was all gaiety during the repast,
laughing at everything, and speaking of Celia and Attilio with
the passionate affection of a woman whose own happiness
delights in that of her friends. Then, just as the dessert had
been served, she turned to the servant with an air of surprise :
' Well, and the figs, Giacomo ? ' she asked.

Giacomo, slow and sleepy of motion, looked at her without
understanding. However, Victorine was crossing the room,
and Benedetta's next question was for her : ' Why are the figs
not served, Victorine ? ' she inquired.

'What figs, Contessina?'

'Why the figs I saw in the pantry as I passed through it this morning on my way to the garden. They were in a little basket and looked superb. I was even astonished to see that there were still some fresh figs left at this season. I'm very fond of them, and felt quite pleased at the thought that I should eat some at dinner.'

Victorine began to laugh: 'Ah! yes, Contessina, I understand,' she replied. 'They were some figs which that priest of Frascati, whom you know very well, brought yesterday evening as a present for his Eminence. I was there, and I heard him repeat three or four times that they were a present, and were to be put on his Eminence's table without a leaf being touched. And so one did as he said.'

'Well, that's nice,' retorted Benedetta with comical indignation. 'What *gourmands* my uncle and Dario are to regale themselves without us! They might have given us a share!'

Donna Serafina thereupon intervened, and asked Victorine: 'You are speaking, are you not, of that priest who used to come to the villa at Frascati?'

'Yes, yes, Abbé Santobono his name is, he officiates at the little church of St. Mary in the Fields. He always asks for Abbé Paparelli when he calls; I think they were at the seminary together. And it was Abbé Paparelli who brought him to the pantry with his basket last night. To tell the truth, the basket was forgotten there in spite of all the injunctions, so that nobody would have eaten the figs to-day if Abbé Paparelli hadn't run down just now and carried them upstairs as piously as if they were the Blessed Sacrament. It's true though that his Eminence is so fond of them.'

'My brother won't do them much honour to-day,' remarked the Princess. 'He is slightly indisposed. He passed a bad night.' The repeated mention of Abbé Paparelli had made the old lady somewhat thoughtful. She had regarded the train-bearer with displeasure ever since she had noticed the extraordinary influence he was gaining over the Cardinal, despite all his apparent humility and self-effacement. He was but a servant and apparently a very insignificant one, yet he governed, and she could feel that he combated her own influence, often undoing things which she had done to further her brother's interests. Twice already, moreover, she had suspected him of having urged the Cardinal to courses which she looked upon as absolute blunders. But perhaps she was wrong ; she did the train-bearer the justice to admit that he had great merits and displayed exemplary piety.

However, Benedetta went on laughing and jesting, and as Victorine had now withdrawn, she called the man-servant: 'Listen, Giacomo, I have a commission for you.' Then she broke off to say to her aunt and Pierre : 'Pray let us assert our rights. I can see them at table almost underneath us. Uncle is taking the leaves off the basket and serving himself with a smile ; then he passes the basket to Dario, who passes it on to Don Vigilio. And all three of them eat and enjoy the figs. You can see them, can't you ? ' She herself could see them well. And it was her desire to be near Dario, the constant flight of her thoughts to him that now made her picture him at table with the others. Her heart was down below, and there was nothing there that she could not see, and hear, and smell, with such keenness of the senses did her love endow her. 'Giacomo,' she resumed, 'you are to go down and tell his Eminence that we are longing to taste his figs, and that it will be very kind of him if he will send us such as he can spare.'

Again, however, did Donna Serafina intervene, recalling her wonted severity of voice : 'Giacomo, you will please stay here.' And to her niece she added : 'That's enough childishness ! I dislike such silly freaks.'

'Oh ! aunt,' Benedetta murmured. 'But I'm so happy, it's so long since I laughed so good-heartedly.'

Pierre had hitherto remained listening, enlivened by the sight of her gaiety. But now, as a little chill fell, he raised his voice to say that on the previous day he himself had been astonished to see the famous fig tree of Frascati still bearing fruit so late in the year. This was doubtless due, however, to the tree's position and the protection of a high wall.

'Ah ! so you saw the tree ? ' said Benedetta.

'Yes, and I even travelled with those figs which you would so much like to taste.'

'Why, how was that ? '

The young man already regretted the reply which had escaped him. However, having gone so far, he preferred to say everything. 'I met somebody at Frascati who had come there in a carriage and who insisted on driving me back to Rome,' said he. 'On the way we picked up Abbé Santobono, who was bravely making the journey on foot with his basket in his hand. And afterwards we stopped at an *osteria*——' Then he went on to describe the drive and relate his impressions whilst

crossing the Campagna amidst the falling twilight. But
Benedetta gazed at him fixedly, aware as she was of Prada's
frequent visits to the land and houses which he owned at
Frascati ; and suddenly she murmured : ' Somebody, somebody,
it was the Count, was it not ? '

' Yes, madame, the Count,' Pierre answered. ' I saw him
again last night ; he was overcome, and really deserves to be
pitied.'

The two women took no offence at this charitable remark
which fell from the young priest with such deep and natural
emotion, full as he was of overflowing love and compassion
for one and all. Donna Serafina remained motionless as if
she had not even heard him, and Benedetta made a gesture
which seemed to imply that she had neither pity nor hatred
to express for a man who had become a perfect stranger to
her. However, she no longer laughed, but, thinking of the
little basket which had travelled in Prada's carriage, she said :
' Ah ! I don't care for those figs at all now, I am even glad
that I haven't eaten any of them.'

Immediately after the coffee Donna Serafina withdrew,
saying that she was at once going to the Vatican ; and the
others, being left to themselves, lingered at table, again full of
gaiety, and chatting like friends. The priest, with his feverish
impatience, once more referred to the audience which he was
to have that evening. It was now barely two o'clock, and he
had seven more hours to wait. How should he employ that
endless afternoon ? Thereupon Benedetta good-naturedly
made him a proposal. ' I'll tell you what,' said she, ' as we
are all in such good spirits we mustn't leave one another.
Dario has his victoria, you know. He must have finished
lunch by now, and I'll ask him to take us for a long drive
along the Tiber.'

This fine project so delighted her that she began to clap
her hands ; but just then Don Vigilio appeared with a scared
look on his face. ' Isn't the Princess here ? ' he inquired.

' No, my aunt has gone out. What is the matter ? '

' His Eminence sent me. The Prince has just felt unwell
on rising from table. Oh ! it's nothing—nothing serious, no
doubt.'

Benedetta raised a cry of surprise rather than anxiety :
' What, Dario ! Well, we'll all go down. Come with me,
Monsieur l'Abbé. He mustn't get ill if he is to take us for a
drive ! ' Then, meeting Victorine on the stairs, she bade

her follow. 'Dario isn't well,' she said. 'You may be wanted.'

They all four entered the spacious, antiquated and simply furnished bed-room where the young Prince had lately been laid up for a whole month. It was reached by way of a small *salon*, and from an adjoining dressing-room a passage conducted to the Cardinal's apartments, the relatively small dining-room, bed-room, and study, which had been devised by subdividing one of the huge galleries of former days. In addition, the passage gave access to his Eminence's private chapel, a bare, uncarpeted, chairless room, where there was nothing beyond the painted, wooden altar, and the hard, cold tiles on which to kneel and pray.

On entering, Benedetta hastened to the bed where Dario was lying, still fully dressed. Near him, in fatherly fashion, stood Cardinal Boccanera, who, amidst his dawning anxiety, retained his proud and lofty bearing—the calmness of a soul beyond reproach. 'Why, what is the matter, Dario *mio*?' asked the young woman.

He smiled, eager to reassure her. One only noticed that he was very pale, with a look as of intoxication on his face. 'Oh! it's nothing, mere giddiness,' he replied. 'It's just as if I had drunk too much. All at once things swam before my eyes, and I thought I was going to fall. And then I only had time to come and fling myself on the bed.'

Then he drew a long breath, as though talking exhausted him, and the Cardinal in his turn gave some details. 'We had just finished our meal,' said he, 'I was giving Don Vigilio some orders for this afternoon, and was about to rise when I saw Dario get up and reel. He wouldn't sit down again, but came in here, staggering like a somnambulist, and fumbling at the doors to open them. We followed him without understanding. And I confess that I don't yet comprehend it.'

So saying, the Cardinal punctuated his surprise by waving his arm towards the rooms, through which a gust of misfortune seemed to have suddenly swept. All the doors had remained wide open: the dressing-room could be seen, and then the passage, at the end of which appeared the dining-room, in a disorderly state, like an apartment suddenly vacated; the table still laid, the napkins flung here and there, and the chairs pushed back. As yet, however, there was no alarm.

Benedetta made the remark which is usually made in

such cases : 'I hope you haven't eaten anything which has disagreed with you.'

The Cardinal, smiling, again waved his hand as if to attest the frugality of his table. 'Oh!' said he, 'there were only some eggs, some lamb cutlets, and a dish of sorrel—they couldn't have overloaded his stomach. I myself only drink water; he takes just a sip of white wine. No, no, the food has nothing to do with it.'

'Besides, in that case his Eminence and I would also have felt indisposed,' Don Vigilio made bold to remark.

Dario, after momentarily closing his eyes, opened them again, and once more drew a long breath, whilst endeavouring to laugh. 'Oh, it will be nothing;' he said. 'I feel more at ease already. I must get up and stir myself.'

'In that case,' said Benedetta, 'this is what I had thought of. You will take Monsieur l'Abbé Froment and me for a long drive in the Campagna.'

'Willingly. It's a nice idea. Victcrine, help me.'

Whilst speaking he had raised himself by means of one arm ; but, before the servant could approach, a slight convulsion seized him, and he fell back again as if overcome by a fainting fit. It was the Cardinal, still standing by the bedside, who caught him in his arms, whilst the Contessina this time lost her head : '*Dio, Dio !* It has come on him again. Quick, quick, a doctor !'

'Shall I run for one ?' asked Pierre, whom the scene was also beginning to upset.

'No, no, not you ; stay with me. Victorine will go at once. She knows the address. Doctor Giordano, Victorine.'

The servant hurried away, and a heavy silence fell on the room where the anxiety became more pronounced every moment. Benedetta, now quite pale, had again approached the bed, whilst the Cardinal looked down at Dario, whom he still held in his arms. And a terrible suspicion, vague, indeterminate as yet, had just awoke in the old man's mind : Dario's face seemed to him to be ashen, to wear that mask of terrified anguish which he had already remarked on the countenance of his dearest friend, Monsignor Gallo, when he had held him in his arms, in like manner, two hours before his death. There was also the same swoon and the same sensation of clasping a cold form whose heart ceases to beat. And above everything else there was in Boccanera's mind the same growing thought of poison, poison coming one knew not whence or how, but

mysteriously striking down those around him with the suddenness of lightning. And for a long time he remained with his
head bent over the face of his nephew, that last scion of his
race, seeking, studying, and recognising the signs of the mysterious, implacable disorder which once already had rent his
heart atwain.

But Benedetta addressed him in a low, entreating voice:
'You will tire yourself, uncle. Let me take him a little, I
beg you. Have no fear, I'll hold him very gently, he will feel
that it is I, and perhaps that will rouse him.'

At last the Cardinal raised his head and looked at her, and
allowed her to take his place after kissing her with distracted
passion, his eyes the while full of tears—a sudden burst of
emotion in which his great love for the young woman melted
the stern frigidity which he usually affected. 'Ah! my poor
child, my poor child!' he stammered, trembling from head to
foot like an oak tree about to fall. Immediately afterwards,
however, he mastered himself, and whilst Pierre and Don
Vigilio, mute and motionless, regretted that they could be of
no help, he walked slowly to and fro. Soon, moreover, that
bedchamber became too small for all the thoughts revolving in
his mind, and he strayed first into the dressing-room and then
down the passage as far as the dining-room. And again and
again he went to and fro, grave and impassible, his head low,
ever lost in the same gloomy reverie. What were the multitudinous thoughts stirring in the brain of that believer, that
haughty Prince who had given himself to God and could do
naught to stay inevitable Destiny? From time to time he
returned to the bedside, observed the progress of the disorder,
and then started off again at the same slow, regular pace, disappearing and reappearing, carried along as it were by the
monotonous alternations of forces which man cannot control.
Possibly he was mistaken, possibly this was some mere indisposition at which the doctor would smile. One must hope
and wait. And again he went off and again he came back;
and amidst the heavy silence nothing more clearly bespoke
the torture of anxious fear than the rhythmical footsteps of
that tall old man who was thus awaiting Destiny.

The door opened, and Victorine came in breathless. 'I
found the doctor, here he is,' she gasped.

With his little pink face and white curls, his discreet
paternal bearing which gave him the air of an amiable prelate,
Doctor Giordano came in smiling; but on seeing that room

and all the anxious people waiting in it, he turned very grave, at once assuming the expression of profound respect for all ecclesiastical secrets which he had acquired by long practice among the clergy. And when he had glanced at the sufferer he let but a low murmur escape him: 'What, again! Is it beginning again!'

He was probably alluding to the knife-thrust for which he had recently tended Dario. Who could be thus relentlessly pursuing that poor and inoffensive young prince? However no one heard the doctor unless it were Benedetta, and she was so full of feverish impatience, so eager to be tranquilised, that she did not listen but burst into fresh entreaties: 'Oh! doctor, pray look at him, examine him, tell us that it is nothing. It can't be anything serious, since he was so well and gay but a little while ago. It's nothing serious, is it?'

'You are right no doubt, Contessina, it can be nothing dangerous. We will see.'

However, on turning round, Doctor Giordano perceived the Cardinal, who with regular, thoughtful footsteps had come back from the dining-room to place himself at the foot of the bed. And while bowing, the doctor doubtless detected a gleam of mortal anxiety in the dark eyes fixed upon his own, for he added nothing but began to examine Dario like a man who realises that time is precious. And as his examination progressed the affable optimism which usually appeared upon his countenance gave place to ashen gravity, a covert terror which made his lips slightly tremble. It was he who had attended Monsignor Gallo when the latter had been carried off so mysteriously; it was he who for imperative reasons had then delivered a certificate stating the cause of death to be infectious fever; and doubtless he now found the same terrible symptoms as in that case, a leaden hue overspreading the sufferer's features, a stupor as of excessive intoxication; and, old Roman practitioner that he was, accustomed to sudden deaths, he realised that the *malaria* which kills was passing, that *malaria* which science does not yet fully understand, which may come from the putrescent exhalations of the Tiber unless it be but a name for the ancient poison of the legends.

As the doctor raised his head his glance again encountered the black eyes of the Cardinal, which never left him. 'Signor Giordano,' said his Eminence, 'you are not over-anxious, I hope? It is only some case of indigestion, is it not?'

The doctor again bowed. By the slight quiver of the

Cardinal's voice he understood how acute was the anxiety of that powerful man, who once more was stricken in his dearest affections.

'Your Eminence must be right,' he said, ' there's a bad digestion certainly. Such accidents sometimes become dangerous when fever supervenes. I need not tell your Eminence how thoroughly you may rely on my prudence and zeal.' Then he broke off and added in a clear professional voice : ' We must lose no time; the Prince must be undressed. I should prefer to remain alone with him for a moment.'

Whilst speaking in this way, however, Doctor Giordano detained Victorine, who would be able to help him, said he ; should he need any further assistance he would take Giacomo. His evident desire was to get rid of the members of the family in order that he might have more freedom of action. And the Cardinal, who understood him, gently led Benedetta into the dining-room, whither Pierre and Don Vigilio followed.

When the doors had been closed, the most mournful and oppressive silence reigned in that dining-room, which the bright sun of winter filled with such delightful warmth and radiance. The table was still laid, its cloth strewn here and there with bread-crumbs ; and a coffee cup had remained half full. In the centre stood the basket of figs, whose covering of leaves had been removed. However, only two or three of the figs were missing. And in front of the window was Tata, the female parrot, who had flown out of her cage and perched herself on her stand, where she remained, dazzled and enraptured, amidst the dancing dust of a broad yellow sunray. In her astonishment, however, at seeing so many people enter, she had ceased to scream and smooth her feathers, and had turned her head the better to examine the new-comers with her round and scrutinising eye.

The minutes went by slowly amidst all the feverish anxiety as to what might be occurring in the neighbouring room. Don Vigilio had taken a corner seat in silence, whilst Benedetta and Pierre, who had remained standing, preserved similar muteness and immobility. But the Cardinal had reverted to that instinctive, lulling tramp by which he apparently hoped to quiet his impatience and arrive the sooner at the explanation for which he was groping through a tumultuous maze of ideas. And whilst his rhythmical footsteps resounded with mechanical regularity, dark fury was taking possession of his mind, exasperation at being unable to understand the why and wherefore of that sickness. As he passed the table he had twice glanced at the things lying on it in confusion, as if seeking some explanation from them. Perhaps the harm had been done by that unfinished coffee, or by that bread whose crumbs lay here and there, or by those cutlets, a bone of which remained? Then as for the third time he passed by, again glancing, his eyes fell upon the basket of figs, and at once he stopped, as if beneath the shock of a revelation. An idea seized upon him and mastered him, without any plan, however, occurring to him by which he might change his sudden suspicion into certainty. For a moment he remained puzzled with his eyes fixed upon the basket. Then he took a fig and examined it, but, noticing nothing strange, was about to put it back when Tata, the parrot, who was very fond of figs, raised a strident cry. And this was like a ray of light; the means of changing suspicion into certainty was found.

Slowly, with grave air and gloomy visage, the Cardinal carried the fig to the parrot and give it to her without hesitation or regret. She was a very pretty bird, the only being of the lower order of creation to which he had ever really been attached. Stretching out her supple, delicate form, whose silken feathers of dull green here and there assumed a pinky tinge in the sunlight, she took hold of the fig with her claws, then ripped it open with her beak. But when she had raked it she ate but little, and let all the rest fall upon the floor. Still grave and impassible, the Cardinal looked at her and waited. Quite three minutes went by, and then feeling reassured, he began to scratch the bird's poll, whilst she, taking pleasure in the caress, turned her neck and fixed her bright ruby eye upon her master. But all at once she sank back without even a flap of the wings, and fell like a bullet. She was dead, killed as by a thunderbolt.

Boccanera made but a gesture, raising both hands to heaven as if in horror at what he now knew. Great God! such a terrible crime, and such a fearful mistake, such an abominable trick of Destiny! No cry of grief came from him, but the gloom upon his face grew black and fierce. Yet there was a cry, a piercing cry from Benedetta, who like Pierre and Don Vigilio had watched the Cardinal with an astonishment which had changed into terror: 'Poison! poison! Ah! Dario, my heart, my soul!'

But the Cardinal violently caught his niece by the wrist, whilst darting a suspicious glance at the two petty priests, the secretary and the foreigner, who were present: 'Be quiet, be quiet!' said he.

She shook herself free, rebelling, frantic with rage and hatred: 'Why should I be quiet!' she cried. 'It is Prada's work, I shall denounce him, he shall die as well! I tell you it is Prada, I know it, for yesterday Abbé Froment came back with him from Frascati in his carriage with that priest Santobono and that basket of figs! Yes, yes, I have witnesses, it is Prada, Prada!'

'No, no, you are mad, be quiet!' said the Cardinal, who had again taken hold of the young woman's hands and sought to master her with all his sovereign authority. He, who knew the influence which Cardinal Sanguinetti exercised over Santobono's excitable mind, had just understood the whole affair; no direct complicity but covert propulsion, the animal excited and then let loose upon the troublesome rival at the moment when the pontifical throne seemed likely to be vacant. The probability, the certainty of all this flashed upon Boccanera who, though some points remained obscure, did not seek to penetrate them. It was not necessary indeed that he should know every particular: the thing was as he said, since it was bound to be so. 'No, no, it was not Prada,' he exclaimed, addressing Benedetta. 'That man can bear me no personal grudge, and I alone was aimed at, it was to me that those figs were given. Come, think it out! Only an unforeseen indisposition prevented me from eating the greater part of the fruit, for it is known that I am very fond of figs, and while my poor Dario was tasting them, I jested and told him to leave the finer ones for me to-morrow. Yes, the abominable blow was meant for me, and it is on him that it has fallen by the most atrocious of chances, the most monstrous of the follies of fate. Ah! Lord God, Lord God, have you then forsaken us!'

Tears came into the old man's eyes, whilst she still quivered and seemed unconvinced: 'But you have no enemies, uncle,' she said. 'Why should that Santobono try to take your life?'

For a moment he found no fitting reply. With supreme grandeur he had already resolved to keep the truth secret. Then a recollection came to him, and he resigned himself to the telling of a lie: 'Santobono's mind has always been somewhat unhinged,' said he, 'and I know that he has hated me ever since I refused to help him to get a brother of his, one of our former gardeners, out of prison. Deadly spite often has no more serious cause. He must have thought that he had reason to be revenged on me.'

Thereupon Benedetta, exhausted, unable to argue any further, sank upon a chair with a despairing gesture: 'Ah! God, God! I no longer know—and what matters it now that my Dario is in such danger? There's only one thing to be done, he must be saved. How long they are over what they are doing in that room—why does not Victorine come for us!

The silence again fell, full of terror. Without speaking the Cardinal took the basket of figs from the table and carried it to a cupboard in which he locked it. Then he put the key in his pocket. No doubt, when night had fallen, he himself would throw the proofs of the crime into the Tiber. However, on coming back from the cupboard he noticed the two priests, who naturally had watched him; and with mingled grandeur and simplicity he said to them: 'Gentlemen, I need not ask you to be discreet. There are scandals which we must spare the Church, which is not, cannot be guilty. To deliver one of ourselves, even when he is a criminal, to the civil tribunals, often means a blow for the whole Church, for men of evil mind may lay hold of the affair and seek to impute the responsibility of the crime even to the Church itself. We therefore have but to commit the murderer to the hands of God, who will know more surely how to punish him. Ah! for my part, whether I be struck in my own person or whether the blow be directed against my family, my dearest affections, I declare in the name of the Christ who died upon the cross, that I feel neither anger, nor desire for vengeance, that I efface the murderer's name from my memory and bury his abominable act in the eternal silence of the grave.'

Tall as he was, he seemed of yet loftier stature whilst with hand upraised he took that oath to leave his enemies to the justice of God alone; for he did not refer merely to Santobono, but to Cardinal Sanguinetti, whose evil influence he had divined. And amidst all the heroism of his pride, he was rent by tragic dolour at thought of the dark battle which was waged around the tiara, all the evil hatred and voracious appetite which stirred in the depths of the gloom. Then, as Pierre and Don Vigilio bowed to him as a sign that they would preserve silence, he almost choked with invincible emotion, a sob of loving grief which he strove to keep down rising to his throat, whilst he stammered: 'Ah! my poor

child, my poor child, the only scion of our race, the only
love and hope of my heart! Ah! to die, to die like this!'

But Benedetta, again all violence, sprang up: 'Die!
Who, Dario? I won't have it! We'll nurse him, we'll go
back to him. We will take him in our arms and save him.
Come, uncle, come at once! I won't, I won't, I won't have
him die!'

She was going towards the door, and nothing would have
prevented her from re-entering the bed-room, when, as it
happened, Victorine appeared with a wild look on her face, for,
despite her wonted serenity, all her courage was now exhausted.
'The doctor begs Madame and his Eminence to come at once,
at once,' said she.

Stupefied by all these things, Pierre did not follow the
others, but lingered for a moment in the sunlit dining-room
with Don Vigilio. What! poison? Poison as in the time of
the Borgias, elegantly hidden away, served up with luscious
fruit by a crafty traitor, whom one dared not even denounce!
And he recalled the conversation on his way back from
Frascati, and his Parisian scepticism with respect to those
legendary drugs, which to his mind had no place save in the
fifth acts of melodramas. Yet those abominable stories were
true, those tales of poisoned knives and flowers, of prelates
and even dilatory popes being suppressed by a drop or a grain
of something administered to them in their morning chocolate.
That passionate tragical Santobono was really a poisoner,
Pierre could no longer doubt it, for a lurid light now illumined
the whole of the previous day: there were the words of
ambition and menace which had been spoken by Cardinal
Sanguinetti, the eagerness to act in presence of the probable
death of the reigning Pope, the suggestion of a crime for the
sake of the Church's salvation, then that priest with his little
basket of figs encountered on the road, then that basket
carried for hours so carefully, so devoutly, on the priest's
knees, that basket which now haunted Pierre like a nightmare, and whose colour, and odour, and shape he would ever
recall with a shudder. Aye, poison, poison, there was truth
in it; it existed and still circulated in the depths of the black
world, amidst all the ravenous, rival longings for conquest and
sovereignty.

And all at once the figure of Prada likewise arose in
Pierre's mind. A little while previously, when Benedetta had
so violently accused the Count, he, Pierre, had stepped forward

to defend him and cry aloud what he knew, whence the poison
had come, and what hand had offered it. But a sudden
thought had made him shiver: though Prada had not devised
the crime, he had allowed it to be perpetrated. Another
memory darted keen like steel through the young priest's
mind—that of the little black hen lying lifeless beside the
shed, amidst the dismal surroundings of the *osteria*, with a
tiny streamlet of violet blood trickling from her beak. And
here again, Tata, the parrot, lay still soft and warm at the
foot of her stand, with her beak stained by oozing blood,
Why had Prada told that lie about a battle between two fowls ?
All the dim intricacy of passion and contention bewildered
Pierre, he could not thread his way through it ; nor was he
better able to follow the frightful combat which must have
been waged in that man's mind during the night of the ball.
At the same time he could not again picture him by his side
during their nocturnal walk towards the Boccanera mansion
without shuddering, dimly divining what a frightful decision
had been taken before that mansion's door. Moreover, whatever the obscurities, whether Prada had expected that the
Cardinal alone would be killed, or had hoped that some chance
stroke of fate might avenge him on others, the terrible fact
remained—he had known, he had been able to stay Destiny
on the march, but had allowed it to go onward and blindly
accomplish its work of death.

Turning his head Pierre perceived Don Vigilio still seated
on the corner chair whence he had not stirred, and looking so
pale and haggard that perhaps he also had swallowed some of
the poison. ' Do you feel unwell ? ' the young priest asked.

At first the secretary could not reply, for terror had gripped
him at the throat. Then in a low voice he said : ' No, no, I
didn't eat any. Ah, Heaven, when I think that I so much
wanted to taste them, and that merely deference kept me back
on seeing that his Eminence did not take any ! ' Don Vigilio's
whole body shivered at the thought that his humility alone
had saved him ; and on his face and his hands there remained
the icy chill of death which had fallen so near and grazed him
as it passed.

Then, twice he heaved a sigh, and with a gesture of affright
sought to brush the horrid thing away while murmuring :
' Ah ! Paparelli, Paparelli ! '

Pierre, deeply stirred, and knowing what he thought of the
train-bearer, tried to extract some information from him :

'What do you mean?' he asked. 'Do you accuse him too? Do you think they urged him on, and that it was they at bottom?'

The word Jesuits was not even spoken, but a big black shadow passed athwart the gay sunlight of the dining-room, and for a moment seemed to fill it with darkness. 'They! ah, yes!' exclaimed Don Vigilio, 'they are everywhere; it is always they! As soon as one weeps, as soon as one dies, they are mixed up in it. And this was intended for me too; I am quite surprised that I haven't been carried off.' Then again he raised a dull moan of fear, hatred and anger: 'Ah! Paparelli, Paparelli!' And he refused to reply any further, but darted scared glances at the walls as if from one or another of them he expected to see the train-bearer emerge, with his wrinkled flabby face like that of an old maid, his furtive mouse-like trot, and his mysterious, invading hands which had gone expressly to bring the forgotten figs from the pantry and deposit them on the table.

At last the two priests decided to return to the bed-room, where perhaps they might be required; and Pierre on entering was overcome by the heartrending scene which the chamber now presented. Doctor Giordano, suspecting poison, had for half an hour been trying the usual remedies, an emetic and then magnesia. Just then too he had made Victorine whip some whites of eggs in water. But the disorder was progressing with such lightning-like rapidity that all succour was becoming futile. Undressed and lying on his back, his bust propped up by pillows and his arms lying outstretched over the sheets, Dario looked quite frightful in the sort of painful intoxication which characterised that redoubtable and mysterious disorder to which already Monsignor Gallo and others had succumbed. The young man seemed to be stricken with a sort of dizzy stupor, his eyes receded farther and farther into the depths of their dark sockets, whilst his whole face became withered, aged as it were, and covered with an earthy pallor. A moment previously he had closed his eyes, and the only sign that he still lived was the heaving of his chest induced by painful respiration. And leaning over his poor dying face stood Benedetta, sharing his sufferings, and mastered by such impotent grief that she also was unrecognisable, so white, so distracted by anguish, that it seemed as if death were gradually taking her at the same time as it was taking him.

In the recess by the window whither Cardinal Boccanera

had led Doctor Giordano, a few words were exchanged in low tones. 'He is lost, is he not?'

The doctor made the despairing gesture of one who is vanquished: 'Alas! yes. I must warn your Eminence that in an hour all will be over.'

A short interval of silence followed. 'And the same malady as Gallo, is it not?' asked the Cardinal; and as the doctor trembling and averting his eyes did not answer, he added: 'At all events of an infectious fever!'

Giordano well understood what the Cardinal thus asked of him: silence, the crime for ever hidden away for sake of the good renown of his mother, the Church. And there could be no loftier, no more tragical grandeur than that of this old man of seventy, still so erect and sovereign, who would neither suffer a slur to be cast upon his spiritual family, nor consent to his human family being dragged into the inevitable mire of a sensational murder trial. No, no, there must be none of that, there must be silence, the eternal silence in which all becomes forgotten.

At last the doctor bowed with his gentle air of discretion. 'Evidently, of an infectious fever as your Eminence so well says,' he replied.

Two big tears then again appeared in Boccanera's eyes. Now that he had screened the Deity from attack in the person of the Church, his heart as a man again bled. He begged the doctor to make a supreme effort, to attempt the impossible; but, pointing to the dying man with trembling hands, Giordano shook his head. For his own father, his own mother he could have done nothing. Death was there. So why weary, why torture a dying man, whose sufferings he would only have increased? And then, as the Cardinal, finding the end so near at hand, thought of his sister Serafina, and lamented that she would not be able to kiss her nephew for the last time if she lingered at the Vatican, the doctor offered to fetch her in his carriage which was waiting below. It would not take him more than twenty minutes said he, and he would be back in time for the end, should he then be needed.

Left to himself in the window recess the Cardinal remained there motionless for another moment. With eyes blurred by tears, he gazed towards Heaven. And his quivering arms were suddenly raised in a gesture of ardent entreaty. O God, since the science of man was so limited and vain, since that doctor had gone off happy to escape the embarrassment of his impotence, O God, why not a miracle which should proclaim the splendour of Thy Almighty Power! A miracle, a miracle! that was what the Cardinal asked from the depths of his believing soul, with the insistance, the imperious entreaty of a Prince of the Earth, who deemed that he had rendered considerable services to Heaven by dedicating his whole life to the Church. And he asked for that miracle in order that his race might be perpetuated, in order that its last male scion might not thus miserably perish, but be able to marry that fondly-loved cousin, who now stood there all woe and tears. A miracle, a miracle for the sake of those two dear children! A miracle which would endow the family with fresh life: a miracle which would eternise the glorious name of Boccanera by enabling an innumerable posterity of valiant ones and faithful ones to spring from that young couple!

When the Cardinal returned to the centre of the room he seemed transfigured. Faith had dried his eyes, his soul had become strong and submissive, exempt from all human weakness. He had placed himself in the hands of God, and had resolved that he himself would administer extreme unction to Dario. With a gesture he summoned Don Vigilio and led him into the little room which served as a chapel, and the key of which he always carried. A cupboard had been contrived behind the altar of painted wood, and the Cardinal went to it to take both stole and surplice. The coffer containing the Holy Oils was likewise there, a very ancient silver coffer bearing the Boccanera arms. And on Don Vigilio following the Cardinal back into the bed-room they in turn pronounced the Latin words:

'*Pax huic domui.*'

'*Et omnibus habitantibus in ea.*' [1]

Death was coming so fast and threatening, that all the usual preparations were perforce dispensed with. Neither the two lighted tapers, nor the little table covered with white cloth had been provided. And, in the same way, Don Vigilio, the assistant, having failed to bring the Holy Water basin and sprinkler, the Cardinal, as officiating priest, could merely make the gesture of blessing the room and the dying man, whilst pronouncing the words of the ritual: '*Asperges me, Domine, hyssopo, et mundabor; lavabis me, et super nivem dealbabor.*' [2]

[1] 'Peace unto this house and unto all who dwell in it.'—*Trans.*

[2] Sprinkle me, Lord, with hyssop, and purify me; wash me, and make me whiter than snow.'—*Trans.*

Benedetta, on seeing the Cardinal appear carrying the
Holy Oils, had with a long quiver fallen on her knees at the
foot of the bed, whilst, somewhat farther away, Pierre and
Victorine likewise knelt, overcome by the dolorous grandeur of
the scene. And the dilated eyes of the Contessina, whose face
was pale as snow, never quitted her Dario, whom she no
longer recognised, so earthy was his face, its skin tanned and
wrinkled like that of an old man. And it was not for their
marriage which he so much desired that their uncle, the all-
powerful Prince of the Church, was bringing the Sacrament,
but for the supreme rupture, the end of all pride, Death which
finishes off the haughtiest races, and sweeps them away, even
as the wind sweeps the dust of the roads.

It was needful that there should be no delay, so the
Cardinal promptly repeated the *Credo* in an undertone, ' *Credo
in unum Deum*——'

' *Amen*,' responded Don Vigilio, who, after the prayers of
the ritual, stammered the Litanies in order that Heaven
might take pity on the wretched man who was about to
appear before God, if God by a prodigy did not spare him.

Then, without taking time to wash his fingers, the Cardinal opened the case containing the Holy Oils, and limiting
himself to one anointment, as is permissible in pressing
cases, he deposited a single drop of the oil on Dario's parched
mouth which was already withered by death. And in doing
so he repeated the words of the formula, his heart all aglow
with faith as he asked that the Divine mercy might efface
each and every sin that the young man had committed by
either of his five senses, those five portals by which everlasting
temptation assails the soul. And the Cardinal's fervour was
also instinct with the hope that if God had smitten the poor
sufferer for his offences, perhaps He would make His indulgence entire and even restore him to life as soon as He
should have forgiven his sins. Life, O Lord, life in order that
the ancient line of the Boccaneras might yet multiply and
continue to serve Thee in battle and at the altar until the
end of time !

For a moment the Cardinal remained with quivering
hands, gazing at the mute face, the closed eyes of the dying
man, and waiting for the miracle. But no sign appeared, not
the faintest glimmer brightened that haggard countenance,
nor did a sigh of relief come from the withered lips as Don
Vigilio wiped them with a little cotton wool. And the last

prayer was said, and whilst the frightful silence fell once more
the Cardinal, followed by his assistant, returned to the chapel.
There they both knelt, the Cardinal plunging into ardent
prayer upon the bare tiles. With his eyes raised to the brass
crucifix upon the altar he saw nothing, heard nothing, but
gave himself wholly to his entreaties, supplicating God to
take him in place of his nephew, if a sacrifice were necessary,
and yet clinging to the hope that so long as Dario retained a
breath of life and he himself thus remained on his knees
addressing the Deity, he might succeed in pacifying the
wrath of Heaven. He was both so humble and so great.
Would not accord surely be established between God and
a Boccanera? The old palace might have fallen to the
ground, he himself would not even have felt the toppling of
its beams.

In the bed-room, however, nothing had yet stirred beneath
the weight of tragic majesty which the ceremony had left
there. It was only now that Dario raised his eyelids, and
when on looking at his hands he saw them so aged and wasted
the depths of his eyes kindled with an expression of immense
regretfulness that life should be departing. Doubtless it was
at this moment of lucidity amidst the kind of intoxication
with which the poison overwhelmed him, that he for the first
time realised his perilous condition. Ah! to die, amidst such
pain, such physical degradation, what a revolting horror for
that frivolous and egotistical man, that lover of beauty, joy,
and light, who knew not how to suffer! In him ferocious
fate chastised racial degeneracy with too heavy a hand. He
became horrified with himself, seized with childish despair
and terror, which lent him strength enough to sit up and gaze
wildly about the room, in order to see if everyone had not
abandoned him. And when his eyes lighted on Benedetta
still kneeling at the foot of the bed, a supreme impulse carried
him towards her, he stretched forth both arms as passionately
as his strength allowed and stammered her name: 'O Benedetta, Benedetta!'

She, motionless in the stupor of her anxiety, had not
taken her eyes from his face. The horrible disorder which
was carrying off her lover seemed also to possess and annihilate her more and more, even as he himself grew weaker and
weaker. Her features were assuming an immaterial whiteness; and through the void of her clear eyeballs one began to
espy her soul. However, when she perceived him thus resus-

citating and calling her with arms outstretched, she in her turn arose and standing beside the bed made answer : ' I am coming, my Dario, here I am.'

And then Pierre and Victorine, still on their knees, beheld a sublime deed of such extraordinary grandeur that they remained rooted to the floor, spell-bound as in the presence of some supra-terrestrial spectacle in which human beings may not intervene. Benedetta herself spoke and acted like one freed from all social and conventional ties, already beyond life, only seeing and addressing beings and things from a great distance, from the depths of the unknown in which she was about to disappear.

' Ah! my Dario, so an attempt has been made to part us ! It was in order that I might never belong to you—that we might never be happy, that your death was resolved upon, and it was known that with your life my own must cease ! And it is that man who is killing you ! Yes, he is your murderer, even if the actual blow has been dealt by another. He is the first cause—he who stole me from you when I was about to become yours, he who ravaged our lives, and who breathed around us the hateful poison which is killing us. Ah! how I hate him, how I hate him ; how I should like to crush him with my hate before I die with you ! '

She did not raise her voice, but spoke those terrible words in a deep murmur, simply and passionately. Prada was not even named, and she scarcely turned towards Pierre—who knelt, paralysed, behind her—to add with a commanding air : ' You who will see his father, I charge you to tell him that I cursed his son ! That kind-hearted hero loved me well—I love him even now, and the words you will carry to him from me will rend his heart. But I desire that he should know— he must know, for the sake of truth and justice.'

Distracted by terror, sobbing amidst a last convulsion, Dario again stretched forth his arms, feeling that she was no longer looking at him, that her clear eyes were no longer fixed upon his own : ' Benedetta, Benedetta ! '

' I am coming, I am coming, my Dario—I am here ! ' she responded, drawing yet nearer to the bedside and almost touching him. ' Ah ! ' she went on, ' that vow which I made to the Madonna to belong to none, not even you, until God should allow it by the blessing of one of his priests ! Ah ! I set a noble, a divine pride in remaining immaculate for him who should be the one master of my soul and body. And

that chastity which I was so proud of, I defended it against
the other as one defends oneself against a wolf, and I defended
it against you with tears for fear of sacrilege. And if you
only knew what terrible struggles I was forced to wage with
myself, for I loved you and longed to be yours, like a woman
who accepts the whole of love, the love that makes wife and
mother! Ah! my vow to the Madonna—with what difficulty
did I keep it when the old blood of our race arose in me like a
tempest ; and now what a disaster!' She drew yet nearer,
and her low voice became more ardent : ' You remember that
evening when you came back with a knife-thrust in your
shoulder. I thought you dead, and cried aloud with rage at
the idea of losing you like that. I insulted the Madonna and
regretted that I had not damned myself with you that we
might die together, so tightly clasped that we must needs be
buried together also. And to think that such a terrible warning was of no avail ! I was blind and foolish ; and now you
are again stricken, again being taken from my love. . . . Ah!
my wretched pride, my idiotic dream !'

That which now rang out in her stifled voice was the
anger of the practical woman that she had ever been, all
superstition notwithstanding. Could the Madonna, who was
so maternal, desire the woe of lovers ? No, assuredly not.
Nor did the angels make the mere absence of a priest a cause
for weeping over the transports of true and mutual love. Was
not such love holy in itself, and did not the angels rather
smile upon it and burst into gladsome song ! And ah ! how
one cheated oneself by not loving to heart's content under the
sun, when the blood of life coursed through one's veins !

' Benedetta ! Benedetta !' repeated the dying man, full of
child-like terror at thus going off all alone into the depths of
the black and everlasting night.

' Here I am, my Dario, I am coming !'

Then, as she fancied that the servant, albeit motionless,
had stirred, as if to rise and interfere, she added : ' Leave me,
leave me, Victorine, nothing in the world can henceforth prevent it. A moment ago, when I was on my knees, something
roused me and urged me on. I know whither I am going.
And besides, did I not swear on the night of the knife-thrust ?
Did I not promise to belong to him alone, even in the earth if
it were necessary ? I must embrace him, and he will carry
me away ! We shall be dead, and we shall be wedded in
spite of all, and for ever and for ever !'

She stepped back to the dying man, and touched him :
' Here I am, my Dario, here I am ! '

Then came the apogee. Amidst growing exaltation, buoyed
up by a blaze of love, careless of glances, candid like a lily,
she divested herself of her garments and stood forth so white,
that neither marble statue, nor dove, nor snow itself was ever
whiter. ' Here I am, my Dario, here I am ! '

Recoiling almost to the ground as at sight of an apparition,
the glorious flash of a holy vision, Pierre and Victorine gazed
at her with dazzled eyes. The servant had not stirred to prevent this extraordinary action, seized as she was with that
shrinking reverential terror which comes upon one in presence
of the wild, mad deeds of faith and passion. And the priest
whose limbs were paralysed felt that something so sublime
was passing that he could only quiver in distraction. And no
thought of impurity came to him on beholding that lily, snowy
whiteness. All candour and all nobility as she was, that
virgin shocked him no more than some sculptured masterpiece
of genius.

' Here I am, my Dario, here I am.'

She had lain herself down beside the spouse whom she had
chosen, she had clasped the dying man whose arms only had
enough strength left to fold themselves around her. Death
was stealing him from her, but she would go with him ; and
again she murmured : ' My Dario, here I am.'

And at that moment, against the wall at the head of the
bed, Pierre perceived the escutcheon of the Boccaneras, embroidered in gold and coloured silks on a groundwork of violet
velvet. There was the winged dragon belching flames, there
was the fierce and glowing motto ' Bocca nera, Alma rossa,'
black mouth, red soul, the mouth darkened by a roar, the soul
flaming like a brazier of faith and love. And behold ! all that
old race of passion and violence with its tragic legends had
reappeared, its blood bubbling up afresh to urge that last and
adorable daughter of the line to those terrifying and prodigious
nuptials in death. And to Pierre that escutcheon recalled
another memory, that of the portrait of Cassia Boccanera the
amorosa and avengeress who had flung herself into the Tiber
with her brother Ercole and the corpse of her lover Flavio.
Was there not here even with Benedetta the same despairing
clasp seeking to vanquish death, the same savagery in hurling
oneself into the abyss with the corpse of the one's only love ?

Benedetta and Cassia were as sisters, Cassia, who lived anew in the old painting in the *salon* overhead, Benedetta who was here dying of her lover's death, as though she were but the other's spirit. Both had the same delicate childish features, the same mouth of passion, the same large dreamy eyes set in the same round, practical and stubborn head.

'My Dario, here I am!'

For a second, which seemed an eternity, they clasped one another, she neither repelled nor terrified by the disorder which made him so unrecognisable, but displaying a delirious passion, a holy frenzy as if to pass beyond life, to penetrate with him into the black Unknown. And beneath the shock of the felicity at last offered to him he expired, with his arms yet convulsively wound around her as though indeed to carry her off. Then, whether from grief or from bliss amidst that embrace of death, there came such a rush of blood to her heart that the organ burst: she died on her lover's neck, both tightly and for ever clasped in one another's arms.

There was a faint sigh, Victorine understood and drew near, while Pierre, also erect, remained quivering with the tearful admiration of one who has beheld the sublime.

'Look, look!' whispered the servant, 'she no longer moves, she no longer breathes. Ah! my poor child, my poor child, she is dead!'

Then the priest murmured: 'Oh! God, how beautiful they are.'

It was true, never had loftier and more resplendent beauty appeared on the faces of the dead. Dario's countenance, so lately aged and earthern, had assumed the pallor and nobility of marble, its features lengthened and simplified as by a transport of ineffable joy. Benedetta remained very grave, her lips curved by ardent determination, whilst her whole face was expressive of dolorous yet infinite beatitude in a setting of infinite whiteness. Their hair mingled, and their eyes, which had remained open, continued gazing as into one another's souls with eternal, caressing sweetness. They were for ever linked, soaring into immortality amidst the enchantment of their union, vanquishers of death, radiant with the rapturous beauty of love, the conqueror, the immortal.

But Victorine's sobs at last burst forth, mingled with such lamentations that great confusion followed. Pierre, now quite beside himself, in some measure failed to understand how it was that the room suddenly became invaded by terrified people

The Cardinal and Don Vigilio, however, must have hastened in from the chapel; and at the same moment, no doubt, Doctor Giordano must have returned with Donna Serafina, for both were now there, she stupefied by the blows which had thus fallen on the house in her absence, whilst he, the doctor, displayed the perturbation and astonishment which comes upon the oldest practitioners when facts seem to give the lie to their experience. However, he sought an explanation of Benedetta's death, and hesitatingly ascribed it to aneurism, or possibly embolism.

Thereupon Victorine, like a servant whose grief makes her the equal of her employers, boldly interrupted him : ' Ah ! sir,' said she, ' they loved each other too fondly ; did not that suffice for them to die together ? '

Meantime Donna Serafina, after kissing the poor children on the brow, desired to close their eyes, but she could not succeed in doing so, for the lids lifted directly she removed her finger and once more the eyes began to smile at one another, to exchange in all fixity their loving and eternal glance. And then as she spoke of parting the bodies, Victorine again protested : ' Oh ! madame, oh ! madame,' she said, ' you would have to break their arms. Cannot you see that their fingers are almost dug into one another's shoulders ? No, they can never be parted ! '

Thereupon Cardinal Boccanera intervened. God had not granted the miracle ; and he, His minister, was livid, tearless, and full of icy despair. But he waved his arm with a sovereign gesture of absolution and sanctification, as if, Prince of the Church that he was, disposing of the will of Heaven, he consented that the lovers should appear in that embrace before the supreme tribunal. In presence of such wondrous love, indeed, profoundly stirred by the sufferings of their lives and the beauty of their death, he showed a broad and lofty contempt for mundane proprieties. ' Leave them, leave me, my sister,' said he, ' do not disturb their slumber. Let their eyes remain open since they desire to gaze on one another till the end of time without ever wearying. And let them sleep in one another's arms since in their lives they did not sin, and only locked themselves in that embrace in order that they might be laid together in the ground.'

And then, again becoming a Roman Prince whose proud blood was yet hot with old time deeds of battle and passion, he added : ' Two Boccaneras may well sleep like that ; all Rome will admire them and weep for them. Leave them, leave them together, my sister. God knows them and awaits them ! '

All knelt, and the Cardinal himself repeated the prayers for the dead. Night was coming, increasing gloom stole into the chamber, where two burning tapers soon shone out like stars.

And then, without knowing how, Pierre again found himself in the little deserted garden on the bank of the Tiber. Suffocating with fatigue and grief, he must have come thither for fresh air. Darkness shrouded the charming nook where the streamlet of water falling from the tragic mask into the ancient sarcophagus ever sang its shrill and flute-like song ; and the laurel bush which shaded it, and the bitter box-plants and the orange-trees skirting the paths now formed but vague masses under the blue-black sky. Ah ! how gay and sweet had that melancholy garden been in the morning, and what a desolate echo it retained of Benedetta's winsome laughter, all that fine delight in coming happiness which now lay prone upstairs, steeped in the nothingness of things and beings ! So dolorous was the pang which came to Pierre's heart that he burst into sobs, seated on the same broken column where she had sat, and encompassed by the same atmosphere that she had breathed, in which still lingered the perfume of her presence.

But all at once a distant clock struck six, and the young priest started on remembering that he was to be received by the Pope that very evening at nine. Yet three more hours ! He had not thought of that interview during the terrifying catastrophe, and it seemed to him now as if months and months had gone by, as if the appointment were some very old one which a man is only able to keep after years of absence, when he has grown aged and had his heart and brain modified by innumerable experiences. However, he made an effort and rose to his feet. In three hours' time he would go to the Vatican and at last he would see the Pope.

XIV

THAT evening, when Pierre emerged from the Borgo in front of the Vatican, a sonorous stroke rang out from the clock amidst the deep silence of the dark and sleepy district. It was only half-past eight, and being in advance the young priest resolved to wait some twenty minutes in order to reach

the doors of the papal apartments precisely at nine, the hour
fixed for his audience.

This respite brought him some relief amidst the infinite
emotion and grief which gripped his heart. That tragic
afternoon which he had spent in the chamber of death, where
Dario and Benedetta now slept the eternal sleep in one
another's arms, had left him very weary. He was haunted by
a wild, dolorous vision of the two lovers, and involuntary sighs
came from his lips whilst tears continually moistened his
eyes. He had been altogether unable to eat that evening.
Ah! how he would have liked to hide himself and weep at
his ease! His heart melted at each fresh thought. The
pitiful death of the lovers intensified the grievous feeling with
which his book was instinct, and impelled him to yet greater
compassion, a perfect anguish of charity for all who suffered
in the world. And he was so distracted by the thought of
the many physical and moral sores of Paris and of Rome,
where he had beheld so much unjust and abominable suffering, that at each step he took he feared lest he should burst
into sobs with arms upstretched towards the blackness of
heaven.

In the hope of somewhat calming himself he began to
walk slowly across the Piazza of St. Peter's, now all darkness
and solitude. On arriving he had fancied that he was losing
himself in a murky sea, but by degrees his eyes grew accustomed
to the dimness. The vast expanse was only lighted by the
four candelabra at the corners of the obelisk and by infrequent
lamps skirting the buildings which run on either hand towards
the basilica. Under the colonnade, too, other lamps threw
yellow gleams across the forest of pillars, showing up their stone
trunks in fantastic fashion; while on the piazza only the
pale ghostly obelisk was at all distinctly visible. Pierre could
scarcely perceive the dim, silent façade of St. Peter's; whilst
of the dome he merely divined a gigantic bluey roundness
faintly shadowed against the sky. In the obscurity he at first
heard the plashing of the fountains without being at all able
to see them, but on approaching he at last distinguished the
slender phantoms of the ever-rising jets which fell again in
spray. And above the vast square stretched the vast and
moonless sky of a deep velvety blue, where the stars were
large and radiant like carbuncles; Charles's Wain, with golden
wheels and golden shaft tilted back as it were, over the roof
of the Vatican, and Orion, bedizened with the three bright

stars of his belt, showing magnificently above Rome, in the
direction of the Via Giulia.

At last Pierre raised his eyes to the Vatican, but facing the
piazza there was here merely a confused jumble of walls, amidst
which only two gleams of light appeared on the floor of the
papal apartments. The Court of San Damaso was, however,
lighted, for the conservatory-like glasswork of two of its sides
sparkled as with the reflection of gas lamps which could not
be seen. For a time there was not a sound or sign of movement, but at last two persons crossed the expanse of the piazza,
and then came a third who in his turn disappeared, nothing
remaining but a rhythmical far-away echo of steps. The spot
was indeed a perfect desert, there were neither promenaders
nor passers-by, nor was there even the shadow of a prowler in
the pillared forest of the colonnade, which was as empty as
the wild primeval forests of the world's infancy. And what a
solemn desert it was, full of the silence of haughty desolation.
Never had so vast and black a presentment of slumber, so
instinct with the sovereign nobility of death, appeared to Pierre.

At ten minutes to nine he at last made up his mind and
went towards the bronze portal. Only one of the folding
doors was now open at the end of the right-hand porticus,
where the increasing density of the gloom steeped everything
in night. Pierre remembered the instructions which Monsignor
Nani had given him; at each door that he reached he was
to ask for Signor Squadra without adding a word, and thereupon each door would open and he would have nothing to do
but to let himself be guided on. No one but the prelate now
knew that he was there, since Benedetta, the only being to
whom he had confided the secret, was dead. When he had
crossed the threshold of the bronze doors and found himself
in presence of the motionless sleeping Swiss Guard, who
was on duty there, he simply spoke the words agreed upon:
' Signor Squadra.' And as the guard did not stir, did not
seek to bar his way, he passed on, turning into the vestibule
of the Scala Pia, the stone stairway which ascends to the
Court of San Damaso. And not a soul was to be seen: there
was but the faint sound of his own light footsteps and the
sleepy glow of the gas jets whose light was softly whitened
by globes of frosted glass. Up above, on reaching the courtyard, he found it a solitude, whose slumber seemed sepulchral amidst the mournful gleams of the gas lamps which
cast a pallid reflection on the lofty glasswork of the façades.

And feeling somewhat nervous, affected by the quiver which pervaded all that void and silence, Pierre hastened on, turning to the right, towards the low flight of steps which leads to the staircase of the Pope's private apartments.

Here stood a superb gendarme in full uniform. 'Signor Squadra,' said Pierre, and without a word the gendarme pointed to the stairs.

The young man went up. It was a broad stairway, with low steps, balustrade of white marble, and walls covered with yellowish stucco. The gas, burning in globes of ground glass, seemed to have been already turned down in a spirit of prudent economy. And in the glimmering light nothing could have been more mournfully solemn than that cold and pallid staircase. On each landing there was a Swiss Guard, halberd in hand, and in the heavy slumber spreading through the palace one only heard the regular monotonous footsteps of these men, ever marching up and down, in order no doubt that they might not succumb to the benumbing influence of their surroundings.

Amidst the invading dimness and the quivering silence the ascent of the stairs seemed interminable to Pierre, who by the time he reached the second-floor landing imagined that he had been climbing for ages. There, outside the glass door of the Sala Clementina, only the right-hand half of which was open, a last Swiss Guard stood watching.

'Signor Squadra,' Pierre said again, and the guard drew back to let him pass.

The Sala Clementina, spacious enough by daylight, seemed immense at that nocturnal hour, in the twilight glimmer of its lamps. All the opulent decorative work, sculpture, painting and gilding became blended, the walls assuming a tawny vagueness amidst which appeared bright patches like the sparkle of precious stones. There was not an article of furniture, nothing but the endless pavement stretching away into the semi-darkness. At last, however, near a door at the far end Pierre espied some men dozing on a bench. They were three Swiss Guards. 'Signor Squadra,' he said to them.

One of the Guards thereupon slowly rose and left the hall, and Pierre understood that he was to wait. He did not dare to move, disturbed as he was by the sound of his own footsteps on the paved floor, so he contented himself with gazing around and picturing the crowds which at times peopled that vast apartment, the first of the many papal ante-chambers.

But before long the Guard returned, and behind him, on the threshold of the adjoining room, appeared a man of forty or thereabouts, who was clad in black from head to foot and suggested a cross between a butler and a beadle. He had a good-looking clean-shaven face, with somewhat pronounced nose and large clear fixed eyes. 'Signor Squadra,' said Pierre for the last time.

The man bowed as if to say that he was Signor Squadra, and then, with a fresh reverence, he invited the priest to follow him. Thereupon at a leisurely step, one behind the other, they began to thread the interminable suite of waiting rooms. Pierre, who was acquainted with the ceremonial of which he had often spoken with Narcisse, recognised the different apartments as he passed through them, recalling their names and purpose, and peopling them in imagination with the various officials of the papal retinue who have the right to occupy them. These according to their rank cannot go beyond certain doors, so that the persons who are to have audience of the Pope are passed on from the servants to the Noble Guards, from the Noble Guards to the honorary *camerieri*, and from the latter to the *camerieri segreti*, until they at last reach the presence of the Holy Father. At eight o'clock, however, the ante-rooms empty and become both deserted and dim, only a few lamps being left alight upon the pier-tables standing here and there against the walls.

And first Pierre came to the ante-room of the *bussolanti*, mere ushers clad in red velvet broidered with the papal arms, who conduct visitors to the door of the ante-room of honour. At that late hour only one of them was left there, seated on a bench in such a dark corner that his purple tunic looked quite black. Then the Hall of the Gendarmes was crossed, where according to the regulations the secretaries of cardinals and other high personages await their masters' return; and this was now completely empty, void both of the handsome blue uniforms with white shoulder belts and the cassocks of fine black cloth which mingled in it during the brilliant reception hours. Empty also was the following room, a smaller one reserved to the Palatine Guards, who are recruited among the Roman middle class and wear black tunics with gold epaulets and shakoes surmounted by red plumes. Then Pierre and his guide turned into another series of apartments, and again was the first one empty. This was the Hall of the Arras, a superb waiting-room with lofty painted ceiling and admirable Gobelins tapestry designed by Audran and representing the miracles of Jesus. And empty also was the antechamber of the Noble Guards which followed, with its wooden stools, its pier-table on the right hand surmounted by a large crucifix standing between two lamps, and its large door opening at the far end into another but smaller room, a sort of alcove indeed, where there is an altar at which the Holy Father says mass by himself whilst those privileged to be present remain kneeling on the marble slabs of the outer apartment which is resplendent with the dazzling uniforms of the Guards. And empty likewise was the ensuing ante-room of honour, otherwise the grand throne-room, where the Pope receives two or three hundred people at a time in public audience. The throne, an armchair of elaborate pattern, gilded, and upholstered with red velvet, stands under a velvet canopy of the same hue, in front of the windows. Beside it is the cushion on which the Pope rests his foot in order that it may be kissed. Then facing one another, right and left of the room, there are two pier-tables on one of which is a clock and on the other a crucifix between lofty candelabra with feet of gilded wood. The wall hangings, of red silk damask with a Louis XIV palm pattern, are topped by a pompous frieze, framing a ceiling decorated with allegorical figures and attributes, and it is only just in front of the throne that a Smyrna carpet covers the magnificent marble pavement. On the days of private audience, when the Pope remains in the little throne-room or at times in his bed-chamber, the grand throne-room becomes simply the ante-room of honour, where high dignitaries of the Church, ambassadors and great civilian personages, wait their turns. Two *camerieri*, one in violet coat, the other of the Cape and the Sword, here do duty, receiving from the *bussolanti* the persons who are to be honoured with audiences and conducting them to the door of the next room, the secret or private ante-chamber, where they hand them over to the *camerieri segreti*.

Signor Squadra who, walking on with slow and silent steps, had not yet once turned round, paused for a moment on reaching the door of the *anticamera segreta* so as to give Pierre time to breathe and recover himself somewhat before crossing the threshold of the sanctuary. The *camerieri segreti* alone had the right to occupy that last ante-chamber, and none but the Cardinals might wait there till the Pope should condescend to receive them. And so when Signor Squadra made up his

mind to admit Pierre, the latter could not restrain a slight
nervous shiver as if he were passing into some redoubtable
mysterious sphere beyond the limits of the lower world. In
the daytime a Noble Guard stood on sentry duty before the
door, but the latter was now free of access, and the room
within proved as empty as all the others. It was rather narrow,
almost like a passage, with two windows overlooking the new
district of the castle-fields and a third one facing the Piazza
of St. Peter's. Near the last was a door conducting to the little
throne-room, and between this door and the window stood a
small table at which a secretary, now absent, usually sat. And
here again, as in all the other rooms, one found a gilded pier-
table surmounted by a crucifix flanked by a pair of lamps. In
a corner, too, there was a large clock, loudly ticking in its
ebony case incrusted with brasswork. Still there was nothing
to awaken curiosity under the panelled and gilded ceiling
unless it were the wall-hangings of red damask, on which
yellow scutcheons displaying the Keys and the Tiara alternated with armorial lions, each with a paw resting on a globe.

Signor Squadra, however, now noticed that Pierre still
carried his hat in his hand, whereas according to etiquette he
should have left it in the hall of the *bussolanti*, only cardinals
being privileged to carry their hats with them into the Pope's
presence. Accordingly he discreetly took the young priest's
from him, and deposited it on the pier-table to indicate that it
must at least remain there. Then, without a word, by a
simple bow he gave Pierre to understand that he was about to
announce him to his Holiness, and that he must be good
enough to wait for a few minutes in that room.

On being left to himself Pierre drew a long breath. He
was stifling ; his heart was beating as though it would burst.
Nevertheless his mind remained clear, and in spite of the semi-
obscurity he had been able to form some idea of the famous
and magnificent apartments of the Pope, a suite of splendid
salons with tapestried or silken walls, gilded or painted
friezes and frescoed ceilings. By way of furniture, however,
there were only pier-table, stools [1] and thrones. And the
lamps, and the clocks, and the crucifixes, even the thrones, were

---

[1] M. Zola seems to have fallen into error here. Many of the seats,
which are of peculiar antique design, do, in the lower part, resemble
stools, but they have backs, whereas a stool proper has none. Briefly,
these seats, which are entirely of wood, are not unlike certain old-
fashioned hall chairs.—*Trans.*

all presents brought from the four quarters of the world in the great fervent days of jubilee. There was no sign of comfort, everything was pompous, stiff, cold and inconvenient. All olden Italy was there, with its perpetual display and lack of intimate, cosy life. It had been necessary to lay a few carpets over the superb marble slabs which froze one's feet; and some *calorifères* had even lately been installed, but it was not thought prudent to light them lest the variations of temperature should give the Pope a cold. However, that which more particularly struck Pierre now that he stood there waiting was the extraordinary silence which prevailed all around, silence so deep that it seemed as if all the dark quiescence of that huge, somniferous Vatican were concentrated in that one suite of lifeless, sumptuous rooms, which the motionless flamelets of the lamps as dimly illumined.

All at once the ebony clock struck nine and the young man felt astonished. What! had only ten minutes elapsed since he had crossed the threshold of the bronze doors below? He felt as if he had been walking on for days and days. Then, desiring to overcome the nervous feeling which oppressed him —for he ever feared lest his enforced calmness should collapse amidst a flood of tears—he began to walk up and down, passing in front of the clock, glancing at the crucifix on the pier-table, and the globe of the lamp on which had remained the mark of a servant's greasy fingers. And the light was so faint and yellow that he felt inclined to turn the lamp up, but did not dare. Then he found himself with his brow resting against one of the panes of the window facing the Piazza of St. Peter's, and for a moment he was thunderstruck, for between the imperfectly closed shutters he could see all Rome, as he had seen it one day from the Loggie of Raffaelle, and as he had pictured Leo XIII contemplating it from the window of his bed-room. However, it was now Rome by night, Rome spreading out into the depths of the gloom, as limitless as the starry sky. And in that sea of black waves one could only with certainty identify the larger thoroughfares which the white brightness of electric lights turned, as it were, into milky ways. All the rest showed but a swarming of little yellow sparks, the crumbs, as it were, of a half-extinguished heaven swept down upon the earth. Occasional constellations of bright stars, tracing mysterious figures, vainly endeavoured to show forth distinctly, but they were submerged, blotted out by the general chaos which suggested the dust of some old planet that had crumbled there, losing its splendour and reduced to mere phosphorescent sand. And how immense was the blackness thus sprinkled with light, how huge the mass of obscurity and mystery into which the Eternal City with its seven and twenty centuries, its ruins, its monuments, its people, its history seemed to have been merged. You could no longer tell where it began or where it ended, whether it spread to the farthest recesses of the gloom, or whether it were so reduced that the sun on rising would illumine but a little pile of ashes.

However, in spite of all Pierre's efforts, his nervous anguish increased each moment, even in presence of that ocean of darkness which displayed such sovereign quiescence. He drew away from the window and quivered from head to foot on hearing a faint footfall and thinking it was that of Signor Squadra approaching to fetch him. The sound came from an adjacent apartment, the little throne-room, whose door, he now perceived, had remained ajar. And at last, as he heard nothing further, he yielded to his feverish impatience and peeped into this room which he found to be fairly spacious, again hung with red damask, and containing a gilded arm-chair, covered with red velvet under a canopy of the same material. And again there was the inevitable pier-table, with a tall ivory crucifix, a clock, a pair of lamps, a pair of candelabra, a pair of large vases on pedestals, and two smaller ones of Sèvres manufacture decorated with the Holy Father's portrait. At the same time, however, the room displayed rather more comfort, for a Smyrna carpet covered the whole of the marble floor, while a few armchairs stood against the walls, and an imitation chimney-piece, draped with damask, served as counterpart to the pier-table. As a rule the Pope, whose bed-chamber communicated with this little throne-room, received in the latter such persons as he desired to honour. And Pierre's shiver became more pronounced at the idea that in all likelihood he would merely have the throne-room to cross and that Leo XIII was yonder behind its farther door. Why was he kept waiting? he wondered. He had been told of mysterious audiences granted at a similar hour to personages who had been received in similar silent fashion, great personages whose names were only mentioned in the lowest whispers. With regard to himself no doubt, it was because he was considered compromising that there was a desire to receive him in this manner unknown to the personages of the Court, and so as to speak with him at ease. Then, all at once, he understood the cause of the noise he had recently heard, for beside the lamp on the pier-table of the little throne-room he saw a kind of butler's tray containing some soiled plates, knives, forks and spoons, with a bottle and a glass, which had evidently just been removed from a supper table. And he realised that Signor Squadra, having seen these things in the Pope's room, had brought them there, and had then gone in again, perhaps to tidy up. He knew also of the Pope's frugality, how he took his meals all alone at a little round table, everything being brought to him in that tray, a plate of meat, a plate of vegetables, a little Bordeaux claret as prescribed by his doctor, and a large allowance of beef broth of which he was very fond. In the same way as others might offer a cup of tea, he was wont to offer cups of broth to the old cardinals his friends and favourites, quite an invigorating little treat which these old bachelors much enjoyed. And, O ye orgies of Alexander VI, ye banquets and galas of Julius II and Leo X, only eight *lire* a day—six shillings and fourpence—were allowed to defray the cost of Leo XIII's table! However, just as that recollection occurred to Pierre, he again heard a slight noise, this time in his Holiness's bed-chamber, and thereupon, terrified by his indiscretion, he hastened to withdraw from the entrance of the throne-room which, lifeless and quiescent though it was, seemed in his agitation to flare as with sudden fire.

Then, quivering too violently to be able to remain still, he began to walk up and down the ante-chamber. He remembered that Narcisse had spoken to him of that Signor Squadra, his Holiness's cherished valet, whose importance and influence were so great. He alone, on reception days, was able to prevail on the Pope to don a clean cassock if the one he was wearing happened to be soiled by snuff. And though his Holiness stubbornly shut himself up alone in his bed-room every night from a spirit of independence, which some called the anxiety of a miser determined to sleep alone with his treasure, Signor Squadra at all events occupied an adjoining chamber, and was ever on the watch, ready to respond to the faintest call. Again, it was he who respectfully intervened whenever his Holiness sat up too late or worked too long. But on this point it was difficult to induce the Pope to listen to reason. During his hours of insomnia he would often rise

and send Squadra to fetch a secretary in order that he might
detail some memoranda or sketch out an encyclical letter.
When the drafting of one of the latter impassioned him he
would have spent days and nights over it, just as formerly,
when claiming proficiency in Latin verse, he had often let the
dawn surprise him whilst he was polishing a line. But,
indeed, he slept very little, his brain ever being at work,
ever scheming out the realisation of some former ideas. His
memory alone seemed to have slightly weakened during recent
times.

Pierre, as he slowly paced to and fro, gradually became
absorbed in his thoughts of that lofty and sovereign personality. From the petty details of the Pope's daily existence,
he passed to his intellectual life, to the *rôle* which he was
certainly bent on playing as a great pontiff. And Pierre
asked himself which of his two hundred and fifty-seven pre-
decessors, the long line of saints and criminals, men of
mediocrity and men of genius, he most desired to resemble.
Was it one of the first humble popes, those who followed on
during the first three centuries, mere heads of burial guilds,
fraternal pastors of the Christian community? Was it Pope
Damasus, the first great builder, the man of letters who took
delight in intellectual matters, the ardent believer who is said
to have opened the catacombs to the piety of the faithful?
Was it Leo III, who by crowning Charlemagne boldly consummated the rupture with the schismatic East and conveyed
the Empire to the West by the all-powerful will of God and
His Church, which thenceforth disposed of the crowns of
monarchs? Was it the terrible Gregory VII, the purifier of
the temple, the sovereign of kings; was it Innocent III or
Boniface VIII, those masters of souls, nations, and thrones,
who, armed with the fierce weapon of excommunication,
reigned with such despotism over the terrified Middle Ages
that Catholicism was never nearer the attainment of its
dream of universal dominion? Was it Urban II or Gregory
IX or another of those popes in whom flared the red Crusading
passion which urged the nations on to the conquest of the
unknown and the divine? Was it Alexander III, who defended
the Holy See against the Empire, and at last conquered and
set his foot on the neck of Frederick Barbarossa? Was it,
long after the sorrows of Avignon, Julius II, who wore the
cuirass and once more strengthened the political power of the
papacy? Was it Leo X, the pompous, glorious patron of the

Renascence, of a whole great century of art, whose mind, however, possessed with so little penetration and foresight that he
looked on Luther as a mere rebellious monk ?   Was it Pius V,
who personified dark and avenging reaction, the fire of the
stakes that punished the heretic world ?   Was it some other
of the popes who reigned after the Council of Trent with faith
absolute, belief re-established in its full integrity, the Church
saved by pride and the stubborn upholding of every dogma ?
Or was it a pope of the decline, such as Benedict XIV, the
man of vast intelligence, the learned theologian who, as his
hands were tied, and he could not dispose of the kingdoms of
the world, spent a worthy life in regulating the affairs of
heaven ?

In this wise, in Pierre's mind there spread out the whole
history of the popes, the most prodigious of all histories,
showing fortune in every guise, the lowest, the most wretched,
as well as the loftiest and most dazzling ; whilst an obstinate
determination to live enabled the papacy to survive everything
—conflagrations, massacres, and the downfall of many nations,
for always did it remain militant and erect in the persons of
its popes, that most extraordinary of all lines of absolute,
conquering, and domineering sovereigns, every one of them—
even the puny and humble—masters of the world, every one
of them glorious with the imperishable glory of heaven when
they were thus evoked in that ancient Vatican, where their
spirits assuredly awoke at night and prowled about the endless
galleries and spreading halls in that tomb-like silence whose
quiver came no doubt from the light touch of their gliding
steps over the marble slabs.

However, Pierre was now thinking that he indeed knew
which of the great popes Leo XIII most desired to resemble.
It was first Gregory the Great, the conqueror and organiser of
the early days of Catholic power. He had come of ancient
Roman stock, and in his heart there was a little of the blood
of the emperors. He administered Rome after it had been
saved from the Goths, cultivated the ecclesiastical domains,
and divided earthly wealth into thirds, one for the poor, one
for the clergy, and one for the Church. Then too he was the
first to establish the Propaganda, sending his priests forth to
civilise and pacify the nations, and carrying his conquests so
far as to win Great Britain over to the divine law of Christ.
And the second pope whom Leo XIII took as model was one
who had arisen after a long lapse of centuries, Sixtus V, the

pope financier and politician, the vine-dresser's son, who, when he had donned the tiara, revealed one of the most extensive and supple minds of a period fertile in great diplomatists. He heaped up treasure and displayed stern avarice, in order that he might ever have in his coffers all the money needful for war or for peace. He spent years and years in negotiations with kings, never despairing of his own triumph; and never did he display open hostility for his times, but took them as they were and then sought to modify them in accordance with the interests of the Holy See, showing himself conciliatory in all things and with every one, already dreaming of an European balance of power which he hoped to control. And withal a very saintly pope, a fervent mystic, yet a pope of the most absolute and domineering mind blended with a politician ready for whatever courses might most conduce to the rule of God's Church on earth.

And, after all, Pierre amidst his rising enthusiasm, which despite his efforts at calmness was sweeping away all prudence and doubt, Pierre asked himself why he need question the past. Was not Leo XIII the pope whom he had depicted in his book, the great pontiff, who was desired and expected? No doubt the portrait which he had sketched was not accurate in every detail, but surely its main lines must be correct if mankind were to retain a hope of salvation. Whole pages of that book of his arose before him, and he again beheld the Leo XIII that he had portrayed, the wise and conciliatory politician, labouring for the unity of the Church and so anxious to make it strong and invincible against the day of the inevitable great struggle. He again beheld him freed from the cares of the temporal power, elevated, radiant with moral splendour, the only authority left erect above the nations; he beheld him realising what mortal danger would be incurred if the solution of the social question were left to the enemies of Christianity, and therefore resolving to intervene in contemporary quarrels for the defence of the poor and the lowly, even as Jesus had intervened once before. And he again beheld him putting himself on the side of the democracies, accepting the Republic in France, leaving the dethroned kings in exile, and verifying the prediction which promised the empire of the world to Rome once more when the papacy should have unified belief and have placed itself at the head of the people. The times indeed were near accomplishment, Cæsar was struck down, the Pope alone remained, and would not the people, the great silent multitude, for whom the two powers had so long contended, give itself to its Father now that it knew him to be both just and charitable, with heart aglow and hand out-stretched to welcome all the penniless toilers and beggars of the roads! Given the catastrophe which threatened our rotten modern societies, the frightful misery which ravaged every city, there was surely no other solution possible: Leo XIII, the predestined, necessary redeemer, the pastor sent to save the flock from coming disaster by re-establishing the true Christian community, the forgotten golden age of primitive Christianity. The reign of justice would at last begin, all men would be reconciled, there would be but one nation living in peace and obeying the equalising law of work, under the high patronage of the Pope, sole bond of charity and love on earth!

And at this thought Pierre was upbuoyed by fiery enthu-siasm. At last he was about to see the Holy Father, empty his heart and open his soul to him! He had so long and so passionately looked for the advent of that moment! To secure it he had fought with all his courage through ever-recurring obstacles, and the length and difficulty of the struggle and the success now at last achieved, increased his feverishness, his desire for final victory. Yes, yes, he would conquer, he would confound his enemies. As he had said to Monsignor Fornaro, could the Pope disavow him? Had he not expressed the Holy Father's secret ideas? Perhaps he might have done so somewhat prematurely, but was not that a fault to be forgiven? And then, too, he remembered his declaration to Monsignor Nani, that he himself would never withdraw and suppress his book, for he neither regretted nor disowned anything that was in it. At this very moment he again questioned himself, and felt that all his valour and determination to defend his book, all his desire to work the triumph of his belief, remained intact. Yet his mental perturbation was becoming great, he had to seek for ideas, wondering how he should enter the Pope's presence, what he should say, what precise terms he should employ. Something heavy and mysterious which he could hardly account for seemed to weigh him down. At bottom he was weary, already exhausted, only held up by his dream, his compassion for human misery. However, he would enter in all haste, he would fall upon his knees and speak as he best could, letting his heart flow forth. And assuredly the Holy Father would smile on him, and dismiss him with a promise

that he would not sign the condemnation of a work in which
he had found the expression of his own most cherished
thoughts.

Then, again, such an acute sensation as of fainting came
over Pierre that he went up to the window to press his burning brow against the cold glass. His ears were buzzing, his
legs staggering, whilst his brain throbbed violently. And
he was striving to forget his thoughts by gazing upon the
black immensity of Rome, longing to be steeped in night himself, total and healing night, the night in which one sleeps on
for ever, knowing neither pain nor wretchedness, when all at
once he became conscious that somebody was standing behind
him, and thereupon, with a start, he turned round.

And there, indeed, stood Signor Squadra in his black
livery. Again he made one of his customary bows to invite
the visitor to follow him, and again he walked on in front,
crossing the little throne-room, and slowly opening the farther
door. Then he drew aside, allowed Pierre to enter, and
noiselessly closed the door behind him.

Pierre was in his Holiness's bed-room. He had feared one
of those overwhelming attacks of emotion which madden or
paralyse one. He had been told of women reaching the Pope's
presence in a fainting condition, staggering as if intoxicated,
while others came with a rush, as though upheld and borne
along by invisible pinions. And suddenly the anguish of his
own spell of waiting, his intense feverishness, ceased in a sort
of astonishment, a reaction which rendered him very calm
and so restored his clearness of vision, that he could see
everything. As he entered he/distinctly realised the decisive
importance of such an audience, he, a mere petty priest in
presence of the Supreme Pontiff, the head of the Church. All
his religious and moral life would depend on it ; and possibly
it was this sudden thought that thus chilled him on the
threshold of the redoubtable sanctuary, which he had approached with such quivering steps, and which he would not
have thought to enter otherwise than with distracted heart
and loss of senses, unable to do more than stammer the
simple prayers of childhood.

Later on, when he sought to classify his recollections he
remembered that his eyes had first lighted on Leo XIII, not,
however, to the exclusion of his surroundings, but in conjunction with them, that spacious room hung with yellow
damask, whose alcove, adorned with fluted marble columns, was

so deep that the bed was quite hidden away in it, as well as other articles of furniture, a couch, a wardrobe, and some trunks, those famous trunks in which the treasure of the Peter's Pence was said to be securely locked. A sort of Louis XIV writing-desk with ornaments of engraved brass stood face to face with a large gilded and painted Louis XV pier-table on which a lamp was burning beside a lofty crucifix. The room was virtually bare, only three arm-chairs and four or five other chairs, upholstered in light silk, being disposed here and there over the well-worn carpet. And on one of the arm-chairs sat Leo XIII, near a small table on which another lamp with a shade had been placed. Three newspapers, moreover, lay there, two of them French and one Italian, and the last was half-unfolded as if the Pope had momentarily turned from it to stir a glass of syrup, standing beside him, with a long silver-gilt spoon.

In the same way as Pierre saw the Pope's room, he saw his costume, his cassock of white cloth with white buttons, his white skull-cap, his white cape and his white sash fringed with gold and broidered at either end with golden keys. His stockings were white, his slippers were of red velvet, and these again were broidered with golden keys. What surprised the young priest, however, was his Holiness's face and figure, which now seemed so shrunken that he scarcely recognised them. This was his fourth meeting with the Pope. He had seen him walking in the Vatican gardens, enthroned in the Hall of Beatifications, and pontifying at St. Peter's, and now he beheld him on that arm-chair, in privacy, and looking so slight and fragile that he could not restrain a feeling of affectionate anxiety. Leo's neck was particularly remarkable, slender beyond belief, suggesting the neck of some little, aged, white bird. And his face, of the pallor of alabaster, was characteristically transparent, to such a degree, indeed, that one could see the lamp-light through his large commanding nose, as if the blood had entirely withdrawn from that organ. A mouth of great length, with white bloodless lips, streaked the lower part of the papal countenance, and the eyes alone had remained young and handsome. Superb eyes they were, brilliant like black diamonds, endowed with sufficient penetration and strength to lay souls open and force them to confess the truth aloud. Some scanty white curls emerged from under the white skull-cap, thus whitely crowning the thin white face, whose ugliness was softened by all this whiteness, this spiritual whiteness in which Leo XIII's flesh seemed as it were but pure lily-white florescence.

At the first glance, however, Pierre noticed that if Signor Squadra had kept him waiting, it had not been in order to compel the Holy Father to don a clean cassock, for the one he was wearing was badly soiled by snuff. A number of brown stains had trickled down the front of the garment beside the buttons, and just like any good *bourgeois*, his Holiness had a handkerchief on his knees to wipe himself. Apart from all this he seemed in good health, having recovered from his recent indisposition as easily as he usually recovered from such passing illnesses, sober, prudent old man that he was, quite free from organic disease, and simply declining by reason of progressive natural exhaustion.

Immediately on entering Pierre had felt that the Pope's sparkling eyes, those two black diamonds, were fixed upon him. The silence was profound, and the lamps burned with motionless, pallid flames. He had to approach, and after making the three genuflexions prescribed by etiquette, he stooped over one of the Pope's feet resting on a cushion in order to kiss the red velvet slipper. And on the Pope's side there was not a word, not a gesture, not a movement. When the young man drew himself up again he found the two black diamonds, those two eyes which were all brightness and intelligence, still riveted on him.

But at last Leo XIII, who had been unwilling to spare the young priest the humble duty of kissing his foot and who now left him standing, began to speak, whilst still examining him, probing, as it were, his very soul. 'My son,' he said, 'you greatly desired to see me, and I consented to afford you that satisfaction.'

He spoke in French, somewhat uncertain French, pronounced after the Italian fashion, and so slowly did he articulate each sentence that one could have written it down like so much dictation. And his voice, as Pierre had previously noticed, was strong and nasal, one of those full voices which people are surprised to hear coming from debile and apparently bloodless and breathless frames.

In response to the Holy Father's remark Pierre contented himself with bowing, knowing that respect required him to wait for a direct question before speaking. However, this question promptly came. 'You live in Paris?' asked Leo XIII.

'Yes, Holy Father.'

'Are you attached to one of the great parishes of the city?'

'No, Holy Father. I simply officiate at the little church of Neuilly.'

'Ah, yes, Neuilly, that is in the direction of the Bois de Boulogne, is it not? And how old are you, my son?'

'Thirty-four, Holy Father.'

A short interval followed. Leo XIII had at last lowered his eyes. With frail, ivory hand he took up the glass beside him, again stirred the syrup with the long spoon, and then drank a little of it. And all this he did gently and slowly, with a prudent, judicious air, as was his wont no doubt in everything. 'I have read your book, my son,' he resumed. 'Yes, the greater part of it. As a rule only fragments are submitted to me. But a person who is interested in you handed me the volume, begging me to glance through it. And that is how I was able to look into it.'

As he spoke he made a slight gesture in which Pierre fancied he could detect a protest against the isolation in which he was kept by those surrounding him, who, as Monsignor Nani had said, maintained a strict watch in order that nothing they objected to might reach him. And thereupon the young priest ventured to say: 'I thank your Holiness for having done me so much honour. No greater or more desired happiness could have befallen me.' He was indeed so happy! On seeing the Pope so calm, so free from all signs of anger, and on hearing him speak in that way of his book, like one well acquainted with it, he imagined that his cause was won.

'You are in relations with Monsieur le Vicomte Philibert de la Choue, are you not, my son?' continued Leo XIII. 'I was struck by the resemblance between some of your ideas and those of that devoted servant of the Church, who has in other ways given us previous testimony of his good feelings.'

'Yes, indeed, Holy Father, Monsieur de la Choue is kind enough to show me some affection. We have often talked together, so it is not surprising that I should have given expression to some of his most cherished ideas.'

'No doubt, no doubt. For instance, there is that question of the working-class guilds with which he largely occupies himself —with which, in fact, he occupies himself rather too much. At the time of his last journey to Rome he spoke to me of it in the most pressing manner. And in the same way, quite

recently, another of your compatriots, one of the best and
worthiest of men, Monsieur le Baron de Fouras, who brought
us that superb pilgrimage of the St. Peter's Pence Fund,
never ceased his efforts until I consented to receive him, when
he spoke to me on the same subject during nearly an hour.
Only it must be said that they do not agree in the matter, for
one begs me to do things which the other will not have me
do on any account.'

Pierre realised that the conversation was straying away
from his book, but he remembered having promised the
Viscount that if he should see the Pope he would make an
attempt to obtain from him a decisive expression of opinion
on the famous question as to whether the working-class
guilds or corporations should be free or obligatory, open or
closed. And the unhappy Viscount, kept in Paris by the gout,
had written the young priest letter after letter on the subject,
whilst his rival the Baron, availing himself of the opportunity
offered by the international pilgrimage, endeavoured to wring
from the Pope an approval of his own views, with which he
would have returned in triumph to France. Pierre conscientiously desired to keep his promise, and so he answered :
' Your Holiness knows better than any of us in which direction
true wisdom lies. Monsieur de Fouras is of opinion that
salvation, the solution of the labour question, lies simply
in the re-establishment of the old free corporations, whilst
Monsieur de la Choue desires the corporations to be obligatory,
protected by the State and governed by new regulations.
This last conception is certainly more in agreement with the
social ideas now prevalent in France. Should your Holiness
condescend to express a favourable opinion in that sense, the
young French Catholic party would certainly know how to
turn it to good result, by producing quite a movement of the
working classes in favour of the Church.'

In his quiet way Leo XIII responded : ' But I cannot.
Frenchmen always ask things of me which I cannot, will not
do. What I will allow you to say on my behalf to Monsieur
de la Choue is, that though I cannot content him I have not
contented Monsieur de Fouras. He obtained from me nothing
beyond the expression of my sincere goodwill for the French
working classes, who are so dear to me and who can do so much
for the restoration of the faith. You must surely understand,
however, that among you Frenchmen there are questions of
detail, of mere organisation, so to say, into which I cannot

possibly enter without imparting to them an importance
which they do not have, and at the same time greatly discon-
tenting some people should I please others.'

As the Pope pronounced these last words he smiled a pale
smile, in which the shrewd, conciliatory politician, who was
determined not to allow his infallibility to be compromised in
useless and risky ventures, was fully revealed. And then he
drank a little more syrup and wiped his mouth with his
handkerchief, like a sovereign whose Court day is over and
who takes his ease, having chosen this hour of solitude and
silence to chat as long as he may be so inclined.

Pierre, however, sought to bring him back to the subject
of his book. ' Monsieur de la Choue,' said he, ' has shown me
so much kindness and is so anxious to know the fate reserved
to my book—as if, indeed, it were his own—that I should
have been very happy to convey to him an expression of your
Holiness's approval.'

However, the Pope continued wiping his mouth and did
not reply.

' I became acquainted with the Viscount,' continued Pierre,
' at the residence of his Eminence Cardinal Bergerot, another
great heart whose ardent charity ought to suffice to restore
the faith in France.'

This time the effect was immediate. ' Ah ! yes, Monsieur
le Cardinal Bergerot ! ' said Leo XIII. ' I read that letter of
his which is printed at the beginning of your book. He was
very badly inspired in writing it to you ; and you, my son,
acted very culpably on the day you published it. I cannot
yet believe that Monsieur le Cardinal Bergerot had read some
of your pages when he sent you an expression of his complete
and full approval. I prefer to charge him with ignorance
and thoughtlessness. How could he approve of your attacks
on dogma, your revolutionary theories which tend to the
complete destruction of our holy religion ? If it be a fact
that he had read your book, the only excuse he can invoke is
sudden and inexplicable aberration. It is true that a very
bad spirit prevails among a small portion of the French
clergy. What are called Gallican ideas are ever sprouting up
like noxious weeds ; there is a malcontent Liberalism rebellious
to our authority which continually hungers for free examination and sentimental adventures.'

The Pope grew animated as he spoke. Italian words
mingled with his hesitating French, and every now and again

his full nasal voice resounded with the sonority of a brass
instrument. 'Monsieur le Cardinal Bergerot,' he continued,
'must be given to understand that we shall crush him on the
day when we see in him nothing but a rebellious son. He
owes the example of obedience; we shall acquaint him with
our displeasure, and we hope that he will submit. Humility
and charity are great virtues doubtless, and we have always
taken pleasure in recognising them in him. But they must
not be the refuge of a rebellious heart, for they are as nothing
unless accompanied by obedience—obedience, obedience, the
finest adornment of the great saints!'

Pierre listened thunderstruck, overcome. He forgot himself to think of the apostle of kindliness and tolerance upon
whose head he had drawn this all-powerful anger. So Don
Vigilio had spoken the truth: over and above his—Pierre's—
head the denunciations of the Bishops of Evreux and
Poitiers were about to fall on the man who opposed their
Ultramontane policy, that worthy and gentle Cardinal
Bergerot, whose heart was open to all the woes of the lowly
and the poor. This filled the young priest with despair; he
could accept the denunciation of the Bishop of Tarbes acting
on behalf of the Fathers of the Grotto, for that only fell on
himself, as a reprisal for what he had written about Lourdes;
but the underhand warfare of the others exasperated him,
filled him with dolorous indignation. And from that puny
old man before him with the slender, scraggy neck of an aged
bird, he had suddenly seen such a wrathful, formidable Master
arise that he trembled. How could he have allowed himself
to be deceived by appearances on entering? How could he
have imagined that he was simply in presence of a poor old
man, worn out by age, desirous of peace, and ready for every
concession? A blast had swept through that sleepy chamber,
and all his doubts and his anguish awoke once more. Ah!
that Pope, how thoroughly he answered to all the accounts
that he, Pierre, had heard but had refused to believe; so
many people had told him in Rome that he would find
Leo XIII a man of intellect rather than of sentiment, a man
of the most unbounded pride, who from his very youth had
nourished the supreme ambition, to such a point indeed that
he had promised eventual triumph to his relatives in order
that they might make the necessary sacrifices for him, while
since he had occupied the pontifical throne his one will and
determination had been to reign, to reign in spite of all, to be

the sole absolute and omnipotent master of the world! And
now here was reality arising with irresistible force and con-
firming everything. And yet Pierre struggled, stubbornly
clutching at his dream once more.

'Oh! Holy Father,' said he, 'I should be grieved indeed
if his Eminence should have a moment's worry on account of
my unfortunate book. If I be guilty I can answer for my
error, but his Eminence only obeyed the dictates of his heart
and can only have transgressed by excess of love for the disinherited of the world!'

Leo XIII made no reply. He had again raised his superb
eyes, those eyes of ardent life set, as it were, in the motionless
countenance of an alabaster idol; and once more he was
fixedly gazing at the young priest.

And Pierre, amidst his returning feverishness, seemed to
behold him growing in power and splendour, whilst behind
him arose a vision of the ages, a vision of that long line of
popes whom the young priest had previously evoked, the
saintly and the proud ones, the warriors and the ascetics, the
theologians and the diplomatists, those who had worn armour,
those who had conquered by the Cross, those who had disposed of empires as of mere provinces which God had committed to their charge. And in particular Pierre beheld the
great Gregory, the conqueror and founder, and Sixtus V, the
negotiator and politician, who had first foreseen the eventual
victory of the papacy over all the vanquished monarchies.
Ah! what a throng of magnificent princes, of sovereign
masters with powerful brains and arms, there was behind that
pale, motionless, old man! What an accumulation of inexhaustible determination, stubborn genius, and boundless
domination! The whole history of human ambition, the
whole effort of the ages to subject the nations to the pride of
one man, the greatest force that has ever conquered, exploited
and fashioned mankind in the name of its happiness! And
even now, when territorial sovereignty had come to an end,
how great was the spiritual sovereignty of that pale and
slender old man, in whose presence women fainted, as if overcome by the divine splendour radiating from his person.
Not only did all the resounding glories, the masterful triumphs
of history spread out behind him, but heaven opened, the very
spheres beyond life shone out in their dazzling mystery. He
—the Pope—stood at the portals of heaven, holding the keys
and opening those portals to human souls; all the ancient

symbolism was revived, freed at last from the stains of royalty here below.

'Oh! I beg you, Holy Father,' resumed Pierre, 'if an example be needed strike none other than myself. I have come, and am here; decide my fate, but do not aggravate my punishment by filling me with remorse at having brought condemnation on the innocent.'

Leo XIII still refrained from replying, though he continued to look at the young priest with burning eyes. And he, Pierre, no longer beheld Leo XIII, the last of a long line of popes, the Vicar of Jesus Christ, the Successor of the Prince of the Apostles, the Supreme Pontiff of the Universal Church, Patriarch of the East, Primate of Italy, Archbishop and Metropolitan of the Roman Province, Sovereign of the temporal Domains of the Holy Church; he saw the Leo XIII that he had dreamt of, the awaited saviour who would dispel the frightful cataclysm in which rotten society was sinking. He beheld him with his supple, lofty intelligence and fraternal, conciliatory tactics, avoiding friction and labouring to bring about unity; whilst with his heart overflowing with love he went straight to the hearts of the multitude, again giving the best of his blood in sign of the new alliance. He raised him aloft as the sole remaining moral authority, the sole possible bond of charity and peace—as the Father, in fact, who alone could stamp out injustice among his children, destroy misery, and re-establish the liberating Law of Work by bringing the nations back to the faith of the primitive Church, the gentleness and the wisdom of the true Christian community. And in the deep silence of that room the great figure which he thus set up assumed invincible all-powerfulness, extraordinary majesty.

'Oh, I beseech you, Holy Father, listen to me,' he said. 'Do not even strike me, strike no one, neither a being nor a thing, anything that can suffer under the sun. Show kindness and indulgence to all, show all the kindness and indulgence which the sight of the world's sufferings must have set in you!'

And then, seeing that Leo XIII still remained silent and still left him standing there, he sank down upon his knees, as if felled by the growing emotion which rendered his heart so heavy. And within him there was a sort of *débâcle*; all his doubts, all his anguish and sadness burst forth in an irresistible stream. There was the memory of the frightful day that he had just spent, the tragic death of Dario and Benedetta, which weighed on him like lead; there were all the sufferings that he had experienced since his arrival in Rome, the destruction of his illusions, the wounds dealt to his delicacy, the buffets with which men and things had responded to his young enthusiasm; and, lying yet more deeply within his heart, there was the sum total of human wretchedness, the thought of famished ones howling for food, of mothers whose breasts were drained and who sobbed whilst kissing their hungry babes, of fathers without work, who clenched their fists and revolted—indeed, the whole of that hateful misery which is as old as mankind itself, which has preyed upon mankind since its earliest hour, and which he now had everywhere found increasing in horror and havoc, without a gleam of hope that it would ever be healed. And withal, yet more immense and more incurable, he felt within him a nameless sorrow to which he could assign no precise cause or name—an universal, an illimitable sorrow with which he melted despairingly, and which was perhaps the very sorrow of life.

'O Holy Father!' he exclaimed, 'I myself have no existence and my book has no existence. I desired, passionately desired to see your Holiness that I might explain and defend myself. But I no longer know, I can no longer recall a single one of the things that I wished to say, I can only weep, weep the tears which are stifling me. Yes, I am but a poor man, and the only need I feel is to speak to you of the poor. Oh! the poor ones, oh! the lowly ones, whom for two years past I have seen in our *faubourgs* of Paris, so wretched and so full of pain; the poor little children that I have picked out of the snow, the poor little angels who had eaten nothing for two days; the women too, consumed by consumption, without bread or fire, shivering in filthy hovels; and the men thrown on the streets by slackness of trade, weary of begging for work as one begs for alms, sinking back into night, drunken with rage and harbouring the sole avenging thought of setting the whole city afire! And that night too, that terrible night, when in a room of horror I beheld a mother who had just killed herself with her five little ones, she lying on a palliasse suckling her last-born and two little girls, two pretty little blondes, sleeping the last sleep beside her, while the two boys had succumbed farther away, one of them crouching against a wall, and the other lying upon the floor, distorted as though

by a last effort to avoid death! . . . O Holy Father! I am
but an ambassador, the messenger of those who suffer and who
sob, the humble delegate of the humble ones who die of want
beneath the hateful harshness, the frightful injustice of our
present-day social system! And I bring your Holiness their
tears, and I lay their tortures at your Holiness's feet, I raise
their cry of woe, like a cry from the abyss, that cry which
demands justice unless indeed the very Heavens are to fall!
Oh! show your loving kindness, Holy Father, show compassion!'

The young man had stretched out his arms and implored
Leo XIII with a gesture as of supreme appeal to the divine
compassion. Then he continued: ' And here, Holy Father,
in this splendid and eternal Rome, is not the want and misery
as frightful! During the weeks that I have roamed hither
and thither among the dust of famous ruins I have never ceased
to come in contact with evils which demand cure. Ah! to
think of all that is crumbling, all that is expiring, the agony
of so much glory, the fearful sadness of a world which is dying
of exhaustion and hunger! Yonder, under your Holiness's
windows, have I not seen a district of horrors, a district of
unfinished palaces stricken like rickety children who cannot
attain to full growth, palaces which are already in ruins and
have become places of refuge for all the woeful misery of
Rome? And here, as in Paris, what a suffering multitude,
what a shameless exhibition too of the social sore, the devouring cancer openly tolerated and displayed in utter heedlessness! There are whole families leading idle and hungry lives
in the splendid sunlight; fathers waiting for work to fall to
them from heaven; sons listlessly spending their days asleep
on the dry grass; mothers and daughters, withered before
their time, shuffling about in loquacious idleness. O Holy
Father, already to-morrow at dawn may your Holiness open
that window yonder and with your benediction awaken that
great childish people, which still slumbers in ignorance and
poverty! May your Holiness give it the soul it lacks, a soul
with the consciousness of human dignity, of the necessary law
of work, of free and fraternal life regulated by justice only!
Yes, may your Holiness make a people out of that heap of
wretches, whose excuse lies in all their bodily suffering and
mental night, who live like the beasts that go by and die,
never knowing nor understanding, yet ever lashed onward with
the whip!'

Pierre's sobs were gradually choking him, and it was only the impulse of his passion which still enabled him to speak. 'And, Holy Father,' he continued, 'is it not to you that I ought to address myself in the name of all these wretched ones? Are you not the Father, and is it not before the Father that the messenger of the poor and the lowly should kneel as I am kneeling now? And is it not to the Father that he should bring the huge burden of their sorrows and ask for pity and help and justice? Yes, particularly for justice! And since you are the Father, throw the doors wide open so that all may enter, even the humblest of your children, the faithful, the chance passers, even the rebellious ones and those who have gone astray but who will perhaps enter and whom you will save from the errors of abandonment! Be as the house of refuge on the dangerous road, the loving greeter of the wayfarer, the lamp of hospitality which ever burns, and is seen afar off and saves one in the storm! And since, O Father, you are power be salvation also! You can do all; you have centuries of domination behind you; you have now-adays risen to a moral authority which has rendered you the arbiter of the world; you are there before me like the very majesty of the sun which illumines and fructifies! Oh! be the star of kindness and charity, be the redeemer; take in hand once more the purpose of Jesus, which has been per-verted by being left in the hands of the rich and the powerful who have ended by transforming the work of the Gospel into the most hateful of all monuments of pride and tyranny! And since the work has been spoilt, take it in hand, begin it afresh, place yourself on the side of the little ones, the lowly ones, the poor ones, and bring them back to the peace, the fraternity and the justice of the original Christian communion. And say, O Father, that I have understood you, that I have sincerely expressed in this respect your most cherished ideas, the sole living desire of your reign! The rest, oh! the rest, my book, myself, what matter they! I do not defend myself, I only seek your glory and the happiness of mankind. Say that from the depths of this Vatican you have heard the rending of our corrupt modern societies! Say that you have quivered with loving pity, say that you desire to prevent the awful impending catastrophe by recalling the Gospel to the hearts of your children who are stricken with madness, and by bringing them back to the age of simplicity and purity when the first Christians lived together in innocent brother-

hood! Yes, it is for that reason, is it not, that you have
placed yourself, Father, on the side of the poor, and for that
reason I am here and entreat you for pity and kindness and
justice with my whole soul!'

Then the young man gave way beneath his emotion, and
fell all of a heap upon the floor amidst a rush of sobs—loud,
endless sobs, which flowed forth in billows, coming as it
were not only from himself but from all the wretched, from
the whole world in whose veins sorrow coursed mingled with
the very blood of life. He was there as the ambassador of
suffering, as he had said. And indeed, at the foot of that mute
and motionless Pope, he was like the personification of the
whole of human woe.

Leo XIII, who was extremely fond of talking and could
only listen to others with an effort, had twice raised one of his
pallid hands to interrupt the young priest. Then, gradually
overcome by astonishment, touched by emotion himself, he
had allowed him to continue, to go on to the end of his outburst. A little blood even had suffused the snowy whiteness
of the Pontiff's face whilst his eyes shone out yet more
brilliantly. And as soon as he saw the young man speechless at his feet, shaken by those sobs which seemed to be
wrenching away his heart, he became anxious and leant forward : ' Calm yourself, my son, raise yourself,' he said.

But the sobs still continued, still flowed forth, all reason
and respect being swept away amidst that distracted plaint of
a wounded soul, that moan of suffering, dying flesh.

' Raise yourself, my son, it is not proper,' repeated Leo
XIII. ' There, take that chair.' And with a gesture of
authority he at last invited the young man to sit down.

Pierre rose with pain, and at once seated himself in order
that he might not fall. He brushed his hair back from his
forehead, and wiped his scalding tears away with his hands,
unable to understand what had just happened, but striving to
regain his self-possession.

' You appeal to the Holy Father,' said Leo XIII. ' Ah !
rest assured that his heart is full of pity and affection for those
who are unfortunate. But that is not the point, it is our holy
religion which is in question. I have read your book, a bad
book I tell you so at once, the most dangerous and culpable
of books, precisely on account of its qualities, the pages in
which I myself felt interested. Yes, I was often fascinated, I
should not have continued my perusal had I not felt carried

away, transported by the ardent breath of your faith and enthusiasm. The subject "New Rome" is such a beautiful one and impassions me so much, and certainly there is a book to be written under that title but in a very different spirit to yours. You think that you have understood me, my son, that you have so penetrated yourself with my writings and actions that you simply express my most cherished ideas. But no, no, you have not understood me, and that is why I desired to see you, explain things to you and convince you.'

It was now Pierre who sat listening, mute and motionless. Yet he had only come thither to defend himself; for three months past he had been feverishly desiring this interview, preparing his arguments and feeling confident of victory; and now although he heard his book spoken of as dangerous and culpable he did not protest, did not reply with any one of those good reasons which he had deemed so irresistible. But the fact was that intense weariness had come upon him, the appeal that he had made, the tears that he had shed had left him utterly exhausted. By and by, however, he would be brave and would say what he had resolved to say.

'People do not understand me, do not understand me!' resumed Leo XIII with an air of impatient irritation. 'It is incredible what trouble I have to make myself understood in France especially! Take the temporal power for instance; how can you have fancied that the Holy See would ever enter into any compromise on that question? Such language is unworthy of a priest, it is the chimerical dream of one who is ignorant of the conditions in which the papacy has hitherto lived and in which it must still live if it does not desire to disappear. Cannot you see the sophistry of your argument that the Church becomes the loftier the more it frees itself from the cares of terrestrial sovereignty? A purely spiritual royalty, a sway of charity and love, indeed, 'tis a fine imaginative idea! But who will ensure us respect? Who will grant us the alms of a stone on which to rest our head if we are ever driven forth and forced to roam the highways? Who will guarantee our independence when we are at the mercy of every State? . . . No, no! this soil of Rome is ours, we have inherited it from the long line of our ancestors, and it is the indestructible, eternal soil on which the Church is built, so that any relinquishment would mean the downfall of the Holy Catholic Apostolic and Roman Church. And, moreover, we could not relinquish it; we are bound by our oath to God and man.'

He paused for a moment to allow Pierre to answer him. But the latter to his stupefaction could say nothing, for he perceived that this Pope spoke as he was bound to speak. All the heavy, mysterious things which had weighed the young priest down whilst he was waiting in the ante-room now became more and more clearly defined. They were, indeed, the things which he had seen and learnt since his arrival in Rome, the disillusions, the rebuffs which he had experienced, all the many points of difference between existing reality and imagination, whereby his dream of a return to primitive Christianity was already half shattered. And in particular he remembered the hour which he had spent on the dome of St. Peter's when in presence of the old city of glory so stubbornly clinging to its purple, he had realised that he was an imbecile with his idea of a purely spiritual pope. He had that day fled from the furious shouts of the pilgrims acclaiming the Pope King. He had only accepted the necessity for money, that last form of servitude still binding the Pope to earth. But all had crumbled afterwards, when he had beheld the real Rome, the ancient city of pride and domination where the papacy can never be complete without the temporal power. Too many bonds, dogma, tradition, environment, the very soil itself rendered the Church for ever immutable. It was only in appearances that she could make concessions, and a time would even arrive when her concessions would cease, in presence of the impossibility of going any further without committing suicide. If his, Pierre's, dream of a New Rome were ever to be realised, it would only be far away from ancient Rome. Only in some distant region could the new Christianity arise, for Catholicism was bound to die on the spot when the last of the popes, riveted to that land of ruins, should disappear beneath the falling dome of St. Peter's, which would fall as surely as the temple of Jupiter had fallen ! And, as for that pope of the present day, though he might have no kingdom, though age might have made him weak and fragile, though his bloodless pallor might be that of some ancient idol of wax, he none the less flared with the red passion for universal sovereignty, he was none the less the stubborn scion of his ancestry, the Pontifex Maximus, the Cæsar Imperator in whose veins flowed the blood of Augustus, master of the world.

'You must be fully aware,' resumed Leo XIII, ' of the ardent desire for unity which has always possessed us. We were very happy on the day when we unified the rite, by imposing the Roman rite throughout the whole Catholic world. This is one of our most cherished victories, for it can do much to uphold our authority. And I hope that our efforts in the East will end by bringing our dear brethren of the dissident communions back to us, in the same way as I do not despair of convincing the Anglican sects, without speaking of the other so-called Protestant sects who will be compelled to return to the bosom of the only Church, the Catholic, Apostolic and Roman Church, when the times predicted by the Christ shall be accomplished. But a thing which you did not say in your book is that the Church can relinquish nothing whatever of dogma. On the contrary, you seem to fancy that an agreement might be effected, concessions made on either side, and that, my son, is a culpable thought, such language as a priest cannot use without being guilty of a crime. No, the truth is absolute, not a stone of the edifice shall be changed. Oh! in matters of form, we will do whatever may be asked. We are ready to adopt the most conciliatory courses if it be only a question of turning certain difficulties and weighing expressions in order to facilitate agreement. . . . Again, there is the part we have taken in contemporary socialism, and here too it is necessary that we should be understood. Those whom you have so well called the disinherited of the world, are certainly the object of our solicitude. If socialism be simply a desire for justice, and a constant determination to come to the help of the weak and the suffering, who can claim to give more thought to the matter, and work with more energy than ourselves? Has not the Church always been the mother of the afflicted, the helper and benefactress of the poor? We are for all reasonable progress, we admit all new social forms which will promote peace and fraternity. . . Only we can but condemn that socialism which begins by driving away God as a means of ensuring the happiness of mankind. Therein lies simple savagery, an abominable relapse into the primitive state in which there can only be catastrophe, conflagration and massacre. And that again is a point on which you have not laid sufficient stress, for you have not shown in your book that there can be no progress outside the pale of the Church, that she is really the only initiatory and guiding power to whom one may surrender oneself without fear. Indeed, and in this again you have sinned, it seemed to me as if you set God on one side, as if for you religion lay solely in a certain

bent of the soul, a florescence of love and charity, which sufficed one to work one's salvation. But that is execrable
heresy. God is ever present, master of souls and bodies; and
religion remains the bond, the law, the very governing power
of mankind, apart from which there can only be barbarism in
this world and damnation in the next. And, once again,
forms are of no importance ; it is sufficient that dogma should
remain. Thus our adhesion to the French Republic proves
that we in no wise mean to link the fate of religion to that of
any form of government, however august and ancient the latter
may be. Dynasties may have done their time, but God is
eternal. Kings may perish, but God lives! And, moreover,
there is nothing anti-Christian in the republican form of
government ; indeed, on the contrary, it would seem like an
awakening of that Christian commonwealth to which you have
referred in some really charming pages. The worst is that
liberty at once becomes licence, and that our desire for conciliation is often very badly requited . . . But ah ! what a
wicked book you have written, my son, with the best intentions, I am willing to believe it, and how your silence shows
that you are beginning to recognise the disastrous consequences
of your error.'

Pierre still remained silent, overcome, feeling as if his
arguments would fall against some deaf, blind and impenetrable
rock, which it was useless to assail since nothing could enter
it. And only one thing now pre-occupied him ; he wondered
how it was that a man of such intelligence and such ambition
had not formed a more distinct and exact idea of the modern
world. He could divine that the Pope possessed much information and carried the map of Christendom with many of
the needs, deeds and hopes of the nations, in his mind amidst
his complicated diplomatic enterprises ; but at the same time
what gaps there were in his knowledge ! The truth, no doubt,
was that his personal acquaintance with the world was confined to his brief nunciature at Brussels.[1]

During his occupation of the see of Perugia, which had
followed, he had only mingled with the dawning life of young
Italy. And for eighteen years now he had been shut up in the
Vatican, isolated from the rest of mankind and communicating
with the nations solely through his *entourage*, which was often
most unintelligent, most mendacious, and most treacherous.

[1] That, too, was in 1843-44, and the world is now utterly unlike what
it was then !—*Trans.*

Moreover, he was an Italian priest, a superstitious and despotic
High Pontiff, bound by tradition, subjected to the influences
of race, environment, pecuniary considerations and political
necessities, not to speak of his great pride, the conviction that
he ought to be implicitly obeyed in all things as the one sole
legitimate power upon earth.   Therein lay fatal causes of
mental deformity, of errors and gaps in his extraordinary
brain, though the latter certainly possessed many admirable
qualities, quickness of comprehension and patient stubbornness
of will and strength to draw conclusions and act. Of all his
powers, however, that of intuition was certainly the most
wonderful, for was it not this alone which, owing to his voluntary imprisonment, enabled him to divine the vast evolution
of humanity at the present day ? He was thus keenly conscious of the dangers surrounding him, of the rising tide of
democracy and the boundless ocean of science which threatened
to submerge the little islet where the dome of St. Peter's yet
triumphed. And the object of all his policy, of all his labour,
was to conquer so that he might reign. If he desired the
unity of the Church it was in order that the latter might
become strong and inexpugnable in the contest which he foresaw. If he preached conciliation, granting concessions in
matters of form, tolerating audacious actions on the part of
American bishops, it was because he deeply and secretly
feared the dislocation of the Church, some sudden schism
which might hasten disaster. And this fear explained his
returning affection for the people, the concern which he displayed respecting socialism, and the Christian solution which
he offered to the woes of earthly life. As Cæsar was stricken
low, was not the long contest for possession of the people
over, and would not the people, the great silent multitude,
speak out, and give itself to him, the Pope ? He had begun
experiments with France, forsaking the lost cause of the
monarchy and recognising the Republic which he hoped might
prove strong and victorious, for in spite of everything France
remained the eldest daughter of the Church, the only Catholic
nation which yet possessed sufficient strength to restore the
temporal power at some propitious moment. And briefly
Leo's desire was to reign. To reign by the support of France
since it seemed impossible to do so by the support of Germany !
To reign by the support of the people, since the people was
now becoming the master, the bestower of thrones ! To reign
by means even of an Italian Republic, if only that Republic

could wrest Rome from the House of Savoy and restore her to him, a federal Republic which would make him President of the United States of Italy pending the time when he should be President of the United States of Europe! To reign in spite of everybody and everything, such was his ambition; to reign over the world, even as Augustus had reigned, Augustus whose devouring blood alone upheld this expiring old man, yet so stubbornly clinging to power!

'And another crime of yours, my son,' resumed Leo XIII, 'is that you have dared to ask for a new religion. That is impious, blasphemous, sacrilegious. There is but one religion in the world, our Holy Catholic Apostolic and Roman Religion, apart from which there can be but darkness and damnation. I quite understand that what you mean to imply is a return to early Christianity. But the error of so-called Protestantism, so culpable and so deplorable in its consequences, never had any other pretext. As soon as one departs from the strict observance of dogma and absolute respect for tradition one sinks into the most frightful precipices . . . Ah! schism, schism, my son, is a crime beyond forgiveness, an assassination of the true God, a device of the loathsome Beast of Temptation which Hell sends into the world to work the ruin of the faithful! If your book contained nothing beyond those words 'a new religion,' it would be necessary to destroy and burn it like so much poison fatal in its effects upon the human soul.'

He continued at length on this subject, while Pierre recalled what Don Vigilio had told him of those all-powerful Jesuits who at the Vatican as elsewhere remained in the background, secretly but none the less decisively governing the Church. Was it true then that this Pope, whose opportunist tendencies were so freely displayed, was one of them, a mere docile instrument in their hands, though he fancied himself penetrated with the doctrines of St. Thomas Aquinas? In any case, like them he compounded with the century, made approaches to the world, and was willing to flatter it in order that he might possess it. Never before had Pierre so cruelly realised that the Church was now so reduced that she could only live by dint of concessions and diplomacy. And he could at last distinctly picture that Roman clergy which at first is so difficult of comprehension to a French priest, that Government of the Church, represented by the Pope, the cardinals, and the prelates, whom the Deity has appointed to govern and administer His mundane possessions—mankind and the earth. They begin by setting that very Deity on one side, in the depths of the tabernacle, and impose whatever dogmas they please as so many essential truths. That the Deity exists is evident, since they govern in His name which is sufficient for everything. And being by virtue of their charge the masters, if they consent to sign covenants, Concordats, it is only as matters of form; they do not observe them, and never yield to anything but force, always reserving the principle of their absolute sovereignty which must some day finally triumph. Pending that day's arrival, they act as diplomatists, slowly carrying on their work of conquest as the Deity's functionaries; and religion is but the public homage which they pay to the Deity, and which they organise with all the pomp and magnificence that is likely to influence the multitude. Their only object is to enrapture and conquer mankind in order that the latter may submit to the rule of the Deity, that is the rule of themselves, since they are the Deity's visible representatives, expressly delegated to govern the world. In a word, they straightway descend from Roman law, they are still but the offspring of the old pagan soil of Rome, and if they have lasted until now and if they rely on lasting for ever, until the awaited hour when the empire of the world shall be restored to them, it is because they are the direct heirs of the purple-robed Cæsars, the uninterrupted and living progeny of the blood of Augustus.

And thereupon Pierre felt ashamed of his tears. Ah! those poor nerves of his, that outburst of sentiment and enthusiasm to which he had given way! His very modesty was appalled, for he felt as if he had exhibited his soul in utter nakedness. And so uselessly too, in that room where nothing similar had ever been said before, and in presence of that Pontiff-King who could not understand him. His plan of the popes reigning by means of the poor and lowly now horrified him. His idea of the papacy going to the people, at last rid of its former masters, seemed to him a suggestion worthy of a wolf, for if the papacy should go to the people it would only be to prey upon it as the others had done. And really he, Pierre, must have been mad when he had imagined that a Roman prelate, a cardinal, a pope was capable of admitting a return to the Christian commonwealth, a fresh florescence of primitive Christianity to pacify the aged nations whom hatred consumed. Such a conception indeed was beyond the comprehension of men who for centuries had regarded themselves as masters of the world, so heedless and disdainful of the lowly and the suffering, that they had at last become altogether incapable of either love or charity.[1]

Leo XIII, however, was still holding forth in his full, unwearying voice. And the young priest heard him saying : ' Why did you write that page on Lourdes which shows such a thoroughly bad spirit ? Lourdes, my son, has rendered great services to religion. To the persons who have come and told me of the touching miracles which are witnessed at the Grotto almost daily, I have often expressed my desire to see those miracles confirmed, proved by the most rigorous scientific tests. And, indeed, according to what I have read, I do not think that the most evilly disposed minds can entertain any further doubt on the matter, for the miracles *are* proved scientifically in the most irrefutable manner. Science, my son, must be God's servant. It can do nothing against Him, it is only by His grace that it arrives at the truth. All the solutions which people now-a-days pretend to discover, and which seemingly destroy dogma, will some day be recognised as false, for God's truth will remain victorious when the times shall be accomplished. That is a very simple certainty, known even to little children, and it would suffice for the peace and salvation of mankind, if mankind would content itself with it. And be convinced, my son, that faith and reason are not incompatible. Have we not got St. Thomas who foresaw everything, explained everything, regulated everything ? Your faith has been shaken by the onslaught of the spirit of examination, you have known trouble and anguish which Heaven has been pleased to spare our priests in this land of ancient belief, this city of Rome which the blood of so many martyrs has sanctified. However, we have no fear of the spirit of examination, study St. Thomas, read him thoroughly, and your faith will return, definitive and triumphant, firmer than ever.'

These remarks caused Pierre as much dismay as if fragments of the celestial vault were raining on his head. O God of truth, miracles—the miracles of Lourdes !—proved scientifically, faith in the dogmas compatible with reason, and the

---

[1] The reader should bear in mind that these remarks apply to the *Italian* cardinals and prelates, whose vanity and egotism are remarkable.—*Trans.*

writings of St. Thomas Aquinas sufficient to instil certainty into the minds of this present generation! How could one answer that, and indeed why answer it at all?

'Yes, yours is a most culpable and dangerous book,' concluded Leo XIII; 'its very title " New Rome " is mendacious and poisonous, and the work is the more to be condemned as it offers every fascination of style, every perversion of generous fancy. Briefly, it is such a book that a priest, if he conceived it in an hour of error, can have no other duty than that of burning it in public with the very hand which traced the pages of error and scandal.'

All at once Pierre rose up erect. He was about to exclaim: ' 'Tis true, I had lost my faith, but I thought I had found it again in the compassion which the woes of the world set in my heart. You were my last hope, the awaited saviour. But, behold, that again is a dream, you cannot take the work of Jesus in hand once more and pacify mankind so as to avert the frightful fratricidal war which is preparing. You cannot leave your throne and come along the roads with the poor and the humble to carry out the supreme work of fraternity. Well, it is all over with you, your Vatican and your St. Peter's. All is falling before the onslaught of the rising multitude and growing science. You no longer exist, there are only ruins and remnants left here.'

However, he did not speak those words. He simply bowed and said: ' Holy Father, I make my submission and reprobate my book.' And as he thus replied his voice trembled with disgust, and his open hands made a gesture of surrender as though he were yielding up his soul. The words he had chosen were precisely those of the required formula: *Auctor laudabiliter se subjecit et opus reprobavit.* ' The author has laudably made his submission and reprobated his work.' No error could have been confessed, no hope could have accomplished self-destruction with loftier despair, more sovereign grandeur. But what frightful irony: that book which he had sworn never to withdraw, and for whose triumph he had fought so passionately, and which he himself now denied and suppressed, not because he deemed it guilty, but because he had just realised that it was as futile, as chimerical as a lover's desire, a poet's dream. Ah! yes, since he had been mistaken, since he had merely dreamed, since he had found there neither the Deity nor the priest that he had desired for the happiness of mankind, why should he obstinately cling to the

illusion of an awakening which was impossible! 'Twere
better to fling his book on the ground like a dead leaf, better
to deny it, better to cut it away like a dead limb that could
serve no purpose whatever !

Somewhat surprised by such a prompt victory Leo XIII
raised a slight exclamation of content. ' That is well said,
my son, that is well said! You have spoken the only words
that can become a priest.'

And in his evident satisfaction, he who left nothing to
chance, who carefully prepared each of his audiences, deciding
beforehand what words he would say, what gestures even he
would make, unbent somewhat and displayed real *bonhomie*.
Unable to understand, mistaking the real motives of this
rebellious priest's submission, he tasted positive delight in
having so easily reduced him to silence, the more so as report
had stated the young man to be a terrible revolutionary. And
thus his Holiness felt quite proud of such a conversion.
' Moreover, my son,' he said, ' I did not expect less of one of
your distinguished mind. There can be no loftier enjoyment than that of owning one's error, doing penance and
submitting.'

He had again taken the glass off the little table beside him
and was stirring the last spoonful of syrup before drinking it.
And Pierre was amazed at again finding him as he had found
him at the outset, shrunken, bereft of sovereign majesty, and
simply suggestive of some aged *bourgeois* drinking his glass
of sugared water before getting into bed. It was as if after
growing and radiating, like a planet ascending to the zenith,
he had again sunk to the level of the soil in all human mediocrity. Again did Pierre find him puny and fragile, with the
slender neck of a little sick bird, and all those marks of senile
ugliness which rendered him so exacting with regard to his
portraits, whether they were oil paintings or photographs, gold
medals, or marble busts, for of one and the other he would
say that the artist must not portray ' Papa Pecci ' but
Leo XIII, the great Pope, of whom he desired to leave such
a lofty image to posterity. And Pierre, after momentarily
ceasing to see them, was again embarrassed by the handkerchief which lay on the Pope's lap, and the dirty cassock soiled
by snuff. His only feelings now were affectionate pity for
such white old age, deep admiration for the stubborn power of
life which had found a refuge in those dark black eyes, and
respectful deference, such as became a worker, for that large

brain which harboured such vast projects and overflowed with such innumerable ideas and actions.

The audience was over, and the young man bowed low: 'I thank your Holiness for having deigned to give me such a fatherly reception,' he said.

However, Leo XIII detained him for a moment longer, speaking to him of France and expressing his sincere desire to see her prosperous, calm and strong for the greater advantage of the Church. And Pierre, during that last moment, had a singular vision, a strange haunting fancy. As he gazed at the Holy Father's ivory brow and thought of his great age and of his liability to be carried off by the slightest chill, he involuntarily recalled the scene instinct with a fierce grandeur which is witnessed each time a pope dies. He recalled Pius IX, Giovanni Mastai, two hours after death, his face covered by a white linen cloth, while the pontifical family surrounded him in dismay; and then Cardinal Pecci, the *Camerlingo*, approaching the bed, drawing aside the veil and dealing three taps with his silver hammer on the forehead of the deceased, repeating at each tap the call, 'Giovanni! Giovanni! Giovanni!' And as the corpse made no response, turning, after an interval of a few seconds, and saying: 'The Pope is dead!' And at the same time, yonder in the Via Giulia Pierre pictured Cardinal Boccanera, the present *Camerlingo*, awaiting his turn with his silver hammer, and he imagined Leo XIII, otherwise Gioachino Pecci, dead, like his predecessor, his face covered by a white linen cloth and his corpse surrounded by his prelates in that very room. And he saw the *Camerlingo* approach, draw the veil aside and tap the ivory forehead, each time repeating the call: 'Gioachino! Gioachino! Gioachino!' Then, as the corpse did not answer, he waited for a few seconds and turned and said: 'The Pope is dead!' Did Leo XIII remember how he had thrice tapped the forehead of Pius IX, and did he ever feel on the brow an icy dread of the silver hammer with which he had armed his own *Camerlingo*, the man whom he knew to be his implacable adversary, Cardinal Boccanera?

'Go in peace, my son,' at last said his Holiness by way of parting benediction. 'Your transgression will be forgiven you since you have confessed and testify your horror for it.'

With distressful spirit, accepting humiliation as well-deserved chastisement for his chimerical fancies, Pierre retired, stepping backwards according to the customary ceremonial.

He made three deep bows and crossed the threshold without turning, followed by the black eyes of Leo XIII, which never left him. Still he saw the Pope stretch his arm towards the table to take up the newspaper which he had been reading prior to the audience, for Leo retained a great fancy for newspapers, and was very inquisitive as to news, though in the isolation in which he lived he frequently made mistakes respecting the relative importance of articles. And once more the chamber sank into deep quietude, whilst the two lamps continued to diffuse a soft and steady light.

In the centre of the *anticamera segreta* Signor Squadra stood waiting black and motionless. And on noticing that Pierre in his flurry forgot to take his hat from the pier-table, he himself discreetly fetched it and handed it to the young priest with a silent bow. Then without any appearance of haste, he walked ahead to conduct the visitor back to the Sala Clementina. The endless promenade through the interminable ante-rooms began once more, and there was still not a soul, not a sound, not a breath. In each empty room stood the one solitary lamp, burning low amidst a yet deeper silence than before. The wilderness seemed also to have grown larger as the night advanced, casting its gloom over the few articles of furniture scattered under the lofty gilded ceilings, the thrones, the stools, the pier-tables, the crucifixes, and the candelabra which recurred in each succeeding room. And at last the Sala Clementina which the Swiss Guards had just quitted was reached again, and Signor Squadra who hitherto had not turned his head, thereupon drew aside without word or gesture, and, saluting Pierre with a last bow, allowed him to pass on. Then he himself disappeared.

And Pierre descended the two flights of the monumental staircase where the gas jets in their globes of ground glass glimmered like night lights amidst a wondrously heavy silence now that the footsteps of the sentries no longer resounded on the landings. And he crossed the Court of St. Damasus, empty and lifeless in the pale light of the lamps above the steps, and descended the Scala Pia, that other great stairway as dim, deserted, and void of life as all the rest, and at last passed beyond the bronze door which a porter slowly shut behind him. And with what a rumble, what a fierce roar did the hard metal close upon all that was within; all the accumulated darkness and silence; the dead, motionless centuries perpetuated by tradition; the indestructible idols, the dogmas, bound round for preservation like mummies; every chain which may weigh on one or hamper one, the whole apparatus of bondage and sovereign domination, with whose formidable clang all the dark, deserted halls re-echoed.

Once more the young man found himself alone on the gloomy expanse of the Piazza of St. Peter's. Not a single belated pedestrian was to be seen. There was only the lofty livid, ghost-like obelisk, emerging between its four candelabra from the mosaic pavement of red and serpentine porphyry. The façade of the basilica also showed vaguely, pale as a vision, whilst from it on either side like a pair of giant arms stretched the quadruple colonnade, a thicket of stone, steeped in obscurity. The dome was but a huge roundness scarcely discernible against the moonless sky; and only the jets of the fountains, which could at last be detected rising like slim phantoms ever on the move, lent a voice to the silence, the endless murmur of a plaint of sorrow coming one knew not whence. Ah! how great was the melancholy grandeur of that slumber, that famous square, the Vatican and St. Peter's, thus seen by night when wrapped in silence and darkness! But suddenly the clock struck ten with so slow and loud a chime that never, so it seemed, had more solemn and decisive an hour rung out amidst blacker and more unfathomable gloom. All Pierre's poor weary frame quivered at the sound as he stood motionless in the centre of the expanse. What! had he spent barely three-quarters of an hour, chatting up yonder with that white old man who had just wrenched all his soul away from him! Yes, it was the final wrench; his last belief had been torn from his bleeding heart and brain. The supreme experiment had been made, a world had collapsed within him. And all at once be thought of Monsignor Nani, and reflected that he alone had been right. He, Pierre, had been told that in any case he would end by doing what Monsignor Nani might desire, and he was now stupefied to find that he had done so.

But sudden despair seized upon him, such atrocious distress of spirit that from the depths of the abyss of darkness where he stood, he raised his quivering arms into space and spoke aloud: 'No, no, Thou art not here, O God of life and love, O God of Salvation! But come, appear since Thy children are perishing because they know neither who Thou art, nor where to find Thee amidst the Infinite of the worlds!

Above the vast square spread the vast sky of dark blue

velvet, the silent disturbing Infinite, where the constellations
palpitated. Over the roofs of the Vatican, Charles's Wain
seemed yet more tilted, its golden wheels straying from the
right path, its golden shaft upreared in the air; whilst yonder,
over Rome towards the Via Giulia, Orion was about to disappear and already showed but one of the three golden stars
which bedecked his belt.

XV

It was nearly daybreak when Pierre fell asleep, exhausted by
emotion and hot with fever. And at nine o'clock, when he had
risen and breakfasted, he at once wished to go down into
Cardinal Boccanera's rooms where the bodies of Dario and
Benedetta had been laid in state in order that the members of
the family, its friends and clients, might bring them their tears
and prayers.

Whilst he breakfasted, Victorine who, showing an active
bravery amidst her despair, had not been to bed at all, told him
of what had taken place in the house during the night and
early morning. Donna Serafina, prude that she was, had
again made an attempt to have the bodies separated; but this
had proved an impossibility, as *rigor mortis* had set in, and to
part the lovers it would have been necessary to break their
limbs. Moreover, the Cardinal, who had interposed once
before, almost quarrelled with his sister on the subject, unwilling as he was that anyone should disturb the lovers' last
slumber, their union of eternity. Beneath his priestly garb
there coursed the blood of his race, a pride in the passions of
former times; and he remarked that if the family counted two
popes among its forerunners, it had also been rendered illustrious by great captains and ardent lovers. Never would he
allow anyone to touch those two children, whose dolorous lives
had been so pure and whom the grave alone had united. He
was the master in his house, and they should be sewn together
in the same shroud, and nailed together in the same coffin.
Then, too, the religious service should take place at the neighbouring church of San Carlo, of which he was Cardinal-priest
and where again he was the master. And if needful he would
address himself to the Pope. And such being his sovereign
will, so authoritatively expressed, everybody in the house had
to bow submissively.

Donna Serafina at once occupied herself with the laying-out. According to the Roman custom the servants were present, and Victorine, as the oldest and most appreciated of them, assisted the relatives. All that could be done in the first instance was to envelop both corpses in Benedetta's unbound hair, thick and odorous hair, which spread out into a royal mantle; and they were then lain together in one shroud of white silk, fastened about their necks in such wise that they formed but one being in death. And again the Cardinal imperatively ordered that they should be brought into his apartments and placed on a state bed in the centre of the throne-room, so that a supreme homage might be rendered to them as to the last scions of the name, the two tragic lovers with whom the once resounding glory of the Boccaneras was about to return to earth. The story which had been arranged was already circulating through Rome; folks related how Dario had been carried off in a few hours by infectious fever, and how Benedetta, maddened by grief, had expired whilst clasping him in her arms to bid him a last farewell; and there was talk too of the royal honours which the bodies were to receive, the superb funeral nuptials which were to be accorded them as they lay clasped on their bed of eternal rest. All Rome, quite overcome by this tragic story of love and death, would talk of nothing else for several weeks.

Pierre would have started for France that same night, eager as he was to quit the city of disaster where he had lost the last shreds of his faith, but he desired to attend the obsequies, and therefore postponed his departure until the following evening. And thus he would spend one more day in that old crumbling palace, near the corpse of that unhappy young woman to whom he had been so much attached and for whom he would try to find some prayers in the depths of his empty and lacerated heart.

When he reached the threshold of the Cardinal's reception rooms, he suddenly remembered his first visit to them. They still presented the same aspect of ancient princely pomp falling into decay and dust. The doors of the three large ante-rooms were wide open, and the rooms themselves were at that early hour still empty. In the first one, the servants' ante-room, there was nobody but Giacomo, who stood motionless in his black livery in front of the old red hat hanging under the *baldacchino* where spiders spun their webs between the crum-

bling tassels. In the second room, which the secretary formerly
had occupied, Abbé Paparelli, the train-bearer, was softly
walking up and down whilst waiting for visitors; and with
his conquering humility, his all-powerful obseqiousness, he
had never before so closely resembled an old maid, whitened
and wrinkled by excess of devout observances. Finally, in
the third anteroom, the *anticamera nobile*, where the red cap
ay on a credence facing the large imperious portrait of the
Cardinal in ceremonial costume, there was Don Vigilio, who
had left his little work-table to station himself at the door of
the throne-room and there bow to those who crossed the
threshold. And on that gloomy winter morning the rooms
appeared more mournful and dilapidated than ever, the hangings frayed and ragged, the few articles of furniture covered
with dust, the old woodwork crumbling beneath the continuous onslaught of termites, and the ceilings alone retaining
their pompous show of gilding and painting.

However, Pierre, to whom Abbé Paparelli addressed a profound bow, in which one divined the irony of a sort of dismissal
given to one who was vanquished, felt more impressed by the
mournful grandeur which those three dilapidated rooms presented that day, conducting as they did to the old throne-room,
now a chamber of death, where the two last children of the
house slept their last sleep. What a superb and sorrowful
gala of death! Every door wide open and all the emptiness
of those over-spacious rooms, void of the throngs of ancient
days and leading to the supreme affliction—the end of a race!
The Cardinal had shut himself up in his little work-room
where he received the relatives and intimates who desired to
present their condolences to him, whilst Donna Serafina had
chosen an adjoining apartment to await her lady friends who
would come in procession until evening. And Pierre, informed
of the ceremonial by Victorine, had in the first place to enter
the throne-room, greeted as he passed by a deep bow from Don
Vigilio who, pale and silent, did not seem to recognise him.

A surprise awaited the young priest. He had expected
such a lying-in-state as is seen in France and elsewhere, all
windows closed so as to steep the room in night, and hundreds
of candles burning round a *catafalco*, whilst from ceiling to
floor the walls were hung with black drapery. He had been
told that the bodies would lie in the throne-room because the
antique chapel on the ground floor of the *palazzo* had been
shut up for half a century and was in no condition to be used,

whilst the Cardinal's little private chapel was altogether too small for any such ceremony. And thus it had been necessary to improvise an altar in the throne-room, an altar at which masses had been said ever since dawn. Masses and other religious services were moreover to be celebrated all day long in the private chapel; and two additional altars had even been set up, one in a small room adjoining the *anticamera nobile* and the other in a sort of alcove communicating with the second ante-room: and in this wise priests, Franciscans, and members of other Orders bound by the vow of poverty, would simultaneously and without intermission celebrate the divine sacrifice on those four altars. The Cardinal, indeed, had desired that the Divine Blood should flow without pause under his roof for the redemption of those two dear souls which had flown away together. And thus in that mourning mansion, through those funeral halls the bells scarcely stopped tinkling for the elevation of the Host, whilst the quivering murmur of Latin words ever continued, and consecrated wafers were continually broken and chalices drained, in such wise that the Divine Presence could not for a moment quit the heavy atmosphere all redolent of death.

On the other hand, however, Pierre, to his great astonishment, found the throne-room much as it had been on the day of his first visit. The curtains of the four large windows had not even been drawn, and the grey, cold, subdued light of the gloomy winter morning freely entered. Under the ceiling of carved and gilded woodwork there were the customary red wall-hangings of *brocatelle*, worn away by long usage; and there was the old throne with the arm-chair turned to the wall, uselessly waiting for a visit from the Pope which would never more come. The principal changes in the aspect of the room were that its seats and tables had been removed, and that, in addition to the improvised altar arranged beside the throne, it now contained the state bed on which lay the bodies of Benedetta and Dario, amidst a profusion of flowers. The bed stood in the centre of the room on a low platform, and at its head were two lighted candles, one on either side. There was nothing else, nothing but that wealth of flowers, such a harvest of white roses that one wondered in what fairy garden they had been culled, sheaves of them on the bed, sheaves of them toppling from the bed, sheaves of them covering the step of the platform, and falling from that step on to the magnificent marble paving of the room.

Pierre drew near to the bed, his heart faint with emotion. Those tapers whose little yellow flamelets scarcely showed in the pale daylight, that continuous low murmur of the Mass being said at the altar, that penetrating perfume of roses which rendered the atmosphere so heavy, filled the antiquated, dusty room with a spirit of infinite woe, a lamentation of boundless mourning. And there was not a gesture, not a word spoken, save by the priest officiating at the altar, nothing but an occasional faint sound of stifled sobbing among the few persons present. Servants of the house constantly relieved one another, four always standing erect and motionless at the head of the bed, like faithful, familar guards. From time to time Consistorial Advocate Morano, who, since early morning had been attending to everything, crossed the room with a silent step and the air of a man in a hurry. And at the edge of the platform all who entered, knelt, prayed and wept. Pierre perceived three ladies there, their faces hidden by their handkerchiefs ; and there was also an old priest who trembled with grief and hung his head in such wise that his face could not be distinguished. However, the young man was most moved by the sight of a poorly clad girl, whom he took for a servant, and whom sorrow had utterly prostrated on the marble slabs.

Then in his turn he knelt down, and with the professional murmur of the lips sought to repeat the Latin prayers which, as a priest, he had so often said at the bedside of the departed. But his growing emotion confused his memory, and he became wrapt in contemplation of the lovers whom his eyes were unable to quit. Under the wealth of flowers which covered them the clasped bodies could scarcely be distinguished, but the two heads emerged from the silken shroud, and lying there on the same cushion, with their hair mingling, they were still beautiful, beautiful as with satisfied passion. Benedetta had kept her divinely gay, loving, and faithful face for eternity, transported with rapture at having rendered up her last breath in a kiss of love ; whilst Dario retained a more dolorous expression amidst his final joy. And their eyes were still wide open, gazing at one another with a persistent and caressing sweetness which nothing would ever more disturb.

Oh, God ! was it true that yonder lay that Benedetta whom he, Pierre, had loved with such pure, brotherly affection ? He was stirred to the very depths of his soul by the recollection of the delightful hours which he had spent with her. She had been so beautiful, so sensible, yet so full of passion! And he had indulged in so beautiful a dream, that of animating with his own liberating fraternal feelings that admirable creature with soul of fire and indolent air, in whom he had pictured all ancient Rome, and whom he would have liked to awaken and win over to the Italy of to-morrow. He had dreamt of enlarging her brain and heart by filling her with love for the lowly and the poor, with all present-day compassion for things and beings. How he would now have smiled at such a dream had not his tears been flowing! Yet how charming she had shown herself in striving to content him despite the invincible obstacles of race, education and environment. She had been a docile pupil, but was incapable of any real progress. One day she had certainly seemed to draw nearer to him, as though her own sufferings had opened her soul to every charity; but the illusion of happiness had come back, and then she had lost all understanding of the woes of others, and had gone off in the egotism of her own hope and joy. Did that mean then that this Roman race must finish in that fashion, beautiful as it still often is, and fondly adored but so closed to all love for others, to those laws of charity and justice which, by regulating labour, can henceforth alone save this world of ours?

Then there came another great sorrow to Pierre which left him stammering, unable to speak any precise prayer. He thought of the overwhelming re-assertion of Nature's powers which had attended the death of those two poor children. Was it not awful? To have taken that vow to the Virgin, to have endured torment throughout life, and to end by plunging into death, on the loved one's neck, distracted by vain regret and eager for self-bestowal! The brutal fact of impending separation had sufficed for Benedetta to realise how she had duped herself, and to revert to the universal instinct of love. And therein, again once more, was the Church vanquished; therein again appeared the great god Pan, mating the sexes and scattering life around! If in the days of the Renascence the Church did not fall beneath the assault of the Venuses and Hercules then exhumed from the old soil of Rome, the struggle at all events continued as bitterly as ever; and at each and every hour new nations, overflowing with sap, hungering for life, and warring against a religion which was nothing more than an appetite for death, threatened to

sweep away that old Holy Apostolic Roman and Catholic
edifice whose walls were already tottering on all sides.

And at that moment Pierre felt that the death of that
adorable Benedetta was for him the supreme disaster. He
was still looking at her and tears were scorching his eyes.
She was carrying off his chimera. This time 'twas really the
end. Rome the Catholic and the Princely was dead, lying
there like marble on that funeral bed. She had been unable
to go to the humble, the suffering ones of the world, and had
just expired amidst the impotent cry of her egotistical passion
when it was too late either to love or to create. Never more
would children be born of her, the old Roman house was
henceforth empty, sterile, beyond possibility of awakening.
Pierre, whose soul mourned such a splendid dream, was
so grieved at seeing her thus motionless and frigid, that he
felt himself fainting. He feared lest he might fall upon the
step beside the bed, and so struggled to his feet and drew aside.

Then, as he sought refuge in a window recess in order
that he might try to recover self-possession, he was astonished
to perceive Victorine seated there on a bench which the hangings
half concealed. She had come thither by Donna Serafina's
orders, and sat watching her two dear children as she called
them, whilst keeping an eye upon all who came in and went
out. And, on seeing the young priest so pale and nearly
swooning, she at once made room for him to sit down beside
her. 'Ah!' he murmured after drawing a long breath, 'may
they at least have the joy of being together elsewhere, of
living a new life in another world.'

Victorine, however, shrugged her shoulders, and in an
equally low voice responded, 'Oh! live again, Monsieur
l'Abbé, why? When one's dead the best is to remain so and to
sleep. Those poor children had enough torments on earth,
one mustn't wish that they should begin again elsewhere.'

This naïve yet deep remark on the part of an ignorant
unbelieving woman sent a shudder through Pierre's very
bones. To think that his own teeth had chattered with fear
at night time at the sudden thought of annihilation. He
deemed her heroic at remaining so undisturbed by any ideas
of eternity and the infinite. And she, as she felt he was
quivering, went on: 'What can you suppose there should
be after death? We've deserved a right to sleep, and
nothing to my thinking can be more desirable and consoling.'

'But those two did not live,' murmured Pierre, 'so why

not allow oneself the joy of believing that they now live elsewhere, recompensed for all their torments?'

Victorine, however, again shook her head, 'No, no,' she replied. 'Ah! I was quite right in saying that my poor Benedetta did wrong in torturing herself with all those superstitious ideas of hers when she was really so fond of her lover. Yes, happiness is rarely found, and how one regrets having missed it when it's too late to turn back! That's the whole story of those poor little ones. It's too late for them, they are dead.' Then in her turn she broke down and began to sob. 'Poor little ones! poor little ones! Look how white they are, and think what they will be when only the bones of their heads lie side by side on the cushion, and only the bones of their arms still clasp one another. Ah! may they sleep, may they sleep; at least they know nothing and feel nothing now.'

A long interval of silence followed. Pierre, amidst the quiver of his own doubts, the anxious desire which in common with most men he felt for a new life beyond the grave, gazed at this woman who did not find priests to her fancy, and who retained all her Beauceronne frankness of speech, with the tranquil, contented air of one who has ever done her duty in her humble station as a servant, lost though she had been for five-and-twenty years in a land of wolves, whose language she had not even been able to learn. Ah! yes, tortured as the young man was by his doubts, he would have liked to be as she was, a well-balanced, healthy, ignorant creature who was quite content with what the world offered, and who, when she had accomplished her daily task, went fully satisfied to bed, careless as to whether she might never wake again!

However, as Pierre's eyes once more sought the state-bed, he suddenly recognised the old priest, who was kneeling on the step of the platform, and whose features he had hitherto been unable to distinguish. 'Isn't that Abbé Pisoni, the priest of Santa Brigida, where I sometimes said mass?' he inquired. 'The poor old man, how he weeps!'

In her quiet yet desolate voice Victorine replied, 'He has good reason to weep. He did a fine thing when he took it into his head to marry my poor Benedetta to Count Prada. All those abominations would never have happened if the poor child had been given her Dario at once. But in this idiotic city they are all mad with their politics; and that old priest, who is none the less a very worthy man, thought he had accomplished a real miracle and saved the world by marrying the Pope and the King as he said with a soft laugh, poor old *savant* that he is, who for his part has never been in love with anything but old stones—you know, all that antiquated rubbish of theirs of a hundred thousand years ago. And now, you see, he can't keep from weeping. The other one came too not twenty minutes ago, Father Lorenza, the Jesuit who became the Contessina's confessor after Abbé Pisoni, and who undid what the other had done. Yes, a handsome man he is, but a fine bungler all the same, a perfect killjoy with all the crafty hindrances which he brought into that divorce affair. I wish you had been here to see what a big sign of the cross he made after he had knelt down. He didn't cry, he didn't : he seemed to be saying that as things had ended so badly it was evident that God had withdrawn from all share in the business. So much the worse for the dead ! '

Victorine spoke gently and without a pause, as if it relieved her to empty her heart after the terrible hours of bustle and suffocation which she had spent since the previous day. ' And that one yonder,' she resumed in a lower voice, ' don't you recognise her ? '

She glanced towards the poorly-clad girl whom Pierre had taken for a servant, and whom intensity of grief had prostrated beside the bed. With a gesture of awful suffering this girl had just thrown back her head, a head of extraordinary beauty, enveloped by superb black hair.

' La Pierina ! ' said Pierre. ' Ah ! poor girl.'

Victorine made a gesture of compassion and tolerance. ' What would you have ? ' said she, ' I let her come up. I don't know how she heard of the trouble, but it's true that she is always prowling round the house. She sent and asked me to come down to her, and you should have heard her sob and entreat me to let her see her Prince once more ! Well, she does no harm to anybody there on the floor, looking at them both with her beautiful loving eyes full of tears. She's been there for half an hour already, and I had made up my mind to turn her out if she didn't behave properly. But since she's so quiet and doesn't even move, she may well stop and fill her heart with the sight of them for her whole life long.'

It was really sublime to see that ignorant, passionate, beautiful Pierina thus overwhelmed below the nuptial couch on which the lovers slept for all eternity. She had sunk down on her heels, her arms hanging heavily beside her, and her hands open. And with raised face, motionless as in an ecstasy of suffering, she did not take her eyes from that adorable and tragic pair. Never had human face displayed such beauty, such a dazzling splendour of suffering and love; never had there been such a portrayal of ancient Grief, not however cold like marble but quivering with life. What was she thinking of, what were her sufferings, as she thus fixedly gazed at her Prince now and for ever locked in her rival's arms? Was it some jealousy which could have no end that chilled the blood of her veins? Or was it mere suffering at having lost him, at realising that she was looking at him for the last time, without thought of hatred for that other woman who vainly sought to warm him with her arms as icy cold as his own? There was still a soft gleam in the poor girl's blurred eyes, and her lips were still lips of love though curved in bitterness by grief. She found the lovers so pure and beautiful as they lay there amidst that profusion of flowers! And beautiful herself, beautiful like a queen ignorant of her own charms, she remained there breathless, a humble servant, a loving slave as it were, whose heart had been wrenched away and carried off by her dying master.

People were now constantly entering the room, slowly approaching with mournful faces, then kneeling and praying for a few minutes, and afterwards retiring with the same mute, desolate mien. A pang came to Pierre's heart when he saw Dario's mother, the ever beautiful Flavia, enter, accompanied by her husband, the handsome Jules Laporte, that ex-sergeant of the Swiss Guard whom she had turned into a Marquis Montefiori. Warned of the tragedy directly it had happened, she had already come to the mansion on the previous evening; but now she returned in grand ceremony and full mourning, looking superb in her black garments, which were well suited to her massive Juno-like style of beauty. When she had approached the bed with a queenly step, she remained for a moment standing with two tears at the edges of her eyelids, tears which did not fall. Then, at the moment of kneeling, she made sure that Jules was beside her, and glanced at him as if to order him to kneel as well. They both sank down beside the platform and remained in prayer for the proper interval, she very dignified in her grief and he even surpassing her, with the perfect sorrow-stricken bearing of a man who knew how to conduct himself in every circumstance of life, even the gravest. And after-

wards they rose together, and slowly betook themselves to the
entrance of the private apartments where the Cardinal and
Donna Serafina were receiving their relatives and friends.

Five ladies then came in one after the other, while two
Capuchins and the Spanish Ambassador to the Holy See went
off. And Victorine, who for a few minutes had remained
silent, suddenly resumed. 'Ah! there's the little Princess,
she's much afflicted too, and, no wonder, she was so fond of
our Benedetta.'

Pierre himself had just noticed Celia coming in. She also
had attired herself in full mourning for this abominable visit
of farewell. Behind her was a maid, who carried on either
arm a huge sheaf of white roses.

'The dear girl!' murmured Victorine, 'she wanted her
wedding with her Attilio to take place on the same day as
that of the poor lovers who lie there. And they, alas! have
forestalled her, their wedding's over; there they sleep in their
bridal bed.'

Celia had at once crossed herself and knelt down beside
the bed, but it was evident that she was not praying. She
was indeed looking at the lovers with desolate stupefaction at
finding them so white and cold with a beauty as of marble.
What! had a few hours sufficed, had life departed, would
those lips never more exchange a kiss! She could again see
them at the ball of that other night, so resplendent and
triumphant with their living love. And a feeling of furious
protest rose from her young heart, so open to life, so eager
for joy and sunlight, so angry with the hateful idiocy of death.
And her anger and affright and grief, as she thus found herself face to face with the annihilation which chills every
passion, could be read on her ingenuous, candid, lily-like
face. She herself stood on the threshold of a life of passion
of which she yet knew nothing, and behold on that very
threshold she encountered the corpses of those dearly loved
ones, the loss of whom racked her soul with grief.

She gently closed her eyes and tried to pray, whilst big
tears fell from under her lowered eyelids. Some time went
by amidst the quivering silence, which only the murmur of
the mass near by disturbed. At last she rose and took the
sheaves of flowers from her maid; and standing on the platform she hesitated for a moment, then placed the roses to the
right and left of the cushion on which the lovers' heads were
resting, as if she wished to crown them with those blossoms,

perfume their young brows with that sweet and powerful
aroma. Then, though her hands remained empty, she did
not retire, but remained there leaning over the dead ones,
trembling and seeking what she might yet say to them, what
she might leave them of herself for evermore. And inspiration came to her, and she stooped forward, and with her whole,
deep, loving soul set a long, long kiss on the brow of either
spouse.

'Ah! the dear girl!' said Victorine, whose tears were
again flowing. 'You saw that she kissed them, and nobody
had yet thought of that, not even the poor young Prince's
mother. Ah! the dear little heart, she surely thought of her
Attilio.'

However, as Celia turned to descend from the platform
she perceived La Pierina, whose figure was still thrown back
in an attitude of mute and dolorous adoration. And she recognised the girl and melted with pity on seeing such a fit of sobbing come over her that her whole body, her goddess-like hips
and bosom, shook as with frightful anguish. That agony of
love quite upset the little Princess, and she could be heard
murmuring in a tone of infinite compassion, 'Calm yourself,
my dear, calm yourself. Be reasonable, my dear, I beg you.'

Then as La Pierina, thunderstruck at thus being pitied
and succoured, began to sob yet more loudly so as to create
quite a stir in the room, Celia raised her and held her up
with both arms, for fear lest she should fall again. And she
led her away in a sisterly clasp, like a sister of affection and
despair, lavishing the most gentle, consoling words upon her
as they went.

'Follow them, go and see what becomes of them,'
Victorine said to Pierre. 'I do not want to stir from here,
it quiets me to watch over my two poor children.'

A Capuchin was just beginning a fresh mass at the improvised altar, and the low Latin psalmody went on again,
while in the adjoining ante-chamber, where another mass was
being celebrated, a bell was heard tinkling for the elevation of
the Host. The perfume of the flowers was becoming more
violent and oppressive amidst the motionless and mournful
atmosphere of the spacious throne-room. The four servants
standing at the head of the bed, as for a gala reception, did
not stir, and the procession of visitors ever continued, men
and women entering in silence, suffocating there for a
moment, and then withdrawing, carrying away with them the

never to be forgotten vision of the two tragic lovers sleeping their eternal sleep.

Pierre joined Celia and La Pierina in the *anticamera nobile*, where stood Don Vigilio. The few seats belonging to the throne-room had there been placed in a corner, and the little Princess had just compelled the work-girl to sit down in an arm-chair, in order that she might recover self-possession. Celia was in ecstasy before her, enraptured at finding her so beautiful, more beautiful than any other, as she said. Then she spoke of the two dead ones, who also had seemed to her very beautiful, endowed with an extraordinary beauty, at once superb and sweet; and despite all her tears, she still remained in a transport of admiration. On speaking with La Pierina, Pierre learnt that her brother Tito was at the hospital in great danger from the effects of a terrible knife-thrust dealt him in the side; and since the beginning of the winter, said the girl, the misery in the district of the castle-fields had become frightful. It was a source of great suffering to everyone, and those whom death carried off had reason to rejoice.

Celia, however, with a gesture of invincible hopefulness, brushed all idea of suffering, even of death, aside. 'No, no, we must live,' she said. 'And beauty is sufficient for life. Come, my dear, do not remain here, do not weep any more; live for the delight of being beautiful.'

Then she led La Pierina away, and Pierre remained seated in one of the arm-chairs, overcome by such sorrow and weariness that he would have liked to remain there for ever. Don Vigilio was still bowing to each fresh visitor that arrived. A severe attack of fever had come on him during the night, and he was shivering from it, with his face very yellow, and his eyes ablaze and haggard. He constantly glanced at Pierre, as if anxious to speak to him, but his dread lest he should be seen by Abbé Paparelli, who stood in the next ante-room, the door of which was wide open, doubtless restrained him, for he did not cease to watch the train-bearer. At last the latter was compelled to absent himself for a moment, and the secretary thereupon approached the young Frenchman.

'You saw his Holiness last night,' he said; and as Pierre gazed at him in stupefaction he added: 'Oh! everything gets known, I told you so before. Well, and you purely and simply withdrew your book, did you not?' The young priest's increasing stupor was sufficient answer, and without leaving him time to reply, Don Vigilio went on : 'I suspected it, but I wished to make certain. Ah ! that's just the way they work ! Do you believe me now, have you realised that they stifle those whom they don't poison ?'

He was no doubt referring to the Jesuits. However, after glancing into the adjoining room to make sure that Abbé Paparelli had not returned thither, he resumed : 'And what has Monsignor Nani just told you ?'

'But I have not yet seen Monsignor Nani,' was Pierre's reply.

'Oh ! I thought you had. He passed through before you arrived. If you did not see him in the throne-room he must have gone to pay his respects to Donna Serafina and his Eminence. However, he will certainly pass this way again ; you will see him by-and-by.' Then with the bitterness of one who was weak, ever terror-smitten and vanquished, Don Vigilio added : 'I told you that you would end by doing what Monsignor Nani desired.'

With these words, fancying that he heard the light footfall of Abbé Paparelli, he hastily returned to his place and bowed to two old ladies who just then walked in. And Pierre, still seated, overcome, his eyes wearily closing, at last saw the figure of Nani arise before him in all its reality so typical of sovereign intelligence and address. He remembered what Don Vigilio, on the famous night of his revelations, had told him of this man who was far too shrewd to have labelled himself, so to say, with an unpopular robe, and who, withal, was a charming prelate with thorough knowledge of the world, acquired by long experience at different nunciatures and at the Holy Office, mixed up in everything, informed with regard to everything, one of the heads, one of the chief minds in fact of that modern black army, which by dint of Opportunism hopes to bring this century back to the Church. And all at once, full enlightenment fell on Pierre, he realised by what supple, clever strategy that man had led him to the act which he desired of him, the pure and simple withdrawal of his book, accomplished with every appearance of free will. First there had been great annoyance on Nani's part on learning that the book was being prosecuted, for he feared lest its excitable author might be prompted to some dangerous revolt ; then plans had at once been formed, information had been collected concerning this young priest who seemed so capable of schism, he had been urged to come to Rome, invited to stay in an

ancient mansion whose very walls would chill and enlighten
him. And afterwards had come the ever-recurring obstacles,
the system of prolonging his sojourn in Rome by preventing
him from seeing the Pope, but promising him the much-
desired interview when the proper time should come, that is
after he had been sent hither and thither and brought into
collision with one and all. And finally, when everyone and
everything had shaken, wearied and disgusted him, and he
was restored once more to his old doubts, there had come the
audience for which he had undergone all this preparation,
that visit to the Pope which was destined to shatter whatever
remained to him of his dream. Pierre could picture Nani
smiling at him and speaking to him, declaring that the
repeated delays were a favour of Providence, which would
enable him to visit Rome, study and understand things, reflect,
and avoid blunders. How delicate and how profound had
been the prelate's diplomacy in thus crushing his feelings
beneath his reason, appealing to his intelligence to suppress
his work without any scandalous struggle as soon as his knowledge of the real Rome should have shown him how supremely
ridiculous it was to dream of a new one!

At that moment Pierre perceived Nani in person just
coming from the throne-room, and did not feel the irritation
and rancour which he had anticipated. On the contrary he
was glad when the prelate, in his turn seeing him, drew near
and held out his hand. Nani, however, did not wear his
wonted smile, but looked very grave, quite grief-stricken.
'Ah! my dear son,' he said, 'what a frightful catastrophe!
I have just left his Eminence, he is in tears. It is horrible,
horrible!'

He seated himself on one of the chairs, inviting the young
priest who had risen to do the same; and for a moment he
remained silent, weary with emotion no doubt, and needing
a brief rest to free himself of the weight of thoughts which
visibly darkened his usually bright face. Then, with a gesture,
he strove to dismiss that gloom, and recover his amiable
cordiality. 'Well, my dear son,' he began, 'you saw his
Holiness?'

'Yes, Monseigneur, yesterday evening; and I thank you
for your great kindness in satisfying my desire.'

Nani looked at him fixedly, and his invincible smile again
returned to his lips. 'You thank me. . . . I can well see
that you behaved sensibly and laid your full submission at his

Holiness's feet. I was certain of it, I did not expect less of
your fine intelligence. But, all the same, you render me very
happy, for I am delighted to find that I was not mistaken
concerning you.' And then, setting aside his reserve, the
prelate went on : 'I never discussed things with you. What
would have been the good of it, since facts were there to convince you? And now that you have withdrawn your book
a discussion would be still more futile. However, just reflect
that if it were possible for you to bring the Church back to
her early period, to that Christian community which you have
sketched so delightfully, she could only again follow the same
evolutions as those in which God the first time guided her ;
so that, at the end of a similar number of centuries, she would
find herself exactly in the position which she occupies to-day.
No, what God has done has been well done, the Church such
as she is must govern the world, such as it is ; it is for her
alone to know how she will end by firmly establishing her
reign here below. And this is why your attack upon the
temporal power was an unpardonable fault, a crime even, for
by dispossessing the papacy of her domains you hand her over
to the mercy of the nations. Your new religion is but the final
downfall of all religion, moral anarchy, the liberty of schism,
in a word, the destruction of the divine edifice, that ancient
Catholicism which has shown such prodigious wisdom and
solidity, which has sufficed for the salvation of mankind till
now, and will alone be able to save it to-morrow and always.'

Pierre felt that Nani was sincere, pious even, and really
unshakable in his faith, loving the Church like a grateful
son, and convinced that she was the only social organisation
which could render mankind happy. And if he were bent on
governing the world, it was doubtless for the pleasure of
governing, but also in the conviction that no one could do so
better than himself.

'Oh ! certainly,' said he, 'methods are open to discussion.
I desire them to be as affable and humane as possible, as conciliatory as can be with this present century, which seems to
be escaping us, precisely because there is a misunderstanding
between us. But we shall bring it back, I am sure of it.
And that is why, my dear son, I am so pleased to see you
return to the fold, thinking as we think, and ready to battle
on our side, is that not so ? '

In Nani's words the young priest once more found the
arguments of Leo XIII. Desiring to avoid a direct reply, for

although he now felt no anger the wrenching away of his dream had left him a smarting wound, he bowed, and replied slowly in order to conceal the bitter tremble of his voice : ' I repeat, Monseigneur, that I deeply thank you for having amputated my vain illusions with the skill of an accomplished surgeon. A little later, when I shall have ceased to suffer, I shall think of you with eternal gratitude.'

Monsignor Nani still looked at him with a smile. He fully understood that this young priest would remain on one side, that as an element of strength he was lost to the Church. What would he do now ? Something foolish no doubt. However, the prelate had to content himself with having helped him to repair his first folly ; he could not foresee the future. And he gracefully waved his hand as if to say that sufficient unto the day was the evil thereof.

' Will you allow me to conclude, my dear son ? ' he at last exclaimed. ' Be sensible, your happiness as a priest and a man lies in humility. You will be terribly unhappy if you use the great intelligence which God has given you against Him.'

Then with another gesture he dismissed this affair, which was all over, and with which he need busy himself no more. And thereupon the other affair came back to make him gloomy, that other affair which also was drawing to a close, but so tragically, with those two poor children slumbering in the adjoining room. ' Ah ! ' he resumed, ' that poor Princess and that poor Cardinal quite upset my heart ! Never did catastrophe fall so cruelly on a house. No, no, it is indeed too much, misfortune goes too far—it revolts one's soul ! '

Just as he finished a sound of voices came from the second ante-room, and Pierre was thunderstruck to see Cardinal Sanguinetti go by, escorted with the greatest obsequiousness by Abbé Paparelli.

' If your most reverend Eminence will have the extreme kindness to follow me,' the train-bearer was saying, ' I will conduct your most reverend Eminence myself.'

' Yes,' replied Sanguinetti, ' I arrived yesterday evening from Frascati, and when I heard the sad news, I at once desired to express my sorrow and offer consolation.'

Your Eminence will perhaps condescend to remain for a moment near the bodies. I will afterwards escort your Eminence to the private apartments.'

' Yes, by all means. I desire every one to know how greatly

I participate in the sorrow which has fallen on this illustrious house.'

Then Sanguinetti entered the throne-room, leaving Pierre quite aghast at his quiet audacity. The young priest certainly did not accuse him of direct complicity with Santobono, he did not even dare to measure how far his moral complicity might go. But on seeing him pass by like that, his brow so lofty, his speech so clear, he had suddenly felt convinced that he knew the truth. How or through whom, he could not have told; but doubtless crimes become known in those shady spheres by those whose interest it is to know of them. And Pierre remained quite chilled by the haughty fashion in which that man presented himself, perhaps to stifle suspicion and certainly to accomplish an act of good policy by giving his rival a public mark of esteem and affection.

'The Cardinal! Here!' Pierre murmured despite himself.

Nani, who followed the young man's thoughts in his childish eyes, in which all could be read, pretended to mistake the sense of his exclamation. 'Yes,' said he, 'I learnt that the Cardinal returned to Rome yesterday evening. He did not wish to remain away any longer; the Holy Father being so much better that he might perhaps have need of him.'

Although these words were spoken with an air of perfect innocence, Pierre was not for a moment deceived by them. And having in his turn glanced at the prelate, he was convinced that the latter also knew the truth. Then, all at once, the whole affair appeared to him in its intricacy, in the ferocity which fate had imparted to it. Nani, an old intimate of the Palazzo Boccanera, was not heartless, he had surely loved Benedetta with affection, charmed by so much grace and beauty. One could thus explain the victorious manner in which he had at last caused her marriage to be annulled. But if Don Vigilio were to be believed, that divorce, obtained by pecuniary outlay, and under pressure of the most notorious influences, was simply a scandal which he, Nani, had in the first instance spun out, and then precipitated towards a resounding finish with the sole object of discrediting the Cardinal and destroying his chances of the tiara on the eve of the conclave which everybody thought imminent. It seemed certain, too, that the Cardinal, uncompromising as he was, could not be the candidate of Nani, who was so desirous of universal agreement, and so the latter's long labour in that house, whilst conducing to the happiness of the Contessina, had been designed to frustrate Donna Serafina and Cardinal Pio in their burning ambition, that third triumphant elevation to the papacy which they sought to secure for their ancient family. However, if Nani had always desired to baulk this ambition, and had even at one moment placed his hopes in Sanguinetti and fought for him, he had never imagined that Boccanera's foes would go to the point of crime, to such an abomination as poison which missed its mark and killed the innocent. No, no, as he himself said, that was too much, and made one's soul rebel. He employed more gentle weapons ; such brutality filled him with indignation ; and his face, so pinky and carefully tended, still wore the grave expression of his revolt in presence of the tearful Cardinal and those poor lovers stricken in his stead.

Believing that Sanguinetti was still the prelate's secret candidate, Pierre was worried to know how far their moral complicity in this baleful affair might go. So he resumed the conversation by saying : 'It is asserted that his Holiness is on bad terms with his Eminence Cardinal Sanguinetti. Of course the reigning Pope cannot look on the future Pope with a very kindly eye.'

At this, Nani for a moment became quite gay in all frankness. 'Oh,' said he, 'the Cardinal has quarrelled and made things up with the Vatican three or four times already. And, in any event, the Holy Father has no motive for posthumous jealousy ; he knows very well that he can give his Eminence a good greeting.' Then, regretting that he had thus expressed a certainty, he added : 'I am joking, his Eminence is altogether worthy of the high fortune which perhaps awaits him.'

Pierre knew what to think, however ; Sanguinetti was certainly Nani's candidate no longer. It was doubtless considered that he had used himself up too much by his impatient ambition, and was too dangerous by reason of the equivocal alliances which in his feverishness he had concluded with every party, even that of patriotic young Italy. And thus the situation became clearer. Cardinals Sanguinetti and Boccanera devoured and suppressed one another ; the first, ever intriguing, accepting every compromise, dreaming of winning Rome back by electoral methods ; and the other, erect and motionless in his stern maintenance of the past, excommunicating the century, and awaiting from God alone the miracle which would save the Church. And, indeed, why

not leave the two theories, thus placed face to face, to destroy
one another, including all the extreme, disquieting views
which they respectively embodied? If Boccanera had escaped
the poison, he had none the less become an impossible candidate, killed by all the stories which had set Rome buzzing;
while if Sanguinetti could say that he was rid of a rival, he had
at the same time dealt a mortal blow to his own candidature,
by displaying such passion for power, and such unscrupulous-
ness with regard to the methods he employed, as to be a
danger for everyone. Monsignor Nani was visibly delighted
with this result; neither candidate was left, it was like the
legendary story of the two wolves who fought and devoured one
another so completely that nothing of either of them was
found left, not even their tails! And in the depths of the
prelate's pale eyes, in the whole of his discreet person, there
remained nothing but redoubtable mystery: the mystery of
the yet unknown, but definitively selected candidate who would
be patronised by the all-powerful army of which he was one
of the most skilful leaders. A man like him always had a
solution ready. Who, then, who would be the next pope?

However, he now rose and cordially took leave of the
young priest. 'I doubt if I shall see you again, my dear
son,' he said, 'I wish you a good journey.'

Still he did not go off, but continued to look at Pierre with
his penetrating eyes, and finally made him sit down again
and did the same himself. 'I feel sure,' he said, 'that you
will go to pay your respects to Cardinal Bergerot as soon as
you have returned to France. Kindly tell him that I respectfully desired to be reminded to him. I knew him a little at
the time when he came here for his hat. He is one of the
great luminaries of the French clergy. Ah! if a man of such
intelligence would only work for a good understanding in our
holy Church. Unfortunately I fear that race and environment
have instilled prejudices into him, for he does not always help
us.'

Pierre, who was surprised to hear Nani speak of the Cardinal
for the first time at this moment of farewell, listened with
curiosity. Then in all frankness he replied: 'Yes, his
Eminence has very decided ideas about our old Church of
France. For instance, he professes perfect horror of the Jesuits.'

With a light exclamation Nani stopped the young man.
And he wore the most sincerely, frankly astonished air that
could be imagined. 'What! horror of the Jesuits! In what

way can the Jesuits disquiet him ? The Jesuits, there are none, that's all over ! Have you seen any in Rome ? Have they troubled you in any way, those poor Jesuits who haven't even a stone of their own left here on which to lay their heads ? No, no, that bogey mustn't be brought up again, it's childish.'

Pierre in his turn looked at him, marvelling at his perfect ease, his quiet courage in dealing with this burning subject. He did not avert his eyes, but displayed an open face like a book of truth. 'Ah !' he continued, 'if by Jesuits you mean the sensible priests who, instead of entering into sterile and dangerous struggles with modern society, seek by human methods to bring it back to the Church, why, then of course we are all of us more or less Jesuits, for it would be madness not to take into account the times in which one lives. And besides, I won't haggle over words ; they are of no consequence ! Jesuits, well, yes, if you like, Jesuits !' He was again smiling with that shrewd smile of his in which there was so much raillery and so much intelligence. 'Well, when you see Cardinal Bergerot tell him that it is unreasonable to track the Jesuits and treat them as enemies of the nation. The contrary is the truth. The Jesuits are for France, because they are for wealth, strength and courage. France is the only great Catholic country which has yet remained erect and sovereign, the only one on which the papacy can some day lean. Thus the Holy Father, after momentarily dreaming of obtaining support from victorious Germany, has allied himself with France, the vanquished, because he has understood that apart from France there can be no salvation for the Church. And in this he has only followed the policy of the Jesuits, those frightful Jesuits, whom your Parisians execrate. And tell Cardinal Bergerot also that it would be grand of him to work for pacification by making people understand how wrong it is for your Republic to help the Holy Father so little in his conciliatory efforts. It pretends to regard him as an element in the world's affairs that may be neglected and that is dangerous, for although he may seem to have no political means of action he remains an immense moral force, and can at any moment raise consciences in rebellion and provoke a religious agitation of the most far-reaching consequences. It is still he who disposes of the nations, since he disposes of their souls, and the Republic acts most inconsiderately, from the standpoint of its own interests, in showing that it no longer even suspects it. And

tell the Cardinal, too, that it is really pitiful to see in what a
wretched way your Republic selects its bishops, as though it
intentionally desired to weaken its episcopacy. Leaving out
a few fortunate exceptions, your bishops are men of small
brains, and as a result your cardinals, likewise mere medio-
crities, have no influence, play no part here in Rome. Ah !
what a sorry figure you Frenchmen will cut at the next
conclave ! And so why do you show such blind and foolish
hatred of those Jesuits, who, politically, are your friends ?
Why don't you employ their intelligent zeal, which is ready to
serve you, so that you may assure yourselves the help of the
next, the coming pope ? It is necessary for you that he should
be on your side, that he should continue the work of Leo XIII,
which is so badly judged and so much opposed, but which
cares little for the petty results of to-day, since its purpose lies
in the future, in the union of all the nations under their holy
mother the Church. Tell Cardinal Bergerot, tell him plainly
that he ought to be with us, that he ought to work for his
country by working for us. The coming pope, why the whole
question lies in that, and woe to France if in him she does
not find a continuator of Leo XIII ! '

Nani had again risen, and this time he was going off.
Never before had he unbosomed himself at such length. But
most assuredly he had only said what he desired to say, for
a purpose that he alone knew of, and in a firm, gentle and
deliberate voice by which one could tell that each word had
been weighed and determined beforehand. 'Farewell, my
dear son,' he said, 'and once again think over all you have
seen and heard in Rome. Be as sensible as you can, and do
not spoil your life.'

Pierre bowed, and pressed the small, plump, supple hand
which the prelate offered him. 'Monseigneur,' he replied, 'I
again thank you for all your kindness ; you may be sure that
I shall forget nothing of my journey.'

Then he watched Nani as he went off, with a light and
conquering step as if marching to all the victories of the
future. No, no, he, Pierre, would forget nothing of his
journey ! He well knew that union of all the nations under
their holy mother the Church, that temporal bondage in
which the law of Christ would become the dictatorship of
Augustus, master of the world ! And as for those Jesuits, he
had no doubt that they did love France, the eldest daughter
of the Church, and the only daughter that could yet help her

mother to reconquer universal sovereignty, but they loved her even as the black swarms of locusts love the harvests which they swoop upon and devour. Infinite sadness had returned to the young man's heart as he dimly realised that in that sorely-stricken mansion, in all that mourning and downfall, it was they, they again, who must have been the artisans of grief and disaster.

As this thought came to him he turned round and perceived Don Vigilio leaning against the credence in front of the large portrait of the Cardinal. Holding his hands to his face as if he desired to annihilate himself, the secretary was shivering in every limb as much with fear as with fever. At a moment when no fresh visitors were arriving he had succumbed to an attack of terrified despair.

'*Mon Dieu !* What is the matter with you ?' asked Pierre stepping forward, ' are you ill, can I help you ? '

But Don Vigilio, suffocating and still hiding his face, could only gasp between his close-pressed hands : 'Ah ! Paparelli, Paparelli ! '

'What is it ? What has he done to you ? ' asked the other astonished.

Then the secretary disclosed his face, and again yielded to his quivering desire to confide in someone. 'Eh ? what he has done to me ? Can't you feel anything, can't you see anything then ? Didn't you notice the manner in which he took possession of Cardinal Sanguinetti so as to conduct him to his Eminence ? To impose that suspected, hateful rival on his Eminence at such a moment as this, what insolent audacity ! And a few minutes previously did you notice with what wicked cunning he bowed out an old lady, a very old family friend, who only desired to kiss his Eminence's hand and show a little real affection which would have made his Eminence so happy ! Ah ! I tell you that he's the master here, he opens or closes the door as he pleases, and holds us all between his fingers like a pinch of dust which one throws to the wind ! '

Pierre became anxious, seeing how yellow and feverish Don Vigilio was : 'Come, come, my dear fellow,' he said, ' you are exaggerating ! '

'Exaggerating ? Do you know what happened last night, what I myself unwillingly witnessed ? No, you don't know it, well I will tell you.'

Thereupon he related that Donna Serafina on returning

home on the previous day to face the terrible catastrophe
awaiting her, had already been overcome by the bad news
which she had learnt when calling on the Cardinal Secretary
and various prelates of her acquaintance. She had then
acquired a certainty that her brother's position was becoming
extremely bad, for he had made so many fresh enemies
among his colleagues of the Sacred College, that his election
to the pontifical throne, which a year previously had seemed
probable, now appeared an impossibility. Thus, all at once,
the dream of her life collapsed, the ambition which she had
so long nourished lay in dust at her feet. On despairingly
seeking the why and wherefore of this change, she had been
told of all sorts of blunders committed by the Cardinal, acts
of rough sternness, unseasonable manifestations of opinion,
inconsiderate words or actions which had sufficed to wound
people, in fact such provoking demeanour that one might
have thought it adopted with the express intention of
spoiling everything. And the worst was that in each of the
blunders she had recognised errors of judgment which she
herself had blamed, but which her brother had obstinately
insisted on perpetrating under the unacknowledged influence
of Abbé Paparelli, that humble and insignificant train-bearer,
in whom she detected a baneful and powerful adviser who
destroyed her own vigilant and devoted influence. And so, in
spite of the mourning in which the house was plunged, she did
not wish to delay the punishment of the traitor, particularly as
his old friendship with that terrible Santobono, and the story
of that basket of figs which had passed from the hands of the
one to those of the other, chilled her blood with a suspicion
which she even recoiled from elucidating. However, at the
first words she spoke, directly she made a formal request that
the traitor should be immediately turned out of the house,
she was confronted by invincible resistance on her brother's
part. He would not listen to her, but flew into one of those
hurricane-like passions which swept everything away, re-
proaching her for laying blame on so modest, pious and
saintly a man, and accusing her of playing into the hands of
his enemies, who, after killing Monsignor Gallo, were seeking
to poison his sole remaining affection for that poor, insignificant priest. He treated all the stories he was told as abominable inventions, and swore that he would keep the train-
bearer in his service if only to show his disdain for calumny.
And she was thereupon obliged to hold her peace.

However, Don Vigilio's shuddering fit had again come back; he carried his hands to his face stammering: 'Ah! Paparelli, Paparelli!' And muttered invectives followed: the train-bearer was an artful hypocrite who feigned modesty and humility, a vile spy appointed to pry into everything, listen to everything, and pervert everything that went on in the palace; he was a loathsome, destructive insect, feeding on the most noble prey, devouring the lion's mane, a Jesuit— the Jesuit who is at once lacquey and tyrant, in all his base horror, as he accomplishes the work of vermin.

'Calm yourself, calm yourself,' repeated Pierre, who whilst allowing for foolish exaggeration on the secretary's part could not help shivering at thought of all the threatening things which he himself could divine astir in the gloom.

However, since Don Vigilio had so narrowly escaped eating those horrible figs, his fright was such that nothing could calm it. Even when he was alone at night, in bed, with his door locked and bolted, sudden terror fell on him and made him hide his head under the sheet and vent stifled cries as if he thought that men were coming through the wall to strangle him. In a faint, breathless voice, as if just emerging from a struggle, he now resumed: 'I told you what would happen on the evening when we had a talk together in your room. Although all the doors were securely shut, I did wrong to speak of them to you, I did wrong to ease my heart by telling you all that they were capable of. I was sure they would learn it, and you see they did learn it, since they tried to kill me. . . . Why it's even wrong of me to tell you this, for it will reach their ears and they won't miss me the next time. Ah! it's all over, I'm as good as dead; this house which I thought so safe will be my tomb.'

Pierre began to feel deep compassion for this ailing man, whose feverish brain was haunted by nightmares, and whose life was being finally wrecked by the anguish of persecution mania. 'But you must run away in that case!' he said. 'Don't stop here; come to France.'

Don Vigilio looked at him, momentarily calmed by surprise. 'Run away, why? Go to France? Why, they are there! No matter where I might go, they would be there. They are everywhere, I should always be surrounded by them! No, no, I prefer to stay here and would rather die at once if his Eminence can no longer defend me.' With an expression of ardent entreaty in which a last gleam of hope tried to assert itself, he raised his eyes to the large painting in which the Cardinal stood forth resplendent in his cassock of red moire ; but his attack came back again and overwhelmed him with increased intensity of fever. 'Leave me, I beg you, leave me,' he gasped. 'Don't make me talk any more. Ah! Paparelli, Paparelli! If he should come back and see us and hear me speak. . . . Oh! I'll never say anything again. I'll tie up my tongue, I'll cut it off. Leave me, you are killing me, I tell you, he'll be coming back and that will mean my death. Go away, oh! for mercy's sake, go away!'

Thereupon Don Vigilio turned towards the wall as if to flatten his face against it, and immure his lips in tomb-like silence ; and Pierre resolved to leave him to himself, fearing lest he should provoke a yet more serious attack if he went on endeavouring to succour him.

On returning to the throne-room the young priest again found himself amidst all the frightful mourning. Mass was following mass ; without cessation murmured prayers entreated the Divine mercy to receive the two dear departed souls with loving kindness. And amidst the dying perfume of the fading roses, in front of the pale stars of the lighted candles, Pierre thought of that supreme downfall of the Boccaneras. Dario was the last of the name, and one could well understand that the Cardinal, whose only sin was family pride, should have loved that one remaining scion by whom alone the old stock might yet blossom afresh. And indeed, if he and Donna Serafina had desired the divorce, and then the marriage of the cousins, it had been less with the view of putting an end to scandal than with the hope of seeing a new line of Boccaneras spring up. But the lovers were dead, and the last remains of a long series of dazzling princes of sword and of gown lay there on that bed, soon to rot in the grave. It was all over ; that old maid and that aged Cardinal could leave no posterity. They remained face to face like two withered oaks, sole remnants of a vanished forest, and their fall would soon leave the plain quite clear. And how terrible the grief of surviving in impotence, what anguish to have to tell oneself that one is the end of everything, that with oneself all life, all hope for the morrow will depart! Amidst the murmur of the prayers, the dying perfume of the roses, the pale gleams of the two candles, Pierre realised what a downfall was that bereavement, how heavy was the gravestone which fell for ever on an extinct house, a vanished world.

He well understood that as one of the familiars of the mansion he must pay his respects to Donna Serafina and the Cardinal, and he at once sought admission to the neighbouring room where the Princess was receiving her friends. He found her robed in black, very slim and very erect in her arm-chair, whence she rose with slow dignity to respond to the bow of each person that entered. She listened to the condolences but answered never a word, overcoming her physical pain by rigidity of bearing. Pierre, who had learnt to know her, could divine, however, by the hollowness of her cheeks, the emptiness of her eyes, and the bitter twinge of her mouth, how frightful was the collapse within her. Not only was her race ended, but her brother would never be pope, never secure the elevation which she had so long fancied she was winning for him by dint of devotion, dint of feminine renunciation, giving brain and heart, care and money, foregoing even wifehood and motherhood, spoiling her whole life, in order to realise that dream. And amidst all the ruin of hope, it was perhaps the nonfulfilment of that ambition which most made her heart bleed. She rose for the young priest, her guest, as she rose for the other persons who presented themselves; but she contrived to introduce shades of meaning into the manner in which she quitted her chair, and Pierre fully realised that he had remained in her eyes a mere petty French priest, an insignificant domestic of the Divinity who had not known how to acquire even the title of prelate. When she had again seated herself after acknowledging his compliment with a slight inclination of the head, he remained for a moment standing, out of politeness. Not a word, not a sound disturbed the mournful quiescence of the room, for although there were four or five lady visitors seated there they remained motionless and silent as with grief. Pierre was most struck, however, by the sight of Cardinal Sarno, who was lying back in an arm-chair with his eyes closed. The poor puny lop-sided old man had lingered there forgetfully after expressing his condolences, and, overcome by the heavy silence and close atmosphere, had just fallen asleep. And everybody respected his slumber. Was he dreaming as he dozed of that map of Christendom which he carried behind his low obtuse-looking brow? Was he continuing in dreamland his terrible work of conquest, that task of subjecting and governing the earth which he directed from his dark room at the Propaganda? The ladies glanced at him affectionately and deferentially; he was gently scolded at times for over-working himself, the sleepiness which nowadays frequently overtook him in all sorts of places being attributed to excess of genius and zeal. And of this all-powerful Eminence Pierre was destined to carry off only this last impression : an exhausted old man, resting amidst the emotion of a mourning gathering, sleeping there like a candid child, without any one knowing whether this were due to the approach of senile imbecility, or to the fatigues of a night spent in organising the reign of God over some distant continent.

Two ladies went off and three more arrived. Donna Serafina rose, bowed, and then reseated herself, reverting to her rigid attitude, her bust erect, her face stern and full of despair. Cardinal Sarno was still asleep. Then Pierre felt as if he would stifle, a kind of vertigo came on him, and his heart beat violently. So he bowed and withdrew : and on passing through the dining-room on his way to the little study where Cardinal Boccanera received his visitors, he found himself in the presence of Paparelli, who was jealously guarding the door. When the train-bearer had sniffed at the young man, he seemed to realise that he could not refuse him admittance. Moreover, as this intruder was going away the very next day, defeated and covered with shame, there was nothing to be feared from him.

'You wish to see his Eminence ? ' said Paparelli. 'Good, good. By-and-by, wait.' And opining that Pierre was too near the door, he pushed him back to the other end of the room, for fear no doubt lest he should overhear anything. 'His Eminence is still engaged with his Eminence Cardinal Sanguinetti. Wait, wait there ! '

Sanguinetti indeed had made a point of kneeling for a long time in front of the bodies in the throne-room, and had then spun out his visit to Donna Serafina in order to mark how largely he shared the family's sorrow. And for more than ten minutes now he had been closeted with Cardinal Boccanera, nothing but an occasional murmur of their voices being heard through the closed door.

Pierre, however, on finding Paparelli there, was again haunted by all that Don Vigilio had told him. He looked at the train-bearer, so fat and short, puffed out with bad fat in his dirty cassock, his face flabby and wrinkled, and his whole person at forty years of age suggestive of that of a very old maid : and he felt astonished. How was it that Cardinal

Boccanera, that superb prince who carried his head so high,
and who was so supremely proud of his name, had allowed himself to be captured and swayed by such a frightful creature
reeking of baseness and abomination? Was it not the man's
very physical degradation and profound humility that had
struck him, disturbed him and finally fascinated him, as
wondrous gifts conducing to salvation, which he himself
lacked? Paparelli's person and disposition were like blows
dealt to his own handsome presence and his own pride. He,
who could not be so deformed, he who could not vanquish his
passion for glory, must, by an effort of faith, have grown
jealous of that man who was so extremely ugly and so extremely insignificant, he must have come to admire him as a
superior force of penitence and human abasement which threw
the portals of heaven wide open. Who can ever tell what
ascendency is exercised by the monster over the hero; by the
horrid-looking saint covered with vermin over the powerful of
this world in their terror at having to endure everlasting
flames in payment of their terrestrial joys? And 'twas indeed
the lion devoured by the insect, vast strength and splendour
destroyed by the invisible. Ah! to have that fine soul which
was so certain of Paradise, which for its welfare was enclosed
in such a disgusting body, to possess the happy humility
of that wide intelligence, that remarkable theologian, who
scourged himself with rods each morning on rising, and was
content to be the lowest of servants.

Standing there a heap of livid fat, Paparelli on his side
watched Pierre with his little grey eyes blinking amidst the
myriad wrinkles of his face. And the young priest began to
feel uneasy, wondering what their Eminences could be saying
to one another, shut up together like that for so long a time.
And what an interview it must be if Boccanera suspected
Sanguinetti of counting Santobono among his clients.
What serene audacity it was on Sanguinetti's part to have
dared to present himself in that house, and what strength of
soul there must be on Boccanera's part, what empire over himself, to prevent all scandal by remaining silent and accepting
the visit as a simple mark of esteem and affection! What
could they be saying to one another, however? How interesting it would have been to have seen them face to face, and have
heard them exchange the diplomatic phrases suited to such an
interview whilst their souls were raging with furious hatred!

All a once the door opened and Cardinal Sanguinetti

appeared with calm face, no ruddier than usual, indeed, a trifle paler, and retaining the fitting measure of sorrow which he had thought it right to assume. His restless eyes alone revealed his delight at being rid of a difficult task. And he was going off, all hope, in the conviction that he was the only eligible candidate to the papacy that remained.

Abbé Paparelli had darted forward : ' If your Eminence will kindly follow me—I will escort your Eminence to the door.' Then, turning towards Pierre, he added : ' You may go in now.'

Pierre watched them walk away, the one so humble behind the other, who was so triumphant. Then he entered the little work-room, furnished simply with a table and three chairs, and in the centre of it he at once perceived Cardinal Boccanera still standing in the lofty, noble attitude which he had assumed to take leave of Sanguinetti, his hated rival to the pontifical throne. And, visibly, Boccanera also believed himself the only possible pope, the one whom the coming Conclave would elect.

However, when the door had been closed, and the Cardinal beheld that young priest, his guest, who had witnessed the death of those two dear children lying in the adjoining room, he was again mastered by emotion, an unexpected attack of weakness in which all his energy collapsed. His human feelings were taking their revenge now that his rival was no longer there to see him. He staggered like an old tree smitten with the axe, and sank upon a chair, stifling with sobs. And as Pierre, according to usage, was about to stoop and kiss his ring, he raised him and at once made him sit down, stammering in a halting voice : ' No, no, my dear son ! Seat yourself there, wait—Excuse me, leave me to myself for a moment, my heart is bursting.'

He sobbed with his hands to his face, unable to master himself, unable to drive back his grief with those yet vigorous fingers which were pressed to his cheeks and temples.

Tears came into Pierre's eyes, for he also lived through all that woe afresh, and was much upset by the weeping of that tall old man, that saint and prince, usually so haughty, so fully master of himself, but now only a poor, suffering, agonising man, as weak and as lost as a child. However, although the young priest was likewise stifling with grief, he desired to present his condolences, and sought for kindly words by which he might soothe the other's despair. ' I

beg your Eminence to believe in my profound grief,' he said.
'I have been overwhelmed with kindness here, and desired
at once to tell your Eminence how much that irreparable
loss——'

But with a brave gesture the Cardinal silenced him. 'No,
no, say nothing, for mercy's sake say nothing!'

And silence reigned while he continued weeping, shaken
by the struggle he was waging, his efforts to regain sufficient
strength to overcome himself. At last he mastered his quiver
and slowly uncovered his face, which had again become calm,
like that of a believer strong in his faith, and submissive to
the will of God. In refusing a miracle, in dealing so hard
a blow to that house, God had doubtless had his reasons,
and he, the Cardinal, one of God's ministers, one of the
high dignitaries of His terrestrial court, was in duty bound
to bow to it. The silence lasted for another moment, and
then, in a voice which he managed to render natural and
cordial, Boccanera said: 'You are leaving us, you are
going back to France to-morrow, are you not, my dear son?'

'Yes, I shall have the honour to take leave of your
Eminence to-morrow, again thanking your Eminence for your
inexhaustible kindness.'

'And you have learnt that the Congregation of the Index
has condemned your book, as was inevitable?'

'Yes, I obtained the signal favour of being received by his
Holiness, and in his presence made my submission and
reprobated my book.'

The Cardinal's moist eyes again began to sparkle. 'Ah!
you did that, ah! you did well, my dear son,' he said. 'It
was only your strict duty as a priest, but there are so many
nowadays who do not even do their duty! As a member of
the Congregation I kept the promise I gave you to read your
book, particularly the incriminated pages. And if I afterwards remained neutral, to such a point even as to miss the
sitting in which judgment was pronounced, it was only to
please my poor, dear niece, who was so fond of you, and who
pleaded your cause to me.'

Tears were coming into his eyes again, and he paused,
feeling that he would once more be overcome if he evoked the
memory of that adored and lamented Benedetta. And so
it was with a pugnacious bitterness that he resumed: 'But
what an execrable book it was, my dear son, allow me to tell
you so. You told me that you had shown respect for dogma,

and I still wonder what aberration can have come over you that you should have been so blind to all consciousness of your offences. Respect for dogma—good Lord! when the entire work is the negation of our holy religion! Did you not realise that by asking for a new religion you absolutely condemned the old one, the only true one, the only good one, the only one that can be eternal? And that sufficed to make your book the most deadly of poisons, one of those infamous books which in former times were burnt by the hangman, and which one is nowadays compelled to leave in circulation after interdicting them and thereby designating them to evil curiosity, which explains the contagious rottenness of the century. Ah! I well recognised there some of the ideas of our distinguished and poetical relative, that dear Viscount Philibert de la Choue. A man of letters, yes! a man of letters! Literature, mere literature! I beg God to forgive him, for he most surely does not know what he is doing, or whither he is going with his elegiac Christianity for talkative working men and young persons of either sex, to whom scientific notions have given vagueness of soul. And I only feel angry with his Eminence Cardinal Bergerot, for he at any rate knows what he does, and does as he pleases. No, say nothing, do not defend him. He personifies Revolution in the Church, and is against God.'

Although Pierre had resolved that he would not reply or argue, he had allowed a gesture of protest to escape him on hearing this furious attack upon the man whom he most respected in the whole world. However, he yielded to Cardinal Boccanera's injunction and again bowed.

'I cannot sufficiently express my horror,' the Cardinal roughly continued; 'yes, my horror for all that hollow dream of a new religion! That appeal to the most hideous passions which stir up the poor against the rich, by promising them I know not what division of wealth, what community of possession which is nowadays impossible! That base flattery shown to the lower orders to whom equality and justice are promised but never given, for these can come from God alone, it is only He who can finally make them reign on the day appointed by His almighty power! And there is even that interested charity which people abuse of to rail against Heaven itself and accuse it of iniquity and indifference, that lacka-daisical weakening charity and compassion, unworthy of strong firm hearts, for it is as if human suffering were not necessary for salvation, as if we did not become more pure, greater and nearer to the supreme happiness, the more and more we suffer ! '

He was growing excited, full of anguish, and superb. It was his bereavement, his heart wound, which thus exasperated him, the great blow which had felled him for a moment, but against which he again rose erect, defying grief, and stubborn in his stoic belief in an omnipotent God, who was the Master of mankind, and reserved felicity to those whom He selected. Again, however, he made an effort to calm himself, and resumed in a more gentle voice : 'At all events the fold is always open, my dear son, and here you are back in it since you have repented. You cannot imagine how happy it makes me.'

In his turn Pierre strove to show himself conciliatory in order that he might not further ulcerate that violent, grief-stricken soul : ' Your Eminence,' said he, ' may be sure that I shall endeavour to remember every one of the kind words which your Eminence has spoken to me, in the same way as I shall remember the fatherly greeting of his Holiness Leo XIII.'

This sentence seemed to throw Boccanera into agitation again. At first only murmured, restrained words came from him, as if he were struggling against a desire to question the young priest. 'Ah yes ! you saw his Holiness, you spoke to him, and he told you I suppose, as he tells all the foreigners who go to pay their respects to him, that he desires conciliation and peace. For my part I now only see him when it is absolutely necessary ; for more than a year I have not been received in private audience.'

This proof of disfavour, of the covert struggle which as in the days of Pius IX kept the Holy Father and the Camerlingo at variance, filled the latter with bitterness. He was unable to restrain himself and spoke out, reflecting no doubt that he had a familiar before him, one whose discretion was certain, and who moreover was leaving Rome on the morrow. ' One may go a long way,' said he, ' with those fine words, peace and conciliation, which are so often void of real wisdom and courage. The terrible truth is that Leo XIII's eighteen years of concessions have shaken everything in the Church, and should he long continue to reign Catholicism would topple over and crumble into dust like a building whose pillars have been undermined.'

Interested by this remark, Pierre in his desire for knowledge began to raise objections. 'But hasn't his Holiness shown himself very prudent?' he asked; 'has he not placed dogma on one side in an impregnable fortress? If he seems to have made concessions on many points have they not always been concessions in mere matters of form?'

'Matters of form; ah, yes!' the Cardinal resumed with increasing passion. 'He told you no doubt, as he tells others, that whilst in substance he will make no surrender he will readily yield in matters of form! It's a deplorable axiom, an equivocal form of diplomacy even when it isn't so much low hypocrisy! My soul revolts at the thought of that Opportunism, that Jesuitism, which makes artifice its weapon, and only serves to cast doubt among true believers, the confusion of a *sauve-qui-peut*, which by and by must lead to inevitable defeat. It is cowardice, the worst form of cowardice, abandonment of one's weapons in order that one may retreat the more speedily, shame of oneself, assumption of a mask in the hope of deceiving the enemy, penetrating into his camp and overcoming him by treachery! No, no, form is everything in a traditional and immutable religion, which for eighteen hundred years has been, is now, and till the end of time will be the very law of God!'

The Cardinal's feelings so stirred him that he was unable to remain seated, and began to walk about the little room. And it was the whole reign, the whole policy of Leo XIII which he discussed and condemned. 'Unity too,' he continued, 'that famous unity of the Christian Church which his Holiness talks of bringing about, and his desire for which people turn to his great glory, why, it is only the blind ambition of a conqueror enlarging his empire without asking himself if the new nations that he subjects may not disorganise, adulterate, and impregnate his old and hitherto faithful people with every error. What if all the schismatical nations on returning to the Catholic Church should so transform it as to kill it and made it a new Church? There is only one wise course, which is to be what one is, and that firmly. Again, isn't there both shame and danger in that pretended alliance with the democracy which in itself gives the lie to the ancient spirit of the papacy? The right of kings is divine, and to abandon the monarchical principle is to set oneself against God, to compound with revolution, and harbour a monstrous scheme of utilising the madness of men

the better to establish one's power over them. All republics
are forms of anarchy, and there can be no more criminal act,
one which must for ever shake the principle of authority,
order, and religion itself, than that of recognising a republic
as legitimate for the sole purpose of indulging a dream of
impossible conciliation. And observe how this bears on the
question of the temporal power. He continues to claim it, he
makes a point of no surrender on that question of the restoration of Rome; but in reality, has he not made the loss
irreparable, has he not definitively renounced Rome, by admitting that nations have the right to drive away their
kings and live like wild beasts in the depths of the forests?'

All at once the Cardinal stopped short and raised his arms
to Heaven in a burst of holy anger. 'Ah! that man, ah!
that man who by his vanity and craving for success will have
proved the ruin of the Church, that man who has never
ceased corrupting everything, dissolving everything, crumbling everything in order to reign over the world which he
fancies he will reconquer by those means, why, Almighty
God, why hast Thou not already called him to Thee?'

So sincere was the accent in which that appeal to Death
was raised, to such a point was hatred magnified by a real
desire to save the Deity imperilled here below, that a great
shudder swept through Pierre also. He now understood that
Cardinal Boccanera, who religiously and passionately hated
Leo XIII; he saw him in the depths of his black palace,
waiting and watching for the Pope's death, that death which
as Camerlingo he must officially certify. How feverishly he
must wait, how impatiently he must desire the advent of the
hour, when with his little silver hammer he would deal the
three symbolic taps on the skull of Leo XIII, while the
latter lay cold and rigid on his bed surrounded by his pontifical Court. Ah! to strike that wall of the brain, to make
sure that nothing more would answer from within, that
nothing beyond night and silence was left there. And the
three calls would ring out: 'Gioachino! Gioachino!
Gioachino!' And, the corpse making no answer, the Camerlingo after waiting for a few seconds would turn and say:
'The Pope is dead!'

'Conciliation, however, is the weapon of the times,' remarked Pierre, wishing to bring the Cardinal back to the
present, 'and it is in order to make sure of conquering that the
Holy Father yields in matters of form.'

'He will not conquer, he will be conquered,' cried Boccanera. 'Never has the Church been victorious save in stubbornly clinging to its integrality, the immutable eternity of its divine essence. And it would for a certainty fall on the day when it should allow a single stone of its edifice to be touched. Remember the terrible period through which it passed at the time of the Council of Trent. The Reformation had just deeply shaken it, laxity of discipline and morals was everywhere increasing, there was a rising tide of novelties, ideas suggested by the spirit of evil, unhealthy projects born of the pride of man, running riot in full licence. And at the Council itself many members were disturbed, poisoned, ready to vote for the wildest changes, a fresh schism added to all the others. Well, if Catholicism was saved at that critical period, under the threat of such great danger, it was because the majority, enlightened by God, maintained the old edifice intact, it was because with divinely inspired obstinacy it kept itself within the narrow limits of dogma, it was because it made no concession, none, whether in substance or in form! Nowadays the situation is certainly not worse than it was at the time of the Council of Trent. Let us suppose it to be much the same, and tell me if it is not nobler, braver, and safer for the Church to show the courage which she showed before and declare aloud what she is, what she has been, and what she will be. There is no salvation for her otherwise than in her complete, indisputable sovereignty; and since she has always conquered by non-surrender, all attempts to conciliate her with the century are tantamount to killing her!'

The Cardinal had again begun to walk to and fro with thoughtful step. 'No, no,' said he, 'no compounding, no surrender, no weakness! Rather the wall of steel which bars the road, the block of granite which marks the limit of a world! As I told you, my dear son, on the day of your arrival, to try to accommodate Catholicism to the new times is to hasten its end, if really it be threatened, as atheists pretend. And in that way it would die basely and shamefully instead of dying erect, proud and dignified in its old glorious royalty! Ah! to die standing, denying nought of the past, braving the future and confessing one's whole faith!'

That old man of seventy seemed to grow yet loftier as he spoke, free from all dread of final annihilation, and making the gesture of a hero who defies futurity. Faith had given him serenity of peace; he believed, he knew, he had neither doubt nor fear of the morrow of death. Still his voice was tinged with haughty sadness as he resumed, ' God can do all, even destroy His own work should it seem evil in His eyes. But though all should crumble to-morrow, though the Holy Church should disappear among the ruins, though the most venerated sanctuaries should be crushed by the falling stars, it would still be necessary for us to bow and adore God, who after creating the world might thus annihilate it for His own glory. And I wait, submissive to His will, for nothing happens unless He wills it. If really the temples be shaken, if Catholicism be fated to fall to-morrow into dust, I shall be here to act as the minister of death, even as I have been the minister of life ! It is certain, I confess it, that there are hours when terrible signs appear to me. Perhaps, indeed, the end of time is nigh, and we shall witness that fall of the old world with which others threaten us. The worthiest, the loftiest are struck down as if Heaven erred, and in them punished the crimes of the world. Have I not myself felt the blast from the abyss into which all must sink, since my house, for transgressions that I am ignorant of, has been stricken with that frightful bereavement which precipitates it into the gulf, which casts it back into night everlasting ! '

He again evoked those two dear dead ones who were always present in his mind. Sobs were once more rising in his throat, his hands trembled, his lofty figure quivered with the last revolt of grief. Yes, if God had stricken him so severely by suppressing his race, if the greatest and most faithful were thus punished, it must be that the world was definitively condemned. Did not the end of his house mean the approaching end of all ? And in his sovereign pride as priest and as prince, he found a cry of supreme resignation, once more raising his hands on high : ' Almighty God, Thy will be done ! May all die, all fall, all return to the night of chaos ! I shall remain standing in this ruined palace, waiting to be buried beneath its fragments. And if Thy will doth summon me to bury Thy holy religion, be without fear, I shall do nothing unworthy to prolong its life for a few days ! I will maintain it erect, like myself, as proud, as uncompromising as in the days of all its power. I will yield nothing, whether in discipline, or in rite, or in dogma. And when the day shall come I will bury it with myself, carrying it whole into the grave rather than yielding aught of it, encompassing it with my cold arms to restore it to Thee, even as Thou didst commit it

to the keeping of Thy Church. O mighty God and sovereign
Master dispose of me ; make me, if such be Thy good pleasure,
the pontiff of destruction, the pontiff of the death of the
world ! '

Pierre, who was thunderstruck, quivered with fear and
admiration at the extraordinary vision this evoked : the last of
the popes interring Catholicism. He understood that Boccanera must at times have made that dream ; he could see him
in the Vatican, in St. Peter's, which the thunderbolts had
riven asunder ; he could see him erect and alone in the spacious
halls whence his terrified, cowardly pontifical Court had fled.
Clad in his white cassock, thus wearing white mourning for
the Church, he once more descended to the sanctuary, there
to wait for heaven to fall on the evening of Time's accomplishment and annihilate the earth. Thrice he raised the large
crucifix, overthrown by the supreme convulsions of the soil.
Then, when the final crack rent the steps apart, he caught it
in his arms and was annihilated with it beneath the falling
vaults. And nothing could be more instinct with fierce and
kingly grandeur.

Voiceless, but without weakness, his lofty stature invincible
and erect in spite of all, Cardinal Boccanera made a gesture
dismissing Pierre, who yielding to his passion for truth and
beauty found that he alone was great and right, and respectfully kissed his hand.

It was in the throne-room, with closed doors, at nightfall,
after the visits had ceased, that the two bodies were laid in
their coffin. The religious services had come to an end, and
in the close silent atmosphere there only lingered the dying
perfume of the roses and the warm odour of the candles. As
the latter's pale stars scarcely lighted the spacious room, some
lamps had been brought, and servants held them in their
hands like torches. According to custom, all the servants of
the house were present to bid a last farewell to the departed.

There was a little delay. Morano, who had been giving
himself no end of trouble ever since morning, was forced to
run off again as the triple coffin did not arrive. At last it
came ; some servants brought it up, and then they were able to
begin. The Cardinal and Donna Serafina stood side by side
near the bed. Pierre also was present, as well as Don Vigilio.
It was Victorine who sewed the lovers up in the white silk
shroud, which seemed like a bridal robe, the gay pure robe of
their union. Then two servants came forward and helped

Pierre and Don Vigilio to lay the bodies in the first coffin, of
pine-wood lined with pink satin. It was scarcely broader
than an ordinary coffin, so young and slim were the lovers
and so tightly were they clasped in their last embrace. When
they were stretched inside they there continued their eternal
slumber, their heads half hidden by their odorous, mingling
hair. And when this first coffin had been placed in the
second one, a leaden shell, and the second had been enclosed
in the third, of stout oak, and when the three lids had been
soldered and screwed down, the lovers' faces could still be seen
through the circular opening, covered with thick glass, which
in accordance with the Roman custom had been left in each of
the coffins. And then, for ever parted from the living, alone
together, they still gazed at one another with their eyes
obstinately open, having all eternity before them wherein to
exhaust their infinite love.

XVI.

On the following day, on his return from the funeral, Pierre
lunched alone in his room, having decided to take leave of
the Cardinal and Donna Serafina during the afternoon. He
was quitting Rome that evening by the train which started at
seventeen minutes past ten. There was nothing to detain
him any longer; there was only one visit which he desired to
make, a visit to old Orlando, with whom he had promised to
have a long chat prior to his departure. And so a little before
two o'clock he sent for a cab which took him to the Via Venti
Settembre. A fine rain had fallen all night, its moisture
steeping the city in grey vapour; and though this rain had
now ceased the sky remained very dark, and the huge new
mansions of the Via Venti Settembre were quite livid, inter-
minably mournful with their balconies ever of the same
pattern and their regular and endless rows of windows. The
Ministry of Finances, that colossal pile of masonry and
sculpture, looked in particular like a dead town, a huge bloodless body whence all life had withdrawn. On the other hand,
although all was so gloomy, the rain had made the atmosphere
milder; in fact it was almost warm, damply and feverishly
warm.

In the hall of Prada's little palazzo Pierre was surprised
to find four or five gentlemen taking off their overcoats;

however, he learnt from a servant that Count Luigi had a meeting that day with some contractors. As he, Pierre, wished to see the Count's father he had only to ascend to the third floor, added the servant. He must knock at the little door on the right-hand side of the landing there.

On the very first landing, however, the priest found himself face to face with the young Count, who was there receiving the contractors, and who on recognising him became frightfully pale. They had not met since the tragedy at the Boccanera mansion, and Pierre well realised how greatly his glance disturbed that man, what a troublesome recollection of moral complicity it evoked, and what mortal dread lest he should have guessed the truth.

'Have you come to see me? have you something to tell me?' the Count inquired.

'No, I am leaving Rome; I have come to wish your father good-bye.'

Prada's pallor increased at this, and his whole face quivered: 'Ah! it is to see my father. He is not very well, be gentle with him,' he replied; and as he spoke, his look of anguish clearly proclaimed what he feared from Pierre, some imprudent word, perhaps even a final mission, the malediction of that man and woman whom he had killed. And surely, if his father knew, he would die as well. 'Ah! how annoying it is,' he resumed, 'I can't go up with you! There are gentlemen waiting for me. Yes, how annoyed I am. As soon as possible, however, I will join you; yes, as soon as possible.'

He knew not how to stop the young priest, whom he must evidently allow to remain with his father, whilst he himself stayed down below, kept there by his pecuniary worries. But how distressful were the eyes with which he watched Pierre climb the stairs, how he seemed to supplicate him with his whole quivering form! His father, good Lord, the only true love, the one great, pure, faithful passion of his life!

'Don't make him talk too much; brighten him, won't you?' were his parting words.

Up above it was not Battista, the devoted ex-soldier, who opened the door, but a very young fellow to whom Pierre did not at first pay any attention. The little room was bare and light as on previous occasions, and from the broad curtainless window there was the superb view of Rome—Rome crushed that day beneath a leaden sky and steeped in shade of infinite mournfulness. Old Orlando, however, had in no wise changed, but still displayed the superb head of an old blanched lion, a powerful muzzle and youthful eyes, which yet sparkled with the passions which had growled in a soul of fire. Pierre found the stricken hero in the same arm-chair as previously, near the same table littered with newspapers, and with his legs buried in the same black wrapper, as if he were there immobilised in a sheath of stone, to such a point that after months and years one was sure to perceive him quite unchanged, with living bust, and face glowing with strength and intelligence.

That grey day, however, he seemed gloomy, low in spirits. 'Ah! so here you are, my dear Monsieur Froment,' he exclaimed ; 'I have been thinking of you these three days past, living the awful days which you must have lived in that tragic Palazzo Boccanera. Ah, God! What a frightful bereavement! My heart is quite overwhelmed; these newspapers have again just upset me with the fresh details they give! ' He pointed as he spoke to the papers scattered over the table. Then with a gesture he strove to brush aside the gloomy story, and banish that vision of Benedetta dead, which had been haunting him. 'Well, and yourself? ' he inquired.

'I am leaving this evening,' replied Pierre, 'but I did not wish to quit Rome without pressing your brave hands.'

'You are leaving? But your book? '

'My book—I have been received by the Holy Father—I have made my submission and reprobated my book.'

Orlando looked fixedly at the priest. There was a short interval of silence, during which their eyes told one another all that they had to tell respecting the affair. Neither felt the necessity of any longer explanation. The old man merely spoke these concluding words : 'You have done well, your book was a chimera.'

'Yes, a chimera, a piece of childishness, and I have condemned it myself in the name of truth and reason.'

A smile appeared on the dolorous lips of the impotent hero. 'Then you have seen things ; you understand and know them now? '

'Yes, I know them ; and that is why I did not wish to go off without having that frank conversation with you which we agreed upon.'

Orlando was delighted, but all at once he seemed to remember the young fellow who had opened the door to Pierre, and who had afterwards modestly resumed his seat on a chair near the window. This young fellow was a youth of twenty, still beardless, of a *blonde* handsomeness such as occasionally flowers at Naples, with long curly hair, a lily-like complexion, a rosy mouth, and soft eyes full of a dreamy languor. The old man presented him in fatherly fashion; Angiolo Mascara his name was, and he was the grandson of an old comrade in arms, the epic Mascara of the Thousand, who had died like a hero, his body pierced by a hundred wounds.

'I sent for him to scold him,' continued Orlando with a smile. 'Do you know that this fine fellow with his girlish airs goes in for the new ideas? He is an Anarchist, one of the three or four dozen Anarchists that we have in Italy. He's a good little lad at bottom, he has only his mother left him, and supports her, thanks to the little berth which he holds, but which he'll lose one of these fine days if he is not careful. Come, come, my child, you must promise me to be reasonable.'

Thereupon Angiolo, whose clean but well-worn garments bespoke decent poverty, made answer in a grave and musical voice: 'I am reasonable; it is the others, all the others who are not. When all men are reasonable and desire truth and justice, the world will be happy.'

'Ah! if you fancy that he'll give way!' cried Orlando. 'But, my poor child, just ask Monsieur l'Abbé if one ever knows where truth and justice are. Well, well, one must leave you the time to live, and see, and understand things.'

Then, paying no more attention to the young man, he returned to Pierre, while Angiolo, remaining very quiet in his corner, kept his eyes ardently fixed on them, and with open, quivering ears lost not a word they said.

'I told you, my dear Monsieur Froment,' resumed Orlando, 'that your ideas would change, and that acquaintance with Rome would bring you to accurate views far more readily than any fine speeches I could make to you. So I never doubted but what you would of your own free will withdraw your book as soon as men and things should have enlightened you respecting the Vatican at the present day. But let us leave the Vatican on one side; there is nothing to be done but to let it continue falling slowly and inevitably into ruin. What interests me is our Italian Rome, which you treated as an element to be neglected, but which you have now seen and studied, so that we can both speak of it with the necessary knowledge!'

He thereupon at once granted a great many things, acknowledged that blunders had been committed, that the

finances were in a deplorable state, and that there were serious
difficulties of all kinds. They, the Italians, had sinned by
excess of legitimate pride ; they had proceeded too hastily with
their attempt to improvise a great nation, to change ancient
Rome into a great modern capital as by the mere touch of a
wand. And thence had come that mania for erecting new
districts, that mad speculation in land and shares, which
had brought the country within a hair's breadth of bankruptcy.

At this Pierre gently interrupted him to tell him of the
view which he himself had arrived at after his peregrinations
and studies through Rome. 'That fever of the first hour,
that financial *débâcle*,' said he, 'is after all nothing. All
pecuniary sores can be healed. But the grave point is that
your Italy still remains to be created. There is no aristocracy
left, and as yet there is no people, nothing but a devouring
middle-class, dating from yesterday, which preys on the rich
harvest of the future before it is ripe.'

Silence fell. Orlando sadly wagged his old leonine head.
The cutting harshness of Pierre's formula struck him in the
heart. 'Yes, yes,' he said at last, 'that is so ; you have seen
things plainly ; and why say no when facts are there, patent
to everybody ? I myself had already spoken to you of that
middle-class which hungers so ravenously for place and office,
distinctions and plumes, and which at the same time is so
avaricious, so suspicious with regard to its money which it
invests in banks, never risking it in agriculture or manufactures
or commerce, having indeed the one desire to enjoy life without doing anything, and so unintelligent that it cannot see it
is killing its country by its loathing for labour, its contempt
for the poor, its one ambition to live in a petty way with the
barren glory of belonging to some official administration.
And, as you say, the aristocracy is dying, discrowned, ruined,
sunk into the degeneracy which overtakes races towards their
close, most of its members reduced to beggary, the others,
the few who have clung to their money, crushed by heavy
imposts, possessing nought but dead fortunes which constant
sharing diminishes and which must soon disappear with the
princes themselves. And then there is the people, which has
suffered so much and suffers still, but is so used to suffering
that it can seemingly conceive no idea of emerging from it,
blind and deaf as it is, almost regretting its ancient bondage,
and so ignorant, so abominably ignorant, which is the one

cause of its hopeless, morrowless misery, for it has not even
the consolation of understanding that if we have conquered
and are trying to resuscitate Rome and Italy in their ancient
glory, it is for itself, the people, alone. Yes, yes, no aristocracy left, no people as yet, and a middle-class which really
alarms one. How can one therefore help yielding at times to
the terrors of the pessimists, who pretend that our misfortunes
are as yet nothing, that we are going forward to yet more
awful catastrophes, as though, indeed, what we now behold
were but the first symptoms of our race's end, the premonitory
signs of final annihilation ?'

As he spoke he raised his long quivering arms towards the
window, towards the light, and Pierre, deeply moved, remembered how Cardinal Boccanera on the previous day had
made a similar gesture of suppliant distress when appealing
to the divine power. And both men, Cardinal and patriot, so
hostile in their beliefs, were instinct with the same fierce and
despairing grandeur.

'As I told you, however, on the first day,' continued Orlando,
'we only sought to accomplish logical and inevitable things.
As for Rome, with her past history of splendour and domination which weighs so heavily upon us, we could not do otherwise than take her for capital, for she alone was the bond, the
living symbol of our unity at the same time as the promise of
eternity, the renewal offered to our great dream of resurrection
and glory.'

He went on, recognising the disastrous conditions under
which Rome laboured as a capital. She was a purely decorative
city with exhausted soil, she had remained apart from modern
life, she was unhealthy, she offered no possibility of commerce
or industry, she was invincibly preyed upon by death, standing
as she did amidst that sterile desert of the Campagna. Then
he compared her with the other cities which are jealous of her ;
first Florence, which, however, has become so indifferent and
so sceptical, impregnated with a happy heedlessness which
seems inexplicable when one remembers the frantic passions,
and the torrents of blood rolling through her history; next
Naples, which yet remains content with her bright sun, and
whose childish people enjoy their ignorance and wretchedness
so indolently that one knows not whether one ought to pity
them ; next Venice, which has resigned herself to remaining
a marvel of ancient art, which one ought to put under glass
so as to preserve her intact, slumbering amid the sovereign

pomp of her annals ; next Genoa, which is absorbed in trade,
still active and bustling, one of the last Queens of that
Mediterranean, that insignificant lake which was once the
opulent central sea, whose waters carried the wealth of the
world ; and then particularly Turin and Milan, those industrial and commercial centres, which are so full of life and
so modernised that tourists disdain them as not being 'Italian'
cities, both of them having saved themselves from ruin by
entering into that Western evolution which is preparing the
next century. Ah ! that old land of Italy : ought one to leave
it all as a dusty museum for the pleasure of artistic souls, leave
it to crumble away, even as its little towns of Magna Græcia,
Umbria, and Tuscany are already crumbling, like exquisite
bibelots which one dares not repair for fear that one might
spoil their character ? At all events there must either be death,
death soon and inevitable, or else the pick of the demolisher,
the tottering walls thrown to the ground, and cities of labour,
science, and health created on all sides ; in one word, a new
Italy really rising from the ashes of the old one, and adapted
to the new civilisation into which humanity is entering.

'However, why despair ?' Orlando continued energetically.
'Rome may weigh heavily on our shoulders, but she is none
the less the summit we coveted. We are here, and we shall
stay here awaiting events. Even if the population does not
increase, it at least remains stationary at a figure of some
400,000 souls, and the movement of increase may set in again
when the causes which stopped it shall have ceased. Our
blunder was to think that Rome would become a Paris or
Berlin ; but, so far, all sorts of social, historical, even ethnical
considerations seem opposed to it ; yet who can tell what may
be the surprises of to-morrow ? Are we forbidden to hope, to
put faith in the blood which courses in our veins, the blood
of the old conquerors of the world ? I, who no longer stir from
this room, impotent as I am, even I at times feel my madness
come back, believe in the invincibility and immortality of
Rome, and wait for the two millions of people who must come
to populate those dolorous new districts which you have seen
so empty and already falling into ruins ! And certainly they
will come ! Why not ? You will see, you will see ; everything
will be populated, and even more houses will have to be built.
Moreover, can you call a nation poor when it possesses
Lombardy ? Is there not also inexhaustible wealth in our
southern provinces ? Let peace settle down, let the South and

the North mingle together, and a new generation of workers grow up. Since we have the soil, such a fertile soil, the great harvest which is awaited will surely some day sprout and ripen under the burning sun ! '

Enthusiasm was upbuoying him, all the *furia* of youth inflamed his eyes. Pierre smiled, won over ; and as soon as he was able to speak, he said : ' The problem must be tackled down below, among the people. You must make men ! '

' Exactly ! ' cried Orlando. ' I don't cease repeating it, one must make Italy. It is as if a wind from the East had blown the seed of humanity, the seed which makes vigorous and powerful nations, elsewhere. Our people is not like yours in France, a reservoir of men and money from which one can draw as plentifully as one pleases. It is such another inexhaustible reservoir that I wish to see created among us. And one must begin at the bottom. There must be schools everywhere, ignorance must be stamped out, brutishness and idleness must be fought with books, intellectual and moral instruction must give us the industrious people which we need if we are not to disappear from among the great nations. And once again for whom, if not for the democracy of tomorrow, have we worked in taking possession of Rome ? And how easily one can understand that all should collapse here, and nothing grow up vigorously since such a democracy is absolutely absent ! Yes, yes, the solution of the problem does not lie elsewhere ; we must make a people, make an Italian democracy.'

Pierre had grown calm again, feeling somewhat anxious, yet not daring to say that it is by no means easy to modify a nation, that Italy is such as soil, history, and race have made her, and that to seek to transform her so radically and all at once might be a dangerous enterprise. Do not nations like beings have an active youth, a resplendent prime, and a more or less prolonged old age ending in death ? A modern democratic Rome, good heavens ! The modern Romes are named Paris, London, Chicago. So he contented himself with saying : ' But pending this great renovation of the people, don't you think that you ought to be prudent ? Your finances are in such a bad condition, you are passing through such great social and economic difficulties, that you run the risk of the worst catastrophes before you secure either men or money. Ah ! how prudent would that minister be who should say in your Chambers : " Our pride has made a

mistake; it was wrong of us to try to make ourselves a great
nation in one day; more time, labour, and patience are
needed; and we consent to remain for the present a young
nation, which will quietly reflect and labour at self-formation,
without, for a long time yet, seeking to play a dominant part.
So we intend to disarm, to strike out the war and naval
estimates, all the estimates intended for display abroad, in
order to devote ourselves to our internal prosperity, and to
build up by education, physically and morally, the great
nation which we swear we will be fifty years hence!" Yes,
yes, strike out all needless expenditure; your salvation lies in
that!'

But Orlando, while listening, had become gloomy again,
and with a vague, weary gesture he replied in an undertone:
'No, no; the minister who should use such language would
be hooted. It would be too hard a confession, such as one
cannot ask a nation to make. Every heart would bound, leap
forth at the idea. And, besides, would not the danger
perhaps be even greater if all that has been done were
allowed to crumble? How many wrecked hopes, how much
discarded, useless material there would be! No, we can now
only save ourselves by patience and courage—and forward,
ever forward! We are a very young nation, and in fifty
years we desired to effect the unity which others have required
two hundred years to arrive at. Well, we must pay for our
haste, we must wait for the harvest to ripen, and fill our
barns.' Then, with another and more sweeping wave of
the arm, he stubbornly strengthened himself in his hopes.
'You know,' said he, 'that I was always against the alliance
with Germany. As I predicted, it has ruined us. We were
not big enough to march side by side with such a wealthy and
powerful person; and it is in view of a war, always near at
hand and inevitable, that we now suffer so cruelly from having
to support the budgets of a great nation. Ah! that war
which has never come, it is that which has exhausted the
best part of our blood and sap and money without the
slightest profit. To-day we have nothing before us but the
necessity of breaking with our ally, who speculated on our
pride, who has never helped us in any way, who has never
given us anything but bad advice, and treated us otherwise
than with suspicion. But it was all inevitable, and that's
what people won't admit in France. I can speak freely of it
all, for I am a declared friend of France, and people even

feel some spite against me on that account. However, explain to your compatriots, that on the morrow of our conquest of Rome, in our frantic desire to resume our ancient rank, it was absolutely necessary that we should play our part in Europe and show that we were a power with whom the others must henceforth count. And hesitation was not allowable, all our interests impelled us toward Germany, the evidence was so blinding as to impose itself. The stern law of the struggle for life weighs as heavily on nations as on individuals, and this it is which explains and justifies the rupture between the two sisters, France and Italy, the forgetting of so many ties, race, commercial intercourse and, if you like, services also. The two sisters, ah! they now pursue each other with so much hatred that all common-sense even seems at an end. My poor old heart bleeds when I read the articles which your newspapers and ours exchange like poisoned darts. When will this fratricidal massacre cease? which of the two will first realise the necessity of peace, the necessity of the alliance of the Latin races, if they are to remain alive amidst those torrents of other races which more and more invade the world?' Then gaily, with the *bonhomie* of a hero disarmed by old age, and seeking a refuge in his dreams, Orlando added: 'Come, you must promise to help me as soon as you are in Paris. However small your field of action may be, promise me you will do all you can to promote peace between France and Italy; there can be no more holy task. Relate all you have seen here, all you have heard—oh! as frankly as possible. If we have faults, you certainly have faults as well. And, come, family quarrels can't last for ever!'

'No doubt,' Pierre answered in some embarrassment. 'Unfortunately they are the most tenacious. In families, when blood becomes exasperated with blood, hate goes as far as poison and the knife. And pardon becomes impossible.'

He dared not fully express his thoughts. Since he had been in Rome, listening, and considering things, the quarrel between Italy and France had resumed itself in his mind in a fine tragic story. Once upon a time there were two princesses, daughters of a powerful queen, the mistress of the world. The elder one, who had inherited her mother's kingdom, was secretly grieved to see her sister, who had established herself in a neighbouring land, gradually increase

in wealth, strength, and brilliancy, whilst she herself declined
as if weakened by age, dismembered, so exhausted, and so
sore, that she already felt defeated on the day when she
attempted a supreme effort to regain universal power. And
so how bitter were her feelings, how hurt she always felt on
seeing her sister recover from the most frightful shocks,
resume her dazzling gala, and continue to reign over the
world by dint of strength and grace and wit. Never would
she forgive it, however well that envied and detested sister
might act towards her. Therein lay an incurable wound, the
life of one poisoned by that of the other, the hatred of old
blood for young blood, which could only be quieted by death.
And even if peace, as was possible, should soon be restored
between them in presence of the younger sister's evident
triumph, the other would always harbour deep within her
heart an endless grief at being the elder yet the vassal.

'However, you may rely on me,' Pierre affectionately
resumed. 'This quarrel between the two countries is certainly a great source of grief and a great peril. And assuredly
I will only say what I think to be the truth about you. At
the same time I fear that you hardly like the truth, for temperament and custom have hardly prepared you for it. The
poets of every nation who at various times have written on
Rome have intoxicated you with so much praise that you are
scarcely fitted to hear the real truth about your Rome of to-
day. No matter how superb a share of praise one may accord
you, one must all the same look at the reality of things; and
this reality is just what you won't admit, lovers of the beautiful as you ever are, susceptible too like women, whom the
slightest hint of a wrinkle sends into despair.'

Orlando began to laugh. 'Well, certainly, one must
always beautify things a little,' said he. 'Why speak of ugly
faces at all? We in our theatres only care for pretty music,
pretty dancing, pretty pieces which please one. As for the
rest, whatever is disagreeable let us hide it, for mercy's
sake!'

'On the other hand,' the priest continued, 'I will cheerfully
confess the great error of my book. The Italian Rome which
I neglected and sacrificed to papal Rome not only exists but
is already so powerful and triumphant that it is surely the
other one which is bound to disappear in course of time.
However much the Pope may strive to remain immutable
within his Vatican, a steady evolution goes on around him,

and the black world, by mingling with the white, has already become a grey world. I never realised that more acutely than at the *fête* given by Prince Buongiovanni for the betrothal of his daughter to your grand-nephew. I came away quite enchanted, won over to the cause of your resurrection.'

The old man's eyes sparkled. 'Ah! you were present?' said he,' 'and you witnessed a never-to-be-forgotten scene, did you not, and you no longer doubt our vitality, our growth into a great people when the difficulties of to-day are overcome? What does a quarter of a century, what does even a century matter? Italy will again rise to her old glory, as soon as the great people of to-morrow shall have sprung from the soil. And if I detest that man Sacco it is because to my mind he is the incarnation of all the enjoyers and intriguers whose appetite for the spoils of our conquest has retarded everything. But I live again in my dear grand-nephew Attilio, who represents the future, the generation of brave and worthy men who will purify and educate the country. Ah! may some of the great ones of to-morrow spring from him and that adorable little Princess Celia, whom my niece Stefana, a sensible woman at bottom, brought to see me the other day. If you had seen that child fling her arms about me, call me endearing names, and tell me that I should be godfather to her first son, so that he might bear my name and once again save Italy. Yes, yes, may peace be concluded around that coming cradle; may the union of those dear children be the indissoluble marriage of Rome and the whole nation, and may all be repaired, and all blossom anew in their love!'

Tears came to his eyes, and Pierre, touched by his inextinguishable patriotism, sought to please him. 'I myself,' said he, 'expressed to your son much the same wish on the evening of the betrothal *fête*, when I told him I trusted that their nuptials might be definitive and fruitful, and that from them and all the others there might arise the great nation which, now that I begin to know you, I hope you will soon become!'

'You said that!' exclaimed Orlando. 'Well, I forgive your book, for you have understood at last; and new Rome, there she is, the Rome which is ours, which we wish to make worthy of her glorious past, and for the third time the queen of the world.'

With one of those broad gestures into which he put all

his remaining life, he pointed to the curtainless window where
Rome spread out in solemn majesty from one horizon to the
other. But suddenly he turned his head, and in a fit of
paternal indignation began to apostrophise young Angiolo
Mascara. 'You young rascal!' said he, 'it's our Rome which
you dream of destroying with your bombs, which you talk of
razing like a rotten, tottering house, so as to rid the world of
it for ever!'

Angiolo had hitherto remained silent, passionately listening to the others. His pretty, girlish, beardless face reflected
the slightest emotion in sudden flushes; and his big blue eyes
also had glowed on hearing what had been said of the people,
the new people which it was necessary to create. 'Yes!' he
slowly replied in his pure and musical voice, 'we mean to
raze it and not leave a stone of it, but raze it in order to build
it up again.'

Orlando interrupted him with a soft bantering laugh:
'Oh! you would build it up again; that's fortunate!' he
said.

'I would build it up again,' the young man replied, in
the trembling voice of an inspired prophet. 'I would build
it up again—oh, so vast, so beautiful and so noble! Will not
the universal democracy of to-morrow, humanity when it is
at last freed, need an unique city, which shall be the ark of
alliance, the very centre of the world? And is not Rome
designated, Rome which the prophecies have marked as eternal
and immortal, where the destinies of the nations are to be
accomplished? But in order that it may become the final
definitive sanctuary, the capital of the destroyed kingdoms,
where the wise men of all countries shall meet once every
year, one must first of all purify it by fire, leave nothing of its
old stains remaining. Then, when the sun shall have absorbed
all the pestilence of the old soil, we will rebuild the city ten
times more beautiful and ten times larger than it has ever
been. And what a city of truth and justice it will at last be,
the Rome that has been announced and awaited for three
thousand years, all in gold and all in marble, filling the Campagna from the sea to the Sabine and the Alban mountains,
and so prosperous and so sensible that its twenty millions of
inhabitants, after regulating the law of labour, will live with
the unique joy of being. Yes, yes, Rome the Mother, Rome
the Queen, alone on the face of the earth and for all
eternity!'

Pierre listened to him, aghast. What! did the blood of Augustus go to such a point as this? The popes had not become masters of Rome without feeling impelled to rebuild it in their passion to rule over the world; young Italy, likewise yielding to the hereditary madness of universal domination, had in its turn sought to make the city larger than any other, erecting whole districts for people who had never come, and now even the anarchists were possessed by the same stubborn dream of the race, a dream beyond all measure this time, a fourth and monstrous Rome, whose suburbs would invade continents in order that liberated humanity, united in one family, might find sufficient lodging! This was the climax. Never could more extravagant proof be given of the blood of pride and sovereignty which had scorched the veins of that race ever since Augustus had bequeathed it the inheritance of his absolute empire, with the furious instinct that the world legally belonged to it, and that its mission was to conquer it again. This idea had intoxicated all the children of that historic soil, impelling all of them to make their city The City, the one which had reigned and which would reign again in splendour when the days predicted by the oracles should arrive. And Pierre remembered the four fatidical letters, the S.P.Q.R. of old and glorious Rome, which like an order of final triumph given to destiny he had everywhere found in present-day Rome, on all the walls, on all the insignia, even on the municipal dust-carts! And he understood the prodigious vanity of these people, haunted by the glory of their ancestors, spell-bound by the past of their city, declaring that she contains everything, that they themselves cannot know her thoroughly, that she is the sphinx who will some day explain the riddle of the universe, that she is so great and noble that all within her acquires increase of greatness and nobility, in such wise that they demand for her the idolatrous respect of the entire world, so vivacious in their minds is the illusive legend which clings to her, so incapable are they of realising that what was once great may be so no longer.

'But I know your fourth Rome,' resumed Orlando, again enlivened. 'It's the Rome of the people, the capital of the Universal Republic, which Mazzini dreamt of. Only he left the pope in it. Do you know, my lad, that if we old Republicans rallied to the monarchy, it was because we feared that in the event of revolution the country might fall into the hands of dangerous madmen such as those who have upset your brain? Yes, that was why we resigned ourselves to our monarchy, which is not much different from a parliamentary republic. And now, good-bye and be sensible; remember that your poor mother would die of it if any misfortune should befall you. Come, let me embrace you all the same.'

On receiving the hero's affectionate kiss Angiolo coloured like a girl. Then he went off with his gentle, dreamy air, never adding a word, but politely inclining his head to the priest. Silence continued till Orlando's eyes encountered the newspapers scattered on the table, when he once more spoke of the terrible bereavement of the Boccaneras. He had loved Benedetta like a dear daughter during the sad days when she had dwelt near him; and finding the newspaper accounts of her death somewhat singular, worried in fact by the obscure points which he could divine in the tragedy, he was asking Pierre for particulars, when his son Luigi suddenly entered the room, breathless from having climbed the stairs so quickly and with his face full of anxious fear. He had just dismissed his contractors with impatient roughness, giving no thought to his serious financial position, the jeopardy in which his fortune was now placed, so anxious was he to be up above beside his father. And when he was there his first uneasy glance was for the old man, to make sure whether the priest by some imprudent word had not dealt him his death blow.

He shuddered on noticing how Orlando quivered, moved to tears by the terrible affair of which he was speaking; and for a moment he thought he had arrived too late, that the harm was done. 'Good heavens, father!' he exclaimed, 'what is the matter with you, why are you crying?' And as he spoke he knelt at the old man's feet, taking hold of his hands and giving him such a passionate loving glance that he seemed to be offering all the blood of his heart to spare him the slightest grief.

'It is about the death of that poor woman,' Orlando sadly answered. 'I was telling Monsieur Froment how it grieved me, and I added that I could not yet understand it all. The papers talk of a sudden death which is always so extraordinary.'

The young Count rose again, looking very pale. The priest had not yet spoken. But what a frightful moment was this ! What if he should reply, what if he should speak out ?

' You were present, were you not ? ' continued the old man, addressing Pierre. ' You saw everything. Tell me, then, how the thing happened.'

Luigi Prada looked at Pierre. Their eyes met fixedly, plunging into one another's souls. All began afresh in their minds, Destiny on the march, Santobono encountered with his little basket, the drive across the melancholy Campagna, the conversation about poison while the little basket was gently rocked on the priest's knees ; then, in particular, the sleepy *osteria*, and the little black hen, so suddenly killed, lying on the ground with a tiny streamlet of violet blood trickling from her beak. And next there was that splendid ball at the Buongiovanni mansion, with all its *odore di femina* and its triumph of love: and finally, before the Palazzo Boccanera, so black under the silvery moon, there was the man who lighted a cigar and went off without once turning his head, allowing dim Destiny to accomplish its work of death. Both of them, Pierre and Prada, knew that story and lived it over again, having no need to recall it aloud in order to make certain that they had fully penetrated one another's soul.

Pierre did not immediately answer the old man. ' Oh ! ' he murmured at last, ' there were frightful things, yes, frightful things.'

' No doubt—that is what I suspected,' resumed Orlando. ' You can tell us all. In presence of death my son has freely forgiven.'

The young Count's gaze again sought that of Pierre with such weight, such ardent entreaty that the priest felt deeply stirred. He had just remembered that man's anguish during the ball, the atrocious torture of jealousy which he had undergone before allowing Destiny to avenge him. And he pictured also what must have been his feelings after the terrible outcome of it all : at first stupefaction at Destiny's harshness, at this full vengeance which he had never desired so ferocious ; then icy calmness like that of the cool gambler who awaits events, reading the newspapers, and feeling no other remorse than that of the general whose victory has cost him too many men. He must have immediately realised that the Cardinal would stifle the affair for the sake of the Church's honour ; and only retained one weight on his heart, regret possibly for

that woman whom he had never won, with perhaps a last
horrible jealousy which he did not confess to himself, but from
which he would always suffer, jealousy at knowing that she
lay in another's arms in the grave, for all eternity. But
behold, after that victorious effort to remain calm, after that
cold and remorseless waiting, Punishment arose, the fear that
Destiny, travelling on with its poisoned figs, might have not yet
ceased its march, and might by a rebound strike down his
own father. Yet another thunderbolt, yet another victim,
the most unexpected, the being he most adored! At that
thought all his strength of resistance had in one moment
collapsed, and he was there, in terror of Destiny, more at a
loss, more trembling than a child.

'The newspapers, however,' slowly said Pierre as if he were
seeking his words, 'the newspapers must have told you that
the Prince succumbed first, and that the Contessina died of
grief whilst embracing him for the last time. . . . As for the
cause of death, *mon Dieu*, you know that doctors themselves in
sudden cases scarcely dare to pronounce an exact opinion——'

He stopped short, for within him he had suddenly heard
the voice of Benedetta giving him, just before she died, that
terrible order : 'You, who will see his father, I charge you to
tell him that I cursed his son. I wish that he should know,
it is necessary that he should know, for the sake of truth and
justice.' And was he, O Lord, about to obey that order?
was it one of those divine commands which must be executed
even if the result be a torrent of blood and tears ? For a few
seconds Pierre suffered from a heartrending combat within
him, hesitating between the act of truth and justice which the
dead woman had called for and his own personal desire for
forgiveness, and the horror he would feel should he kill that
poor old man by fulfilling his implacable mission which could
benefit nobody. And certainly the other one, the son, must
have understood what a supreme struggle was going on in the
priest's mind, a struggle which would decide his own father's
fate, for his glance became yet more suppliant than ever.

'One first thought that it was merely indigestion,' continued Pierre, 'but the Prince became so much worse, that
one was alarmed, and the doctor was sent for——'

Ah ! Prada's eyes, they had become so despairing, so full
of the most touching and weightiest things, that the priest
could read in them all the decisive reasons which were about to
stay his tongue. No, no, he would not strike an innocent old

man; he had promised nothing, and to obey the last expression of the dead woman's hatred would have seemed to him like charging her memory with a crime. The young Count, too, during those few minutes of anguish, had suffered a whole life of such abominable torture, that after all some little justice was done.

'And then,' Pierre concluded, 'when the doctor arrived he at once recognised that it was a case of infectious fever. There can be no doubt of it. This morning I attended the funeral; it was very splendid and very touching.'

Orlando did not insist, but contented himself with saying that he also had felt much emotion all the morning on thinking of that funeral. Then, as he turned to set the papers on the table in order with his trembling hands, his son, icy cold with perspiration, staggering and clinging to the back of a chair in order that he might not fall, again gave Pierre a long glance, but a very soft one, full of distracted gratitude.

'I am leaving this evening,' resumed Pierre, who felt exhausted and wished to break off the conversation, 'and I must now bid you farewell. Have you any commission to give me for Paris?'

'No, none,' replied Orlando; and then, with sudden recollection, he added, 'Yes, I have though! You remember that book written by my old comrade-in-arms, Théôphile Morin, one of Garibaldi's Thousand—that manual for the bachelor's degree which he desired to see translated and adopted here? Well, I am pleased to say that I have a promise that it shall be used in our schools, but on condition that he makes some alterations in it. Luigi, give me the book; it is there on that shelf.'

Then, when his son had handed him the volume, he showed Pierre some notes which he had pencilled on the margins, and explained to him the modifications which were desired in the general scheme of the work. 'Will you be kind enough,' he continued, 'to take this copy to Morin himself? His address is written inside the cover. If you can do so you will spare me the trouble of writing him a very long letter; in ten minutes you can explain matters to him more clearly and completely than I could do in ten pages. . . . And you must embrace Morin for me, and tell him that I still love him—oh! with all my heart of the bygone days, when I could still use my legs and we two fought like devils side by side under a hail of bullets.'

A short silence followed—that pause, that embarrassment tinged with emotion which precedes the moment of farewell. 'Come, good-bye,' said Orlando; 'embrace me for him and for yourself, embrace me affectionately like that lad did just now. I am so old and so near my end, my dear Monsieur Froment, that you will allow me to call you my child and to kiss you like a grandfather, wishing you all courage and peace, and that faith in life which alone helps one to live.'

Pierre was so touched that tears rose to his eyes, and when with all his soul he kissed the stricken hero on either cheek, he felt that he likewise was weeping. With a hand yet as vigorous as a vice, Orlando detained him for a moment beside his armchair, whilst with his other hand waving in a supreme gesture, he for the last time showed him Rome, so immense and mournful under the ashen sky. And his voice came low, quivering and suppliant. 'For mercy's sake swear to me that you will love her all the same, in spite of all, for she is the cradle, the mother! Love her for all that she no longer is, love her for all that she desires to be! Do not say that her end has come; love her, love her so that she may live again, that she may live for ever!'

Pierre again embraced him, unable to find any other response, upset as he was by all the passion displayed by that old warrior, who spoke of his city as a man of thirty might speak of the woman he adores. And he found him so handsome and so lofty with his old blanched, leonine mane and his stubborn belief in approaching resurrection, that once more the other old Roman, Cardinal Boccanera, arose before him, equally stubborn in his faith and relinquishing nought of his dream, even though he might be crushed on the spot by the fall of the heavens. These twain ever stood face to face, at either end of their city, alone rearing their lofty figures above the horizon, whilst awaiting the future.

Then, when Pierre had bowed to Count Luigi, and found himself outside again in the Via Venti Settembre, he was all eagerness to get back to the Boccanera mansion so as to pack up his things and depart. His farewell visits were made, and he now only had to take leave of Donna Serafina and the Cardinal, and to thank them for all their kind hospitality. For him alone did their doors open, for they had shut themselves up on returning from the funeral, resolved to see nobody. At twilight, therefore, Pierre had no one but Victorine to keep him company in the vast, black mansion; for when he expressed a desire to take supper with Don Vigilio she told him that the latter had also shut himself in his room. Desirous as he was of at least shaking hands with the secretary for the last time, Pierre went to knock at the door, which was so near his own, but could obtain no reply, and divined that the poor fellow, overcome by a fresh attack of fever and suspicion, desired not to see him again, in terror at the idea that he might compromise himself yet more than he had done already. Thereupon it was settled that, as the train only started at seventeen minutes past ten, Victorine should serve Pierre his supper on the little table in his sitting-room at eight o'clock. She brought him a lamp and spoke of putting his linen in order; but he absolutely declined her help, and she had to leave him to pack up quietly by himself.

He had purchased a little box, since his valise could not possibly hold all the linen and winter clothing which had been sent to him from Paris as his stay in Rome became more and more protracted. However, the packing was soon accomplished; the wardrobe was emptied, the drawers were visited, the box and valise filled and securely locked by seven o'clock. An hour remained to him before supper, and he sat there resting, when his eyes, whilst travelling round the walls to make sure that he had forgotten nothing, encountered that old painting by some unknown master, which had so often filled him with emotion. The lamplight now shone full upon it; and this time again as he gazed at it he felt a blow in the heart, a blow which was all the deeper, as now, at this parting hour, he found a symbol of his defeat at Rome in that dolent, tragic, half-naked woman, draped in a shred of linen, and weeping between her clasped hands whilst seated on the threshold of the palace whence she had been driven. Did not that rejected one, that stubborn victim of love, who sobbed so bitterly, and of whom one knew nothing, neither what her face was like, nor whence she had come, nor what her fault had been—did she not personify all man's useless efforts to force the doors of truth, and all the frightful abandonment into which he falls as soon as he collides with the wall which shuts the unknown off from him? For a long while did Pierre look at her, again worried at being obliged to depart without having seen her face behind her streaming golden hair—that face of dolorous beauty which he pictured radiant with youth and delicious in its mystery. And as he gazed he was just fancying that he could see it, that it was becoming

his at last, when there was a knock at the door and Narcisse
Habert entered.

Pierre was surprised to see the young *attaché*, for three
days previously he had started for Florence, impelled thither
by one of the sudden whims of his artistic fancy. However,
he at once apologised for his unceremonious intrusion. 'Ah!
there is your luggage!' he said; 'I heard that you were going
away this evening, and I was unwilling to let you leave Rome
without coming to shake hands with you. But what frightful
things have happened since we met! I only returned this
afternoon, so that I could not attend the funeral. However,
you may well imagine how thunderstruck I was by the news
of those frightful deaths.'

Then, suspecting some unacknowledged tragedy, like a
man well acquainted with the legendary dark side of Rome,
he put some questions to Pierre, but did not insist on them,
being at bottom far too prudent to burden himself uselessly
with redoubtable secrets. And after Pierre had given him
such particulars as he thought fit, the conversation changed
and they spoke at length of Italy, Rome, Naples and Florence.
'Ah! Florence, Florence!' Narcisse repeated languorously.
He had lighted a cigarette, and his words fell more slowly as
he glanced round the room. 'You were very well lodged
here,' he said; 'it is very quiet. I had never come up to
this floor before.'

His eyes continued wandering over the walls until they
were at last arrested by the old painting which the lamp
illumined, and thereupon he remained for a moment blinking
as if surprised. And all at once he rose and approached the
picture. 'Dear me! dear me!' said he, 'but that's very
good, that's very fine!'

'Isn't it?' rejoined Pierre. 'I know nothing about painting,
but I was stirred by that picture on the very day of my
arrival, and over and over again it has kept me here with my
heart beating and full of indescribable feelings.'

Narcisse no longer spoke, but examined the painting with
the care of a connoisseur, an expert, whose keen glance
decides the question of authenticity, and appraises commercial
value. And the most extraordinary delight appeared upon
the young man's fair, rapturous face, whilst his fingers began
to quiver. 'But it's a Botticelli, it's a Botticelli! There can
be no doubt about it,' he exclaimed. 'Just look at the hands,

and look at the folds of the drapery! And the colour of the hair, and the technique, the flow of the whole composition. A Botticelli, ah! *mon Dieu*, a Botticelli!'

He became quite faint, overflowing with increasing admiration as he penetrated more and more deeply into the subject, at once so simple and so poignant. Was it not acutely modern? The artist had foreseen our pain-fraught century, our anxiety in presence of the invisible, our distress at being unable to cross the portal of mystery which was for ever closed. And what an eternal symbol of the world's wretchedness was that woman, whose face one could not see, and who sobbed so distractedly without it being possible for one to wipe away her tears! Yes, a Botticelli, unknown, uncatalogued: what a discovery! Then he paused to inquire of Pierre: 'Did you know it was a Botticelli?'

'Oh no! I spoke to Don Vigilio about it one day, but he seemed to think it of no account. And Victorine, when I spoke to her, replied that all those old things only served to harbour dust.'

Narcisse protested, quite stupefied: 'What! they have a Botticelli here and don't know it! Ah! how well I recognise in that the Roman princes who, unless their masterpieces have been labelled, are for the most part utterly at sea among them! No doubt this one has suffered a little, but a simple cleaning would make a marvel, a famous picture of it, for which a museum would at least give——'

He abruptly stopped, completing his sentence with a wave of the hand, and not mentioning the figure which was on his lips. And then, as Victorine came in, followed by Giacomo, to lay the little table for Pierre's supper, he turned his back upon the Botticelli and said no more about it. The young priest's attention was aroused, however, and he could well divine what was passing in the other's mind. Under that make-believe Florentine, all angelicalness, there was an experienced business man, who well knew how to look after his pecuniary interests and was even reported to be somewhat avaricious. Pierre, who was aware of it, could not help smiling therefore when he saw him take his stand before another picture—a frightful Virgin, badly copied from some eighteenth century canvas—and exclaim: 'Dear me! that's not at all bad! I've a friend, I remember, who asked me to buy him some old paintings. I say, Victorine, now that Donna Serafina

and the Cardinal are left alone, do you think they would like
to rid themselves of a few valueless pictures ? '

The servant raised her arms as if to say that if it depended
on her, everything might be carried away. Then she replied :
' Not to a dealer, sir, on account of the nasty rumours which
would at once spread about, but I'm sure they would be happy
to please a friend. The house costs a lot to keep up, and
money would be welcome.'

Pierre then vainly endeavoured to persuade Narcisse to
stay and sup with him, but the young man gave his word of
honour that he was expected elsewhere and was even late.
And forthwith he ran off, after pressing the priest's hands
and affectionately wishing him a good journey.

Eight o'clock was striking, and Pierre seated himself at
the little table, Victorine remaining to serve him after dismissing Giacomo, who had brought the supper things upstairs in a basket. ' The people here make me wild,' said the
worthy woman after the other had gone, ' they are so slow.
And besides, it's a pleasure for me to serve you your last
meal, Monsieur l'Abbé. I've had a little French dinner
cooked for you, a *sole au gratin* and a roast fowl.'

Pierre was touched by this attention, and pleased to have
the company of a compatriot whilst he partook of his final
meal amidst the deep silence of the old, black, deserted
mansion. The buxom figure of Victorine was still instinct
with mourning, with grief for the loss of her dear Contessina,
but her daily toil was already setting her erect again,
restoring her quick activity ; and she spoke almost cheerfully
whilst passing plates and dishes to Pierre. ' And to think,
Monsieur l'Abbé,' said she, ' that you'll be in Paris on the
morning of the day after to-morrow ! As for me, you know,
it seems as if I only left Auneau yesterday. Ah ! what fine
soil there is there ; rich soil, yellow like gold, not like their
poor stuff here which smells of sulphur ! And the pretty
fresh willows beside our stream, too, and the little wood so
full of moss ! They've no moss here ; their trees look like tin
under that stupid sun of theirs which burns up the grass.
Mon Dieu ! in the early times I would have given I don't
know what for a good fall of rain to soak me and wash away all
the dust. Ah ! I shall never get used to their awful Rome.
What a country and what people ! '

Pierre was quite enlivened by her stubborn fidelity to
her own nook, which after five and twenty years of absence

still left her horrified with that city of crude light and black
vegetation, true daughter as she was of a smiling and tem-
perate clime which of a morning was steeped in rosy mist.
'But now that your young mistress is dead,' said he, 'what
keeps you here? Why don't you take the train with me?'

She looked at him in surprise: 'Go off with you—go back
to Auneau! Oh! it's impossible, Monsieur l'Abbé. It
would be too ungrateful to begin with, for Donna Serafina is
accustomed to me, and it would be bad on my part to forsake
her and his Eminence now that they are in trouble. And
besides, what could I do elsewhere? No, my little hole is
here now.'

'So you will never see Auneau again?'

'No, never: that's certain.'

'And you don't mind being buried here, in their ground
which smells of sulphur?'

She burst into a frank laugh. 'Oh!' she said, 'I don't
mind where I am when I'm dead. One sleeps well everywhere. And it's funny that you should be so anxious as to what
there may be when one's dead. There's nothing, I'm sure.
That's what tranquillises me, to feel that it will be all over
and that I shall have a rest. The good God owes us that,
after we've worked so hard. You know that I'm not devout
—oh, dear, no! Still that doesn't prevent me from behaving
properly, and, true as I stand here, I've never had a lover.
It seems foolish to say such a thing at my age; still I say it
because it's the sober truth.'

She continued laughing like the worthy woman she was,
having no belief in priests, and yet without a sin upon her
conscience. And Pierre once more marvelled at the simple
courage and great practical common sense of this laborious and
devoted creature, who for him personified the whole unbelieving
lowly class of France—those who no longer believe and will
believe never more. Ah! to be as she was, to do one's work
and lie down for the eternal sleep without any revolt of pride,
satisfied with the one joy of having accomplished one's share
of toil!

When Pierre had finished his supper Victorine summoned
Giacomo to clear the things away. And as it was only half-
past eight she advised the priest to spend another quiet hour
in his room. Why go and catch a chill by waiting at the
station? She could send for a cab at half-past nine, and as
soon as it arrived she would send word to him and have his

luggage carried down. He might be easy as to that, and need trouble himself about nothing.

When she had gone off Pierre soon sank into a deep reverie. It seemed to him, indeed, as if he had already quitted Rome, as if the city were far away and he could look back on it, and his experiences within it. His book, 'New Rome,' arose in his mind; and he remembered his first morning on the Janiculum, his view of Rome from the terrace of San Pietro in Montorio, a Rome such as he had dreamt of, so young and ethereal under the pure sky. It was then that he had asked himself the decisive question: Could Catholicism be renewed? Could it revert to the spirit of primitive Christianity, become the religion of the democracy, the faith which the distracted modern world, in danger of death, awaits in order that it may be pacified and live? His heart had then beaten with hope and enthusiasm. After his disaster at Lourdes, from which he had scarcely recovered, he had come to attempt another and supreme experiment by asking Rome what her reply to his question would be. And now the experiment had failed, he knew what answer Rome had returned him through her ruins, her monuments, her very soil, her people, her prelates, her cardinals, her Pope! No, Catholicism could not be renewed: no, it could not revert to the spirit of primitive Christianity; no, it could not become the religion of the democracy, the new faith which might save the old toppling societies in danger of death. Though it seemed to be of democratic origin, it was henceforth riveted to that Roman soil; it remained kingly in spite of everything, forced to cling to the principle of temporal power under penalty of suicide, bound by tradition, enchained by dogma, its evolutions mere simulations, whilst in reality it was reduced to such immobility that, behind the bronze doors of the Vatican, the papacy was the prisoner, the ghost of eighteen centuries of atavism, indulging the ceaseless dream of universal dominion. There, where with priestly faith exalted by love of the suffering and the poor, he had come to seek life and a resurrection of the Christian communion, he had found death, the dust of a destroyed world in which nothing more could germinate, an exhausted soil whence now there could never grow aught but that despotic papacy, the master of bodies as it was of souls. To his distracted cry asking for a new religion, Rome had been content to reply by condemning his book as a work tainted with heresy,

and he himself had withdrawn it amidst the bitter grief of
his disillusions. He had seen, he had understood, and all had
collapsed. And it was himself, his soul and his brain, which
lay among the ruins.

Pierre was stifling. He rose, threw the window overlooking the Tiber wide open, and leant out. The rain had
begun to fall again at the approach of evening, but now it
had once more ceased. The atmosphere was very mild, moist,
even oppressive. The moon must have arisen in the ashen
grey sky, for her presence could be divined behind the clouds
which she illumined with a vague, yellow, mournful light.
And under that slumberous glimmer the vast horizon showed
blackly and phantom-like: the Janiculum in front with the
close-packed houses of the Trastevere; the river flowing
away yonder on the left towards the dim height of the
Palatine; whilst on the right the dome of St. Peter's showed
forth, round and domineering in the pale atmosphere. Pierre
could not see the Quirinal, but divined it to be behind him,
and could picture its long façade shutting off part of the sky.
And what a collapsing Rome, half-devoured by the gloom, was
this—so different from the Rome, all youth and dreamland,
which he had beheld and passionately loved on the day of his
arrival! He remembered the three symbolic summits which
had then summed up for him the whole long history of Rome
—the ancient, the papal, and the Italian city. But if the
Palatine had remained the same discrowned mount on which
there only rose the phantom of the ancestor, Augustus
emperor and pontiff, master of the world, he now pictured St.
Peter's and the Quirinal as strangely altered. To that royal
palace which he had so neglected, and which had seemed
to him like a flat, low barrack, to that new Government which
had brought him the impression of some attempt at sacrilegious
modernity, he now accorded the large, increasing space that
they occupied in the panorama, the whole of which they would
apparently soon fill; whilst, on the contrary, St. Peter's, that
dome which he had found so triumphal, all azure, reigning
over the city like a gigantic and unshakable monarch, at
present seemed to him full of cracks and already shrinking,
as if it were one of those huge old piles which, through the
secret, unsuspected decay of their timbers, at times fall to the
ground in one mass.

A murmur, a growling plaint, rose from the swollen Tiber,

and Pierre shivered at the icy abysmal breath which swept past his face. And his thoughts of the three summits and their symbolic triangle aroused within him the memory of the sufferings of the great silent multitude of poor and lowly for whom pope and king had so long disputed. It all dated from long ago, from the day when, in dividing the inheritance of Augustus, the emperor had been obliged to content himself with men's bodies, leaving their souls to the pope, whose one idea had henceforth been to gain the temporal power of which God, in his person, was despoiled. All the middle ages had been disturbed and ensanguined by the quarrel, till at last the silent multitude, weary of vexations and misery, spoke out; threw off the papal yoke at the Reformation, and later on began to overthrow its kings. And then, as Pierre had written in his book, a new fortune had been offered to the pope, that of reverting to the ancient dream, by dissociating himself from the fallen thrones and placing himself on the side of the wretched in the hope that this time he would conquer the people, win it entirely for himself. Was it not prodigious to see that man, Leo XIII, despoiled of his kingdom, allowing himself to be called a Socialist, assembling under his banner the great flock of the disinherited, and marching against the kings at the head of that fourth estate to whom the coming century will belong? The eternal struggle for possession of the people continued as bitterly as ever, even in Rome itself, where pope and king, who could see each other from their windows, contended together like falcon and hawk for the little birds of the woods. And in this for Pierre lay the reason why Catholicism was fatally condemned; for it was of monarchical essence to such a point that the Apostolic and Roman papacy could not renounce the temporal power under penalty of becoming something else and disappearing. In vain did it feign a return to the people, in vain did it seek to appear all soul; there was no room in the midst of the world's democracies for any such total and universal sovereignty as that which it claimed to hold from God. Pierre ever beheld the Imperator sprouting up afresh in the Pontifex Maximus, and it was this in particular which had killed his dream, destroyed his book, heaped up all those ruins before which he remained distracted without either strength or courage.

The sight of that ashen Rome, whose edifices faded away into the night, at last brought him such a heartpang that he

came back into the room and fell on a chair near his luggage.
Never before had he experienced such distress of spirit, it
seemed like the death of his soul. After his disaster at
Lourdes he had not come to Rome in search of the candid and
complete faith of a little child, but the superior faith of an
intellectual being, rising above rites and symbols, and seeking
to ensure the greatest possible happiness of mankind based
on its need of certainty. And if this collapsed, if Catholicism
could not be rejuvenated and become the religion and moral
law of the new generations, if the Pope at Rome and with
Rome could not be the Father, the arch of alliance, the
spiritual leader whom all hearkened to and obeyed, why then,
in Pierre's eyes, the last hope was wrecked, the supreme
rending which must plunge present day society into the abyss
was near at hand. That scaffolding of Catholic socialism which
had seemed to him so happily devised for the consolidation of
the old church, now appeared to him lying on the ground ; and
he judged it severely as a mere passing expedient which might
perhaps for some years prop up the ruined edifice, but which
was simply based on an intentional misunderstanding, on a
skilful lie, on politics and diplomacy. No, no ; that the people
should once again, as so many times before, be duped and
gained over, caressed in order that it might be enthralled—this
was repugnant to one's reason, and the whole system appeared
degenerate, dangerous, temporary, calculated to end in the
worst catastrophes. So this then was the finish ; nothing
remained erect and stable ; the old world was about to disappear amidst the frightful sanguinary crisis whose approach
was announced by such indisputable signs. And he, before
that chaos near at hand, had no soul left him, having once
more lost his faith in that decisive experiment which, he
had felt beforehand, would either strengthen him or strike
him down for ever. The thunderbolt had fallen, and now, O
God, what should he do ?

To shake off his anguish he began to walk across the
room. Aye, what should he do now that he was all doubt
again, all dolorous negation, and that his cassock weighed
more heavily than it had ever weighed upon his shoulders ?
He remembered having told Monsignor Nani that he would
never submit, would never be able to resign himself and kill
his hope in salvation by love, but would rather reply by a
fresh book, in which he would say in what new soil the new
religion would spring up. Yes, a flaming book against Rome,

in which he would set down all he had seen, a book which
would depict the real Rome, the Rome which knows neither
charity nor love, and is dying in the pride of its purple! He
had spoken of returning to Paris, leaving the Church and
going to the point of schism. Well, his luggage now lay
there packed; he was going off, and he would write that book;
he would be the great schismatic who was awaited! Did not
everything foretell approaching schism amidst that great
movement of men's minds, weary of old mummified dogmas
and yet hungering for the divine? Even Leo XIII must be
conscious of it, for his whole policy, his whole effort towards
Christian unity, his assumed affection for the democracy had
no other object than that of grouping the whole family around
the papacy, and consolidating it so as to render the Pope
invincible in the approaching struggle. But the times had
come; Catholicism would soon find that it could grant no
more political concessions without perishing, that at Rome it
was reduced to the immobility of an ancient hieratic idol, and
that only in the lands of propaganda, where it was fighting
against other religions, could further evolution take place. It
was, indeed, for this reason that Rome was condemned, the
more so as the abolition of the temporal power, by accustom-
ing men's minds to the idea of a purely spiritual papacy,
seemed likely to conduce to the rise of some anti-pope, far
away, whilst the successor of St. Peter was compelled to cling
stubbornly to his Apostolic and Roman fiction. A bishop, a
priest would arise—where, who could tell? Perhaps yonder
in that free America, where there are priests whom the
struggle for life has turned into convinced socialists, into
ardent democrats, who are ready to go forward with the
coming century. And whilst Rome remains unable to
relinquish aught of her past, aught of her mysteries and
dogmas, that priest will relinquish all of those things which
fall from one in dust. Ah! to be that priest, to be that great
reformer, that saviour of modern society, what a vast dream,
what a part, akin to that of a messiah summoned by the
nations in distress! For a moment Pierre was transported as
by a breeze of hope and triumph. If that great change did
not come in France, in Paris, it would come elsewhere, yonder
across the ocean, or farther yet, wherever there might be a
sufficiently fruitful soil for the new seed to spring from it in
overflowing harvests. A new religion! a new religion! even
as he had cried on returning from Lourdes, a religion which,

in particular, should not be an appetite for death, a religion
which should at last realise here below that Kingdom of God
referred to in the Gospel, and which should equitably divide
terrestrial wealth, and with the law of labour ensure the rule
of truth and justice.

In the fever of this fresh dream Pierre already saw the
pages of his new book flaring before him when his eyes fell
on an object lying upon a chair, which at first surprised him.
This also was a book, that work of Théôphile Morin's which
Orlando had commissioned him to hand to its author, and he
felt annoyed with himself at having left it there, for he might
have forgotten it altogether. Before putting it into his valise
he retained it for a moment in his hand, turning its pages
over, his ideas changing as by a sudden mental revolution.
The work was, however, a very modest one—one of those
manuals for the bachelor's degree containing little beyond the
first elements of the sciences ; still all the sciences were
represented in it, and it gave a fair summary of the present
state of human knowledge. And it was indeed Science which
thus burst upon Pierre's reverie with the energy of sovereign
power. Not only was Catholicism swept away from his mind,
but all his religious conceptions, every hypothesis of the
divine tottered and fell. Only that little school book, nothing
but the universal desire for knowledge, that education which
ever extends and penetrates the whole people, and behold the
mysteries became absurdities, the dogmas crumbled, and
nothing of ancient faith was left. A nation nourished upon
Science, no longer believing in mysteries and dogmas, in a
compensatory system of reward and punishment, is a nation
whose faith is for ever dead : and without faith Catholicism
cannot be. Therein is the blade of the knife, the knife which
falls and severs. If one century, if two centuries be needed,
Science will take them. She alone is eternal. It is pure
naïveté to say that reason is not contrary to faith. The truth
is, that now already in order to save mere fragments of the
sacred writings, it has been necessary to accommodate them
to the new certainties, by taking refuge in the assertion that
they are simply symbolical ! And what an extraordinary
attitude is that of the Catholic Church, expressly forbidding
all those who may discover a truth contrary to the sacred
writings to pronounce upon it in definitive fashion, and order-
ing them to await events in the conviction that this truth will
some day be proved an error ! Only the Pope, says the

Church, is infallible ; Science is fallible, her constant groping is exploited against her, and divines remain on the watch striving to make it appear that her discoveries of to-day are in contradiction with her discoveries of yesterday. What do her sacrilegious assertions, what do her certainties rending dogma asunder, matter to a Catholic since it is certain that at the end of time, she, Science, will again join Faith and become the latter's very humble slave ? Voluntary blindness and impudent denial of things as evident as the sunlight, can no further go. But all the same the insignificant little book, the manual of truth, travels on, continuing its work, destroying error and building up the new world, even as the infinitesimal agents of life built up our present continents.

In the sudden great enlightenment which had come on him Pierre at last felt himself upon firm ground. Has Science ever retreated ? It is Catholicism which has always retreated before her, and will always be forced to retreat. Never does Science stop ; step by step she wrests truth from error, and to say that she is bankrupt because she cannot explain the world in one word and at one effort is pure and simple nonsense. If she leaves, and no doubt will always leave, a smaller and smaller domain to Mystery, and if supposition may always strive to explain that Mystery, it is none the less certain that she ruins, and with each successive hour will add to the ruin of the ancient hypotheses, those which crumble away before the acquired truths. And Catholicism is in the position of those ancient hypotheses, and will be in it yet more thoroughly to-morrow. Like all religions it is, at the bottom, but an explanation of the world, a superior social and political code, intended to bring about the greatest possible sum of peace and happiness on earth. This code which embraces the universality of things thenceforth becomes human, and mortal like everything that is human. One cannot put it on one side and say that it exists on one side by itself, whilst Science does the same on the other. Science is total and has already shown Catholicism that such is the case, and will show it again and again by compelling it to repair the breaches incessantly effected in its ramparts till the day of victory shall come with the final assault of resplendent truth. Frankly, it makes one laugh to hear people assign a rôle to Science, forbid her to enter such and such a domain, predict to her that she shall go no further; and declare that at this end of the century she is already so weary that she abdicates ! Oh ! you little men of shallow or distorted brains, you politicians planning expedients, you dogmatics at bay, you authoritarians so obstinately clinging to the ancient dreams, Science will pass on, and sweep you all away like withered leaves!

Pierre continued glancing through the humble little book, listening to all it told him of sovereign Science. She cannot become bankrupt, for she does not promise the absolute, she is simply the progressive conquest of truth. Never has she pretended that she could give the whole of truth at one effort, that sort of edifice being precisely the work of metaphysics, of revelation, of faith. The *rôle* of Science, on the contrary, is only to destroy error as she gradually advances and increases enlightenment. And thus, far from becoming bankrupt, in her march which nothing stops, she remains the only possible truth for well-balanced and healthy minds. As for those whom she does not satisfy, who crave for immediate and universal knowledge, they have the resource of seeking refuge in no matter what religious hypothesis, provided, if they wish to appear in the right, that they build their fancy upon acquired certainties. Everything which is raised on proven error falls. However, although religious feeling persists among mankind, although the need of religion may be eternal, it by no means follows that Catholicism is eternal, for it is, after all, but one form of religion, which other forms preceded and which others will follow. Religions may disappear, but religious feeling will create new ones even with the help of Science. Pierre thought of that alleged repulse of Science by the present-day awakening of mysticism, the causes of which he had indicated in his book: the discredit into which the idea of liberty has fallen among the people, duped in the last social reorganisation, and the uneasiness of the *élite*, in despair at the void in which their liberated minds and enlarged intelligences have left them. It is the anguish of the Unknown springing up again; but it is also only a natural and momentary reaction after so much labour, on finding that Science does not yet calm our thirst for justice, our desire for security, or our ancient idea of an eternal after-life of enjoyment. In order, however, that Catholicism might be born anew, as some seem to think it will be, the social soil would have to change, and it cannot change; it no longer possesses the sap needful for the renewal of a decaying formula which schools and laboratories destroy more and more each day. The ground is other than it once was, a different oak must spring from it. May Science therefore have her religion, for such a religion will soon be the only one possible for the coming democracies, for the nations whose knowledge ever increases whilst their Catholic faith is already naught but dust.

And all at once, by way of conclusion, Pierre bethought himself of the idiocy of the Congregation of the Index. It had condemned his book, and would surely condemn the other one that he had thought of, should he ever write it. A fine piece of work truly! To fall tooth and nail on the poor books of an enthusiastic dreamer, in which chimera contended with chimera! Yet the Congregation was so foolish as not to interdict that little book which he held in his hands, that humble book which alone was to be feared, which was the ever triumphant enemy that would surely overthrow the Church. Modest it was in its cheap 'get up' as a school manual, but that did not matter : danger began with the very alphabet, increased as knowledge was acquired, and burst forth with those *résumés* of the physical, chemical, and natural sciences which bring the very Creation, as described by Holy Writ, into question. However, the Index dared not attempt to suppress those humble volumes, those terrible soldiers of truth, those destroyers of faith. What was the use, then, of all the money which Leo XIII drew from his hidden treasure of the Peter's Pence to subvention Catholic schools, with the thought of forming the believing generations which the papacy needed to enable it to conquer ? What was the use of that precious money if it was only to serve for the purchase of similar insignificant yet formidable volumes, which could never be sufficiently 'cooked' and expurgated, but would always contain too much science, that growing science which one day would blow up both Vatican and St. Peter's? Ah! that idiotic and impotent Index, what wretchedness and what derision !

Then, when Pierre had placed Théophile Morin's book in his valise, he once more returned to the window, and while leaning out, beheld an extraordinary vision. Under the cloudy, coppery sky, in the mild and mournful night, patches of wavy mist had risen, hiding many of the house-roofs with trailing shreds which looked like shrouds. Entire edifices had disappeared, and he imagined that the times were at last accomplished, and that truth had at last destroyed St. Peter's dome. In a hundred or a thousand years, it would be like that, fallen, obliterated from the black sky. One day, already, he had felt it tottering and cracking beneath him, and had foreseen that this temple of Catholicism would fall even as Jove's temple had fallen on the Capitol. And it was over now, the dome had strewn the ground with fragments, and all that remained standing, in addition to a portion of the apse, were five columns of the central nave, still upholding a shred of entablature, and four cyclopean buttress-piers on which the dome had rested—piers which still arose, isolated and superb, looking indestructible among all the surrounding downfall. But a denser mist flowed past, another thousand years no doubt went by, and then nothing whatever remained. The apse, the last pillars, the giant piers themselves were felled! The wind had swept away their dust, and it would have been necessary to search the soil beneath the brambles and the nettles to find a few fragments of broken statues, marbles with mutilated inscriptions, on the sense of which learned men were unable to agree. And, as formerly, on the Capitol, among the buried remnants of Jupiter's temple, goats strayed and climbed through the solitude, browsing upon the bushes, amidst the deep silence of the oppressive summer sunlight, which only the buzzing flies disturbed.

Then, only then, did Pierre feel the supreme collapse within him. It was really all over, Science was victorious, nothing of the old world remained. What use would it be then to become the great schismatic, the reformer who was awaited? Would it not simply mean the building up of a new dream? Only the eternal struggle of Science against the Unknown, her searching, pursuing inquiry which incessantly moderated man's thirst for the divine, now seemed to him of import, leaving him waiting to know if she would ever triumph so completely as to suffice mankind, by satisfying all its wants. And in the disaster which had overcome his apostolic enthusiasm, in presence of all those ruins, having lost his faith, and even his hope of utilising old Catholicism for social and moral salvation, there only remained reason that held him up. She had at one moment given way. If he had dreamt that book, and had just passed through that terrible crisis, it was because sentiment had once again overcome reason within him. It was his mother, so to say, who had wept in his heart, who had filled him with an irresistible desire to relieve the wretched and prevent the massacres which seemed near at hand; and his passion for charity had

thus swept aside the scruples of his intelligence. But it was
his father's voice that he now heard, lofty and bitter reason
which, though it had fled, at present came back in all
sovereignty. As he had done already after Lourdes, he protested against the glorification of the absurd and the downfall
of common sense. Reason alone enabled him to walk erect
and firm among the remnants of the old beliefs, even amidst
the obscurities and failures of Science. Ah! reason, it was
through her alone that he suffered, through her alone that
he could content himself, and he swore that he would now
always seek to satisfy her, even if in doing so he should lose
his happiness.

At that moment it would have been vain for him to ask
what he ought to do. Everything remained in suspense, the
world stretched before him still littered with the ruins of the
past, of which, to-morrow, it would perhaps be rid. Yonder,
in that dolorous Faubourg of Paris, he would find good Abbé
Rose, who but a few days previously had written begging him
to return and tend, love and save his poor, since Rome, so
dazzling from afar, was dead to charity. And around the
good and peaceful old priest he would find the ever-growing
flock of wretched ones; the little fledgelings who had fallen
from their nests, pale with hunger and shivering with
cold; the households of abominable misery in which the
father drank and the mother became a prostitute, while the
sons and the daughters sank into vice and crime; the
dwellings too through which famine swept, where all was
filth and shameful promiscuity, where there was neither
furniture nor linen, nothing but purely animal life. And
then there would also come the cold blasts of winter, the
disasters of slack times, the hurricanes of consumption
carrying off the weak, whilst the strong clenched their fists
and dreamt of vengeance. One evening, too, perhaps, he
might again enter some room of horror and find that another
mother had killed herself and her five little ones, her last
born in her arms clinging to her drained breast, and the
others scattered over the bare tiles, at last contented, feeling
hunger no more now that they were dead! But no, no, such
awful things were no longer possible: such black misery
conducting to suicide in the heart of that great city of Paris,
which is brimful of wealth, intoxicated with enjoyment, and
flings millions out of window for mere pleasure! The very
foundations of the social edifice were rotten; all would soon

collapse amidst mire and blood. Never before had Pierre so acutely realised the derisive futility of Charity. And all at once he became conscious that the long awaited word, the word which was at last springing from the great silent multitude, the crushed and gagged people was *Justice*! Aye, Justice not Charity! Charity had only served to perpetuate misery, Justice perhaps would cure it. It was for Justice that the wretched hungered; an act of Justice alone could sweep away the olden world so that the new one might be reared. After all, the great silent multitude would belong neither to Vatican nor to Quirinal, neither to pope nor to king. If it had covertly growled through the ages in its long sometimes mysterious, and sometimes open contest; if it had struggled betwixt pontiff and emperor who each had wished to retain it for himself alone, it had only done so in order that it might free itself, proclaim its resolve to belong to none on the day when it should cry Justice! Would to-morrow then at last prove that day of Justice and Truth? For his part, Pierre amidst his anguish—having on one hand that need of the divine which tortures man, and on the other sovereignty of reason which enables man to remain erect—was only sure of one thing, that he would keep his vows, continue a priest watching over the belief of others though he could not himself believe, and would thus chastely and honestly follow his profession, amidst haughty sadness at having been unable to renounce his intelligence in the same way as he had renounced his flesh and his dream of saving the nations. And again, as after Lourdes, he would wait.

So deeply was he plunged in reflection at that window, face to face with the mist which seemed to be destroying the dark edifices of Rome, that he did not hear himself called. At last, however, he felt a tap on the shoulder : ' Monsieur l'Abbé ! ' And then as he turned he saw Victorine, who said to him : ' It is half-past nine ; the cab is there. Giacomo has already taken your luggage down. You must come away, Monsieur l'Abbé.'

Then seeing him blink, still dazed as it were, she smiled and added : ' You were bidding Rome good-bye. What a frightful sky there is.'

' Yes, frightful,' was his reply.

Then they descended the stairs. He had handed her a hundred-franc note to be shared between herself and the other servants. And she apologised for going down before him with the lamp, explaining that the old palace was so dark that evening one could scarcely see.

Ah! that departure, that last descent through the black and empty mansion, it quite upset Pierre's heart. He gave his room that glance of farewell which always saddened him, even when he was leaving a spot where he had suffered. Then, on passing Don Vigilio's chamber, whence there only came a quivering silence, he pictured the secretary with his head buried in his pillows, holding his breath for fear lest he should speak and attract vengeance. But it was in particular on the second and first-floor landings, on passing the closed doors of Donna Serafina and the Cardinal, that Pierre quivered with apprehension at hearing nothing but the silence of the grave. And as he followed Victorine, who, lamp in hand, was still descending, he thought of the brother and sister who were left alone in the ruined palace, last relics of a world which had half passed away. All hope of life had departed with Benedetta and Dario, no resurrection could come from that old maid and that priest who was bound to chastity. Ah! those interminable and lugubrious passages, that frigid and gigantic staircase which seemed to descend into nihility, those huge halls with cracking walls where all was wretchedness and abandonment! And that inner court, looking like a cemetery with its weeds and its damp porticus, where remnants of Apollos and Venuses were rotting! And the little deserted garden, fragrant with ripe oranges, whither nobody now would ever stray, where none would ever meet that adorable Contessina under the laurels near the sarcophagus! All was now annihilated in abominable mourning, in a death-like silence, amidst which the two last Boccaneras must wait, in savage grandeur, till their palace should fall about their heads. Pierre could only just detect a faint sound, the gnawing of a mouse perhaps, unless it were caused by Abbé Paparelli attacking the walls of some out-of-the-way rooms, preying on the old edifice down below, so as to hasten its fall.

The cab stood at the door, already laden with the lugagge, the box beside the driver, the valise on the seat, and the priest at once got in.

'Oh! You have plenty of time,' said Victorine, who had remained on the foot-pavement. 'Nothing has been forgotten. I'm glad to see you go off comfortably.'

And indeed at that last moment Pierre was comforted by the presence of that worthy woman, his compatriot, who had

greeted him on his arrival and now attended his departure.
'I won't say "till we meet again," Monsieur l'Abbé,' she
exclaimed, 'for I don't fancy that you'll soon be back in this
horrid city. Good-bye, Monsieur l'Abbé.'

'Good-bye, Victorine, and thank you with all my heart.'

The cab was already going off at a fast trot, turning into
the narrow sinuous streets which lead to the Corso Vittorio
Emmanuele. It was not raining, and so the hood had not been
raised, but although the damp atmosphere was comparatively
mild, Pierre at once felt a chill. However, he was unwilling to
stop the driver, a silent fellow whose only desire seemingly
was to get rid of his fare as soon as possible. When the cab
came out into the Corso Vittorio Emmanuele, the young man
was astonished to find it already quite deserted, the houses
shut, the footways bare, and the electric lamps burning all
alone in melancholy solitude. In truth, however, the temperature was far from warm and the fog seemed to be increasing, hiding the house-fronts more and more. When Pierre
passed the Cancelleria, that stern colossal pile seemed to him
to be receding, fading away ; and farther on, upon the right,
at the end of the Via di Ara Cœli, starred by a few smoky
gaslamps, the Capitol had quite vanished in the gloom. Then
the thoroughfare narrowed, and the cab went on between the
dark heavy masses of the Gesù and the Altieri palace ; and
there in that contracted passage, where even on fine sunny
days one found all the dampness of old times, the quivering
priest yielded to a fresh train of thought.

It was an idea which had sometimes made him feel anxious,
the idea that mankind, starting from over yonder in Asia, had
always marched onward with the sun. An east wind had
always carried the human seed for future harvests towards the
west. And for a long while now the cradle of humanity had
been stricken with destruction and death, as if indeed the
nations could only advance by stages, leaving exhausted soil,
ruined cities, and degenerate populations behind, as they
marched from orient to occident, towards their unknown
goal. Nineveh and Babylon on the banks of the Euphrates,
Thebes and Memphis on the banks of the Nile, had been
reduced to dust, sinking from old age and weariness into a
deadly numbness beyond possibility of awakening. Then
decrepitude had spread to the shores of the great Mediterranean lake, burying both Tyre and Sidon with dust, and afterwards striking Carthage with senility whilst it yet seemed in

full splendour. In this wise as mankind marched on, carried
by the hidden forces of civilisation from east to west, it
marked each day's journey with ruins ; and how frightful was
the sterility nowadays displayed by the cradle of History, that
Asia and that Egypt, which had once more lapsed into childhood, immobilised in ignorance and degeneracy amidst the
ruins of ancient cities that once had been queens of the world !

It was thus Pierre reflected as the cab rolled on. Still he
was not unconscious of his surroundings. As he passed the
Palazzo di Venezia it seemed to him to be crumbling beneath
some assault of the invisible, for the mist had already swept
away its battlements, and the lofty, bare, fearsome walls
looked as if they were staggering from the onslaught of the
growing darkness. And after passing the deep gap of the
Corso, which was also deserted amidst the pallid radiance of
its electric lights, the Palazzo Torlonia appeared on the right
hand, with one wing ripped open by the picks of demolishers,
whilst on the left, farther up, the Palazzo Colonna showed its
long, mournful façade and closed windows, as if, now that it
was deserted by its masters and void of its ancient pomp, it
awaited the demolishers in its turn.

Then, as the cab at a slower pace began to climb the
ascent of the Via Nazionale, Pierre's reverie continued. Was
not Rome also stricken, had not the hour come for her to
disappear amidst that destruction which the nations on the
march invariably left behind them ? Greece, Athens, and
Sparta slumbered beneath their glorious memories, and were
of no account in the world of to-day. Moreover, the growing
paralysis had already invaded the lower portion of the Italic
peninsula ; and after Naples certainly came the turn of Rome.
She was on the very margin of the death spot which ever
extends over the old continent, that margin where agony
begins, where the impoverished soil will no longer nourish and
support cities, where men themselves seem stricken with old
age as soon as they are born. For two centuries Rome had
been declining, withdrawing little by little from modern life,
having neither manufactures nor trade, and being incapable
even of science, literature, or art. And in Pierre's thoughts
it was no longer St. Peter's only that fell, but all Rome—
basilicas, palaces, and entire districts—which collapsed amidst
a supreme rending, and covered the seven hills with a chaos
of ruins. Like Nineveh and Babylon, and like Thebes and
Memphis, Rome became but a plain bossy with remnants,

amidst which one vainly sought to identify the sites of ancient edifices, whilst its sole denizens were coiling serpents and bands of rats.

The cab turned, and on the right, in a huge gap of darkness Pierre recognised Trajan's column, but it was no longer gilded by the sun as when he had first seen it; it now rose up blackly like the dead trunk of a giant tree whose branches have fallen from old age. And farther on, when he raised his eyes while crossing the little triangular piazza, and perceived a real tree against the leaden sky, that parasol pine of the Villa Aldobrandini which rises there like a symbol of Rome's grace and pride, it seemed to him but a smudge, a little cloud of soot ascending from the downfall of the whole city.

With the anxious, fraternal turn of his feelings, fear was coming over him as he reached the end of his tragic dream. When the numbness which spreads across the aged world should have passed Rome, when Lombardy should have yielded to it, and Genoa, Turin and Milan should have fallen asleep as Venice has fallen already, then would come the turn of France. The Alps would be crossed, Marseilles, like Tyre and Sidon, would see its port choked up by sand, Lyons would sink into desolation and slumber, and at last Paris, invaded by the invincible torpor, and transformed into a sterile waste of stones bristling with nettles, would join Rome and Nineveh and Babylon in death, whilst the nations continued their march from orient to occident following the sun. A great cry sped through the gloom, the death cry of the Latin races! History, which seemed to have been born in the basin of the Mediterranean, was being transported elsewhere, and the ocean had now become the centre of the world. How many hours of the human day had gone by? Had mankind, starting from its cradle over yonder at daybreak, strewing its road with ruins from stage to stage, now accomplished one half of its day and reached the dazzling hour of noon? If so, then the other half of the day allotted to it was beginning, the new world was following the old one, the new world of those American cities where democracy was forming and the religion of to-morrow was sprouting, those sovereign queens of the coming century, with yonder, across another ocean, on the other side of the globe, that motionless Far East, mysterious China and Japan, and all the threatening swarm of the yellow races.

However, while the cab climbed higher and higher up the Via Nazionale, Pierre felt his nightmare dissipating. There was here a lighter atmosphere, and he came back into a renewal of hope and courage. Yet the Banca d'Italia, with its brand new ugliness, its chalky hugeness, looked to him like a phantom in a shroud; whilst above a dim expanse of gardens the Quirinal formed but a black streak barring the heavens. However, the street ever ascended and broadened, and on the summit of the Viminal, on the Piazza delle Terme, when he passed the ruins of Diocletian's baths, he could breathe as his lungs listed. No, no, the human day could not finish, it was eternal, and the stages of civilisation would follow and follow without end! What mattered that eastern wind which carried the nations towards the west, as if borne on by the power of the sun! If necessary, they would return across the other side of the globe, they would again and again make the circuit of the earth, until the day should come when they could establish themselves in peace, truth, and justice. After the next civilisation on the shores of the Atlantic, which would become the world's centre, skirted by queenly cities, there would spring up yet another civilisation, having the Pacific for its centre, with seaport capitals that could not be yet foreseen, whose germs yet slumbered on unknown shores. And in like way there would be still other civilisations and still others! And at that last moment, the inspiriting thought came to Pierre that the great movement of the nations was the instinct, the need which impelled them to return to unity. Originating in one sole family, afterwards parted and dispersed in tribes, thrown into collision by fratricidal hatred, their tendency was none the less to become one sole family again. The provinces united in nations, the nations would unite in races, and the races would end by uniting in one immortal mankind—mankind at last without frontiers, or possibility of wars, mankind living by just labour, amidst an universal commonwealth. Was not this indeed the evolution, the object of the labour progressing everywhere, the finish reserved to History? Might Italy then become a strong and healthy nation, might concord be established between her and France, and might that fraternity of the Latin races become the beginning of universal fraternity! Ah! that one father-land, the whole earth pacified and happy, in how many centuries would that come—and what a dream!

Then, on reaching the station, the scramble prevented Pierre from thinking any further. He had to take his ticket and register his luggage, and afterwards he at once climbed into the train. At dawn on the next day but one, he would be back in Paris.

THE END.

LOURDES

ÉMILE ZOLA

In *The Three Cities*, Zola moves from a study of France's Second Empire past to the Republican present, and directly addresses the religious and social issues of his age. Set at the turn of the century, the three-part itinerary of Lourdes, Rome and Paris can be regarded as an updated pilgrim's progress.

A pilgrim indeed is Pierre Froment, a young Catholic priest in a state of spiritual crisis, when he travels to Lourdes in a train of sufferers and helpers. Here he witnesses the disturbing venality of the spa tourist industry that has developed in the thirty-five years since the vision of Bernadette, and senses the underlying ecclesiastical interests. He is sad but unsurprised that the fond hopes of many, be they devout or superstitious, are sorely deceived, but the pious young woman whom in other circumstances he might well have loved appears to make a miraculous recovery from paralysis.

Will this be the sign that will quell his nagging scepticism and restore his wavering faith in God?

PARIS

ÉMILE ZOLA

In *The Three Cities*, Zola moves from a study of France's Second Empire past to the Republican present, and directly addresses the religious and social issues of his age. Set at the turn of the century, the three-part itinerary of Lourdes, Rome and Paris can be regarded as an updated pilgrim's progress.

Three years after returning empty-handed from Rome, Abbé Pierre Froment's ceaseless missions, in which the reader follows him from finely depicted slum, boudoir and salon to intrigue-ridden Parliament itself, have convinced him of the uselessness of practical charity. He is reunited with his brother, Guillaume, whose anarchist acquaintances believe that terrorism is the means whereby society will be generated, and in his fiancée, Marie, meets a woman who seems unconsciously to prefer the troubled priest.

Will the tranquil scientific rationalism of this family home help Pierre at last to lay down the burden of his cassock?

THE FORTUNE OF
THE ROUGONS

ÉMILE ZOLA

This volume is the first of the monumental series of novels with the collective title *Les Rougon-Macquart* which occupied Zola for over twenty years and was to take his chosen family through all the ups and downs of the Second Empire. The rich gallery of characters he created has its origins defined in the self-contained *Fortune of the Rougons*. Set in Plassans (Aix-en-Provence) it evokes the colourful life of this cloistered town, revealed during a period of insurrections, revolutionary movement and violent clashes between peasantry and cavalry.

Aunt Dide, Pierre Rougon, Macquart and all the other members of this ravenous, neurotic and yet humorous family are brought to life in a book which should be read for its own sake. As a bonus it is also the perfect introduction to the whole series of novels which includes *Nana*, *Earth* and *Doctor Pascal*.

THE FAT AND THE THIN

ÉMILE ZOLA

The Fat and the Thin, the third novel in Zola's *Les Rougon-Macquart*, is an epic poem to the physical environment of the Halles, the newly built and technologically advanced central market of Paris, and to the wide range of products that are sold there, enumerated in descriptive passages that have often been likened to symphonies.

It is this setting of coarse, throbbing vitality that greets one of Zola's wide-eyed newcomers. Florent, a political deportee after Louis Bonaparte's *coup d'etat*, returns to the pork butcher's shop presided over by his smug Macquart sister-in-law, and to gainful employment as a market inspector. But the joy of the long-lost brother's homecoming is short-lived on both sides; as one of the eponymous 'thin', he soon feels submerged and asphyxiated beneath the bourgeois complacency of the 'fat', and begins to plot against the regime that has legitimized their plunder.

But is this republican agitator the true villain of the piece?

DOCTOR PASCAL

ÉMILE ZOLA

*D*octor Pascal is the final novel in the twenty-volume *Rougon-Macquart* series which follows the fortunes of this family of disparate characters through the Second Empire in France. It is, in Zola's own words, 'a scientific work, the logical deduction and conclusion of all my preceding novels', in which he presents a final formulation of his theories on atavism, and the role of heredity in shaping men's lives.

In *Doctor Pascal*, Zola creates a vivid and moving picture of passionate love between an old man and a young girl, and of the persecution of an ageing savant by his own family. Most of all, however, *Doctor Pascal* offers a fascinating and thought-provoking discourse on the social and religious issues surrounding the lives of the characters, many of which are as relevant to today's readers as those when Zola was writing towards the end of the last century.

HIS MASTERPIECE

ÉMILE ZOLA

The story of Claude Lantier, a great painter, one of the crucified martyrs of art, who adored women and sacrificed his wife, Christine, so loving and, for a time, so loved.

His Masterpiece is a strikingly accurate picture of artistic life in Paris during the latter years of the Second Empire. Amusing at times, extremely pathetic and even painful at others, it not only contributes a necessary element to the *Rougon-Macquart* series of novels but also represents a particular period of Zola's own career and work.

This is the Parisian art world as it really was, brought to life in a fine novel by one who had 'lived' it.